THIS ONE IS MINE

THIS ONE IS MINE

A Novel

MARIA SEMPLE

Little, Brown and Company

New York   Boston   London

Little, Brown and Company
Hachette Book Group
237 Park Avenue, New York, NY 10017
Visit our Web site at www.HachetteBookGroup.com

First Edition: December 2008

Little, Brown and Company is a division of Hachette Book Group, Inc. The Little, Brown name and logo are trademarks of Hachette Book Group, Inc.

This book is a work of fiction. The events described are imaginary, and all of the characters are fictitious. Some celebrity names appear in the novel in order to place the story in a modern cultural perspective, but these names are used fictitiously and in an imaginary context. Any resemblance in this novel to real events or people, living or dead, is coincidental and not intended to portray any actual persons or to suggest that any of the incidents ever happened.

The author is grateful for permission to use excerpts from the following works:
"This One Is Mine," from the Penguin publication *The Gift: Poems by Hafiz,* copyright © 1999 by Daniel Ladinsky and used with his permission. "Enter Sandman," written by James Hetfield, Lars Ulrich, and Kirk Hammett. Lyrics reprinted with permission of Creeping Death Music © 1991. "Whiskey River," words and music by J. B. Shinn III. Copyright © 1972 (Renewed 2002) Full Nelson Music, Inc. All rights controlled and administered by EMI Longitude Music. All rights reserved. International copyright secured. Used by permission. "Losing My Mind" from *Follies,* written by Stephen Sondheim. Used by permission of Herald Square Music, Inc., on behalf of Range Road Music, Inc., Jerry Leiber Music, Mike Stoller Music, Rilting Music, Inc., and Burthen Music Company, Inc. "My Funny Valentine," music by Richard Rodgers, lyric by Lorenz Hart. Copyright © 1937 Chappell & Co., Inc. Copyright renewed. Copyright assigned to Williamson Music and WB Music Corp. for the extended renewal period of copyright in the USA. International copyright secured. All rights reserved. *Goodnight Moon* © 1947 by Harper & Row. Text © renewed 1975 by Roberta Brown Rauch. Illustrations © renewed 1975 by Edith Hurd, Clement Hurd, John Thacher Hurd, and George Hellyer, as Trustees of the Edith & Clement Hurd 1982 Trust. Used by permission of HarperCollins Publishers. "Sultans of Swing," by Mark Knopfler. Copyright © 1978 Straitjacket Songs Ltd. (PRS). All rights for the US and Canada administered by Almo Music Corp. (ASCAP). Used by permission. All rights reserved. "Not While I'm Around" from *Sweeney Todd.* Music and lyrics by Stephen Sondheim. Copyright © 1979 Rilting Music, Inc. All rights administered by WB Music Corp. All rights reserved. Used by permission of Alfred Publishing Co., Inc. *Scarface,* courtesy of Universal Studios Licensing, LLLP. "Tiny Dancer," by Elton John and Bernie Taupin. Copyright © 1970 Dick James Music Ltd. (PRS). Copyright renewed. All rights for the US and Canada administered by Universal—Songs Of PolyGram Int., Inc. (BMI). Used by permission. All rights reserved. "Now" from *A Little Night Music.* Words and music by Stephen Sondheim. Copyright © 1973 (Renewed) Rilting Music, Inc. All rights administered by WB Music Corp. All rights reserved. Used by permission of Alfred Publishing Co., Inc. "Company" and "Sorry-Grateful" from *Company,* written by Stephen Sondheim. Used by permission of Herald Square Music, Inc., on behalf of Range Road Music, Inc., Jerry Leiber Music, Mike Stoller Music, and Rilting Music, Inc.

Library of Congress Cataloging-in-Publication Data
Semple, Maria.
     This one is mine : a novel / Maria Semple.—1st ed.
       p. cm.
     ISBN 978-0-316-03116-5
     1. Couples—Fiction. 2. Music trade—Fiction. 3. Hollywood (Los Angeles, Calif.)—Fiction. 4. Adultery—Fiction. 5. Need (Psychology)—Fiction. 6. Domestic fiction. I. Title.
     PS3619.E495T48 2008
     813'.6—dc22   2008015329

10 9 8 7 6 5 4 3 2 1

RRD-IN

Designed by Meryl Sussman Levavi

Printed in the United States of America

For my little family

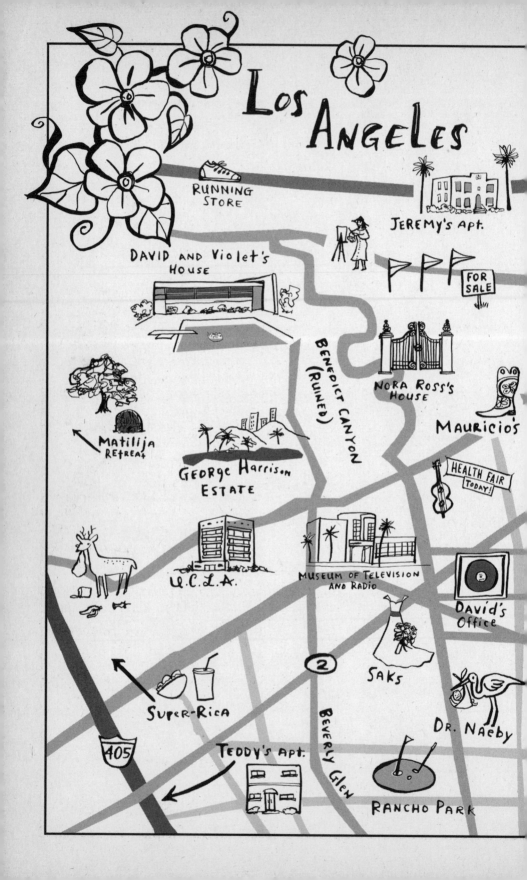

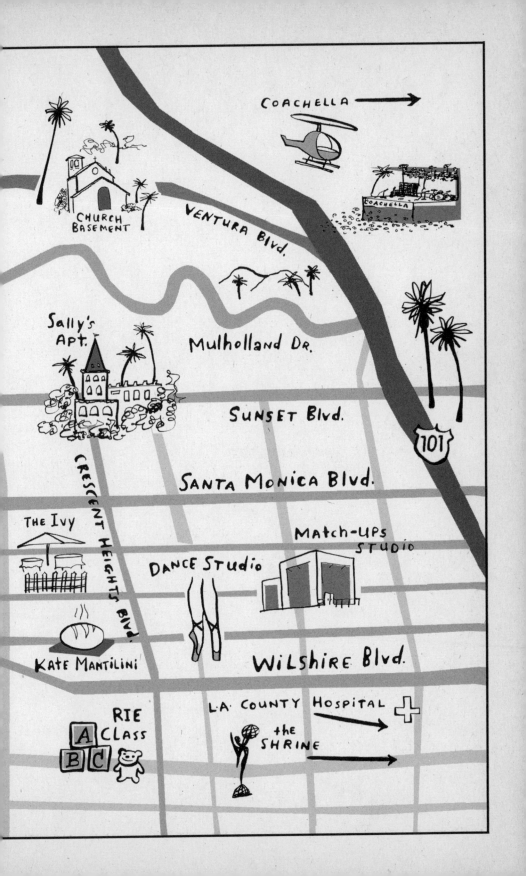

Someone put
You on a slave block
And the unreal bought
You

Now I keep coming to your owner
Saying,
"This one is mine."
You often overhear us talking
And this can make your heart leap
With excitement.

Don't worry,
I will not let sadness
Possess you.

I will gladly borrow all the gold
I need

To get you
Back.

— Hafiz

THIS ONE IS MINE

CHAPTER ONE

DAVID STOOD AT THE SINK, A PINE FOREST TO HIS LEFT, THE PACIFIC OCEAN to his right, and cursed the morning sun. It beat through the skylight and smashed into the mirror, making it all but impossible to shave without squinting. He had lived in Los Angeles long enough to lose track of the seasons, so it took glancing up at CNBC and seeing live images of people snowshoeing down Madison Avenue for it to register: it was the middle of winter. And he determined that all day, no matter how bad things got, at least he'd be grateful for the weather.

His pool shimmered. Stone Canyon Reservoir shimmered. The ocean shimmered. He cocked his head and flicked his wrist, skipping an imaginary stone from the pool to the reservoir. It split some Westwood high-rises, then landed in the Santa Monica Bay. He wound up again—this time to clear Catalina—then stopped.

There was a furry...brown...*thing* floating in the Jacuzzi.

"Honey!" He walked into the bedroom. "There's something in the Jacuzzi." He paused, waiting for the daylight in his eyes to fade.

His wife was in bed, her back to him, her hair seeping from under the pillow she'd taken to putting over her head at night.

"Ma-ma, Ma-ma." A squawk erupted from the baby monitor. There was a cough, then a bleat.

But Violet didn't move. What was her plan? Who did she think was going to get the baby? Was a standoff really so necessary that Violet would let Dot cry like this? *Jesus Christ.* David marched by the bed, skirting the rug so his bare heels struck the hardwood.

"Aggh." Violet pulled the pillow off her head. And there they were, the reason he fell in love with her almost twenty years ago in front of the Murray Hill Cinema: the violets tattooed behind her ear.

David's dog walker, a friend of Violet's from Barnard, had set them up. David managed two bands at the time—big ones, but still, only two. He'd been told Violet worked for a legendary theater producer and was the daughter of some obscure intellectual he'd never heard of. The plan was to meet half an hour before *Full Metal Jacket.* David arrived on time, but the movie had already sold out. He spotted Violet—she had said she'd be the one wearing red plastic sandals—sitting on the sidewalk in the ticket holders' line, engrossed in the *New York Times,* and listening to a Walkman. Two movie tickets were tucked under her leg. She wasn't a knockout, but wasn't fat either, and had a face you wanted to look into. She turned the page of the business section and folded it, then folded it again. An artsy chick who read the business section? Who was responsible enough to have arrived early and bought tickets? With enough Ivy League pluck to sit on a dirty sidewalk and not care who saw her? It was done and done. He had to have her. As he stepped forward, she absentmindedly twisted her long hair off

4

her neck. That's when he first glimpsed the tattoo behind her ear, teasing him from the edge of her hairline. He found it wildly sexy. But something inside him sank. He knew then there'd be a part of her he'd never possess.

"I'll get her, I'll get her, I'll get her." Violet threw off the covers and trudged to Dot's room without looking up.

The violets. *Those fucking violets.*

DAVID headed to the kitchen, comforted by the sounds of the morning: babbling Dot, the hiss of brewing coffee, the crunch of Rice Krispies underfoot. These days, there were two kinds of Rice Krispies, those waiting to be stepped on and those that already had been.

Pffft. He landed on some Krispy dust.

"Dada!" Dot shouted. She sat with perfect posture at her miniature wooden table, covered head to toe in croissant flakes, a darling, crusty monster.

"Aww, good morning!" David said, stepping on some Krispy virgins. "That's what I like to see, my girls!" A carafe of coffee and his newspaper awaited. "Honey," he said to Violet, "there's something floating in the Jacuzzi."

Violet opened the fridge. "What?"

He walked to the window. "It looks like a dead gopher."

"Then it's probably a dead gopher." She rooted around in the fridge. "Ah! There it is." She tore white butcher paper from a hunk of cheese. At least she still did that for him, got him the good cheese.

"How long has it been there?" David asked.

"Mama, what's dat?" said Dot.

"It's cheese, sweetie." Violet sliced some off.

"Want dat."

"I'll get you some. First, I'm making Dada his breakfast."

"How long has the gopher been there?" David repeated.

"I don't know. This is the first I've heard of it." Violet placed

David's breakfast on the counter: wheat toast, sheep's-milk cheese, sliced apples sprinkled with lemon juice and freshly grated nutmeg. "Are we good?"

"You didn't notice it when you looked out the window this morning?"

"Apparently not," Violet said. "Oh! Your milk." She removed a small pitcher from the microwave, set it next to the coffee, and surveyed David's domain. "Okay, that's everything."

"It doesn't upset you that there's a dead animal in our Jacuzzi?"

"I guess it does, a little. For the gopher."

"What gopher?" asked Dot.

"That water could have dysentery in it." David sat down. "What if Marta took Dot in there to swim?" To underscore the seriousness of his point, he had called their nanny by her real name, Marta, not their nickname for her, LadyGo.

"Mama! Want cheese," said Dot.

"I'm getting you some." Violet walked a piece of cheese over to Dot, then sat down on a tiny stool beside her and looked up at David. "Marcelino is coming today. I'll have him fish out the gopher, drain the Jacuzzi, and disinfect it." There was no discernible edge to her voice. This was one of Violet's most bedeviling tactics, acting as if she was being completely reasonable and it was David who was hell-bent on ruining a perfectly fine morning.

"Thank you," he said. "Look, I'm sorry. Today's big. KROQ is debuting the Hanging with Yoko single at nine. I've got tickets going on sale at the Troubadour at ten—Shit."

"What, Dada?"

"Yesterday was my sister's birthday," he said to Violet. "I totally spaced it. That must have been why she kept calling the office."

"I'll get her something and have it messengered over," Violet said. "I'll make sure it's expensive enough so she can't complain."

"Really? Thanks." David was heartened. This was the Violet he loved, the Violet who took care of business. He jiggled the mouse on his laptop and clicked open his brokerage account. Up from yesterday, and the Dow was down eighty points. The hard part wasn't *making* the money, it was *keeping* the money. And he had his gold stocks, his little fighters, to thank for that. He opened the chart for Nightingale Mining and sang its theme song. (After all, what would a stock be without its own theme song?) For Nightingale Mining—symbol XNI—he sang Metallica's "Enter Sandman." "X-N-I. X-N-I. Take my hand. Off to never-never land."

Plunk. Something landed on the newspaper. David ignored it and clicked the chart for Wheaton River Minerals. "Now, that's what you want a chart to look like." To the tune of "Whiskey River," David sang, "Wheaton River, take my mind. Don't let memories torture me. Wheaton River, don't run dry. You're all I got, take care of me."

"Good morning, *Meester* David." It was LadyGo, sliding open the back door. She carried clippers and a canvas gardening bag.

"Good morning," he said, then resumed singing. "I'm drowning in a Wheaton River—"

Plunk. David looked over. The *Los Angeles Times* was covered in something sticky. "Violet? What is this?"

"What is what?" She was lost in thought, staring at the floor.

"What's all over the newspaper?"

Violet blinked, then got up. She stuck her finger in the goo, smelled it, then raised it to her mouth.

"Don't eat it—"

Too late. "It's honey," she said. "That's weird. I didn't put any honey out." She looked up. "There must be a beehive in the crawl space." There was, in fact, a dark stain between two cedar ceiling planks.

"What do you mean, There must be a beehive in the crawl space?"

"Well, I don't know."

"You act like that's something that always happens."

7

"Want honey," said Dot.

"No, sweetie," Violet said. "This honey is not for you." She turned to David. "Perhaps because it's been so unseasonably hot, the honey melted and dripped through the ceiling." She shrugged and returned to the little stool. "But I don't know anything."

The only reason Violet dared say something so self-pitying and provocative was that she knew David wouldn't get into it in front of LadyGo. LadyGo, the human shield! David glared at Violet, but she wouldn't look at him.

"*Meesuz*, look," the nanny said to Violet, a glint in her eye. "The animals. They eat all the vegetables." LadyGo held out a handful of sugar snap peas. Each pod had tiny holes bored in it. "I ask Javier. LadyGo, What animal is it? LadyGo, I spray next time."

"No," said Violet. "I don't want Javier spraying the vegetables."

"What animals?" asked Dot.

"Maybe *las ratas*. All the carrots? *No mas*."

"That's probably gophers," Violet mused. "Oh well. I'll just have to get carrots and peas at the farmers' market tomorrow." She got up. "Okay, I'm going to take a shower."

David stared at the floor, took a long breath, and clenched his jaw. What the fuck was going on around here? Was this his house or a goddamned wild-animal sanctuary?

"I'll call the gopher guy and the bee guy at nine," Violet said. "There's nothing I can do but deal with it, right?"

"Those are your vegetables. You planted them from seeds. They're ruined. Why doesn't that upset you? I don't understand you sometimes."

"I'll try to be more upset, then."

"What kind of a thing is that to say?"

"David," Violet said. "Please, I can't."

"Where *las ratas*?" squeaked Dot.

"You can't *what*?" David asked.

"I can't," Violet said. "I can't…nothing."

"You can't *nothing!* Great. Thanks for the fucking insight."

"Why Dada sad?" asked Dot.

"Dada's happy," Violet said quickly.

David got up. At the sound of the stool skidding, Violet flinched. LadyGo swooped up Dot and carried her away. *For fuck's sake.*

A drop of honey landed on David's shoulder. He pinched it off and grabbed his car keys. "I'm going to fucking Starbucks."

SALLY awoke to the rising sound of the "babbling brook" feature on her alarm clock, which, like "bamboo waterfall" and "ocean waves," just sounded like an airplane flying overhead. She hit the snooze button and braced herself. It wasn't yesterday, her birthday, that had worried her. That was filled with phone calls, funny cards, a cake at work, and margaritas at El Coyote. It was today she feared, the day *after:* when everyone's attention drifted elsewhere and she woke up in her same one-bedroom apartment on a noisy street, one year older. She took a breath, then another, then smiled. Thirty-six she could manage.

Moving on to today. Sally was teaching back-to-back ballet until Maryam picked her up for the party where Sally would finally be introduced to Jeremy White. Her husband to be. Since today was so jam-packed, Sally had done her bring-a-new-guy-home sweep of the apartment last night. She went over the list in her head one last time.

> Waste baskets: empty
> Box of tampons: off the toilet
> Dishes: washed and put away
> Floors: vacuumed
> Medicine: tucked away in the fridge
> Credit card bills: in the back of the desk drawer
> Candles: everywhere

Sally sprang up. The gossip magazines she had plucked from the studio's recycling basket were still visible on the coffee table. She didn't want Jeremy White to think she was shallow, so she'd bought a *New Yorker* to place on top of them. She got out of bed, then tripped on something.

A wisteria vine from the balcony had crept under the door, across the carpet, and under Sally's bed. She had noticed it last night when she was vacuuming. Thinking it a carefree touch—a thing Holly Golightly might have let grow wild in *her* first apartment—Sally had vacuumed around it. Now something terrible occurred to her. As of eleven o'clock last night, she'd been able to pick up the whole branch; this morning it was stuck to something. She dropped to her hands and knees and traced the vine under the Laura Ashley dust ruffle. A lime green tendril was coiled around the leg of her bed. That meant the vine had snaked around it *while she was sleeping.*

Sally shuddered. She yanked the wisteria, but that only tightened its grip on the metal rod. She clawed off the wet young growth with her fingernails, then threw open the door and hurled the awful branch off the balcony. But the door wouldn't close. The stupid knob had been painted over too many times. She kicked the wood frame until the lock clicked. Her hands trembled as she checked to make sure her manicure wasn't wrecked.

The *tap, tap, tapping* of tangled backstage passes hanging from the doorknob slowed until there was silence. Def Leppard, the Rolling Stones, Commonhouse, the Red Hot Chili Peppers. All bands managed by David at some point. All more important than his little sister's birthday.

The babbling brook started up again. *The New Yorker.* She couldn't forget *The New Yorker.*

TUESDAYS in Los Angeles made Violet sad. It always caught her by surprise, the sadness, like today, as she was driving, safe and alone in her car after another revolting morning with David. Then she'd see the open-house signs and would remember: Tuesday, open-house day.

She stopped at the light at Beverly Glen and watched Gwen Gold struggle to haul a sign from her white Lexus SUV and place it strategically to block the other signs. (Who cared if a dozen cars saw her, she had a house to sell, baby!) Gwen stuck several eye-catching GWEN GOLD flags in the hard earth, careful not to muss her Chanel knockoff pantsuit. She wore a grimace, and unlaced hiking boots over her hose, saving her smiles and good heels for later, when she'd be all poise as she presented the peekaboo city views and granite countertops, trying to concentrate on the client and not the math in her head—*listed at 1.65, half of 3 percent of 1.5 is 30,000, if I can get five of these a year, that's 150 before taxes, I could pay off the face-lift and put ten down on a condo. That's good, that's enough....*

Violet knew the type, and they made her sad. Those divorcées who had staked it all on being the perfect wife and mother. Nothing evil in that, nothing that everyone else wasn't doing, nothing to be punished for. But something had gone awry, and now these women were single, fifty, and forced to earn a living without any discernible skills. So they became realtors. How had Gwen played her cards wrong? Had she let herself go after giving birth to four boys? Had that driven her husband into the arms of his hard-bodied young secretary? Had the pressures of a disabled child been too much for even a solid marriage? Or had Gwen had the affair? A desperately needed fling with a young green-eyed man who worked at J. Crew? And her husband, Stan—Violet thought Gwen would be married to a Stan—Stan had caught them and thrown Gwen out, just when her preppy lover got scared away by her need. Whatever Gwen had done, she didn't deserve the indignity of this; of that Violet was certain.

The light turned green. Just past Deep Canyon, a woman

wearing a puffy straw hat and a billowy white linen dress painted a picture of the valley, taking advantage of this especially crisp day. Violet caught a glimpse of the oil as she drove past. It wasn't very good. It would never sell. How sad for this woman, who obviously imagined herself on Nantucket the way she was dressed, not choking on fumes overlooking Sherman Oaks. Would she try to get into a group art show with her series of unremarkable landscapes? Would a friend buy a few to make her feel good? Violet had an impulse to turn around and buy the painting on the spot, but she'd never make the U-turn. The traffic on Mulholland had gotten so relentless. She always felt as though someone was about to ram into her while she snaked along the only street in LA she had ever lived, the spine of the city.

Floating past the gatehouse guarding the swollen mansions of Beverly Park, Violet remembered words spoken by her father at this same spot, decades before the mansions. "When you get older," he had said, "you will learn there are two kinds of people. Those who grew up listening to Sondheim on Mulholland, and those who didn't." Years later, he'd lose control of the convertible Jaguar on another part of Mulholland and sail to his death. A drunk-driving accident? A final attempt to make a splash—any splash would do—after never fulfilling the promise of his youth? It was unclear. Violet had hardly spoken to him toward the end.

She flowed with traffic down Coldwater Canyon. A cement truck was backing out of a driveway up ahead. Violet stopped for it, making the driver tailgating her slam on his brakes and hit his horn for a good ten seconds. But he didn't know Violet had nowhere to go. A little shopping. Sally's present. A movie by herself, perhaps. The *New York Times* at a sushi bar. Dot needed socks.

At the weird, long park along Santa Monica Boulevard, some workers had just raised a banner that read BEVERLY HILLS HEALTH FAIR. A dozen card tables anchored bunches of colorful balloons. But there were no people! How sad for the organizers, who had no doubt spent months planning this event. Violet wanted to reassure them that the crowds would come, just wait until lunchtime. A band was setting up on the grass. A brown-skinned man wearing a black suit sound-checked his upright bass. Poor dear. He probably had no idea how hot it was expected to be when he got dressed this February morning.

David had always accused Violet of feeling sorry for the wrong people. She could cry at the mere thought of Buzz Aldrin's having to endure a lifetime of being known as merely the *second* man on the moon. "Ultra," David would say—it was the nickname he gave her on their first date, as in Ultra Violet—"you really don't need to feel sorry for Buzz Aldrin." But once Violet saw the inherent sadness in one thing, she couldn't stop.

That is why, when she walked into the French chocolate shop on Little Santa Monica, the tiny one that was always empty, the one that sold the gorgeous, bitter truffles, she couldn't help it. She felt unbearably sad. The heaviness filled Violet's stomach, then her chest. She grabbed a small wooden crate of truffles and placed it on the counter. At thirty-five dollars, no wonder there were no customers! The saleslady, her hair pulled severely back and tied with a silk scarf, looked up from her Sudoku book. Her sevens and ones were unmistakably French. This made Violet even sadder. She grabbed two giant crates and placed them on the counter. Perhaps this act of charity would stanch the sadness rising in her chest and prevent it from spilling out her eyes.

"*Bonjour, madame,*" Violet managed to say.

"*Bonjour, madame,*" answered the woman in that curt way of the French.

A pregnant woman announced her entrance with a singsong "Hi!"

Violet could tell she was eager to talk about her pregnancy, and obliged. "Is it your first?" she asked.

"Yes." The woman touched her stomach. "Cody. A boy."

This poor woman. She had no idea how hard it was going to be, even if she loved her baby as much as Violet did Dot. And how Violet did love Dot, was possessed by her. Not a night went by without Violet uttering her name, Dot, just before slipping off. Even if Cody was this woman's blood and heart and every thought, did she know that love wouldn't be enough? Love wouldn't make being a mother any less boring or draining or bewildering. Love wouldn't prevent her from, some mornings, standing at the bottom of the driveway, like Popeye, a wailing Swee'Pea dangling from stiff arms, waiting for the arrival of the nanny.

For too many years, Violet had identified with the comic-book lady on that eighties T-shirt—the one everyone thought was a Lichtenstein but wasn't—who realizes, to her horror, OH NO, I FORGOT TO HAVE CHILDREN! But these first years of motherhood made Violet think there should be a follow-up T-shirt. On it, the same woman is finally cradling her prized baby. But she's still stricken, and her thought bubble now reads IT'S ALL ADDING UP TO NOTHING! There was no reward, no thank-you, no sense of accomplishment, no sustaining happiness. Often, Violet would find herself standing in a room, having no idea what she had gone in to do. It reminded her of the great Stephen Sondheim line…

> Sometimes I stand in the middle of the floor
> Not going left. Not going right.

Then she'd realize that Dot was back in the other room. And Violet's only purpose in leaving had been to *get out of the same room as her baby*. It was truly astonishing that something as unremarkable as having a kid would be the thing that had finally felled Violet Grace Parry.

"Congratulations," Violet told the expectant mother.

"*Et voilà*." The saleswoman handed Violet a sales slip.

"*Merci, madame*."

There was a sticker on the French lady's black cardigan. It was of a bear with a Band-Aid on its arm. I GAVE BLOOD, it read. That did it. Violet was about to start crying. She signed the sales slip without really looking at the amount. It began with a three.

SALLY was sitting on the edge of the tub inspecting her feet when the phone rang. It was her best friend. "Hi, Maryam, I don't have much time." Her toes looked good, no cuts, no blisters.

"I just want to give you directions to the party," said her friend.

"I thought you were going to pick me up." Sally admired her naked body in the mirror. How many thirty-six-year-olds could say there was *nothing* they'd want to change about their body? Heart-shaped ass, delts to die for, not a whisper of ab flab.

"But the party's in Marina del Rey," Maryam started in. "And I am, too, so it doesn't make sense for me to drive all the way to West Hollywood at rush hour to pick you up, then have to drive you back after the party."

Sally knew all this. But she needed Maryam to drive. That way, after Sally captivated Jeremy White at the party, she could tell him that Maryam had left without her, then innocently ask him for a ride home. She'd invite him up, tease him with the best kiss of his life, and abruptly send him on his way. Always leave them wanting more.

"Then I just won't go," Sally said.

"You can't not go!" Maryam cried. "Jeremy never goes to parties. The only reason he's coming tonight is to meet *you*. And my boss invited a bunch of people to impress them. If Jeremy shows up and you're not there, he'll turn around and go home, then I'll look like an idiot."

"You know I hate going to parties alone—" Sally practically dropped the phone: there was a red bump on her bikini line. Please, she prayed, not an ingrown hair. She took a closer look. It was. *Fudge*. If she didn't get the hair out, it would get all gross and infected.

"I *would* pick you up," Maryam said, "but I'm on location in the desert and I need to shower and change when I get home."

"Unlike you, I'd never make *my* best friend do something she's not comfortable with, so I just won't go." Sally squeezed the bump. Nothing came out. She pinched it between her fingernails. Blood collected under the purplish crescent indentations. What a freaking disaster! "Have a nice day," she said. "Good-bye."

"No, Sally—"

Sally hung up. Ice might keep it from getting infected. She went to the kitchen and popped an ice cube out of the tray, then placed it on the splotch.

When Sally moved into this delightful one-bedroom on Crescent Heights Boulevard, she had discovered a bunch of baskets that the previous tenant had left behind in a closet. Full of confidence and whimsy, she hung the baskets from her new kitchen ceiling. But the whole Shabby Chic craze came and went; still, there were the baskets. Except for the two or three she had to throw away because they got infested with those horrible moths that got into her cereal, too. She'd arrived in LA feeling so full of promise. Her career as a dancer hadn't worked out, but that was okay. She invented a ballet-inspired workout, named it Core-de-Ballet, and within a month was teaching classes. All without any help from David.

David. She couldn't believe he forgot her birthday yesterday. She had called to remind him, for his sake. Three times. A snooty secretary answered. "May I tell Mr. Parry your last name?" she asked. "It's the same as his," Sally said. "I'm his *sister*." David still didn't take her call! When she had returned home from her birthday dinner, there was a message on her machine. "I have David Parry returning," said the witch. David always used to remember Sally's birthday. But now he was too busy up there in his zillion-dollar house with that baby of his, who'd won the lottery of the universe just by being born. And Violet, always throwing dinner parties for rock stars, most of them single, and not inviting Sally. Sally knew David way before Violet did, and now Violet acted like she owned him.

Sally's phone rang. "Hello?" It would have been cruel to answer, Hello, Maryam.

"I'll pick you up at six," said her defeated friend.

"Oh, Maryam!" Sally gushed. "You're the best!"

"But I'm going to be wearing hiking boots, and my hair will be caked with dust. Just so you know, my cat will probably pee on my pillow again to punish me for not coming home to feed her—"

Sally jumped in before the subject of the cat could take hold. "Thanks sooo much," she said. Sally loved Maryam but wished she'd change her name to something less Persian. *Maryam* practically begged to be *Marianne*. She was, after all, born in LA and completely American. Sally had brought it up several times, but Maryam got all touchy because her name meant "sweet-smelling flower" or something. Sally wouldn't have been so hung up on it if it weren't for Maryam's surliness and disregard for her personal appearance. She had a nice face and a good body. A little makeup and better clothes could kick her up to a whole other level. Sally herself didn't care one way or the other. She was only thinking of Maryam. As the pretty friend, Sally felt it her obligation.

She checked the ingrown hair. The ice seemed to be working.

VIOLET walked as fast as she could down Little Santa Monica. If she ran, she'd feel her ass jiggle, and that in itself might let loose the tears. She turned down Beverly Drive, then stopped. She was parked back on Camden. But she couldn't just turn around. Someone she knew might see her flailing. Her heart was full-blown in her chest, fluttering, double and triple beating. The tingling bled down her inner arms to her hands, then got trapped in her fingertips, which felt as if they might burst. The heat prickled in her jaw and rose up her cheeks. Oh God, she had to get off the street.

The Museum of Television and Radio was right there. Violet flung open the heavy glass door and entered the hushed travertine lobby. An elderly docent didn't look up from her knitting. Violet remembered her from a few years back.

It was when *Mann About Town* was being inducted. During the screening of an episode—it was one Violet had written—she had stepped out to read the paper but ended up stuck in a conversation with the excitable docent, who recounted all the famous TV people she'd met. Violet acted impressed, but TV never really interested her. She had always considered her destiny to be more noble, like writing plays or teaching English. But a one-act she had written in college had gotten noticed by a TV writer who quickly hired her. She and David hadn't even been dating a year, but he could manage bands from LA just the same as from New York, so he was happy to relocate. One thing led to another, and there she had found herself, almost twenty years later, being honored at a museum for crap.

But today, even the most innocuous conversation with this docent might cause Violet to collapse, or scream, or die, even. She nestled her face in her shoulder and made a break for the bathroom.

The antechamber was softly lit, with beige walls and comfy carpet. Violet crumpled onto a tufted Knoll bench and allowed the tears to flow. *Why don't you get the baby—you're already awake! I was up all night because of your snoring. If you're so upset about the gopher, get it out of the Jacuzzi yourself! I'm making breakfast for you and Dot. Why don't you figure out what the sticky stuff is in the ceiling? The gophers and rats already ate the damn vegetables—bitching about it isn't going to bring them back. You're not the only one living in this house. Have some consideration before you ruin everybody's morning. See! It's not just me. Dot and LadyGo are scared of you, too!* These were all things Violet would never actually say to David. It was easier to nod.

Violet wiped her nose on her sleeve. There was some pink Play-

Doh on the lapel of her corduroy jacket. She scraped it off with her front teeth; the salt tasted good. A crack of light on the carpet widened into a wedge. A silhouette stepped into it. Violet raised her eyes. A man stood in the door that led to the bathroom proper. Behind him were urinals.

"Oh God," she said. "I'm in the men's room."

"I'm sorry," he said.

"No, it's my fault. I didn't look."

The man wore black, had brown skin and moppish black hair. "Hey," she said. "You're the one playing bass at the health fair."

"Are they looking for me?" Fear danced in his eyes. "They said we were on a fifteen-minute break."

"No, I noticed you when I drove by, that's all." It was rather dear, how worried he was. Violet figured he didn't frequent Beverly Hills and might be intimidated. She felt an odd responsibility to put him at ease. "Are you having fun?" she asked.

"What are you, the ambassador of Beverly Hills?"

"No," she said with a laugh, startled by his acuity, or her transparency, she didn't know which.

"Since you asked," he said, "my answer is no. The Jew bandleader won't give me gas money. It's my fault because I wrote it down wrong. And I show up and see it's a fucking blood drive so there's no tip jar. Not to mention the shit going on with my car, which probably won't start. So here I am, a one-man charity event for a bunch of Beverly Hills receptionists raking in sixty G's a year."

"Jew bandleader, huh?" Violet couldn't tell if he was Jewish himself or some other kind of ethnicity.

"What," he said. "Are you Jewish?"

"No, but I could be."

"Come on, I was just saying that. You seemed cool."

"I am cool."

"Anyway, he's a nigger. I just called him a Jew because he's so cheap."

"My God," she said. "Did you miss the memo? These aren't words people use anymore. Who raised you?"

"Wolves." He sat down beside her. He had bloodshot eyes and lint in his hair. It was hard to tell if it was full of gel or in need of a shampoo. His clothes smelled like a Goodwill. "Really, though," he said. "Are you okay? I'm a good listener."

"I'm fine."

"Nigger, please. What kind of future can we expect when you lie to me like that?"

"Future?" She felt mortified by how besotted she sounded and lowered her voice a register. "I mean it. I have a car that starts. That's something to be grateful for, right?"

"Amen to that." His pants were shiny and polyester. Neat rows of staples held up the hems. On his feet were stiff black-and-white shoes. He must have bought golf shoes without knowing it, probably at a thrift store. "My tires are the thickness of rolling paper, and when I turn on the engine, there's a weird chugging. I think the axle is bent, because it pulls to the left. The whole thing's about to die, I can feel it."

Violet's tunic was twisted so it exposed the elastic panel of her pants. She quickly yanked down her shirt. Jesus, Dot was almost two and Violet was still wearing maternity jeans. Last night, during the Clippers-Nuggets game, a horrifying fact had flashed on the screen: Allen Iverson weighed 165 pounds. In other words, Violet was one pound heavier than the NBA's star point guard. She was completely disgusting.

"And if my car dies," he continued, "I'm dead. I have no cash to fix it. I'd have to leave it on the street. No more gigs, because I can't haul my upright around on a fucking bus. Then I'd lose my apartment, so I might as well be back in Palm Springs." He ran his fingers forcefully through his hair. "Okay," he said, talking himself down, "I have to stop thinking like that. I've got to have faith that God will take care of me."

"Aren't we full of contradictions?" Violet said. "Talking about God now."

He gnawed at a cuticle.

"Stop biting your nails."

"I know, thanks." He leaned back and turned so he could get a square look at her. "So. Are your problems worse than mine?"

"My problems." Violet stared at the three hundred dollars' worth of chocolate nestled between her four-hundred-dollar loafers. "My problems are all problems I'm lucky to have. And I know it, so therein lies the rub."

"You know what we say. If you're alive, all problems are quality problems."

"We say that, do we?"

"How about you and me trade? Your problems for my problems."

"No, thanks," she said.

"You didn't even think about it!" he said. "You bitch!"

Violet laughed loudly.

"Wow, there's a laugh," he said. "Am I good or am I good?"

"You're good." Violet handed him the bag. "I can pay you for your services in chocolate."

"I don't eat chocolate."

"It cost three hundred dollars."

"Are you fucking high?" He rifled through the bag. "How do you blow three Benjamins on chocolate?"

"I got it for this salesman at Hermès. Ten years ago, I bought a hat at Hermès in Paris, which I absolutely cherished. But it blew off when I was flying in a small plane over the Pantanal. We were looking for tapirs. Anyway, I went to the Hermès here in Beverly Hills to replace it, but it had been discontinued. So ever since, the salesman, Daniel, calls me any time a similar hat comes in. Resulting in me not only buying hats that I never wear, but also feeling an insane obligation to get him this ridiculously overpriced chocolate that ironically only a salesman at Hermès would appreciate. And he's not even French, but *Australian,* if you can believe it."

"Okay," said the bass player. "My price just went up for having the shit bored out of me."

Violet gave him a shove. "Good-bye. We wouldn't want you to be tardy for the light-headed secretaries."

He laughed. One of his teeth was missing, not a front tooth, or the one over, but the one beside that. Still, it was a shock. Violet had never been this close to a grown person with a missing tooth. He stood up and looked in the mirror. Violet expected a gasp when he beheld the state of his hair. Instead, he gave himself a churlish smile. Then, without warning, he dropped to one knee and took her hand. "It was a pleasure to meet you, milady."

His skin was so rough. Violet turned her hand up so his rested in it. His nails were savaged, the cuticles stained black. "Do you garden?" she asked.

"Listen to you. Do I garden."

There was a calm in his face, an invitation to linger. She lowered her eyes. His hand, scarred with worry. Hers, plump from herbal-infused creams. The only way people like them were meant to meet was across a counter. She wasn't supposed to be alone with him in a lavishly appointed men's room, a black American Express card in her wallet, a month's rent worth of artisan truffles at her feet. If the chatty docent came upon them and caught the foul-mouthed bass player from Palm Springs holding Violet Parry's hand, it would be within reason for her to call security.

Violet placed her other hand on top of his, cupping it as she would a cricket that had made its way inside the house and she had to return to the safety of the wild. The bass player looked up. She met his green eyes, daring him to do something. But he looked down. She quickly let go of his hand. "Blood," she said.

"What?"

"There, where you were biting your nails." A poppy seed of

blood rested on his cuticle. Violet went to wipe it off, but he jerked his hand away before she could touch it. Violet was momentarily confused, then it occurred to her: he must have just noticed her five-carat diamond ring. "I'm married," she said.

He rose to his feet. "Stay happy," he said. "You twinkle when you're happy." A blast of sunlight blinded her, and the bass player was gone.

SALLY pulled up to the gate off Mandeville Canyon, early for her one o'clock, a private ballet class for three-year-old twins. She got out of her Toyota RAV4—her "truck" as she liked to call it—with the CORE-DE-BALLET placard in the window and picked up the newspaper. She had made sure to arrive early because Jeremy White's column ran Tuesdays in the *Los Angeles Times* and she wanted to appear informed when she finally met him tonight. Sally scooched the paper out of its plastic so she'd be able to return it undetected. The parents were super-nice and would have let her read it if she had asked, but one of the things that made Sally so successful as a private instructor was knowing her boundaries.

She opened the sports section and found "Just the Stats" by Jeremy White. Jeremy's column had started running last fall, and since then he'd predicted the winner of some amazing number of football games. So amazing, apparently, that Maryam, a producer for ESPN, was giving him a segment on their Sunday-morning show beginning next month. That's why tonight was so important. Sally had to get a ring on her finger *before* Jeremy became famous and started earning the big bucks. That's how they never leave you. Because no matter what happens, they know you loved them for them and not for their money.

Her phone rang. She recognized the number as David's office and wasn't thrilled at the prospect of another unpleasant exchange with his secretary. "Hello."

"Hey, Sal, it's me!"

"Oh—David—Hi!"

"Happy birthday. I'm sorry we didn't connect yesterday."

"That's okay," Sally said, unable to resist the surge of love her brother's voice always triggered. "I know how super-busy you are."

"Thirty-six," he said. "That's a big one."

"Yeah, I went out with friends. How are you—"

"You're good?" he asked. It was more of a statement than a question. "Health's good? Work's good?"

"Yeah, fine. What are you up to?"

"Same old—Violet, Dot, my bands. Hey, I saw the Bolshoi is coming. I thought you'd like to go."

"Wow, I'd love to. When is it?"

"April something," he said. "I'll be out of town, but I'll get you tickets—"

Caw! Caw! A screech echoed through the breezy canyon. Sally covered her free ear.

"Well, sounds like you're busy," David said with a laugh.

"No, I'm not, it's just—"

"Call if you need anything."

Then—*splat!* And another *splat.* Out of nowhere, the hood of Sally's truck was freckled with white. And in the tree overhead, parrots! A whole flock of them! "Aaaah!" Sally shut her phone and shielded her hair with the *LA Times. Splat-splat. Splat-splat. Splat-splat-splat-splat.* Wet bird poop machine-gunned the flimsy newsprint. She jumped into her truck, turned on the engine, and drove into the clear. She opened the door and ditched the gross newspaper on the driveway. Always one to learn from her mistakes, Sally resolved to never again park under a tree without first looking for parrots.

OVER the past several hours, Violet had found many excuses to wander the streets of Beverly Hills, the jazz music beckoning her through the mash of traffic. At one point, she had stood across from the park and watched him. The song was "My Funny Valentine," whose lyrics always broke Violet's heart.

Your looks are laughable,
Unphotographable,
Yet you're my fav'rite work of art.

The bass loomed over the bass player. His stance was wide, aggressive, and his arms snaked around the instrument's neck as if trying to wrestle it to its death. But the bass was surely older than the musician who slapped it. It would survive long after he was dust. Between songs, the wizened black drummer said something to the bassist, who in turn laughed. His same laugh from the bathroom. Violet had felt jealousy, stacked with the preposterousness of such jealousy. She had shaken it off and headed to her car.

Yet here she was again, an hour later, pulled toward the park and the dismantled health fair. She didn't realize it until her heart quickened. There he was, getting into a car across Santa Monica Boulevard. Violet hustled through traffic, then flat-out ran up the block to the fenderless Mazda hatchback.

"Fuck! Fuck!" He pounded the wheel with both hands.

Violet tapped on the window. Still looking down, he smiled, then cocked his head and met Violet's eyes. He nodded, as if he'd been expecting her. She motioned for him to roll down the window. He turned the crank with one hand and hooked his finger over the top of the glass.

"Push down," his muffled voice instructed Violet. She flattened both hands against the window and pushed. Their combined effort lowered it six inches. "Did I fucking predict this?" he said with a great big laugh. "My car won't start."

"Can I give you a ride home?" she asked. The passenger seat was fully reclined. On it rested the upright bass in a black bag.

Violet imagined him tenderly laying the instrument on the tattered seat, and blushed.

"I need this fucking car," he said. "I have a champagne brunch gig in Agoura Hills on Sunday, and the rest of the band lives in Ventura, so if someone comes to pick me up, I'll have to give them gas money, and I'm only making fifty bucks for the gig."

"Oh my God. It's like every other word out of your mouth is gas money."

"Excuse me if my biggest concern in life isn't chocolate and hats."

"I have a great mechanic," she said. "I can have your car towed there. He'll arrange for a rental and make sure your car is fixed in time for your gig."

"Really?" he asked.

"Really."

"That's the way it's going to happen?"

"That's the way it's going to happen," Violet said, "because I'm going to pay for it." She felt as though she had just hurled herself off a cliff. He looked away, unable to see she was falling, falling. He started chewing his nails. "Stop that," she said, eager to change the subject.

"Thanks." He pulled his finger out of his mouth. "Why are you doing this?"

"Noblesse oblige?"

"Heh?"

"Never mind. It was—it's just my way of saying thank you. For cheering me up in the men's room."

"Don't let your rich husband hear you say that."

"Whatever it's going to cost, it's an insignificant amount of money."

"Say that again."

"What?"

"Insignificant amount of money."

Violet did. The bass player looked off and thought about it. "I might never be able to pay you back," he said.

"Think of it as me *miracling* you."

"*Miracling* me?"

"It's a Deadhead thing," Violet said. "At Grateful Dead shows, there'd be all these nasty hippies walking around holding up one finger, saying, I need a miracle, which was meant to take the form of someone giving them a free ticket."

"You're a Deadhead?" he asked skeptically.

"I was."

"I feel less guilty accepting your money knowing you have such shitty taste in music."

"I'll call our car service to pick you up," she said. "The mechanic will take care of you."

"Do you think one day *I'll* ever say, Our car service?"

"Most likely no."

"Man, as hippie chicks go, you have one hell of a mean streak."

"The best ones always do."

He got out of the car. His black shirt was wet and stuck to his back. Violet resisted the urge to peel it off.

"You do know how to get shit done," he said. "Are you sure you're not a cokehead, too?" He had changed into flimsy flip-flops. His feet were small and delicate, with black hairs sprouting from the tops of his toes.

Violet fumbled for her cell phone. "What's your name?"

He pulled out a stiff leather wallet chained to his belt loop and removed a business card.

TEDDY REYES
BASS PLAYER
11838 Venice Blvd.
Los Angeles, CA 90066
(310) 555-0199

Reyes. It meant "kings" in Spanish. That answered it; he must be Mexican. Violet pictured Venice Boulevard but could see only oil-change places, strip malls, and junk shops. She didn't know people actually lived on Venice. The zip code—90066—meant nothing to her. Bordering the card were colorful dancing pharmaceutical pills. "What are you, some kind of pill freak?"

"I was," he said. "Among other things. I've been clean almost three years."

"So that's the royal we? AA?"

"I'm Teddy and I'm an alcoholic."

"I'm Violet," she said. "And I'm…I'm happy to meet you."

Teddy gave a big laugh. There it was, his laugh: her laugh. "Of course you're a Violet," he said. "Nice to meet you, too, Violet. I need a miracle."

SALLY followed Maryam into her boss's Marina del Rey condo. It was packed, loud and overlit with twenty-dollar halogen torch lamps you could get at any drugstore. Sally couldn't believe that after all these years in LA, she was still stuck at the level of party where they served baby carrots and Trader Joe's hummus. Since she had the best arms in the room, Sally took off her coat and pushed it into Maryam. "Could you put this somewhere?"

Maryam dutifully did as told and disappeared into the crowd.

"You must be Maryam's friend," a voice called, "the beautiful Sally."

"And you must be our gracious host!" Sally handed the sweaty man two crates of chocolate. She couldn't figure out why Violet had sent over seven pounds of chocolate for her birthday. (The card had read "Love, David and Violet," but Sally knew Violet's writing.) It was a thoughtless, bizarre choice. Sally was about to chuck the bag in the trash, but then saw the round orange box.

In it was a gorgeous Hermès belt. She could forgive Violet the chocolate.

"May I get you a drink?" asked the host.

"No, thanks. I'll just wander." Sally scanned the crowd for Jeremy White. Not wanting to appear too eager, she had never pumped Maryam about Jeremy's looks. All Maryam had said was "He's actually kind of cute." *Actually* kind of cute. Sally wondered, Why the *actually*?

"Hey! Look who it is!" Maryam had reappeared and was spinning Sally around by her shoulders. "Jeremy! This is my friend Sally." Sally found herself, without ceremony, face-to-face with Jeremy White. He was pressed against a wall, a beer high to his chest.

He stuck out his hand. "Nice to meet you, Sally."

Sally shook it. Clammy. "Likewise," she said.

"I can't believe you came to a party," Maryam said, and punched Jeremy in the shoulder.

"You told me I had no choice." He shot a glance at Sally, but before she could engineer a seductive smile, he looked down.

The tension that had been building in Sally's neck and shoulders all day swooshed down her spine and disappeared. Tonight would be easy-peasy-lemon-squeezy. "I'm a big fan of your column," she said. "I don't know how you do it."

"I have a secret system," Jeremy said.

Sally pantomimed pointing a gun at him. "We have ways of making you talk."

"I'm scared," he replied to her left cheek. She worried a zit had sprung up.

Maryam laughed. "You guys are totally made for each other."

Sally felt a flush of excitement that what she was thinking had just been spoken aloud. "Maryam, look! They have five-layer dip." Sally gave her a little wave. "*Your favorite.*" Maryam glowered and walked off.

"It involves finding the value in a spread," Jeremy was saying. "Even a half-point discrepancy—especially if it's a valuable half point from three to three and a half—can be statistically significant." It took Sally a second to realize he was still talking about his betting system.

For a geek. That's what Maryam must have meant: he's actually kind of cute *for a geek.* Jeremy had perfect posture. His chin was tucked in, as if to create an extra half-inch distance between himself and the world. He had pale skin and lots of sandy hair, with no signs of balding. He looked slender under a crumply button-down and wide-wale cords. It was a good start, something Sally could work with. "I think it's so amazing you work at the *LA Times,*" she said.

"I work at home. I've only been to Spring Street once."

"Even better! Working at home!"

"Gee. Everything makes you happy," he said.

"I guess I'm just one of those types of people."

"I've never heard of the type who is happy one hundred percent of the time."

"Try me."

"That would require spending every day and night with you."

A joyous "Aah—" was all that came out.

A dumpy, unattractive woman in sweatpants butted in. "Let me know when you're ready to go," she said to Jeremy.

Sally waited for an introduction, but there was none. "Hi, I'm Sally Parry," she had to say.

"I'm Jeremy's neighbor." She had a big mole on her cheek.

"Jennifer drove me here," Jeremy said. "I don't drive."

Jeremy didn't drive here? What about Sally's plan? If he didn't drive her home, she couldn't bring him upstairs. If she couldn't bring him upstairs, she couldn't tease him. If she couldn't tease him, she couldn't send him away, flummoxed and erect. This was a four-alarm disaster! "That's so fascinating!" Sally squealed. "I wish I had a neighbor to chauffeur me!"

"There you go again," he said. "Happy about everything."

"Whatever," Jennifer said. "I'm ready when you are."

"I'm having fun," he said to Jennifer. "Do you mind staying?"

The neighbor girl looked Sally up and down. Sally stood her ground with confidence. Jennifer turned to Jeremy. "Let me know when you're ready. I have to get up early."

Sally had to think fast. Jeremy was totally flirting with her, but were just five minutes face-to-face enough for him to ask her out? This blind date had taken three whole months to maneuver. Sally had only six weeks before Jeremy became a TV star. She grabbed his hand. "Come with me."

VIOLET found David in the bathroom, flossing his teeth in his boxers. At forty-six, his physique was as good as when Violet had first met him.

"Pick a number," he said. Floss hung from either side of his mouth, like a brontosaurus. "From one to five."

"Why?"

"Just pick one and I'll tell you if you're right."

"I don't know...."

"One to five. It isn't hard."

Violet stiffened. She had an eighty percent chance of saying the wrong thing. "Two."

"Five! That's the number of nights we sold out at the Troubadour. They played the single on KROQ. It was massive. By noon we sold out five nights."

"No kidding!" Violet said. David was legendary when it came to breaking new bands, but with the music business imploding, all the old methods were being challenged. "You're the greatest, baby!"

"You better believe it."

Violet removed her hat from the Hermès bag and cut off the

tag. Six hundred dollars. Daniel had seen it in the spring *chapeaux* catalogue and declared a "shopping emergency"—those words were actually preprinted on a slip of paper. The hat was Fed-Exed from Paris to Beverly Hills for Violet's perusal, "no obligation to buy, of course." It wasn't a great hat. But, trapped in a friendship with scented Daniel, Violet gave him the small crate of chocolates and bought it anyway.

"I met the sweetest guy today," Violet said. "A bass player."

All day Violet had been analyzing what had happened between her and Teddy. All day she had reached the same conclusion: nothing. Their meeting was purely accidental. She had made it clear she was married. She'd probably never see him again. But paying to have his car fixed was trickier to rationalize. Technically, it was David's money. But he had just given a bunch to a charity for struggling musicians. And if he did happen across the mechanic's bill—which he wouldn't, as all the bills went straight to the accountant—Violet would say she'd helped a struggling musician.

Still, as Violet kept combing over the details of her strange encounter—Teddy's soulful eyes, the way he kept repeating what she said as if she were the most mesmerizing person in the world, how safe she felt when he took her hand, how their banter made her twinkle, how she practically dared him to kiss her, the desperation she felt offering to fix his car, and the insanity as she tried to play it down—her shame intensified. She kept having to remind herself that nothing illicit had happened. No self-exculpation was necessary. If it were, would she be telling her husband?

"He was playing at a health fair," she added. "I helped him get his car fixed."

"I'm going to get Tara McPherson to do some artwork for the Troubadour shows," David said. He shot antiplaque rinse into his mouth and swished it around.

"That's a great idea." Violet stepped into the closet. She quickly changed into her pajamas while David was occupied with his teeth, to ensure he wouldn't see her naked. "Oh," she said, emerging from the closet, "I sent Sally a belt from Hermès. One of those orange ones with the H buckles. It's a bit arriviste for me, but she likes that kind of thing."

"I'll get Tara to do some T-shirts for the guys at KROQ," David said. "They did me a real solid playing that single."

Violet felt a pang every time David ignored what she said. In a college psych book, she once read that conversations were like contracts between people. Everyone would prefer to talk *all* the time, but if they did, the person they were talking to would lose interest and end the conversation. Therefore, in order to keep talking, a person had to stop talking and listen to the other person. Then, and only then, could they continue talking themselves. At the time, Violet had found it cynical. But after sixteen years of marriage, what she would give! She didn't expect David to genuinely care about a person she'd helped, or a present she'd bought for his sister, but he could at least act as if he cared. One time, as an experiment, Violet had decided to only listen to what he said and never bring anything up about herself. After a couple of days, he grew depressed and became hostile toward her. Still, he had never asked a single question about her day or how she was. Violet had secured her proof that he was a selfish asshole, but she felt terrible to have been responsible for any strife. The whole thing taught her to every day volunteer something about herself. Even knowing it would be met with indifference.

Violet put on her new hat.

"Hey, look at you in that hat," David said. "What a cutie you are." He blew her a kiss in the mirror and headed off to bed.

JEREMY didn't protest as Sally led him to the bedroom and shut the door. "Do you have to use the restroom?" he asked.

That's what was so weird about the way he spoke, Sally realized.

His voice had no inflection. She was about to change that, and how. She took the beer out of his hand and set it on the dresser.

"Forgive me," she said, "but there's something I have to do." She kissed him. He stood there with frozen eyes. She kissed him again.

This time he puckered back with a loud "Mmwwaa." *Mmwwaa* was the sound your grandmother made when she kissed you. Sally tickled his lips with her tongue, caught an opening between his teeth, and wedged them apart. She went in for a slow, sensual kiss. His tongue flapped wildly in her mouth. "Mmwwaa." He pulled his head back and wiped the saliva off his face. "What?" He was breathing heavily. "What do you have to do?"

"Make love." Sally kissed him again and undid his top button.

"Here?" His voice cracked.

"That's right." She walked him to the foot of the bed and pushed him onto the mountain of purses and coats. She straddled him with straight legs to showcase her flexibility. He grabbed her ass. She gave him a few seconds to register the firmness of her glutes. She slalomed her tongue up his cheek to his ear, then recoiled when she hit something synthetic. Weird, he had earplugs in. "Take off your pants," she whispered. She climbed off the bed and locked the door. When she turned around, his tighty-whities were nestled in his cords at his ankles. Everything about him was reedy and pale: his dick, his thighs, his pubic hair.

Sally unwrapped her dress, appreciating how sexy it must look as it poured onto the floor. Because of her firm, small breasts, she could get away with going braless. In thong and heels, she sashayed toward Jeremy in big pronounced steps. (It was a walk she had learned at a bridal shower years ago, where a stripper had been hired to give the girls lessons.) In one move, Sally slipped one leg out of her underwear and raised her turned-out leg so her foot was next to Jeremy's waist. Not something he got the pleasure of seeing every day, she was sure of that. He grabbed a breast in each hand and pulsed them. She smiled once, then again to mask a wince. The last thing Sally needed was for Jeremy to come before they made love, which she knew was a serious possibility. Therefore, she couldn't risk licking or even touching his penis. She wanted them to come together this time, their first time, for the romance.

"You turn me on so much," she said. "I swear, I think I might come as soon as you stick it in me." She picked up his dick, now thick and vanilla, like a Twinkie, and lowered herself onto it. Jeremy's eyes rolled back in his head. She knew it—he was coming! She let out a yelp and faked it, "Jeremy! Jeremy!" He closed his eyes and gulped. "Oh God," she said. "Did you come, too?"

"Yes." His eyes were still closed.

Sally rolled onto her side and covered her face with her hands. "I'm so embarrassed."

His eyes flew open, but he didn't look over.

"I've never done that before," she said. "I bet you do that to all the girls, naughty boy."

"Do what?" His eyes moved across the ceiling, as if he were counting the white cork tiles.

"Drive the girls crazy with your statistics."

"No girl has ever done that to me." Jeremy pulled his pants up and shuddered, as if the cheapness of what happened had just penetrated him. He fixed his eyes on the floor.

Sally could tell she was losing him. They had both partaken in the desperate act of a middle-aged woman in a Marina del Rey condo. She was lying naked, a stranger's sperm dripping out of her onto someone's jean jacket. All because she had played it wrong too many times before. The married travel agent who didn't leave his wife for her like he had promised; the Pepperdine law student who had moved in with her for two years, then dumped her the day he passed the bar for some paralegal who "was a better fit intellectually"; the would-be garment king who had talked her into bankrolling his leather jacket business, then dumped her, along with twenty-six grand of credit card debt in her name.

This one Sally would play right. She pulled her knee into her chest, then twisted so her back was arched and her breasts were well showcased. A classic sexy pose, like those early shots of Marilyn Monroe, only Sally wasn't so fat. "Well, did you like it?" she purred.

"Yes."

"Don't make me do it again," she said with a tease. She didn't want a big wet spot on her dress. She grabbed something from the bed and cleaned herself off. Whoops. It was Maryam's scarf. Sally kicked it under the bed and got dressed.

There was a knock on the door. The knob rattled. Sally ignored it. "Would you like to do it again sometime?" she asked.

"Yes." Jeremy patted his pockets. Sally could relax: he wanted a pen to write down her number.

"Sally! Jeremy! Are you in there?" It was Maryam, of course.

"Maybe we could go on a date." Sally fixed Jeremy's collar. "You could send a car to pick me up."

"That could happen." Jeremy had a sweet submissiveness that was starting to grow on her. Sally's type was usually hot guys with hot cars. Like Kurt and his white Jeep Wrangler. How she had loved driving around LA with him, her hair flapping in the wind, a Starbucks *venti* in one hand, the other clinging to the roll bar for dear life. If Don Henley had ever seen them, she was convinced he would have starred them in his next music video. Sally smiled now just remembering it.

"Sally! Are you in there?" Maryam again.

Sally grabbed her coat and swung open the door. "There you are!" she said. "Jeremy had to pee and I was just getting my coat." Sally turned. Jeremy stood in the dim light, flipping a quarter in the air, slapping it on his hand, then doing it again. He must have not found that pen after all....

"If you want a ride home," Maryam said, "we have to leave now. I'm sure my cat is peeing all over my comforter as we speak."

"God, okay. I'm ready." Sally tossed Maryam her jacket. "Here you go."

"Where's my scarf?"

"You didn't have it on when you came in," said Sally.

"But—"

"It's in the car," Sally snapped. She reached into her pocket and found the single business card she'd tucked in especially for this occasion. She slipped it to Jeremy. "Call me." She gave him a peck on the cheek.

"Mmwwaa," he said.

CHAPTER TWO

From One to Ten

THE SPLASH OF COLD WATER HELPED. AT LEAST IT WOULD MASK THE TEARS streaming down her cheeks. Violet opened her eyes and stared at herself in the mirror, something she normally took great pains to avoid. She obviously wasn't beautiful, or people would have said so. But was one feature in particular the culprit? She had big eyes, long lashes, high cheekbones, a nice-enough nose. Maybe it was her mouth. Her mouth might be too small, her lips too thin. Or was it her chin? In some pictures it looked pointy and witch-like. Violet had always wanted to know what number she'd be on a scale from one to ten. She once asked David. "Whoooaaa," he had said, "there's no right answer to that question." She promised not to get all weird on him. He relented and told her she was an eight. She thanked him for the compliment but secretly went wild with insecurity. Why just an eight? Was she really a six, and he added two to keep the peace? Would he someday leave her for a nine? God knows he was surrounded by them. Years back, when one of his bands was playing the Coliseum, Violet went to find David in his makeshift office, the production trailer. In the tiny bathroom, she saw a *Perfect Ten* magazine. It made her want to collapse.

Thump. Thump. Thump. The swift pounding of David's heels heralded a confrontation. This one promised to be a doozy. An hour ago, in the middle of their private yoga class, David had spotted the dead gopher at the bottom of the Jacuzzi. The one Violet had completely forgotten to take care of. David castigated her in front of the yoga teacher. Ten minutes later, Violet excused herself to the bathroom, and had been here ever since.

"Honey!" David entered, sweaty from yoga. "What happened? Why didn't you come back?"

"I couldn't deal with yoga today." Violet blotted her face.

David took a breath. She knew he was trying to control his temper. All she could do was wait and hope. "Shiva wanted to confirm our place at the yoga retreat next month," he said.

"I'll call her about it later." Violet opened the shower door and turned on the steam.

"Wait a second," he said. "Are you crying?"

"No, I'm fine."

"Is it the gopher?"

"No, it's—"

"What the fuck else am I supposed to do? I'm standing there trying to balance on one leg, and Shiva says pick a spot to focus on. So I look into the Jacuzzi and I see the *same dead gopher* that was there—what—two weeks ago?"

"You were right to yell," Violet said, instantly regretting it.

"Yell? I would hardly call that yelling."

"I know, I know."

"Really. Let's get Shiva on the phone and ask her if I *yelled* at you.

I was merely expressing my very authentic and justifiable shock. You said you'd take care of it *two weeks ago*. Come on, Violet, what's going on? I used to be able to rely on you."

"I'll go fish it out now." Violet headed out.

"Violet, stop." She froze in place, as if playing red-light-green-light. "Every time I come home," he said, "there's some truck in the driveway and a Mexican I've never seen before walking around scowling. Have one of *them* get the gopher out of the Jacuzzi."

Violet couldn't stand him looking at her fat ass anymore. She turned around and walked toward the shower. "Okay, I will."

David intercepted her and gave her a big hug. She stood on her tiptoes and looked into his eyes. They were so gorgeous and mournful, even when he was angry. "It's just that I trust you," he said. "When you say you're going to do something, you usually do it. I've grown to expect it from you. Remember, you're UV-A, not UV-B."

UV-B: Violet despised being called that. David's first nickname for her, Ultraviolet, was endearing. Ultraviolet had morphed into Ultra, and then UV-A. One day, many years ago, when she accidentally locked her keys in her car, Violet had jokingly referred to herself as UV-B. Even though it had originated with her, UV-B struck her as unspeakably cruel coming from her husband.

David got undressed and stepped into the steam. The door sealed shut behind him.

Violet knew she deserved this. She hadn't worked in five years. She didn't *have* to quit her job, but the hours were brutal and she had grown to despise the executives with their idiotic notes. As David had put it, she was too rich to let people dumber than she was have power over her. Plus, it was time to get serious about getting pregnant. She'd been off the pill for a year and nothing had happened. Before she resorted to in vitro, Violet decided to quit her job. A week later, driving down Mulholland, she saw an open-house sign at the bottom of a long driveway she'd always wondered about. On a lark, she went up. She got out of the car and found herself pulled up the exposed aggregate stepping-stones, through the Aleppo pines, and into a glass box on five acres overlooking Stone Canyon Reservoir. The realtor was in the yard talking to a client, so Violet walked through the house alone. It was as if a benevolent force guided her from room to room. Violet had been in a few Richard Neutra houses before and knew instinctively that this was his and arguably one of his best. The place had been neglected since the sixties and needed a ton of work. Still, she raced down the hill to David's office, alive with images of David and her living in the house, entertaining in the house, bringing their elusive baby home from the hospital to the house. Without removing his headset, David had said that if she really wanted it, she could offer full asking price. He didn't need to see it. He trusted her. She was UV-A.

How could she have foreseen that the house would be her undoing? The restoration and addition cost four times the estimate and took three times as long. Overnight, Violet shape-shifted from in-demand, Emmy-winning writer to resident dunce. Every day David pummeled her with questions she couldn't know the answers to. Why didn't the electrician show up? Who scratched the brand-new floors? Why did the decorator charge twenty grand for a throw rug? How did that window get broken? Why did they deliver the wrong tile? But the house was Violet's big idea, so she stoically accepted her role as human bucket for David to vomit into. In addition to the daily drubbings, she was paying for the remodel with her own money and ended up burning through her entire savings. When they finally moved in, Violet was pregnant and, for the first time in her life, unemployed and without a penny to her name. David had no reaction to the news that she'd need to start sending her bills to his accountant. She knew it was a fair trade. Lots of women would gladly get called a dumb fuck a couple times a week in exchange for not having to work.

Steam hissed from the cracked shower door. "Ultra?" David stuck his head out. "Aren't you coming in?"

"One second." Violet opened the medicine cabinet and lifted the colorful Venetian glass votive they'd gotten on their honeymoon, crammed tight with Q-tips. Underneath was the business card she couldn't throw away but hadn't dared touch.

TEDDY REYES
BASS PLAYER

Violet closed the cabinet door and gave her face a hard look. Her skin was holding up well. From one to ten, she'd give herself a seven, with room for improvement.

CHAPTER THREE

SALLY WAS FOUR BLOCKS FROM JEREMY'S BUILDING WHEN SHE STARTED LOOKING for a parking space. His street was nothing but apartments, which meant there was never any place to park. It made Sally want to scream. She trolled the endless stretch of crammed cars and had to remind herself: when Jeremy became a giant TV star and they were married and living in Beverly Hills, she'd be *nostalgic* for the days she fretted over finding a parking space in the valley.

A car pulled out—smack in front of Jeremy's building! Sally gunned it and waved to the exiting Cadillac. The old boat had left so much room that Sally was able to glide right in, headfirst, without having to go into reverse even once. She turned off the ignition, then thought of something: if this was her one allotment of good luck for the day, did she really want to waste it on a parking space? Maybe she should park somewhere else. A car pulled up alongside her. The driver gave Sally an exasperated are-you-staying-or-are-you-going look and threw up her hands. That settled it. No way was Sally going to gift this biotch with a primo parking space. She pulled the key out of the ignition.

In Jeremy's courtyard, she came upon the mailman sorting mail. "Apartment Two G?" she asked. "I'll take that." She plucked Jeremy's bundle and rolled off the rubber band. Bulk mail coupons, a reminder from his dentist, a Visa bill—Sally felt a pang at the mere sight of a boyfriend's Visa bill.

Once, during the final throes of her relationship with Kurt, she had steamed open his Visa bill. Orders for the leather jackets weren't coming in as expected, and Sally had been forced to take out a second credit card to pay off the first. Then one day, lo and behold, Kurt—whose signature look was vintage Hawaiian shirts—traipsed out of the bedroom wearing a new one. "Where did that come from?" she asked. "I've had it forever," he said, rattling the pen cup for the black Sharpie he used to paint his gray hairs. "Well, why haven't I seen it before?" "Maybe you weren't looking." After Kurt left for work, Sally ransacked their wastebaskets and even the big cans in back to find proof he'd recently bought the shirt, but came up empty. Then his Visa bill appeared in the mail. She steamed it open and discovered an eighty-five-dollar charge from Wasteland, his favorite vintage-clothing store. She drove to the boot shop where he worked and confronted him. But he totally turned it around and used this "invasion of privacy" as his basis to dump her!

Sally tucked Jeremy's Visa bill into his other mail and knocked on 2G.

Jeremy opened the door. "You don't have to knock," he said. "You have a key."

"I know." She gave him a big kiss. "I just don't want to barge in on anything."

"There's nothing to barge in on. You've already seen me naked."

Sally laughed. "You're so sweet. Here's the mail."

"How was your class this morning?"

"I had forty-five people," Sally said. "They were spilling next door into the hip-hop class. My manager couldn't believe it."

"That's really great," he said. He tried to shut the door, but it caught on his shoe. Sally wished he'd get rid of those clunky docksiders with the gigantic gummy soles. But he had resisted her attempts to make him over. She finally had to resort to stuffing his *really* geeky clothes between his mattress and box spring. Unfortunately, the dumb shoes were too bulky to hide. Maybe if they went to a shoe store together, Sally could innocently suggest he try on some cross-trainers....

"Hey, I need some new sneakers," she said. "After lunch maybe we could drive to that running store."

"I write my column after lunch."

As if she hadn't noticed! Every day, Jeremy woke up, read two newspapers, ate his breakfast, checked his sports websites, walked to Hamburger Hamlet for lunch, came home, wrote his column, then walked to El Torito and watched sports at a corner table while he ate a cheese quesadilla. Yes, it was boring. On the upside, Sally didn't have to spend her whole life driving around to check if he really was where he said he was.

"Of course *after* you write your column, silly."

There was a knock. It was Jeremy's friend Vance, who joined them for lunch every Wednesday.

"Surprise, surprise," she said.

Vance had been Jeremy's roommate at Cal Poly Pomona. An inveterate gambler, Vance would drag Jeremy to Santa Anita, where he had discovered Jeremy's genius at handicapping horses. It was

Vance who had persuaded a friend at the *LA Times* to give Jeremy a column.

"You're three minutes late," Jeremy said to Vance.

"I know. Traffic." Vance winked at Sally. Not a lascivious wink, but in shared appreciation of Jeremy.

The trio walked down Van Nuys Boulevard, Jeremy working himself up about the upcoming NCAA tournament while Vance listened. Sally could understand why, when it was just Jeremy and her, he did all the talking about sports. The odd thing was, even when Jeremy was with someone who shared his interest in sports, he still did all the talking. And so loudly, at that. She wished he'd stop wearing earplugs.

They passed the usual line of people waiting to get into a hole-in-the-wall falafel place. "Hey, guys!" Sally called ahead. "I want to try this place for a change."

She entered the tiny restaurant, put her warm-up jacket on the only empty table, then went back outside to stand in line. Jeremy and Vance weren't there. To her astonishment, she spotted them across Ventura, heading into Hamburger Hamlet. Without her! Sally went to the corner and shouted across the boulevard. "Jeremy!"

He stopped and turned.

"Didn't you hear me? I want to eat here."

"I always go to Hamburger Hamlet," he shouted back. The signal invited him to WALK across the street, but he stayed on the curb.

"I know that!" she yelled over the crossing pedestrians. "But I want to try someplace new."

"Okay," he said. "We'll be at Hamburger Hamlet."

"Jeremy!" she screamed.

"Do you need money?" he asked.

"I have money! I thought we were going to have lunch *together*."

"Me, too," he said. "But you want to go to lunch by yourself."

Jeremy turned and walked inside Hamburger Hamlet. Vance ran through the blinking DON'T WALK sign.

"Falafel is a great idea," he told her. "Let's go."

"I don't want to have lunch with you!"

Vance looked as if he was formulating something to say, then sucked in his lips. "Okay, then." He crossed the street and disappeared into Hamburger Hamlet.

Sally felt as if she might faint. What was happening? It didn't make sense. She and Jeremy had been going out three whole weeks, and he still hadn't said "I love you." And now this? Didn't Jeremy realize he'd never do better than Sally? She was thin—and sweet! She was a dancer! Why wasn't he terrified of letting her get away? She didn't understand. It literally left her dizzy. She braced herself against a lamppost.

The first time she had felt this way, she was three and David was reading her *Goodnight Moon*. They bid goodnight to the various things in the room. "Goodnight kittens / And goodnight mittens. Goodnight mush / And goodnight to the old lady whispering 'hush.'" Then, they turned the page and it was blank. The words read "Goodnight nobody." What did that mean? How did you say goodnight to *nobody*? Was *nobody* in the room with them now? After David put her to bed, would *nobody* still be there? That night, Sally couldn't sleep, imagining *nobody* settling in, breathing up all her air; not knowing if, at any moment, *nobody* would swallow her up.

Not knowing. It was the one thing Sally couldn't tolerate. Then something occurred to her: she had a way of finding out.

She let go of the post, retrieved her warm-up jacket from the restaurant, and headed back to Jeremy's apartment. She only had forty-five minutes until they returned. She decided to run.

VIOLET arrived at Kate Mantilini before one so she could score a booth. The busboy brought some of their fabulous sourdough bread. A week ago, Violet would have slathered it with butter and wolfed down the entire half loaf. But not today. Today she was flying. Today she was meeting Teddy. Her pulse raced. She felt utterly relaxed. This was where she belonged, right here, sitting in this booth, waiting for him.

The glass door opened. Through the sea of waiting people flashed pieces of Teddy. He made his way to the hostess and said something. She threw back her long, flat hair and laughed. Violet waved, but couldn't tell if Teddy saw her. He wore lopsided mirrored sunglasses that were too big for his face. Violet waved again. Teddy leaned in to the hostess and whispered. She whispered back. Teddy lifted his shirt. His stomach was a rich brown, with a treasure trail of dark hair running from his belly below the waist of his pants. The hostess slapped Teddy's hand and giggled. Violet sprang to her feet, but the edge of the thick table rammed her gut. She waved both hands. Finally, Teddy surveyed the room and spotted her. He stuffed his pockets with mints and toothpicks and pointed Violet out to the hostess, who shoved him on his way.

Violet got her first clean look at her lunch date. His hair was unbrushed. He wore a sleeveless cowboy shirt, long black sweat shorts, and…huaraches. His shirt had fresh threads hanging from the armholes, as if he'd ripped off the sleeves on the car ride over. Violet had picked this bustling showbiz watering hole because there might be people she knew here, as if to prove there was nothing sneaky about her rendezvous. But as Teddy neared, her terror grew. What if someone she knew *did* see her with this motley character? She needed an alibi: he could be a friend of a friend—who wanted to break into TV—who had just gotten out of rehab—and couldn't afford clothes—it was charity work for the Writers Guild Foundation—mentoring at-risk minorities—

"I figured out about you." Teddy slid into the booth across from her. "You're a Deadhead who took some really good acid, and your life is now one big magical hallucination."

Violet caught that Goodwill whiff again. "I'll think about that," she said, breathing through her mouth. A waitress passed carrying plates of food. Violet practically yelled, "Hi! We're in a hurry!"

"What can I get you to drink?" asked the waitress.

"Some codeine cough syrup," Teddy said.

"If we had any," the waitress replied, "it would be long gone by now."

"Don't I know it." Teddy held up his hand. The waitress transferred the plates to one arm and high-fived him.

"I'll have an iced tea," Violet said flatly.

"Make that two." Teddy watched the waitress leave, then stretched his arms across the back of the booth. "So, Baroness, what brings you here?"

"How's your car driving?"

"Fucking awesome. You have no idea what it's like for me to not have to worry about it breaking down."

"Your mother never taught you to write thank-you notes?"

"I had no way to get in touch with you."

"The mechanic knows my phone number and address. You could have asked him."

"Wow," Teddy said. "You really wanted to be thanked, didn't you?" His hair was ripe with grime and flecks that shimmered pink and blue under the hot halogen bulbs.

"I'm just saying it's kind of white trash of you."

"I'm the only thing worse than white trash," Teddy said. "Half-Mexican white trash."

Violet found herself smiling.

"You totally did miracle me," Teddy said. "I have no idea how I can ever repay you."

"One day you're going to have to step up."

"Shit," Teddy said with a twitch. "What does that mean?"

"I'm not sure," she answered. "It doesn't necessarily have to be with money. At some point, you'll just step up and do the right thing. When the time comes, you'll know."

"You mean like one day I'll have to drive you to the airport?"

"Oh, it's going to be a lot more than a ride to the airport."

The hostess led several black people to a table. Teddy waited for them to pass, then leaned in. "You know what I ask myself when I see niggers eating in a place like this?"

Violet quickly looked around to make sure nobody had heard. "I hope you ask yourself, Why do I keep using that word?"

"I know," he said. "It's bad. But when I was a junkie, that's who I'd hang around with. Everything was, nigger this, nigger that. I was living on the streets, so I was lower than a nigger. I forget I'm not there anymore."

"On behalf of Emily Post? Try keeping it to a minimum."

"Yes, ma'am."

"Thank you. Now, you were saying...."

"You want to know what I think when I see niggers eating in a place like this?"

Violet buried her smile in her hands and peered up. "You seemed determined to tell me."

"I think, How did they get this kind of money?"

"Money? This place is just for assistants and development girls."

"Gee, thanks a lot for the invite!" He laughed.

Violet studied him. "Do you have a girlfriend?"

"Yeah. I have this crazy girlfriend who I'm about to break up with. She's a performance artist. Her name's Coco." Teddy raised his eyebrows and added, "Coco *Kennedy*."

"Of the Hyannisport Kennedys?"

"Of the John-John Kennedys. He was her cousin."

It all clicked for Violet: her attraction to Teddy *wasn't* an aberration. He was objectively charming and desirable: to the hostess, to the waitress, even to American royalty. Coco Kennedy most likely had a plethora of glamorous suitors, yet she chose Teddy. "Really? A Kennedy?"

"Don't tell me you're obsessed with John-John, too?" he said.

"I met him a few times in New York, like everybody did. But I'd hardly consider myself obsessed."

"Good. Because I would barf if someone classy like you fell for those Kennedy poseurs."

"I'm not sure the first word that comes to mind to describe the Kennedys is *poseurs*."

Teddy rolled his eyes. "Why does God keep bringing people into my life who don't see bullshit for what it is?"

"JFK was responsible for the space program and oversaw the civil rights movement. That's more than posing."

"What are you, a fucking historian?"

"My father was." The colorful and dissipated Churchill Grace. He had moved to Hollywood in the sixties and kept company with his fellow countrymen Aldous Huxley and Christopher Isherwood. *Jam Today,* his slim but prescient jeremiad against all that Americans held dear, caused a minor stir when it was published in 1965. He was able to string together writing assignments, guest professorships, and Esalen weekends until his death thirty years later. His wife, Violet's mother, left and moved to Hawaii when Violet was just a baby. Churchill's devotion to his little daughter allowed him second and third chances with friends and benefactors. But finally, booze, regret, and anger were greater than his love of Violet. She had learned of his death from one of her father's devotees. The memorial service was at Churchie's favorite watering hole, Chez Jay in Santa Monica. Violet could have imagined nobody showing up, or five hundred. Twenty people did. That was the saddest part of all.

"How's she related to the Kennedys?" Violet asked. "Through Teddy or Bobby? Aren't they the only brothers?"

"Who the fuck knows? I try not to listen." Teddy ran his hands through his hair and checked his reflection in the window, then turned to Violet. "Anyway. Miss Kennedy aborted my baby this morning in Palm Springs."

"God…"

"Yeah, well. What are you going to do?"

"Why Palm Springs?"

"That's where she grew up," he said.

"How did a Kennedy grow up in Palm Springs?"

"Jesus. What does it fucking matter? She aborted my baby!"

"I'm sorry."

"I'm waiting a couple of hours until her sister drives her home from the baby-killing center, then I'm going to call her and break up with her. It's like the fourth kid of mine a chick has aborted."

"*Like* the fourth?" asked Violet. "You've lost count?"

"Four that I know of. I'm sure there are a dozen more." Teddy poured some salt on the table. He grabbed a sugar packet and started cutting the salt into lines. "Make me a promise." He looked up. "No matter what, never let me get back together with her. Okay?"

"I promise."

The booths, that's why Violet must have picked this restaurant. She knew they would be cocooned in one of these dark booths with the high backs that shut out the rest of the world.

"You seem to do okay for yourself," she said. "Sounds like you'll be onto the next in no time."

"No nice girl will ever go out with me."

"What makes you say that?"

"I'm broke, I'm an addict who will probably use again, and I have hepatitis C."

Violet blurted, "What's hepatitis C?"

"It's the consolation prize God gives the junkies he spares from AIDS."

"Did you share needles?"

"Ha! That's the *best* thing I did when I was a junkie. I'd cook heroin on a Christmas tree ornament and shove that up my vein if it meant getting high."

"Gee," Violet said lamely.

"I guess God gives you what you can handle."

"Then God must have a low opinion of me," she said. "He's given me money, health, the easiest baby in the world, and I *still* can't deal."

"Fuck off, you can't believe that. You're a saint. You know that, right? You're like this Johnny Appleseed of joy and light. Anyone who gets to feel your love is lucky. And I don't just mean lucky. I mean *one of the lucky*. The cosmically lucky."

"Are you dying?" she asked.

"Not really." He brushed the sugar onto the floor. "Hep C fucks up your liver and eventually you die of cancer. But if I eat right I'll be okay. I just get really fucking tired sometimes."

"You know what I'd do if I found out I was dying?" Violet asked. "I'd spend my last hours smoking cigarettes and listening to Stephen Sondheim."

"What, no Percocet?"

"Percocet would ruin the Sondheim. You've got to be all there for Sondheim."

"The Grateful Dead and 'Send in the Clowns'? That's a fucked-up combo."

Violet felt a ripple of relief that Teddy knew who Stephen Sondheim was. Not so much for Teddy as for Sondheim. It always made Violet sad when people didn't know who he was. It happened surprisingly—outrageously—often.

"Are there dating groups for people with hepatitis C?" she asked.

"It's called AA," he said with a laugh.

"How are you impregnating all these girls? Don't you use condoms?"

"I hate condoms."

"Oh man. I am sorry, but that is not cool."

"The doctors say you can't catch hep C from hetero sex."

"Are you sure about that?"

"You're totally disgusted by me, aren't you? See, this is AA at work. Three years ago, I never would have said that to anyone. Now I'm all like, Hi, I'm Teddy, I'm a junkie, I have hep C, and I don't use condoms. What's your name?"

"You're certainly honest," she said. "I have to give you that."

"*Certainly*. Listen to you with your five-dollar words."

"Wait until you hear me use the word *insouciant*."

"Break me off a piece of that."

She assumed airs and said, "Your prejudice against condoms whilst infected with hepatitis C would indicate an insouciant disregard for safe sex."

The waitress had walked up. "I'll come back," she said, and pivoted away.

"Whoops," said Violet.

Teddy let loose a big, appreciative laugh, then stared into her eyes. She sunk deeper into his. Was he jaundiced? She couldn't tell. His bloodshot green eyes with the angry dark circles couldn't be considered beautiful. But they were arresting. And she couldn't look away.

"You're the one who's honest, Violet. You have this natural honesty that erupts from your heart then straight out of your mouth. I'm a manipulative junkie. Any kind of honesty I have has to be drummed into me by going to meetings every day. With you, it's pure."

Violet lolled in this gorgeous moment. Then she said, "You bring it out in me. I'm like this naturally, I suppose. But with you it's extreme."

"Jesus. I don't even know you and you're already using the word *extreme*. See what I do to people?"

"No, no, no," Violet said. "Extreme is good. We like extreme."

"No, we don't. Extreme is bad. I'm over extreme. I just want to play my music and write poetry."

"You're a poet?" Violet's heart swelled.

"Yeah, I'm always writing poetry," he said. "Poetry keeps me sane. And golf keeps me present."

"Golf?"

"I always start the day with golf. It pimp-slaps me into the here and now. There's no such thing as the past or the future when it's just you and the next shot."

Violet frowned. "I can't picture you on the links."

The waitress returned. "Have you decided?"

"Whatever she orders, I'll have the same," Teddy said. "And make it quick, because we've got somewhere to be."

SALLY already felt better. Concrete action was the only thing that worked in times like these, and here she was, taking it. The teakettle whistled. Sally held Jeremy's Visa envelope an inch over the steam. If she got one edge loose and peeled the flap from there, she'd stand a chance of not mangling this one the way she had Kurt's.

She realized this was not her finest hour, but she wouldn't have been reduced to standing here if what had happened back on the street were an isolated incident. No, a troubling pattern had formed. Jeremy always put his routine above her. He had difficulty looking her in the eye. He never shared his innermost feelings. What was he hiding? Another girlfriend? Could he be one of those men who had another secret family? Could he be opening up emotionally with his *wife*? Of course not! That's what was so maddening. Jeremy was faithful and predictable. Sally had never caught him in a lie or whispering into the phone, and his e-mails were all spam or work related. With Jeremy, what you saw was what you got.

Sally had once broached the subject with Maryam. "Compared to my other boyfriends," Sally had said, "I feel like there's something with Jeremy that's…missing." Maryam shot back, "The asshole part? If you're having problems with a guy who has a job and isn't running around on you, maybe *you're* the problem. Some girls can't be happy unless a man is treating them like garbage." Sally couldn't dismiss Maryam's analysis, as coarse as it was. Still, she didn't quite know what to make of Jeremy.

She tested the flap of the envelope. It lifted right off. She scanned the first page of the bill:

> Hamburger Hamlet
> El Torito
> Hamburger Hamlet
> El Torito
> Hamburger Hamlet
> El Torito
> Hamburger Hamlet

In case anyone didn't believe the man loved his routine! She turned to the second page.

> El Torito
> Hamburger Hamlet
> El Torito
> Hamburger Hamlet
> El Torito
> Cabot & Sons
> Hamburger Hamlet
> El Torito
> Hamburger Hamlet
> El Torito

She would have missed it if the dollar amount in the right column hadn't popped out: *$8,800.* Cabot and Sons was the jeweler just around the corner on Ventura! Sally neatly folded the bill and surrendered it to its envelope. The adhesive stuck, leaving no trace of her minor trespass.

"FOLLOW me" was all Teddy said when Violet asked where they were going. She found herself zooming along Wilshire Boulevard, lacing amid traffic, gunning through yellow lights, swerving into bus lanes—anything to keep up. The battered Mazda teased her late-model Mercedes through the Beverly Hills corridor, turned left at what was once CAA, then left again through Century City. Teddy's speed and recklessness were a throw-down, a sexual tease. Pure adrenaline, Violet was right there with him, proving herself worthy of the challenge. Approaching a red light, Teddy sharked into the left lane, as if to turn east on Pico. Violet, two cars behind, put on her blinker. But when the light turned green, Teddy lurched right. A car screeched to a stop and its engine died. Violet rammed into reverse, then drive, and stepped on the gas. She glimpsed Teddy's tail a long block ahead, sailing west, making no concessions to her. The light was green, but the walk signal a solid red. Violet was four cars back. She swerved into the right-turn-only lane and made it through the intersection. Violet neared Twentieth Century Fox. Right now, writers in smelly rooms were slogging through rewrites, eating take-out, unbuttoning the top button of their pants, putting in their order for the afternoon's coffee run, and debating where they'd order dinner. None of them had a clue that right now, Violet was airborne. She looked up. The light at Motor was red—it was too late to stop.

Fifteen years old: Violet's father drove her from the Zurich airport, up a verdant Alps road, for her first year of boarding school at Le Rosey. They entered a particularly long mountain tunnel. As they emerged from it, her father's eyes were closed. Violet screamed. "My dear," he said, in that blasé way of his, "when in the dark, it's easier to see with your eyes closed."

Now Violet closed her eyes and flew through the red light. She opened them. She had cleared the intersection unharmed. Teddy turned left into a parking lot outside Rancho Park. Just as she had thought…he was taking her golfing. Her phone rang.

"Have you arrived at the undisclosed location?" he asked.

"I'm here." Violet looked for a parking spot.

"May I draw your attention to the office building across the street."

Violet passed his car. It looked like he was taking off his shirt. "What are you doing in there?"

"Hey!" he said. "Don't look."

She found a space. "Okay, what?" she said.

"My ex-wife, Vanessa, used to work there while I stayed home smoking crack. And I wanted to fuck her, so I'd call her at work every five minutes saying, When-are-you-coming-home-when-are-you-coming-home-when-are-you-coming-home? She was busy, so I just sat on the couch all day, smoking crack and watching *Sanford and Son*."

"Come on. *Sanford and Son*?"

"You didn't love *Sanford and Son*?"

"I never saw it," she said. "I was at Le Rosey."

"What you say?"

"Forget it. Okay, I'm parked. Where do I go now?"

"Stay right where you are," said Teddy. "So there I was, out of my mind on crack, wanting to fuck my wife for sixty-five hours straight, but she was in a meeting all afternoon. And see that Jewish synagogue next door? Well, they were all worried about terrorist threats because it was right after September eleventh." There was considerable grunting coming from the other end of the phone.

"What are you doing?" Violet got out and walked toward his car, looking down.

"Stop. Hang on a second." After a long pause, Teddy resumed.

"Okay. Anyway, I wanted Vanesa to come home, so I called up the lobby of the building and said there's a bomb. And they evacuated like a mile of Pico. Everyone who worked up and down here was out on the sidewalk."

"Jesus! I remember that. I was working at Fox. It was after lunch, right? I was off the lot and couldn't get back on."

"Yeah! They evacuated the movie studio, too."

"That was you? You could have been arrested for calling in a bomb threat. That's a federal offense."

"See how far I'll go for the love of a woman?"

"I should be mortified to be having a conversation with you."

"But you're not," he said. "You think it's rad."

"It's pretty rad."

"Ha-ha. I just got you to use the word *rad*."

"It was my first time," Violet admitted.

"Okay, you can look." Teddy had changed into long black pants, a short-sleeved black knit shirt, and the black-and-white golf shoes. Topping it off was a straw porkpie hat. He leaned against a golf bag and had one of the toothpicks from the restaurant sticking out the side of his mouth. It was hard not to love him, standing there, jaunty and confident.

"Dress more like that," she said.

"Oh man. You don't get it."

Violet walked toward him, still talking on their cell phones. "Frayed clothes?" she said. "Who doesn't get it?"

"Maybe I get it on a whole other level that you don't."

"We can stipulate that. All I'm saying is this is one natty look."

"Who you calling natty?" Teddy barked, as Red Foxx. "And whatchyou doing wasting my minutes, woman?"

Violet snapped her phone shut. "Hey, look." A BMW had pulled into the space next to hers, about five cars down. A plump man had squeezed out and was writing something in the dirt on her window.

"What's he doing?" asked Teddy.

L-E-A-R-N T-O, the hothead spelled in the dirt. *Learn to park,* probably," Violet said. "The car next to me was parked over the line, so I had to park over the line, too." Indeed, the next word was P-A-R-K.

"There's more," said Teddy. They watched, side by side, Teddy leaning into Violet's arm. It was all she could do to concentrate on the man finishing his sentence: Y-O-U D-U-M-B A-S-S-H-O-L-E.

"That's amazing," Violet said. "Not only did he know I'm an *asshole,* but a *dumb* asshole, too!"

The guy got his golf clubs out of his trunk and stomped off. Teddy stormed over to Violet's car and wiped the words off the window. "That's not right," he said, blackening. "Hacker with his brand-new Pings." Teddy returned to his car, Violet at his heels.

"Once," she said, "I worked on a show on the Radford lot, and my parking spot was outside the *Seinfeld* writers' offices. They got so traumatized by my dirty car, which they had to stare at all day, that they wrote all over it 'Eat more meat, I love chicken.' Because I'm a vegetarian and they knew it was the only way to get me to wash my car."

"What a fucking hard-on," Teddy muttered. "I'll meet him on the dance floor." He pulled a ratty putter from his golf bag, then opened his trunk and threw the rest of the clubs back in. He choked the putter and headed toward the clubhouse, a wild look in his eye.

WHERE would it be? Sally had already scoured Jeremy's dresser, medicine cabinet, and jacket pockets. She pulled open his bedside drawer, which was filled with loose earplugs and scraps of paper scrawled with variations of "H-H-H-T-T-T-H." Jeremy had a habit of flipping a coin, then marking down if it was heads or tails. To what purpose, she had no idea. Why he kept them, still no idea.

Sally sifted through the fluff and shuddered: it was like running her fingers through the bottom of a hamster cage. She returned to the living room and opened his desk drawer.

There it sat, a pink velvet cube. She cracked it. Inside was a diamond ring. She opened it all the way. Her spirits flattened. She had always imagined nothing smaller than a four carat, and this was barely a two. Sally bucked herself up. The ring was gorgeous. Classic. Tasteful. And if anyone gave her attitude about the size, she could say it had belonged to his mother—

"Sally?"

She spun around. It was Vance. She dropped the ring box on the desk. "Vance! Hi! I thought you were at lunch!"

"I wanted to see how you were." He stepped closer.

"I'm dandy." Sally hopped up onto the desk to block his view of the ring, and closed the drawer with a calf as she twisted her legs.

"I know sometimes Jeremy can be tough. Today—the thing with lunch. Well, that's going to happen. But it's nothing personal."

"Couples disagree. It's healthy." She reached behind her, closed the ring box, and tented it with her hand.

"I know," he said. "And I'm glad you do, too. I always knew he'd find someone who appreciates him as much as I do."

"I'm an appreciator!" she said with a laugh.

Thump. Thump. Thump. Jeremy's big shoes pounded the stairs. His shadow rippled across the venetian blinds.

"Oh look, Jeremy's home!" Sally pointed. Vance turned. Sally opened the desk drawer, dropped in the ring, and slammed it shut just as the door opened. "Welcome home, my love!" she cried.

VIOLET followed Teddy through the cheesy wood-paneled clubhouse and out to the putting green. The darkness that had befallen Teddy in the parking lot was still in effect. His jaw worked the toothpick; his lion eyes scoped out the scene. Then Violet understood: the man from the parking lot was practicing his putts on the far side of the green.

"That guy thinks he can buy game," Teddy grumbled. "He doesn't have game." Teddy's animal spirits were on the rise, and Violet rose with them. He reached into his pocket and removed a ball. In one sinuous movement, he let it roll down his fingers and onto the tight grass. He gripped the putter with one hand, then the other, then snuggled both hands to form a grip on his old familiar friend. Violet caught herself staring and had to remember to breathe. She looked up. Teddy had seen her hunger. Violet waited—forever, it seemed—for him to call her on her carnal desire, to sentence her, humiliate her. Instead, he winked.

"So?" He putted the ball. He was loose, confident, unbelievably sexy. "What about you?" he said, his eyes never leaving the ball.

"What about me?" She looked around, hoping all could see that he was hers, and she, his.

"What's a rich husband doing letting you spend the afternoon with a guy like me?"

"*Letting* me?"

"No woman of mine would ever be allowed to eat at a restaurant like that with another man."

"Is that so?"

"It's my pimp nature," he said. "If you were my woman, there's no way I'd let you run around the way you do."

"It's lucky I'm not your woman," she said. "Because I don't like being told what to do."

"You would with me, though."

"I would not," she said.

"Oh, you would like it."

"I would not."

"Okay, then, you wouldn't." Teddy pointed to a hole about thirty feet away. "You think I can make it?" He hit the ball. It stopped just short.

Violet followed him to the cup. "Wait a second. You *do* realize that no guy will ever break me of my independence."

Teddy tapped the ball in and retrieved it. "I'll give you that one." He let the ball roll down his forearm, then snapped it high in the air. He spun around and caught it behind his back.

"Deal with it," said Violet. "You could never break me."

Teddy flashed a smile. "I already have." He hit his ball and called to someone, "Whoa! Look out!" His crusty ball knocked into a gleaming one, causing it to ricochet off course.

"What the fuck!" It was the BMW guy. He dropped his putter and glared at Teddy.

"Sorry about that, bro." Teddy made the putt.

"Are you done?" said the guy, yet to pick up his fallen club.

"I don't know." Teddy picked up the sparkling putter and returned it to its owner. "This hole is lucky for me. How about we putt for it?"

The guy picked up both balls and threw them fifteen feet away. "Happy to," he said.

"Jesus, here we go." Teddy shook his head. He putted his ball, and it swerved to the right. His rival made the shot. "Lucky shot!" cried Teddy. "Bet you a buck you can't do it again."

The guy reached into his pocket and rummaged through some bills. "All I got is a ten."

"If we're talking real money, I'll have to use your putter."

"Since when is ten bucks real money?"

"I'm not the only one playing at a public course. What, were there no tee times at Riviera?"

The guy took some phantom strokes, then lined up his shot and missed. "Fuck!"

He handed Teddy the overengineered putter.

Teddy marveled at its feel. "Sharp!"

Violet quickly looked away. The eroticism of Teddy handling another golf club was more than she could take.

Teddy putted; his ball rolled swiftly and directly into the hole.

Violet folded her hands behind her back so she wouldn't spontaneously embrace him.

Teddy plucked the ten from the guy's shirt pocket. "Thank you, ma'am." He led Violet off. "I'm going to buy you something pretty with this."

"Double or nothing," called the man.

Teddy stopped. He smiled at Violet, waited a beat, then turned on his heels. "You *do* know this time we're going to be shooting for that badass putter."

"It's an eighty-dollar Callaway."

"I'm good for the money." Teddy turned to Violet. "You got eighty bucks?"

"I got eighty bucks."

"One putt," said the man. "Eighty bucks or the putter." He went through the usual tortured deliberations and stood over his ball. Just as he was about to hit it, Teddy said, "You ever watch *The Partridge Family*?"

"What?" asked the man.

"I used to love that show when I was a kid. Especially the end, where Keith would sing the song. Then, one night, I'm sitting there watching the one where they all go to SeaWorld. And at the end, the mom starts walking around Shamu's tank, singing a love song about *whales*. The song ends, and I'm waiting for Keith to start singing, you know, the *real song* with his brothers and sisters. Then you know what happens?"

"What?"

"The show ends," Teddy said. "That was the song! The mother singing to a goddamned whale!"

"What's your point?" asked the man.

"It's just fucked up, is all."

The man took his shot.

As the ball swerved right, Teddy said, "Yippee kay yay!" The man hurled his club to the ground.

It was Teddy's turn. He picked up the putter, then stood over the ball. He turned his head to either side to loosen up his neck. He took an exaggerated backstroke, froze, then looked up at Violet. "This one's for you, baby." He hit the ball. Violet locked eyes with Teddy. Her father, her education, her husband, her career, motherhood, it all molted away. For this, Violet had driven through red lights, eyes closed. She looked. Teddy didn't have to. His ball was rattling in the cup.

"Jesus fuck me!" cried the man. He wheeled his bag away. "Fucking hustler."

Teddy turned to Violet. "Jesus fuck me? I'll have to remember that one." He handed Violet the club. "My gift to you, Baroness."

"In other words, you *do* know how to play golf."

"I shoot low seventies. When I was a kid, I spent all day on the links. My uncle was a greenskeeper at a public course and got me on the Junior Circuit. I placed top ten in enough tournaments to earn a golf scholarship to USC."

"I didn't know you went to SC." Violet sat down on a bench. "What did you major in?"

"I only lasted a semester. Not even. Couldn't deal with all those rich assholes. By Thanksgiving I was shooting up every day and stopped showing up for classes."

"But you could play professionally now, right? I mean, what was that?" She pointed to the putting green.

"That, my friend, was hustling." Teddy stood with one foot on the bench beside her. "That guy, I watched him. He's probably not a bad player. But when I asked him to putt me for the hole, everything about him changed. Sure, he made the shot, but I could tell he was feeling the heat. You want me to drop some science on you?"

"Go ahead, drop some science."

"When there's something on the line, when there's real heat, I play better than my abilities. Good players, even world-class sticks, can't do that."

"Can I just say, that was one of the coolest things I've ever experienced. And this from someone who saw the Clash at Bonds in '81."

Teddy took a seat beside her. Their legs touched, and stayed touched. "Do you have any idea what you've done to me?" he asked.

Violet braced herself. What he said next would lock them into a marvelous adventure, their future together, with Teddy calling the shots. "What?" she asked.

"Do you know what I'm going to spend all night doing?"

"Tell me."

"A tenth-step inventory."

"A…what?"

"An inventory. The tenth step: 'continued to take personal inventory and when we were wrong promptly admitted it.'"

"But—you didn't drink."

"You don't have much experience with alcoholics, do you?"

"My father was a drunk and died from it, if that's what you mean." Teddy threw his head back and laughed. Violet couldn't help but be charmed by such a wildly inappropriate reaction. "Thanks for the sympathy."

"I'm sorry. People like me and people like you…" Teddy trailed off.

"What?"

"We don't mix. Or, should I say, we mix way too well."

"Well, which is it?" she asked.

There was a long silence. "Hey, wanna see my track marks?" He held out his arm. There were some candle drips of scar tissue on the inside of his elbow. "First thing, when I meet people?" he said. "I check to see if they have track marks."

"That seems a bit self-defeating, doesn't it?"

"Meh?"

"You're clean now," she said. "You're living an honorable life. That kind of thinking just perpetuates the junkie mentality, which you've clearly outgrown."

"You may not believe it, but there are a few things I may be smarter about than you, Miss Violet."

She ran her finger along his track marks. Teddy lifted her dark glasses and looked into her eyes. She smiled. "What?" he asked. "What are you thinking?"

"I'd like to kiss you," she said.

"That probably wouldn't be cool, though." Teddy shuddered and scooched away.

"Oh—" Violet's hand was stranded in the air. She tucked it under her leg.

"Don't worry about it." He was plastered to the far side of the bench.

Violet had to get away before the skin on her face peeled off from her scorching humiliation. "I've got to get home." She stood up.

"Where do you live?" Teddy asked idly.

"Excuse me?"

"Where's home?" It was true! He hadn't a clue that he had just driven their budding affair into the ground. And with it, any hope of friendship.

"Up on Mulholland, with my husband and child."

"Who's your husband?"

"His name is David Parry." Violet waited for the inevitable.

"Holy shit! David Parry, the Ultra Records guy?" There it was, the inevitable. The intellectuals had this reaction when they found out who her father was. Most others had it for her husband.

"So you've heard of him."

"No fucking way! Ultra has the sickest jazz catalog. Ray Charles, Stan Getz, John Coltrane."

"Yep," Violet said. "Back in 2001, David saw into the future that the kids and every generation thereafter wouldn't pay for music. So he set about buying publishing catalogues and jazz labels. Old people's music. He's done quite well." It felt good, sticking it to Teddy with David's accomplishments.

"But he's also a big rock-and-roll manager."

"Yes, David is the star."

"Fuck. I can't believe David Parry's wife just tried to kiss me!"

"I've got to go to the market. David said he wanted pasta for dinner." Violet fished the keys from her pocket.

"I'm fucking depressed," Teddy said.

Her heart leapt: had he already regretted letting the moment pass? Would he try to win her back? "I'd give anything for a home-cooked meal," he said.

"Here's your putter. Sell it for gas money." Violet checked her watch. It was four o'clock. She could easily make it to the market and get dinner on the table by the time David returned home. She walked off, with a lightness to her step, immensely relieved that her abasement, though grotesque, was so short-lived.

FIRST people said "I love you," *then* they get engaged. It was this sequence of events Sally pondered as she sat in the teetering forest of shoe boxes stacked from floor to ceiling. She had already picked out some cross-trainers for herself. (That was ninety-five dollars she'd never see again!) Now it was time for the true purpose of the foray....

"Hey," she said to Jeremy. "While we're here, maybe *you'd* like some new shoes!"

"I already have these."

"I think you need some new ones," volunteered the marathon-running hippie who had been helping Sally. He had long hair, leathery skin, and an emaciated body. He looked like someone who'd been stranded on a desert island. "See how you're over-pronating your right foot?" The castaway pointed to the sole of Jeremy's gigantic docksider, which had, in fact, worn out at the inner heel.

Jeremy studied it. Sally liked where this was going. Her best strategy was to hang back and let the castaway fight this battle for her. "But these shoes are perfectly comfortable," Jeremy said.

"*Now,* maybe," said the castaway. "But if you don't get some stability in that right heel, you're looking down the barrel of a lifetime of heel spurs, plantar fasciitis, and shin splints. If you're lucky."

"Really?" Jeremy said.

"Absolutely. What size are you?"

"Ten," Sally said. The castaway disappeared into the back. She called after him, "Make sure they're dark! With dark soles!"

I love you. How would Sally get Jeremy to say the words? He was a man of habit. Saying "I love you" wasn't part of his habit.

He took a quarter out of his pocket and started flipping it. "Do you have a pen?" he asked.

"I love you!" Sally said, mortified at what had just squirted out of her mouth. "I mean—"

Jeremy looked at her. "Me, too."

"What—you do?"

"Of course I do."

"Well, when were you going to tell me?"

"I thought it was obvious."

This was all too odd and fabulous. But Sally couldn't rest. Jeremy still hadn't said the words. "You thought *what* was obvious?"

"I love you."

She gave him a shove. "You are *such a guy!* Do you realize how much of a guy you are?"

"Yes."

"Jeremy?"

"Sally?"

"Does it scare you?" She took his hand. "Our love?"

"No."

"I'm not scared, either."

"You shouldn't be," he said. "Real love, like the kind we have, is hard to find. We should be happy."

Sally's heart swelled with tenderness. It filled this cluttered little store, bursting through the wall, spilling out into Encino, and expanding up into the heavens. Everything that just moments earlier had annoyed her—the sun blisters on the castaway's cheekbones, the turned-over shopping cart blocking the good parking space, the drizzle that had started out of nowhere and would cause her hair to frizz—all of it was dissolving fabulously skyward.

Jeremy got a pen from the counter and fished out a piece of paper from the trash. He flipped his quarter several times and wrote out the results. T-H-T-T-T-H-H-T.

An image came to Sally, something she remembered from childhood. It was from the Carl Sagan series *Cosmos*, something called Flatland. Flatland was this two-dimensional world where everything was flat, even the Flatlanders who lived there. They could only perceive left and right, front and back, but no above or below. One day, a potato flew over from another dimension— really, Carl Sagan had said it was a potato—and this potato looked down and said, "Hello." The Flatlanders couldn't see it because it was hovering over them and they had no up or down. And when the potato entered their two-dimensional world, all the Flatlanders were able to see was this weird changing potato slice appearing from nowhere. It totally blew their minds because they had no concept this other dimension even existed. Then, when the potato went home and the Flatlanders who witnessed it tried to explain it to their friends, they couldn't. Because they literally didn't have words for it. Jeremy's "I love you" was like the potato materializing out of nowhere. Sally realized she had been living in a world where love equaled scheming, second-guessing, and game playing. Now she understood that there was a whole other dimension where love simply...*was.*

The castaway returned with a pair of dark brown hiking boot–sneakers with black soles.

Jeremy put them on and stood up. He smiled and turned to Sally. "These are more comfortable than any shoes I've ever worn," he said. "Thanks for making me come here."

Sally caught a glimpse of the two of them in a mirror. Jeremy and Sally. Sally and Jeremy. How she loved Jeremy, the kind genius. And how she loved that she loved a kind genius. And how she loved that the kind genius would no longer be galumphing around in those awful shoes.

VIOLET crawled up traffic-clogged Benedict Canyon, the words "I can't believe David Parry's wife just tried to kiss me" strangling her brain. Back at Whole Foods, she had to ask someone three times where the capers were, when she had been staring straight at them. She had to pull it together before she got home. What was she thinking asking Teddy to lunch? She'd never had an affair. If she did, it would certainly be with some genius rock star like Thom Yorke, not *Teddy Reyes.* She sat in traffic, her embarrassment so visceral she felt as if she were about to suffocate. She rolled down the windows. Her cell phone rang.

"It got pretty intense back there, didn't it?" It was him.

"It really didn't."

"Do you have Sprint?" Teddy asked.

"I don't know."

"You don't know? What do you mean, you don't know?"

"I don't concern myself with such things. We have people for that," she said, pleased with how haughty she just sounded. "What's it to you?"

"You're so fucking rich," he said. "I can talk for free to people who have Sprint. That's why."

"Do you work for them?" she asked.

"Do I work for them? It's my phone plan! What does your phone say?"

It said Sprint.

"Good," Teddy said. Without missing a beat, he started in. "How scary was that? Every time we see each other we almost fuck."

"Hardly." There was roadwork ahead. Hopefully, traffic would loosen once Violet passed it.

"I'm telling you, I'm totally hardwired for sex. Remember how you held my hand in the museum?"

"Yes." She sighed.

"After I left you, I went to the men's room in the park and jerked off."

"You did?" This was difficult for Violet to imagine. Twenty years ago, maybe. But after sixteen years of marriage,? And that stomach! A few weeks after giving birth, Violet had been taking a shower and accidentally ran her hand over it and nearly shrieked at how squishy it had become. Sometimes she found herself actually tucking her stomach into her pants! What had once been an admittedly curvy body was now the shape of a troll doll, with fat showing up in the most dispiriting places, like her upper back! The thought of a stranger—a young stranger with a Kennedy for a girlfriend, no less—jerking off to that? Okay, she liked it.

"You like that, don't you?" he asked.

"Are you a sex addict?"

"I don't concern myself with such things. I have people for that." Repeating what she said, that's what made her twinkle. "What positions do you like?" he asked.

"Have we already graduated to ribaldry—if there's such a word?" A horn blared. There wasn't a car ahead of her. Violet stepped on the accelerator, rounded the bend, and caught up with traffic.

"You love this, coming down off your mountain and giving the junkie a hard-on. Tell me. What positions do you like?"

"I don't know."

"Do you like doggy style?"

"I guess."

"Say certainly."

"I certainly like doggy . . . you know."

"You know what you like even more?" he asked.

"What?"

"Getting fucked in the ass."

"I should say not! I've never had the dubious honor."

"That's such a lie," he said.

"It's true."

"Then you've got a real treat coming to you. Chicks like you who think they're in charge are the ones who love taking it up the ass the most. What's your pussy like?"

"I don't know." She rolled up the windows and checked her mirror to make sure nobody she knew was in the car behind her.

"Do you shave it?" he asked. "Is it big and hairy?"

"Big? You mean like men have big dicks?"

"Is it hairy?"

"I wax it a bit. Not too much."

"David Parry likes hairy pussies! Ha! I knew we were brothers. Ask me some questions."

"Where are you?" Violet turned a sharp corner. A cheery patchwork ball that belonged to Dot jingled under her feet. She picked it up and tossed it over her shoulder.

"What do you mean?" he asked.

"You have conversations like this while you're driving, or are you behind a tree on the back nine?"

"I'm driving," he said impatiently. "Ask me a question."

"Will you recite a poem you wrote?"

"Not that kind of question!"

"Please?"

"Hey!" he said. "I have an idea. You put me on the payroll, and I'll write poems for you."

"I can be your Maria de' Medici," she said.

"Huh?"

"You know, the Medicis of Florence. During the Italian Renaissance they were patrons of Michelangelo and everyone. Rubens did those paintings of her that are hanging in the Louvre."

"Four out of five dentists surveyed said"—Teddy went into a Red Foxx impression—"*What you just say?*"

"Never mind," said Violet.

"Don't you worry. I'll be writing plenty of poems for you, Violet." She gripped the wheel with both hands so the flood of joy wouldn't knock her car off the road. He continued, "Ask me something."

"Why are you so broke all the time when you have an obvious talent for golf? Why don't you become a golf pro?"

"Are you trying to make me lose my erection?"

"You're driving with an erection? I didn't know such a thing was possible."

"Of course it is. Oh, my fucking God, will you just ask me about my cock?"

"I don't know. What's it like?" A fuzzy lamb stared at Violet from the passenger seat. She scowled and chucked it over her shoulder. When it landed, it emitted an ugly "Ba-ah! Ba-ah!"

"What the fuck was that?" asked Teddy.

"Nothing."

"Well, what about my cock? Ask me some questions."

"Is it…big?"

"Jesus, you have a lot to learn. Ask me if it's hard. Ask me if I'm stroking it. Ask me what I want to do with it."

"Can't you at least become a caddy? They do well with tips, from what I gather."

"I've been a caddy, and it doesn't do it for me, okay? Tips! Thanks a fucking lot."

"Aren't we in high dudgeon over a perfectly reasonable suggestion? Couldn't you—you know—do what you did today with that guy for money?"

"Hustle? That's not exactly what we at Alcoholics Anonymous call 'a manner of living which demands rigorous honesty.' What we're trying to do is live the life we're meant to live, which requires a restoration of ethics and morals. My cock is waiting."

"By the way, thanks for telling me that I'm responsible for you having to do an inventory."

"Oh man!" Teddy laughed. "You should have seen your face! You looked totally…" He kept laughing.

"The word is *chagrined*."

"You totally wanted me to say I was going to jerk off to you."

"I can just hang up. You are aware that cell phone technology makes such a thing possible."

"I'm sorry. You're right. You didn't make me do anything. I'm responsible for my own actions."

"He said, as if trying to convince himself." Violet neared her house and slowed down.

"Hey, I want to apologize for not thanking you for fixing my car. You're right, that was ghetto. So, thank you."

"You're welcome."

"I just didn't know how. You don't realize how much sixteen hundred bucks is to me. I mean, the most I've ever had at one time was eight hundred dollars. I had a real job, selling sunglasses on the Venice boardwalk. And one day a bus of Japanese tourists gets out and buys my entire inventory. When I got home, I spread all the money out on the floor and just stared at it."

"*Then* you spent it on drugs."

"No! I was clean then. I bought a sleigh bed."

"For the first time in your life you have money, and you go out and buy a sleigh bed?" Violet howled. "That has got to be the most low-rent thing I've ever heard!"

"Do you even know what a sleigh bed *is?*" he asked. "Those rad wooden beds with the iron metalwork."

"Of course!" Violet couldn't stop laughing.

"What's so funny?"

"It's just so nineties!"

"It was the fucking nineties. What do you want?"

"Where's the sleigh bed now?"

"I sold it for drugs two months later."

"How much did you get for it?"

"Fuck you." He sounded hurt.

"Two hundred bucks?"

"Can we change the subject?"

"One hundred?" Violet found a shoulder and pulled over behind a guy selling fruit from a truck.

"Is your husband always going out of town?"

"We're supposed to go to a spring equinox yoga retreat in Ojai. But I don't feel like going."

"So *that's* when we're going to fuck."

"You're pretty sure of that, aren't you?"

The fruit guy shuffled over, holding a three-pack of strawberries in one hand and a bag of oranges in the other. Violet waved him off.

"Just stepping up and doing the right thing like you asked," Teddy said.

"God! You totally don't get what I meant by that."

David's Bentley whizzed by. He seemed to be on the phone himself and didn't slow down. He probably hadn't seen Violet. She fumbled for the gearshift and jerked the car into drive. "I've got to go," she said.

"Why? What happened?"

"Don't you have a Kennedy to dump?" Violet waited for the Flying Spur to disappear up their driveway, then merged onto Mulholland.

"I get it," Teddy said. "Bye, Violet Parry."

"Bye, Teddy Reyes." Violet pushed the warm phone to her cheek. Her whole face ached from smiling so much. She drove through the Aleppo pines, making figure eights with her jaw to counter the cramps forming in her cheeks. If David asked—and she knew he wouldn't!—she'd say she had pulled over to finish up a phone conversation before she got home. That wasn't lying.

CHAPTER FOUR

Control It or It Controls You ✾ And the Sultans Played Creole

"You're doing great," Sally told Nora Ross, the thick-waisted wife of Jordan Ross, head of one of the big talent agencies. Nora was doing some of the most pathetic *grande pliés* Sally had ever witnessed. "*Plié, relevé, plié, relevé.* Now with arms over the head."

"Ugh!" Nora's pudgy arms fell to her sides and she flopped breathlessly against the wall. "I am so stressed out. The guest list for tonight's party keeps *ballooning.*"

An army of Mexicans carrying heat lamps passed by the bay window.

"Next to the pool!" Nora shouted. "*Junto la piscina!*" She turned to Sally. "Is that how you say it?"

"I think so. How about we switch to *demi pliés?*"

"I hate you," said the wealthy butterball. "Can't I just do those kicky things?"

"Fine. *Dégagé,* with foot flexed. Third position." Sally set her feet and floated her arms into *grande pose.* "Right foot to the front. *Tendu* and *dégagé.* Heel leads the toe."

Nora flung her leg forward with all the grace of kicking a cat. "Please tell me these will get rid of my fat ass."

"You know what I say, Control it or it controls you." That was Sally's motto, from a bumper sticker she had on her three-ring binder in high school. "And one way to control your tush is *dégagé.* To the back. Toe leads heel. *Dégagé.*"

The phone rang. Happy to bail, Nora unlatched a cabinet door and answered it.

Since the Rosses' only child, J.J., had been diagnosed with autism, any object that could conceivably be picked up and hurled by a tantruming child—framed photos, telephone, ceramic bowls—had been secured behind custom-built glass-fronted cabinets. Last year, Sally had shown up to find the glass shattered and all the treasured memories in a million pieces in a heap on the floor. (Nora sent Sally home that day but still paid for the whole hour, which was really classy.) The following week, the glass had been removed and in its place, chicken wire. Behind which were imprisoned the images of Nora and Jordan smiling on the Great Wall, arms around Bill Clinton, huddled with Jack Nicholson at the *Vanity Fair* Oscar party, Nora, happy and pregnant on a yacht off Croatia. Before the diagnosis, before they stopped taking pictures.

Nora hung up and locked the phone back in the cabinet. "Can we just do abs and call it a day?" She kicked open the mat Sally had brought and sprawled out on it. "Jordan put the arm on all his big stars to show up. And word got out, so everybody, I mean *everybody,* wants to come." She rolled on her side and curled up. "That's what happens when you're only charging five hundred bucks a plate. Live and learn, am I right?"

"Let's try for twenty leg darts," said Sally.

"I hate those." Nora yelled out, "Zdenka!"

Sally braced herself for the entrance of the young Czech nanny, who clearly outranked her in the Ross household.

"Yes?" asked Zdenka in her hard accent. She nursed a bottle of exotic water. Anytime Nora outgrew a piece of clothing, it ended up on Zdenka. Today she sported a Dolce & Gabbana silk shirt, True Religion jeans, and Hogan shoes. Sally would have looked totally hot in that shirt, belted over leggings with her new Hermès belt. But did Sally ever get a crack at any of Nora's discards? No.

"The gals are coming to put together the goody bags in the dining room," Nora said. "Don't let J.J. anywhere near that, please."

"Of course," answered the nanny, and left.

Nora raised a leg in the air, an indication that she wished to be stretched out. Sally complied. Her student groaned with pleasure, then asked, "So. What's the latest on your beau?"

Sally had hoped Nora wouldn't ask. It had been two weeks since Sally had seen the ring. Still, Jeremy hadn't proposed. Sally was completely flummoxed. "We're doing fine," she said.

"I don't see a ring on your finger."

"If he proposes, he proposes. If he doesn't, I'm fine with that, too." This was what Sally had started to tell those who asked.

Nora yanked her leg free. "What do you mean? Two weeks ago you raved about what a good fit you two were."

"I know. But I think I'm looking for someone more…emotionally available."

"Please!" Nora crossed one leg over the other. Sally pushed the stuffed sausages into Nora's chest. "Men don't care about how you feel. That's what girlfriends are for. If you're waiting around for a guy who will share his feelings, you'd better pack Proust, because you're going to be waiting a mighty long time."

"I like that," Sally said.

"You don't have to like it or dislike it. You just have to accept it.

Jordan and I have a great marriage. But does he ever have a clue what I'm *feeling?* Never! That doesn't mean he's a bad husband."

"And you're a great wife."

"Well, thank you. I try to be. Sure, in the early days, we were screwing three times a day and making spectacles of ourselves in public and it was all very dramatic. But time passes. He has his career. I have my causes. We have a special-needs kid. We're partners who love each other."

Partners who love each other. Sally's thoughts quickened. It was as if she and Jeremy had fast-forwarded past the fireworks phase straight to the partner phase. And if she wanted to talk about feelings, she had friends for that. *Feelings.* They suddenly seemed so trivial in the context of a whole *life* together. "Can you finish off with ten basic crunches?" She really wanted to help Nora with that waist.

"Fine," moaned Nora. "But only ten."

Sally lay on the hardwood floor and led Nora in some crunches. "One, two, three—" The overhead lights flashed. Sally squeezed her eyes shut, then squinted. J.J. stood in the doorway, flipping the switch and staring expressionless into the bulbs. On the outside, J.J. was a beautiful eight year old with long blond curls. There was no way of knowing how damaged and creepy he was on the inside. Sally closed her eyes. The hot rays burned through her eyelids and into her retina, on-off-on-off-on-off. She shielded her eyes and shot a look at J.J., but he was transfixed by the repetition.

"Could someone get him to stop that?!" Sally cried. "My God! Stop it! Where's his nanny—"

Zdenka stared down at her. "I'm right here."

Sally quickly turned to Nora. "I'm sorry...." For all of Nora's complaining, she *did* pay cash and worked out in the middle of the day when the dance studio was closed. And Nora never once put up a fight about paying for canceled sessions. Sally couldn't afford to lose Nora, one of her bread-and-butter clients. "I apologize." Sally's voice trembled. "My eyes are just really sensitive."

"Zdenka, take him to the park or something, will you?" Nora said, unfazed by Sally's freak-out.

Sally flopped into a forward bend, fully aware she had just dodged a bullet. The Jeremy situation was beginning to affect her work. *Control it or it controls you.* It was time to apply her motto to Jeremy.

How do you look when you're interested? Violet tried to remember, as she and David drove up Beverly Glen, Dot a bubbly passenger in her car seat.

"…Capitol is trying to get us to rerecord two of the tracks," David was saying. "So contractually, I can shop the record. I've got Columbia frothing at the mouth."

"Sultans of Swing" came on the radio. Violet loved this song. She was about to turn onto Mulholland, and music sounded better on Mulholland. She started to reach for the volume, but David was still talking; such an act on Violet's part ran the risk of igniting a conflagration.

"The question is," he said, "do we stay with Capitol and force them to release the tracks? Or would that make them lose enthusiasm for the single?"

A question. He had just asked her a question. Thank God it was still buffered in her short-term memory. Violet rewound it in her head and replied, "Is one of the tracks in question the first single?" Violet felt good about her reply; it was quick and informed, the reply of someone who cared.

"Yes. They gave me a list of producers. George Drakoulias was at the top."

"We love George," Violet said.

"Maybe I'll give him a call."

"Want dat. Want dat." Dot had spotted Violet's cell phone in the cup holder. Violet slipped it back to Dot, her gaze never deserting her husband.

"But all this—Hanging with Yoko, the record label, the catalogues—it's all starting to look like a fucking hobby compared to what the gold stocks are doing. You know what I say. Gold, it's the king of money. When it starts to run, it's going to be scary."

"I'm so happy for you," Violet said.

"Be happy for us. It's ours." David kicked at something on the floor. "What's this?"

"Oh," she said, "when I subscribed to *Cook's Illustrated,* without realizing it, I signed up for some cookbook-of-the-month thing. And most of the recipes involve meat, so I can't use them."

"Have you gotten off the list, at least?"

"I tried, but it's such a pain. So I thought I'd just give them to LadyGo."

David picked up a cookbook and leafed through it. "She can't understand this."

"I know, but there was a monster line at the post office when I went to return them. I'm sure LadyGo knows somebody who wants them."

David stared at her, jaw hanging. "That's your solution? For every month for the rest of my life, I'm going to pay, what"—he looked for a price on the book—"thirty-nine bucks for a cookbook that you're giving to someone who doesn't speak English, in hopes that she'll find someone who wants it? Come on, Violet."

"I'm sorry." She should have known this would happen. She should never have left these books in her car.

"It's not about the money," he said. "It's just—how are we living, here?"

"You're right. I'll get off the list and return the books on Monday."

David wasn't happy, but at least he had stopped talking. Just in time for Violet's favorite part of the song.

And a crowd of young boys, they're fooling around in the corner
Drunk and dressed in their best brown baggies and their platform soles
They don't give a damn about any trumpet playing band
It ain't what they call rock and roll....

Violet held her breath to better hear her favorite line, the one that never failed to slay her:

And the Sultans played Creole.

Violet's eyes welled up.

"Get that cell phone out of Dot's hand!" It was David, talking again. "She could get brain cancer."

"It's not on." Violet turned and held out her hand for Dot. "Mommy needs that back, sweetie."

"That's not the point. I don't want her in the habit— Shit— Violet, are you crying? What's going on?"

"I just really love this song."

"'The Sultans of Swing'?" David frowned and his head jerked back slightly, as if he was jolted by that fact. "Really?"

"Have you ever listened to the words?"

"No."

"It's about these working stiffs who play in a band every Friday night. And when they're onstage, nobody appreciates them. But they don't care. Because for those few hours, they're...free."

David looked alarmed. "Maybe you can go see Dire Straits next time they're in town. Or, you know what, Mutt Lange is friends with Mark Knopfler. We can all go to dinner next time we're in London."

Teddy hadn't called for two weeks! Two weeks tomorrow. Who jerks off to you five minutes after they meet you and asks what your pussy is like and doesn't call you for two weeks? Violet had called him. Twice. Left messages both times, but nothing. Who winds someone up like that just to go AWOL? Where was he? Did he know how much pain she was in? How she jumped any time she heard her cell phone ring? How his absence made time crawl? Was he dying of hepatitis C somewhere? Had he not broken up with the Kennedy girl after all? Were *they* somewhere fucking, him repeating everything *she* said, him laughing at *her* jokes? Did being in his aura make *her* drunk with submission? He had told Violet she was the most pure thing he had ever experienced. Didn't that merit a return phone call? She had gotten the mechanic's bill. Sixteen hundred dollars to fix his shitty car, and no phone call? He was going to write poems for her! He wanted to fuck her in the ass! Call her back! She wanted to twinkle! But ever since the putting green, ever since that thrilling phone call on Benedict Canyon, ever since all she had to do was close her eyes and he was there, she couldn't twinkle on her own.

David typed into his BlackBerry and flashed Violet a triumphant smile. "Mark Knopfler's number. I e-mailed it to you. You can call him when we get home. Done and done."

David had no idea. The last person Violet wanted to talk to was Mark Knopfler.

CHAPTER FIVE

The Ferrari

"TODAY WE'RE PROUD TO INTRODUCE OUR NEW COLLEAGUE, JEREMY White." A hot guy Sally recognized from TV—Jim Something-or-Other—spoke directly into the camera. "Many of you know the name from his 'Just the Stats' column, which appears in over a dozen newspapers nationwide. Beginning today, the big man himself will be joining the *Match-Ups* team every Sunday morning. Welcome, Jeremy."

Jeremy's face appeared on the dozen monitors throughout the dark soundstage. Sally's fingers were crossed in her pocket. She closed her eyes: her entire future hinged on the next three minutes.

"Hi, I'm Jeremy White. Let's take a look at one of sports' most exciting events, the NCAA Sweet Sixteen. First off, the matchup between heavily favored Georgetown and the little team that could, Canisius College…." The voice filling the air was soothing, almost musical. Sally opened her eyes. Yes, it was Jeremy, aglow on the enormous screen overhead, his face relaxed, his eyes gazing directly and calmly into hers. Finally, he wasn't wearing those dirty earplugs. His jacket and tie added a sexy look of authority. Sally blinked. It was as if she was beholding the man she *imagined* Jeremy to be when they were apart, only to have her heart sink when she saw how awkward he was in person. She turned around. In the booth, Maryam and the executives muttered excitedly, equally transfixed by this suddenly charismatic apparition.

"And who do you belong to?" Hot, wet breath tickled Sally's ear. It was Jim, the anchorman who had introduced Jeremy. Without waiting for an answer, he ambled over to the food table.

Sally scurried to keep up. "I'm a friend of Maryam and Jeremy's."

"Shush!" said a voice.

"First time on a set?" Jim whispered, shaking sugar to the bottom of five packets.

"No!"

"Shhh!" Maryam stepped out of the booth and shot Sally a nasty look.

"We're all heading to Marie Callender's after this." Jim poured the sugar directly into his mouth and took a hard swallow. "Maybe you'd like to join."

"I'm more Jeremy's friend than Maryam's. If you know what I mean."

"Say it isn't so." Jim's eyes slid down Sally, coming to rest on her ass. "Jeremy White picks seventy percent and gets to bang the likes of you? This dude is my idol."

Sally threw back her head and laughed. "He should be." Her long hair felt so soft against her bare back.

Jim reached forward and cupped the ballet slippers dangling from Sally's necklace. "Don't even tell me you're a dancer."

"Three years with the Colorado Ballet. I would have made principal, but I got injured."

He quickly dropped the necklace. "Here comes the queen bitch."

"You guys!" Maryam got in their faces and whispered, "Keep it *down*."

"She's *your* friend," said Jim. "It's not my fault she's never been on a set before."

"You!" Sally knuckled Jim in the shoulder.

"Easy," he said. "We're not in bed yet."

"That's the head of the network in there," Maryam hissed. "Are you trying to ruin Jeremy's screen test?"

"Of course not," Sally shot back.

"Then *shut up!*" Maryam headed to the booth, walking on the back edges of her heels so her footsteps didn't echo.

Sally returned her eyes to Jeremy and tried really hard not to giggle at Jim, who she felt watching her, maybe even making faces at her.

"...That's why I like Arizona's chances to upset Villanova," Jeremy was saying. "Until next week, I'm Jeremy White."

"Cut!" Applause erupted throughout the studio. Maryam received hearty congratulations from her beloved bigwigs as they all poured onto the set.

"You sure backed the winning horse, didn't you?" Jim said. Sally flashed him a saucy smile.

She was *so glad* she had called in sick to the ballerina birthday party this morning to drive Jeremy to this screen test. For the past week, she had withheld sex, not spent the night, and waited twelve hours to return his calls. It hadn't resulted in getting the ring on her finger, but she needed to give it time. She was, after all, a Flatlander going up against a mysterious potato.

"Jeremy?" the director asked over the PA system. "Next week, when we're live, I want you and Jim to do some happy talk. Jim, where did you go?"

"I'm right here!" Jim boomed from Sally's side.

Jeremy jumped out of his chair and headed straight for Sally, not even stopping to shake the hands of a dozen well-wishers. Sally got goose bumps; it was like the end of *Rocky*, when Sylvester Stallone called out, "Adrian!"

"Congratulations, sweetie!" Sally gave him a peck on the cheek.

Jeremy reared his head and turned to Jim. "What's happy talk?" he asked, rolling an earplug between his fingers, then sticking it into his ear.

"I'm sure this little lady knows a thing or two about happy talk."

Sally punched Jim in the arm.

"I don't understand what that means," Jeremy said to Jim.

"You know, banter," Jim said.

"Can you write it out for me?"

"Then it wouldn't be banter, would it?" Jim patted Jeremy on the butt. "Relax, big guy." He gave Sally a wink and walked away.

"Uh, hello?" Sally stepped into Jeremy's line of vision. "Sweetie?"

"I don't know what they mean by banter." Jeremy reached into his pocket, took out a quarter, and started flipping it.

"You just say stuff to each other," she said. "You know, chitchat. You see it all the time on TV."

"My contract says nothing about chitchat. Do you have a pen and some paper?"

"Jeremy!" She grabbed the quarter out of the air. "I congratulated you."

"Thanks. Everyone seemed happy."

Maryam rushed over. "We're all going to Marie Callender's. Do you want to come?"

Sally had resigned herself to the fact that spontaneity such as this wasn't possible with Jeremy. "Thanks," she said, "but no."

"Sure!" said Jeremy.

"Wha—" Sally said.

"Great!" said Maryam. "It's the one on Wilshire, west of La Brea." She ran off.

A woman with overprocessed hair plopped down a canvas gardening bag with pockets full of makeup brushes. "Hi, I'm Faye." She sidled up to Jeremy and started wiping foundation off his face. "Looks like we'll be spending lots of time together."

"Honey," Sally said, "they don't have anything you like at Marie Callender's."

"It's for my work," Jeremy said. "You don't have to come if you don't want to."

Faye brushed her fingers through Jeremy's hair. "There you are." Out of the side of her mouth, she added, "I've been doing this a lot of years. When the president of the network delays his flight back to New York to eat buffalo wings with a new guy—well, you better show up." Faye gave Sally the stink eye and walked away.

A fuming Sally led Jeremy through the studio and outside to the sunny parking lot in the gross part of Hollywood. The gigantic double-hatch doors sealed shut behind them. She spun around. "Jim asked me out just now."

"Are you going?" Jeremy asked.

"On a date. He asked me out *on a date*."

"But you're my girlfriend." He walked to Sally's car and waited at the passenger door.

"*Am* I your girlfriend, Jeremy?"

"Of course you are."

"Because I just don't know anymore. We haven't spent the night together in one whole week."

"You're the one who wanted it that way."

"Why would I want that?" She stood an inch from his face.

"You said you're on your menstrual cycle."

Everything with Jeremy was so frigging *literal*. It was impossible to give him a hint. Yes, Sally had told him she was having her period. But the last time she had her period, during the "honeymoon phase," she had given him blow jobs every night and slept over. Shouldn't the numbers guy be able to put two and two together?!

"What do *you* want, Jeremy?" Sally felt herself entering that zone that scared off all the other boyfriends, the one that gave her the reputation for being "crazy."

"I want you to stop getting mad."

"Then stop making me mad!"

"I want to. But I never know how."

"You're so freaking selfish, Jeremy."

"I don't understand. When I met you, everything made you so happy."

"I *was* happy. But you just manipulate me and walk all over me like I'm a doormat!"

"Do you need something to eat?" he asked.

"I'm sorry I'm not a *number*, Jeremy. Because you'd probably pay more attention to me. I'm sorry I'm not a hamburger at Hamburger Hamlet! I'm sorry I'm not a cheese quesadilla! I'm a human being who has feelings, who just wants to connect. But trying to connect with you is like trying to connect to a robot!" Sally shrieked and sobbed all at the same time.

Technically, she could rein herself in. But once she started losing control, she enjoyed the release and didn't want to pull back. It's what she imagined car buffs meant when they said high-performance cars "liked" to be taken out and opened up on an empty highway. Like the finest Ferrari, Sally enjoyed pushing the envelope of her emotional pain to see how far she could take it.

The horror on people's faces as she did—and it was always boy-friends who were on the receiving end of these spectacles—only reinforced her humiliation, which made her want to go further.

"I'm sorry I'm not a makeup whore or a television camera or a *quarter,* you bastard! I'm sorry I'm in love with you and turn down dates for you. I'm sorry I crushed the dreams of a dozen little bal-lerinas this morning so I could drive you here! *I'm sorry I exist!* I'm sorry I ever met you! Oh God, look what you've done to me! What have I become? I'm sorry I was ever born!"

Jeremy looked utterly bewildered. "I'm glad you were born."

"Don't lie to me!"

"If you weren't born, I wouldn't know you. And then what would I do?"

"Huh?"

"You're my life, Sally. I'll do anything for you. If you don't want to go to Marie Callender's, we don't have to."

"Really?" Sally looked up, her eyes moist. "But what about your career?"

"Television is just television. I can live without television. You, Sally, you're a person. A person I love."

"I love you, Jeremy." She hugged him. It was four o'clock. She *did* need some food in her. "Let's go to Marie Callender's."

CHAPTER SIX

Spring Equinox ❖ Thank God It's Just Diabetes ❖ Super-Rica

This Is It? ❖ Just the Check ❖ Standing There ❖ Ho!

TODAY HE WOULD CALL. SPRING EQUINOX. VIOLET HAD TOLD TEDDY THAT WAS when David would be out of town. It seemed so obvious when she had figured it out. Once she did, her torment gave way to the calm of having the upper hand in a delicious game of cat and mouse.

So Violet had spent the past two weeks preparing. Embracing the hunger pains she carried to the hairdresser, the waxing place, the facialist, the nail salon. Actually looking at herself in a full-length mirror while David was at work to see which outfits made her ass look the least gigantic. The expedition to a mall deep in the valley to buy size-large lingerie, then stashing it in the back of her T-shirt drawer. The body scrubs and cellulite massages using serum made of sheep colostrum.

While Violet attended to her body, she'd slip off into her life with Teddy—the one she'd lovingly write and rewrite. They'd live near the ocean in Santa Monica. On Georgina or Alta (west of Lincoln, of course!), where they could walk down the steps and across PCH to the Jonathan Club. Violet would fix up an old Craftsman. They'd buy the house next door and tear it down so they'd have a bigger yard and room for Teddy's studio. She'd fix him up as well—his teeth, his hair, his wardrobe. Because of her age, they'd have to have a baby soon. Maybe they'd get married. Maybe not. Paperwork might befoul the purity of their love. People would talk; Violet accepted that. But once they got to know Teddy, and watched her blossom, they'd wildly approve.

Violet had asked around about golf. It turned out that anyone, for a smallish fee, could sign up for amateur tournaments. If Teddy won enough—which he surely would—he would graduate onto increasingly larger circuits and ultimately the PGA. Even though he was no spring chicken—how old was he, anyway, thirty-something probably, she'd have to remember to ask—the main indicator for success in golf was that you started young, which Teddy had. How she'd burst with pride, standing by his side as he vanquished all nonbelievers. Their charity golf event would be the talk of the town. Lots of rock stars and movie stars, raising money for hepatitis C. That's right; Violet would not be ashamed of his disease. She had researched it online and was relieved to see that Teddy was correct: the virus was transmitted only by the exchange of blood, such as sharing needles, not from kissing or vaginal sex. There was even a cure for it, interferon, which was a long and expensive regimen, but one Violet would valiantly nurse Teddy through.

And of course, there was Teddy's poetry. He'd write epic, scrappy poems about Violet and their baby, Lotus. Lotus and Violet, his two flowers. (And Dot, of course, never forgetting Dot!) He could turn his poems into songs, which would lead to a robust music career. Ideally, Teddy wouldn't go on the road. He probably was a sex addict, and Violet didn't need to add that to her list of worries. So preferably he'd become a local sensation.

She sought solitude so she could filigree this future with Teddy. When David came home, she'd invent an excursion to the market. While there, she'd imagine the guest list for Teddy's listening party. Something low-key, a clambake perhaps? And David, happily remarried, would come with his new wife and give blessing.

Soon, Violet's high-flying life with Teddy was so vivid that the drudgery of her life with David and Dot felt like the distraction. A simple act such as David's popping his head into the steam shower—her beloved isolation chamber—asking, "Honey, have you seen my car keys?" felt like an act of violence. When conversation with David was unavoidable, she would still think about Teddy. That morning at breakfast, as David bitched about something, Violet had to check the urge to half-close her eyes, as she felt the softness of Teddy's tongue in her mouth, kissing her for the first time.

But there was a catch.

It was three in the afternoon on March the twenty-first, and Teddy hadn't called. Violet had carried her cell phone all day so as not to miss their assignation. Equally problematic, David refused to accept that his wife was not accompanying him to the yoga retreat. He was now standing at the car, ready to go.

"Where's your stuff?" he asked as he threw his duffel bag and yoga mat into the Prius—he knew enough not to drive his Bentley to a yoga retreat.

"I'm not going," Violet said for the tenth time.

"You planned it."

"I want to spend the weekend alone. Dot's with LadyGo, and I just want to relax."

"Thus, the yoga retreat."

"It will be more relaxing for me to be home alone," she said.

"You're always alone." He opened the front door of Violet's

Mercedes and popped the trunk. The obstinate bastard then grabbed her yoga mat, some sweats and tossed them in the Prius. "There. You're packed. Let's go before we hit weekend traffic."

Violet dug her fingers into her face. Teddy hadn't called yet. Should she just go with her husband?

David exploded, "What kind of face is that? I'm asking you to go away for the weekend like we planned, and you look like I just punched you in the stomach!"

Violet's cell phone rang. Her body knew it was Teddy before she saw the incoming phone number: 310-555-0199. Violet could have collapsed with relief. But she couldn't answer it in front of David. He grabbed the phone out of her hand. "Will you talk to me?!" It rang again. What if Teddy didn't leave a message?—oh God—"Say something, Violet!"

"I never said I was going with you!" she screamed. "I want a break!"

"From what? What do you need a break from? Spending my money? Spacing out? Driving off by yourself to God knows where? What do you even fucking do? I make the money. LadyGo raises your child. You do nothing! You're not necessary!"

"From that! You treat me like I'm a gigantic fuckup!"

"Does it occur to you that maybe it's because you're *fucking up?!* You're constantly out of the house but never doing anything. You're spending less and less time with Dot. We are your family. Live your fucking life. You haven't been UV-A for three years. You're not even UV-B. You're more like UV-Z."

"Don't call me that!" The phone! It had rung twice, now three times.

"What the fuck happened to you? You used to be a writer. Why don't you write anymore?"

"You know why," she said. "I don't want to be stuck on a show for sixty hours a week with Dot at home."

"Who said you have to write for TV? Write in your fucking

diary! But write. Why am I even having to tell you this? You used to know these things. You used to be a dynamo."

"Those days are over."

"As your husband, don't I get a fucking vote on that?"

"No!"

"That's your solution? For me to just go about my business while you slip away?"

Violet knew it was her turn to say something. But the phone had stopped ringing. Would Teddy leave a message? She was stranded on the silence, staring at the phone in David's hand without shame, like a dog fixated on the slimy tennis ball he wants you to throw.

"Your silence speaks volumes," David said.

The tinny trumpets of Pachelbel's Canon in D heralded. A voice mail! Violet panted, her eyes locked on the little blinking mailbox.

David opened his hand. "Your phone." She snatched it. "I hope you realize how much you stand to lose, Violet." He slammed the trunk, got into the car, and peeled out.

Violet's fingers trembled as she hit the voice mail button. *One new message.* "Hi, it's your spring equinox call." Teddy's voice was higher and more nasal than she'd remembered. "I need a favor from you. And ask me what I did last night."

Violet hit the reply button.

"That didn't take long," Teddy said. "Aren't you impressed that I know when the spring equinox is?"

"What did you do last night?" Violet said, feral with impatience.

"I downloaded pictures of chicks who looked like you and jerked off to them."

Violet swirled with delight. "Really?"

"I thought you'd like that."

"What favor do you want?"

"I'd like Geddy Lee's 4001 Rickenbacker bass."

"When's your birthday?"

"Listen to you," he said. "Like you're going to get it for me."

"We know Geddy Lee."

"*We* know Geddy Lee! Ha!"

"We used to spend every Christmas with him in Anguilla."

"Do you have any idea how much I love Rush?"

"And you're giving *me* shit about being a Deadhead? When's your birthday?"

"May first is my AA birthday. I'll have three years."

"May Day," Violet said.

"What's that supposed to mean?"

"May Day. It's a pagan celebration where children with ribbons dance around a maypole."

"Are you tripping on that hippie acid again?"

"All I meant is, congratulations on being sober for three years." There was a puddle of oil on the floor. Violet grabbed a rag from the tool bench and started to mop it with her foot.

"If I make it."

"Of course you'll make it."

"We have to stay humble in the program," Teddy said.

"Let's have a birthday party for you."

"We can't do that."

"Why?"

"Because it's my sponsor's birthday, too. And he always wants to have our birthdays together."

"That's cool." Violet picked up the dirty rag with her fingertips. "I can throw a party for both of you."

"He doesn't exactly know about you."

"Why not?" Violet headed toward the trash cans.

"He's this very by-the-book AA dude and he'd be really down on our relationship."

"Why?" She froze.

"You're a rich married lady I jerk off to who gives me money. That's not exactly part of the program."

"Oh." Violet dropped the rag.

"Don't worry. I've got it figured out, though. What's your address?"

"Why?"

"So I can come over tonight. Don't you love it how little old junkie me knows when David Parry's going to—" A roar from his end overpowered his voice.

"Where are you?" Violet asked.

"I just dropped off Her Majesty Coco Kennedy at the airport. Her sister is going on tour with the *Cats* of Japan and she got Coco a free plane ticket. Don't ask, because it doesn't make sense to me, either. You should hear her voice mail. It's filled with all these producers who want to make her a celebutard reality star. What a crazy bitch." Violet was speechless. "What's wrong?" he asked.

"I thought you broke up with her. Is she still your girlfriend?"

There was a pause. *No; that's all he had to say, no. Come on, say it: no.*

"Yes." There must have been another pause, because Teddy was now saying, "Violet? Does this upset you? Hello?"

Violet's throat throbbed. "No."

"Great. You're upset," he said.

"You made me promise I wouldn't let you get back together with her, that's all."

"Oh that. I forgot. Well, relationships are complicated. Am I right, Mrs. David Parry?"

"So you still have a girlfriend."

"I'm only eighty-five percent faithful to her."

If Violet could just hit "pause," she might be able to separate out the vagaries tangling up her brain.

"Hit me with the deets," he said. "What's your address? All I've been eating are blueberry bagels. I need some healthy food or my liver's going to balloon. You have no idea what it's like. I have the body of an eighty year old. You're a vegetarian. You can make me some healthy grub, right? Come on, where do you live?" Violet was too addled to do anything other than recite her address. He'd be there at eight. "And Violet?"

"Yeah?"

"We're just going to hang out. No funny stuff." Teddy hung up.

Violet felt repellent, like a duped sex predator slavering over the phone in a grimy carport. Her Mercedes was right there. She could jump in and catch up with David. She called Teddy back to tell him not to come. But his phone rang and rang and rang, then went to voice mail. She was certain he had seen it was her and not picked up, figuring she was trying to cancel. She closed her phone. The only thing to do was to have him over, whip up some spinach from the garden, and never see him again. Tomorrow morning, she would drive up to Matilija and make things right with David.

SALLY, Jeremy, and his two lesbian neighbors were gathered around his kitchen counter. "To Jeremy!" Jennifer raised a plastic cup of two-buck chardonnay she and Wendy had brought over in celebration.

"Good luck on Sunday," Wendy said, digging into the super-market veggie-and-dip platter. She was the guy in this relationship, judging from her bulging khakis and rugby shirt. "We'll always be able to say we knew you when!"

Sally bristled at the sense of ownership these girls felt over Jeremy. Sure, they used to drive him places, but Sally did the driving now.

"Come on, Sally!" said one of the gals. "Have some wine."

"I'll stick to Diet Coke," she said. Wendy and Jennifer launched into reminiscences about the old days. Sally excused herself. "I have to use the little-girls' room."

"Don't forget your purse," Jennifer said. Wendy stifled a giggle.

"Thanks for reminding me." Sally smiled and grabbed her purse. Apparently dykes thought it was the height of uptightness to bring one's purse to the bathroom. They had commented on it before. But Sally wasn't offended. Jeremy had asked her to pick a romantic restaurant where they could have dinner later tonight. Deviating from his routine could only mean that he was finally going to pop the question. Sally had picked the Ivy, a place she had always imagined herself getting engaged. Soon enough, she and Jeremy would be kissing off Jennifer, Wendy, and this whole crappy apartment complex for a new life over the hill.

Sally shut the bathroom door, unzipped her Liberty of London cosmetic bag, and got out her lancet and glucometer. She washed her hands with soap and hot water. In honor of the occasion, Sally pricked the ring finger on her left hand. She stuck a test strip into the glucometer, squeezed her finger, and touched the blood to the plastic. The meter beeped. She sucked her finger and waited seven seconds for the reading. She had to smile: diabetes didn't know happy days from sad ones. It didn't care if she was getting engaged to Jeremy or dumped by Kurt, rejected by Juilliard or dancing the part of Giselle: ten times a day she'd still have to prick her finger and inject herself in the stomach.

The glucometer read 230. Sally had counted on her blood sugar being lower, considering her three o'clock injection and forty-five minutes of cardio. She would definitely want at least half a tarte tatin, the Ivy's signature dessert. Plus, the maître d' would probably send over champagne when he heard the joyous hullabaloo. That would give Sally another ten grams of carbs. Should she take some Humalog now and not have to worry about it until tonight's dose of Lantus? But her sugar levels might spike from the champagne and excitement. Then, if she ate even a couple bites of tarte tatin, she might feel too crashed to make love later. And tonight was a night she and Jeremy had to make love.

Sally decided to be safe and take a shot now, then test herself at the restaurant. She removed the tiny cushioned bottle of Humalog and the syringe dedicated to it, then drew out four units. She lifted her dress, felt her stomach for a spot that wasn't tender, and injected herself.

One of the things Sally loved most about Jeremy was the way he had reacted when she told him she was type one diabetic. And that she had lost half of her little toe to it. He frowned and said he was sorry, then never brought it up again. Everyone else got so maudlin when they found out. (Especially about the toe!) Sally knew from that point on, she'd be "poor diabetic Sally." So she never brought it up. And always wore closed-toe shoes.

As much as she would have liked to say to Jennifer and Wendy, Hey ladies, I bring my purse to the bathroom because I'm *diabetic,* Sally never once used the diabetic card for sympathy. Not even with her boyfriends, who might have forgiven her some of her histrionics had she blamed low blood sugar. Diabetes was simply something she was born with. Her eyes were blue, her teeth were straight, and her pancreas didn't produce insulin. If Sally didn't deviate from her four-hour plan, she was no different from anybody else. Control it or it controls you.

When Sally was three, she fainted while Mom videotaped her practicing her mouse dance for *The Nutcracker.* David and Mom rushed her to the hospital. When she was diagnosed with juvenile diabetes, her mother said, "Thank God it's just diabetes." The one and only time Sally went to a shrink, she recounted this story. He was astonished at Sally's unwillingness to allow that diabetes was something she should feel anger or sadness over. She left before the hour was up.

If anything, diabetes taught her the self-discipline necessary to excel at ballet. She attended the Academy of Colorado Ballet, then joined the company. Years passed as Sally watched her fellow graduates make coryphée, soloist, and principal, while she remained stuck in the corps. But then she got lucky. A guest choreographer from Russia was so inspired by her that he created a ballet around her in celebration of the hundredth anniversary of women's suffrage in Colorado. A month before Sally's premiere (the governor was scheduled to attend, and Don Johnson!), a blister on her little toe split open. She practiced through the pain, then the tingling, then the numbness. She ignored the black spots. The swelling and stiffness spread to her foot. She wrapped it tight, which bought her a couple of rehearsal days. Then her ankle started to swell. By the time Sally made it to the hospital, the toe was mottled white and scarlet, and even light blue. It looked like an exotic coral. The infection had spread to the bone. They had no choice but to amputate. A dancer four years Sally's junior ended up dancing the part and was now a principal with the San Francisco Ballet.

Sally prided herself on her ability to bounce back—indeed, what else was there to pride herself on?—and she considered it a badge of honor when someone close to her didn't know she was diabetic. None of her students had a clue. Her manager at the dance studio had no idea. When Violet sent over those crates of chocolate, it made Sally think *she* didn't know, either. Sally had certainly never brought it up with her sister-in-law. But she found it hard to believe that after seventeen years, David had never mentioned it to his wife. It had been such an enormous part of his life, too. He still paid Sally's insurance and doctors' bills. That would be one of the sweetest aspects of marrying Jeremy: getting on his insurance, so David could finally stop paying her bills.

Sally withdrew the needle from her stomach and returned the syringe to the section of her cosmetic bag where she kept the Humalog syringes to reuse. Even though they said you shouldn't reuse syringes, all diabetics did, because of the cost. Insurance didn't cover five needles per day, which Sally averaged, so it made sense to use one until the tip became so blunt it made her bruise. She did it as a courtesy to David.

"Let's see." It was Jennifer's muffled voice from the other room. Jeremy clomped across the floor. Even with his new shoes, his walk was loud and clumsy! Sally held her breath and leaned against the door. The desk drawer slid open and shut. Jeremy clomped back to the kitchen. Sally cracked the door. Jennifer and Wendy leered at the ring. Jeremy closed the velvet cube and dropped it in his jacket pocket. Sally flushed the toilet to make it seem as if she had been peeing, then rejoined the party.

SUPER-RICA, a funky taco stand on the outskirts of Santa Barbara, was a favorite of David and Violet's. It wasn't on the way to the yoga retreat, but it was worth the half hour detour. David stood, puzzling over the hand-painted menu board above the window. Violet always ordered for them, and none of this looked familiar. The line behind David was long and impatient: UCSB students and NPR-listening foodies who had made the pilgrimage to Super-Rica and knew precisely what they would order when they finally arrived at the window.

"There's some melted-cheese thing?" David asked.

"*Queso de cazuela,*" the Mexican said.

"Fine. And a horchata." The man gave David a number and a cup of the rice drink he'd been craving on the drive up. David handed the guy a twenty. "Keep it." He sat down under the tented dining area and, in its blue glow, thought about Violet.

She had sought refuge and stability after being raised by an unreliable father. Done. She wanted to move to LA. Done. She wanted to quit her job. Done. She wanted a fabulous house. Done. She wanted a baby. Done. She wanted a full-time nanny. Done and done.

And I'm the fucking asshole?

Did she have any idea how it stung when David said something and she met him with silence? At best, she'd fake it with a zombie smile or a vacant "Really?" He knew what it was like to have Violet head over heels for you. There was nothing like it. When he met her, she was a bubbly, brilliant chatterbox, always with a million questions. Now she was remote, weepy, mute.

What was her fucking excuse? That the pregnancy was *hard*? That she had a baby over a year ago and the adjustment was *hard*? That the house she had found was *harder* to remodel than she thought? That she stuffed her face during her pregnancy and it was so *hard* to lose the weight? That having a husband support her lavish lifestyle was just so *hard* on her self-esteem? That making two breakfasts in the morning, one for David and one for Dot, and not having time to make one for herself was so darned *hard*?

How about spending high school waking up at four AM to deliver newspapers in a shitty blizzarding Denver neighborhood, then doing the afternoon *and* evening shifts at Baskin-Robbins to work a forty-hour week to qualify for benefits? That was pretty *hard*. How about a teenager filing for legal guardianship of his diabetic sister so she could be covered by his health insurance? Or never going to college, getting an accounting degree through the mail, and now sitting on $32.8 million, liquid. With compounding interest, probably $32.85 after the car ride up here. Last time David checked, that was a *hard* thing to do. How about being a goddamned visionary and seeing the music business about to fall off a cliff, then leveraging everything to buy publishing catalogues that had since grown into cash cows? He had done it, and would consider it *hard*. How about booking a band whose debut album hadn't even been released to open for Green Day this summer? David had finalized that just this morning. These days, that was a mighty hard thing to pull off. How about the forty e-mails that came in on the drive up? From bands and record executives and road managers and art directors and the friend of a friend of a friend who didn't want much, just help becoming a *gigantic rock star!* Handling all that with grace only to come home to a crazy cunt of a wife was *pretty fucking hard!*

Were any of these people e-mailing or calling just to check on how David was doing? Or to thank him for always being there? No. They wanted jobs or favors or rescuing from some fuckup. Since David was a teenager, he'd been the daddy. To his mother, to Sally. Now to Violet, to Dot, to his bands, and to the hundred or so people he employed at any given time. David would consider that *harder* than making a pot of coffee in the morning and handing a baby off to LadyGo.

Earlier, in the carport, his wife couldn't take her eyes off her cell phone as it rang in his hand. Just six months ago, he had to persuade her to carry one. Now she was Susie-fucking-cell-phone. Her peculiar fixation on it had made him look down at the incoming number. Bad news for Violet, David was good at memorizing numbers.

310-555-0199.

It wasn't one he recognized. Who could have reduced Violet to such possum-eyed stupidity? A lover? That would explain a lot. But Violet fucking somebody? It wasn't the Violet he knew. If he called the number from his cell phone, whoever it was could trace it back to him, so David went to the pay phone and dialed it.

"Please deposit two dollars, fifty cents."

David smashed the receiver against the phone and let it dangle. A bunch of jocks, finishing up their lunch, snickered at him. On their table, among the empty red plastic baskets, was a cell phone. David pulled a fifty from his money clip and slapped it down. "I have to make a call. Keep the change."

"Wow, sure." A kid wearing a Def Leppard *Hysteria* T-shirt handed over his phone. David had managed that tour. He dialed the number. It went straight to voice mail.

"Dude, it's Teddy. Leave a message."

David tossed the phone back onto the table. The kids looked up, hushed. "Here, you want to use mine?" said one. The others exploded in dumb laughter.

David returned to his chair. Teddy. The name sounded familiar.

He navigated his BlackBerry to e-mail, then searched for "Teddy."
One message came up, last month from his assistant.

> To: David@ultra.com
> From: Kara@ultra.com
> Re: mechanic bill
> Hi David,
> The accountant just called about a bill for $1588.04 for
> repair work on a 1989 Mazda 323 belonging to a Teddy
> Reyes. We don't show you owning a Mazda 323 and
> there's no one by that name on the payroll, so we wanted
> to make sure this bill wasn't sent in error.
> Kara ☺

David scrolled through Kara's other e-mails. He found one
from later that day:

> To: David@ultra.com
> From: Kara@ultra.com
> Re: Re: mechanic bill
> Hi David,
> I just spoke to Violet and she cleared up the charge. She
> said you were super busy and I shouldn't bother you with
> this kind of stuff. Sorry about that. ☹
> Kara ☺

So. Violet had fixed a car belonging to some guy named Teddy
Reyes. David vaguely remembered being in the bathroom a while
back and Violet saying she had helped someone whose car had
broken down. She had failed to mention the part about paying for
it. Then she tried to hide it from David. And now Teddy Reyes was
calling.

"Fifteen!" shouted the man from the window. "Fifteen! You
number fifteen, mister?"

David checked his ticket and got his tray of food. It wasn't the thing he liked, the thing that Violet ordered for them.

THE tofu was grilled; the rice had about ten more minutes; the fresh ginger was grated into the soy and rice-vinegar mixture; the garlic cloves were fried and awaiting the spinach Violet had picked. She popped a jar of peanut butter into the microwave. Fifteen seconds should soften it sufficiently to whisk into the sauce.

Her cell phone rang. "I have to tell you something before I see you." It was Teddy. Violet had been so absorbed in her preparations, she'd almost forgotten for whom she was cooking.

"Okay." The microwave beeped. Violet tested the peanut butter. It needed thirty more seconds. She put it back in.

"My mother's in jail," he said.

"Oh." Violet frowned, not quite sure how this concerned her.

"She tried to kill one of her boyfriends," he said haltingly. "You know what I mean."

Violet didn't, nor did she want to imagine.

"There was this main one who'd beat the shit out of her. And I was around for a lot of it. For all of it."

"Oh," she said.

"You think I'm totally disgusting and beneath you, don't you?"

"No!" she said, too brightly.

"I get really weird after I fuck a chick. My relationship with Coco is totally abusive. I'd never want to do that to you. It's such a gift from God to have you in my life."

Finally, a judo moment, where Violet could use his words against him. "Thank you for telling me," she said. "Because it's abundantly clear we should just be friends."

"Why? Because I'm so gross?"

"Because, if I'm inferring correctly, you have mother issues and I'm an older woman who has recently stopped breast-feeding."

"Hot. Do you still have milk in your tits?"

"No!" Violet said as she fluffed the rice. "I've cared for you in a way a mother would and you sexualized it. It's classic repetition compulsion."

"The doctor is *in!* I've never met anyone like you before. Dig?"

"Yes," Violet said, almost wistful for the time when these words would have thrilled her. "I dig."

"You can't say, Yes, I dig. You have to just say, Dig."

"Dig." For Violet, his attempt at badinage had all the lightness of a protein bar.

"Nobody's ever been nice to me like you have," he said. "I've never felt this loved by somebody." The creature now sounded needy. Violet was sick at herself for what she had allowed to develop between her and this…person. She needed therapy. She'd get it, starting Monday. She owed it to David.

"Now, open up these gigantic gates." He was outside! There was no point in panicking. Violet simply had to make it through dinner, bid him adieu, and change her cell phone number. She pushed the button to open the gate and waited at the front door. "Jesus Christ," he said from the darkness as he tripped on something.

"Sorry. I should have turned on the lights."

Teddy emerged wearing jeans, a T-shirt, and a dark wool coat. His face was much more prepossessing than she had remembered. It filled her with calm, knowing she'd cast him back out into the world so handsome. He'd find another girl in no time.

"Don't kiss me," he said. "I have a sore on my mouth."

"Is it herpes?" Violet retracted the mixing bowl into her body.

"No, I don't have herpes yet. Ha! Listen to me. I don't have herpes *yet*. Aren't you glad you know me?"

He beat her to her own thoughts; Violet had to give him that. Standing there tentatively in his secondhand clothes, Teddy reminded Violet of that line in *Sweeney Todd* where Mrs. Lovett says to Toby, the street urchin who has developed a fondness for her,

What a lovely child it is. A rush of warmth filled Violet. For Stephen Sondheim, for putting it all down in words. And for her father, for telling her he would.

"Welcome," she said.

Teddy stood in the foyer and scoped out the place. "This is it?"

"It's not the biggest house. But it's by a good architect and we like the spot."

"You're seriously apologizing for this house? Jesus Christ. The view out this window is like a fucking airplane." Teddy followed Violet into the kitchen and sat at the counter. He checked out the valley lights to his right and the city lights to his left. "Okay, I just got a contact high from that magical acid you and David took." He opened a *New York Post*.

"David gets the New York edition Fed-Exed to him." Violet turned on the burner for the spinach. "He likes it better than the national edition."

"When I get to be a rich rock star, I'll have to start doing that with the *Desert Sun*." Teddy twirled around on the kitchen stool. "What's for dinner, Lucy?"

"I might have conjured up some brown rice, sautéed spinach, and tofu. Oh! I forgot the peanut butter." Violet opened the microwave and removed the jar. She dug in a spoon and plunked some into the ginger-soy mixture.

"Wait," he said. "You're putting peanut butter in spinach?"

"It's a ginger-soy-peanut sauce." She pulled a small whisk from a Tuscan ceramic.

"Peanut butter? I don't think so."

"It's a common ingredient in Asian cuisine."

"I can't eat sugar," he said. "It's bad for my liver."

"Who's talking about sugar?"

"There's a ton of sugar in peanut butter."

"Peanuts are nuts. Nuts are fat and protein. Not sugar."

"You're so fucking out of touch up here in your glass castle that

110

you don't even know what's in peanut butter!" Teddy gave her a lusty laugh and did another 360.

"*Peanuts* are in peanut butter." Violet wondered what the Kennedy girl must think of her boyfriend's intelligence, or lack of it.

"Say what you want," Teddy said. "All I know is spinach and peanut butter don't go together."

"They do, though." Violet stabbed the glob of peanut butter with a fork and raised it in the air. "But it's up to you. In or out, just tell me."

"Out."

Violet pitched the fork into the sink.

"Ha!" Teddy said. "Did I tell you I have a pimp nature?"

Violet threw the spinach in the pan. The flash of steam caused her glasses to fog. She didn't bother wiping them.

"WE'D like the tarte tatin, please," Sally said. "To share."

"Right away." The waiter withdrew the menu and retreated.

"Are you nervous about Sunday, my love?" she asked.

"Not really." He patted his jacket. "I was wondering. Do you—"

"Yes, Jeremy?"

"Have a pen? I wish I knew the breakdown of viewers in terms of sharps and squares. I want to remember to ask the producers tomorrow."

Sally knew herself well enough to know she was on the verge of one of her "Crazy Sally" episodes. The dinner wasn't over, she reminded herself. Perhaps Jeremy needed some space to gather his thoughts before he proposed. It was time to check her blood sugar anyway.

"Excuse me," she said.

To get to the bathroom, Sally had to walk through two rooms and a patio. She wasn't sure, but she thought that meant they had a bad table. In the front room, Sally came upon the entire band

Aerosmith, dining with some music business types. She could introduce herself as David's sister.

When David was just eighteen, he had joined a corporate accounting firm in Denver. Soon after, Aerosmith had come to play Red Rocks, where the band's manager had discovered someone was embezzling money from the tour. The manager called David's firm to send over their "most straitlaced" auditor. David ran the numbers and found a rat's nest of improprieties. The manager was so impressed he hired David to join the tour the next day. A year later, in a hotel lobby in Sydney, some local kids saw David emerge from a limo with Aerosmith and gave him a demo tape of their band. Not knowing what else to do with it, David passed the demo to a guy from the record label. That's how David had "discovered" Commonhouse. His reputation as a no-nonsense manager with an ear for music was on its way. Her geeky brother, David! The only record he'd ever bought was a Beach Boys greatest-hits album.

The guys in Aerosmith would certainly remember David if Sally dropped his name. But any time she had tried it in the past, a pall settled over the conversation. People still had to be civil to her—David's stature required it—but it was obvious what they were really thinking: David was an asshole. Sally opted to let Aerosmith dine in peace, and continued to the patio.

Adam Sandler was eating with his posse. He locked eyes with Sally, then returned his attention to his friends. Sally felt a jolt of humiliation that he had seen her emerge from Social Siberia. But, then again, for all he knew, she could have been eating with Aerosmith. Sally knew he'd glance back up at her, so on her way to the bathroom, she made sure to sway her hips.

Sally sat down on a toilet seat and took out her diabetes kit. She pricked her finger, dabbed the drop of blood on the test strip, and stuck it in the glucometer. Her seven o'clock reading had been a low 79, but with the swordfish and rice she'd just eaten, she had figured on something between 90 and 110. The glucometer read 260. *Dang*. It might be a false reading, considering she'd just eaten. Under normal circumstances, she'd hold off until her nighttime shot of Lantus. But not tonight. If Sally was going to indulge in a couple of bites of tarte tatin and a real sip of champagne, not a fake one, she'd have to counteract it with three units of Humalog. She washed her hands, dug out her syringe and insulin bottle, and lifted her dress. Her stomach had begun to bruise, which wasn't the most romantic sight in the world. She'd better take this shot in the leg. She drew out the insulin and stabbed herself in the quad. It hurt. The needle was dull. Time to throw it away. She applied pressure to the injection site. If she stood still for about a minute, it would help with the bruising.

Sally had to be especially vigilant about keeping her blood sugar near 100 because she'd gone off her birth control pills without telling Jeremy. This morning she had peed on the ovulation wand and it had come up pink, which meant she was in the all-important forty-eight-hour window. If the egg traveling down her fallopian tube was to get fertilized tonight, her sugar levels had to be absolutely consistent.

She recapped the syringe and returned it to the cosmetic bag, where she put the needles to throw away when she got home. She checked her smile in the mirror from the right, the side Adam Sandler would see as she returned to her table.

The maître d' stood at the star's table, blocking her line of vision. Sally considered it inappropriate for a maître d' to bother a celebrity like that. She paused.

"Excuse me." The hostess gently touched Sally's arm. "Can I help you with something?"

Sally jerked from the woman's touch and returned to her table. Jeremy was flipping a quarter and scribbling the outcome on a scrap of paper. The tarte tatin had been split onto two plates, and Jeremy had already wiped his clean. She waited for him to acknowledge her, but he didn't. She sat down, cut into her dessert, and took a bite. There goes thirty carbs for nothing, she thought.

"Try it with the whipped cream," Jeremy said eagerly. *The whipped cream!* That was it! He had hidden the ring in the whipped cream.

Sally gave him a beguiling smile. "I think I just might." The joy she'd kept bridled for the past month broke free. She had to steady her hand as she sliced across the dollop. The edge of her fork clinked against the hand-painted plate. Sally's eyes, her face, her past and future, fell on the fork positioned over the only remaining portion of whipped cream big enough to contain a ring. She slowly lowered her fork. It hit ceramic. She mashed the whipped cream. Once, twice—

"Just get a little bit." Jeremy helpfully stuck his fork on her plate. She attacked his fork with hers and smashed flat the whipped cream and the apple tart. Growls came out of her mouth. "Sally?" Jeremy asked. "Are you okay?"

"Sorry to interrupt," said a familiar voice behind Sally.

Jeremy looked up. "Hi," he said.

Sally spun around. Adam Sandler had come to their table! Had their chemistry in that one glance been so powerful that he'd brazenly ask her out right in front of her boyfriend?

"Look who's here!" she gargled.

"Sorry to interrupt." Adam Sandler shifted his weight and looked down bashfully. What a sweetie!

"Not at all," she said.

His eyes still on the floor, Adam Sandler said, "You're—"

"Sally!"

"Jeremy White," said Adam Sandler.

"Huh?"

"The maître d' tipped me off. You've got to believe there's like nobody I'd come up and bother while they're eating. Basically, you and any Pittsburgh Steeler. And Al Gore. But that's because I heard he was talking trash about my mother."

"What did he say about your mother?" Jeremy asked.

"He's joking!" howled Sally, rolling up her eyes.

"I've got to thank you for your Rose Bowl pick last year," the movie star said.

"Number one versus number two is a terrific angle," Jeremy said. "Works nine percent better in bowl games than regular season."

"I bet the money line," said Adam Sandler.

"You got plus one fifty, then. One sixty at kickoff."

"You're a fucking genius." Adam Sandler turned to Sally and said, "May I?"

"Sure." She had no idea what she had just permitted.

Adam Sandler grabbed Jeremy's cheeks and shook his face. "I love this guy," he said. "If you didn't have a girlfriend, I'd kiss you." He let go of Jeremy's face. "Good luck Sunday, by the way. They've been promo'ing the shit out of you."

"Thanks," said Jeremy.

"I'll let you go," Adam Sandler said, and walked off.

"Don't!" cried Sally after him.

The waiter swung by. "Would you be needing anything more this evening?"

"Just the check," Jeremy said.

DINNER was delicious and the conversation, covering topics from Teddy's favorite movie (*Vanilla Sky*) to his theory on the origin of hepatitis C (invented by drug companies), airless. Violet had let Teddy's misnomers, conspiracy theories, and harebrained schemes go undisputed, and even feigned interest in his idea for a TV show he proposed they team up to write.

"I can't believe it's almost ten o'clock," Violet finally said.

"What is that, a hint?"

"Not at all." She stood up and cleared their plates. He had eaten around the cloves of garlic. She didn't trust people who didn't like garlic, especially big fried pieces.

"It is a hint!" he said with a laugh. "Look at you. You're throwing me out."

"If that's what you want to call it."

"Well, thanks for dinner." He reluctantly got up. "I haven't had a home-cooked meal in years. I hope David realizes what a cool chick you are."

"Who knows anymore." Violet walked to the front door, but Teddy lingered at a painting.

"Is that you?" he asked.

"It's a portrait David had commissioned for our anniversary. That's me at the pool. You'll recognize the view."

"Coco's family is totally into art, too," he said. "They just sold a Picasso for like seventeen grand."

"Seventeen grand? It must have been a print."

"No, it was a painting. It was just really small."

Violet let that one go, and opened the door.

"So, we'll hang out again?" he said. "Maybe with your husband?"

Teddy and David friends? David would last about two seconds in conversation with this jejune nitwit.

"Teddy?" Violet said.

Teddy twitched.

"What's wrong?" she asked.

"That's like the second time I've heard you actually say my name. I still kind of can't believe I know you."

"I was about to say something intimate."

"Shit," said Teddy. "What?"

"I want you to know that the intensity I felt for you wasn't something that had ever happened to me before." Hopefully, Teddy would find comfort in these words when she stopped returning his calls.

"Hey," he said. "What are you doing tomorrow? You want to see me play in this gooney Rolling Stones cover band in Long Beach? We totally rock, even though the lead singer is a fucked-up junkie. I'm going to fire him after the show." He couldn't have known that David had once managed the Rolling Stones, and Violet had spent her honeymoon jetting through South America on the *Steel Wheels* tour.

"Really?" she said. "Bill Wyman kicking Mick Jagger out of the Stones? That can happen?"

"Shut up. Just come check us out."

"I wish," said Violet. "But I'm driving up to meet David at the yoga retreat in the morning."

"I thought he was going alone."

"I decided to join him."

"While we were having dinner? Jesus. Am I really that dull? I told you I'm tired, right?"

"Like you said, relationships are complicated." She kissed him on the cheek and closed the door. She returned to the kitchen and started the dishes.

Then her cell phone rang.

Without even looking at the number, she went to the front door and opened it. Standing there, phone in hand, was Teddy.

To be on the road with a rock band was to become intimately familiar with *Scarface*. The movie was on a constant loop in tour buses, dressing rooms, and hotel suites. Roadies had *Scarface* tattoos. Production offices were indicated by life-size cutouts of Al Pacino in that white suit. The video game was a recent annex to the riders of David's bands. Snippets of the movie's dialogue were played between songs on the precurtain mix tape. David knew them all: "First you make the money, then you get the power, *then* you get the women." "You think you can take me? You need a fucking army if you gonna take me!" "You're all a bunch of fucking assholes. You know why? You don't have the guts to be who you wanna be.... You need people like me so you can point your fucking fingers and say, 'That's the bad guy.'... Well, say good night to the bad guy." "I never fucked anybody over in my life didn't have it coming to them." Before their encore, Commonhouse would blast, "You wanna fuck with me? Okay. You wanna play rough? Okay. Say hello to my little friend!" Then they'd rip into "Light Sweet Crude."

David's personal favorite moment was when a business associate suggested doing something that displeased Tony Montana. Tony considered it, then said, "So that's how you wanna play it?" One of the most sinister lines in the history of cinema.

So that's how you wanna play it?

Violet had sent David off to a yoga retreat so she could fuck some guy named Teddy Reyes in David's ten-million-dollar house while their daughter slept at LadyGo's in Pasadena. Did Violet take him for a fucking chump? Had lust damaged her brain? Didn't she realize that David had spent the past fifteen years beating off groupies? What did she think happened on the road, anyway? But had he ever cheated on his wife? Never once.

When David had first met Violet, he was seeing a girl in Sacramento whom, to this day, he had never told her about. Sacramento Sukey, she was known to any band that rolled through town. She was famous for the blow jobs she generously bestowed, not only on the band members but roadies, too. No doubt, she was a skank. Still, David found her kindhearted and a good listener. She had a kid and cut hair or something. David found himself spending hours on the phone with her every night. He even flew her to Japan and Australia on one of the tours. He kept her quarantined in his hotel room, of course, for fear of getting ruthlessly teased if anyone discovered he'd developed bona fide feelings for the blow job queen of central California. In the early days of Violet, David had rendezvoused with Sukey a few times. But the moment he got engaged, he cut Sukey off. And now, sixteen years into a marriage, fresh from weaning their baby daughter, Violet was cheating on *him?*

So that's how you wanna play it?

David zoned out into the wet tea bag stuck to the side of his handmade cup. Dinner was over and everyone had trickled outside for the sweat lodge ceremony. He was alone in the mess hall, frozen, a state he had found himself in more than once since his arrival at the Matilija Retreat Center. During the afternoon yoga class, Shiva had asked David if he was okay. Only then had he realized he'd been standing, lost in a knot in the wood floor, while the other students were arched in backbends at his feet.

David looked up from his tea. A hand-painted sign on the wall read ONLY TAKE WHAT IS FREELY GIVEN.

Did Violet think David had earned eight million dollars last year in a music industry that had turned to shit because he didn't enjoy a *street fight?* For starters, he'd throw her out of the house. Change the locks. Cancel the credit cards. Shut off her cell phone. Impound her Mercedes. Send LadyGo and the rest of the minions packing. Then he'd kick the party into high gear and go about winning sole custody of Dot.

You wanna fuck with me? Okay. You wanna play rough?

All it would require was money. Any judge would sympathize with hardworking David, whose stay-at-home wife spent more time with her south-of-the-border lover than with the baby she could barely conceive.

Her womb is so polluted she can't even make a fucking baby.

David couldn't wait for the scabrous trial so he could enumerate Violet's maternal transgressions. The time she was changing the battery on a smoke alarm and Dot swallowed a bunch of pennies and David had to perform the Heimlich in order to save her life. When Violet had left Dot unattended in the rocking chair while she went outside to show the phone guy some junction box. Or when Violet was in another room and Dot had sucked on an indelible-ink marker, which left her with a sickening black mouth and tongue for a week. The jury would gobble that shit up. David wasn't the one who had been desperate for a baby, but at least he understood that once she was born he had an obligation to keep her alive!

The table David sat at was made of wood. Burned into its surface in wavy lettering were the words THIS PLACE OF FOOD, SO FRAGRANT AND APPETIZING, ALSO CONTAINS MUCH SUFFERING. David pondered its meaning, then caught himself softening and looked away: anger reloaded.

So that's how you wanna play it?

Did Violet actually think she could get by without David? The most she'd ever earned in a year was a million. And that was before she took five years off. The television business, like the music business before it, was fucked. If she was even able to get a job, she'd be lucky to make two hundred grand, one hundred after taxes. He'd love to see her try to scrape by on that! Private trainers, nannies, assistants, maids, first-class travel, limos, restaurants, shopping sprees whenever she got bored. That cost *real* money. Their nut was a million a year. Did Violet even know that? Had she ever thought to ask? Did she fucking care? She'd start caring come Monday, when she'd return home from some goddamned manicure and her gate clicker wouldn't work. When she finally tracked down a pay phone—she'd have to, as he'd have canceled her cell phone—David would be unreachable because he'd be out to lunch with one of the long list of women who would die to be seen with him. And how old would they be? Twenty-five. What would they look like? A perfect ten.

I never fucked anybody over in my life didn't have it coming to them. You got that?

She thought things were rough now? She didn't know the half of it. Her life would be spent *never knowing*. Would Dot get dropped off for her supervised visit? Would the alimony be there this month? Sometimes yes, sometimes no. David would fuck with her payments as much as possible without getting hauled into court. There were pettifoggers who specialized in shit like that. Violet would become one of those divorcées deformed by plastic surgery who descended into madness and isolation because all they could talk about was how evil their ex was. Violet would be forced back into the workplace. She liked houses; she could always become a realtor. He pictured her face on the bus bench, VIOLET PARRY, THE CONDO QUEEN OF ENCINO!

You think you can take me? You need a fucking army if you gonna take me!

What did Violet think was so great out there for a fat, divorced, forty-two-year-old woman with a kid? Oh, that's right, some guy who didn't have the wherewithal to fix his own car! For that Violet had sabotaged sixteen years of marriage and a family? For that she was willing to abdicate all claims to David's riches?

Say good night to the bad guy.

David hoped Teddy the King would still be there for Violet when the money dried up and the friends mysteriously scattered. LA wasn't kind that way. All their friends would fall in line behind legendary impresario David Parry, not his aging, unemployable wife. How long would it take Violet to realize that all she was to Teddy Reyes was a rich lady who paid to have his car fixed? If *Señor Reyes* could stomach fucking *Señora Gorda,* there might be more bills paid. Perhaps a new cell phone. He'd gladly eat some stretched-out gabacho pussy for one of those stylin' Apple phones! Was Violet deluded enough to think Teddy Reyes was in it for her sparkling personality?

"David?" It was Shiva. She stood in the open door. "Are you going to join us for the sweat lodge?"

"I'll be right there."

And David *would* be there. He honored his commitments. Violet had been the one to sign up for the yoga retreat, but she apparently preferred staying home and getting fucked by a beggar!

David brought his cup to the kitchen. Above the sink hung a colorful sign, WASHING THE DISHES IS LIKE BATHING A BABY BUDDHA. THE PROFANE IS SACRED. He smashed his cup in the sink and went outside.

The night sky was not an LA night sky, where streetlights hit the haze and ricocheted back a constant glow. It was a night sky that meant business: black, the stars-you-could-touch each had their own twinkle. David walked under the canopy of ancient California oaks and startled as the stars popped out from between the web of branches. The roar of the water sliced into his ears. He had noticed a river before, but only now really heard it. David hung at the perimeter of affluent yogis and yoginis who, like him, had driven up from the city. They stood around a roaring fire, attention rapt on Ruth, an abdominous woman with tough skin and scarecrow hair.

"The ceremony will last for roughly an hour and a half," she said. "Hot stones will be brought in between each prayer round...."

"Can I see your wrist?" whispered a young guy with a scraggly beard who wore pajama bottoms. "This sweet grass will form a band of protection around your heart."

"If it's supposed to protect my heart, why are you putting it around my wrist?" asked David.

"It's to protect *your heart*," the kid said. He was either stoned or stupid. David offered his arm. The hippie, tongue hooked over his lip in concentration, braided some grass around David's wrist and gave it a tug. "Make sure you let this fall off naturally. If you cut it off, everything you receive tonight from the Great Spirit will disappear."

"Thanks for the tip."

"There are about thirty of us," Ruth was explaining. "That means we'll need to have an inner and an outer circle. It's going to be a tight fit." She nodded to a chest-high dome constructed from branches; it measured about twelve feet in diameter and was covered in animal hides.

Tight fit? When Shiva had said there'd be a sweat lodge, David pictured a *lodge* lodge, like an Ahwahnee or an El Tovar. Not as grand, obviously, but something wood paneled, with a place to sit, like a big sauna. *That puny twig thing was* the *fucking sweat lodge?* During the evening yoga class, David had contemplated some hippies pulling pelts out of a plastic storage bin, the kind Violet kept stacked in the carport to store Christmas decorations and the like. The hippies had laid the pelts across this wood structure. David had assumed there'd be one structure per person. *Jesus,* they were all expected to fit into this *one?* And hot stones, too?

"The temperature will reach a hundred and fifty degrees," said Ruth, oblivious to the growing terror in the Westsiders' eyes. "I will pour water onto the stones throughout the ceremony, which will make it about two hundred degrees with humidity."

There was no way Violet would have been able to take this. David remembered when she was pregnant and she tried to cajole him into letting her have a home birth. He pointed out that she had once complained for three days after swallowing a piece of gum. "I have a high tolerance for pain but a low tolerance for discomfort," she had explained. It was very Violet, and David was charmed, as ever.

"Earth Mother," Ruth intoned to the night sky, "we ask you to accept us into your womb and return us to our innocence. Please cleanse us of our ignorance and spiritual *dis-ease....*"

Dis-ease. This, too, would have sent Violet fleeing to the nearest Four Seasons. Nothing vexed her like hippies mangling the English language. Once, during a yoga class at home, Shiva had said,

"We're all members of the *one song*." She repeated it several times, *one song* this, *one song* that. Finally, Violet couldn't take it anymore. She stood up out of her Warrior II pose and demanded, "Why do you keep saying that? What is that? *One song?*" Shiva answered, "Uni-verse. *Uni* means one and *verse* means song. One song. Uni-verse." Violet rolled her eyes. "Oh, for God's sake," she said, always her father's daughter!

Ruth started banging on a drum. "We call upon the spirit guides of the Four Directions. We beseech you to grant us your wisdom so we may be re-birthed into the world with a healed heart."

A pleasing array of yoga asses swayed to Ruth's *a capriccio* drumbeat. David used to fetishize yoga chicks for their hot bodies and free-loving spirits. But enough yoga classes had made him realize these hotties were no less crazy or manipulative than strippers. Both were willfully ignorant and directed their limited intelligence into their bodies. There was a yin-yang to it. Yoga chick on the one side, crazy stripper on the other.

"Now that we've blessed the stones," Ruth said, "it's time for us to take off our clothes and enter the lodge." She ripped off her T-shirt and sarong. David wasn't the only one to quickly look away.

If Violet were here, she'd have been having a complete breakdown. He'd have to go through the whole rigmarole about how she wasn't fat. A lie! But what else could he say? David had never pressured his wife to lose the baby weight. He was painfully aware of the looks on people's faces any time Violet stopped by the office, their eyes aglimmer because the almighty David Parry's wife had gone fat on him. He had been heartened this past month to see Violet exercising and losing weight—for Teddy! *It was for her new lover, Teddy.*

"Aaagggh!" He punched a nearby tree. The skin across his knuckles split open. He felt the sting but didn't bother to look.

Apparently, nobody wanted to be the first to strip. All just stood there, eyes downcast. At least nut job strippers had no problem getting naked! David pulled off his T-shirt, stepped out of his shorts, and walked over to Ruth.

"What is it you want us to do?" he said.

"Enter the lodge on your hands and knees, prostrating yourself to Earth Mother. Crawl counterclockwise until you're nearest to the door on the other side."

David spiked his clothes, dropped to his hands and knees, and hightailed it into the so-called lodge. Inside, he hesitated. It was darker than dark, the dark of nothingness, and impossible to determine where his body ended and the blackness began. He proceeded gingerly, the twig wall brushing his right side. Suddenly, a pain pierced his knee. A sharp rock was sticking out of Earth Mother. David's hand was already raw and throbbing from the tree. He didn't want to fuck up his knee, too. He stood up, and the whole lodge popped off the ground with him. He fumbled for a branch to balance the sweat lodge before the whole goddamn hunk of junk capsized.

"Jesus Christ!" He dropped to his knees, and the structure crashed down on his back. "Fuck me!"

"Hey, what happened?" called Ruth. "Stay prostrated close to Earth Mother."

David continued crawling, then felt something soft on his face. Before he realized it, he was inhaling a musty animal pelt. "Gaaah!" He slapped the germs off his face, then a head rammed his legs.

"Did someone up there stop?" asked a voice.

David decided to bail on this perimeter bullshit. He clambered across to where he sensed the door would be. But then his arm buckled and his face was planted in some loose dirt: he had fallen into a pit. "Cock-sucking fucking shit cock motherfucker." David spit out a mouthful of dirt and licked the rest onto his forearm.

"I think someone's hurt," called a frightened woman.

"I'm fine!" David lifted himself back on all fours. He had lost any sense of direction. He decided to crawl until he reached the wall, then hang a left. He put one hand in front of the other until the crown of his head tapped a branch. He turned to the left. He felt something soft and fuzzy against his arm. Only when it pressed harder against him did he realize he had brushed up against a dick and some hairy balls. "Aah!" David jerked his arm away.

"Just breathe in, buddy."

"Yeah, I'm trying."

"One hand, then one knee," offered another voice.

"Then the other hand and then the other knee," someone else pitched in. "Break it down."

How had this fucking happened? Just this morning, David had booked Hanging with Yoko to open fifty dates on the Green Day tour. And now a mob of new age dipshits was instructing him on the finer points of *crawling?* These privileged half-wits who drove up for the weekend in their Mercedes Kompressors, did they actually think they had money? David would put his portfolio up against theirs any day. *Bring it, motherfuckers!*

"Why are we stopped?" squeaked a woman.

"I thought we were supposed to go counterclockwise," said a deep voice.

"Is something wrong?" It was Ruth. She must have stuck her head in. "You've got to keep moving in there. Is someone confused?"

"It's the guy who punched the tree," volunteered a woman.

Anger ripped through David. Violet would pay for this. He would put a dollar amount on his rage and humiliation and deduct it from her settlement. He took a deep breath, then knocked heads with somebody.

"Ouch!" cried a woman.

At least it meant he'd reached the door. David felt for the edge, then planted himself beside it and pulled his legs into his chest. The dick-and-balls guy plastered himself next to David. Why didn't he just lean in for a kiss while he was at it? David attempted to get comfortable, but a knot from a branch poked into his upper back. He reached around and broke it off. It didn't do any good. He shifted his weight and nestled between some bigger branches. He licked his injured knee and sucked the dirt from the raw wound. Big salty flaps of skin came off in his mouth. If Violet were here, she'd give him a peck on the cheek. She understood how hard his days were....

A fleshy ass dropped onto David's feet. He quickly widened his stance to avoid his toe up someone's butt. A slender back leaned into his shins. He scrunched his legs closer, but the person just pushed deeper into them.

Something heavy landed in his lap. Jesus Christ, it was a *braid*. One of the yoga-chick-slash-strippers had a big one. He had marveled at its lack of hygiene in the dinner line. David lifted the braid with his thumb and index finger and dropped it off to the side. In an instant, it was back in his lap. Once again, David picked up the braid.

"Excuse me," whispered a woman. "It throws off my alignment if my braid falls to the side."

"How's that my problem, Rapunzel?" David tossed the braid off to the side.

"I need it to fall straight back," she said. The braid-that-wouldn't-die landed in David's lap.

"Cut your hair, why don't you?" David chucked the braid to the side, making sure to yank the woman's head in the process.

"Ouch!"

"Fuck you!"

"Hey—" admonished someone. "Language."

"That energy is totally inappropriate," said another.

The fetid thing once again appeared in David's lap. He wiped his bloody hand and knee on it.

"What are you doing?" said the woman.

"Nothing." David spit into his palm and smeared that on the braid, too.

Violet would have found this hilarious. If she were here, this incident would be added to their rich annals of happiness: how the sweat lodge kept getting worse and worse and then…the hippie braid fight. Knowing it was being shared with the woman he loved would have made David's increasing misery almost thrilling. But no, it was just David, alone in the dark with a bunch of strangers.

Fat-lady grunts announced the arrival of Ruth. "O Great Spirit of Life," she adjured, "we are gathered below in our pitiful little lodge on Earth Mother." Ruth needed to read that book of Dot's about using your "inside voice." If David had whispered that to Violet, she would have cracked up. He smiled. Violet had a zesty, unapologetic laugh. After all these years, it still took him by surprise.

"We shall invite the helpers of the Great Spirit to enter our lodge," said Ruth, who continued on with some mumbo jumbo. The drum sounded three times, then there was silence. Not even the river could be heard. Did their bodies absorb its roar? The hides deflect it? David couldn't comprehend the physics of it. A glowing orange orb floated past him. Smooth wood touched his shoulder. The fire guy must have been using a pitchfork to lay down the hot stones. Three more were brought in and lowered into the pit. Sweat dripped down David's face. A hiss filled the darkness. Wet heat blasted him.

"O Wakan Tanka," Ruth said, "we thank you for providing us with life-giving rains, which this water symbolizes." Her voice had become low and spooky, like Sally and her little friends when they'd put on séances.

David closed his eyes. It seemed no darker than before. He opened his eyes to make sure. Indeed, there was no difference. His eyelids fell and, in turn, his body levitated slightly. He knew it wasn't levitating. Obviously, his body wasn't levitating. Still, he kept his eyes closed to enjoy the strange sensation.

"We will now begin our four rounds of prayer," said Ruth. "I will begin, then we will go around one by one, starting with the first gentleman who entered." That would be David. He smiled as he imagined Ruth's words entering through his legs and traveling up to his brain that way. "When you are finished praying, you are to say, Ho! Then, as a way of acknowledging your prayer, the group answers, Ho! That will indicate that it's time for the next person to speak." David didn't really understand what he was supposed to do and didn't really care. "Great Father Sky," entreated Ruth, "you are the protector of Mother Earth. We call upon your power to heal our hearts. May we be free from danger. May we be free from *dis-ease*. Until we feel happiness and peace ourselves, we will be unable to walk down your great Red Path. Kindly listen as we go around the circle and pray for ourselves." Ruth shook her rattle. "Great Father Sky, I ask you, please free me from depression," she said. "Ho!"

"Ho!" answered the chorus of yogis.

Shit, that was quicker than David had expected. It was now his turn to pray for himself. What did he want? The man who had everything. David liked to tell people that the only thing money couldn't buy was poverty. Maybe he could lay that line on these new age bozos. Or, better, he could say, "My wife's back home fucking a Mexican. What does that make her? A…" And then they'd answer, "Ho!"

Instead, David found himself saying, "To be understood. Please, let me be understood. Ho!"

Violet thought he was an asshole. Everyone at this retreat thought he was an asshole. LadyGo walked around on eggshells because she thought he was a big asshole. Hanging with Yoko had signed with him because, after meeting with all the top managers, they said, We wanted an asshole on our team. None of them understood: David was no asshole. He was responsible.

"Free me from attachment," said the man to his left. "Ho!"

"Please," said a woman, "let me live in a world…" She paused to gather her thoughts, then continued, "…not *without* men, but with men who are more in touch with their inner woman."

David had taken care of Sally since she was two. Their dentist father had died suddenly of a heart attack, leaving the family shockingly in debt. Their mother's response was a rapid descent into frailty: physical, mental, emotional. Twelve-year-old David had no choice but to quit sports and devote his afternoons and weekends to working. A year later, Sally was diagnosed with juvenile diabetes.

"Money problems," someone was saying. "I promise I will get everything under control if you remove my debt. Ho!"

It was up to David to take Sally to her doctors, check her heartbreakingly tiny feet for cuts, monitor her blood sugar, ride his bike to the pharmacy to get her insulin, cut the Chemstrips in thirds to save money, fill out reams of insurance forms. And always, the shots. Any kiddie birthday party, David would take the bus to the only bakery in Denver that carried sugar-free desserts. It was down on Colfax and Franklin, the one that stuck day-old doughnuts on tree branches for the birds. He'd buy something for Sally so she wouldn't feel any more ripped off by life. On Halloween, he would tie ribbons around baggies of celery and deliver them on his paper route with a note that read "When the drum majorette trick-or-treats tonight, please give her this. She's diabetic." He'd stay with her at ballet class, long past the age when the other girls got dropped off, making sure she ate, and ate properly. But he never saw Sally as a burden. It filled him with lofty purpose, doing the work of Sally's pancreas so she could remain a child.

"Free me from fantasy," a voice cried in the dark. "Ho!"

But everything changed when Sally turned eleven. David had driven her to Dr. Turner to discuss recent advancements in diabetes treatment. The doctor asked Sally about her regimen and David jumped in with the answers. The doctor instructed David to step into his office, where he called the Denver Children's Hospital and requested a bed for the next week. "It's time Sally learned for herself how to be a diabetic." David said, "But I'm her big brother; I want to help her." The doctor replied, "Help her, you'll kill her." David didn't visit Sally once that week, as she learned for herself to count carbs, prick her finger, read a glucometer, and give herself multiple shots. A month later, Aerosmith offered him the job. David's first call was to Dr. Turner. He said leaving Sally would be the best thing for her. So David left. She didn't tell him about the amputation until after it happened, after she moved to LA. He could see the terror in her eyes as she pshawed it as a silly inconvenience. His heart broke for her, so he went along with the charade. A charade he'd kept up for the past ten years.

The drum sounded again. More rocks were brought in. David leaned into their unbelievable heat. It was soothing in the same way that biting down on a sore tooth made it feel better.

"Now that Great Father Sky has healed our hearts," said Ruth, "we ask Earth Mother to do the same for a beloved friend. May this beloved friend be happy. May they be physically well. May they feel safe. May they know peace." The rattle sounded. "To the man out there who hasn't found me yet," she said. "You, beloved life partner, may you feel joy. I love you so. Ho!"

It was David's turn. He had only one beloved friend. "My wife," he said. "Please help her. She is suffering. Ho!"

Why else wouldn't she be here? The Violet he knew and loved showed up. The first time he had laid eyes on her, she was sitting in that ticket holders' line ahead of time. She was a stand-up chick. She didn't bail. She didn't lie. She certainly didn't *cheat*.

"My children," another voice said. "Ho!"

Violet must have been suffering. What else could explain her behavior? She had wanted a baby more than anything. But she seemed to be running away from little Dot. That must have been so confusing to Violet. Violet, who was so intelligent and empathetic.

Violet, who had said just the right thing innumerable times to all different types of people. This time, Violet was unable to help herself.

"I pray my boyfriend finds the clarity to accept my love," said
someone. "Ho!"

Violet was radiant and honest and impeccable with her word
and serious and vulnerable and remembered things you said ten
years later and played the piano and could quote Shakespeare and
wrote thank-you notes and once even a letter to the boss of the
guy at the airline counter who had been especially helpful on their
way to Aspen and she kept secrets and listened to what you were
saying not just with her ears but with her eyes and also her smile
and she left five dollars in the hotel for the maids and knew a hit
song the first time she heard one and baked teething biscuits for
Dot and grew the most lovely smelling roses and knew how to cro-
chet and spoke four languages and when someone complimented
her on her perfume she'd send them a bottle the next day and anytime David looked across a crowded party and saw her talking to
somebody he had no doubt they'd adore her just like he did and
she never wore makeup and people remembered her for her dinner parties and big crazy words and without her he was just an
asshole rock-and-roll manager that's why the guys from Hanging
with Yoko said he was an asshole because they hadn't met Violet
yet and when people met Violet they realized there must be something more to David because why would such a successful and
worldly and gorgeous, he couldn't forget gorgeous, woman be married to David if that was all he was, an asshole? To the uninitiated,
David seemed like the star of the marriage. This was the truth,
though: people came for David, but they stayed for Violet. And
now she was gone.

David wept. Others did, too. More stones had been brought
in. Water had been splashed on them. More steam arose. These
things must have happened, for Ruth was praying again.

"O Great Spirit," Ruth said, "we give thanks for the rich bounty that results from the water of springtime. You have heard our prayers for ourselves. You have heard the prayers for our dear friends. Now let us summon the Buffalo Calf Woman to send similar healing to a teacher. A difficult person who has been placed on our path to teach us compassion. The rains of the Great Spirit are not selective. They fall equally on one and all, and so should our love. We now ask the Buffalo Calf Woman to birth this equanimous love and let it rain on this difficult person who has caused us so much suffering."

David's head flopped down and landed squarely on the wet braid across his knees. He smiled and up bobbed his head.

"To my father, who beat me," Ruth said. "I hope he feels safe. I hope he feels free. Ho!"

"Teddy Reyes." David spoke the forbidden name. "Ho!"

David knew what it felt like to have Violet's eyes fall on you and you alone. It was as if you'd been singled out for life's greatest honor. Just minutes into their first date, in line for popcorn, David had felt it, and it made him believe he could accomplish anything. And he had! To meet Violet for the first time was to be seduced by her strange brew of curiosity and high-mindedness. Now Teddy, whoever he was, had gotten a hit of it, too. Of course he was calling. He needed another fix! Maybe he thought he was rescuing the rare, exotic Violet. From her asshole husband.

Because David was an asshole. He was mean to her. The shameful part was, he had only started being mean when she began to show signs of weakness. When she had trouble conceiving, then the remodel, and finally the pregnancy. With no money and no job of her own, David only bullied her more.

In the delivery room: Violet had been in labor for twelve hours, refusing the epidural. (She had been right; her tolerance for pain *was* high!) Violet, writhing and grimacing. David, horrified at his helplessness. In front of Dr. Naeby and the nurses, Violet said to her husband, "Please, don't be mean to me anymore. Look at me. See how hard I'm trying? Please don't be so mean, especially now, with the baby." Having watched his wife endure such pain, David had already resolved to do the same. But to be called out by a woman in labor, in front of a roomful of strangers, was unendurably humiliating. David rolled his eyes to Dr. Naeby and the nurses. The good doctor smiled, oh-the-things-I've-seen, and shrugged. Despite Violet's plea—indeed, perhaps because of it—David had, if anything, been crueler to her since she became a mother.

What had happened to them? When he met her she was Ultraviolet. That's why he loved her. Not for the fantasia of good food and laughter and sex that had become their life together. But for her supreme confidence. Her boundless energy. He had found a teammate who, like himself, could take care of business. For their one-year anniversary, right after they had moved to LA, he had bought her a gold necklace from the Elvis Presley estate with Elvis's "TCB quick as a flash" logo encrusted in diamonds. Sure, even in those early days, Violet would break down when it all got to be too much. She'd cry some mornings. But before noon there would invariably be a call. "I'm okay!" she would declare, and the sparkle was back. The mojo intact.

But this time Violet wasn't bouncing back. She had escaped into the arms of Teddy Reyes. Poor bastard. He probably thought he had a chance with her! He may have even convinced himself that he understood her. But before Violet was David's wife, she was her father's daughter. David knew the stories well. Had Teddy heard them, too? Of the often drunk and always grandiose Englishman driving his erudite little girl around Los Angeles in a convertible Jag, quizzing her on Greek versus Roman gods, or the legacy of Sputnik, or devouring the latest Broadway cast album? Did Teddy know Churchill Grace once sent his daughter to bed without pudding because she didn't know the exact round in which Muhammad Ali knocked out George Foreman in Zaire? David understood only too well that Violet was an inveterate snob. She would protest wildly when accused of such a thing. This blind spot was her most charmingest of charms. Soon, David knew, the snob in Violet would stir from its slumber and forbid her from spurning her Croesus husband and heiress daughter for a man incapable of scraping together sixteen hundred dollars to fix a car!

The drum sounded. Ruth spoke, "Now we will begin our final round of prayer. Let us commit ourselves to the transformative love we have generated and which connects us to the Great Spirit."

Right now, at this moment, David loved Violet.

And now he loved Violet.

And now he loved her, too.

The marriage had turned to shit. At least Violet was doing something about it. She was taking a leap. So David would take one, too: no matter what Violet said or did, from this moment on, he would love her as he loved her now.

Ruth shook the rattle. "I promise to slow down and appreciate life's precious gifts," she said. "Ho!"

It was David's turn. "I will love her. Ho!"

CHAPTER SEVEN

Present/Wonderful Moment ❧ I'm Hearing Something ❧ The Message

The *Pietà* ❧ Ritz-Carlton ❧ Elephant Slaying ❧ *Mas*

The Dress Hollow ❧ God Is for Poor People

VIOLET CARRIED DOT INTO THEIR SUNDAY MORNING RIE CLASS. RESOURCES for Infant Educarers, or RIE, was a parenting approach that Violet had flipped over. It was founded in the sixties by a Hungarian, Magda Gerber, and based on the research of Dr. Emmi Pikler, a Budapest pediatrician. RIE held that all babies were born competent, inner directed, and confident. Only by well-intended but misguided parenting in which babies were wheedled, praised, and entertained did they become insecure, overly dependent, and quick to bore. Unlike in other mommy-and-me-type classes, in RIE class, parents were asked not to initiate conversation with their babies, so the teachers could model how and when to respectfully communicate. Thus RIE classes were rather solemn affairs.

"Good morning, Dot," said Sharon, the serious but gentle teacher. Violet found it demoralizing that a woman in her sixties had a better body than she did.

Violet put Dot down and joined the wall of trendy moms. One man was there, a young tattooed father who took every opportunity to mention that he had directed an episode of *Entourage*.

Dot stood at the door, watching the group of infants play with wooden toys, plastic kitchen items, and such. She took a deep breath and looked at Violet. Violet nodded. Dot took a deeper, quivering breath.

"Ball," she said. Violet acknowledged this with a smile. Dot bustled over and picked up the ball.

"What we just saw was wonderful parenting on the part of Violet," said Sharon. "Dot was able to choose *on her own terms* when to initiate play. Violet did not order Dot to go play. How wonderful life would be if, as adults, we could take a couple of deep breaths to assess *our* comfort level before *we* jumped into a strange new situation."

Violet nodded. She hadn't heard a word of what Sharon had just said.

TEDDY *stood in the door, his hands nestled in the pockets of his pill-covered peacoat. His downcast eyes said he well understood that what they were about to embark on was grave and dishonorable. He entered the house and hesitated. Violet removed her glasses and placed them on a table alongside her car keys, some dry-cleaning tickets, and Dot's spare EpiPen. She locked the door, then walked to the couch and sat on its edge. Teddy followed and sat beside her, his head down, his hands still in his pockets. His profile betrayed his inferior breeding: weak chin, narrow nose, no cheekbones to speak of. Ashy skin, sparse eyelashes.*

He turned to Violet. "So?" he asked. Through a crack in his jacket, Violet saw his beating T-shirt. She moved closer and touched both palms to his cheeks, then ran her fingers through his thick, unclean hair.

"Oh Jesus." Unloosed, Teddy kissed Violet. She released into the pillows. They searched each other's mouths. Tenderly, roughly, trading off leads, as if to say, This is who you are? Well, this is who I am. *All with the aching thrill that is impossible with a husband of sixteen years.*

A blond-haired boy wearing a Hanging with Yoko T-shirt and kabbalah bracelet struggled to fit a hair curler into the wide mouth of a water jug. When he finally succeeded, the *Entourage* director glanced up from his text-messaging and said, "Good job, Django!"

Sharon smiled. Violet braced herself. She knew this guy was going to get it.

"In RIE," Sharon told him, "we think of praise as sugarcoated control. Django was peacefully enjoying the challenge of putting the roller in the jug. By telling him, Good job, you sent the message that something arbitrary to him is of great import to you. Not only does this confuse a child, but it also erodes his inner peace. Pretty soon, you will have a praise junkie on your hands whose only motivation in life will be to perform for other people because it's the only way he knows how to feel good about himself." Violet had never much cared for the *Entourage* director, and even secretly hoped he'd get on Sharon's bad side. But now that it had happened, it made her kind of sad.

VIOLET *luxuriated in the teenage playfulness of making out with Teddy. With her tongue, she explored the gap in his teeth. On one side was the sharp edge of his front tooth. On the other side, the flat, smooth molar.*

"I know," Teddy said. "When I first lost that tooth, I always did that myself."

"How did you lose it? Did a dealer beat you up?"

"I'm such a fucking cliché. You know me too well."

Violet kissed him again. He answered back. "Oh God," she said. "Can we kiss forever?"

"No!" Teddy laughed and pushed his hand down her pants, beneath her underwear, and slid his fingers up inside her. "God, your pussy's wet." For years, Violet couldn't get like that for David. It was unspoken, that they needed to use spit to fuck. It had been awkward and embarrassing at first; now it was just fact. "Take off your clothes," Teddy said, and pulled his T-shirt over his head.

Violet undid one button on her shirt, then the other. Luckily, she was wearing one of her new bras, a lacy confection that smooshed her breasts together to yield a fulsome, almost cartoonish cleavage. "Take that fucking thing off," he said. "Hurry it up."

"I have a question," said a young mother. "Tess fusses when I'm at my computer doing e-mail."

"What's your question?" Sharon said.

"I feel bad. I mean, I need to check my e-mail—and I never do it for more than fifteen minutes—but Tess hates it. And I want her to be happy."

"Wanting your child to be happy is a misguided goal," said Sharon. "The goal shouldn't be to raise a constantly *happy* child. The goal should be to raise a child who is capable of dealing with reality. Reality is boring. Reality is frustrating. Reality isn't about getting everything you want the second you want it. Even a one year old is capable of handling these things."

Violet was back in the living room with Teddy.

He undressed with frenetic purpose, as if stripping in the snow before jumping into a hot tub. It allowed Violet to match his lack of shame with her own. Naked, supine on the velvety couch, she felt giddy nonchalance. She was Manet's Olympia, sumptuous, alert, being attended to by a dark figure. More shocking than the tableau was the trust she felt in the supplicant standing before her with the big erection.

"I can't believe how hard I am right now," he said, stroking himself. "Jesus, you have great tits." He reached down and cupped one of her breasts, her soft

white skin super-sensitive to his every hangnail and cracked cuticle. Teddy sidestepped between the couch and the coffee table until he stood squarely before her, then dropped to his knees. Violet pushed the table away with her heels.

"Thanks," he said. "I didn't know if it was a million-dollar antique or something."

It was a Donald Judd and it cost fifteen grand, but Teddy didn't need to know that. He sucked her breast. His hands moved to her legs. He pushed them apart, wide. Violet smiled-winced at the pleasure-pain of her ligaments stretching. Teddy sat back on his heels and examined her. "Your pussy is more gorgeous than anything on the internet. You just ruined jerking off to porn forever."

"I think that makes me happy."

"You little minx," he said. He gave her inner thigh a sweet kiss.

"That's me all right. A little minx."

He rammed his face between her legs and worked his fingers, his tongue, even his teeth, it seemed, only coming up for air, face shiny, to exclaim, Fuck, or, Jesus.

For fun, Violet said, "Jesus, fuck me," but Teddy didn't get the reference.

OLIVER, a darling two year old, shook the water bottle full of hair rollers. Dot ran to look and tripped over a plastic bucket.

"Dot, I saw that," said Sharon. She walked over and sat near Dot, who was about to cry, or maybe not. "You fell and hit your head." Sharon picked up the bucket and showed it to Dot. "This bucket. You tripped on it."

Dot took in Sharon's words, then sprang up and ran to join Oliver.

"All Dot needed," Sharon said to the parents, "was acknowledgment that someone saw what had happened to her. Parents think they need to fix every little painful thing that happens to a child. Children are born with an incredible capacity to get over things.

They just need to know that someone saw it. It is evident to me that Violet is adhering to the RIE principles at home."

"Thank you," Violet said.

KNOWING that Teddy preferred going without, Violet was relieved when he dug through his pants and pulled out a condom. "Just happened to have one handy?" she teased.

"I never know who I'm going to run into. One time, I was coming out of the men's room in Beverly Hills, and there was this hot lady just sitting there."

"Oh yeah?"

"I totally could have fucked her."

"You think?" Violet watched Teddy put on the condom. She had been married and faithful for so long that sex with a condom was a racy novelty.

She lay back and hung one leg over the back of the couch. Deep in a trance, Teddy positioned himself and thrust inside her. Once, twice. He brushed his hair out of his face and pushed himself up on his hands and looked down. He was transfixed by the rhythmic penetration. Like a stupid animal, his mouth hanging open, watching.

"Fuck," he kept saying. "You're so fucking hot."

Now Violet knew: this was all she'd ever needed. Not the money, not the career, not the landmark aerie. The moment she recognized it, a panic filled her: it wasn't enough. Teddy was on top of her, fucking her hard, grunting with each thrust. They were sticky with sweat. She breathed him in. It still wasn't enough. Violet pulled his body close into hers and stuck her tongue in his mouth. It still wasn't enough. She clawed her nails deep into his back. He reached for her hand, singled out her index finger, and pushed it toward his asshole.

"Do that," he said. She stuck her finger in deep. "Like that," Teddy whispered. "I like that." She grabbed his hair with her free hand. "You fucking whore," he whispered. Teddy's cock was in her, his tongue in her mouth, her finger up his ass. There was nothing more she could do. This had to be enough. She closed her eyes.

Present Moment, Wonderful Moment.

That was a mantra the Vietnamese monk Thich Nhat Hanh had given at a teaching in France. Each time Teddy pulled out, Violet thought, *Present Moment.* Every thrust in, *Wonderful Moment.*

Present Moment, Wonderful Moment. She finally understood what the simple Buddhist had meant.

There was one problem: the future.

Violet opened her eyes. What would she do with all the moments that weren't this present moment, this wonderful moment? There would be so many, too many to endure. She was forty-two. If she lived to eighty, there would be almost forty years of moments that wouldn't be this wonderful. Violet closed her eyes. She had to stop thinking that way. *Be present,* she scolded herself. *In. Out. In. Out. Present Moment, Wonderful Moment.*

"Get on your hands and knees," Teddy said. She did, and he pushed deep inside her. The force of it sent her face into the arm of the couch. Violet grabbed onto it for support. He reached under her and lifted her so they both stood on their knees. Their reflection in the sliding glass door was beautiful, haunting. Violet naked, hair cascading down. Behind her, Teddy, his dark arms entwined around her luminous skin, playing her like his upright bass, attuning himself to her subtleties. The overlay of dappled moonlight reflecting off the pool reminded Violet of that Gustav Klimt painting The Kiss. Once, in Vienna, it was on some rock tour, she couldn't remember which, she had gone to see it three days in a row. There it was, in the reflection.

Suddenly, Teddy stopped. "Is that a tat?"

"A what?"

Teddy lifted her hair off her ear. "It is. Ha! It's a fucking tattoo."

"Oh yeah. Violets."

"When did you get all tatted up?"

"In Amsterdam, one spring break."

"You hung out in Amsterdam? With the hash and hookers?" He pulled out and turned her around.

"With the Anne Frank house."

"The what?"

"Anne Frank House."

"Who's that?"

"The Jewish girl who hid from the Nazis in the attic and then died in the Bergen-Belsen concentration camp."

"Hey, nice thing to bring up while you're getting fucked."

"You're the one who brought it up."

"I just asked about your tattoo." He kissed her neck.

"It seemed like the punk thing to do at the time."

"Do you think I should get a tattoo?" He sat down on the couch to give it serious consideration.

"No." She flopped on her back, her legs straddling him. "I think they're pretty reductive."

"Heh?"

"I can either fuck you or give you a vocabulary lesson. What's it going to be?"

"Jesus, look at you."

"Are you kidding?" she asked. "Look at you."

"I need to come on you." He ripped off his condom.

"Be my guest." In his animal trance, that Violet felt so privileged to be part of, Teddy jerked off on her stomach.

RIE class was over. Violet was collecting her things when the *Entourage* director approached. "Hey, I saw on the class roster, you're Violet Parry."

"Yeah," she said. Here it comes, Violet thought.

"I directed an *Entourage* once."

"Really?"

"Yeah. So I'm sure we know lots of the same people. Are you working on anything now?"

"Nope," Violet said. "I'm out of TV. You know, raising the kid."

"Your husband's David Parry?"

"Yeah." No matter how successful she was, it always came around to David.

"Did you see Django's T-shirt?"

"It's cute."

"Maybe we can have a playdate sometime," he said. "Django is always talking about Dot."

"Maybe." Violet pulled out her cell phone to make busy, then saw it: a red message light. She practically yelped. "I'll get your number next week. Dot! Hurry!"

"We're one minute away!" alerted the assistant director.

Jeremy sat at the anchor desk, all alone under the bright lights. He was full-fledged handsome in his Zegna suit and tie. Faye finished powdering his nose, then checked his hair. Jim sat at the next desk and gabbed on his cell phone.

And like a big dummy with nothing to do, Sally stood at the snack table, free falling. She had exhausted her arsenal of threats and emotional stunts. Never before had her wiles failed her like this. No matter how bad things had gotten in the past, she always had one more trick up her sleeve. Not this time. It had left her in such a state of panic that last night she needed something to help her sleep. But when she searched her medicine cabinet for a sleeping pill, anti-anxiety drug, or antidepressant—things she'd been prescribed over the years by doctors but had never actually taken—Sally remembered all the bottles were empty. Years back, she had dumped the contents of every one into her cupped hands and threatened to swallow them in front of Kurt. His reaction? He barely looked up from the TV. "Go ahead, take them. You don't have nearly enough there to kill yourself. They might make you more tolerable." In a frustrated rage, Sally had flushed them down the toilet.

So today, she came armed with her old standby, the single business card in her jacket pocket. She ran the edge of it between the flesh of her thumb and fingernail as she tried to catch Jim's eye. Coming to her boyfriend's first day of work with the purpose of hitting on his coworker: it wasn't Sally's proudest moment. But Jeremy had given her no choice.

"Twenty seconds!"

Maryam and her bosses settled onto their thrones in the control booth.

"Ten seconds!"

Jim, who hadn't even seen Sally yet, clicked his cell phone shut. Like a quarterback, he held the phone behind his head with one hand, pointed forward with the other hand, then…spiraled it right at Sally! She snatched it out of the air like a bride's bouquet and hugged it into her chest, suppressing a squeal of delight.

"Five, and four, and three," the director announced.

One second before the light went on, Jim winked at Sally, then turned to the camera. "This week," he said, "we have the pleasure of introducing our new feature, 'Just the Stats.' It's brought to you courtesy of Jeremy White. And if you've never heard of Jeremy White, lucky you. You don't have a gambling problem. Welcome, Jeremy."

The red light on Jeremy's camera came on. "Thank you, Jim," he said.

Maryam flew onto the set. Since gambling was illegal, it was a humongous no-no to use words such as *betting, point spread,* or *money* on *Match-Ups.* Jim must have ad-libbed that part. Sally, who loved the bad boys, found it an auspicious start to their future together.

"With their rebound-to-turnover ratio," Jeremy said, "I'd give Duke a big edge."

Maryam stared daggers at Jim, who mocked her with a schoolmarm face, then winked at Sally. Maryam spun around and caught Sally mid-giggle. Sally quickly turned to watch Jeremy.

"My picks are Duke and Villanova," he was saying. "Until next week, I'm Jeremy White and those are Just the Stats."

Jim's camera light came on and he turned to Jeremy. "I'm with you, Professor. The Duke D was impressive against the Wildcats."

Jeremy responded by silently staring into his own camera.

"Yoo-hoo!" Jim gave Jeremy a wave. "Over here, Professor."

An eternity passed as the studio hung on Jeremy's silence.

"Hey." Jim's voice was tense. "You okay over there?"

"Jim, you know what they say," Jeremy finally said. "Don't get on the bus with Cinderella."

"There you have it, boys and girls," Jim said. "Jeremy White has spoken. Call your bookies before the line moves."

"Cut!" boomed the director's voice.

"Jim!" shrieked Maryam. "You can't mention bookies!"

"Whoopsie daisy!" Jim cracked up.

"It's not funny," Maryam said.

"She thought it was hilarious." Jim pointed at Sally. All eyes turned to her.

"I did not!" Sally shook Jim's cell phone at him. She marched over to whack him, but tripped over Jeremy, who hadn't budged from his chair. His face was twisted, his eyes fixed to the floor. "Jeremy," Sally said, "the segment is over." He was unresponsive. She jiggled his chair. "Get up."

"I'm hearing something," yelled a sound guy. "It started at the end of the last segment. I need everyone to be quiet." The studio went silent and everybody stood still. "There it is," said the sound guy.

First, Sally smelled it: a pungent odor.

Then she heard it: a strange gurgling sound…

Sally looked down. It was coming from Jeremy. A brown stain spread down the inside of his pant leg. He looked up at her, helpless.

In an interview about his secret to success, David said that you only needed to get lucky once; after that, you had to get really smart, really fast. Sally had gotten lucky by capturing the imagination of that visiting Russian choreographer. But she hadn't followed David's advice. It was a mistake she was still paying for.

Standing in the studio, Sally recognized that luck had once

again presented itself. This time, she was going to get really smart, really fast.

"My bad!" she said to the crew as she touched her stomach. "I forgot to eat this morning." With a big smile, she tossed her purse into Jeremy's lap. "Let's go get some breakfast, sweetheart." She swiveled his chair and gave it a playful push toward his dressing room.

THE SUV that had been lurking for Violet's parking space honked, and honked again. Violet didn't care how long the bitch had been waiting, nor that Dot was crying because her shoe had fallen off, nor that it was boiling hot in the car with the windows rolled up. Teddy had finally called after thirty-six long hours. Violet replayed the message, to pillage it for meaning.

"Violet, Violet, Violet," her lover said. "Poor little rich Violet. Where y'at, woman? I just set up for my nonpaying big-band gig at a totally lame AA Sober Picnic in the valley. We're going on at eleven and playing for half an hour. There are like a thousand people here, and that rocks, but I had to haul my upright and amp across an entire soccer field to set up. These morons found the place farthest from the parking lot and decided, Hey, let's put the stage here. That's alcoholics for you. Maybe if David Parry managed me he could get some roadies written into my contract. But what am I saying? La la la la la la. I'm saying that I'm going to marry you. And you're going to cook for me and I'll golf in Pebble Beach and I'll never have to suffer through these ridiculous gigs again. Holler back, baby."

Violet shifted into drive and headed up the hill.

SALLY stood at the teeny sink in Jeremy's dressing room and scrubbed his underwear with warm water and a bar of soap.

Jeremy sat on the loveseat, a throw pillow covering his manhood. "I was fine when I was looking at the camera," he said to the floor.

"This is nothing to be ashamed of, my love." Sally rinsed and wrung out his underwear, then rifled through the drawers for a hair dryer. "Bingo!"

"I like looking at the camera," Jeremy said. "It was when I had to look over at Jim—"

Sally turned on the hair dryer and aimed it at the undies. Jeremy sat frozen, as if in a shock-induced trance. She held the underwear to her cheek. They were dry enough. "Here you go," she said. She glanced up and caught her reflection in the mirror.

Her face, tilted slightly downward and her arms outstretched, reminded her of the replica of Michelangelo's *Pietà* in St. Martin's church in Denver. As a child, Sally would stare at it during mass. She'd grow enraptured by the Virgin's look of sorrow, cradling her dying son. After receiving communion, Sally would pass by the statue and try to stop in Mary's direct line of vision. But the Virgin's flat marble eyes made it impossible. Sally spent her whole life secretly cuddling the feeling that love such as Mary's was her destiny.

Sally turned to Jeremy. He still wasn't getting dressed. "Get up," she clucked. "Turn around. I want to make sure all the poop is off." Jeremy shuddered, then complied. There was a trace of brown on the inside of his right knee. She wetted a paper towel and scrubbed it. "As good as new," she said. "I think it's best if we bring the suit to the dry cleaners ourselves. She stuffed the offending Zegna into a plastic shopping bag." Jeremy stepped into his khakis. Sally removed his blazer from the hook and helped him into it. She felt the pocket. The ring box was still there.

She led Jeremy to the parking lot. Words weren't necessary. From this point on, no matter how rich or famous Jeremy became, Sally would be the only one who knew that he had diarrhea on camera and she had saved him from career-ending public humiliation. He knew that she knew. It never had to be spoken of again.

Sally drove them straight to the Ivy. The maître d' had seen Jeremy on TV this morning. With great fanfare, he led them to a table, on the patio this time, where they dined on crab legs and mimosas. Over dessert of flourless chocolate cake—the tarte tatin wasn't as great as everyone had made it out to be—Jeremy proposed.

VIOLET stepped out of the shower and did the unthinkable: stood squarely in the mirror and examined her naked body. Over the years, she had perfected the art of getting out of the shower without catching even a fleeting glimpse of herself in the mirror. But it was imperative to know what Teddy would be seeing tonight so she could offer him only the most flattering angles. She had lost fifteen pounds in the past month and a half, but God she was fat! She might *feel* thinner, but that didn't mean she was objectively *thin*. And the skin on her cheeks hung off her high cheekbones. Sometimes her face looked plump and youthful; sometimes it looked like an arid hide. This is what happened when you were forty-two: sometimes it all came together and you looked okay; sometimes you looked fifty.

It was noon. On his message, Teddy had said he was going onstage at eleven to play for half an hour. It would take another half hour to load his gear back into his car. He was in the valley, but where exactly? Violet figured it would take him half an hour to drive home. Assuming that he *didn't* loiter at the gig—and why would he, he had called it lame in his message—that would put his estimated time of arrival back home anywhere between twelve thirty and one. Violet had to leave pronto if she wanted to catch him.

She picked up the phone on the wall to call him. The message light was flashing. Violet's whole body seized up.

"Hi, girls." It was David! "I'm leaving early so I can come home and see my two favorite people. I miss you both and can't wait for a group hug." *Beep.* "Received Tuesday, 4:35 AM." *Shit.* Violet hadn't reset the date and time since the power went out last month. If David had left this message an hour and a half ago, she was in good shape. But if he had called just after she left for RIE class, he might burst through the door any minute.

"LadyGo!" Violet screamed. "LadyGo!" She had told the nanny to pack the car for a trip, but there was no way to tell how much LadyGo actually understood. LadyGo's English seemed to have somehow gotten worse over the past fifteen years. All Violet could do was instruct her and hope. Violet called LadyGo's cell phone. The one reliable law of the universe: nothing got between LadyGo and her cell phone.

"*Allo?*" LadyGo said.

"Could you please come into my bathroom?" Violet hung up. She grabbed a duffel bag and pell-mell crammed it with handfuls of underwear, pants, and shirts.

LadyGo plodded in. "Yes, *meesuz?*" Violet had relinquished command of the household to the El Salvadorian, who hadn't missed a day of cleaning in fifteen years and who now reigned supreme as the nanny. Violet had never enjoyed a relationship as simple as this, where the more she paid someone, the happier they were. Most people turned on her and got resentful for the vulgar wealth on display, but never LadyGo. She lived in an apartment in Pasadena with a rotating cast of sisters and cousins fresh from, as she'd wistfully say, "my country."

"When did Mister David call?" Violet asked. "Did you hear the message?"

"I don't know, *meesuz.*" LadyGo smiled. Violet never knew what LadyGo was always smiling about. It had even occurred to her that LadyGo wasn't smiling at all. Rather, it was just the deepening contours of her Indian face. There was no use trying to wring information out of the inscrutable nanny.

"Did you pack Dot's things like I asked?"

"Yes, *meesuz.*"

"Please have her in the car and ready to go in five minutes."

"Yes, *meesuz.*"

"We're going away in the car. For a trip. In five minutes. You understand?"

"Yes, *meesuz.*" LadyGo wasn't moving.

"We're going to the Ritz-Carlton." Perhaps the lure of purloined shoe mitts and sewing kits would light a fire under LadyGo's ass.

"Ritz-Carlton, *meesuz?*" Indeed, the name enlivened LadyGo. "Ritz-Carlton is *spencie.*"

"Yes, very expensive."

"Club floor?" asked LadyGo. The club floor with its twenty-four-hour buffet of shrimp, Coca-Cola, and miniature pastries was a veritable pleasure dome to the El Salvadorian.

"Yes. And we need to be out the door in five minutes." Violet held up five fingers.

"No *Meester* David?"

"No Mister David." Violet then noticed LadyGo's T-shirt. It read HOLD MY PURSE WHILE I KISS YOUR BOYFRIEND. It was a mystery to Violet where LadyGo got these things. (They seemed to have a connection to her prodigal nephew, Marco, who LadyGo was constantly bailing out of jail.) It mortified Violet to be seen at the Brentwood Country Mart or the Wednesday farmers' market alongside LadyGo pushing the stroller, wearing one of her bizarre T-shirts. The best/worst was last summer at an engagement party for someone from David's office. LadyGo had worn one that read ASS IS THE NEW MOUTH. Violet thought it was hilarious and dragged David over to see. David exploded; Violet had been apologizing for it ever since.

Violet grabbed a fleece and tossed it to LadyGo. "Here. Put this on."

"For me?" LadyGo smiled big.

"For you. Now go!"

"We go now?" asked LadyGo.

"We go now."

"Why you call me for?"

"Just be ready to go in five minutes."

LadyGo left and Violet took a breath. She had her phone, cash, clothes. She raced down the hall and found Dot in the middle of the kitchen, completely naked and eating a bag of Flamin' Hot Cheetos.

"LadyGo!" called Violet. LadyGo *knew* Dot shouldn't eat processed food; it made her eczema flare up. More important, Violet needed Dot hungry for the hour-plus drive down to Laguna. That way, she could ward off Dot's fussing with grapes and juice. The last thing Violet wanted was to scare off Teddy with a crying kid in the backseat. Violet squatted down and held out her hand. "Dot, sweetie? I don't want you eating Cheetos. Please give me the bag."

"*Want* Cheetos," replied Dot.

"I know you do. You can have some grapes later, when we're in the car."

The back door creaked open. Violet jumped. It was just LadyGo, speaking animatedly into her cell phone in Spanish, something about the Ritz-Carlton.

"Please, would you put a diaper on Dot," Violet said. "I want to leave in five minutes."

"Yes, *meesuz*." LadyGo took Dot's hand. "Come, *Mama*."

Violet grabbed hold of the counter and pulled herself up. She dialed Teddy on her cell phone. It went straight to voice mail. *Shit.* Violet dialed his number again. Voice mail. Again. Violet closed her phone.

The orchid on the counter. It was abloom in scowling, pinched faces! Slanted black eyes and yellow puckering mouths teetered under gigantic velvety white headdresses.

"Gaah!" Violet chucked the plant into the sink. She called Teddy again. Voice mail. She knew it was risky to show up without notice to whisk him off. But what qualm could he possibly have about an ocean-view suite at a five-star hotel? Violet dialed his number again. Voice mail. She hung up.

Dot emerged from the bathroom, dressed but still clutching the bag of Cheetos.

"Honey, give those to me," demanded Violet.

"*Want* dem," said Dot.

"You can't have them!" Violet tore the bag from Dot's hands. Angry red Cheetos flew all over the floor. "LadyGo!"

"Cheetos!" wailed Dot.

The back door opened. "LadyGo!" Violet scooped up the Cheetos. "Dot can't have these. It's what causes that rash on her feet—"

"*Meesuz,* you want LadyGo put Miss Dot in car seat now?" LadyGo appeared from the bathroom.

Violet froze. Who, then, had just entered through the back door?

"Knock-knock," a woman's voice chirped. "Anybody home?"

Violet spun around. Walking toward her were Sally and some guy she'd never seen before.

"Hello!" Sally called. "David? Dotty Dot? Anyone here?" She breezed down the hall, Jeremy right behind.

Finally, it was Sally's chance to prove *there was nothing wrong with her.* Not that her brother or sister-in-law had ever come out and said as much, but it was what that shrink one time called "the elephant in the room." The elephant in Sally's room was that something must be wrong with her if she was so pretty and thin and still single. It was also why Sally had stopped telling people she was David's sister. At first, they'd be impressed. But then, the elephant in the room: that there must be something wrong with Sally if David Parry was her big brother and she was still driving around with a trunk full of tutus. This engagement ring would slay both those elephants, and even a third: that Violet was somehow better than Sally. Now Sally would also be the wife of a rich guy. Plus, hers was on TV.

Sally stopped. Violet was in a dogfight with her wailing baby over a bag of chips. Dot's face and hands were covered in red dye, and that awful nanny just lurked and smiled.

"Hi, sis," Sally said.

"Sally. How did you get in?"

"I know the code to the gate." Sally prayed she was wearing enough foundation to hide that her face was most likely as red as Dot's. "From when I house-sat for you. I just wanted to stop by so you could meet my fiancé."

"David's not with you?" Violet asked.

"No." Sally hooked her arm in Jeremy's. "Violet, this is my fiancé, Jeremy White."

"Oh." Violet stuck out her hand. "Nice to—" She looked down. Her hand was covered in red dye. She wiped it on her pants. "Shit," she said.

There was a long pause. "Where are you going?" Sally asked.

"What?"

"Your car is packed."

"Ritz-Carlton, meesuz," chimed the nanny. "They give you steak and shrimp all day. I bring my wallet, but lady go, If you have special key, you no pay. No charge extra, nothing."

Violet told the nanny, "Put Dot in her car seat, please," then turned to Sally. "I'm sorry," Violet said, "but this isn't a good time to chat."

This wasn't a flipping *chat!* Sally had just announced she was getting *married.* Wasn't the big whoop about Violet that she was so classy with her fancy-pants upbringing? Sure, Violet was *rich.* The kitchen alone screamed money. The French sea salt in the silver dish. The Montblanc pens, some without their caps, stuffed into a Rolling Stones mug. The Cartier watch tossed into a bowl of miniature red bananas. The slim basket of boysenberries they wanted ten bucks for at Whole Foods. The shoes with the red soles that Nora Ross sometimes wore, so they had to cost a fortune, just kicked into the corner. But *class?*

Violet was a wreck! Her home was a pigsty. There was a two-hundred-dollar orchid—that their "orchid guy" came once a week to "switch out"—crashed in the sink. Her brat was screaming. The word *congratulations* had yet to be uttered! She was probably a size twelve. What was the use of having money and health if you weren't grateful? If you didn't look good? If you were going to act so weird and rude?

"We didn't want to stay long, anyway." Sally tightened the grip on her purse. "We just wanted to share the good news."

"I'm glad you did. But we're in a rush. I'll make it up to you."

"That won't be necessary," Sally said with a swallow. She took Jeremy's hand and turned to leave. "Oh, and Violet?" Sally added. "You look *amazing.* When I get pregnant, I want all your secrets so I can be tiny like you a year after giving birth."

"Oh, yeah…" Violet said. Then her face dropped.

Sally turned. David had entered, an uncharacteristic spring in his step. "David," she said. "Hi!"

"Dada!" Dot raced into his arms.

"Hey, beautiful!" David scooped up his daughter. "The whole gang's here! All my Parry girls! What's the occasion? Where's everyone going?"

"Ritz—" the nanny started in.

"David!" Violet jumped in. "Sally got engaged."

"Wow! You what?"

"I'd like you to meet my fiancé, Jeremy White."

"Wait," David said. "Jeremy White from the *LA Times?*"

"And now TV." Sally demurely held out her left hand.

"How about that sparkler! Jeremy White part of the family; who would have thunk such a thing? Welcome."

David grabbed Jeremy's hand, then winced in pain. David's hand was bandaged and he wore some hippie-looking braid around his wrist. "I forgot," he said. "I messed up my hand." Both knees were cut and swollen, too. "Honey," he said to Violet, "you know who Jeremy is. He's the one who picks the NFL games. He had an amazing run last year."

"A zillion percent or something," Sally mooned.

"Seventy-one against the spread," Jeremy said.

"Yeah, right." Violet's words looked like torture to get out.

"Hi, gorgeous." David walked over and hugged Violet. But she just stood with dead arms, car keys in one hand, cell phone in the other. David then announced, "There's something outside I want everyone to see."

Violet grabbed Dot and said, "We'll be right there."

Sally and Jeremy followed David outside. David stood at the edge of the lawn and pointed toward the horizon. "See them? Painted lady butterflies." Indeed, butterflies, in groups of a dozen, were flying in a straight line. "They're migrating from Mexico," he said. "They'll end up in the Pacific Northwest. It only happens once a decade. See them, Sally?"

This was the David she knew. The David who loved nature. The David who had been an Eagle Scout. The David who had taken her overnight camping in the Rockies and hung their food from a tree so bears couldn't eat it. The David who had brought her to a pond to study the movement of frogs for her solo in *The Frog Prince*. But *that* David left home the first chance he got, never to return. Now theirs was strictly a business relationship. David paid Sally's medical insurance and she kept away. Another elephant in the room.

"Yeah," Sally answered. "There are hundreds of them."

"Back in '98, Violet and I drove to this spot in Topanga that the entomologists projected would be on the migration path. It was like a Dead show. There were a hundred cars on the side of the road, and people were hanging out, listening to music. But the butterflies ended up migrating about five miles east. By the time everyone packed up and caravanned down Topanga, across PCH and up some other canyon, it was too late. The butterflies had gone. Just now, when I pulled up, I saw them. Of all places, of all times, they chose Stone Canyon, right now. What are the odds?"

"I've been trying to calculate them," said Jeremy.

"I bet you have!" David let out a big laugh, then turned to Sally. "Maybe these butterflies are a sign that you two should get married here."

In all of Sally's fantasies about her wedding, she had never allowed herself to imagine getting married at David's house. It was so obvious and within reach that for it *not* to happen would have been too cruel to endure. She looked up at Jeremy. "What do you say, sweetie?"

"Anything you want."

"Isn't this wild?" David said. A butterfly had just landed on his hand. "It's a chemical that builds up in their brains. Every ten years, the switch is flipped and nothing can stop them. Who ever thinks of a butterfly on a mission?"

Sally saw it before David did. She didn't know what it was exactly, but she wanted to protect him from it: Violet was in the car with Dot and the nanny, screeching onto Mulholland.

VIOLET felt LadyGo staring daggers at her from the backseat. "This Ritz-Carlton?" Violet said. She adjusted her mirror, but LadyGo averted her eyes. "It's supposed to be the best. Beautiful beach. Big pool…" Unimpressed, LadyGo shook an elephant rattle in front of Dot.

The scene back at the house was certainly inelegant. Sally barging in trailed by that sportswriter with the earplugs. And David. Bounding in, wearing a grass thing around his wrist, acting like Mr. Natural? His last words before he had driven off for the weekend were, You're not necessary. That's what Violet was fleeing, a dead marriage with a cruel husband who raged at her. His bruised knuckles told the real story. The peace-and-love David would soon revert to the volatile wall-punching David. Violet ached for Teddy—to be entwined in his dark, scarred arms, treated rough, exalted, laughing, kept guessing but always knowing. She crossed the double yellow line to enter the car pool lane.

"Truck with cars!" Dot pointed to a transporter loaded with Mini Coopers.

"That's right," Violet said. "A truck with cars."

"*Mas!*" Dot said. It had been her first word, *mas.* "More" in Spanish.

"It's right there," said Violet.

"*Mas!*" said Dot. "*Mas!*" She started to cry.

Violet slowed down so Dot was abreast of the transporter. "See it? It's right there. You don't need *mas.*" But Dot was implacable. "Baby, what's wrong?"

"Right turn ahead," said the computer lady on the GPS.

"*Mas!*" wailed the little girl.

"Give her some juice or something," Violet told LadyGo, and exited onto Sepulveda, then turned left on Venice.

"Your destination is ahead on your left."

Violet cruised past a ninety-*eight*-cent store. A place to refill your water jugs. Piñatas hung from a bodega's tattered awning.

"SpongeBob!" said Dot.

"*Sí, Mamacita,* SpongeBob!" LadyGo said, full of pride. "Miss Violet, the baby is too much intelligent." How would Dot know about SpongeBob? Violet and David didn't let her watch TV. LadyGo must be plopping Dot in front of it while Violet was away.

"You have arrived at your destination," announced the voice with an almost grotesque calm. Next to a Mexican dentist's office with bars on the windows, set back from a patch of dead grass, was a small two-story building.

Violet pulled an illegal U and parked the car. "I'm going to run in and pick up my friend," she told LadyGo. "*Then* we'll go to the Ritz-Carlton."

"Miss Dot stay in Mercedes car," said the nanny. Violet had seen where LadyGo lived and it was no step up from this. But get LadyGo in a Mercedes with a blue-eyed child and she became the queen of England.

"I'll be right back," said Violet.

There were two units in the stucco building, one above and one below. 11838 was upstairs. Violet passed some rusted rosebushes and climbed the steps. She opened the screen door and knocked. No footsteps, nothing. She knocked again. She scanned the street for Teddy's car. LadyGo pointed up to Violet. Dot waved. Violet waved back. She walked to the rear of the landing to see if there was parking behind the building.

"*Allo.*" A black man with braids, wearing just athletic shorts, appeared behind the screen. Violet remembered Teddy once saying he had a roommate named Pascal, someone from AA, who worked in catering.

"Hi," she said. "Is Teddy here?"

"*Zey* went out this morning."

Violet wondered, Did he say *they* or was it just his accent? "You must be Pascal?"

"*Oui.*"

"My name is Violet Parry." She held out her hand.

"The lady who paid to have his car fixed."

That wasn't exactly how she would have put it. "Yes," she said.

Pascal opened the door but wasn't happy about it. "Does Teddy know you're coming?"

"Not exactly." As Violet passed Pascal, she got the strong sense he was checking her out. She was overcome with guilt for letting Teddy down with her fat ass.

The apartment was bright and uncluttered. The beige wall-to-wall carpet—while beige wall-to-wall carpet—was surprisingly unworn. Violet was emboldened by the restraint of the decor. It struck her as adult and lent her confidence in having chosen Teddy.

"I'll call him to see where he is," Pascal said.

"I already tried. His phone is turned off."

"Let me try." Pascal disappeared to his bedroom and closed the door. Violet devoured her surroundings. An unobjectionable sectional sofa they had probably found on the curb. Some book-shelves made of cinder blocks and two-by-fours. French gangster movie posters on the wall. Teddy's golf bag. A boom box with lots of cheesy flashing lights. Jazz CDs. Rush CDs. Free weights in the corner. An unopened Homer Simpson Chia Pet.

"Teddy will be here in five minutes," Pascal returned to announce.

"Great, thanks."

"So, your husband is David Parry?"

"Yep." Violet went to the window.

"Must be nice, eh?"

"It's okay." LadyGo and Dot kicked a ball on the lawn. Violet had to give that to LadyGo: she never went anywhere without a ball. "My daughter and nanny," Violet explained.

Pascal looked out the window. "That's your S600?"

"My what?"

"S600."

"Oh, right. My Mercedes."

"Must be *very* nice."

Violet's cell phone rang. She checked the number. It was David. "I'm not going to get it."

The screen door creaked open and slammed shut. "Wazzup, bro?" There he was, Teddy, in the room with her.

Violet's intention had been to act cool, but a gigantic smile hijacked her face. "Nice to see you," she said.

"Look who found her way into Beaner Central. I hope you left some bread crumbs so you can find your way back."

"I have to change for work," Pascal said.

"Thanks, man." Teddy gave him a jive handshake and seemed to whisper something, then turned to Violet. "To what do I owe this honor?"

"I have a surprise for you."

"I'll say! Is that your kid and nanny outside?"

"Yes."

"Your daughter's beautiful. What's her name again?"

"Dot."

"That's right, Dot. Anyway." Teddy put his hands on Violet's hips. This was what it felt like to belong to Teddy. She didn't want to talk, just sink deeper and deeper until she no longer existed. "I'm waiting," he said.

"Oh—" she said. "Pack your bags. I got us two rooms at the Ritz-Carlton in Laguna Niguel, where we can eat healthy food and you can play golf at Torrey Pines."

"Wow!" Teddy's hands flew apart.

"Like you said, I make shit happen."

"Yeah... but I can't go."

"Why not?"

Teddy looked perplexed. "I have a job."

"You do?" Violet felt the blood rising in her cheeks.

"I'm not just a pickup cat. I work at a music store."

"Oh—I—"

"That's why my fingernails are black. It's ebony dust. I repair guitars. What? Did you think I was just *dirty*?"

"No—I—" Violet sputtered. "Can't you call in sick?"

"Not if I want to keep my job!" Teddy laughed. "Plus I have a commitment at an AA meeting tonight."

"Oh."

"My sponsor has me on a ninety-in-ninety. I have to do ninety meetings in ninety days. And I don't know any meetings down there."

"The concierge can help us find them," she said.

"The concierge can help us find them! Jesus Christ, I've arrived."

Violet felt like she was finally establishing a beachhead and carefully moved forward. "The concierge can also tell us where to buy you a new bass," she said. "Rickenbacker 4001, if my memory serves me."

"You get some serious points for remembering that." Teddy crept closer. "It can't be a new one, though. You've got to get me a vintage."

"Done."

"*Pura vida,* baby." He stepped in and gave her a rough kiss. There it was. She kissed back, matching his aggressiveness. "Shit, you're a good kisser," he said.

"How about we leave tomorrow?".

He pulled her head close and stood on his toes to kiss her again. David was six foot two and Violet had to stand on *her* tiptoes to kiss him. It seemed unnatural to lean down to kiss a man. Teddy suddenly jumped back.

Dot was climbing the stairs, LadyGo's head bobbing behind her. Neither had seen Violet and Teddy.

"Thanks," whispered Violet. She opened the door for her daughter and nanny. "Dot and LadyGo, this is Teddy. Teddy, this is Dot and LadyGo." Teddy and LadyGo exchanged pleasantries in Spanish. Violet was encouraged by how swimmingly it was all going, until Pascal emerged from the bedroom. LadyGo stiffened. She had made it clear on numerous occasions that she didn't care for the company of *los negros.*

"Hey, Pascal, where are you working today?" Teddy said, for everyone's benefit.

"Brian Grazer's house in Malibu." Pascal buttoned his white shirt and tucked it into his pressed black pants.

"Pascal's father was a slave," said Teddy. "A real bona fide slave from Africa. He escaped and moved to France. Am I right, brother?"

Pascal grunted in affirmation. He walked to the door and lit a Gauloise.

"Kunta Kinte, I wish you wouldn't smoke those things," Teddy said. "There's a fucking baby here."

Pascal waved him off and exhaled through the screen door. "I feel like shit."

"Then stop smoking cigarettes." Teddy turned to Violet. "When he was a kid he sold incense in the Paris flea market."

"*J'aime bien le marché aux puces à Paris,*" Violet said to Pascal.

"*Vous été allée à Paris, eh?*" he asked with a bright smile.

"*Parfaitement,*" answered Violet. "*Et même plusieurs fois. Je suis allé à l'internat en Suisse. A Le Rosey.*"

"I love it." Teddy beamed with pride. He punched Pascal's shoulder. "Listen to her. I told you she was the real deal."

"So," Violet asked Teddy, "are you coming with us?"

"I don't know...." Teddy bit his nails.

Violet slapped his hand down. "Don't do that. I'm going to spray you with skunk oil so you don't chew your fingernails."

"How did I all of a sudden go from a five-thousand-dollar bass to skunk spray?"

"Come here," Pascal said to Dot. "I want to show you something outside."

"Go with them, please," Violet ordered LadyGo.

LadyGo, who had probably pictured herself being offered a complimentary fruit drink at the Ritz-Carlton right about now, did not take kindly to being ordered outside a run-down apartment to play with a black man. "Yes, *meesuz.*" She heroically followed them outside.

The door slammed and Violet turned to Teddy. "We can stay here tonight and go down tomorrow, if that would be easier."

"I can't have you and your posse crash here. It's not fair to Pascal. He paid my rent this month. I'm lucky he didn't kick me out."

"I'll send Dot and the nanny down in my car now, then you and I can take a limo down tomorrow," she said.

"Where's your fucking husband during all of this?"

"He's still out of town," she said quickly.

Teddy gnawed at his fingernails. It was impossible to tell what he was thinking. "Fine," he said. "But I have to leave for a little while to take care of some stuff."

"Now?"

"I have a commitment."

"At the music store?"

"No, not at the music store. I'll meet you back here in two hours. Let's walk out together." Violet wanted to interrogate him about where he was going, but thought better of it. Tomorrow they would be in a suite on the Ritz-Carlton club floor. That was all that mattered.

Outside, Dot and Pascal were running around, trying to catch something in the air. "Bugs!" cried Dot. Violet took a closer look. They weren't bugs. They were painted lady butterflies.

SALLY floated up the escalator to the bridal salon. It had felt wrong to be cooped up in Jeremy's apartment watching basketball on the first day of her engagement, so she left him there and raced over the hill to Saks.

She opened the door and discovered a plush forest of glimmering mannequin brides. In the corner was an antique desk where an okay-looking brunette and her mother quietly flipped through a gilded leather portfolio.

An impeccably groomed salesman stepped toward Sally. "Hello," he said.

"Hi! I'm here to buy a wedding dress."

His eyes darted to her ring finger, then back to her face. "I'm with a customer," he said with finality.

Sally shot a glance at the other bride's ring. It was gigantic. Sally lifted her eyes. The woman had also spotted Sally's measly ring. Sally's hand twitched. "That's okay," she told the salesman. "I'll wait." How Sally would have loved to show them all who they were dealing with and buy the most expensive dress on the spot! But long ago, she had stopped carrying credit cards.

The money she had taken out to start Kurt's leather jacket business had mushroomed from the original six thousand to forty-nine thousand, spread across eight credit cards. Sally would never forgive Kurt for sticking her with the debt, then changing his phone number and telling everyone *she* was the psycho.

She had called the credit card companies in an attempt to negotiate the runaway debt. They'd offer the option of making a small down payment, which would lock her into a fixed interest rate that was only one-tenth of a percentage higher than the current one. She would make the payment only to discover that the new "fixed interest rate" was just fixed for fifteen days. And then *it* shot up eight whole points. Once, she had Fed-Exed a payment to arrive on the due date, March 12, so the "penalty rate" wouldn't kick in. But she hadn't seen the fine print that stated it had to be received by *seven AM* on the twelfth. So it triggered something called "universal default," where all the credit card companies talked to one another, and once you defaulted on one payment, they *all* went into penalty rate. Before Sally knew it, she had eight credit cards, each at 29.9 percent interest. She felt so stupid and alone; the shame compounding inside her like the interest itself.

Last year, she had screwed up the courage to ask Maryam if she knew of any credit consolidation places. "Why?" snapped Maryam. "You're not in credit card debt, are you?" "Of course not,"

Sally replied. "It's for a student." Maryam said, "Good. Because only morons get into credit card debt." Sally never mentioned it again to Maryam or anyone else. She'd lie in bed at night, with open eyes, the weight bearing down on her chest from above. When it got too great, she'd roll onto her stomach. But the debt would push up through the mattress. She'd turn onto her side, but it squeezed her like a vise grip.

She wandered through the glittery dresses and stopped at a gorgeous lace-upon-lace creation. She then realized it was an A-line cut. A-lines were for fatties. She wanted a super-fitted, strapless, low-back mermaid cut.

The really annoying thing about Sally's financial straits was that she made good money! After taxes, forty-five grand a year. Her rent was two thousand a month. Her living expenses another fifteen hundred, which left her a three-thousand-dollar cushion. But she always managed to spend that, too. A friend would get married in Seattle, and she had to fly there and buy a bridesmaid's dress. Or her laptop would get a virus and crash. Or, to keep up with the trends, she needed to replace all her birthday party tutus with princess dresses.

For the past couple of years, Sally's whole focus had been on trying to find a rich husband. Now that it was a reality, Sally saw that what may have been sound in concept was vague in execution. Did she have to have an actual conversation in which she'd tell Jeremy she was fifty grand in debt because of an ex-boyfriend and please pay it off? The thought of it made Sally sick. Literally. She closed her eyes.

David had generously offered to "take care of the wedding." Could Sally ask him for cash, then siphon off fifty grand to pay off her credit cards? Perhaps, but it would mean skimping on her big day. She deserved to have the wedding of her dreams, nothing less. Maybe she could tell guests that instead of presents, she wanted cash. That might be considered tacky, though, getting married at David's fabulous house and asking the guests for envelopes of money....

Or. Or. Or. There was personal bankruptcy. People on the radio were constantly singing its praises. Sally had looked into it once but decided against it because it would show up on her credit report for ten years. That meant she couldn't get a new car or move into a better apartment. But...after she married Jeremy, she could use *his* credit cards. Married couples did that all the time. And he would pay for their new house. She could get him to buy her a new car. So, really, there was nothing to prevent her from filing for bankruptcy. And Jeremy would never know....

"Are you okay, miss?" the brown-haired bride asked Sally with sweet concern.

"I'm fine." Sally opened her eyes and straightened. She must have been leaning against the wall for some time, because the bride was touching her back. The mother and salesperson were looking over. "I'm fine!" Sally said with a wave. "Nothing to look at!"

The other bride returned to the desk.

Sally made a show of spotting a dress in the center of the salon and walked toward it. Just the couple of steps were enough to make Sally feel like fainting. What was wrong? Hypoglycemia or hyperglycemia never made her feel sick in this way. And her blood sugar was 120 when she left the apartment half an hour ago.

The trio were whispering and glancing over.

Did that mean Sally looked as sick as she felt? She smiled, but the effort almost made her barf. She touched the first gown she saw. "Aaah." She stepped behind the mannequin, as if to inspect the back of the dress. She was now in a secret hollow of outward-facing headless brides.

Oh God. Tulle, bows, rhinestones, flowers, crystals, glass slippers, necks, corsages — they all spun fantastically around her. Sally had trouble fighting her way out of the kaleidoscope of dreams. One mannequin teetered. Sally was about to be sick. But not all over the beautiful dresses! She fumbled her purse open, buried her head in it, and hoped she wouldn't vomit.

It had been two and a half hours since Teddy's car disappeared down Venice Boulevard. Violet had dispatched LadyGo and Dot to the Ritz-Carlton with a credit card, then trekked to the Whole Foods on National. She now sat on Teddy's steps, teeming grocery bags against her shins, and brooded over whether Pascal had said *they* went out this morning or *he* went out this morning.

Zey, he. Zey, he. Zey, he.

The words did sound similar. For argument's sake, if Pascal had said *they,* who would *they* be? Teddy and who? Surely not Coco. As of Friday night, she was on a plane to Japan. And it didn't make sense for her to be back in Los Angeles two days later.

"Sick!" Teddy leapt up the stairs and stood over the groceries. "You have no idea how hungry I am. Whole Paycheck is like Oz for an evil junkie like me."

"Hello." Violet closed her eyes and surrendered herself to the possibilities. They had the apartment to themselves. What would it be? Would Teddy drag her by the arm into his bedroom, pimp-style? Would he take her right here on the steps? Would it start with a tender kiss?…She opened her eyes.

Teddy was hoisting himself up by the handrail, clearing Violet and three steps' worth of groceries. He let himself into the apartment.

"Oh," Violet heard herself say.

She gathered the bags and deposited them in the kitchen. Teddy was splayed on the couch, chimplike with one arm stretched overhead, listening to his cell phone messages. Terror shot through Violet: something had happened, something terrible.

"I can't wait to crash after I eat." Teddy kicked off one motorcycle boot, then the other, and scowled at their smell. He shut his phone. "That was my white-trash aunt from Palm Springs." *Palm Springs.* The words scalded Violet, a cruel reminder of the history Teddy shared with Coco. "My aunt has this son who wants to learn to play bass, and she asked me if I could find him a used one. I said I had an extra I'd sell to her for forty-five bucks. So, I box it up and stand in this long fucking line at the post office, and then they tell me it's gonna cost *twenty-five* bucks to ship. So I call my aunt and ask if she'll pay that, and she says no. She wants me to *drive* it out. Sure, I say, if she pays for gas—"

"Where did you go?" Violet said.

"Huh?"

"I'll pay to mail the bass, if that's what you're getting at."

"Fuck you." He looked genuinely hurt. "That's not why I was telling you. I was sharing something that was going on in my life. Or isn't that something the hoi polloi like you and David Parry concern yourselves with?"

He had confused *hoi polloi* with *hoity-toity,* but this was no time to scrap it out over a malapropism. "I'm sorry," Violet said. "What did your aunt say?"

"It doesn't fucking matter."

"That was rude of me," she said. "I duly apologize. Let's have some dinner and start over."

"Do-over granted."

"Good." Violet retreated to the kitchen and emptied a still-warm container of brown rice and vegetables into a clean-enough bowl and placed it on the counter. "So," she asked, "how are you?"

"I had a really rough time last night." Teddy pinched some rice in his fingers and ate it standing up.

"Why?" Violet handed him a fork. "What happened?"

"I came this close to using. It was like three in the morning, and Pascal had some Almond Roca and I ate the whole fucking can." Teddy pulled out a julienned green pepper and flung it on the counter. "Next time, don't buy me anything with peppers.

Peppers make me fart. Anyway, I started going through the trash to see if there were any nuts left in the foil. That's what you do with crack. You go through the packets of foil to see if you missed any. I felt like I was on the verge of slipping."

"Why?" Fearing a body blow, Violet crouched down and made busy with the groceries. "What happened?"

"I cheated on my girlfriend, that's what happened." Teddy stood agape. A square of tofu rested on his tongue. "God, am I that bad in bed? Did you forget?"

"But you said you were only eighty-five percent faithful to her."

"Ha! Did I say that?"

"Yes."

"I'm such an alcoholic! No wonder I'm on a ninety-in-ninety." He chuckled and took a giant bite of food.

"So what happened?" Violet asked. "Did you drink last night?"

"Jesus! Of course not."

"So stop calling yourself an alcoholic."

"We don't say, 'Hi, I'm Teddy, I *used* to be an alcoholic.' We say, 'Hi, I'm Teddy, I'm an alcoholic.' It's a progressive disease."

"Whatever."

"Whoa, whoa." Teddy pointed at the bag. "What's that I see?"

"Rice cakes?" She had debated buying them, on account of their being so cheap and ordinary.

"I fucking love rice cakes. You have no idea how many of those babies I can scarf down." Teddy's vim was appreciably on the rise.

Violet decided to ride its momentum. "But Friday night," she said, "didn't you have fun…you know…?"

"Fucking you? Of course." He let out a loud belch. "I'm a sex fiend. I guess I'm just not mature enough to fuck a married woman and not feel like shit afterwards."

"I don't think it's a matter of maturity." Violet pulled out a spray of ranunculus and stuck them in a pitcher.

"You and me can fuck," he said. "And it's instant gratification and all, but eventually I end up back in my shitty apartment with the chain-smoking Nigerian and I have to go for days eating the free shit they put out at AA meetings just to pay my cell phone bill."

Violet dithered. This might be the perfect time to announce she had left David. Or might that spook Teddy? She needed to work on him a little more. She held up a pastry bag. "Sugar-free vegan ginger cookies."

"You have no idea what you've done for me," he said. "You've opened the door to everything I've been praying for my whole life. To be a famous musician, to eat good food, to have a friend I can count on." *Friend:* the word was an arrow slung into Violet's chest. She opened the refrigerator door and stood behind it for cover. "Our friendship is a gift from God," he said. "I don't want it to get all muddy from fucking. I think I told you, I'm a much better friend than boyfriend."

Violet was in that *Far Side* cartoon where the man scolded his dog, Ginger, but all the dog heard was: *Blah, blah, blah, Ginger, blah, blah, blah, Ginger.* All Violet could hear was *friend.* She felt like screaming for Teddy to stop, but the words caught in her throat.

"God has blessed me with your friendship and generosity," he continued. "He's blessed me with Coco, who's so beautiful. It's ridiculous to think I have to choose. So I want to offer you my friendship. I usually charge a million bucks. But I'll give it to you for the low price of five hundred grand."

"Wait," Violet said. "She aborted your baby."

"I don't really know if that happened."

"You mean she's still pregnant?"

"Fuck no," Teddy scoffed.

"What are you saying? She *lost* the baby?"

"You never know with Coco Kennedy."

"What does that mean?" A torrent was rising within Violet and she was powerless to quell it. "You're either pregnant or you're not. You have an abortion or you don't. Those things are immutable."

"You sure like to concern yourself with stuff that's none of your beeswax, don't you, Baroness? That's what I should start calling you, Baroness von Beeswax."

"It *is* my fucking business!" Violet slammed the refrigerator door. "Two hours ago you were shoving your tongue in my mouth and now I'm a *treasured friend!*" Violet picked up the box of milk thistle tea bags that the lady who worked in the nutrition aisle had said helped balance the liver. Not the three-dollar box of tea bags, or the eight-dollar box, or even the twelve-dollar box, but the *sixteen-dollar box of milk thistle tea bags because only the best for the king of 90066!* She threw it full force at Teddy's head. He swerved just in time.

"Gee, Violet," he said, "have you communed with God yet today?"

"I don't believe in God." She looked around Teddy's apartment, with its thrift shop decor and Holy Bible on the table, and thought, God is for poor people.

"Godless Violet. It's all starting to make sense." Teddy picked up the tea bags and walked over. Violet took them. His hand and hers, not even touching, just touching the same dented box, it was enough to make her melt. Teddy brushed his hand across her cheek and pushed her hair behind her ear. "Let me see that ink again," he said. Violet lowered her head and leaned into his hand. "That is so fucking rad."

Violet was mute, a beggar. This was Teddy's chance to erase the past ten minutes. She'd forgive him everything if he'd just kiss her....

"Do you think I should get a tattoo?" he said. "They say you should get one on the best part of your body." He turned to a wall of mirrored tiles and lifted his shirt. "I'm so fucking obese."

Violet blinked. She breathed in through her nose. She touched the counter. Yes, it was true: she was standing in squalor, and the bootless pauper who had just rejected *her* preened in a mirror. She opened her phone and dialed LadyGo.

"I need you to come back," she told the long-suffering nanny. "Pick me up at the empanada place on Venice. The one we went to that time after the beach." Violet hung up.

"You let a fucking beaner drive your car?" Teddy still hadn't peeled his eyes off his reflection. He held his hair in a topknot, which he admired. "That car costs a hundred and fifty grand."

"Probably."

"What do you pay her, like a million a year? Oh Violet. Why did we fuck? Now I can never be your nanny. It wouldn't be clean." He dropped the clump of hair.

Violet folded the grocery bags, stacked them on the counter, and headed for the door.

"Wait, you're going?" He dove into the grubby sectional. "Come on. Just because we fucked once doesn't have to change anything. I'll always love you."

"At last," Violet said. "My poem. I thought you had forgotten." Her phone rang. She didn't look to see who it was. Anybody would be better than this vainglorious dirtbag.

Of all people, it was Sally. "Don't you go to that fabulous hard-to-get-into gyno, Dr. Naeby?" she asked breathlessly. "The one who's really good with delivering babies? Well, could you get me an appointment? I've tried in the past and the nurse said he wasn't taking any new patients." Violet said she would and hung up.

Teddy examined something he'd mined from between his toes. "Does this mean we won't be spending Christmas with Geddy Lee?"

"Affirmative." Violet opened the door.

"Are you okay?"

"I'm more than okay. In fact, this moment marks the end of my self-immolation and the rehabilitation of my *amour propre*. If you don't know what those words mean—and why would you, they have nothing to do with seventies television—I invite you to look them up in a dictionary."

The screen door slammed behind Violet. She didn't bother looking back to see if Teddy would come after her. She knew he wouldn't.

CHAPTER EIGHT

Fantastic Voyage

IT WAS A SUNNY DAY, BUT SALLY KEPT THE WINDOWS OF HER TRUCK ROLLED UP to seal herself into her hothouse of happiness. Was it possible? Was she really out of debt? *Out of debt!* If she'd known that declaring personal bankruptcy would be this easy, she'd have done it years ago. After the debacle in the bridal salon, she'd spent all week downloading forms and gathering her financial records. She made an appointment at an out-of-the-way law office and had just dropped off the paperwork with a check for three hundred dollars. It took all of ten minutes. The only thing left to do was attend a hearing—which, she'd been assured, was a mere formality—and the whole nightmare would be in the past. She could now indulge herself in her delicious future.

"Woo!" Sally screamed as she reached Santa Monica Boulevard. "Woo-hoo!" But she was too happy to go home. She wanted to keep going. At the top of La Cienega, she got in the left lane and headed west down the curvy part of the Strip. Mulholland, PCH, Sunset: driving these streets made Sally feel as if she *was* Los Angeles. Like in that movie *Fantastic Voyage*—where shrunken scientists were injected into a dying man's bloodstream—Sally zoomed along Sunset with the flow of traffic. She caught the light at Sunset Plaza, then surged ahead with the pack. She felt integral to the city she loved, as if her driving were keeping it alive.

In that interview David had given, another thing he said was "Go with the green lights. Don't try to make people do things they don't want to do." Sally finally understood what he meant. She was literally going with the green lights, and her courtship with Jeremy had been just the same. Their setup, their humble life at his apartment, his audition, the proposal, there was such a beautiful inevitability to it all. And now she was going to be a mother!

Dr. Naeby had accepted Sally as a patient and confirmed that the episode in the bridal salon was morning sickness. So Sally was carrying the ultimate accessory, a Naeby baby. Sally loved, loved, *loved* Dr. Naeby. He was so handsome and relaxed. During her appointment, he'd accidentally left the image of Sofia Coppola's uterus up on the ultrasound monitor. So that was cool. Sally hadn't yet shared the news of her pregnancy with Jeremy. The books said not to tell people until the second trimester, in case something happened.

She adjusted her hand on the steering wheel so the diamond looked bigger than two carats. "Woo-hoo!"

Could it be that not having to worry about money was really this transformative? Back in the days, Kurt began every morning by chanting. It was part of the Buddhism he was into where you'd chant for money. Sally didn't think it was all that Buddhist to have your one wish in life be to get rich. But Kurt had explained he was only chanting for money so, once he had it, he could devote himself to world peace. Money first, world peace second. Sally was suspicious. Still, as a show of support for his spiritual journey, she went to Pottery Barn and bought big golden letters that spelled out the words WISH and DREAM and hung them from fishing line over his altar.

Traffic slowed as Sally passed what used to be Le Dôme. Once, when she had her convertible Rabbit, some men had pulled up alongside her and asked if she'd like to have a drink at Le Dôme. They were Seiko reps in town for a jewelry show. Over drinks, they opened a display box and offered Sally her pick of glittery watches. She chose a gold with mother-of-pearl inlay. She hadn't had to "do anything" for it, because she told the guys she had to run home and change before meeting them back at their hotel. She slipped them a wrong phone number and never saw them again. Later that night, she told Kurt the watch had been a gift from David.

Kurt…Kurt… Now that Sally was free of his debt, she felt a pang of guilt about how psycho she'd gone when he dumped her. Was it really necessary for her to have retaliated by hacking into his e-mail program and sending a group message to his entire address book, as him, saying he liked to have sex with dogs? Now that she had some perspective, it did seem immature. Sally rounded the bend where Tower Records used to be and found herself stopped at the first red light. Right outside Mauricio's Boot Shop. Where Kurt worked. There was a parking spot smack in front. With time left on the meter. This had to be some kind of sign. Sally glided into the space.

She entered the tiny atelier wedged between Duke's Diner and the Whiskey. Mauricio was a quiet man who made custom cowboy boots for rock stars, socialites, and Japanese tourists. The walls of the shop were plastered with framed magazine covers, autographed pictures, even gold records given to Mauricio as thanks for his master craftsmanship. All boots were handmade to order and started at eight hundred dollars. For the truly hip, it was never a question of *if* you owned a pair of Mauricio's but *how many*. Get some margaritas in Kurt and he'd be hi-larious about the "shit that went on." Sally thought he should partner with Violet on a sitcom about Mauricio's. Kurt had considered it but decided he didn't want someone to rip off his stories and steal all the credit.

The store was empty. Part of Mauricio's mystique was that there were no boots on display, just a wood bench that ran the length of the narrow store. Kurt would chat up the customers and determine whether they were worthy of Mauricio's. If Kurt deemed them unhip, he'd say Mauricio was backed up for three years. Japanese tourists were preapproved because they'd pay three grand for a pair of eight-hundred-dollar boots.

Kurt emerged from the workroom carrying a box. He wore one of his vintage Hawaiian shirts and the Peter Criss cat boots Mauricio had made for the 2004 KISS reunion tour, which Kurt got to keep when Peter Criss quit the band. Kurt's shoulder-length ringlets were as perfect as ever, just blacker. He looked up and saw Sally, but nothing registered on his face. He was always so cool, so Zen. He stepped behind the counter and shelved some bottles of leather conditioner. Sally wished she could just turn around. But she was stranded in the middle of the empty store.

"If it isn't Sally Parry," Kurt finally said, barely opening his mouth. "Or maybe it's not Parry anymore?"

"Not for long." She swatted the air with her left hand.

"Who's the lucky guy?"

"Just a TV personality." Sally narrowed her eyes. "How are *you?*"

"Could be better, could be worse," he said, always the Buddhist. "How's your brother?"

"He's great. We were just up at his house."

"Was he out of town?" The corners of his mouth curled.

"He was there," snapped Sally.

"I checked out Hanging with Yoko at the Troubadour. I was going to go up and say hi to David, but the band was so derivative. I mean, give me the Velvet Underground any day." Kurt stepped out from behind the counter to check the display. His shirt was tight around his gut. Sally, on the other hand, had maintained her figure.

"You look great," she said.

"Flea was in here the other day. I delivered his boots because the Chili Peppers are like family. Has David ever taken you over to Flea's house?"

"No," Sally said.

"You should ask him to, because it's really cool." He used both palms to line up the bottles.

"Are you still living over on Curson?" she asked.

"Nah, I moved."

"Are you still a Buddhist?" she asked.

"Oh yeah. I chanted this morning for forty-five minutes. You should try it. It can really transform your life."

"I'm doing fine," she said.

"Still, never hurts to make the world a better place."

"I am making the world a better place," Sally said. "I'm getting married."

"Well, good luck." Kurt picked up the empty box and headed to the back. "Tell David I said hey."

"Kurt!" she said. He turned around. "I—I wanted to invite you to my wedding." His eyebrows lifted, but just barely. She added, "It's going to be at David and Violet's house."

Kurt rested the corner of the box on the counter. "Do they still live in that place near Coldwater?"

"Oh no!" Sally said with a guffaw. "They bought an important architectural house and spent two years restoring it. It's been in all the magazines. Anonymously, of course. You'd have no way of knowing it was theirs."

"Let me give you my new address."

"I'll mail the invitation here. If there's one thing I know, it's that you'll always be working here." She spun around to leave. Kurt was an ass man, and Sally wanted to make sure he saw that hers was better than ever.

CHAPTER NINE

Gilbert Osmond ❀ Better and Better, Faster and Faster ❀ Mayday

ALL THAT MATTERED WAS THAT VIOLET GET THROUGH TODAY WITHOUT CALL-
ing him. The past five weeks had left her sleep deprived and shaky.
But she hadn't gone and done anything crazy. Sure, she had called
Teddy a hundred times, but she had never left a message or uttered
a peep when she heard his voice, Hello...hello...hello?

There were, however, other lapses. Every few days, Violet had
found herself buying a present to give him today, May 1, his three-
year AA birthday. There was the cell phone, the golf clubs, the
1980 Rickenbacker bass she'd had Geddy Lee sign and send her.
The moment she'd purchase one of these lagniappes, hope and
self-loathing would ricochet within, leaving her jumpy and demor-
alized. But the important thing was: she hadn't made contact. If
she could just survive today, she'd be over a significant hurdle. To

ensure success, Violet had composed an itinerary, one to which she would adhere no matter what.

7–9 AM:	Wake up, make breakfast.
9 AM:	LadyGo arrives. Say good-bye to David.
9:20 AM:	Go down to garden. Dig cell phone out of hole. DON'T TURN ON PHONE TO CHECK TO SEE IF TEDDY HAS CALLED. HE HASN'T. Give phone to Dot.
9:30 AM:	Leave for LA Mission.
10 AM–6 PM:	LA Mission: Feed homeless. Disperse Teddy's presents to homeless.
7 PM:	Pick up David at office. Take one car to Paul McCartney at Hollywood Bowl.
8–11 PM:	Paul McCartney concert.
11 PM:	Get David's car back at office. Drive home.
12 AM:	Sex with David. Sleep.

So far, Violet hadn't deviated from the plan. It was 9:30 and she'd made it out of the house and into the car ahead of schedule, sans cell phone. The phone had been her most formidable adversary in her attempt to banish Teddy from her thoughts.

A week into her travail, Violet had announced to David that she wanted to change her phone number. "Why?" he asked, glancing up from his breakfast. Violet blanked. She couldn't remember what she had just said. That's how bad it had gotten. She'd often start a sentence and, midway through, realize she had no idea what she had just set out to say. That's where Teddy lived, in the interstices. Between sentences, between words, between thoughts. "Never mind," she told her husband. "I don't care one way or another," David said with uncharacteristic alacrity, which only served to rattle Violet further. He continued, "I'm just asking because if there's a problem with Sprint, I'll have Kara get on it."

"No, I was just thinking about it." Violet knew it wasn't an answer. But now she was trapped into keeping her phone number, a cruel reminder that Teddy had forsaken her. All she could do was change her ringer, so it wouldn't turn her into a Pavlov dog and unleash a stampede of hope every time it rang. Last night, she had woken up at four in the morning and gone to the kitchen, where her cell phone was charging, and checked for messages. She called voice mail over and over in a sickening loop, in case Teddy had called while she was dialing. Then she'd heard a voice. "No!" it said, "No! No! No!" It was Dot, from the baby monitor. She was scolding her dolls, something she was into these days. Violet then realized it was daylight. She'd been standing there for two hours! Disgusted with herself, she walked to the garden, dug a hole, and buried her phone.

She turned south onto Beverly Glen and passed a cluster of real estate signs. She remembered: it was Tuesday. The morning rush clogged the canyon road, but Violet eschewed the quicker Benedict Canyon because that's where she was driving when Teddy had called her after their idyll at the putting green. It was in front of the shoddy alcazar, with the flesh-colored VW bus abandoned halfway up the curb, that Teddy had made it known he'd jerked off to her the day they met. It was while she was driving by the once-proud family of deep green palms, now stiff and cappuccino colored since the cold shock a month ago, that Teddy had asked her to say, I *certainly* like doggy style. It was as she was passing the Craftsman with the sycamore trees, strange ones that grew more horizontal than vertical, that Teddy had said he would write plenty of poems for her. Because of Teddy, Benedict Canyon was now ruined. So were Wilshire, Beverly Drive, RIE class, the 405. And Sondheim. The know-nothing had even managed to ruin Sondheim!

A few weeks back, Violet had made an appointment with a shrink she'd seen on and off. But his earliest availability was two weeks away. "I can come in early one morning if it's an emergency," the therapist had offered. "No!" Violet answered. She hung up and decided to cut through the yackety-yak and get on some fucking meds. She called her agent—who had frequently spoken of the rainbow of pills he popped—to get the name of his psychopharmacologist. Violet was tickled to be put right through, even though she hadn't worked in several years. "Oh God, don't tell me it's you, too?" the agent had said on speaker. "I've got a thousand former show runners who will work for nothing just to keep their houses. Don't tell me I have to find work for the wife of a billionaire." His laughter and that of others filled his office. Violet said she was calling to secure an item for the RIE auction, and quickly hung up. Two weeks later, she drove to the therapist's office but never got out of her car. What would she tell him anyway? He'd never understand Teddy. There was no way to convey his laugh, what a great kisser he turned out to be, so playful, so obliging…

Violet snapped the rubber band on her wrist and said, "Gilbert Osmond Gilbert Osmond Gilbert Osmond."

This morning, she had written GO on a rubber band and put it around her wrist. Any time she thought about Teddy, she was to snap it and repeat her mantra: Gilbert Osmond Gilbert Osmond Gilbert Osmond. Were their affair to proceed, that's what Teddy would have been, Gilbert Osmond to her Isabel Archer. Invoking *The Portrait of a Lady,* one of Violet's favorite novels, gave her strength and clarity. Everyone but Violet would see that Teddy was utterly beneath her and only interested in her money. At least Gilbert Osmond was a suave aesthete. Teddy didn't know who the Medicis were!

Crawling to the intersection where the Four Oaks restaurant used to be, Violet saw an open-house sign. Taped to it was a handwritten piece of paper: LAND!!! She checked her watch. She had time, and it was always fun to look.…

She followed the signs up a mile of increasingly narrow streets, through the land that curb appeal forgot, and arrived at a dirt cul-de-sac. Among a forest of blue-and-white GWEN GOLD flags was a white Lexus SUV with the driver's door open. Inside was a woman in her sixties who wore a dowdy Ann Taylor suit. She seemed utterly surprised to see Violet.

"Pull up behind me," Gwen shouted. "Make sure you turn your wheel to the right." Gwen pantomimed turning the wheel. A former actress, Violet thought. Violet introduced herself as a neighbor in an attempt to quell any hope of a sale on the part of the eye-lifted realtor.

"It has fabulous estate potential," Gwen said. "Ten acres, which is unheard of in 90210." Two huge gates, held together by a rusty chain, lay in the dirt at the bottom of the hill. "As you can see," Gwen said, "the driveway needs some work."

"What was once here?" asked Violet. "Was there a house?"

"Over the hill. It's the old George Harrison estate. He lived here in the seventies. The next owner tore the house down and never rebuilt."

George Harrison. The name sent a bolt through Violet.

Five years ago, in a book of Linda McCartney photographs, Violet had seen a photo of George Harrison sitting in a Los Angeles house that overlooked a lake. She and David couldn't figure out where in LA it was. Violet had even asked Barbara Bach about it at a dinner party; she said the house was in Beverly Hills. Violet knew there wasn't a lake in Beverly Hills, but felt it would be insolent to challenge the wife of a Beatle.

"The house—or what's left of it—is it up there?" asked Violet.

"You can hike up if you'd like." Gwen handed Violet a spec sheet. "I wore the wrong shoes. I have a meeting with a mediator at noon. I thought it was next week, but my ex's lawyer informs us this morning that it's *today*."

Violet headed up the rocky path. At the first switchback, she stopped to catch her breath. Below were tightly packed hippie shacks. It was quite charming, this incognito hamlet. She continued her ascent. The driveway, if widened and stabilized, could be stunning blanketed with acacia groundcover and Aleppo pines. She reached the top of the rise. Stone Canyon Reservoir shimmered below. She made her way down the cushiony gopher hole–riddled hillside to the foundation of the former house. There wasn't a building in sight. The reservoir was so close, it bounced sunlight onto her face. The water lapped against the shore. It felt like Lake Tahoe. David loved Lake Tahoe. She could build a Lake Tahoe retreat in the middle of the city.

Violet owed it to David. When she had arrived home with LadyGo and Dot after her humiliating trip to Teddy's, Violet explained her sudden disappearance with a convoluted story involving a birthday party at Chuck E. Cheese, a freeway closure, and a note she thought she'd left on the counter. She had expected a merciless interrogation, which she was only semi-prepared for. Instead, David gave her a big hug, then took Dot and did her night-night all by himself.

Could it really be? Had David become more loving and patient than ever since the night of her betrayal? Or was it a cruel illusion, another facet to her madness? She didn't know anymore. A week ago she'd left her credit card at a restaurant on purpose just to provoke some of David's good old-fashioned rage. But he had patted her on the head and driven back to get it himself. Had there never been any basis for escaping into Teddy's arms? If there was a God, Violet was convinced it was a cruel one, for turning her husband nice on her.

Building a house. It was a huge project, but she needed a huge distraction. The other house was cursed. Violet's unemployment, miserable pregnancy, empty bank account: these could all be traced back to the Neutra house. She had to get away from the front door she had opened to Teddy. The living room ceiling she had stared at, trying to coax Father Time into making the sex last forever. The bed of roses where Teddy had taken her, his brown body with its huge cock, ramming into her from behind, her pussy throbbed now just thinking about it, God, if she could only feel it again, just one more time, she'd tried to replicate it, lying in bed while David slept, touching herself with one hand, pulling her hair with the other, but she couldn't, she needed Teddy, oh, to be on her knees, sucking that cock, that's all she needed, to feel her mouth around that glorious—

Violet snapped her rubber band. *Gilbert Osmond Gilbert Osmond Gilbert Osmond.* She forced a breath through her pounding chest.

The spec sheet said there were ten acres of land. For $1.9 million, it was a steal. David, a huge Beatles fan, would heartily endorse buying a part of Beatles history. And how fortuitous that tonight was the Paul McCartney concert? Violet needed to get to David's office ASAP. She clambered up the hill, her feet sinking into the rodent-softened soil a good six inches with each step.

IF the past five weeks were any indication of what the rest of her life would be like, Sally hoped to live a long, long time. Between planning the wedding, Jeremy's growing fame, and her pregnancy, things were getting better and better, faster and faster. Life was a thrill ride, and Sally's hands were up in the air.

"Will all debtors please stand up?" It took Sally a second to realize this meant her. The two hundred others who had appeared for their 341 bankruptcy hearing in this ballroom-turned-courtroom stood up. Sally sprang to her feet.

"Do you solemnly swear," said the bailiff, "to tell the truth, the whole truth, and nothing but the truth, so help you God?"

"Yes," answered the cacophony.

A small Japanese woman had taken "the bench." The bailiff said, "Bankruptcy court under the Honorable Aiko Yashima on this first day of May, is now in session."

"You may all be seated," said the tiny judge.

The notice had said to plan on being here all day. Sally had come prepared with wedding-related paperwork. Even her bankruptcy hearing, which she had imagined as a bunch of towering figures with distorted faces hissing indignities at her, turned out to be altogether civil. Most of her fellow "debtors" were white, middle-aged, and looked pleasantly bored. Sally untied the ribbon on her wedding organizer and spread out her flowchart, bridal magazines, and RSVPs on the empty chairs beside her.

Who knew that planning a wedding could be this deeply satisfying? David had told her to spare no expense, so Sally had hired the wedding planner to the stars. Under Pam's guidance, Sally had discovered she possessed a unique talent for picking the rarest lily, the most sought-after calligrapher, the tip-top-of-the-line tent. Any time Pam presented Sally with makeup artists or photographers from which to choose, she would pick the most expensive. "Why do I bother?" Pam would ask, shaking her head. It became one of their many hilarious inside jokes.

Sally dove into the RSVPs that had arrived yesterday. The first one she opened—wouldn't you know—was an acceptance from Kurt. Sally's heart sank. How would she ever explain his presence to her friends? Sally had attempted to work Kurt into conversation. "I thought it would be fun to wear white cowboy boots with my wedding dress," she had said to the gang at their girls night out at the Laugh Factory. Maryam barked, "Don't tell me you're even *considering* talking to that creep Kurt again." Sally blushed. "Of course not!" When she returned home, she called Kurt to disinvite him, but got the machine. The outgoing message was normal enough, "Hi, it's Kurt. I'll catch you later." Then a woman giggled in the background. With laughter in his voice, Kurt seemed to turn to her and say, "Wha—?" *Beep.* Sally was so flustered that she hung up. The best option at this point was to act indignant that Kurt was there and blame his presence on Violet.

"That's me, Your Honor." A man in the row behind Sally stood up using the back of her envelope chair, which caused them to spill all over the worn carpet. Sally shot him a dirty look and gathered her RSVPs.

"Is this a complete list of your assets?" asked the judge. "A 2006 Formula Sun Sport boat, a 2005 Porsche Cayman S, adjoining properties at 2860 and 2862 North Beverly Drive in Beverly Hills."

"That's right, Your Honor," answered the man.

Sally looked around for someone to exchange an eye roll with. But most were too absorbed with text-messaging to even be listening.

"The court will appoint a trustee to sell your nonexempt assets. Once you complete the required course in personal-finance management, you will receive a notice informing you that your debts are hereby discharged."

And that was it! The guy with the speedboat, Porsche, and not one but *two* houses in Beverly Hills made his way down the row of chairs and out the door!

Dum-dum da-dum-dum-dum-dum. The wedding march trilled from Sally's cell phone. It was her new BFF, Pam. NO CELL PHONES signs hung everywhere. Sally crouched down and whispered, "Hi, Pam."

"What's this message about you inviting the entire Lakers franchise to the wedding?"

Jeremy's star was rapidly rising, and with it, the number of guests. Jeremy would never think of inviting his new business associates, but as his better half, Sally considered it her duty. What had started out as a once-a-week spot on *Match-Ups* had turned into a nightly appearance on *SportsCenter*. Jeremy had just been assigned to broadcast from the floor of the NBA semifinals. So on their first day as man and wife, they'd be crisscrossing the country, first-class.

"Don't kill me." Sally giggled to Pam. "But we just found out that Jeremy is doing some print ads for the Gap!"

"Get out!" squealed Pam.

"I know. They're doing a new campaign called 'You Will Be Famous,' starring people who just got famous. Jeremy's going to be on billboards!"

"Girlfriend, you have landed yourself such a hottie."

"I know. But it means I have to invite the Gap people *and* his commercial agents."

"Oh God. How many?"

"Ten," Sally said in an itty-bitty voice.

"Can I renegotiate my deal so I'm paid by the guest?"

"Shut up!"

"You'd better not stop by any Starbucks between now and then," Pam said, "because you'll invite all of *them* to this thing, too." Sally loved Pam. She was so salty.

"Sally Parry," the bailiff called. "Sally Parry!"

"Gotta run," Sally whispered, then sprang up. "I'm right here!"

"I see you have no assets," said the judge without looking up. "Your debts total forty-nine thousand dollars to eight credit card companies. Is that accurate?"

"Yes." Sally straightened herself. Compared to that last guy, she felt a flush of pride over her fiscal responsibility.

"You want to reaffirm the debt on your 2006 Toyota RAV4. Is that car insured?"

"Yes, Your Honor."

"Have you cut up all your credit cards?"

"Yes."

"The court has received certification that you completed the personal-finance-management course," said the judge with an impressed pout, "ahead of schedule. Your debts are hereby discharged. You will receive a written notice within thirty days."

"Randall Kline," said the bailiff. Just like that, it was over. Sally collected her wedding stuff and skipped out. What did she care if Kurt came to the wedding?

VIOLET stood outside David's glass-fronted office. His newish assistant, Kara, sat at her desk. "So, what's it like out there?" she asked Violet. "Did it ever start raining?"

"What—oh, no," Violet answered.

"I'm from Arizona, and every morning I think it's going to rain, but it never does."

"Yeah...." Violet would normally make small talk with an assistant, especially one this mousy and sweet, but she had the rare opportunity to observe David at work. He was on his headset, elbows on his knees, looking out the floor-to-ceiling window behind his desk. No checking e-mail or leafing through *Billboard* while on the phone. Completely tuned in. A rare quality in this day of multitasking, it had impressed Violet seventeen years ago.

She'd never forgotten that conversation outside the Murray Hill Cinema. "*You're* Violet Grace?" David had said, as if in disbelief. "Yes." Violet scrambled to her feet, peeled off her Walkman, and tucked the newspaper under her arm. "You already bought the tickets?" he asked, with a bluntness that belied his sad eyes. The incorrigibly self-possessed Violet found herself stammering, "I—I thought it might sell out. I got here early. I hope that's okay." He looked deep into her face and said, "I'm surprised." "Good surprised or bad surprised?" Violet was born with an instinct for people. Sure, she had the education and worldliness that was out of reach of an accountant-turned-rock-manager from Denver. But she somehow knew that David was a better person than she. "Good surprised." The glint in his eye said he was wild with approval. She craved more. She'd been chasing it ever since.

David finished his call and removed his headset. This was his element, making big decisions. All of them the right decisions, for his clients, for his record label, for his family. He never once let them down.

"Hey, look who's here!" He jumped up.

Violet pushed open the heavy door. "Hi, sweetie. Sorry to bother you."

"Of course not!" David gave her a hug and held the door open with his foot. "Kara, you've never met the beautiful Ultraviolet herself."

"I have just now, Mr. Parry," said Kara. "I mean, we've talked on the phone. And I *feel* like we've met—"

"Hold my calls," David said, and let the door close. He took Violet's hand. "I'm glad to see you. What's the good word?"

The office had been the same for ten years. Shelves crammed with books, stacks of CDs everywhere. Good, not great stereo. Violet had resisted the wifely urge to storm in, decorator in tow, and put her stamp on his domain. Like her husband, the office was what it was: no airs, all business.

"I came upon something that might intrigue you," she said.

"I'm listening."

"You know behind the Four Oaks, where that preschool is? Well, there's a lot for sale that overlooks Stone Canyon Reservoir."

"Okay…" David said.

"Not high above it like we are now. Just thirty feet above the water. There's not another house in sight."

"Are we in the market for a new house?" he asked.

"I was driving by and I saw the sign. Ten acres for one point nine."

"How much is buildable?"

"About an acre. It's the old George Harrison estate."

"Really." David blinked, big.

"You have that book here, don't you?" Violet went to the bookshelf. "Remember, we were looking at that picture, wondering where it was, and I asked Barbara Bach about it?" David pulled out the Linda McCartney book. "That's it!" Violet found the photograph of George Harrison sitting in a bay window. He had scruffy clothes and long hair, so youthful and at peace. Behind him were pine trees and a body of water.

David studied the photograph. "That *is* Stone Canyon," he said. "We can see that curve from the bathroom. Son of a gun."

"Isn't that wild? There's no house there now. Just the foundation. The city would probably make us build within the footprint."

"So we're buying the land?"

"It seems to happen any time I stop by," Violet said. "Maybe next time you won't be so pleased to see me."

On his desk was a framed picture of Violet and David holding Dot. They had been on vacation in Lake Tahoe. Violet was smiling so hard her face looked like a fun-house distortion of happiness. Was there really a time when standing in the snow with David and Dot could have made her so happy? That was the last weekend in January. She had met Teddy on February 1, a Tuesday. Little did she know when this picture was taken that just three days later, she would desecrate a good life. Of all that Teddy had absconded with, that was the cruelest. Worse than her self-worth—he could have that!—he had robbed her of any proclivity to find joy in life's simple pleasures.

"You keep saying fixing up the Neutra house almost killed you," David said.

"I know."

"One question. Why isn't this that definition of insanity, doing the same thing over and over and expecting different results?" David studied her. He was direct. He was even. But he was saying something Violet didn't want to hear, and this is what made him seem like an asshole. It wasn't fair, but Violet understood the reputation.

"I know what you mean," she conceded.

"I'm amenable to it," said David. "We have the dough. If every five years you fix up a house, there are worse vices in the world. I just need to know *you've* thought it through." The phone rang. One of David's rules was to never go home without returning every call, which often meant staying in the office until late in the evening. Knowing the exigencies were piling up in the outer office made Violet anxious. "Don't worry about the phones," David said. He ran his finger along the grass bracelet around his wrist. "Do *you* understand why you want to do this?"

Violet's heart skipped. For the first time, it occurred to her that David knew about Teddy. He sees it all, thought Violet. My ecstasy, my shame, my madness. It was so obvious that she feared she might explode in laughter. What else would explain the queer expansiveness that had befallen David since the yoga retreat? Was it part of a twisted game? Was he waiting to pounce? Would the dreaded confrontation happen here, now? Violet had rehearsed for this moment. "I fell in love," she would say, "or thought I did." "With whom?" he'd want to know. "A musician, no one you've heard of. It's over now." Violet wouldn't attempt to gainsay any of her husband's accusations. How could she possibly defend her swath of destruction? *Nostalgie de la boue* run amok? Sure, David had lost his temper every now and then, but that surely didn't justify Violet's going off and fucking someone with hep C and trying—unsuccessfully!—to buy his affections with David's money. "It's not your fault," she would tell her husband. "It's all on me. I went crazy or something. I developed a frantic attachment to the first person who showed some interest. I know how feeble that sounds, but I don't know how else to put it. I love you, and I want our family to work. If you don't, I understand. But please know I will spend the rest of my life making it up to you, if you'll let me."

The glass door opened. Kara entered. "I'm sorry—"

"I'm talking to my wife," David said.

"It's just—I finally tracked down Yuri. He's on his cell phone for the next ten minutes and then he's getting on a plane—"

"Take it, take it, take it," Violet said.

"I'm talking to my wife," David repeated to Kara. She slunk away and shut the door, trapping Violet in the phantasmagoria that David's office had become.

"So?" he asked. "Do you know *why* you want to buy this land? Yes or no."

"Yes, yeah," Violet stammered. "I do."

"Okay, then." David had chosen to spare her. She could breathe again. "Do you want me to call the broker and get into it?" he asked.

"I know what to do."

"Truer words were never spoken," he said.

Violet laughed. David was her salvation. Love would come. "You keep saving me, David."

"Thanks for noticing."

"I'll see you tonight," said Violet.

"Yeah," he said. "Paul McCartney. Oh! I got us the fresh hookup." It was something that had always endeared David to her. He was an accountant by nature, yet used phrases like "fresh hookup" with perfect ease. "If we go back before the show, Paul will take a picture with Dot."

"You're kidding!"

"LadyGo can bring her over for the photo op, then take her home. She'll be going to bed late, but it's worth it for a picture with a Beatle, am I right?"

"I love you, David."

"I know that. And I love you."

"I don't know why sometimes. But thank you."

"I knew you were complicated from the start," he said. "You announced as much when you wanted that song sung at the wedding."

Violet cringed. He was referring to Stephen Sondheim's "Sorry-Grateful," from *Company*. It was what she had been listening to on her Walkman outside the movie theater that day, so she always considered it "their song." Violet had asked Def Leppard to play it at the wedding. When the band saw the lyrics, they checked with David. He confronted Violet and she quickly withdrew the request.

"That's the best thing Def Leppard ever did," she said now. "*Not sing that song. I don't know what I was thinking.*"

Violet was shaky as she walked out of David's office and down the hallway. She took Gwen Gold's card out of her pocket, then remembered she didn't have her cell phone. She opened the door to the conference room.

A couple of interns unpacked the day's lunch. MR. CHOW, the thick glossy bags read.

"I need to use the phone," Violet said. "I'm David's wife." Neither reacted. They wouldn't get far in the business. She reached for the phone. Her fingers dialed a number.

310-555-0199.

"Hello?" It was Teddy.

"Happy birthday." Violet panted like a sick animal. With dead eyes, she gazed at the rubber band on her wrist. GO, it said.

"I knew you'd remember," he said. "You looking for that ride to the airport?"

CHAPTER TEN

KURT SLITHERED UP ROSCOMARE IN HIS CHARTREUSE DODGE SATURN. HE had closed Mauricio's early to get a chant on before the wedding. Kneeling at his altar, Kurt had chanted *Nam myōhō renge kyō* for an hour, then shampooed his hair. While his curls air dried, he chanted the Lotus Sutra ten times before heading out.

The song "Tiny Dancer" came on the radio.

> *Blue jean baby, LA lady,*
> *Seamstress for the band*
> *Pretty eyed, pirate smile,*
> *You'll marry a music man.*

Last year, before Kurt kicked his chanting up a notch, this song would have made him go postal. *What the fuck was "Tiny Dancer" doing on KLOS? Since when did some fruit's B-side take over for "Stairway to Heaven" as the quintessential classic rock anthem?* The dudes next door at Duke's Diner would blast "Tiny Dancer" just so Kurt would come over and honor them with his genius rant.

But now "Tiny Dancer" played and Kurt had equanimous mind. *Nam myōhō renge kyō* once again delivering the goods. In a video-taped speech, President Ikeda had said the universe's offerings were abundant. Most people walked around in delusional states and couldn't see what was theirs for the taking. Only by chanting *nam myōhō renge kyō* could they transform their karma.

If someone had told Kurt a year ago that he'd one day drive to David Parry's house and *not* seethe with revenge fantasies, he would have told them to take another hit of crack. When the custom leather jacket business didn't take off, Kurt had a brainstorm. He'd introduce a cheaper line of ready-to-wear and sell them at rock concerts. He had dragged his sample case to David's office for a meeting. The deal was simple: Kurt would set up a booth at David's gigs and kick him twenty percent of his profit. But before Kurt even got a chance to unlatch the trunk, David shook his head. "Kurt, it doesn't fly. I have an exclusive agreement with my merchandiser. I'd have to pay you and him. That's just not gonna happen." Kurt said, "You don't understand—" But David cut him off. "As a favor to Sally, I'll give you an internship if you're interested in learning how the music business works." Kurt *knew* how the business *worked*. For the past ten years, he'd seen it firsthand from the boot shop. He wanted to be David's *partner,* not the guy who brought him coffee!

But, like President Ikeda said, painful experiences were necessary to motivate us. Once you devoted yourself to the Mystical Law, the hidden connections of the universe started working for you. And he was right. Kurt had chanted for months to live in an apartment without roommates. One day, he saw a giant balloon that read CONDOS FOR SALE, ZERO DOWN. It was a brand-new building with a pool on the roof. Kurt took out an interest-only mortgage for three hundred dollars a month more than his rent. Within a week, he had moved in, set up his Gohonzon, and hung the letters WISH and DREAM.

Turned out, three hundred bucks was more of a dent than he'd imagined. After a couple of months, things were getting dire. In order to make the April mortgage, Kurt had been forced to sell all his CDs, disconnect his Internet, and never set foot in a Jamba Juice. He kept chanting, but with a fierceness he'd never before applied to anything in his life. He'd show up for work barely able to speak, his voice was so hoarse. And then what happened? Crazy Sally Parry walked through the door. At first, Kurt was terrified. He knew he'd stuck her with massive credit card bills. He had been haunted by the prospect of the cops coming after him, or worse: her brother. Every time the sleigh bells on the shop door jingled, Kurt jumped, fearing it was David Parry coming to kick his ass. Kurt's paranoia had consumed him to the point where he had to take codeine cough syrup to get the edge off. But what did Sally do? Invited him to her wedding. *Nam myōhō renge fucking kyō.*

Kurt stopped at the light at Mulholland and checked his hair. His curls always looked sharpest two weeks after a perm. And the goatee was a nice addition. The single gold hoop earring was pure inspiration, which came to him while chanting. This Captain Morgan look was a keeper.

> *Hold me closer, tiny dancer*
> *Count the headlights on the highway*
> *Lay me down in sheets of linen*
> *You had a busy day today.*

The light turned green. Kurt trusted that the universe was leading him to David Parry's for a reason. He just needed to stay openhearted when the opportunity presented itself. He turned off the radio and chanted the rest of the way there.

"*Nam myōhō renge kyō, nam myōhō renge kyō, nam myōhō renge kyō*...."

WHEN Violet had offered Sally and her entourage the "spare bedroom" to use as her bridal suite, Sally couldn't picture it. That's because there was nothing to picture! The room was the size of a postage stamp, barely big enough for the measly twin bed shoved in the corner. Here Sally sat, having her hair ironed by Clay, a ghoulishly Botoxed, brow-lifted, and spray-tanned hairdresser.

"Ouch! That burned my scalp!" Sally swatted his hand away.

The door opened, knocking into a tiny Vietnamese manicurist who carried a pan of swaying soapy water. A caterer, balancing plastic-wrapped cookie sheets, entered and zeroed in on a small dresser piled with purses. "Whose are those?"

"Mine," offered the old-lady makeup artist from the bed, where she lounged on her side, recovering from "the altitude." Her name was Fern and she smelled musty. Who knew where Pam had dug her and the rest of these clowns up?

"I'm going to need to move them," announced the caterer.

"Wait a second!" Sally jumped up and accidentally flipped over the pan of water.

"Oh no!" squawked the manicurist.

"This is the *bridal suite*!" Sally blocked the caterer from the flat surface. "You can't put those here."

"Is that sushi?" asked Fern, coming to life.

"Soft-shell crab rolls," said the caterer. "Have one."

"No!" Sally said. "Stop that! They're all about to touch me. Put those somewhere else! Where's Pam? Could someone get Pam!"

"Honey, I need you to sit down," said the hairdresser.

"Is my scalp burned?" Sally patted her forehead.

"Your scalp is not burned."

"It's still stinging." Sally went to the teensy bathroom and examined her hairline in the mirror. She could make out a faint red mark. "There it is," she told Clay, not a little triumphantly. "A burn."

"So Fern will fix it with powder," he said.

"Hunh?" Fern looked up from her deteriorating sushi roll and touched Sally's face with roe-speckled fingers.

Sally yelped. "Wash your hands! They're covered in fish!" She felt her face. Tiny orange fish eggs stuck to her fingers. "Oh, my God! Where's Pam? Or Maryam or anyone? I need help! Did someone call Pam?"

"Everyone looks so beautiful," hummed Fern, perched at the window.

"My guests are arriving?" Sally jumped out of her chair.

"I *will* burn you next time you do that." Clay slung the curling iron over his shoulder.

Sally peeked through the blinds. A familiar Escalade pulled up to the valets.

"Nora and Jordan Ross are here!" Sally cried.

Nora emerged, draped in yards and yards of chiffon. Sally prayed that Nora would identify herself as Sally's friend, not a Core-de-Ballet student. Sally wanted no accountability for *that* body. Nora had some kind of Band-Aid on her cheek. Why was it that you reached a certain age and you suddenly had no qualms about leaving the house with Band-Aids on your face? The passenger door opened, and out climbed Nora's son, J.J.

"I didn't invite *him!*" Sally's eyes widened. "Where's Jordan? Don't tell me *that boy* is Nora's plus one!" The valet got in the car and zoomed away.

"Relax!" laughed the hairdresser.

"You have no idea!" spit Sally. "That boy is autistic."

"He looks very sweet," said Fern.

"Yes, but he could throw a fit and ruin everything!"

The manicurist, ready with a pair of cuticle scissors, tapped one of Sally's feet. Sally would be wearing closed-toe pumps, of course. Still, she wanted her feet to be beautiful underneath.

"No cut cuticles," Sally said. "Only polish."

The hairdresser opened the door and shouted into the hallway, "Can someone please tranquilize the bride? And me, too, while you're at it!"

"That is *not* funny!" Sally fought back tears. She had made a special trip to the foot doctor yesterday to get her nails cut. "I just want nail polish."

"Polish?" asked the Vietnamese woman. Her accent made it sound as if she were talking around a big ice cube in her mouth.

"Polish only. No cutting."

Finally, Pam traipsed in, swinging a glass of champagne. "The peach Bellinis are to die for," she said. "I'm taking orders."

"Get us all doubles!" said the hairdresser. "With a Valium chaser."

"Pam!" Sally grabbed the wedding planner. "We've got to move Nora Ross. She brought her son instead of her husband."

"No Jordan Ross?" Pam pouted. "Boo-hoo. I hear he messes around."

"Put them at table sixteen," Sally said, "with Maryam and the people from the gym."

"I'll figure something out."

"There's nothing to *figure out*. I told you, table sixteen."

A sweaty man carrying a video camera poked his head in. "I'm looking for Pam. I'm here to videotape."

"*C'est moi*," said Pam.

"You haven't started yet?" Sally shrieked to the man.

"I kept going up and down Mulholland, trying to find the house. It isn't very well marked."

"Everyone else has managed to find it," Sally said. "I want you out there shooting the arrivals!"

"The *arrivals!*" hooted the hairdresser.

Pam swallowed a guffaw and lunged for the door. "I'll show you where to set up," she told the videographer.

"Don't go!" Sally seized Pam's arm and whispered, "Don't leave me alone with him."

"Who?" Pam blurted, "Clay?"

"Everybody's treating me like I'm a *C-U Next Tuesday*."

"A what?"

"A *C-U Next Tuesday*," Sally whispered. "Spell it out."

"A cunt? Darling, just say it. A cunt."

"Now I'm a *cunt,* am I?" The hairdresser scratched the air. "Mee-oww!"

Sally turned to Pam. "Have you found out what band is playing?"

Although David had given Sally carte blanche to throw the wedding she wanted, she put him in charge of the band. She'd taken every opportunity to hint at how much she loved Coldplay. Def Leppard had played at Violet and David's wedding. Why not Coldplay at hers?

"I'll go check," said Pam.

The videographer hadn't moved from the doorway. Sally asked, "What are you doing standing there?"

"You're right. I should get some balloons."

"What?"

"To put out. So people can find the wedding."

"People are finding the wedding," Sally said. "People have found the wedding. We need that fact videotaped. The ceremony is going to start in forty-five minutes and you're not shooting videos!"

"What's important," Pam said, "is that you relax, Miss Beautiful Sally Parry-soon-to-be-White. Now, you kids play nice." She left.

The hairdresser turned to Sally. "Honey, you need to let me

finish your hair so I can grab a cupcake and go to the gym to work it off."

"Those cupcakes are the wedding cake. You can't eat them now!"

"Everyone else is."

"What do you mean? Who's eating them?"

"They have cupcakes?" Fern rose from the bed.

They were interrupted by an echoing screech. Sally ran to the bathroom window. A banged-up van had pulled into the adjoining carport.

"The band!" Sally eagerly watched as some middle-aged men tumbled out. None looked like Chris Martin, but he'd probably arrive separately, in his own limo. Sally turned and opened the door to the hallway.

David happened to be passing by. He wore a blue suit and a floral tie. It was the first time in forever she'd seen her brother in a suit, and she was struck by how handsome he was. "David!"

"Hey, don't you look beautiful?"

"I can't stand the suspense." She pulled him into the room. "You have to tell me."

"What?"

"Who's the band?" Sally prepared to explode in excitement.

"I have no idea." David looked confused. "I told Violet to take care of it. I don't know any wedding bands."

"Oh." Sally's mouth trembled. "Of course."

"Let's clear the area!" Pam was in the hallway herding out David, the video guy, and several caterers who had somehow packed themselves in. Sally found herself marooned with the original gang of idiots.

"Was that really David Parry?" asked Fern. "He's just a baby."

Sally returned to the bathroom window. The band was mostly in their thirties or forties. Long hair, tight jeans, all pretty skeevy to be playing at a wedding. The van door slid open to reveal a drum. On it was the famous lip logo of the Rolling Stones! Sally's heart jumped. On another drum was printed THE ROLLING STONERS. THE WORLD'S GREATEST ROLLING STONES TRIBUTE BAND.

VIOLET zipped up her dress. She had told Sally she'd be a brides-maid only if she could give Sally's fabric to her own dress designer. The result was a chic A-line gown. Violet grabbed one boob and hiked it so it sat high in her bra, then the other boob. Everything is okay, she reminded herself, and slipped on her shoes. Hiring Teddy's band to play the wedding was *not* a desperate attempt to win back her ungovernable lover. It was a tender beneficence for a dear friend who had sounded despondent when she called him on his birthday.

May Day, when Violet phoned Teddy in the conference room, she had asked, "How are you?" Teddy's voice was scratchy and slow. "My bones ache and I want to sleep all the time. My boss sent me home last week because he said I was depressing the custom-ers." Violet smiled for the benefit of the interns setting out the Chi-nese food. She asked, "Is he paying you?" "Is he paying me?" Teddy laughed. She'd forgotten about the laugh. She asked, "What are you doing about money?" "Pascal paid the rent for May. I'm eating at AA meetings. Plus, there's this store in Malibu that gives away oranges. Sometimes I drive up there, but with gas, it's cheaper to eat at the Ninety-Nine-Cent Store even though the food there fucks up my liver." If this was legerdemain on Teddy's part—working in the rent, AA, gas money, and the condition of his liver in one breath—Violet would have to give him a ten. "Why didn't you call me?" she asked. "Because you made it more than clear that unless I fucked you, you didn't want to know me." Violet felt as if she'd been punched in the throat. It all flooded back, the scorching humiliation. She had somehow blocked out how dour and recal-citrant he could be. Put the phone down, she said to herself. But now that Teddy had injured her so grievously, Violet couldn't stop until she'd reclaimed some dignity. What came out of her mouth was "Oh." She dug her fingers into the back of a conference chair. "My hep C is fucking *on*," he said. "Have you seen a doctor?" One of the interns was looking at her. Violet met the kid's gaze, and he quickly resumed stuffing chopsticks into an NPR mug. "I'm not going to LA Country," Teddy said. "Which is the only place that will take me. It's fucking gross." "You're such a prince." "Make fun of me," he said, "but people die there." "Are you collecting unemployment?" "I was thinking about applying for SSI." "What's that?" "You're so fucking rich," he said. "I can't talk to you." She asked, "You mean, like welfare?" "Yes, I mean like welfare. Thanks a fucking lot for making me say it." "What about golf? Can't you get some money that way?" He scoffed, "I told you, that's not part of the program. I have to live my life with rigorous honesty." "I don't mean *hustle*. Can't you get a job as a caddy?" "What's up with you?" he said. "You suddenly have a thing for niggers?" "What?" He shot back, "Then stop trying to turn me into one." That's when Violet had devised the plan to hire Teddy's band to play at the wedding. The Rolling Stoners charged a thousand dollars. She'd give Teddy three thousand in cash. "You can disperse the moneys at your discretion," she told him. "Now, those are two words that have never been spoken to me in one sentence: *money* and *discretion*." "What do you say?" Violet asked with a laugh. He answered, "I can eat your pussy a couple of times for three grand." Violet thought she would vomit. The interns had just opened a container of that crispy orange tofu Mr. Chow made especially for her and David. She knew she'd never be ordering it again. "I hope you're joking," she said with faux gaiety. "Of course I'm joking," he said. "You're just doing what friends do, watch each other's backs."

The din of the wedding guests grew louder. Violet ran her fingers through her wet hair and headed into the bedroom, then stopped.

A man in a tuxedo sat perfectly upright on an Eames bench in the sitting area.

"Jeremy?" she asked.

He lifted his eyes, then gazed down. His hands were clutched tightly together. Fluorescent earplugs stuck out of both ears.

"I can't do it," he said to the floor. "It's a big mistake. I know I'm lucky to marry anybody. Especially Sally. But she doesn't care about me. It's like I don't exist."

"Okay...." Violet sat down beside him.

"She doesn't love me. She tolerates me. There's nothing worse."

"It's intolerable being tolerated."

"What?" Jeremy flashed her a look.

"Stephen Sondheim. From *A Little Night Music*. 'As I've often stated, it's intolerable being tolerated.'"

Jeremy doubled over and hugged himself. "I only bought her the ring because Vance made me. I tried not to give it to her. But she's too strong. She scares me. I don't know why I have to get married. I don't know why anyone has to get married."

"Jeremy?" Violet wanted to take his hand, but he still hadn't looked up. "What do you want to do?"

"I tried not giving her the ring, but she's too strong. I can't stop the wedding."

"You *can* stop the wedding, though." Violet knew the customary course of action would be to deliver a buck-up speech about pre-wedding jitters. But she could attest to Jeremy's fears. Sally always stood a little too close when she talked to you. Her eyes sparkled a little too brightly. Her makeup was too dewy perfect. She would frequently touch Violet's shoulder in sympathy when there was nothing to be sympathetic about. Violet was always at ease around aberrant personalities. As a girl, her father's coterie had made it a necessity. But with Sally, Violet felt as if she were being manipulated, to what purpose was never clear. It terrified Violet.

"I can't stop the wedding," said Jeremy.

"Jeremy. You have no idea how hard-core I am. If you want me to go out there right now and announce that the wedding is canceled, I will do it."

"Really?" He finally held her gaze. His eyes flickered hazel with hope.

"Absolutely." Violet took his hand. "I just need to make sure it's what you want to do."

"What about Sally?"

"You will have to go talk to her."

Jeremy quaked. "I can't. She'll start screaming. Or ignore me. She won't let me cancel the wedding."

"It's not up to her," said Violet. "It's up to you. Sally has lots of friends who can help her through this."

"I'm scared," said Jeremy.

"I'm scared for you. This is a big move. But it's imperative you do what's right for *you*. Ultimately, it will be what's right for Sally. She deserves better than to marry someone who feels this way about her."

"That's true," said Jeremy.

"Do you want some time alone while you think about it?" Violet stood up.

"No!" Jeremy pulled her arm. "Stay here."

Violet placed her other hand over his and sat down. She turned her head to give him some privacy.

Out on the lawn, fifty people sipped Bellinis and plucked appetizers off silver trays. Some admired the view, others the house, all giddy at finding themselves surrounded by such impeccable taste. But then, a piece of seared tuna flew off a woman's cocktail napkin. A man grabbed an old lady who had suddenly tipped over. A plume of champagne shot through the air.

Then: a young woman, wild with anger, ripped through the crowd. And in the girl's chaotic wake: Teddy. He seized the girl with the short black hair and porcelain skin.

Violet watched the ruckus, unable to hear any of it behind glass.

Teddy—ludicrously attired in lopsided mirrored aviators, red-white-and-blue terry-cloth headband, and shiny shirt unbuttoned to his waist—lunged at the lithe girl. The crowd widened around them. She pushed Teddy. He yanked her. She fell sloppily to the ground. She leapt up. Teddy grabbed her face with one hand. He snared his arms around her waist and grimaced. The black from his missing tooth screamed, *This is who you chose to fuck, a wino from the gutter!* Violet squeezed Jeremy's hand, lest she fly apart. Teddy dragged the girl away. One of her Ugg boots dropped to the ground.

And they were gone. With a collective shrug, the guests resumed their enjoyment of the party.

Dot, festooned with colorful pipe cleaners, skipped through the crowd, followed by LadyGo, who nibbled on a bouquet of satay. Violet had averted disaster earlier today by giving LadyGo a blouse to wear over her JOHN TRAVOLTA IS A HUGE FAG T-shirt.

Violet shook loose Jeremy's hand. "Excuse me," she said. "I have to ask my nanny a question." Violet opened the door and waved. "LadyGo! LadyGo! Come here!"

"Mommy!" Dot charged over and mightily hugged Violet's legs.

"Hi, sweetie." LadyGo walked over at funereal pace. Violet grabbed her arm. "Who was that girl who just ran through?"

LadyGo needed a few seconds to gulp down the chicken. "I don't know, *meesuz*," she said. "Somebody ask and lady go, I'm a friend of the band. Lady who plan the party? Lady go mad."

Jesus Christ, Violet thought, could it be Coco?

"I want you to go find that girl and ask her what her name is." Violet dug her nails into LadyGo's jiggly upper arm. LadyGo looked down. Violet released her grip. "You must find out that girl's name. Do you understand?"

"Yes, *meesuz*." LadyGo brushed the phantom wrinkles from her sleeve and made a big show of regaining her composure. She trudged out the door.

"Faster!" Violet said. "Run!"

"Who dat, Mommy?" Dot pointed at Jeremy.

He was stuck in some kind of sickening loop. "She screams and I keep talking until I say the right thing, then she's fine, then she screams and I keep talking and then it stops when I say the right thing, she screams—"

"That's Jeremy!" Violet half-squealed. "He's a friend of Aunt Sally's!"

"And I keep talking until I say the right thing, then she's fine, then—"

"Jeremy?" asked Violet.

He looked up, his eyes flashed a plea for Violet to help him stop. Then he looked down. "It's nice for a while and we have fun and I say the wrong thing and then it starts over—"

"Jeremy!" Violet dropped to her knees and grabbed his cheeks. "Stop it!"

"And then she keeps talking and I talk and then she says something and then I say the right thing—"

"Stop it!" parroted a delighted Dot.

"Dot, it's not funny. Mommy needs to talk to Jeremy. Go look at the books." Violet nudged Dot in the direction of the coffee table, then turned back to Jeremy. "You are going to call off this wedding."

"I want that," he said.

"I want dat!" chuckled Dot, pushing the art books onto the floor. The Robert Williams book thumped down; so did the first edition of *Uncommon Places* by Stephen Shore.

"You need to find Sally and tell her," Violet told Jeremy.

Dot found the book she wanted, the Andreas Gursky with that marvelous photograph of the Ninety-Nine-Cent Store. "Dot has those chairs." She pointed to the chair that she did indeed have.

Violet dipped her head so she was in Jeremy's line of vision. "You have to do it now. The wedding is in ten minutes." She stood up, hoping he would follow her lead, but he didn't.

"Candy." Dot pointed to some licorice in the photograph. "Dat candy has no nuts."

Violet pulled Jeremy up by a dead arm. "Do you know where Sally is?" she asked.

"No."

"Off the garage, in the guesthouse. It's where the wedding party is gathering."

"*Meesuz?*" LadyGo rushed in, her eyes dancing with excitement.

Violet held up a finger to LadyGo while she dispensed with Jeremy. "Go talk to Sally. Don't make it more complicated than it has to be. Just say the words, I want to call off the wedding."

"I want to call off the wedding," he repeated.

"That's right. That's all."

"You'll be here?" asked Jeremy.

"I'll be here. Everything is okay."

"*Meesuz,*" said Violet's agent provocateur, unable to contain her reconnaissance. "Lady go name is *Coco Kennedy.*" The Spanish accent made the name even more grotesque.

"Lollipops!" said Dot.

LadyGo noticed the wreckage of expensive books. "Miss Dot! Very bad girl." LadyGo dropped to her knees and matched the books to their jackets.

Jeremy just stood there. "You'll be here?" he asked Violet.

"I'll be here," Violet said flatly.

"Everything is okay?"

"Everything is okay."

SALLY, an opaline vision of silk and lace, navigated the carport, careful not to brush against the dirty Bentley and Mercedes. Maryam dutifully followed, holding the bride's five-foot train.

"Careful of the bikes," Sally warned, then stopped suddenly

before she stepped in a puddle of oil. Maryam smacked into her. "Watch out!" said Sally.

"What are you doing?"

"Uh, trying not to ruin my dress?"

"Tell me next time if you're going to stop," said Maryam. "I can't see anything."

"You know this wouldn't be happening if I was getting married at the Bel-Air Hotel," Sally said to Maryam's tulle head. "Where is Violet, anyway? *She* should be the one helping me."

"I don't know," Maryam said, with a tinge of sullenness.

"You're not still steamed about me making Violet the maid of honor, are you?" Sally asked. "It's her house. I had no choice." The tulle mushroom cloud was silent. Sally lifted her dress with one hand and reached for the Mercedes mirror with the other, careful to keep arm's length from the dusty car. She hurdled the oil spill. One foot landed. Just before the other one did, her body jerked back. "Aaah!" Sally's leg swung in the air, but she miraculously regained her balance.

"Oh God!" cried Maryam.

Sally turned. Her follower was splayed on the concrete, Sally's train triumphantly overhead. Sally grabbed the wad of lace.

"Did I get dirty?" Maryam scrambled to her feet. Black goo covered one side of her dress, arm, and leg.

"Not too," Sally chirped. But she couldn't keep a straight face as Maryam registered the extent of the disaster. A laugh escaped Sally's pursed lips.

"It's not funny!" Maryam said.

"I'm sorry—it's just—how did you possibly get that—it's in your *hair!*"

Maryam started crying. "How can you laugh? In five minutes I have to get up in front of everyone."

"You don't have to get up in front of everyone if you don't want." Sally prayed Maryam would take the hint.

"If I don't want?!" Tears streamed down Maryam's face. "I'm a bridesmaid! I spent a hundred dollars on my hair and three hundred dollars on this ugly dress I'll never wear again. You're such a fucking bitch!"

Sally gasped. "I can't believe you just said that."

"I swear, I hate you sometimes." Maryam stood on one leg like a flamingo, using her clean leg to wipe her dirty one. "You wouldn't even know Jeremy if it weren't for me."

"What does that have to do with anything?" Sally said. "Are you jealous?"

"Of you?" Maryam cried. "Give me a break."

"You *are* jealous! Because now you're the only one who's not married."

"Can you stop being a selfish bitch for one minute of your life? I'm covered in black engine oil!"

Sally took a deep breath. "Maybe Violet has a robe you can wear over your dress."

"I'm not walking around all night in a robe!"

"Or you could turn the dress inside out?" Sally offered.

"Fuck you." Maryam stormed into the guesthouse.

Sally called after her, "How dare you! After I paid to have your makeup done with my own money! And you *know* how much trouble I went to picking out bridesmaid dresses that you *can* wear again!" The door slammed. Sally stood there, red faced, holding her own train. She stomped into the guesthouse.

Jennifer, Jim, David, Vance, Clay, Fern, and Pam were in a tizzy over Maryam. Not a word about how magnificent Sally looked. And still no trace of Violet, her maid of honor!

Sally went into the bathroom, shut the door, and screamed in frustration. She pulled her diabetes kit from her garter belt and checked her blood sugar. She wanted to inject herself at the last possible minute so she could enjoy a four-hour stretch of unadulterated bliss. Her glucose was 210, on the high side. With the champagne and wedding cake and pure joy, it was certain to climb. Sally drew four units of Humalog into her syringe. Suddenly the door swung open.

It was Jeremy.

"Oh!" Sally fumbled to hide her diabetes kit, but it fell from the edge of the sink. Syringes, glucose strips, and insulin bottles showered the floor. Sally swept them into a pile with her foot and stood over it. "Jeremy!" she said. "What a lovely surprise!"

Sally saw the look on Jeremy's face and she knew: *he wants to call off the wedding.* She was so sure of it that a strange calm befell her. She gingerly closed the door behind him. "You know it's bad luck to see the bride before the wedding," she tut-tutted.

"I have something to tell you." He met her eyes with a coldness she'd never before seen.

"Well, I have something to tell *you*," she said.

"No. I have something to tell you."

"I want to tell you mine first." She scrunched her nose.

"I have something to—"

"Jeremy—" she said.

"I don't want to get—"

"I'm pregnant!"

"What?"

Sally closed the toilet lid. She tapped Jeremy's chest and he dropped onto it. "Dr. Naeby confirmed it yesterday," she lied. "I wanted to surprise you tonight."

"I didn't know," Jeremy sputtered.

"We're going to have a baby!" She took his hand. It was heavy and cold. Her heart began to race. *He still wants to call off the wedding.*

"I don't want to—" he attempted again.

Sally kissed him, stuffing the words back in his mouth. "Darling," she said, her lips still pressed against his, "I've been so emotional this past month, wanting our wedding to be perfect. And now that all our friends are here, some of them flying in from all over the country, I'm so glad that I *did* make it perfect. And all your colleagues are here and they're going to be so impressed. I know I've been a little crazy. But now we know it was the pregnancy hormones that made me act a teensy bit cuckoo."

Sally withdrew her face just enough to see that Jeremy had the wild, defiant look of a caged animal. He was calm now, but sometimes caged animals looked defeated when they still had one flurry of fight left in them.

"I don't want to worry you," Sally said, hating herself for the lie she was about to tell, "but my diabetes has been out of control this past month. My doctor wanted to hospitalize me. There's an ambulance waiting on Mulholland, just in case."

"There is?" Jeremy said. "What's wrong?"

"I'm stabilized now, so there's nothing to worry about."

Jeremy stared at the floor.

Sally felt a rush of relief. "It's six o'clock!" she said. "You'd better go and take your position."

"Okay." Jeremy got up, shoulders still slumped.

"You look gorgeous, my love," she said. "Or should I say, Dad!" She plucked the earplugs out of his ears. "Not today."

Jeremy zombie-walked back into the main room. Just then, Violet breezed in with wet hair. She stopped and gave Jeremy an urgent, quizzical look. Sally withdrew into the bathroom to watch. Jeremy said something to Violet. Violet grabbed him by the shoulders. Sally could read Violet's lips. *What happened?* So that's where her maid of honor had been this whole time! Jeremy walked off without responding to Violet, who looked up and spotted Sally.

"There you are!" Sally said, arms swept outward, like a soap opera *grande dame.*

"Sally!" Violet said. "Is there something I can help you with?"

"Thank you," Sally said. "But you've already done so much."

THE ceremony, in all its banal splendor, had come and gone. Dinner, too. After the meal, Violet had found herself maundering drunkenly to some Gap executive, so she plopped herself down at a deserted table, content to be the requisite drunk whom all others avoided.

The guests were spilled across the lawn, basking in the balmy night and jetliner views. Some had been drawn to the edge by the sound of coyotes attacking an animal. The terrifying screeches and even more terrifying high-pitched clicking sounds were nothing new to Violet, who had grown up in the hills. Tonight, there seemed to be some meows thrown into the clamor. Perhaps the wild things had scored a neighbor's cat.

Teddy's band wasn't scheduled to begin until after the cake ceremony. Just before, Violet would blame a migraine and slip off to the Beverly Hills Hotel, where she and David had booked a room to avoid the racket of the cleanup. Violet hadn't seen Teddy since he had dragged off Coco, caveman-style. At first, Violet was appalled that her beneficiary hadn't come looking for her. But after six Bellinis, she no longer gave a shit.

She fished the booze-soaked peaches out of her glass and closed her eyes, willing the fruit to deaden her emotions even further. She grabbed an abandoned glass from across the table and scooped the peach mash from it, too.

In lieu of a wedding cake, Sally had opted for the *de rigueur* tower of cupcakes. Several caterers had just carried it out and nervously lowered it onto a rose-petal-covered table. The tower, topped by a groom and ballerina, reigned over the crowd, its frosted finery beckoning all to come hither and have a taste. But a caterer-sentinel was positioned nearby to prevent any such thing.

Guest after guest was politely but firmly rebuffed. Violet lived for shit like this. She couldn't stop grinning.

But the cake ceremony was nearing, time for Violet to make her escape. First, she needed one of those cupcakes. She pushed herself up, then grabbed the table to steady herself. She wobbled to the cupcake tower and reached for a chocolate with coconut frosting.

"I'm going to have to ask you to wait," the caterer said, "until the cake ceremony."

"I won't be here for the cake ceremony." Violet snatched a cupcake.

The caterer grabbed her arm.

"It's my house," she said.

The caterer instantly released his grip. Violet smiled. Aah, how cozy it was, being David Parry's wife with all its attendant perks. She ripped the top off the cupcake and crammed it in her mouth. All she needed now was a blast of caffeine to sober her up for the drive. She stepped unevenly to the bar and ordered a Diet Coke.

A partygoer approached, eyes on Violet's cupcake. "Oh! Are they letting us eat those now?"

"Knock yourself out." Violet stuffed the bottom half of the cupcake into her mouth, but had forgotten to peel off the paper. She pulled it out, saliva and cake spilling onto her chest. She needed a trash can.

On the bar sat an empty jar. Taped to it, a grainy color Xerox of a British flag. Written in big letters, the word TIPS. Beside it, a fan of business cards that read "The Rolling Stoners."

"Wait—what are these?" Violet said to the bartender.

"Some guy started putting them around. He said David Parry, whose house this is, said it was cool."

Violet scanned the soirée. Tip jars had sprung up on every conceivable flat surface! She stuffed the business cards into the tip jar and thrust it at the bartender. "Throw this away!"

"But David Parry said—"

"I'm his wife. Go. Get rid of all of them. Now!"

"Aaaaah!" A shriek erupted from inside the house. A woman's voice? Coco's voice? Violet staggered toward it.

"Aaaaah!" There it was again, coming from the master bedroom. Violet flung open the door. The bedroom was quiet, tranquil. But someone was in the bathroom—a woman—and sobs, too.

"It's okay, don't worry," said a soothing voice.

Violet hurtled through the door.

A whimpering boy stood in the corner. A woman with kind eyes stroked his hair. "Hi," she said to Violet. "I apologize. J.J. was using the bathroom and saw a spider."

"Oh!" Violet laughed with relief. "A spider!"

"It's there! It's there!" J.J. pointed to the bathtub.

"That's a big scary one, all right," Violet said. "Do you know what we do with spiders here?" The boy was silent. "We help them." Violet picked up a newspaper and brushed the spider onto it. "If you open the window, I can put him outside." The boy did. Violet shook the newspaper and the spider fell off. "Now he's back with his friends."

His mother stuck out her hand. "I'm Nora Ross. Thanks for your patience. He's on the autism spectrum and can get a little fixated."

"He's a sweetheart," Violet said.

"He's my teacher, that's for sure!" Nora tousled the beautiful boy's hair.

Violet wanted to hug this shell-shocked woman who still somehow managed to radiate such tenderness. The boy sprinted through the bedroom and out into the thick of the party.

"I'd better go," Nora said, and followed.

Violet stepped into the yard. People were being herded in the direction of the cupcake tower. Violet needed to split. She didn't need to say good-bye to David. And Sally, well, who cared about Sally?

"Violet!" It was David. He was holding Dot, who devoured a cupcake the size of her face.

"Hi. I was about to come find you. You know what? I'm not feeling well...." Violet trailed off. Under Dot's arm was a dirty pink Ugg boot.

"Violet, what's going on?" David asked.

"What—what do you mean?" Her stomach tightened.

"Did you book this band?"

"A friend of mine plays in it." Shit. She'd forgotten to lie. "Why?"

"Apparently there's a girl with them who's in the house causing some kind of commotion. The wedding planner tried to kick her out, but she claimed she was a friend of yours."

"Shit. I'll take care of it."

"Shit," said Dot in her small voice.

"Since when do you have a friend who plays in a Stones cover band?" David asked, incredulous.

"He's the nice guy I met on the street that day. He's a nice guy, a friend, who needs the money. His name is Teddy."

David practically dropped Dot. "Teddy Reyes?"

"Yeah," Violet said as casually as possible. She furiously tried to remember if she'd ever mentioned Teddy's last name. Oh God, David's face was reddening. His jaw was working. His neck was tensing.

"That's it," he said. "I'm done." He shook his head and walked away.

Violet caught up and grabbed his arm. "David! David!" A nearby group of Sally's girlfriends glanced over. Violet lowered her voice. "What do you mean?"

"You're smart about some things," David said, heedless of the girls who had paused their conversation to listen. "But you're not smart about others. You grew up around intellectuals and loveable eccentrics. I grew up around poor people. What do I always say?"

There was no way Violet could answer that. David was always inculcating her on so many different topics.

"Troubled people are trouble," he said.

It was one of their common themes: that Violet didn't understand people. Sure, she floated with ease among the most rarefied strata of society. But her idea of a scary lowlife was someone walking around with JUICY COUTURE emblazoned across their ass.

David continued, "Some people think the worst thing in life is to wear white after Labor Day. Others think nothing of throwing their babies into dumpsters."

"What babies, Dada?" Dot asked.

"Down-and-out people are down-and-out for a reason." David's voice spewed venom. "They're drunks. They're liars. They're lazy. They're insane. If you want to pay to have their car fixed or whatever the fuck you're doing with them, do it on your own time." And now he started screaming, "But don't let them into my house! Don't let them near my fucking daughter! Do you hear me?! What is wrong with you?!"

Dot began wailing. The guests, who had only moments ago taken pleasure in watching the rich people fight, scurried away.

"You're right," Violet said. "I'm sorry. I'll change."

"You'll change." He spit out a laugh. "I really tried, Violet."

Dot tried to worm out of David's grasp. "Mama!"

"Come to me, sweetie," Violet held out her hands, but David jerked Dot away.

"I want Mama," Dot cried. "I want Mama!"

"It's okay, Dot," Violet said. "Mommy and Daddy are happy."

"Don't lie to her!" David raged. "Will you stop lying for once in your fucking life?! Lie to yourself. Lie to me. But don't lie to Dot!"

"What should I do?" Violet pleaded. "Tell me what you want me to do."

"What you always seem to do: whatever the fuck you want." He stormed off with Dot. Violet swayed like sea grass in the ocean of the lawn.

The bartender came over with a glass. "Your Diet Coke."

"Whoooooaaaa!" A collective moan rose from the crowd. The cupcakes had tumbled to the ground. Nearby, J.J. was crying in shame. Nora was on her hands and knees, frantically picking up cupcakes.

EVERYONE'S attention diverted by the cupcake avalanche, Kurt skulked into the house. David Parry was the kind of macher who was probably swimming in codeine cough syrup or better. Rich people, they got a hangnail and some Beverly Hills doctor was writing them a scrip.

He cased the living room. Nice shit they had here. Smaller than their other place, but right out of *Dwell*. In the corner was a door. Kurt scuttled toward it.

Shit, his head ached. His hands felt arthritic. A swig of codeine should lube the joints just right. It was a sweet party. Except for Maryam, who kept shooting him dirty looks, or at least tried to through her crazy makeup. He got a ton of compliments on his Peter Criss boots, but that was to be expected. He was seated at a table with a bunch of people from the Lakers. Maybe he could do a search-and-replace on that leather jacket proposal he wrote up for David and give it to them. Selling leather jackets at Lakers games... Kurt was warming to the idea.

He closed the door and flipped on the light. It was a fucking kid's room. Crib, quilts on the wall, a stuffed rocking hippo in the corner. Kids got coughs, too, right? Maybe they gave the brat codeine cough syrup. Kurt entered the bathroom and shut the door. In the medicine cabinet sat a promising-looking bottle. Zyrtec. Kurt had never heard of it. He chugged the whole thing and stuck the empty bottle in the pocket of his Hawaiian shirt. If he caught a buzz, he could call into the pharmacy and get the refills.

Something slammed. At the other end of the bathroom was

an open door Kurt had missed. His instinct was to beat it, but he paused. A familiar voice drifted in from the other room.

"How could you show up here with her?" It was Violet; he'd know her voice anywhere. Even though she was a heifer, he wouldn't mind hitting some of that million-dollar snatch. She always smelled so nice.

Kurt crept closer to the door.

"Did I tell you she was crazy?" A man was talking now.

Kurt couldn't resist taking a peek. The guy was short, had dark skin and good hair. Kurt drew back.

"She doesn't belong here!" Violet screamed. "I don't care if she is a fucking Kennedy."

"Well, good. Because she probably isn't."

"What did you just say?"

"Her driver's license says Carolyne Portis. She just goes around posing like a Kennedy because people are lame enough to be impressed with it. Personally, I always had my doubts. I mean, think about it. What's a Kennedy doing growing up in Palm Springs?"

"You asshole!" There was a struggle. Violet was trashing the poor fucker with both arms. In Kurt's humble opinion, she needed to start altering her life state big-time. Violet screamed, "How could you invite her up here?"

"I didn't *invite* her. She hacked into my e-mail and found out where the gig was. She walked here from the Greyhound station."

"And that's meant to mollify me? Jesus Christ!"

"She's gone now. She bit one of your caterers, so I had a friend pick her up and bring her back to my apartment."

"She's biting people now?! What the fuck is going on? Do you realize my life is over? And for what?" Violet started really crying. "What happened that day? Was *she* there? Is that where you disappeared for those two hours? To find your girlfriend and tell her to give you a minute, the rich lady just showed up and you needed to string her along? Do you have any idea how infected my brain has become because of that night? Right now, the trunk of my car is full of presents for you. Golf clubs, a cell phone, even a bass I had Geddy Lee sign, waiting to give you when you finally called me to tell me that *you felt it, too!*"

Kurt shivered. The connections were flying, just like President Ikeda said they would.

Violet continued, through tears, "Do you realize what you've done to me? I grind out my days with my husband and child, but by night, I'm yours. I'm yours, but you don't want me. Thanks to you, I'm a ghost, drifting through life, craving something I'll never taste again."

"Violet, I didn't know."

"David is going to leave me."

"I'm sorry. I really am."

"Why didn't you at least fight for me?" she asked. "Aren't I worth a fight? Or a poem? You never wrote me a poem. Do you think about me? Every day, every waking hour? Tell me the truth."

"No."

Violet laughed and shrieked at the same time. It was more fucked-up sounding than those coyotes.

"I think about my rent and my car and getting laid and staying sober and how shitty I feel and my roommate who's always coming home after work and calling France while I'm trying to sleep."

"So in the end it all comes down to your shitty little existence? Is that who I was to you, then? A cash cow? Well, cash cows have feelings, too."

"Tell me," he said. "What can I do? I want to make amends."

"You can think about me every day until you die."

"Of course I think about you."

"And you can suffer!"

"Ha! That can be arranged."

"You smelly creep. You shiftless fucker. This is not a joke. I am not a joke. You watch out for me. You fear me. I'm so vast you'll never know. I'm the weather."

The door slammed. It was like the universe had dumped a fucking fruit basket in Kurt's lap. He had to hightail it to Violet's car before the other dude did. That shit could pay his mortgage for the entire year.

SALLY had imagined dancing and being serenaded by Coldplay until the wee hours. Instead, it was 9:45, most of the guests were gone, and a no-name band played "Street Fighting Man" to a deserted dance floor. Sally stood at the front door, Nora holding both her hands. "I am so, so sorry about the cupcakes."

"Don't worry about it," said Sally. "It wasn't J.J.'s fault." It was *Violet's* fault. She was the one who had grabbed the first cupcake before it was time. From that point on, the wedding was doomed. With no cake ceremony, the release of the doves and the center-piece raffle stood no chance of being magical.

"Where are you two newlyweds off to?" Nora asked.

"We're back and forth, traveling with the NBA for the month...." Sally trailed off. She couldn't remember what month it was....

"Oh!" Nora grabbed an envelope from her purse. "I wanted to give you this. It's a save-the-date card for a thing I'm having on June first, if you're in town."

"Ooh." Sally took the envelope, with the faint realization that she had in her hand something she'd wanted ever since she started working with Nora—an invitation to one of her parties. But Sally's mouth was so dry. She wandered away from Nora and bumped into a man.

"Hey, nice party, babe," he said. Sally couldn't remember his name. He worked with Jeremy.

"Right..." said Sally. She needed some water. And someplace to lie down.

"I've never heard a whole Stones set without a bass player."

Who was this guy? Jim. That's right, Jim. When did she last eat? Some fruit, a bite of cupcake. She'd raised a champagne flute to her lips during the toasts, but hadn't swallowed any. Was she low or high? When did she take her last shot…?

"I asked Jeremy how it felt to be married," Jim said, "but he was neither zero nor one about it." He cracked up. "Come on, that's hilarious. Jeremy has two emotions, zero and one."

Sally hiked the hem of her dress, felt for her garter, and pulled out the diabetes kit she'd had made in matching satin just for the occasion. She stabbed her finger with the lancet and squeezed some blood out.

"Oh—what are you—I'll just give you some privacy." Jim slunk off.

Sally pressed the blood onto a test strip and stuck it in the glucometer.

Beep.

404.

That couldn't be right. Sally blinked. 404. She pulled out a fresh test strip and tested her blood again. 412.

Oh God! She'd never taken that shot before the wedding. Jeremy had come in and she'd totally forgotten! At over 400, she risked slipping into ketoacidosis. She could go into a coma. What if she passed out here? *Please, no. Not at my wedding, not in front of the guests.* She needed some insulin now! Her medicine was in the guesthouse. Sally staggered down the hall, her heart rampaging throughout her body.

Her baby! What if she had ketones in her urine? If any passed into her placenta, it might damage the baby's developing organs. Sally picked up her pace. Oh God, how could she have let this happen?!

Sally flew into the carport and beheld a sight that under any other circumstance would have bowled her over.

Kurt stood at the open trunk of Violet's Mercedes. When he

saw Sally, his jaw dropped and eyes flew open. In the whole five years they were together, Sally had never seen so much…*expression* on Kurt's face.

"Sally!" he yelped.

But Sally kept running, her dress dragging across the oily floor. She tumbled into the guesthouse and lunged for the bathroom door.

It was locked.

"Hello!" She knocked on the door. "Please hurry! I have to get in." She pounded it with both fists. "It's the bride; I need to get in!" She rattled the knob. "Hello! This is an emergency! Please!"

The door opened. A man stood there, nobody she recognized. A red-white-and-blue terry-cloth headband tamed his unruly hair. He looked sleepy, as if he'd just woken up. His green eyes, sickly and bloodshot, stared into hers. Sally froze, as if this man were a portent of evil.

"Who are you?" she asked. But he just walked away.

Sally shut herself in the bathroom. Her Liberty of London bag was on the floor behind the toilet, where she had kicked it when Jeremy burst in. She'd forgotten to put it away! Bottles of insulin, test strips, caps, lancets, alcohol wipes, were scattered everywhere. She grabbed the Humalog. Now she needed a syringe. She couldn't find one. She shook her bag and turned it inside out, then dropped to her knees and checked behind the toilet. She picked up the rug, turned over the trash can—there it was: a syringe! Among the tissues—in the trash can! Sally laughed. It must have landed there when Jeremy surprised her!

Sally jammed the needle into the little jar. Her hand shaking, she drew out ten units. She didn't bother lifting her wedding dress. She stabbed the syringe through the satin and injected herself in the stomach. She could finally breathe. Her baby was going to be fine.

CHAPTER ELEVEN

Double Secret Probation ❦ The Game Show ❦ Coachella

Now Do You Believe Me? ❦ I Never Really Liked You

"TEN FIVE PER EPISODE?" VIOLET SAID TO HER AGENT AS SHE BACKED OUT OF the carport. Violet's friend Richard had just gotten a pilot picked up. There was a bit of money left in the budget, and he had asked if she'd consult a couple days a week. "We can close the deal," she told her agent. "Let me know my start date." She hung up, tickled to be once again employed.

The night of the wedding, Violet had stayed up for David in their hotel room, bracing herself for his excoriation, but he never appeared. Instead, he had checked into his own bungalow. It was where he'd been living for the past month, coming and going from the house only to see Dot, get the mail, and drop off laundry. He was always perfectly agreeable, exchanging pleasantries with

Violet, who trepidatiously followed his lead. It was as if she were on some type of double secret probation.

All Violet could do as she awaited her sentence was live her life, their life. She kept the house in order and tended to Dot. Every night, she'd snuggle in bed with her little girl and, after the books, tell her, "Mommy loves you. And Daddy loves you. And Mommy loves Daddy. And Daddy loves Mommy."

Teddy rarely appeared in her thoughts. When he did, it was so benign—she'd read a reference to JFK and think, Oh—that Violet would smile at the utter lack of emotional charge.

However, there were some loose ends. First, she had to wiggle out of the George Harrison estate. The geology report was a disaster, which gave her an excuse to cancel the purchase. The paperwork had to be signed and delivered by five o'clock tomorrow.

The second issue was a bit more unsettling. The myriad of gifts stashed in her trunk had disappeared the night of the wedding. Violet resisted calling Teddy, not only because she didn't want any contact with him, but because her gut said he didn't do it. His code of honor was rife with nuance, to be sure. But burglary was something that just didn't fit. There was the additional matter of hepatitis C. She and Teddy had used a condom. Still, she would get a blood test, just to be sure.

Violet reached the bottom of the driveway and stopped at the mailbox. Despite all of David's success, his face would fill with child-like anticipation at the sight of the mail. She'd bring him the mail, the lunch she had made him, the escrow cancelation papers, and word of her new job. David had wanted her to start writing again. Perhaps he'd be so happy he'd sleep at home tonight. Perhaps he'd already made up his mind to throw her out. There was no way to tell. Yesterday at the market, she had reached for a dozen eggs, and realized they had a good chance of lasting longer at her house than she did.

She dialed David's office.

"Violet!" burst the startled voice of David's assistant.

"David's wife."

"I know. He was out of the office all morning, I have no idea where, and I've got a million people trying to get a hold of him."

"Oh," Violet said. "He's not around?"

"He just got on a helicopter to Coachella. Even though the concert's not until Saturday, he went today to make sure the sound from the main stage won't drown out the second stage—" The assistant gasped.

"What?" asked Violet.

"Nothing," said the girl. "I don't know why I'm telling you all this."

Violet had been thinking the same thing. "Well, just tell David I called." She hung up, disappointed she would miss him.

SALLY ascended the steps of her Crescent Heights apartment. Strewn on the landing was a month of mail laced with shriveled wisteria blossoms. The state seal of California jumped out at her. She opened the envelope. "Sally Miller Parry, this letter informs you that your debts have been discharged, blah, blah, blah...." Could she have really gotten away with the whole thing? She was out of debt, married, and pregnant, all in four months. She gathered the mail and opened the door.

Before her was a wonderland of wedding presents, all shapes and sizes. They were just gigantic chunks of cardboard, of course, but Sally's X-ray eyes saw the light blue Tiffany boxes, gold Geary's ones, and more! It was as if she had opened door number two and won the grand prize. She half-expected Bob Barker to step in and hand her the keys to a brand-new convertible. The audience would lustily applaud, knowing Sally deserved it all.

She could have ripped open every box on the spot, but she had to organize her medicine before the car arrived. Game One of the NBA Conference Finals was tonight in Houston, and the plane left in two hours. Sally picked her way to the kitchen, where she loaded medicine into her extra diabetes kit for the plane. Hopefully, Houston would be more fun than Sacramento. It ended up that there was only so much you could do, or charge, at the Sheraton Grand Sacramento. She and Jeremy had ventured out once, to the California State Railroad Museum. At the ticket booth, Jeremy got recognized by a bunch of scary black people wearing Kings jerseys. They kept shouting, Hey, Professor! and taking pictures with their cell phones. The newlyweds left before the guide showed up for their VIP tour.

Sally zipped the kit shut, then couldn't help it. She had to open just one present.

She raced into the living room and chose a giant box from Tiffany. She yanked off the red ribbon. Inside was a peacock cachepot. Sally's spirits sank. She *had* registered for it, but what would she do with a five-hundred-dollar cachepot? Maybe start a charity where people gave away their wedding presents to those less fortunate. Sally had once read in *Town & Country* that Jessica Seinfeld, Jerry's wife, founded a charity that distributed baby stuff that her friends didn't want. Now that she was Sally White, she needed to start taking herself seriously like that, too.

Sally looked at the mail. Maybe there was something good *there*. She recognized a return address as belonging to Nora Ross. The envelope was heavy, the paper thick and expensive. Sally opened it and removed a little book bound with red silk cord. On the cover were the words:

Brilliant
Absentminded
Mathematically Inclined
Structured

That was a perfect description of Jeremy! This must be some kind of personalized thank-you note for the wedding. She turned the page.

Repetitive
Clumsy
Literal Minded
Socially Inept
Obsessive

Sally frowned. Sure, all those things applied to Jeremy, but they were hardly appropriate for a thank-you note. And where was the part about *her*? She turned the page.

ASPERGER'S SYNDROME

A Pervasive Developmental Disorder
that has reached
epidemic proportions.

Please join
Nora and Jordan Ross
as they Shine a Spotlight
on the Autism Spectrum.

There was a Web address on the bottom of the invitation. Sally went to her laptop and typed it in. A blare of words and phrases appeared on the screen.

> Asperger's syndrome is considered to be a lesser form of AUTISM…

Wait, Sally thought, J. J. has autism. Jeremy is nothing like J.J.

> Asperger's syndrome is often marked by high intelligence and a tendency to become abnormally fixated on one subject. This often results in a successful career in that field.…

That did describe Jeremy, but lots of people were successful.

They have trouble empathizing and reciprocating emotion.... Their speech often lacks inflection....

Sally? She could hear Jeremy's flat voice as if he were right there in the room.

Many people with Asperger's syndrome have difficulty making eye contact....

Sally.

They have an unusually low tolerance of loud noises.

Sally.

They rigidly adhere to specific arbitrary rituals, any deviation from which can cause significant anxiety....Despite their intelligence, everyday activities such as driving a car can seem impossibly complicated....

Sally!

Asperger's is highly hereditary. One in three girls born to a parent with Asperger's will inherit it. Double that with boys.

Sally grabbed her stomach and closed her eyes. Jeremy's horrible voice echoed in her brain. *Sally. Sally. Sally.*

"Stop it!" She covered her ears.

"Sally. The car is waiting." She turned. Instead of Bob Barker standing among the boxes, it was Jeremy. "Sally," he said, "it's time to go."

"Jeremy. Is something wrong with you?"

"No."

"Why do you always wear earplugs?" Sally had never even asked him this, always having attributed it to the delightful eccentricity of a genius.

"Do you want some?" He reached into his pocket and offered her a pair. She hit them to the floor.

"Look at me," she said. He flashed her a glance, then looked down. "Look me in the eyes." She stepped toward him. He didn't look up. "What is wrong with you?"

"Our plane leaves at twelve fifty and it's eleven now. The driver said there's lots of traffic."

"Why don't you drive?"

"I don't have a license," he said.

"Have you ever tried to get one?"

"Six times."

"What happened?" Her voice trembled.

"It didn't work out."

"*What* didn't work out?"

"I scored a hundred on the written, but I didn't like the driving portion."

"Don't you think it's weird," she said, "that you got your PhD in a week, but you can't drive a car?"

"I got my PhD in five semesters."

Then it occurred to her. "That's why you pooped that day. You can look into a *camera* just fine. But when it came time to look into Jim's *eyes*, you got so nervous, you shit your pants!"

Sally had played everything right. The dating, the proposal, the pregnancy, the wedding. The one thing she had overlooked was that Jeremy was retarded. And chances were, the baby in her belly was, too.

"Go," she said. "Go to Houston by yourself."

"You have a plane ticket."

"Get out!" Sally said. Jeremy turned and walked out of the apartment.

THE helicopter began its descent. David stared out the window. The Coachella Valley looked as if someone had begun to methodically stick postage stamps in different shades of green to the desert floor, only to abandon the task halfway through. He could make out the festival site up ahead, its monster main stage and dozen white tents scattered on the hyper-green polo field. David's Black-Berry vibrated. There it was.

> To: David@ultra.com
> From: BartonC@TMBB.com
> Re: divorce papers
> Just been filed. Let me know when you want them served.

David contemplated the grass bracelet that still clung to his wrist.

At the fire pit, the stoned kid had cautioned that the sweet grass must fall off naturally, otherwise the transformative power of the sweat lodge would be lost. Over the past months, David had grown increasingly preoccupied with the bracelet, never tugging on it, careful not to get it wet, even wearing his watch on his right hand so it wouldn't rub against it. He hated himself for his superstition. What had happened there anyway, other than David and a bunch of strangers getting really, really hot together? Still, he hung on to the hope that something life-changing had actually taken place.

Indeed, compassion had flowed in the weeks after the yoga retreat. How couldn't it have? David had returned home to find Violet a lying, distracted wretch. Pity was a cinch. Until Sally's wedding.

David had been prepared to storm into the hotel room that night and announce he was leaving her. Heading down the palm-plastered corridor, Dot in his arms, thoughts ablaze with the invective he'd been rehearsing for the past five hours, he held the door open for a couple of women. "Awwww," they both cooed, in such a maudlin way that David almost turned to see what it could be. But of course it was Dot. Bundled up in her quilt, clutching her froggie, her fancy dress stained with berries and chocolate, God, what could compare to the peacefulness of that sleeping face? And David thought: *Violet had turned him into a chump and a cuckold, but there was no way she was going to turn him into a man who walked out on his child.* He turned right around and checked into a bungalow.

And amazingly, this past month, Violet had seemed to find her way back. But with every wifely duty she performed, David's rage grew. He could get his own lunch. He had an assistant for that. How about a fucking apology with his tofu and brown rice? Violet was perfectly plucky to go about her business as if nothing had ever happened! Which meant that *David* would be the one stuck suffering a lifetime of suspicion and betrayal.

The helicopter touched down on the empty polo field. All but one strand of the bracelet had frayed. He would serve the divorce papers when it finally fell off.

The pilot opened the door. David was met by a woman who worked for the promoter.

"David! Hi!" she said. Thirties, skinny, in jeans and tank top showing off great arms. "We've got the whole Ultra village set up. Five Airstreams, all with wireless and *Scarface*."

"How about Guitar Hero?"

"Guitar Hero on big screens. I had to lock up the mini guitars because the crew won't stop messing around with them." She laughed and touched his shoulder and kept it there a second too long. He knew that word had leaked out that he was living apart from his wife. The promoter chick wore too much makeup but had full lips, the kind that never quite closed. "Are you staying through Saturday," she asked, "or going back to LA tonight?"

"I don't know," he said. "It depends how it goes."

SALLY sat across from Dr. Naeby at his cluttered desk.

"What's up?" he asked.

"I'd like to get an abortion," she said. "Now."

Dr. Naeby's eyebrows jumped. The walls of his office were covered with framed pictures of his own children. The lyrics of "Teach Your Children Well" were handwritten and signed by David Crosby, with a personalized thanks to the OB/GYN.

"You're not going to tell me why," he said.

"No," said Sally.

Dr. Naeby flipped through her chart and looked up. "You never called us back about the blood test."

Sally now remembered receiving a message from him last week about needing to draw more blood for some routine tests. "I was out of town," she said.

The doctor pushed a button on the intercom. "Diana? Could you get room four ready? And tell Marcella we're going to need some blood." Dr. Naeby paused at a flimsy ultrasound of Sally's fetus that was stapled to her chart. He appeared lost in thought for a moment, then shook his head wistfully and looked up. "Okay." He hit his hands on the desk. "See Marcella first and I'll meet you in room four."

Compared to her other two, this abortion was pure class. Dr. Naeby, Diana, Marcella, they all struck the perfect tone, not too solemn, not too cheery. Basketball was discussed as Sally got the IV of Valium, and the whole thing was over before she knew it had started.

"Stay as long as you like," Diana said, removing the IV. "We don't need the room. You have someone to drive you home?"

"Yes." It was easier to lie.

"Here are some pads and some pills," Diana said. Sally didn't bother looking. "These are to help your uterus contract. And some painkillers for cramping. Give us a call if the bleeding doesn't stop by tomorrow."

"Thanks." The door opened and shut. Sally lay there, comfy-cozy, drifting in and out. She thought it was funny when people talked about abortions as though they were so tragic. If only she could have one every day. Nothing could compare to the satisfaction of knowing a potentially ruinous situation had been averted.

On the wall was a photograph of a cheetah or a leopard, peering out over some green hills. It must have been a cheetah. Cheetahs were the ones that looked as if they were crying black tears. The picture was signed in the corner, Charles Naeby. Dr. Naeby probably took it when he was on safari with his family. Sally loved Dr. Naeby.

She would tell Jeremy that she had lost the baby due to diabetic complications. She could fly to Houston in time for tonight's game. Wait—what was she thinking?—the secret was out—there was something wrong with Jeremy. She had no choice but to divorce him. A good lawyer could prove that Sally was the only reason he had gotten the ESPN job, which would entitle her to half of his contract. But that might get canceled once everybody found out he had...whatever that thing was he had. All she'd need was enough for her apartment—no—she had given up the apartment, and somebody else was set to move in on the first. And now she couldn't get a new one because she'd declared bankruptcy. Plus, she'd given up all her classes and privates, so her career was dead. And she'd canceled her health insurance through David. The wedding presents! The presents must be worth thirty grand. She could return them for cash—no, probably not; most were engraved. God, did that mean she had to stay with Jeremy? How could she not have seen what was wrong with him? All the signs had been there on the very first night! Jeremy was so literal minded. He didn't drive. He didn't look her in the eye. He wore earplugs. She always knew there was something a little *off* about him, but she was happy to live with it. Now that it had a name, now that it was all over the internet, now that Nora Ross was having parties celebrating it—Sally sat up.

Weird hospital-issued maxi pads the size of bricks were stacked on the counter. She looked down. They had put one of those abortion garter belt things on her. Sally's thighs were smeared with blood. Dr. Naeby and the nurses had just left her there, bottomless. The paper sheath she wore from the waist up had shadows of blood on it, too. She ripped it off. Here she was again. It didn't matter what movie star was in the next room, an abortion was an abortion. A jumbo maxi pad was a jumbo maxi pad.

The first abortion Sally had, she was fifteen years old. Def Leppard had just played the first of four sold-out shows at McNichols arena. After flirting with Joe Elliott, the lead singer, at the Brown Palace bar, Sally went upstairs with him to his room. He was practically passed out on the bed, wearing the same ripped jeans and Mott the Hoople T-shirt from the show. She was a virgin and didn't have a clue how to proceed when he unzipped his tight pants and peeled them down to his knees. He never took his eyes off the *Top 10 Video Countdown* on MTV. Sally locked her mouth around his uncircumcised thingy—it was the first and last time she'd seen one of those!—and blew, while he yelled instructions in a stupid Eliza Doolittle accent. "Suck! Slower. Softer. Watch your teeth. Suck. Deeper." *Deeper?* Sally was already worried she might gag. Still, he kept barking at her, "Deeper, deeper." Sally knew there were a dozen girls at the bar who would take her place in a second. So she slowed down, sucked, shielded her teeth with her lips, and pushed her mouth down as far as she could without gagging. "I'll do it myself." He pushed her out of the way and grabbed his pecker. The VJ had just announced the most requested video of the day, "Pour Some Sugar on Me" by Def Leppard. "It's okay!" Sally said. "I'll do it!" She stuck his dick as far down her throat as she could, and something came up. She couldn't stop herself. She vomited on his stomach. Not too much, though. "What was all that?" He rose to his elbows. "Nothing!" Sally pushed him back and frantically licked up her vomit. He shoved her aside and passed out. The next day, the roadies made a big deal out of giving her a special laminated pass with her picture on it. She proudly flashed it to all the yellow jackets at that night's show. At the after party, David marched over and ripped off her lanyard. "Give me that thing," he said. The whole party went silent. "You fucking assholes," David shouted to the crew members. "She's just a child!" He spiked the pass onto the concrete floor and stormed out. Sally picked it up. Above her picture, it didn't say DEF LEPPARD. In the same triangular letters as their logo, it said BAR FEEDER. Sally didn't see anything wrong with being called that. "Bar feeder," she said to herself. Then, the kick in the stomach: it *read* "Bar Feeder." But spoken, it *sounded like* "Barf Eater." The roadies burst into laughter. The only one who took pity on her was the one-armed drummer. An hour later, she lost her virginity to him and got pregnant. That's how pathetic her one attempt as a groupie had been; she couldn't even fuck somebody with two arms.

Her second abortion had been paid for by the travel agent who didn't leave his wife for her. He drove Sally to and from some clinic by the airport and never spoke to her again.

Tears flowed down Sally's cheeks and tickled the back of her neck. *Drip, drop.* They landed on the paper covering the exam table.

Throughout her childhood, all the other kids were frightened of her. She was the weirdo who couldn't eat sweets and had to go to the nurse's office to test her blood sugar. The isolation she felt only made her try harder, which only further repelled her class-mates. The one person who understood her isolation was David, but he left home. So Sally marshaled her fear into ballet. The better she got, the more the teachers yelled at her, the bigger her smile. But then "3 mm X 3 mm" of her toe was taken. All she had to show for her years of grueling practice was the lying smile on her face. When she just wanted to tell someone, "I'm scared."

Nobody could understand how much she hurt, how hard she tried, for how little she was asking. She'd have been happy to stay in the *corps de ballet* at a regional company. It would have been fine to marry a guy who worked in a boot shop. She knew her place.

Now, fresh from abortion number three, she had nowhere to go. "I'm scared," she whimpered.

She had always ached for a baby, just so she could hold it and say, "I know you're scared. I'm scared, too." And now that baby was dead in the wastebasket. Why had she run out and had another abortion? From now on, she'd be a girl who had gotten three abortions. Prostitutes and sluts had three abortions, not nice girls. Maybe this was her last chance to have a baby and she'd just murdered it. Maybe it wasn't even a boy, and chances were there was nothing wrong with it. What if she'd murdered her daughter for no reason? God, she had to check to make sure it wasn't a little ballerina—Sally jumped off the table and her legs gave out. She crawled to the trash can and smashed the pedal with her hand. It was full of white shiny paper. She reached in and touched something small, hard, and slimy—it stuck to her hand.

"Aaaah!" Sally shook her hand wildly. It was just a piece of gum, which went flying. "I'm scared," she sobbed. "Now do you believe me?"

"She's right in here." The nurse's voice grew louder from the hallway.

"Who?" said another voice.

The door swung open.

"Violet?" Sally said.

"Sally?" said Violet.

"Oh shit." Diana, the nurse, turned white and ran to help Sally to her feet. "Are you okay?"

"I'm fine, I'm fine."

"I'm sorry," said Diana. "I assumed she was here to take you home."

"No," said Violet, who had a cotton ball and white tape on the inside of her elbow.

"I'm so sorry," said Diana. "This has never happened. I mean, I just assumed, since you're family—"

"It's okay," Violet told her. "It's okay." Diana left. Violet stepped into the room and closed the door. "Are you okay?" she asked Sally.

"I'm fine. I'm great, really. I had no choice but to get a little abortion." Sally grabbed her jeans and stepped into them. "Because of my diabetes."

"I'm sorry—I—" Violet stammered. "I didn't know. Here, let me help you."

"I can manage." Sally slipped her shirt over her head.

"Gestational diabetes?" Violet asked. "I thought they tested for that later."

"Regular diabetes. *My* diabetes."

"You're diabetic? Since when?"

"Since I was three. Type one."

"Jesus Christ," said Violet. "I had no idea. David never told me."

"He didn't?"

"I'm sorry. I don't want to make it about me. But I'm just kind of reeling here." Violet gulped. "Let me drive you home."

"I'm fine." Sally grabbed the handful of pads.

"Where's Jeremy?" asked Violet.

"He's in Houston. He knows, and all. I'm just going home. I'll be fine." The stupid pads wouldn't fit in her purse. No matter how hard she crammed them, they fell to the floor.

"Here." Violet took Sally's purse. "I'm going to drive you to our house. You can spend the night there."

"I don't want David to know," Sally said.

"He won't."

They walked down the hall to Diana's desk. "I am so sorry, you guys," she said. "Nothing like that has ever happened before."

"Don't worry about it," said Violet. "How are we paying for this?"

"I'll send a bill to the Crescent Heights address," said Diana, off Sally's chart.

Before Sally could protest, Violet handed Diana a black American Express card. "How about we put it on this?"

VIOLET drove up the canyon, Sally curled in the passenger seat, her back to Violet. Violet reached for the Tupperware container containing David's lunch, pulled off the top, and offered it to Sally. "If you're hungry, I made them."

Sally took it.

"And for the tenth time, I can't believe David never told me you were diabetic." Then it struck her. "Oh, my God. I sent you *chocolates* on your birthday!"

"I thought that was pretty insensitive." Sally bit into one of the fritters. "You made these?"

"Chard and quinoa. They're better when they're hot."

Sally rolled onto her back and wolfed down another one. Violet felt Sally studying her face. Sally finally said, "I didn't have an abortion because I was diabetic. I had an abortion because I found out there's something wrong with Jeremy. It's something called—I don't even know how to pronounce it—it's a syndrome or something."

"Asperger's?"

"You knew?" Sally looked stricken.

"Well, no. But now that you mention it, I'm not surprised."

"I'm the only one who didn't know he was retarded?"

"He's not retarded!" Violet couldn't help but laugh. "It's a spectrum disorder. Our accountant definitely has it. People speculate that Bill Gates has it, and Albert Einstein probably did, too. Seriously, it's no big deal." Sally stared out the window. Violet continued, "Every woman in America at some point must think her husband has it. You think I never wanted to throw myself off a cliff because David is so unemotional? I mean, not telling his own wife that his sister is diabetic. What is that?"

"Everyone knew but me!" Sally dropped the Tupperware.

"Nobody *knows*," Violet said. "And if they did, they wouldn't care. I think it was Oscar Wilde who said, You wouldn't care about what other people thought about you if you realized how seldom they actually did."

There was silence. Then Sally said, "Why did you tell Jeremy to call off our wedding?"

For a moment, Violet was speechless. "I just happened upon him. There was no treachery on my part. He said you scared him."

"That's the best you can do?" Sally said.

Sally had been painfully honest with Violet. Now it was Violet's turn. "I never really liked you," she said.

"I never really liked you, either," Sally shot back.

"Thank you!" Violet laughed. "That makes me feel so much better. From the first day I met you, I could tell something was off. And I thought I was crazy. I mean, this whole time, I thought it was me."

"It *was* you," said Sally. "I didn't like you. I thought you were a snob masquerading as a nice person."

Violet was impressed. "I've never heard it put that way before." She drove past a eucalyptus grove on Mulholland. "When I was a little girl," she said, "I remember driving by this exact spot with my father. He was shit-faced as usual, and he told me, If there's one thing I know how to do, it's drive these canyon roads drunk."

Sally forced a smile.

"From now on," Violet said, "it will always be the spot where you said, I never really liked you."

CHAPTER TWELVE

Geddy Lee / eBay / Bass ❀ What Bills?

Get It Done ❀ So That's How You Wanna Play It? ❀ Poison into Medicine

The Number *i* ❀ The Story

KARA DROPPED HER PURSE ON HER DESK WHEN THE PHONE RANG. SHE WOULD have let it go to voice mail, but it was five after ten, and it might be David calling in for messages. She grabbed the phone, making sure she didn't sound out of breath. "David Parry's office."

"Hi, is David there? It's Geddy Lee."

Geddy Lee. The name sounded familiar, but Kara couldn't place it. "He's not in yet. May I take a message?"

"I'm calling to razz him about my bass showing up on eBay. Tell him if he's really that cheap, I'll give his wife the money."

Kara didn't have a pen and her computer was asleep. There was no way she would remember what this guy had just said. "Do you want me to try him at home?" she asked, then gasped. David never wanted people put through to his house. "Or," she said, "maybe he's in his car, but I can't reach him because it's hard to get reception in the canyons." Kara cringed at how lame that just sounded.

"Just give him the message when he gets in."

"He's usually in by now," she said. "But he was at Coachella for a sound check yesterday and probably got back late to the—" Oh God! Kara had almost told this Geddy guy that David was living at the Beverly Hills Hotel! Even Kara wasn't supposed to know. "I'll give him the message," she said.

"He knows my numbers."

Now Kara was back at square one. Who was Geddy Lee? How did you spell Geddy Lee? And what was the message? Something about eBay and a bass. She *so* didn't want to get fired for this.

"KNOCK, knock."

Sally roused from an oozy semi-slumber and found herself back in the bridal suite.

"I'm sorry if I woke you." Violet entered with a breakfast tray. "Egg white omelet with low-fat Jarlsberg, sautéed mushrooms, and ten blueberries. Everything low in sugar for my diabetic sister-in-law."

"Yeah, thanks." Sally sat up. On the tray were a vase of flowers and some gossip magazines.

"Your medicine is in the bathroom. Your mail is in the kitchen, and your clothes are there." Two of Sally's velour sweat suits were folded on a chair, along with her washed and ironed clothes from yesterday. Sally vaguely remembered having changed into Violet's silk pajamas and giving her keys to her apartment.

"I really appreciate it," Sally said. "I'll be out of here this morning."

"Don't even think about it. You're staying the night."

Dot, the shiny-eyed force of nature, hurtled in. Nothing had ever gone wrong for this quizzical girl in the crooked pigtails.

"Hi, Dot." Sally tried not to smile too big.

Last month, when she was planning the wedding, Sally had made an extra effort to connect with her niece. Dot had hidden her face in her hands and told Violet, Mommy, tell the lady to stop smiling at me.

"You read me a book?" Dot handed Sally a stiff copy of *Goodnight Moon*.

"What," Violet said, off of Sally's look. "You don't like *Goodnight Moon*?"

"It was a little weird," Sally admitted.

"Goodnight nobody. Don't you love that? It's so random." Violet turned to Dot. "I'll read it to you later, sweetheart."

"Uppy, uppy." Dot raised her arms. Violet scooped her up.

"Well, we're off. I have errands and a playdate, then the realtor wants to meet me at that land we're not going to buy. Be here when I get back."

"I will." Sally watched Violet leave and couldn't resist. "Violet, those cargo pants…"

"I know, I know. They make my ass look gigantic, but I trekked to Everest Base Camp in them a million years ago and I have a sentimental attachment."

"Wear them around here if you have to," Sally said, "but get some low-rise jeans to wear in public."

"I'm starting a new job next week. We can go to Barney's and blow my paycheck before I get it. You can be my stylist." Violet left.

Sally picked up a magazine. It was brand-new and didn't have an address label on it. Neither did the other magazines. Violet must have picked them up especially for Sally. Maybe Sally had it backward: Violet was a nice person masquerading as a snob.

Sally ate her breakfast and took a shower. She carried her tray to the kitchen and tripped on something. An overstuffed laundry bag from the Beverly Hills Hotel had appeared in the hallway.

"Sally." David stood at the kitchen counter. Violet had said he was out of town. "Are you feeling better? Violet left a note."

"Hi! Yeah, I'm fine. I hope it's all right that I spent the night."

"I have to talk to you about something."

Sally opened the dishwasher. "Sure, what?"

"I was looking through the mail, and before I realized it was *your* mail, I saw this." Swinging between his thumb and index finger was her bankruptcy letter. "You declared bankruptcy?"

"Oh, my God—" Sally dropped a glass in the sink.

"The creditors listed are credit card companies," David said. "What do I need to do?"

"Nothing. It's over. The bankruptcy went through. Isn't that what the letter says?"

"How were you able to file for Chapter Seven? After the Bankruptcy Act a couple of years ago, didn't they make that more difficult?"

"I get paid in cash, so most of my income didn't show."

David considered this and nodded. "Remember that correspondence course I took to get my accounting degree?"

"Yeah."

"Here's what it taught me. Those who understand compound interest earn it; those who don't, pay it. Got that?"

"Yes."

"Next time, come to me, will you?"

"There won't be a next time," she said.

David handed her the discharge letter. "On another unpleasant topic: my wife called me last night, none too pleased that I never told her about your diabetes."

"Oh."

"You made me promise not to tell anyone, right?"

"Right." She had, but that was way back in high school.

"Could you clarify that fact for Violet next time you see her?"

"I'm sorry," said Sally. "I just assumed, because you were married, it would come up."

"A promise is a promise, unless I'm instructed otherwise."

"Well, what do you tell her when the bills come?" Sally asked.

"What bills?"

"My doctors' bills."

"I'm paying your doctors' bills?" David's head jerked back ever so slightly. She'd forgotten he did that.

"And my insurance."

"That's news to me."

"Wait," Sally said. "You didn't know?"

"I believe you," said David. "Anyone who screws in a lightbulb around here ends up on my insurance."

The phone rang. David answered it. Sally held herself up, both hands on the counter. Her insides stung as if she'd just been eviscerated.

David handed her the phone. "Dr. Naeby, for you."

"Oh," said Sally.

"Okay. I'm going to the office. See you later." David left. She waited for the door to shut, then took the call.

"Hi, Sally," said Dr. Naeby. "How are you this morning?"

"Fine."

"No cramping or excessive bleeding?"

"No, everything's fine."

"That's the good news." Dr. Naeby changed gears. "Now, about your blood test. Something of concern showed up in the first one, and that's why I wanted to run another...."

KARA stood proudly before David. Not only had she pieced together Geddy Lee's message, but she'd also found the eBay auction and e-mailed David the link. David seemed unusually interested in it and had asked her to get Geddy Lee on the phone. David had just hung up and called Kara in.

"The bass?" he said.

"Yes?" Kara had pen in hand, ready to take notes.

"Pay for it with cash. I want that bass, the seller's name, and where he lives on my desk before lunch."

It took Kara a second to realize she was committing the number one cardinal sin of an assistant: standing there with the deer-in-headlights look. She had to say something, but all that came out was "Muawh—"

"Get it done," David said.

"Of course." Kara calmly walked down the hall to the office of the guy who did the bookings. "Hi, would you mind covering David's phones?" she asked his secretary.

"Sure," said the older Hillary, who had no choice. As David's assistant, Kara outranked her.

Kara returned to her computer and found the auction. There was an option that let you "Buy It Now." Which was a whopping $10,000. The actual auction had only reached $1,200 and it closed at five. It seemed stupid to pay $10,000 now, when David could probably buy the bass in a few hours for much less. Kara rose from her chair to point this out, then sat back down. It wasn't her job to second-guess David. She bought the bass, contacted the seller, and got his address. He wanted to know more about her, but she said nothing. Any information was too much information.

The messenger from the bank arrived with the cash, and Kara walked him into David's office. David tore open the plastic envelope, counted the money, and signed for it.

"I have the address and I'll leave now to get the bass," Kara said.

"Where is it?" he asked.

"Really close: 8907 Sunset Boulevard."

David's head shot back. "That's on the strip, right?"

"A place called Mauricio's Boot Shop."

David blinked. And blinked again. "Mauricio's?"

"Yeah."

David stood up. "I'll get it myself." He started out. The brick of hundreds was still on his desk.

"Don't forget the money!" said Kara.

"Go to the bank and deposit it back into the account."

"Of course," said Kara.

Now she's fucking Kurt Pombo! David fishtailed onto Sunset Boulevard. All he could figure was that Violet had moved on to Kurt Pombo and was funneling him rock memorabilia to sell on eBay. Had the great Violet Grace Parry truly stooped this low? It was impossible to fathom. David double-parked outside Mauricio's and left the front door of his Bentley open. He flew into the boot shop. If he had a baseball bat he would have been wielding it.

The joint was empty. But not for long. Kurt entered from the back room. "Hey, David," he said with a yip. "What's up, bro?"

"So that's how you wanna play it?" It must have come out pretty fucking menacing, because Kurt fled into the back like the little bitch he was. "You want to fuck with me?" David charged him. Kurt had nowhere to run in the tiny workroom. He cowered in the corner. David grabbed him by the Hawaiian shirt and threw him against the wall.

"I'm sorry," Kurt yowled. He slid to the floor. "I'll give it back. It's right there—"

"I don't give a fuck about the bass." David kicked Kurt in the gut. After two lonely months of Saint David, kicking the shit out of a wannabe lowlife sure hit the spot. "I'm here because of my *wife,* you asshole. But I don't want her back, either. Whatever the fuck you two are doing together, she's all yours." He kicked him again.

"I swear—I didn't—I swear. I'm not the one fucking your wife." David stopped.

"I just stole that shit from the car." Kurt stood up. "I took the shit she was about to give to that other dude—the guy in the Stones cover band."

David cocked his head and walked himself through the logic of this new information.

"I promise you, man," Kurt said, "I never touched your wife. Take the bass. And the phone and the golf clubs. It's all there. And your kid's cough syrup."

On the cobbler's bench, among cowboy boots in various stages of finish, sat Dot's eczema medicine. David had to smile. He extended his hand to Kurt, who recoiled. David grabbed his daughter's medicine and left.

VIOLET sat in her car at the bottom of George Harrison's former drive-way, flipping through the escrow papers. Gwen had insisted on meeting at the property before Violet made any "rash decisions." Violet had finally acquiesced. She felt a strange tenderness toward this older divorcée, her very own Ghost of Christmas Future. Violet then noticed that David had forgotten to sign the middle of page four.

"Shit," she said.

"Shit," said Dot.

"No, darling, we don't say shit."

"Mama? Out. Out."

"We can't get out." Violet turned on the stereo.

> Bobby...Bobby...Bobby...Bobby...Bo-bo-bo-bo-bo-bo-bo-bo-Bobeeeee.

Violet checked the rearview mirror. Dot was mesmerized, as always, by the opening number from *Company*.

> Bobby, baby. Bobby, Bubby. Robby. Robert, darling. Robbo.
> Bobby, baby. Bobby, Bubby.

Dot whispered along, keeping up as best she could. Violet smiled. It was never too early to indoctrinate Dot into the glories of Stephen Sondheim. Dot, named after the artist's muse from *Sunday in the Park with George*. David was dismissive of Sondheim, saying, He can't write songs. Violet fervently disagreed. She didn't care if other children grew up to the Wiggles or Dan Zanes. Hers would adore Sondheim. Violet had declared it that joyous day of the first ultrasound. David conceded her Sondheim if she'd give him the Mets. They shook on it in front of Dr. Naeby, who raised his brow and went about his business.

There was a knock on the window. "Ooh, you brought the munchkin!"

"Gwen, hi." Violet turned down the volume.

"I have my walking shoes on!" Gwen lifted a hiking boot to the window. Perhaps she'd been a dancer once.

"I really can't," started Violet. "I have the baby. You know how enthusiastic we were, but the geology report leaves us no choice but to cancel. You understand."

"Oh." Gwen's face came crashing down.

"Mommy?" said Dot.

"Yes, sweetie?"

"Shit."

"I'm ignoring that," Violet informed Gwen. "Thanks for everything, but our decision is made. Here are the papers. David didn't sign page four, but he signed everywhere else—"

Gwen swung her hands up, as if avoiding being served. "Nope. Can't accept those. No point in trying. Papers gotta be signed. No can do."

It was impossible to hate Gwen. Violet would send her a check, or a client, even see if there was a one-line part for her in the new TV show.

"I understand," Violet said. "I'll fax them to your office by five." Gwen pivoted, climbed into her car, and drove off.

"Out!" said Dot. "Mommy, want out!"

Dot had been a trouper all day, plus it would be good to burn off energy before the nap. "Just for five minutes."

A green car crunched up the dirt road and stopped. "Green car," said Dot.

"Yes," Violet said. "That's a green car."

"What dat man's name?" asked Dot.

"I don't know," Violet said. "Now run around and then we're going to go home and take a nap."

A door slammed. The green car's trunk was open. Behind it was that guy Sally used to date, with the hair and the Hawaiian shirts.

Violet's instinct was to protect Dot. "Honey, don't go far."

Then, this guy—Kurt, she thought—loaded his arms with Geddy Lee's bass, the set of Callaway golf clubs, and the bag from the Apple store. He walked over and dumped them at Violet's feet.

"Take them," he said. "Get them out of my life. I don't need the karma." He turned around.

"Where did you get these?"

"I took them out of your car."

"Oh." Violet said. "Wait—" She glanced at Dot, who was climbing the nearby hill. It was rocky and steep, but thanks to RIE, Dot had good balance. Violet turned to Kurt. "How did you know I was here?"

"I went to your house and Sally told me. I'm sorry. I'm a fucking moron. If suffering serves as a springboard to expand your life state, then I'm going to have the biggest life state in the universe." His Hawaiian shirt was torn, his hand bandaged, and one eye was starting to swell.

"What happened?" she asked.

"Ask your fucking husband."

"Oh God." Violet's stomach roiled.

Dot was squatting, completely absorbed in some discarded

strawberry baskets. "Bobby baby, Bobby bubby," she sang to herself as she filled a basket with rocks.

"He thought I was fucking you or something," said Kurt.

"Why would he think that?"

"Don't ask me. What goes on between you and your husband is your business. My only business is to chant until I transform my destructive tendencies from poison into medicine. I'm like Pigpen with a black cloud of bad karma following me everywhere."

"Hang on a second." Violet frantically tried to calculate the bits of information. "How did you even know this stuff was in my car?"

"I overheard you telling the guy you were fucking."

"Is that what you told David?!"

"I really don't remember. I was too busy trying not to get my face kicked in." He turned to leave.

"No—you can't go—tell me." She grabbed both of his arms. "What did you hear? What did you tell David—"

"I told him I'm not the guy you were fucking."

"What?!" Violet's whole body throbbed. "What did he say? What did you tell him—"

A shriek echoed across the canyon. It was Dot. No *Mommy*, no *Mama*, just one cry, then silence. It was what Violet had always feared the most, silence.

"Dot!" she screamed. Her daughter had vanished from the hill. Blades of grass and fragile California poppies swayed in the breeze. It was silent and idyllic, like the day-after scenes of Chernobyl.

"Shit," Kurt said. "She was right here. Where did she go?"

"Dot! Baby! Say something!" Violet fought her way up the hill. "Dot! Mommy's here. Dot! Where are you?!" Violet screamed to Kurt, who stood at the bottom of the hill, "Help me! Maybe she's down on the street. Or in a house. Knock on the doors. Oh God—"

Violet thought she might vomit: the reservoir. "No, no." She scrambled to the top of the rise.

Twenty feet below, splayed among the rocks, was the still body of little Dot, facedown, pigtails askew, wearing her beloved Spider-Man T-shirt and the frilly pants Violet had sewn for her just last week.

JEREMY entered his Sherman Oaks apartment. "Sally?" It had been twenty-nine hours since she had told him to get out. She never arrived in Houston, as he figured she would. She hadn't called once.

He removed the pad of graph paper he kept in his jacket. After the wedding, Jeremy had begun to graph Sally's moods. He entered the intensities and frequencies onto a basic Cartesian graph. He had intended, through Fourier analysis, to break the master waves into component waves and extend the graph out to predict Sally's mood swings. But he could only realistically predict sixty-three percent. Although that may have been an impressive number for sports handicapping, it didn't help when applied to the person you were married to. He then came up with the idea of inputting his own actions into the sine-cosine equation in an attempt to see if he was indeed responsible for his wife's terrifying moods. She always said they were *his* fault, for being so selfish. But what was he so selfish about? Wanting to go to a restaurant he liked? Wanting to walk instead of drive? Wanting to read the papers every morning in silence? Why wouldn't *she* be considered equally as selfish for wanting to go to the restaurants *she* liked? Or wanting to drive everywhere? Or blathering on about some television show while he was trying to read the paper? How did that make *him* selfish and not her?

Jeremy had tried to make this point many times, but how did you prove to someone that you felt as much as they did? All the feelings Sally was always accusing him of not feeling—love, anger, fear—he *felt* them. He just didn't feel the need to talk about them. That was a feeling, too, not feeling like talking about your feelings. If all feelings were so great, why didn't that one count? Besides, whenever he did try to talk about his feelings, she told him he was stupid to feel what he was feeling. In Jeremy's opinion, the things *Sally* felt were stupid. Therefore, they should just cancel each other out.

But Jeremy had taken Sally as his wife. All he could do now was try to figure her out. Coin flipping, formulas, first-order discrete differential equations, propositions: all had proven to be dead ends. But Jeremy had noticed that, like his favorite number, the imaginary number i, Sally's moods were cyclical. So he decided to graph them out.

Even though the graphs were ultimately of no use, entering data points and curve-fitting served to calm him. Over the last couple of days, he had recognized that Sally was nearing an instantaneous inflection point and he had braced himself for an outburst. But yesterday's tirade was a true anomaly. He tried to input it, but the curve had gone parabolic!

He looked through the mail. Among the rectangles was a square. A pamphlet. He flipped it open and read:

Repetitive
Clumsy
Literal Minded
Socially Inept
Obsessive

On the last page, it said, "To learn more about Asperger's syndrome, please call Nora Ross at..."

Jeremy picked up the phone and dialed the number.

VIOLET took a deep breath, then walked steadily toward the Ultra office, Dot on her hip. It was imperative that David sign the escrow papers in the next fifteen minutes, or they'd lose their $50,000 deposit. If pressed, Violet could attribute her shakiness to such a tight deadline. Before she opened the door, she ran through the story one last time.

I was meeting Gwen Gold at the George Harrison property when I discovered you forgot to sign page four. Dot wanted to chase butterflies. I let her, never being more than two steps away. All of a sudden, the ground gave way. She must have stepped into a gopher hole. The geology report talked about them, remember? Next thing I knew, Dot rolled down the hill. I was right there. There was a little blood, but she hardly cried. On my way over, I stopped by Dr. Naeby's, just in case. He thought Dot needed a couple of stitches and offered to do it there. I tried calling you, but Kara said you couldn't be disturbed.

It was a good story. The only collateral damage would be to Kara. David would demand to know why she hadn't put Violet through when his daughter was getting stitches. Kara would claim no such thing had happened. Ultimately, it would come down to Violet's word against the assistant's. Kara was young; she'd find another job.

Violet entered the office.

"Mommy, down," said a squirmy Dot. "Down, Mommy."

"In a second, sweetie."

Even though Dot's CAT scan and neurological had been normal, the ER doctor had said it was imperative for Violet to monitor her for drowsiness, headache, balance issues, or vomiting. Any of these symptoms could indicate a hematoma and would require immediate surgery.

David was behind glass at his desk, his back to them.

Kara was at hers, taping receipts to a sheet of paper. "Mrs. Parry, hi!" she said. "Finally, I get to meet Miss Dot. Hi there!" She gave Dot's hand a squeeze. "Aren't you beautiful? And isn't that the cutest hat ever?"

"Mommy, what's dat?" asked Dot with an impish smile. She pointed to a can of Coke on Kara's desk.

"What do you think it is?" Violet said.

"*Coca-Cola*," said Dot, in an unmistakable Spanish accent. "Want dat."

"Just this once." Violet put Dot down. Kara punched something into her computer and led Dot toward the kitchen. David switched to a wireless headset and walked over. Violet took a deep breath: this was it.

When Violet had reached the bottom of the hill, Dot was whimpering. Violet scooped her up. Dot's mouth was full of blood; it flowed down her chin and onto Violet. Dot looked at her mother, indignant, as if to say, How dare you allow such a thing to happen to me? Violet wept with relief and cradled Dot's head. Instantly, Violet's hand became soaked. Blood flowed from a gash behind Dot's ear. Violet pressed her fingers against the cut and ran to the Mercedes. On the drive down to UCLA, Violet had phoned their neighbor, the head of surgery there. By the time mother and daughter arrived at the emergency room, a team was mobilized and waiting on the curb. It reminded Violet of when she would arrive early for a party and there were too many valets.

David muted his headset and stuck his head out of the office. "What's up?" he asked.

"I need you to sign page four in the next fifteen minutes and fax it back." Violet handed him the papers.

"I'll be right there." He shut the door. Violet welcomed the chance to review her story one last time.

Dot tripped in a gopher hole. She didn't cry. Only upon Dr. Naeby's insistence did I let her get a couple of stitches. I tried to call, but Kara wouldn't put me through. It was over before Dot even knew what happened.

Dot and Kara returned, Dot holding a can of Coke with both hands. Her balance, vision, and mental acuity all appeared perfect.

"Dot," Kara said, "do you want to see pictures of my nephew? His name is Lucas. He was only four pounds when he was born, teeny tiny." The screen saver on the assistant's computer was of a curled newborn covered with monitoring devices. "I'm so excited," Kara told Violet. "I get to go to Coachella this weekend. David said he'd let me stand on the stage for Hanging with Yoko. I'm going to totally wave to all my friends."

"Come here, baby doll." Violet adjusted Dot's cashmere cap so it hid the inch-long tape protecting her stitches.

Kara said, "And next week is going to be crazy with drummer auditions."

Violet thought of something. Coachella was this weekend, so David would probably spend at least two nights there. And with Yoko drummer auditions all week, his nights would be tied up. There was a good chance he wouldn't be dropping by the house at all. Dot's stitches were coming out in five days. If Violet could keep David from Dot, he might never know about the stitches. Violet's new story was:

Dot fell into a gopher hole while we were walking around the George Harrison property and—

Actually, there was no reason to tell David any of it!

In the UCLA parking garage, Violet had changed into some yoga clothes she always kept in the trunk. She didn't have clean clothes for Dot, so she had called Daniel at Hermès. Fifteen minutes later, he was standing on the curb with a six-hundred-dollar (!) ensemble for Dot. And hats for Violet, of course. Other than the tiny stitches that were hidden by the Hermès knit cap, Dot betrayed no evidence of the fall. David always went out of his way to avoid talking to the neighbors, so he wouldn't find out about the accident from the surgeon. And if Violet brought cash to UCLA, she could pay the bill and there'd be no paper trail!

David was now off the phone.

One last time, Violet ran through the story—there was no story! And sweet Kara would be spared! If David confronted Violet about the stuff Kurt stole, she would say she'd gotten it for the RIE silent auction and figured a valet at the Beverly Hills Hotel had stolen it.

David opened his office door and handed Kara the papers. "Fax these immediately and get a time-stamped confirmation they were received. Thanks."

Dot galloped into David's office and jumped up and down upon seeing all the pictures of her. "Dot!" she exclaimed. Dot's favorite subject was Dot. She was like a miniature rapper, always referring to herself in the third person.

"I have lots of pictures of my girls here," David said.

"Daddy?" Dot held up a framed picture. "*Dat* man eating nuts?"

"No, that's Dada."

"*Dat* man eating nuts," Dot insisted.

David studied the picture, then laughed. "How about that?" It was the photograph of them at Lake Tahoe, the one where Violet looked so incomprehensibly happy.

They had flown up to ski and had watched the Super Bowl while playing Texas Hold 'Em at a casino. Violet was up two grand at one point, then gave it all back and more. David won a monster pot early and cashed out. Violet's style was to raise and bluff, even when she knew she'd been beat. At halftime, when her stack had started to dwindle, David had come by and whispered, "Learn the thrill of a smart lay-down."

"Do you see that?" David asked Violet. "In the corner. See that man eating a Mr. Goodbar?" He turned to Dot. "You're just a little smartie, aren't you?" David swept up his daughter and emitted a roar of love. "God, I love this little girl. I'm never going to let anything bad happen to you."

Back in the hospital examining room, Violet had held her bloody daughter. Their neighbor Dr. Driscoll entered. A highly decorated Vietnam vet, the surgeon commanded fear from the orderlies. "Thank you so much for coming, Dr. Driscoll," she said. "I really appreciate it." "What's going on?" he asked. "It's right above her ear. A cut." Dot's hair obscured the injury. Violet lifted it, but the blood had dried, sticking strands of hair to the wound. "Owww!" howled Dot. The surgeon shot a withering look at the nurse and growled, "Will someone get me a sponge with some warm water?" The nurse did, and Violet pressed it against Dot's head. "How did it happen?" asked Dr. Driscoll. "We were walking on a hill and she fell—I was right there." "With kids," the surgeon said, "the worst ones happen when you're right there. Jonah fell off the changing table when he was three months. I swear, I had my hand on him!" He smiled at the recollection, then looked at the cut and frowned. "I'm going to have to sew this shut." Violet trembled as the nurse prepped the forceps, needle, and syringe. "Relax, Mom," laughed the doctor. "I'll have her looking like she went to a Beverly Hills plastic surgeon." The nurse popped her head into the bustling hallway. "I'm going to need all hands," she called. "We've got a baby." It required four nurses, as well as Violet, to hold Dot down for the lidocaine shot and the stitches. Violet repeatedly telling her daughter, "It's okay, Dot. Mommy's here." Then whispering: "I'm sorry I didn't want to be with you. I'm sorry you weren't enough." It was the only time during the ordeal Violet had cried. Once the final suture was in, Dot's shrieks abruptly turned into strange high-pitched barks, "Oof! Oof!" Violet panicked that her daughter's brain had been damaged. "What, Dot?" Violet looked desperately into her daughter's eyes. Dot pointed to a wall where a calendar of West Highland terriers hung. "Doggies. Oof! Oof!"

Violet watched Dot now, sitting in her Dada's lap, playing with his headset.

"Mine," Dot said.

"Mine," David teased back.

Dot grabbed the grass bracelet around David's wrist. "Mine," she said.

"Mine," David parroted back.

Dot yanked the bracelet, and it came off in her hand. "Mine!" She squealed with delight.

David looked up at Violet. His eyes, always so sad and incongruous with his temper, finally looked like they belonged on his face.

And Violet knew it was over.

She walked to her husband and daughter, then even closer so that all three touched. God, she loved her little family. And Dot, what a scrapper! She had barely cried when she was born. She came out eyes open, as if not wanting to miss any opportunity to drink in life. David had said if there was a thought bubble over Dot's head those first moments, it would have been, What else ya got? He also said he would entirely trust Violet's instincts when it came to raising Dot. All he asked in return was that Violet keep her safe.

Violet fell to her knees. Dot cupped her mother's cheeks with her small hands. Violet closed her eyes. Dot's impossibly soft skin on her face, it felt like being held by little whispers.

"Ultra?" David was calling her name. "Ultra?"

The door opened. Someone entered.

"Kara?" he said. "Could you take Dot?"

"Of course."

The door closed.

"Violet? Ultra?"

Violet looked up. "David," she said. "I have something to tell you."

"I know you do." His eyes swelled with understanding.

"I'm scared."

"I know you are." He took her hands in his.

"I got really off track, baby."

"I know you did."

And she told David the story.

CHAPTER THIRTEEN

Surprise Me ❀ Thank You ❀ Surprise!

Reyes, T. ❀ Genotype Two

FOR THE PAST SIX MONTHS, SALLY HADN'T MUSTERED THE COURAGE TO RAISE her hand. But last week, out of nowhere, Flicka, the eighties runway model who ran the group, approached Sally and asked if she would "tell her story."

The eight double-spaced pages quivered so in Sally's hands that the words darted about in a game of catch-me-if-you-can. In an attempt to steady them, Sally dug her elbows into her sides. Don't look up, she reminded herself.

"I was born in Denver. And I had a happy childhood. I loved ballet and I had diabetes and I collected horses." Sally stopped, realizing how that sounded. "Not *real* horses. Those plastic Breyer ones. You know what ones I'm talking about." She looked up. The dozen or so people in the room, most of them familiar, appeared baffled and bored. Flicka winced. Sally quickly dropped her eyes, but had lost her spot on the page. She vamped as she tried to find it. "Horses…diabetes…ballet…Everything was great.…I was happy." She turned the paper over. "I'm sorry. I'm new at this."

None of the others had ever written out their speeches, but most of them were seasoned AA people and seemed perfectly at ease with offering up the most humiliating version of themselves to complete strangers.

Sally still couldn't find her place, and now all the pages were out of sequence—she'd have to do without. She quickly fixed her gaze on a smoke alarm above the sea of eyes.

"Like I was saying, I had a happy childhood and everything was great. Even the diabetes wasn't so bad. I don't remember a time when I didn't have it. And if you think like a pancreas, you'll be fine. And I was. I had friends, a job teaching ballet, a husband."

Sally's eyes drifted down. Flicka picked at a thread on her jeans. A man stood at the coffeemaker, and several people waved to him to get them some coffee, too. Most other eyes were on a baby a lady bounced on her lap.

In one breath, she looked at the audience and said the dreaded words, "I'm Sally and I have hep C."

Everyone swung their attention to her. Instantly, their faces were filled with that combination of curiosity and sympathy that had kept Sally coming back to this little church basement in the valley.

"I found out I had the virus six months ago," she said, "during a routine blood test when I was pregnant. I don't even know why they tested for EIA, but I guess they test for everything these days. And I tested positive. And then I retested positive. And then I reretested positive. Because, you see, if it wasn't for my denial, my life would have been crap."

Sally heard a guffaw that was unmistakably Simon's. She stole a peek at the Irish motorcycle mechanic who was covered in tattoos and got infected, like almost everyone here, from sharing needles. He was the only one to make small talk with Sally at that first meeting, the one Violet had dragged her to, the day of her diagnosis. Simon had asked Sally if she was new and given her his phone number, right in front of his hot girlfriend, Petra, who, like Simon, was also HIV positive. Sally hesitated before touching the piece of paper, which only seemed to endear her more to the couple.

"So, I went to a hepatologist and I tested positive for EIA, CIA, and RIBA. Luckily, my viral load was low. My ALT levels were normal." Sally scrunched her shoulders to her ears and spoke in a small voice. "And please don't hate me, you guys, but I'm genotype two."

The vast majority of those infected with hep C were genotype one, which responded poorly to interferon treatment. Only fourteen percent were genotype two, which had an eighty-one percent cure rate.

"Listen to me," Sally said. "I feel guilty because I have the *less* deadly form of hep C!" If there was one thing she had learned from the denizens of this room, it was gallows humor. "I started the twenty-four-week course of Pegasys and ribavirin. I went in last week and..." Sally paused. She hadn't included this part in her written speech, for fear of seeming cruel. "I tested clear."

Her friends applauded. Sally, an expert in detecting mixed emotion, knew their happiness was pure. "Oh, you're just clapping because you want to get rid of me."

"We do!" called a leather-faced granny.

"Not more than me!" said Sally. But really, she rued the thought of saying good-bye to these people, her unlikely tribe. Although she'd never be far. David had given her money to start the Sally Parry Foundation, which would raise money for hep C research by staging marathons. The first event would be a 10K run/walk whose finish line would be in David and Violet's yard.

"I still need to wait another six months before I'm declared virus free," she said. "And even then, it could reappear as another genotype. But I can't help it, I feel lucky." Sally laughed. "Not *too* lucky, mind you. The interferon just about killed me. I couldn't work, which was especially horrible, because I'd just declared bank-ruptcy—" Sally couldn't believe she'd actually admitted that. "That's right. I'm diabetic, hep C positive, bankrupt, *and* single! Men in the audience, I'm *available!*" Once again, the group laughed.

Sally was still waiting for the complete nervous breakdown to hit her because of the divorce. As Violet had put it, You can't secretly abort your husband's baby because you think he's retarded and expect to stay happily married. Tonight would be hard. Sally would be seeing Jeremy for the first time since they broke up.

Sally sighed. "I know as the speaker I'm supposed to share my difficulties. In my speech, I wrote about how horrible the inter-feron treatment was, with the vomiting and the fever and my sister-in-law having to hold me still while my brother gave me my insulin shots. And I became severely anemic, so I had to get blood transfusions, which terrified me. I think I ended up in the hospital four or five times. I lost count. But really, that was nothing." She looked up. She'd lost the crowd again. "Okay, don't believe me, but I'm diabetic. I had to have one of my toes amputated." She shook her left flip-flop at the crowd. Several people craned their necks to get a look at her half-toe, the one with the ring on it. "It cost me my career as a ballerina. Next to that, interferon was a breeze!" She paused. "I didn't plan on telling you about the hardest part for me, because it's going to sound so stupid." She looked at the faces. Nobody was going to make her say it. And so she said it. "The hardest part for me"—Sally's voice filled with tears—"is not knowing how I got it." She didn't try to stop the tears. She knew nobody minded. Mascara was a thing of the past, anyway. "Most of you are ex-junkies, so *you* know how you got your hep C. And I'm just telling you, be grateful, okay? I'm serious. I'm sure you're all thinking, Oh, she's diabetic; she probably got infected from a needle. But I promise you, I never shared a needle once. I've never had a blood transfusion. Diabetics never even *hear* about hep C. It's not something that happens."

Sally sensed a presence. Violet had appeared and was standing against the back wall. Today was one of Violet's workdays, an important one, as they were shooting an episode she had written. Sally had begged her not to drive all the way out to the valley just for this, but there she was, beside the sign that read BETWEEN BLACK AND WHITE ARE ALL THE COLORS OF THE RAINBOW. Violet winked.

Sally continued, "I would give anything to find out how this disease happened to me. I know it's stinking thinking to say all I need is this one thing and *then* I can be happy. But I swear, if I could just know how I got infected, then I'd be okay." Nobody in the room seemed to hold this against her. "Can I just say? When I first got here, I really hated you people." Everyone laughed, Violet the loudest. "See! That's why. You all laughed too much. Some of you looked so sick and scary, and I hated you for it. But I really, *really* hated those of you who *didn't* look sick. I thought, How dare you walk around in your nice clothes and try to pass yourselves off as *normal*. Don't you just love how I thought that?" Sally laughed. "I couldn't see what was so funny about a bunch of dying people. Worse, a bunch of dying people who talked about how hep C was some frigging *gift from God*."

Sally smiled at the housepainter who had spoken at that first meeting. "God is the ultimate physician," he had said. "He is open for business twenty-fours hours a day and he still makes house calls." At all the God talk, atheist Violet had twisted so much in her chair she practically tumbled to the floor.

"When I first came to this room," Sally said, "I knew better than everyone. I had all the answers. I woke up every morning with a plan. But now…" Sally started crying again. "I hate you guys—you've turned me into one of *you!* Because I *do* feel so blessed by this disease. And for the first time in my life, I wake up and I don't care what happens. I'm just so happy to be alive. Now I wake up and I say…" She raised her eyes, as if talking to God.

"Surprise me."

VIOLET had been to enough Emmy ceremonies to know her way around the Shrine Auditorium. She hurried along the deserted red carpet, brandishing her jumbo ticket to the security people, who, at this late hour, just talked among themselves.

The banquet room was hushed and dim. Violet looked for her table number atop the wilted centerpieces. These weren't the Prime-time Emmys or the Technical Emmys, which had been held over the weekend. These were the Sports Emmys, held on the following Monday night. Regardless, it was a bunch of people in black-tie, unimpressed with the food. A familiar voice from the stage caught Violet's attention.

"Seventeen years ago, our son Michael was diagnosed with autism." It was Dan Marino.

Violet wove through the tables and slipped into the empty seat beside David. He'd saved her the best one, facing the stage. "Nice to see you, Ultra," he whispered. "How was work?"

"It went well, thanks." She kissed his cheek.

"Since 1992," Dan Marino was saying, "the Dan Marino Foundation has raised over twenty million dollars to fund spectrum disorder research."

Violet reached across David and squeezed Sally's hand. In support of Jeremy, David had bought a table. It was brave of Sally to come. She flashed a smile at Violet, then returned her attention to the stage.

"Tonight," said Dan Marino, "to present the First Annual Dan Marino Humanitarian Award, I'd like to introduce a tireless warrior in the fight for spectrum awareness."

A waiter set a plate in front of Violet. "Spinach, potatoes, grilled mushrooms, and Diet Coke," he said, then turned to David with trepidation. David nodded. Everyone else was eating dessert. David must have ordered it especially for Violet. She smiled. She was cared for.

"Please welcome Nora Ross," Dan Marino said, then stepped back.

Violet's heart still broke for Dan Marino's Super Bowl loss to the Forty-Niners, his second year as a pro. "Never made it back to the Super Bowl," Violet whispered to David. "Isn't that so sad?" David shook his head in mock exasperation and gave her a kiss.

Nora looked as disheveled and fabulous as ever. She stood at the podium and spoke extemporaneously. "My husband and I are proud parents of a son who has autism. As Dan alluded to, I spend every waking minute raising money, having meetings, going in front of Congress, and in general, haranguing anyone who crosses my path into helping us find a cure. So you can imagine how pleased I was, six months ago, when I received the most extraordinary phone call. It was Jeremy White, saying he wanted to know more about Asperger's." Nora dropped her jaw and affected an exaggerated look of amazement. "I had met Jeremy a few times. He wasn't one for chitchat, so of course I thought he was on the spectrum. But ask my husband; I think every neuro-typical is on the spectrum. I *did* know Jeremy was a television personality, so I asked him if we could use him as the face of our SOS campaign. He obliged, and we coordinated the media message with his Gap ad."

Jeremy's ad appeared on the screen. In it, he wore khakis and a button-down shirt, and flipped a coin. Across the top were the words YOU WILL BE FAMOUS. It was the same giant Jeremy that graced Sunset Boulevard, Times Square, and every other bus in America.

Nora continued, "I got Jeremy in touch with a fabulous cognitive therapist. A few months later, he started driving for the first time in his life!"

Violet knew how hard this must be hitting Sally. She looked over. Sally's smile was huge, her eyes fixed on Jeremy. She wore the same look as Dot did when she'd spot a woman breastfeeding in the park. Dot would walk over and stand an inch away, enthralled, delighted, not knowing it was socially unacceptable to look so nakedly interested in another person.

"The *New York Times* picked up the story," Nora said, "and it's been the most e-mailed article of the past month. That shows you just how hungry people are to learn about spectrum disorders. Jeremy White's brave 'coming out' has been the tipping point that made people realize a person can be brilliant, successful, *and* still be on the spectrum. Ladies and gentlemen, please welcome this year's recipient of the Dan Marino Humanitarian Award, Jeremy White."

Sally jumped to her feet and applauded. David and Violet did, too.

The day Violet had gone to Sally's apartment to pick up her medicine and clothes, she came across the Hermès belt she had given her for her birthday. To Violet, it was an afterthought, something she'd thrown in because she knew Daniel would deliver the chocolates if she bought a gift from Hermès. There was the belt, proudly displayed on a shelf in Sally's closet. It was coiled in the original orange box, the brown ribbon neatly tied around it. Seeing the tender care Sally had taken of a dumb belt somehow repelled Violet. She decided then to step up and love Sally well.

Everyone in the ballroom was on their feet. Although Jeremy had continued to write his column and appear as a commentator, he had never publicly addressed his Asperger's. Jeremy stepped to the podium. There was a palpable sense in the room that tonight they would all witness a small piece of history. He leaned in to the microphone.

"Thank you," he said, then turned and walked off the stage.

Dan Marino stepped up to the mike. "And people say there's no difference between typicals and spectrum disorders!"

Nora thwacked Dan Marino with a program.

"Hey!" Dan Marino said. "I can joke. The guy picked twelve-and-two against the spread yesterday."

Nora shoved Dan Marino, who sheepishly spoke in to the mike. "You're cool, Jeremy?" he asked. "Right? You can take a joke."

"Yes," Jeremy said, off stage. Everyone applauded. Sally covered her face with her hands, smiling and shaking her head. The next presenter took the stage.

"I have to pee," Violet told David. "Don't let them take my food." Violet passed the staging area where a regiment of caterers loaded coffee onto silver trays.

She stopped. Pascal was one of the waiters, his dreads tied back with a black ribbon. He saw Violet and smiled as if it were yesterday. She bounded over. *"Pascal, bonsoir. Ça va bien?"* She kissed him on both cheeks.

"Oui, Violet," he said. *"Et vous?"*

"Ça va bien, merci."

"Avez vous entendu qui est arrivé à Teddy?" he said.

"No!" Violet froze. "What happened?"

Sally appeared, grabbed Violet's arm, and hung from it. "I'm freaking out," Sally said. "Jeremy was so adorable. I want to go say hi. Will you come with me?"

"Sally—" Violet shook her arm loose.

"I'm sorry." Sally stepped back with a frown.

"Did something happen?" Violet studied Pascal. He hesitated and threw a glance toward Sally. Violet said, "She's okay."

"It happened a couple of days ago," Pascal said. "He was on the bus and started vomiting blood. An ambulance took him to the hospital."

"Why?" Violet said. "What was wrong?"

"He went out."

"Where did he go?"

"He got high, got drunk," Sally volunteered. "That's what they say. Who are you talking about?"

"My friend Teddy, the one with hep C." It had been of great comfort to Sally when Violet first mentioned she had a friend who was infected and living a full life. Violet had marveled at the coincidence that *two* people she knew could have the virus. It made her especially grateful that her own test was negative. Sally had questioned Violet on and off about this infected friend, but out of respect for David, Violet kept it vague.

"First he shot drugs," Pascal said. "Then he started drinking. And now he's in LA County."

"LA County?" Violet's chest froze. "He hates LA County. He says people die there."

"That's what happens if you drink with hep C," Sally said. "It's a real no-no."

"It was because of me." Violet gulped. "Because of what I said at the wedding. Oh God, I should have apologized. It's my fault."

"He started shooting drugs for one reason," Pascal said.

"Because of me," Violet said.

"Because he had the cash."

"What?" Violet asked.

"He had three thousand dollars cash in his junkie hands, and he went out and got high. It's as simple as that."

"I have to go," Violet said.

"Violet, don't," Pascal said.

"I need to do this." Violet took Sally's hand. "I have to get David and I have to go." She started off, then stopped. "Pascal?"

"Yes."

"Thank you."

SALLY watched Violet hustle off and stood there with the French waiter....

Violet's mysterious friend with hep C.

He was shooting drugs.

He was at Sally's wedding.

The frightening man who emerged from the bathroom.

272

The syringe in the wastebasket.

It had no cap on it.

That's how Sally had contracted hep C.

He used my needle to get high at my wedding.

The waiter looked at Sally, as if waiting for her to speak. There was nothing to say. This guy—Teddy was his name—the one responsible for infecting Sally. He was now at LA County Hospital.

VIOLET ran-walked-ran down the hall of the ICU, reading the patients' names off the doors. The nurse had told her Teddy's room number less than a minute ago, but she'd already forgotten.

FLORES, L.

This is all my fault. Before you met me, you were playing jazz, golf, going to AA meetings. I shouldn't have given you the money. I meant well, but I didn't know. You were right; there's a lot I'm not very smart about.

IDELSON, E.

This was my fault. I won't stop until you're sober and healthy again. I promise.

TOLL, J.

David can help your career. You can audition for one of his bands. Or, if touring would be too hard on you, you could be a session musician. That pays great.

REYES, T.

Violet stopped.

She'd gone back to the table to tell David the news. "What do you want me to do?" he asked. He didn't press her for details. He didn't get angry. He didn't point out that in a marriage, you take care of the marriage, not the people outside the marriage. "I want to go," she said. David put down his napkin and stood up. "I'm going with you."

Teddy was on a respirator, a tube sloppily taped to his mouth with too much tape, in a too-big X. Both arms were tucked under a thin blanket. A bag of brown liquid hung from the bed rail. He was awake and staring at the ceiling. Several clear bags of drugs hung from an IV drip, their contents landing in his vein. Was one of them morphine? She hoped so; she knew how fond he was of the opiates. At Kate Mantilini, Violet had studied the whites of his eyes to see if she could detect jaundice. Now they were a solid yellow. Yellow and green, Green Bay Packer colors…

Teddy slowly turned his head in her direction, just like the first day they met, when she had run to his parked car. He had known it was her then; he had known that she would come. As he did now. And just like then, he nodded.

"Oh, fuck you," Violet said with a laugh. With that laugh, Teddy's laugh, warmth filled her body. She sprang closer to the bed. Pieces of his hair were braided with colorful beads. "*There's* your look," she said. "It took you a while, but you finally found it."

He rolled his eyes but didn't try to speak. He studied her face. On the TV, Jay Mohr told Conan an unremarkable story about being given the wrong hotel room in Vegas. Violet let Teddy's eyes wash over her, savoring what felt like his touch.

"You paged me?" A sandy-haired doctor breezed in.

"Hi," Violet said, startling. "Yeah. Could you tell me what happened?"

The doctor looked at Teddy, then back at Violet. "I can only discuss a patient's care with immediate family."

"I'm his aunt," Violet said.

The doctor frowned and turned to Teddy. "Do I have your consent to discuss your case with this woman?"

Teddy nodded.

"Is he going to be okay, Dr. —" Violet looked at the doctor's name tag. "Dr. Molester?"

The doctor quickly corrected, "*Moleester.*"

Violet didn't dare look at Teddy for fear they'd both erupt in laughter.

Dr. Molester unhooked Teddy's chart from the foot of the bed and gave it a cursory look. "He was brought in two days ago with acute esophageal variceal hemorrhage, caused by alcoholic hepatitis."

"I'm sorry, you're going to have to dumb it down."

"Mr. Reyes's liver was already compromised from hepatitis C. Excessive alcohol consumption caused the liver to enlarge and block certain veins from draining. Pressure built up in the esophagus to the point where his esophageal veins popped, causing a massive bleed. He's lucky he didn't bleed to death."

Teddy stared at the ceiling, a majestic beast, caged, yet not deigning to make eye contact with his captor.

"Why is he on a respirator?" Violet asked.

"We inserted a Blakemore tube in his esophagus to put pressure on the varices to stop the bleeding. It's coming out tomorrow."

"So it's not a permanent condition? He'll be off the respirator and able to talk?"

"That's correct."

She grabbed Teddy's foot and gave it a shake. "I guess it's premature to break out the cigarettes and 'Send in the Clowns.'"

The doctor scowled.

"What, no Sondheim fans?" asked Violet.

"There's not a lot to joke about," he said. "A biopsy indicated his liver is severely cirrhotic."

"Oh God." Cirrhotic livers, this was her father's bailiwick. "How bad is it?"

"The liver is a regenerative organ. Sometimes it can recover from the injury of alcohol. Unfortunately, the scarring is permanent, so it remains vulnerable to any alcohol and infections."

"But if he doesn't drink, he'll be fine," Violet said.

"If he doesn't drink, he might get better. We don't know yet. If he drinks again, he'll probably die."

"That's easy enough." She looked at Teddy. "Right? You can stop drinking."

Teddy raised his eyebrows skeptically.

"Oh, come on. That's the easy part. I can get you one of those minders David hires to go on tour with his bands." She turned to the doctor. "Can I sign him up for a liver transplant?"

"They don't put active alcoholics on the transplant list." He looked Violet up and down with disapproving eyes. "As you know, livers are hard to come by. You have to show that you want to live enough to not drink."

"But if he stays sober, he can get on the list."

"I'm not sure." The doctor clanked the chart back onto the rail. "There's a screening process that I'm not completely familiar with."

"So tomorrow I'll talk to someone and get you on the list," she told Teddy. "I know the best hepatologist in the city. Dr. Beyrer. We'll have her take over your case."

"If you really want to help?" said the doctor.

"Yes," said Violet eagerly.

"I suggest you donate blood. When Mr. Reyes came in, his liver was unable to manufacture the compounds required for clotting, so he required a massive blood transfusion. The hospital is always in need of blood."

"Oh," Violet said, deflated by the meagerness of the request.

"Unless, of course..." he said.

"What?" she asked, brightening.

"You're infected, too."

Violet felt a stab of humiliation. "No," she said. "Of course I'm not infected."

"Good. Then you can give blood on the fourth floor. They're open all night. Is that all?"

"When will he be released?" Violet asked.

"He's on a strong regimen of somatostatin to lower the pressure within the portal system. Also, his abdomen was showing preliminary signs of ascites, which caused an infection to develop. We've got him on diuretics and broad-spectrum antibiotics."

"Well, whatever. The important thing is he won't drink again and we'll get him a new liver."

The doctor raised his eyebrows. "Excuse me, but we're short staffed here."

"Of course. Thank you, Dr. Mol-*eester*."

The doctor departed. Teddy laughed, and coughed so hard he was thrust upright. The respirator tube snared him back like a fish on a hook.

"Jesus! I'm sorry!" Violet frantically pushed her fingertips into the milky tape to keep the breathing tube affixed. She placed one hand on Teddy's chest to push him back down, and left it there. He closed his eyes.

"Don't worry," she said. "The Baroness von Beeswax is in the house. I'm going to make sure you stay clean and get you a new liver." Violet quoted Shakespeare, "Come, let's away to prison; We two alone will sing like birds in the cage." Teddy opened his eyes. "You do know where that quote is from," she said. "It's what Shirley Jones sang to Shamu in your favorite *Partridge Family* episode."

Teddy laughed again and started coughing.

"Stop it, stop it," she said.

And then: in traipsed Coco.

On a chair and table were a mangy rabbit-fur coat, cans of Red Bull, and a *Vogue*. They'd been there the whole time; Violet just hadn't noticed.

Coco was dressed the part, in all black. Laced into her black bob were braids with colorful bangles. Also on the table was a Ziploc bag of beads. Coco must have woven them into his hair. Her doll.

"Who are you?" Coco's voice was breathy and her words choppy. Her eyes, evacuated. There wasn't even the slightest attempt at affability. Violet stared into the face of crazy. Not good-crazy. Mean, hard, mentally ill crazy. Violet looked to Teddy. His eyes were closed.

"I'm his aunt," Violet said, the words getting stuck in her throat.

"No, you're not." Coco sat down on the bed. She took a swig from a can of apricot juice, then tore open some Oreos. "That lady in the blood place was a real bitch," she told Teddy. "She wouldn't let me give blood because of the hep C. But I stole some cookies and juice." She seemed to have completely lost interest in Violet.

Teddy opened his eyes but stared at the ceiling. He wouldn't look at Violet. The fucking coward.

Coco was a crazy liar who didn't love Teddy, yet he kept coming back for more.

Teddy was a crazy liar who didn't love Violet, yet she kept coming back for more.

So who was Violet, other than a crazy liar…who kept David coming back for more?

But Violet could change that. She would make herself worthy of David. It might be the only thing of note she would do for the rest of her life.

It would have to be enough.

She hoped it would be enough.

"Turn it up," Coco said to no one in particular. "I love this commercial."

Violet looked at Teddy one last time, his eyes still closed. She turned and walked out of his room and down the corridor.

She thought about the zucchini in the garden. Winter weather hadn't yet arrived, so the summer vegetables were still thriving in December. Tomorrow, she'd pick some and make David that pasta he liked, the Marcella Hazan recipe with the mint and garlic and red wine vinegar. She picked up her pace; she couldn't wait to tell David about the dinner she was going to make. She'd fry green tomatoes, too, with herb aioli. Because of the heat, the dill and cilantro Violet had planted last month were beginning to bolt and needed to be picked. Dot could help Violet. She loved helping her mama in the garden.

Violet turned into the waiting room. David sat cross-legged on the floor, playing dominoes with a black family. She had no idea her husband knew how to play dominoes.

He looked up. "What?" he asked.

She decided against telling David about the pasta. It would be better to surprise him.

SALLY watched, undetected, from across the nurses' station, as Violet left. Once the coast was clear, Sally moved to a chair beside Teddy Reyes's room. She didn't know what she'd been waiting for, but when the girl in black left, Sally floated to her feet and entered.

The respirator was so loud it seemed to overpower the patient asleep in bed. Sally walked closer. Yes, this was the man from the wedding. Not that she had doubted it, but seeing him gave her the serenity of knowing she'd put the pieces together correctly.

Sally glanced at his chart. There it was, hepatitis C, genotype two. Fourteen percent of all hep C cases were genotype two. At least he'd given her the *good* hep C.

He was beautiful. Gorgeous fuzzy eyebrows, the kind you wanted to gently brush your lips across. A crooked nose. Sweet ears. One had been pierced several times but was now free of adornment. Short, sparse eyelashes. His forehead smooth, kissable. His arms rested above the blankets. So tanned, the jaundice only showed on the inside of his elbows. He must have loved the sun—a day laborer, a beach rat, a water baby?

A tattoo peeked above the blood pressure cuff and continued down his inner arm. Sally couldn't tell if it was a vine or some kind of snake.

His thumb bled at the fingernail. He must have chewed it just before he fell asleep. Poor guy. What had he been so worried about that he pushed the respirator tube away and risked his life just to chew his nails? Was it something Violet had said? On the blanket, near his right hand, was a bright red dot. Fresh, virus-infected blood. Before Teddy, Sally might have been afraid of it. Tonight, she touched it. She leaned over to behold his face. Her hair brushed his cheeks.

"It's okay," she whispered. She reached under his neck and felt the warmth of his skin, happy warmth. She slipped her fingers farther down his back and felt the ripple of his ribs. In his slumber, his head rocked, then lolled on her arm.

"You did the best you could," she said.

Sally's free hand was slightly cupped and turned upward. She closed her eyes. Teddy was alive in her. As was the person he had contracted the virus from. And the person who'd given it to them. And anyone else who had hep C. Or any other disease. Or who'd ever been delivered impossible news. Or whose life was not what they'd hoped it would be. They all rested in the palm of her hand.

"I know you're scared," she said. "I'm scared, too."

When Sally opened her eyes, his were open and gazing into hers. Their yellow glow only added to their beauty, such a gorgeous icy green.

"I forgive you," she said.

His eyes absorbed her with such courage. His lower lids rose slightly. He was smiling. And then he closed his eyes.

CHAPTER FOURTEEN

Those Violets

DAVID HADN'T TOLD HIS WIFE WHERE HE WOULD BE TODAY. IF VIOLET CALLED, Kara was under strict orders to tell her he was unreachable, not back at the hospital.

"What's the name of this ambulance service?" asked the woman in the billing office. She was fat and peppy, a combination David found endearing.

"It's called Private Ambulance Providers of Los Angeles," he said.

"And it's not one of ours?"

"It's a private ambulance service."

"You know insurance isn't going to cover that?"

"I know."

"Can't be cheap." The woman shook her head.

"It isn't." David had arranged for Teddy to be transferred to Cedars and to be cared for by Sally's hepatologist, Dr. Beyrer. David would pay the bill, no questions asked.

"Okey dokey," said the lady. "We're just about ready. Let me get one more authorization." She pushed herself up with a celebratory groan.

"Take your time," David said.

Last night, when Violet had found David in the waiting room—he was playing dominoes with the father of a guy who'd been shot—there was a peculiar look on her face. David knew what it looked like to be wildly loved by Violet, he could tell by the twinkle in her eyes, and for the first time in years, he saw it. He had no idea what had transpired in that hospital room. But David's final act of faith in Violet, and he knew it was the last one that would be required, was loving those she loved.

In the sweat lodge, David had chosen to believe in her. It had brought him the truth that day in his office. What she told him, the depths to which she had sunk, and in the name of what, he still couldn't comprehend; it nauseated him. What she described, not the details as much as the madness of the affair, was all too familiar.

Back when David and Violet were newly engaged, Sacramento Sukey had called David's office every day and every night. He never took her calls, naively willing her to just go away. His heart still raced, remembering that white-knuckle moment when he was heading out to meet Violet at Orso, before *Falsettos*. His secretary had buzzed him, "David, it's Sukey again." "Tell her I'm out of the office." "She's out *here*," whispered the secretary, "*in my office*." David slipped out the back door and raced down the thirty-eight flights of stairs, to Seventh Avenue. Somehow, there stood Sukey, jangly, puffy faced, *desperate*, outside a souvenir shop. She held the hand of her little boy. David wrote Sukey a check for five grand, right there on the sidewalk—for what, he didn't know, but he became unglued by the prospect that Violet would surprise him at his office, as she sometimes did, and discover he was a cheat. Sukey never called again. Still, David hadn't set foot in Sacramento for seventeen years. In fact, when Violet landed her first TV job and wanted to move to LA, the only hesitation on David's part was that it was too close to Sacramento. This was why he hadn't cheated since. Not because fidelity was sacrosanct, but because infidelity turned good people bad. David sometimes wished he could give himself points for his rectitude. But he had made up his mind, so it wasn't even a choice. Other people apparently had a harder time sticking to things. Not David.

On the hospital worker's desk was a clownish ceramic bowl with pinched edges. In it were fifty cards the size of shirt labels. David grabbed a bunch and fanned through them, reading the single word calligraphed on each.

Gratitude
Healing
Compassion
Play
Tenderness

"I see you found my angel cards," sang the woman.

"Oh. Yeah."

"Every morning you're supposed to pick one and use it for inspiration."

"Ahh," said David.

"Pick one."

He tossed the cards back into the bowl, stirred them with his finger, and picked one. "*Courage,*" he read. Beside the word was a drawing of an angel in a bathing suit, jumping off a high dive.

"Do you like it?" asked the lady. "Because if you don't, you can take another one. I do it all the time."

"Courage is fine."

"You, young man," the lady said, handing him some papers, "have gorgeous credit."

"I get that a lot." David filled out a check for a whopping $23,545.99.

"Come with me," she said conspiratorially. David followed her down the corridor. "I sprained my ankle a couple of months ago." She winced with each step. "It keeps flaring up. I guess I should have taken better care of it."

"Rice," said David.

"What?"

"It's an acronym. Rest, Ice, Compression, Elevation. It's what you should do for an ankle sprain."

"You'd think working at a hospital, someone would have told me that!" She laughed. "Here you are, room 833."

David hadn't realized it, but she had escorted him to a door that read REYES, T. David balked. "Oh."

"Have a nice day, Mr. Parry," she said, and hobbled off.

"Yeah, you, too."

Last night, David and Violet had taken his car to and from the hospital. Back home, Violet slept, but David couldn't. He had called a taxi to take him to the Shrine to get Violet's car. That was LA for you—a voracious gobbler of time and energy over car logistics.

The best example had been ten years ago, at a Grammy party at the old Morton's. David couldn't leave until he had said hi to Mick Jagger, who was in serious conversation with some chick. David lingered a few minutes. Then, to give Mick a hint, he sat on the edge of the banquette. David overheard them fervently debating whose car to take home. They could take both cars, but if they did, Mick would have to park his Bentley on the street, which wasn't safe, but if they left his car at Morton's, the valet would be closed in the morning, so maybe they should park one car on the street now, but this neighborhood had overnight parking by permit only, so they would risk getting towed...Christ, it went on for an eternity! David realized that if Mick Jagger wasn't immune to LA car bullshit, nobody was. From then on, David had always found it amusing.

Driving Violet's car home on the 405 early this morning, David had the freeway to himself. The shoulder was dotted with tough orange garbage bags. Parolees in stenciled vests picked up trash in the dry hills. A deer had one of the bags in its teeth and shook it with a dumb violence not usually associated with Bambi. David smiled. He'd have to tell Dot about it. He turned on the stereo. A CD was playing, something Violet must have been listening to on the way to the Shrine last night.

> *You're always sorry,*
> *You're always grateful...*

It was that Sondheim song she had wanted sung at their wedding. David couldn't remember exactly what about the lyrics had made him so upset. It was some song where married men explain to a bachelor what it was like being married. David turned up the volume.

> *You're always sorry.*
> *You're always grateful.*
> *You hold her thinking,*
> *"I'm not alone."*
> *You're still alone....*
>
> *You're sorry-grateful*
> *Regretful-happy.*
> *Why look for answers*
> *Where none occur?*

You'll always be
What you always were,
Which has nothing to do with,
All to do with her.

It had taken him long enough, but driving north on the 405, just past the Getty, David finally got Sondheim.

A man coughed. A dry cough that wouldn't stop. Teddy Reyes. David stood at the open door. Courage, the angel card had counseled.

Teddy Reyes sat on the bed, his back to David, naked it appeared, his hospital gown in one hand. His hair was shaggy, his back brown and slight. Seeing the skin his wife had touched, loved once, it made David's stomach tighten. Teddy Reyes pulled a T-shirt over his head. Before he stuck his hands through the armholes, he rested, depleted from the exertion. The small man who had sundered David's marriage barely had the strength to put on a T-shirt! Still, he had somehow managed to wrest Violet's sanity. David knew she wouldn't have relinquished it without a fight. Teddy got his arms through the shirt and sat there, slumped.

That's when David saw them: the violets tattooed on Teddy's arm. A garland, exactly like those behind Violet's ear. They snaked from the inside of his wrist, up his arm, around his elbow, then disappeared inside his shirtsleeve. The violets. *Those fucking violets.*

LATER that day, David was returning calls at his desk when Kara entered with a Post-it: "The driver from PAPLA." It took David a second to register, Private Ambulance Providers of Los Angeles.

"Get him on the phone," David said. As he waited, there was a terrific squawking through the double-paned window.

A flock of birds, big ones, swooped down Beverly Drive and, in a glorious watery movement, alighted on the cheesy Santa sleigh that spanned Wilshire Boulevard. David knew from their silhouettes that the birds were Amazon parrots, giant and Christmas colored. He had never seen them before, but there was much lore surrounding this flock of LA parrots. Some believed them to have escaped from the set of *Doctor Dolittle* in the sixties. Here they were now, shimmering red and green in the tinsel under the harsh December sun. Marvelous!

The phone rang. "This is David Parry."

It was the ambulance driver. Teddy Reyes was nowhere to be found. David got his friend with the sprained ankle on the phone. She was as surprised as anyone. When nobody was looking, Teddy Reyes had unhooked the IVs, gotten dressed, and walked out of the hospital. The only trace of him was a note on the bed. It read "Went to pick up a friend at the airport."

TEDDY

I GIVE YOU THIS GIFT. COME CLOSER. ALL I HAVE TO GIVE IS THIS, AND I GIVE it to you.

I'm a know-nothing, my ignorance is immense. (You would call me a philistine.)

I'm a jailed crazy, a sobbing drunk in the garden, a diseased pirate, the scorpion king of Venice. Still you come, basket in hand, to collect more of my booty.

Come closer....

I gave until you lit up the night sky. I took until you were a madwoman wandering the canyons.

Oh, how your basket trembles for my gifts.

Shall I fill it with my sick roses and counterfeit coins, my long nights, my sweet heart, and the birdsong of my brilliant parrots circling overhead cawing your name?

Look at your displeasure! How you hate to wait, plump, spoiled, bejeweled queen of the glass castle. I apologize.

I won't make you wait any longer, darling, dear, sweet-smelling co-conspirator of mine. Here is my gift.

Come closer....

I am gone.

Don't be angry. Since that first too-hot morning, I am your laughing puppet, your dance floor caddy, and my heart leaps only for you.

Soon, you will wake up from a well-deserved afternoon nap. For one moment, you experience that wonder of not knowing who you are or where you are, or if it's day or night. You could be, and are, anyone.

Then: the lake out the window, the newspaper beside you on the bed, the glasses in your hand, your daughter's laughter swirling up up up through the pines.

And you remember, *I am Violet Parry.*

But this time: you rejoice. Throw your basket in the air! Know I am by your side. See, I am branded, my arm forever abloom in your name.

I know you're scared, so am I.

I have stumbled enough. I am forgiven. I am abundant. I am certainly insouciant. I'm not your tar baby. You're the star, baby. Love the lucky well.

Maria Semple wrote for television shows including *Arrested Development, Mad About You,* and *Ellen.* She has escaped from Los Angeles and lives with her family on an island off Seattle. This is her first novel.

Writing in Nonacademic Settings

Perspectives in Writing Research
LINDA S. FLOWER AND JOHN R. HAYES, EDITORS

Writing in Nonacademic Settings
LEE ODELL AND DIXIE GOSWAMI, EDITORS

When a Writer Can't Write: Studies in Writer's Block and Other Composing-Process Problems
MIKE ROSE, EDITOR

New Directions in Composition Research
RICHARD BEACH AND LILLIAN S. BRIDWELL, EDITORS

In Preparation

Protocol Analysis
LINDA S. FLOWER AND JOHN R. HAYES

Writing in Nonacademic Settings

EDITED BY

Lee Odell
RENSSELAER POLYTECHNIC INSTITUTE

Dixie Goswami
CLEMSON UNIVERSITY

The Guilford Press
NEW YORK • LONDON

© 1985 The Guilford Press
A Division of Guilford Publications, Inc., 200 Park Avenue South, New York, N.Y.
10003

Printed in the United States of America

Library of Congress Cataloging in Publication Data
Main entry under title:

Writing in nonacademic settings.

(Perspectives in writing research)
Includes index.
1. English language—Rhetoric—Study and teaching. 2. English language—Business English—Study and teaching. 3. English language—Technical English—Study and teaching. 4. Technical writing—Study and teaching. 5. Report writing—Study and teaching. I. Odell, Lee, 1940–   . II. Goswami, Dixie. III. Series.
PE1404.W726 1985   808'.042'07   85-27239
ISBN 0-89862-252-2

Contributors

PAUL V. ANDERSON, PhD, Department of English, Miami University, Oxford, Ohio

ROBBIN M. BATTISON, PhD, Document Design Center, American Institute for Research, Washington, D.C.

GREGORY G. COLOMB, PhD, University of Chicago, Chicago, Illinois

BARBARA COUTURE, PhD, Director, Writing Program, Department of English, College of Liberal Arts, Wayne State University, Detroit, Michigan

DAVID DOBRIN, PhD, Massachusetts Institute of Technology, Cambridge, Massachusetts

STEPHEN DOHENY-FARINA, PhD, University of North Carolina at Charlotte, Charlotte, North Carolina

LESTER FAIGLEY, PhD, Department of English, The University of Texas, Austin, Texas

EDWARD S. GOLD, MA, Document Design Center, American Institute for Research, Washington, D.C.

JONE RYMER GOLDSTEIN, PhD, Department of English, Wayne State University, Detroit, Michigan

DIXIE GOSWAMI, PhD, Department of English, Clemson University, Clemson, South Carolina

JEANNE W. HALPERN, PhD, Department of English, Purdue University, West Lafayette, Indiana

DAVID A. LAUERMAN, PhD, Department of English, Canisius College, Buffalo, New York

ELIZABETH L. MALONE, PhD, Department of English, Wayne State University, Detroit, Michigan

CAROLYN R. MILLER, PhD, Department of English, North Carolina State University, Raleigh, North Carolina

RICHARD MILLER, PhD, Exxon Chemicals Corporation, Houston, Texas

DENISE E. MURRAY, PhD, Department of Linguistics, Stanford University, Stanford, California

BARBARA NELSON, PhD, Department of English, Wayne State University, Detroit, Michigan

LEE ODELL, PhD, Rensselaer Polytechnic Institute, Troy, New York

JAMES PARADIS, PhD, Director of Technical Communication, Massachusetts Institute of Technology, Cambridge, Massachusetts

SHARON QUIROZ, PhD, Department of English, Wayne State University, Detroit, Michigan

JANICE C. REDISH, PhD, Director, Document Design Center, American Institute for Research, Washington, D.C.

MELVIN W. SCHROEDER, PhD, Department of English, Canisius College, Buffalo, New York

JACK SELZER, PhD, Department of English, Pennsylvania State University, State College, Pennsylvania

KENNETH SROKA, PhD, Department of English, Canisius College, Buffalo, New York

E. ROGER STEPHENSON, PhD, Department of English, Canisius College, Buffalo, New York

DWIGHT W. STEVENSON, PhD, Professor of Technical Communication, College of Engineering, The University of Michigan, Ann Arbor, Michigan

JOSEPH M. WILLIAMS, PhD, Department of English, University of Chicago, Chicago, Illinois

Preface

In the summer of 1977, the editors of this book were team-teaching in an NEH summer institute on "Writing across the Curriculum." At one point, we began discussing the sort of writing college students might have to do once they finished their schooling and began their careers as, say, engineers or lawyers or business executives. The discussion was brief. We quickly realized that we didn't know enough even to speculate about the writing people had to do in business, government, and industry. Indeed, we were not entirely sure that many people did, in fact, have to do much job-related writing. We assumed that some people were hired specifically for their writing skill—speechwriters, for example, or technical writers. But we had no idea how many people, apart from those specifically hired as writers, had to do much writing as a routine part of their day-to-day work. And we had no personal knowledge about the forms this writing took, about the diverse rhetorical and conceptual demands it entailed, or about the kinds of sophistication these writers possessed (or lacked).

Our acute awareness of how little we knew led us to conduct a series of studies, funded by the National Institute of Education, of writing in nonacademic settings. As we began these studies, it was clear that colleagues in rhetoric and composition had been slow to follow the lead of researchers in other areas—principally technical writing—who had already begun to study writing in the workplace. During the past ten years or so, however, researchers in composition and rhetoric have begun to recognize the diversity and importance of writing in nonacademic settings and have begun to study this writing, drawing heavily on rhetorical theory and using ethnographic as well as quantitative and experimental research methodologies. Consequently, a body of scholarship is beginning to develop in this area.

Our intent in this volume is to represent some of this current scholarship and to suggest ways it might become the basis for teaching and for further research. Thus all the chapters in this book include discussions of needed research, and most chapters suggest pedagogical applications of the topics they discuss. Part I of this book consists of a single chapter, Paul V. Anderson's "What Survey Research Tells Us about Writing at Work." In addition to reporting findings from his own survey of writing in the workplace, Anderson provides a comprehensive summary of the principal conclusions we can draw from other surveys. Where these conclusions are most solidly substantiated, Anderson suggests implications for teaching. And in noting limitations of existing surveys, Anderson helps us see where further research is needed.

In Parts II and III, chapters deal with the structure of discourse and with the ways writers are influenced by new technologies. (We have not included discussions of style in nonacademic writing because this topic has been dealt with at length in such recent works as Joseph Williams's *Style: Ten Lessons in Clarity and Grace*.) The section on the structure of written discourse begins with "Perceiving Structure in Professional Prose: A Multiply Determined Experience" by Gregory G. Colomb and Joseph M. Williams. In this chapter, Colomb and Williams describe characteristics of form that appear at all levels of discourse, ranging from individual sentences to a complete text. In their essay "Making Information Accessible to Readers," Janice C. Redish, Robbin M. Battison, and Edward S. Gold draw heavily on recent work at the Document Design Center. They show how writers can structure a text so that readers can use it as efficiently as possible. They also consider some of the reasons that nonacademic writing is poorly organized.

Part III, on the influence of new technologies, begins with "An Electronic Odyssey" by Jeanne W. Halpern. She visited a number of corporations, conducting surveys and interviewing workers to determine how new technologies (word processing, electronic mail, dictation) influence the composing process. Halpern describes these technologies, identifies advantages and disadvantages of each, and identifies factors that influence people's willingness to use these technologies. The subsequent chapter by Denise E. Murray ("Composition as Conversation: The Computer Terminal as Medium of Communication") focuses on a much more limited topic, computer conversation. Murray examines a series of communications between two computer users, bringing rhetorical and sociolinguistic theory to bear on a form of communication that displays characteristics of both spoken and written discourse. Since this is likely to become a widely used form of communication among computer users, Murray's chapter helps us rethink our notion of what it means to be "computer literate."

Part IV, "Viewing Writing from a Social/Institutional Perspective," illustrates a point that seems absolutely essential to research on writing both in schools and on the job: writing and reading are social activities. In creating and shaping a message and in understanding a message, both writers and readers draw on a variety of social resources, including personal interaction and the culture of the organization in which they read and write. Lester Faigley's "Nonacademic Writing: The Social Perspective" contrasts the social perspective with two others (the textual perspective and the individual perspective) that have, in the past, dominated research on writing. Faigley provides a theoretical justification for adopting this perspective and suggests some of the research it might engender. The subsequent chapters reflect this perspective, even though they were written before the authors had read Faigley's chapter. In "Beyond the Text: Relations between Writing and Social Context," Lee Odell uses both interviews and analyses of conversations to show how the process of inquiry, central to both reading and writing, can be a social process, one that is informed by interpersonal communication and by the shared knowledge, interests, and procedures that characterize a particular group of writers in a particular office. In "Writing at Exxon ITD: Notes on the Writing Environment of an R&D Organization," James Paradis, David Dobrin, and Richard Miller explore: (1) the roles writing can play in a nonacademic setting (in this instance, a research and development organization); and (2) the ways people in an organization interact to produce written documents. In contrast with chapters by Odell and by Paradis et al., the chapter by Carolyn R. Miller and Jack Selzer does not focus on the process of composing but, rather, on the features of written texts. In "Special Topics of Argument in Engineering Reports," Miller and Selzer show how arguments in these texts reflect not only general forms of argument (the common topics) but also *special topics*, the types of argument that are characteristic of specific genres and specific institutions or organizations.

Part V addresses questions that are becoming increasingly popular in our field: How can we teachers of writing use our knowledge and skill in working with writers in business, industry, and government? How can our understanding of the workplace affect what we do in our on-campus writing classes? In "The Writing Teacher in the Workplace: Some Questions and Answers about Consulting," Dwight W. Stevenson identifies some of the benefits and drawbacks associated with consulting on writing in the workplace. He also suggests ways teachers might make the kinds of contacts that can lead to consulting work. The next two chapters describe ways in which a medium-sized state university and a relatively small liberal arts college have made connections between their undergraduate writing programs and the larger communities in which the two schools exist. The chapter by Barbara Couture, Jone Rymer Goldstein, Elizabeth L. Malone, Barbara Nelson, and Sharon Quiroz ("Building a Professional Writing Program through a University/Industry Collaborative") describes procedures used at Wayne State University to involve local business people in a collaborative effort to devise a writing curriculum. In "Workplace and Classroom: Principles for Designing Writing Courses," David A. Lauerman, Melvin W. Schroeder, Kenneth Sroka, and E. Roger Stephenson describe specific teaching procedures used in advanced composition courses at Canisius College. All these procedures are based on the authors' study of writing in the workplace. The chapter also suggests principles that can help teachers structure courses that emphasize job-related writing assignments.

The final section, part VI, contains two discussions of research methodology. In the first, Paul Anderson provides an introduction to survey methodology and suggests ways we could: (1) become better analysts of published research, and (2) initiate our own surveys of research on writing. In the following chapter, Stephen Doheny-Farina and Lee Odell describe some of the assumptions and methodologies that are important in conducting ethnographic research on writing.

It seems appropriate that this book should conclude with discussions of research methodology; we still have much to learn about writing in the workplace. But despite the limitations of our present knowledge, we have encouraged contributors to this book to speculate about ways their work might have implications for teaching. We have done so with this reservation: one must be careful not to equate *what is* with *what ought to be*. Even if our profession had developed a very comprehensive, well-documented picture of writing in the workplace, it would be foolish to assume that every existing practice necessarily represents ideal or even adequate practice. And there is no basis for assuming that everything we know about writing outside schools is directly applicable to student writers and student writing. Whatever we learn about writing in nonacademic settings must be tested against current theory and research; it must be reconciled with our experience and our goals as educators. But even in acknowledging this reservation, we believe that writing in the workplace can be important both pedagogically and theoretically. Some job-related writing tasks entail rhetorical problems that concern writers at many age levels; by including some of those problems in the courses they teach, composition teachers can help students prepare for their careers while also conveying basic rhetorical principles. Moreover, writers in the workplace can display considerable astuteness and sensitivity. As we learn from these writers, our profession can refine our basic conceptions about, say, the composing process or the definition of *maturity* in reading and writing. In brief, studies of writing in the workplace can contribute to the advancement of knowledge in our discipline.

LEE ODELL
DIXIE GOSWAMI

Contents

Writing in Nonacademic Settings

Surveying the Field I

What Survey Research Tells Us about Writing at Work

1

PAUL V. ANDERSON
Miami University, Ohio

A survey is an empirical investigation in which naturally occurring phenomena are studied by asking predetermined sets of questions. When properly designed, a survey enables researchers to generalize about the attributes, attitudes, and activities of large groups of people by gathering information from a relatively small number of individuals in those groups. The most familiar type of survey is the pre-election poll, in which researchers use information gathered from a few thousand people to predict with considerable accuracy the voting patterns of millions. Surveys have also been used to study a wide variety of other human phenomena, as in marketing research to predict the likely reception by consumers of new packages and products, and in sociological research to investigate such things as the location in Chicago of juvenile gangs (Thrasher, 1927) and bordellos (Reckless, 1933), the sexual behavior of American males (Kinsey & Associates, 1948) and the attitudes of men and women toward crime (Stinchcombe et al., 1980). One of the many human phenomena that have been studied by means of surveys is the writing people do at work.

In this chapter, I explore the knowledge that survey research has so far provided to us concerning the writing people do on the job. Derived from the fifty studies discussed in this chapter, this knowledge is of interest for two reasons: it constitutes a very substantial part of what we know through empirical research about writing in nonacademic settings, and it provides teachers with important insights they can use as they design courses in business, technical, and other forms of career-related writing.

Although a discussion of a body of survey research might be organized into a series of abstracts of individual surveys, I have chosen instead to organize around the various topics investigated by one or more surveys. For instance, in a section on the importance of writing, I discuss the results on that subject obtained by all the surveys that inquired about it. In this way I attempt to present a single, coherent account of the issues that have been studied by those surveys and of the conclusions that we may draw (sometimes with more confidence, sometimes with less) from the surveys.

Organizing in this way, I necessarily atomize the surveys, focusing on the individual result, not on the whole study. Readers, however, should keep in mind that each individual survey result takes its specific meaning from the details of the survey that produced the result. That is, the response to a particular survey question must be interpreted in terms of such variables as: the characteristics of the individuals (called *respondents*) who provided the responses; the way the respondents were chosen by the researcher; the way the question was posed to them (in person, in writing); how the question was phrased; what statistical procedures were used to analyze the responses and their relations with the answers to other questions; and the use the researcher desired to make of the result. All these variables (and more) affect the meaning of a survey's results and influence the amount of confidence we can place in any conclusions drawn from these results. I have taken these variables into account when presenting each individual survey result, but I have not reported all the variables to my readers. Readers who want to determine the full meaning of any of the individual results I present must turn to the full report of the survey that produced the result.

In this chapter, I have three objectives:

- To illustrate the way all the variables in survey design work together, thereby showing how these variables affect the meaning of the results obtained from a survey. (I pursue this objective by reporting a previously unpublished survey that concerns the writing done on the job by graduates of seven departments of a single university.)

- To review the entire corpus of published surveys of writing in the workplace and to summarize the general conclusions we may draw from those surveys.
- To discuss the implications of these survey results for teachers of business, technical, and other career-related writing courses.

Readers may find it helpful to refer to chapter 13, in which I discuss the theoretical and technical aspects of survey methodology and explain more fully the technical terms and concepts briefly described in this chapter.

BACKGROUND: GENERALIZING ABOUT SURVEY RESULTS

As a prelude to the three major topics just outlined, I want to address two questions that necessarily arise in an attempt to interpret a corpus of survey literature:

- How far can the results of a particular survey be generalized?
- What are we to think when one survey produces results that appear to conflict with the results of another survey?

Generalizability

The very purpose of most surveys is to enable researchers to generalize the results they obtain from their respondents (collectively called a *sample*) to some larger group of people (called a *population*). Researchers and readers of research, however, need to consider carefully how far these generaliztions can be extended.

In the abstract, results obtained from a small group of people can be generalized to any larger group that is *accurately represented* by that small group. The narrowest definition of the conditions under which a sample accurately represents a population is the operational definition provided by survey methodology: a sample represents a population if it is chosen by using the accepted practices for constructing samples (those procedures are called *sampling methods*). The most widely known (but not the most widely used) sampling method is the procedure used to select a *random sample*; in that procedure, the researcher does the following:

1. Obtains a list of every individual in the population of interest (e.g., every graduate of a particular university),
2. Assigns a unique number to each individual,
3. Draws numbers randomly,
4. Includes in the sample each person whose number is drawn.

For various practical reasons, true random sampling is rarely used in survey research, usually because of the difficulty or impossibility of obtaining a list of all members of the population. Regardless of the practical difficulties involved, however, persons trained in social science research generally use *some* commonly accepted procedure for constructing a sample that, *in a technical sense*, represents the population the researchers wish to study.

There is also a less technical, more commonsensical view of the conditions under which a sample accurately represents a population. Suppose, for instance, that a team of researchers surveyed the graduates of three science departments at a particular university. If they used an accepted sampling method, these researchers could justifiably generalize the results obtained from their sample to the entire population of graduates of those three departments. At the same time, the researchers (and the readers of their report) would undoubtedly be aware that the population of graduates of those three departments resemble—more or less—some other populations, such as graduates of other science departments at the same university. Although they have no *technical* justification for generalizing their results to these other populations, they might reasonably claim that they have a commonsense justification. After all, a sample that accurately represents one population also accurately represents other, similar populations, provided there is not some telling difference between the populations.

Of course, the researchers would be more confident about generalizing to some populations than to others. For example, suppose that all three departments whose graduates constitute the *study population* (i.e., the population technically represented by the sample) are in the life sciences; then the researchers would be more certain about generalizing the results to the graduates of other life sciences departments than they would be about generalizing the results to graduates in the physical sciences.

Lest this distinction between the technical definition and the commonsensical definition seem sharper than it actually is, I want to point out that even according to the theory that underlies survey sampling methods, researchers can never be completely certain that the responses they obtain from the survey sample correspond directly to the results they would obtain by querying the entire study population. Furthermore, as mentioned earlier, the most rigorous sampling procedures are seldom used because of practical difficulties in employing them.

Thus, even when evaluating the generalizability of sample results to a study population, researchers and readers must use their judgment (based partly on technical considerations, partly on common sense). On the other hand, all generalizations beyond the study population are less certain than those made to the study population, partly because inconspicuous—but telling—differences may exist between the study population and the other populations. If someone wishes to achieve greater certainty concerning the application of a study's results to some population other than the study population, he or she can conduct another survey, using the appropriate procedures for selecting a sample that, in technical terms, represents that other population.

In fact, the desire to be more certain about the applicability of a study's results to some other population is one of the chief reasons that surveys are conducted. For example, Barnum and Fischer (1984) conducted a survey of writing at work largely to determine if the information obtained by Davis (1977) from people listed in *Engineers of Distinction* would also apply to graduates of the engineering technology programs at their own university. In such situations, if the results from the second survey agree with those of the first survey, the researchers may feel even more confident about generalizing the results of the *two* surveys to still other, similiar populations. If the results of the two surveys do *not* agree, the researchers must undertake to understand why.

Conflicting Results

When two surveys produce conflicting results, researchers face a particularly knotty problem of interpretation because these differences may have any of several different causes.

One possible cause of conflicting results is that the two surveys deal with distinct populations that differ substantially with respect to the phenomenon under study. In some cases a distinction between the two populations is readily apparent, as when one survey studies graduates of two-year colleges and the other studies graduates of four-year colleges. In other cases, however, one must look further to spy a possible distinction between the two populations. In either case, when researchers speculate that their conflicting results are caused by differences in populations, they generally present their thoughts as hypotheses to be tested, not as facts to be accepted. They know that conflicting results can arise not only from real differences in populations but also from any of many sources involved with survey design and administration.

One of these sources is *sampling error*. Sampling error can be explained most readily through an example. Suppose a teacher of business writing wants to learn the average amount of time the twenty-two students in her class spend per week preparing the course assignments. She could ask a sample of five students to tell her how much time each of them spends and then calculate the average for the five. It is improbable that this average would be precisely the same as the average she would obtain if she had randomly selected a different group of five students. It is also unlikely that either of these groups would report an average that is precisely the same as the average for the entire class. These differences between the averages obtained from the samples of five students and the average the teacher would obtain from the entire population of twenty-two students are examples of sampling error. In a similar way, two separate surveys asking the same question to different samples from the same population could obtain different—and even conflicting—responses.

Differences due to sampling error should not be confused with differences that arise from the use of unsound sampling methods. Theoretically, sampling error is always present, even in the most perfectly designed survey; sampling error cannot be eliminated. In contrast, the errors that arise from careless sampling can be avoided. When two equally well designed surveys produce conflicting results, there is no way to decide which results are the more accurate. Researchers, however, usually place more confidence in the results of a survey with a sound sampling design than in the results of a survey with an unsound sampling design.

Conflicting results may also arise from any of a host of *response effects*, factors that can influence the way respondents reply to survey questions. Response effects include the place of a question in the overall survey, the phrasing of the question, and the way in which the interviewer poses the question. (These and other response effects are discussed in chapter 13). Thus, when apparently conflicting results are obtained, the surveys must be examined to determine whether some response effect accounts for the discrepancy.

So far, my examples of conflicting results have dealt with the responses that respondents in two different surveys make to a single question. Conflicting results can be even more difficult to interpret when the surveys are studying relationships between two or more variables, such as the relationship between attitude toward writing and the amount of writing the respondent reports that he or she does. Errors arising in the responses to any one of the questions involved can affect the outcomes of such analyses.

As this brief discussion demonstrates, researchers and readers of research cannot easily determine the best way to interpret conflicting results from different surveys. Even in an apparently clear-cut case, where one survey uses sound sampling methods and the other does not, there is a chance that the survey with the unsound sample design has obtained the result that most closely approximates the result that would be obtained if the entire population were queried. In the end, the best way to determine which of the conflicting results is the more accurate is to conduct a third survey.

Summary

As indicated by this brief discussion of the relationships among surveys, all decisions about how far to generalize a survey's results require judgment, and these decisions are subject to uncertainty. This discussion also indicates that researchers may have many different reasons for undertaking additional surveys of areas—writing, for example—that have already been investigated by other surveys. Of course, the researchers may want to investigate some research question that has never been studied before, but they may also want to ask familiar questions to a population not surveyed before, or they may want to verify results already obtained by another survey, or they may want to explain the differences between conflicting results of two or more previous surveys.

A SURVEY OF GRADUATES OF SEVEN
DEPARTMENTS THAT SEND STUDENTS
TO A TECHNICAL WRITING COURSE

In this section, I report on a survey in which I asked graduates of
seven departments at Miami University (Ohio) about the writing they
do at work. As mentioned earlier this report is intended to serve two
purposes. First, it illustrates the ways the various elements of a
survey—including purpose, research questions, procedure, respondents, data analysis, and interpretation—all work together to give the
particular meaning that is acquired by the responses to any particular
question or set of questions asked in the survey. In the next section of
this chapter, after the report of my survey, I provide a digest of the
results of fifty surveys that inquire about writing at work; readers
should remember that each of the individual results mentioned there
likewise takes its specific meaning from the various elements of the
survey that produced it.

The second purpose of this report of my survey is to provide an
account of a previously unpublished survey about writing in the
workplace.

Purpose

My purposes in reporting this study here may be distinguished, to
some extent, from my purposes in conducting it. I undertook this
survey project primarily because I wanted to gather information that
could be used to refine the basic technical writing course at Miami
University (Ohio). This course is taught to juniors and seniors from a
variety of majors, including some in the sciences, applied sciences,
and service professions. Because the course is intended to prepare
students for the writing they will do at work, I reasoned that I could
improve the course if I knew more about the writing those students
would do in their careers. Further, I believed that graduates of the
very departments in which my students are now studying could
provide the most accurate information possible about that writing.

As I began this project, I knew that some other researchers had
already conducted surveys similar to mine. I was uncertain, however,
whether the results of those surveys could be generalized to graduates
of my school. Two of these surveys, by Skelton (1977) and by Glenn
and Green (1979), involved people who had earned associate degrees
in technical and occupational programs; my students are all studying

for their bachelor's degrees. A third study, by Davis (1977), involved people listed in *Engineers of Distinction*; although my classes include some engineers—even some who might become engineers of distinction—my classes also include students in service professions (e.g., home economics) and the sciences. The remaining surveys of writing at work involved graduates of schools of business—people who likewise seem as though they might hold jobs substantially different from those my students will fill.

I had a second reason for wanting to undertake my own survey: the existing studies had not investigated some matters that interested me. For example, I wanted to learn more about the readers my students would write to on the job, about the forms they would use, and about the reasons they would have for writing at work. Assumptions about all three of these aspects of the rhetorical situation at work shape the topics covered and the assignments made in many technical writing courses, including my own.

Frequently, teachers of technical writing make the following assumptions about the *readers* that technical writing students will address on the job:

- The readers will be inside the organization that employs the student.
- They will be higher than the student in the organization's managerial hierarchy.
- They will be outside the student's specialty (or from that specialty but out of touch with it, as is the case with some managers).

As a way of preparing their students to write to such readers, some teachers ask the students to write *all* their assignments to the "intelligent but uninformed lay person" (often meaning the teachers themselves). If my students would actually write to other readers or to a broader array of readers (including fellow specialists, subordinates, and clients), then I wanted to know, so that I could emphasize a broader array of rhetorical strategies and make a broader array of assignments than I otherwise would.

I had a similar reason for wanting to learn what *forms* my students will use on the job: I wanted to be sure I provided them with instruction and practice in using the forms they would need to employ most regularly. Discussion of forms is unpopular at present because of the movement in composition pedagogy (and, more recently, in technical writing pedagogy) away from an approach that focuses on the formal characteristics of good writing to one that focuses on the processes by which good writing is created. As a result, discussion of the forms of writing tends to be scorned. But there are good reasons for considering form. Both in their writing class and on the job, students are going to have to write in some form—whether it be one they are already familiar with (such as the academic term paper) or one that is more novel to them (such as the technical report). Moreover, a person's mastery of the forms used in the workplace can contribute to his or her success as a writer in that setting. For one thing, a writer's ability to use conventional forms in the customary way shows that he or she is a bona fide member of the culture of the workplace; a person who cannot use these forms may appear to readers to be generally unqualified. In addition, the forms used in the workplace are functional; they help writers communicate effectively and efficiently. From a cognitive point of view, van Dijk (1980) makes this point by explaining how conventional forms provide cognitive frames that readers can use to process the information the forms contain. From a rhetorical point of view, Miller (1984) makes a similar point by explaining how the forms of technical and business writing are actually genres of communication that have been developed as effective modes of organizing and presenting discourse in recurring types of rhetorical situations. Finally, Winkler (1983) has argued, from a theoretical point of view, that a writer's use of his or her knowledge about forms is an integral part of the composing process. By conducting my own survey, I hoped to learn what forms I should be preparing my students to use.

For a similar reason, I was interested in knowing why my students will write on the job. A common assumption of courses and textbooks in technical writing is that college graduates almost always write on assignment from other people. As a result, instruction in technical writing often scants the writing strategies that are effective in the very different situations in which the writer is proffering an unsolicited communication. I wanted to conduct my own survey in order to learn whether I should be including that instruction in my class.

Besides wanting to learn about the readers, forms, and reasons for writing that my students will encounter on the job, I also wanted to gain some basic information about the amount of writing they might expect to do at work and its likely importance to their careers. Such information would help me explain to students the relevance of my class.

Furthermore, I wanted to learn whether or not some groups of alumni differed from others in terms of the factors I have just described. For example, I wanted to know whether the readers, forms, and reasons for writing would be different for graduates of some departments than for graduates of other departments. At some schools, technical writing courses are divided into sections, one for students in each major; learning about the differences and similarities among the writing experiences of the graduates of various departments at Miami would help the other technical writing faculty and me decide whether to segregate our course in the same way. In addition, this knowledge would alert me to the special needs of students from various departments.

Also, I wanted to learn whether the readers, forms, and reasons for writing would be different for new employees than they would be for those who had been on the job longer. This information would let me know whether there were special writing tasks I should emphasize because they would be particularly important to my students during the first years of their careers. Finally, I wanted to learn whether the readers, forms, and reasons for writing would be different for graduates who went on to earn advanced degrees than for those who did not. This knowledge would help me learn whether students headed for graduate school had special needs that I should address in my course.

In sum, I undertook this survey primarily out of a desire to gain information that would help me teach my class in technical writing at Miami University. The research questions I framed, the survey population I defined, the sample I constructed, the questionnaire I created, and the data analysis I performed were all directed to that end. Naturally, I believed I was asking questions of general interest, and I hoped that other teachers and others studying writing at work would find my results valuable, but these were secondary concerns to me.

Research Questions

Given the purposes just described, I formulated the following research questions for my survey.

1. How much writing is done at work by alumni from a heterogeneous group of seven departments selected from the sciences, social sciences, and service professions?
2. How important to these alumni is the writing they do at work?
3. What are some of the major features of the rhetorical situations in which these alumni write at work? In particular:

- To whom do they write?
- What forms do they use?
- Why do they write?

4. With respect to the questions asked here, what important differences (if any) are to be found in the following comparisons:

- When the graduates of any one of the seven departments are compared with the graduates of the others?
- When the alumni who have been on the job for only a few years are compared with those who have been on the job longer?
- When the alumni who went on to earn graduate degrees are compared with the alumni who did not?

Procedure

To answer those research questions, I designed a four-page questionnaire, containing twenty-eight questions, which I mailed to 2,335 alumni of Miami University (Ohio) who met all the following criteria: (1) earned a baccalaureate from one of seven selected departments (to be listed), (2) received the baccalaureate at least one year earlier, and (3) had a U.S. address listed in the files of the university's alumni office.

The people on the mailing list for the questionnaire included every graduate of the Manufacturing Engineering, Office Administration, Paper Science and Engineering, and Systems Analysis departments. The mailing list also included every other person on a roster of Home Economics graduates and every fourth person on rosters of Chemistry and Zoology graduates. (For a discussion of the use of rosters to select samples, see Sudman, 1983).

The questionnaire was mailed along with a letter in which I explained the purpose of the survey and asked the alumni to cooperate by returning their responses in the enclosed prepaid envelope. Ten days later, I mailed a postcard to the alumni, reminding them to return the questionnaire.

Respondents

In all, 1,052 alumni returned the questionnaire. For a variety of reasons, however, 211 of the questionnaires were unusable. The 841 alumni who returned usable questionnaires were distributed among the seven departments in the following way:

Department	Number
Science:	
Chemistry	52
Zoology	60
Applied science:	
Manufacturing Engineering	143
Paper Science and Engineering	93
Systems Analysis	230
Service professions:	
Home Economics	163
Office Administration	100
Total	841

When asked how many years they had been employed since obtaining their baccalaureates, the alumni provided the information shown in figure 1-1. Overall, the alumni constitute a young group, probably because some of the departments in the survey are relatively new at Miami and because the university itself expanded rapidly in the 1960s. For each question on the survey, I compared the responses of the 201 alumni who had been on the job for fewer than three years with the responses of the 640 who had been on the job longer.

When asked how much additional education they had received since earning their baccalaureates, the respondents provided the information shown in figure 1-2. The alumni who placed themselves in the "some" category had engaged in wide variety of educational activities, such as earning a second baccalaureate, taking additional college courses without receiving a degree, completing flight-training

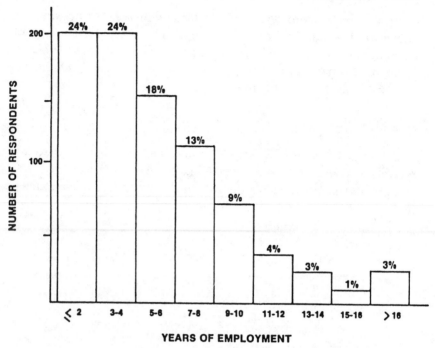

Figure 1-1 Years of Employment

school or an American Dietetics Association Internship, and participating in in-house courses offered by their employers. The 39
respondents with doctorates earned the following degrees: PhD (17),
MD (11), DDS (5), JD (3), DO (2) and DVM (1). For each question in the
survey, I compared the responses from the 173 alumni who indicated
they had earned graduate degrees after receiving their baccalaureates
at Miami with the responses of the 650 who indicated they had
not.

Results and Discussion

The following subsections outline the major results of the
survey.[1] For all statistical tests, I used the .05 level of significance.
Throughout the following discussion, Duncan's multiple-range test
for variable response is referred to simply as Duncan's test.

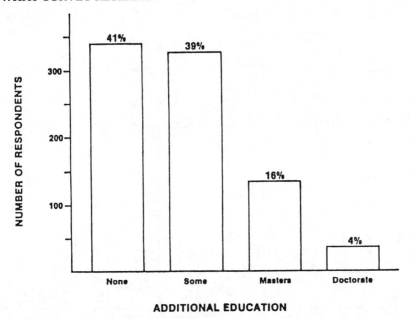

Figure 1-2 *Additional Education since Receiving Baccalaureate*

HOW MUCH TIME DO THEY SPEND WRITING? The alumni indicated the percentage of their time at work that they spend writing by checking one of seven alternatives: 0 percent, 1–10 percent, 11–20 percent, 21–40 percent, 41–60 percent, 61–80 percent, and 81–100 percent. For statistical analyses, the responses were coded on a six-point scale for which 0 percent = 0, 1–10 percent and 11–20 percent = 1, 21–40 percent = 2, 41–60 percent = 3, and so on.[2]

As figure 1-3 shows, the 841 alumni spend a substantial amount of their time at work writing. Sixty-nine percent reported spending more than 10 percent, which is equivalent to saying that on the average they write more than one-half day in every forty-hour week. Thirty-eight percent reported writing more than 20 percent of their time (more than one day a week), and 15 percent reported writing more than 40 percent of their work time (more than two days a week).

Writing is a major activity for *all* subgroups of the sample. Whereas I had guessed that graduates of some of the seven departments would spend more time writing than would the gradu-

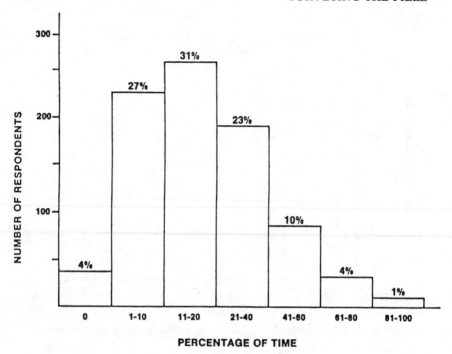

PERCENTAGE OF TIME

Figure 1-3 Time Spent Writing

ates of the others, an analysis of variance (one way) found *no significant difference* among the seven departments, $F(6, 829) = 1.40$, $p = .211$. Similarly, a Student's *t*-test found no significant difference between the alumni who earned graduate degrees and those who had not. In contrast, another Student's *t*-test showed that the alumni who had been on the job for three years or more spent a significantly greater amount of their time writing than do those who have been on the job less than three years, $t (834) = 2.04$, $p = .042$, $\bar{X}_{lje} = 1.42$, $\bar{X}_{mje} = 1.58$ ($\bar{X}$ indicates the mean response; *lje* means *less job experience*; *mje* means *more job experience*). Even among the alumni with less job experience, however, 53 percent reported they write more than 10 percent of their time at work, and 32 percent reported they write more than 20 percent of that time.

HOW IMPORTANT IS WRITING? Of course, a person could devote a large portion of his or her time to an activity that is unimportant. But that is not the case with writing. To determine how important the ability to write well (not just write, but write *well*) would be to someone who wanted to perform his or her present job, I asked the alumni to check one of five levels of importance: negative, minimal, some, great, and critical. For statistical analyses, the responses were coded on a five-point scale (negative = 0, critical = 4).

As figure 1-4 shows, 93 percent said the ability to write well would be of at least "some importance." Fifty-seven percent stated that it would be of "great" or "critical importance."

Additional examination of the respondents' replies indicates that writing is an important activity for alumni in all the subgroups of the sample, and that it is even more important for some subgroups than for others. In terms of the importance they assign to the ability to write well, a Student's t-test found no significant difference between the alumni who had been on the job for three years or more and those who had been on the job for less time; both groups appear to find writing about equally important. In contrast, a Student's t-test indicated that the alumni with graduate degrees perceive writing to be significantly more important than do the alumni without graduate degrees, $t(795) = 4.97$, $p = .0001$, $\bar{X}_{gd} = 2.95$, $\bar{X}_{ngd} = 2.60$ (gd means graduate degree; ngd means no graduate degree). Even so, 83 percent of the alumni without graduate degrees reported that writing is of at

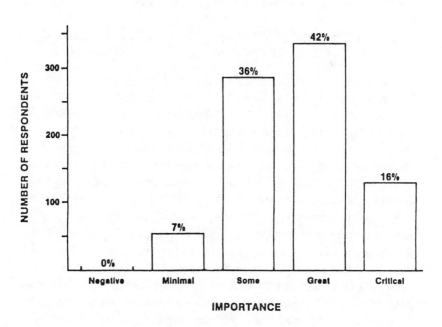

Figure 1-4 Importance of Writing

least "some importance," and 54 percent reported that writing is of at least "great importance."

Similarly, an analysis of variance (one way) showed that a difference exists among the alumni of the seven departments in terms of the degree of importance they assign to writing, $F(6, 793) = 4.97$, $p = .0001$. A Duncan's test revealed the details of this difference: alumni from five of the departments (Chemistry, Manufacturing Engineering, Office Administration, Paper Science and Engineering, and Systems Analysis) find writing well to be significantly more important than do the alumni of the other two departments (Home Economics and Zoology). But even Zoology alumni—the group who placed the least importance on writing—still reported that they find it to be very important: 84 percent of the Zoology alumni indicated that the ability to write well is of at least "some importance," and 42 percent indicated that it is of at least "great importance."

WHO READS THEIR WRITING? A series of eleven questions asked the alumni to tell how often their communications are read by various kinds of readers. They answered by checking one of five responses: "never," "rarely," "sometimes," "often," "always." For statistical analyses, the responses were coded on a five-point scale ("never" = 0, "always" = 4).

The most important finding is that the alumni's writing, overall, is read not by any single kind of reader, but by a variety of kinds.

Readers' Knowledge. First the alumni indicated how often their writing is read by readers with various levels of knowledge of the alumni's specialties: those who know more than the alumni about those specialties, those who know about the same amount, those who are familiar with the specialties but know less, and those who are completely unfamiliar with them. All four groups of readers were checked either "sometimes," "often," or "always" by at least 60 percent of the alumni. Furthermore, each of the subgroups of alumni provided essentially similar information. At least 50 percent of the alumni from each of the seven departments, at least 59 percent of both the alumni with graduate degrees and those without graduate degrees, and at least 54 percent of both the alumni with less than three years of job experience and those with three years or more of job experience reported that their communications are read at least "sometimes" by all four groups of readers.

To be sure, the alumni of these seven departments do write to some of these groups of readers more often than they write to others, as indicated by the results of an analysis of variance (randomized complete block), $F(3, 2376) = 117.01$, $p = .0001$. Which groups do they address more often? The first important finding of a Duncan's test is that there is not a significant difference between the frequency with which they address writers who are merely familiar with their specialties and those who know about as much as the alumni do about their specialties. This finding provides a significant comment on the assumption held by many students that in their careers they will communicate almost exclusively with fellow specialists. The second important finding of the Duncan's test is that the alumni write significantly more often to each of the two groups just mentioned (familiar, know as much) than the alumni write either to readers who know more than the alumni do about their own specialties or to readers who are completely unfamiliar with the alumni's specialties.

In examining the responses from the various subgroups of alumni, I found some results that surprised me. Whereas I expected that the alumni with graduate degrees would surely write more often than alumni without graduate degrees to their fellow specialists, a Student's t-test found no significant difference between the two groups of alumni in terms of how often their communications are read by either those who know as much as or those who know more than the alumni do about the alumni's specialties. Even more to my surprise, the alumni with graduate degrees write significantly more often to readers who are completely unfamiliar with their specialties, $t(789) = 2.15$, $p = .032$, $\bar{X}_{ngd} = 1.98$, $\bar{X}_{gd} = 1.79$. Similarly, the alumni with three years or more of job experience write significantly more often than do the alumni with less job experience to readers who are completely unfamiliar with their specialies, $t(792) = 2.50$, $p = .013$, $\bar{X}_{lje} = 1.66$, $\bar{X}_{mje} = 1.88$.

These differences among the subgroups of alumni should not obscure the major conclusion that *all* the alumni—regardless of department, regardless of the amount of additional education they have had, and regardless of the amount of job experience they have gained—need to be able to address readers across the full range of levels of knowledge of their specialties.

Readers' Level in Organizational Hierarchy. The respondents also answered questions about how often the communications they prepare are read by persons at each of three levels *within* the organizations that employ the alumni: a level higher than the alumni's, the alumni's own level, and a lower level. An analysis of variance (randomized complete block) indicated that there were significant differences in the alumni's responses to these three questions, $F(2, 1,582)$ 145.74, $p = .0001$. A Duncan's test showed the nature of that difference: the alumni's writing is read significantly more often by people at their own level than by people below. Even people at a lower level, however, read the writing of 70 percent of the alumni at least "sometimes."

Likewise, the alumni in each of the subgroups write very frequently to readers at all three levels. At least 48 percent in each of the seven departments (69 percent of all except Office Administration) reported that they write to all three groups at least "sometimes," as did 66 percent of both the alumni with and without graduate degrees and 57 percent of both the alumni with more and with less job experience.

Readers outside Writer's Organization. The alumni also indicated how often the communications they prepare are read by each of four groups of readers *outside* the organizations that employ them: customers, vendors (who sell products to the alumni's organizations), legislators and other government officials, and the general public.

Analyses of the alumni's responses produced three major findings. First, the alumni write significantly more often to readers at every one of the three levels within their own organizations than to any of these four outside groups. This is shown by a Duncan's test that was applied after an analysis of variance (randomized complete block) indicated signficant differences in the response to the seven questions involved, $F(6, 4736) = 569.58$, $p = .0001$. The second major finding is that, of the four outside groups, the most important is generally customers. Third, how frequently the alumni address any of these four outside groups depends largely on the department from which the alumni graduated. For example, whereas only 6 percent of the Systems Analysis alumni reported that their writing is read at least "sometimes" by the public, 50 percent of the Home Economics alumni reported that theirs is.

WHAT FORMS OF COMMUNICATION DO THEY WRITE? Besides telling how often their communications are read by each of a variety of kinds of readers, the alumni also indicated how often they prepare

Table 1-1

How Often Respondents Prepare Eleven Forms of Written Communication

Form	N	Never	Rarely	Sometimes	Often	Always	Mean[a]	Grouping[b]
				Percentage of Respondents				
Memoranda	793	5	9	23	53	10	2.55	
Letters	800	5	11	30	46	8	2.42	
Step-by-step instructions	796	7	13	31	44	5	2.28	{
General instructions	794	11	14	34	38	3	2.09	{
Preprinted forms (to be filled out by respondent)	793	12	21	33	26	8	1.97	{
Proposals for funding or approval of projects	795	24	18	30	24	4	1.64	{
Formal reports (with title page or special cover sheet)	793	22	24	33	19	2	1.55	{
Minutes of meetings or conversations	795	26	27	28	17	2	1.42	{
Scripts for speeches or presentations	795	31	27	30	11	1	1.25	{
Advertising	785	70	14	10	5	1	0.54	
Articles for professional journals[c]	791	68	19	9	3	0	0.48	{

[a]Responses coded on a five-point scale (0 = never, 4 = always).
[b]Brackets enclose means that are not significantly different at the $\alpha = .05$ level of significance as calculated by a Duncan's test. The results of an analysis of variance F test on these data are as follows: $F (10,7919) = 461.86$, $p = .0001$.
[c]Row does not add to 100 percent because of rounding.

each of the eleven forms of communication listed in table 1-1. Admittedly, two of these forms—letters and memoranda—overlap with each other and with some of the others. For example, alumni could request funding or approval for a project in a letter or memorandum as well as in a special form called a *proposal*. In contrast, some of the other forms I asked about perform a narrower range of functions. No one is likely to ask for funding or approval in a set of step-by-step instructions. Despite the fuzziness of the distinctions among some of the forms, a question about forms seemed well worth asking for the reasons I outlined in discussing my purpose in conducting this study.

Five of the eleven forms are used regularly by many of the alumni. At least 50 percent of the alumni from every one of the seven departments indicated that they write the following five forms at least "sometimes": memoranda, letters, step-by-step instructions, general instructions, and preprinted forms to be filled out by the alumni.

On the other hand, one form that sometimes receives special emphasis in technical writing courses is seldom used by these alumni: Duncan's tests showed that for six of the seven departments, articles for publication in professional journals are written significantly *less* often than are any of the other ten forms. In the seventh department (Zoology), the only form that is not written significantly *more* often than articles for publication is advertising. Even alumni with graduate degrees do not often write articles for publication in professional journals. Although the alumni with graduate degrees write such articles significantly more often than do alumni without graduate degrees, they too write journal articles significantly less often than they write every other form except advertising; that is true for every one of the seven departments, *including* the two science departments, Zoology and Chemistry.

Of course, it is possible that for at least some alumni a form like articles for publication may be quite important to their careers, even though it isn't written very often. My survey does not provide information about that possibility. Certainly, however, these articles can't be very important to the 68 percent of the alumni who reported that they "never" write them. (Only 9 percent report that they "sometimes" do, a mere 3 percent that they "often" or "always" do.)

As the two preceding paragraphs indicate, there is clear agreement among the alumni of the seven departments about which forms they write most often and which they write least often. At the same time, there are substantial differences among departments with respect to how often their alumni write some of the other forms. For example, whereas only 39 percent of the Systems Analysis alumni reported that they "sometimes," "often," or "always" complete preprinted forms, more than twice as many (80 percent) of the Office Administration alumni reported that they complete preprinted forms "sometimes," "often," or "always," t (310) = 4.37, p = .0001, $\bar{X}_{sa}$ = 1.72, X_{oa} = 2.32 (sa means Systems Analysis; oa means Office Administration). Similarly, whereas only 4 percent of the Chemistry alumni "sometimes," "often," or "always" write advertising, more than ten times as many (41%) of the Home Economics majors write advertising "sometimes," "often," or "always," t (170) = 5.34, p = .0001, $\bar{X}_{chem}$ = .21, $\bar{X}_{he}$ = 1.22 (chem means Chemistry; he means Home Economics).

WHY DO THE ALUMNI WRITE? By answering the final two questions on the survey form, the alumni indicated how often they write for each of two reasons: because someone else asked them to and because they decided to write on their own initiative. A paired t-test found no significant difference between the responses to the two questions, t (792) = 1.48, p = .14, $\bar{X}_{ser}$ = 2.49, $\bar{X}_{oi}$ = 2.55. (ser means someone else's request; oi means own initiative.). Ninety-two percent of the alumni indicated that they write at someone else's request at least "sometimes," and 53 percent indicated that they do so either "often" or "always." Similarly, 90 percent of the alumni indicated that they write on their own initiative at least "sometimes," and 59 percent indicated that they do so either "often" or "always." Analyses of the responses from each of the subgroups of alumni produced similar results. At least 87 percent of the alumni from every one of the seven departments said that they write at someone else's request at least "sometimes," and at least 84 percent said that they write on their own initiative at least "sometimes." A Student's t-test showed that the alumni without graduate degrees write significantly less often on their own initiative than do those with graduate degrees, t (351.9) = 4.35, p = .0001, $\bar{X}_{gd}$ = 2.74, $\bar{X}_{ngd}$ = 2.50, but even then 89 percent of the alumni without graduate degrees do so at least "sometimes." Similarly, another Student's t-test indicated that alumni with three years or more of job experience write significantly more often on their own initiative than do alumni who have been on the job less than three years, t (791) = 3.87, p .0001, $\bar{X}_{lje}$ = 2.37, $\bar{X}_{mje}$ = 2.61. Even then, 86 percent of the alumni with less job experience do so at least "sometimes."

Conclusions

The information provided by the 841 respondents to this survey affords substantial insights into the writing done at work by graduates of seven departments that send their juniors and seniors to the introductory technical writing course at Miami University (Ohio). *The major conclusion to be drawn from this information is that these graduates of programs in science, applied science, and service professions are called on to be versatile communicators who can use a variety of forms to address a variety of readers who may or may not have asked the graduates to write.* Seven specific conclusions are suggested by this survey.

1. *Writing is a major activity for these graduates.* Regardless of their department, regardless of whether they are new or experienced employees, regardless of whether or not they have earned graduate degrees, the respondents reported that they write a very considerable portion of their time at work and that the ability to write well is important in their jobs.

2. *In terms of the writing they do on the job, the typical graduates of all seven departments are very similar.* There is no significant difference among the graduates of the various departments in terms of the *amount* of writing they do on the job. Furthermore, although there are significant differences among them in terms of the *importance* they attach to writing, the graduates of all seven find writing to be very important. In addition, the graduates of all seven departments are very similar in terms of the readers they address and the five forms of communications they use most often. Finally, they all write very often on their own initiative as well as at the request of someone else. These results indicate that there is no need to create special sections for students in one or another of the departments represented by these graduates.

3. *Likewise, the typical graduates who are new on the job and those with more experience report generally similar writing experiences, as do the typical graduates with and without graduate degrees.* A well-designed class for students in departments represented by these graduates will teach writing skills that will be useful to the students throughout their careers, whether or not they go to graduate school.

4. *The typical graduates of all seven departments write regularly to a variety of kinds of readers.* These graduates regularly address

readers who (like their professors) know more than they do about their specialties, but they also write regularly to readers who know only as much as they do, to readers who know less, and to readers who are completely unfamiliar with their specialties. In addition, they write regularly to readers at their own level within their organizations as well as to readers at higher and lower levels. Finally, many of the graduates write regularly to various kinds of readers outside their organizations. Writing classes for students who will enter jobs like the ones held by these graduates should provide instruction and practice at writing to many of these kinds of readers.

5. *The typical graduates of these departments write significantly more often to readers inside their organization than to writers outside.*

6. *The typical graduates write in a variety of forms.* Five of the eleven forms treated in this survey are written at least "sometimes" by at least 50 percent of the respondents from every department; the forms are: memoranda, letters, step-by-step instructions, general instructions, and preprinted forms that the writer must fill out. These five forms deserve serious consideration for being included in a writing course for students in the departments represented in the survey.

7. *The typical graduates write about as much on their own initiative as at someone else's request.* Writing classes for students in the departments represented by these graduates should teach the rhetorical strategies appropriate in each of these very different situations.

As indicated at the beginning of this section, one purpose of this report of my survey is to illustrate the ways that the various elements of a survey work together. From the point of view of survey design, a key element is the researcher's purpose, which determines the research questions that will be asked, the sample that will be constructed, the questions that are framed, and the analyses that are applied to the data. In the case of my survey, the initial purpose was my desire to obtain information that I thought would help me improve my technical writing course. I selected a sample that represented people working in the kinds of jobs my students would hold, and I framed questions that would investigate the aspects of writing that I thought to be important to my purpose. For example, the sets of questions about readers (level of knowledge, level in the organization, etc.) focused on the characteristics of readers that I thought salient. Similarly, the statistical procedures I selected were designed to make the kinds of comparisons I believed would be informative (e.g., comparisons between the responses about readers inside and outside the respondent's organizations, and between answers given by graduates of one department and the graduates of another). Even the conclusions I drew circled back to my initial purpose, centering on the implications of what I found for the teaching of my students.

The sharp focus of any survey (particularly, the specific characteristics of the survey sample) influences the extent to which the survey results can be generalized beyond the population focused on in the study. Questions of generalizability are fundamental to the next section of this chapter, where I explore the broad generalizations that may be derived from fifty surveys of writing at work. Many of those surveys focus on populations as small as the population studied in the survey I have just described.

SUMMARY OF SURVEY FINDINGS

In this section, I discuss the findings of fifty surveys that have asked one or more questions concerning the writing people do at work.[3] In order to provide a unified account of those findings, I have organized this discussion around general conclusions rather than around the studies from which the conclusions are derived.

I have usually stated the conclusions themselves in tentative terms, using such words as *seem* and *may*, for two reasons. The first arises from the nature of survey research. As discussed at the beginning of this chapter, the results obtained from the particular individuals in a survey sample may be generalized to the study population from which the individuals were selected, if those individuals were selected according to a technically sound method. Further, the results obtained from those individuals may be generalized to still other populations if there is a good reason to believe that the other populations closely resemble the study population. Differences between populations, however, are not always readily apparent. For that reason, all generalizing beyond the study population must be relatively tentative, at least until other studies of the same phenomena have produced similar results, thereby supporting the wide applicability of the results. This caution about generalizing too widely beyond the study population is especially relevant when discussing surveys of writing at work, because most of them involve very narrow study populations: the graduates of *one* school, the employees of *one* company, the managers in *one* city. Further, almost all concern *college-educated* workers, so that even when similar results are obtained by two or more of the studies, generalizations based on them might have to be limited to the college-educated portion of the work force in the United States.

My second reason for stating conclusions tentatively in the following discussion is that many of the surveys of writing on the job are flawed. The most common methodological problem involves the use of inappropriate sampling methods. Many studies use *convenience samples*: samples composed of people who came readily to hand (for instance, the people at a conference the researcher attended). Convenience samples are similar to street-corner samples, in which someone tries to generalize about attitudes of all U.S. citizens by standing on a street corner and asking questions of the people who pass by. Clearly, the results obtained by the researcher will depend on what corner the researcher chooses—whether in a city or a town, whether in the Northeast or the Southwest, whether in a wealthy neighborhood or a poor one. The careless construction of a sample can be a particularly serious flaw: unless the sample has been carefully constructed, there is no certainty that the results obtained from the sample can be generalized to the study population, much less any other population.

A second problem found in many of the surveys to be cited is that researchers do not always use appropriate procedures for analyzing the data collected from the respondents. For instance, many of the studies involve at least some comparisons between the responses to two or more questions (e.g., "How often do you write memos?" and "How often do you write proposals?"). If the results of such comparisons are to be generalized beyond the sample to the population, the researchers should use inferential statistics. Many of these studies fail to do so—and some that do use inferential statistics fail to report the results of the inferential procedures the researchers used.

In fact, sketchy reporting is a third major problem encountered in many of the studies. In some cases, the researchers report their study designs so sketchily that readers are left asking basic questions: Exactly how was the sample chosen? Exactly how was the question worded? Exactly what were the alternative responses from which respondents were asked to choose?

Despite their shortcomings, even the most seriously flawed surveys of writing at work deserve mention in this chapter. At the very least, they illustrate the kinds of topics that can be investigated through surveys, and they indicate the kinds of results that might be obtained through more soundly constructed studies.

In sum, in the discussion that follows I have stated very tentatively most of the conclusions that might be drawn from the existing surveys of writing at work. I do this, in part, because even the most soundly designed studies of this subject concern narrowly defined populations, from which one would generalize to large segments of the U.S. work force only with considerable temerity. And I state conclusions tentatively, in part, because many of the studies of writing at work are flawed. Nevertheless, fairly firm conclusions can be drawn on some points—those on which several different surveys have obtained similar results. Further, even the most tentative conclusions given here can serve as a spur to further research and as a hint at what we have yet to learn.

I have gathered the conclusions under the following headings: time spent writing, importance of writing, composing processes used, writing skills needed, audiences addressed, kinds of written communications prepared, functions of writing, quality of writing, workers' perception of their own writing ability, and workers' attitudes and beliefs concerning education about writing.

Time Spent Writing

More than twenty surveys have inquired about the amount of time at work that workers spend writing. The results of these surveys lead to five conclusions.

1. *Writing consumes a substantial portion of the working day for almost all college-educated workers.* All the surveys that have inquired about the matter find that the respondents spend, on average, approximately 20 percent of their time at work writing. The highest average (25 percent) that respondents have reported concerning *their own* writing was obtained in three studies: Spretnak's (1982) survey of 595 graduates of the College of Engineering at the University of California at Berkeley, Storms's (1983) survey of 837

graduates of the School of Business Administration at Miami University (Ohio), and Cox's (1976) survey of 150 people who had taken his business communication class over the past fifteen years and had earned an A or a B in it. Stine and Skarzenski (1979) obtained a somewhat higher average estimate of time spent writing when they asked 83 executives of companies with businesses in Iowa to tell about the time spent writing by *other* people: the respondents reported that they thought that the people working for them spend about 28 percent of their time writing. The lowest average (16 percent) was obtained by Rader and Wunsch (1980) in a survey of 93 workers who earned undergraduate degrees from the College of Business Administration at Arizona State University. The range of times reported by individual respondents is very great, however—from 0 percent, reported by very few, to nearly 100 percent, also reported by very few.

Other surveys that have inquired about the amount of time workers spend writing are: Barnum and Fischer (1984); Bataille (1982); Davis (1977); Erickson (1975); Harwood (1982); Faigley, Miller, Meyer, and Witte (1981); Flatley (1982); Hinrichs (1964); Klemmer and Snyder (1972); Paradis, Dobrin, and Bower (personal correspondence, 1984); Van Dyck (1980); Weinrauch and Swanda (1975); and my survey (reported earlier).

In addition, apparently unreliable estimates of time spent writing were obtained in surveys by Persing, Drew, Bachman, Eaton, and Galbraith (1976), and Persing, Drew, Bachman, and Galbraith (1977); both surveys used the same respondents, who estimated that they spend 134 percent of their time in various communication activities. I discuss the accuracy of estimates of time spent writing later.

2. *As much time as college-educated workers spend writing, they generally spend more in oral communication.* Many surveys have asked the respondents to indicate how much time they spend writing and how much they spend communicating orally. These surveys indicated that the time spent in oral communication is greater—in a few cases, much greater. Comparisons of time spent writing with time spent speaking, however, can be misleading because of the different relationships these two ways of *sending* messages have with ways of *receiving* messages. In oral communication (especially in one-to-one conversation), speaking and listening are interwined in a way that writing and reading seldom are. This problem is worth noting because some studies compare the amount of time the

respondents spend *writing* against the amount they spend *communicating orally*—without distinguishing between the speaking and listening components of oral communication.

In a study that did observe the distinction between speaking and listening, Rader and Wunsch (1980) found that 93 business graduates of Arizona State University spend an average of 37 percent of the working day speaking and only 16 percent writing; they spend 19 percent listening and 13 percent reading. Blue, Breslin, Buchanan, and Leingany (1976) obtained similar results when investigating the ways people send messages in eight occupational areas entered by graduates of two-year vocational college programs. The respondents in seven of these areas spend more of their time sending messages orally than they spend writing. These areas are: agricultural, distribution and marketing, health, home and family life, technical, and trade and industrial. The one area in which the respondents write (slightly) more often than they speak is business and office occupations.

Other studies that have inquired about time spent in both written and oral communication include: Bennett (1971), Cox (1976), Hinrichs (1964); Huegli and Tschirgi (1974); Persing, Drew, Bachman, and Galbraith (1977); Skelton (1977); Stine and Skarzenski (1979); and Weinrauch and Swanda (1975).

3. *When deciding whether to communicate in writing or orally, workers may be influenced by their apprehensions concerning the alternative communication channels available.* In a study involving 53 faculty at a large public university and 15 faculty at a vocational-technical school, Reinsch and Lewis (1984) investigated how much their respondents' decisions to write rather than to communicate in other ways are determined by the following forms of apprehension: speech apprehension (i.e., apprehension of giving speeches), communication apprehension (i.e., apprehension of communicating face to face), telephone apprehension, and writing apprehension. Interestingly, the researchers found a positive correlation between writing apprehension and each of the other three forms of apprehension: people who are apprehensive about writing are likely to be apprehensive about communicating by other means as well. Even so, the researchers found that writing apprehension scores constituted a significant predictor of the respondent's answer to the question: "In general, would you rather write or call?"[4]

4. *The total amount of time spent writing may be related to a number of factors, including job category, college major, amount of*

graduate education, level in the organization, and years of work experience. Investigating how the amount of time spent writing is related to various factors, researchers have produced evidence of a general relationship for only one factor, *job category.* In contrast, they have obtained conflicting results concerning these other factors: college major, amount of graduate education, level in the organization, and years of work experience. Even these conflicting results are worthy of examination, partly because they suggest areas for further study and partly because they hint at some of the many factors that may influence all aspects of the writing experiences of college-educated workers.

JOB CATEGORY. In their survey of 93 people who earned undergraduate degrees from the College of Business Administration at Arizona State University, Rader and Wunsch (1980) found a statistically significant relationship between job category and the percentage of the average day spent writing. For example, accountants spend a significantly greater percentage of their time writing (25 percent) than do people in four other job categories for which the survey sample contained enough respondents to make comparison possible: banking/finance (15 percent), production/plant management (14 percent), marketing (12 percent), and office/general management (9 percent).

The existence of a relationship between job category and time spent writing appears to be supported by Faigley, Miller, Meyer, & Witte (1981) in a study involving a sample of 200 college graduates in four cities in Texas and Louisiana; this sample had the same proportion of college-educated persons in various job categories as does the U.S. work force at large.[5] Although Faigley et al. did not use inferential statistical procedures to analyze their data, their results suggest that the average time spent writing varies greatly from one job category to another. For instance, they found that professional and technical employees spend 29 percent of their total work time writing, more than seven times the amount spent by college-educated blue collar workers (4 percent). Incidentally, Faigley et al. also found some large differences among types of employers: government and service organizations require the most writing (29 percent), whereas wholesale and retail trades require the least (13 percent).

COLLEGE MAJOR. Conflicting results have been obtained by studies that have sought to determine whether there is a relationship between college major and percentage of time spent writing.

Rader and Wunsch (1980) found that the percentage of the average work day spent in writing is significantly related to the major taken by graduates of Arizona State University's School of Business Administration. Finance majors and accounting majors reported spending a significantly greater percentage of their time writing (28 percent and 23 percent respectively) than did majors from two of the three other departments with enough respondents to make statistical comparisons possible: marketing (12 percent) and general business (12 percent). Similarly, in a survey of a random sample of about 250 graduates of Christopher Newport College (Virginia), Harwood (1982) found that the quantity of writing his respondents had done during a two-week period was significantly related to undergraduate college major. The alumni who had majored in the humanities wrote the least.

In contrast, two surveys involving graduates of Miami University (Ohio) found no significant difference among departments in terms of the time spent writing on the job. In the first, Storms (1983) surveyed 837 graduates of six departments in the School of Business Administration: accountancy, economics, marketing, finance, general business, and management. In the second (reported earlier), I surveyed 841 graduates of seven science, applied science, and service departments.

As mentioned at the beginning of this chapter, it is possible to speculate about the causes of conflicting results from different surveys, but it is not possible to explain the conflicts for certain without conducting a further study that treats these speculations as hypotheses to be tested. Any hypothesis developed to explain the conflicting results concerning the relationship between college major and time spent writing should take into account that two of the studies—those by Storms and by Rader and Wunsch—involved graduates of the same kinds of programs—schools of business administration. (One possible explanation of that difference is discussed later, in the section on the relationship between time spent writing and the number of years of work experience.)

AMOUNT OF GRADUATE EDUCATION. Two surveys have produced conflicting results concerning the relationship between amount of time spent writing and amount of graduate education. In his survey of about 250 graduates of Christopher Newport College, Harwood (1982) found that the amount of postbaccalaureate education is significantly related to the amount of writing the respondents did during a two-week period: the more postbaccalaureate education, the more writing the person did. In contrast, in my survey (reported earlier) of 841 graduates of science, applied science, and service departments at Miami University (Ohio), I found that there is not a statistically significant difference between the amount of writing done by respondents who had earned graduate degrees and those who had not.

Perhaps Harwood and I obtained different results because we surveyed graduates of different schools or graduates of different kinds of departments (his sample included humanities majors, for instance; mine did not). On the other hand, the differences may arise from our different ways of measuring "amount of writing"—or from any of many other causes. There seems to be no single, most-likely explanation.

LEVEL IN THE ORGANIZATION. Surveys have also produced conflicting results concerning the relationship of level in the organization to amount of time spent writing. Rader and Wunsch (1980) found no significant difference among business graduates of Arizona State University at the four levels they inquired about (top management, middle management, supervisory, other).

In contrast, three other studies all seem to indicate that there is a relationship between organizational level and time spent writing. In the first, Davis (1977) asked 245 people listed in Engineers of Distinction how the amount of time they spent writing changed as their responsibilities increased. Sixty-five percent reported that as their responsibilities increased, so did the amount of time they spent writing; however, 32 percent reported that as their responsibilities increased, the amount of time they spent writing decreased. Only 3 percent reported that they continued to write about the same amount. Similarly, in Barnum and Fischer's (1984) survey of 305 graduates of Southern Technical Institute (most earned the Bachelor of Engineering Technology degree), 73 percent of the respondents reported that as they have advanced they have written more; 24 percent reported that they have written about the same amount; and only 3% reported that they have written less. Finally, in Spretnak's (1982) survey of 595 people who had graduated from the College of Engineering at the University of California at Berkeley between one and thirty years earlier, 79 percent of the respondents said that as they advanced in their careers the amount of writing they did increased; 32 percent said it increased "greatly."

These conflicting results raise two questions. The first, obviously, is this: Why does one survey find no relationship between level in the organization and time spent writing, while three others find evidence that there is a relationship between the two variables? One possible explanation lies in the different methods used for gathering information. Rader and Wunsch asked their respondents to report their current behavior; then they grouped the responses according to the respondent's levels and compared the groups of data against one another. In contrast, Davis, Barnum and Fischer, and Spretnak asked their respondents to rely on memory, which may be an unreliable source for this sort of information.

The second question is: Why did 32 percent of the respondents in Davis's survey report that they have written less as they have advanced, while only one-tenth that amount (a mere 3 percent) of the respondents in the Barnum and Fischer survey reported writing less as they have advanced? One possible explanation of these results is presented in the next section.

YEARS OF WORK EXPERIENCE. Because it is possible that differences in the average number of years on the job may explain some of the conflicting results just mentioned, it would be desirable to know for certain if there is a relationship between years of job experience and amount of writing done at work. Unfortunately, the two studies that have investigated this relationship have provided conflicting results. In this case, both of the studies surveyed graduates of Miami University (Ohio), and both found statistically significant relationships—but in opposite directions. In his survey of 837 graduates from all departments in the School of Business Administration at Miami University (Ohio), Storms (1983) found that as years on the job increase, time spent writing decreases, at least to a point. Respondents with more than five years of job experience write significantly less than do graduates with five years experience or less. (With respect to the time spent writing, he found no significant difference between respondents with six to twenty years of experience and those with more than twenty years.) In contrast, as reported above, in my study of the 841 graduates of seven science, applied science, and service departments at Miami University (Ohio), I found that as years on the job increase, so does time spent writing:

respondents with more than three years on the job write significantly *more* often than do graduates with three years or less. One possible explanation of this conflict is that the two groups represented in the two surveys may differ substantially in terms of the way the amount of writing they do changes as they gain additional years of job experience. Another possibility is that, ironically, the conflicting results may arise from a difference in the average number of years of job experience in Storms's sample and mine: whereas the average number of years of job experience for Storms's sample was 15, 96 percent of my respondents had less than 15 years of job experience. Perhaps during the *early* years of a person's career the amount of time spent writing typically increases (as I found), but *later* in the person's career the amount of time spent writing typically decreases (as Storms found).

If there is such a relationship between years of job experience and time spent writing, it might help explain two of the sets of conflicting results mentioned earlier. First, Storms's (1983) study found no significant difference among graduates of various business departments in terms of time spent writing, whereas Rader and Wunsch's (1980) study did find a significant difference among majors in terms of that factor. The samples used in these two studies differed substantially with respect to the typical respondent's number of years of work experience: no respondent in the Rader and Wunsch survey had been on the job more than six years, whereas the *average* number of years of job experience for the respondents in Storms's sample was fifteen. Perhaps there are differences among majors that appear early in people's careers but disappear as people gain additional experience.

A possible relationship between time spent writing and years of job experience may also explain the conflicting results concerning the relationship between level in the organization and time spent writing. As mentioned earlier, Davis (1977) found that 32 percent of his respondents have written *less* as they have advanced, whereas only 3 percent of the respondents in the Barnum and Fischer (1984) survey have written less as they have advanced. Again, the samples used in these two surveys are very different from each another in terms of their average number of years of job experience: Barnum and Fischer's had *at most* fifteen years; Davis's had an *average* of thirty-three. Thus it is possible that very few of the respondents in the Barnum and Fischer study had yet had a chance to advance to the kinds of positions that presumably were held by many of Davis's prominent engineers—positions in which (perhaps) a substantial number of workers write less often than they did five, ten, or fifteen years earlier in their careers.

In any event, it appears that the relationship between time spent writing and number of years of job experience is worth further investigation.

5. *Research has yet to define the precise configuration of the factors that affect the total amount of time spent writing.* Assuming that all the studies mentioned earlier used truly representative samples and that they all produced valid, reliable results, there is no clear explanation for the conflicting results obtained concerning the relationships that time spent writing has with college major, amount of graduate education, level in the organization, or years of work experience. Further, it is certainly possible that some of the major factors that affect the amount of time workers spend writing have not yet been investigated by any survey. It seems possible, for instance, that the amount of time a person spends writing is partly determined by the amount of pleasure the person finds in writing. That possibility gains some plausibility from a finding in my survey (reported earlier) that workers appear to be able to "volunteer" for at least some of the writing they do (or don't do): the 841 graduates of the science, applied science, and service departments at Miami University (Ohio) who responded to my survey write about as much on their own initiative as they do at someone else's request.

It is also possible that the amount of time that college-educated workers spend writing is determined in part by the colleges the workers attended. That could be the case if some colleges typically send graduates to jobs or employers that require a great deal of writing and others send their graduates to jobs or employers that require less writing. The possibility of a relationship between college attended and time spent writing on the job gains some plausibility from the observation that graduates of the School of Business Administration at Miami University (Ohio) spend 50 percent more of their time at work writing than do graduates of the School of Business Administration at Arizona State University; these results are from the studies by Storms (1983), who found that Miami graduates spend an average of 25 percent of their time at work writing, and by Rader and Wunsch (1980), who found that Arizona State graduates spend an average of 16 percent of their time at work writing.

FINAL REMARKS: Any discussion of time spent writing needs to include a few general observations about the results obtained on this matter through surveys. First, although the "average" is the statistic usually reported to describe a typical response, it may not be the best statistic to use. The average can be changed noticeably by only a few responses that are extremely far above or below the "average." In contrast, the median (the number above and below which 50 percent of the responses fall) is not susceptible to extreme values and may therefore be a better descriptive statistic to use. In their survey of 200 college-educated workers in a cross-section of job categories, Faigley et al. (1981) found that the average time spent writing was 23 percent whereas the median was only 17 percent.

Second, there may be a tendency for people to overestimate the time they spend in communication activities. In a study involving 232 supervisory and technical employees (primarily chemists and chemical engineers) in a large research and development organization, Hinrichs (1964) found that his respondents, who were from a variety of levels in the organization, provided estimates of their time spent writing that exceeded by 2 percent to 7 percent the time they were found to be writing when a systematic auditing technique was used. Similarly, in Klemmer and Snyder's (1972) study of the communication practices of a large research and development center, 2,626 employees in a wide variety of jobs (e.g., clerks, technicians, engineers) reported spending 22 percent of their time writing, but were observed to be writing only 14 percent of their time. A tendency to overestimate may account for the surprising results that some studies have produced when inquiring about the time respondents spend communicating. As mentioned earlier, in a study by Persing, Drew, Bachman, Eaton, and Galbraith (1976) 49 workers who had taken a business communication course while undergraduates said they spend an average of 13 percent of their time in communication activities. Similarly, in Weinrauch and Swanda's (1975) study of businesspersons in the South Bend, Indiana, area, the 46 respondents reported spending an *average* of 10.9 *working* hours *per day* in various forms of direct and indirect communication (including oral communication).

The question of a possible tendency toward overestimation is related to a third point: it isn't clear how the respondents to survey questions define the term *writing* (an observation made by Faigley et al., 1981). For example, a scientist might define writing as the act of putting words on paper—a definition that contradicts the one currently held by most scholars of composing, who would include as writing such activities as figuring out what to say, analyzing the audience, and so on. On the other hand, if the scientist considers writing to be everything he or she does (including laboratory research) that relates to the reports he or she prepares, then there is scarcely any part of the scientist's work that isn't writing, and the question, "What percentage of your time at work do you spend writing?" becomes meaningless.

Differences in the definition of writing may account for the differences, mentioned earlier, that Hinrichs (1964) and Klemmer and Snyder (1972) found between the amount of time their respondents *said* they spend writing and the amount of time they were *observed* to be writing. Whereas the observers may have counted only the time the respondents were engaged in a physical activity associated with writing (e.g., holding a pencil), the respondents may have counted the time they spent planning without pencil in hand or, perhaps, the time they spent gathering necessary information from their files.

It is clear from all the surveys that have inquired about the matter that writing (however that term is defined) consumes a substantial part of the time at work of the typical college-educated worker.

Importance of Writing

1. *Writing is one of the most important job-related skills for most college graduates.* Storms (1983) asked 837 business graduates of Miami University (Ohio) how important the ability to write well would be to someone who wanted to perform the respondent's present jobs; respondents were asked to check the appropriate response on a five-point scale: unimportant, not very important, important, very important, and critically important. Seventy-four percent replied that the ability to write well would be at least "very important," and 30 percent said that it would be "critically important." These results are typical of those obtained by other researchers who have asked similar questions: Barnum and Fischer (1984), Bataille (1982), Davis (1977), Flatley (1982), and my own study (described earlier).

Some perspective on the importance of writing can be gained from studies that have compared its importance with that of other job-related skills. They show that writing is one of the most important skills for college-educated workers to have. For example, Simonds (1960) asked 133 upper-level managers to tell how often they use the specific knowledge provided by each of 62 college courses. About 80 percent of the respondents put skill in business writing at the top of their list. Similarly, in a survey by Traweek (reported in Penrose, 1976), business administration alumni who graduated from the University of Texas between 1917 and 1954 rated business writing as the second most important course they had taken, placing it behind accounting, with English rated third. Likewise, when the American Society for Engineering Education asked 4,057 engineers to identify subjects needed for professional careers in industry, more respondents named technical writing than named any other subject except management practices (reported in Middendorf, 1980).

In two other surveys, the respondents placed writing somewhat lower on lists of important job-related skills. Penrose (1976) sent a survey questionnaire to every tenth business listed in the yellow pages of the Austin, Texas, telephone book, asking them to rate each of twelve business-related abilities on a seven-point scale (from "very valuable" to "not valuable"). The 157 respondents gave business writing their sixth-highest rating. Even so, writing received a very high rating: 2.32 on the seven-point scale; public relations, the ability rated highest, received 1.84. Furthermore, the respondents with college degrees (about 55 percent) gave business writing a higher rating, placing it third, in a tie with accounting and behind public relations and marketing. Similarly, Elfert asked 166 engineering graduates of McNeese State University (Louisiana) to rate nine courses in terms of the courses' contribution to their professional development. The respondents gave technical writing the eighth-highest rating, behind all the other courses listed except chemistry. The seven courses rated higher were all technical: calculus, engineering economics, fluid mechanics, physics, statics, thermodynamics, and engineering graphics. Nevertheless, 51 percent of Elfert's respondents rated technical writing as making an "above average" contribution to their professional development, which was relatively close to the proportion (64 percent) who gave above-average ratings to the highest-rated course, calculus. (Neither Penrose nor Elfert performed the inferential statistical procedures required to determine whether the differences they found were significant.)

Other evidence that writing is an important skill in the workplace was discovered in a survey of 1,139 corporate academic leaders by the Accreditation Research Committee of the American Assembly of Collegiate Schools of Business (1980). The committee asked these respondents to indicate the amount of time they would devote (if they were deans of schools of business) to each of thirteen major knowledge areas. Written communication was not one of the major knowledge areas listed on the survey. However, it was mentioned more often than any other area in the place on the questionnaire form where respondents could name knowledge areas that should be included in business curricula but were not mentioned in the researchers' list.

As these studies indicate, whether or not writing is *the* most important job-related skill, it certainly is one of the most important.

2. *Writing ability appears to affect a worker's prospects for advancement.* In an attempt to assess the importance of writing, several researchers have tried to ascertain the extent to which a person's writing ability affects his or her chances for advancement. All reach the same conclusion: it does. For example, in Davis's (1977) survey of 245 people listed in *Engineers of Distinction*, 96 percent of the respondents said that the ability to communicate on paper had "helped" their own advancement, and 89 percent reported that the ability to write is usually an "important" or "critical" consideration when someone is being evaluated for advancement.

Similar results were obtained in two other studies that posed similar questions to people presumably in technical fields: Spretnak's (1982) survey of 595 people who graduated during the past thirty years from the College of Engineering at Berkeley, and Barnum and Fischer's (1984) survey of 305 people who had graduated during the past fifteen years from Southern Technical Institute (mostly with bachelor's degrees in engineering technology). Finally, in their survey of 181 people who had earned associate degrees at Cincinnati Technical College, Glenn and Green (1979) asked whether it was necessary to know how to write each of three kinds of communications in order to advance or be promoted. Sixty-one percent said it was necessary to know "how to write about processes." Much smaller percentages said it was necessary to know how to write business letters and informal reports.

Most of the surveys described in the preceding paragraph involve people in technical fields. Researchers surveying people in business fields have also found that writing can affect advancement. For example, in Storms's (1983) survey of 837 graduates of the School of Business Administration at Miami University (Ohio), 88 percent of the respondents indicated that the ability to write well has at least "some effect" on advancement. Fifty-four percent said it has at least a "great effect," and 14 percent said it is essential to advancement. Similar testimony concerning the relationship of writing ability to advancement is found in the following surveys concerning people working in business fields: Belohlov, Popp, and Porte (1974); Cox (1976); Hetherington (1982); Stine and Skarzenski (1979); and Van Dyck (1980).

3. *The importance of writing may be related to college major, years of work experience, and level in the organization.* Three of the five factors that have been studied in relation to the amount of time spent writing have also been studied in relation to the importance of writing: college major, years of work experience, and level in the organization. (No one has investigated the relationship of the importance of writing to job category or to amount of graduate education.) The results are as follows.

COLLEGE MAJOR. Conflicting results have been obtained by the two surveys that investigated the relationship between college major and importance of writing. In terms of their responses to the question, "How important would the ability to write well be to someone who wanted to perform your present job?" Storms (1983) found no significant difference among the alumni of seven business departments at Miami University (Ohio). Nor did he find a significant difference among the six departments in terms of their responses to this question: "What effect does the ability to write well have on advancement in your organization?" In contrast, in my survey (reported earlier) of 841 graduates of seven departments in science, applied science, and service professions at Miami University (Ohio), I found that graduates of various departments differed significantly in their answer to the question about the importance of writing to someone who wanted to perform the respondent's job. I asked no question comparable to Storms's question about advancement.

One possible explanation for the conflicting results obtained by Storms's survey and mine is that a real difference exists: perhaps college major is not significantly related to the relative importance of writing for graduates of business departments, but is related for graduates of the departments I surveyed.

YEARS OF WORK EXPERIENCE. Storms and I also obtained conflicting results in our analyses of the relationship between years of work experience and the importance of writing. In this case, however, Storms found the significant difference and I found none. He was comparing business graduates with six years or less of job experience against those with more experience, whereas I was comparing science, applied science, and service graduates with three years or less against those with more.

LEVEL IN THE ORGANIZATION. No one has conducted a survey in which inferential statistics were used to compare people at various levels within an organization in terms of the importance they attribute to writing. There is, however, some evidence that people at higher levels in an organization attribute more importance to writing than do people at lower levels. Flatley (1982) asked 89 managers who work at three levels in various private companies in the San Diego area to indicate how important they consider written communication to be as a management tool. Sixty-three percent of the upper-level managers said it was "extremely" important, whereas only 39 percent of the middle-level managers and 44 percent of the lower-level managers said that it was. This difference among levels may be explained by some results obtained by Cox (1976) in a survey of 150 people who had earned an A or a B in his business communication class over the preceding fifteen years. When Cox asked these respondents whether a person's need for writing ability increases as he or she is promoted, 89 percent said it does.

4. *As important as writing ability is, it seems to be less important than ability in oral communication.* When writing is compared with oral communication, oral communication is almost always rated as more important. For instance, when Rader and Wunsch (1980) asked 93 business graduates from Arizona State University how important the ability to communicate *in writing* is to their jobs, 62 percent gave it the highest rating ("very important"), and only 4 percent said it was not important. Schiff (1980) obtained similar results when he asked 367 alumni of seven engineering departments at Michigan Technological University to rate thirty skills in written and oral communication. On a seven-point scale (from "not important" to "critically important"), Schiff's respondents gave an average rating

of 4.75 to all the oral communication skills listed and only 4.33 to all the writing skills listed.

In comparison, 90 percent of the respondents rated the ability to communicate *orally* as "very important," and only 1 percent said it was not important. In a survey of 45 executives from *Fortune 500* firms, Swenson (1980) gathered information about the relative importance of eighteen *specific* writing and speaking skills. At the top of a ranked list are two oral communication skills (face-to-face communication within the firm and small-group communication within the firm). Next on the list are the ability to write each of the following forms of communication: memos, short reports, letters, final reports, proposals, and progress reports. These writing skills received higher ratings than any of the remaining oral communication skills, which included speaking to large groups within the organization and speaking with individuals and groups outside the organization.

Similarly, in a survey involving presidents of 51 of the 100 largest corporations in the United States, Lull, Funk, and Piersol (1955) asked whether oral communication was more important or less important than written communication. Ninety-eight percent of the presidents said oral communication was at least as important, and 40 percent said it was even more important. Further, Lull, Funk, and Piersol presented the respondents with a list of five alternative methods of communication and asked the respondents to place a check by the two that would be most likely to get the best results if "very important policy" is to be transmitted. The presidents preferred calling a meeting (44 checks) and holding personal interviews with key personnel (27 checks) to the two forms of written communication included in the list: announcing policy in a management bulletin (16 checks) and explaining the policy in an interoffice memo (14 checks). In a survey involving 84 large organizations in the private sector, Belohlov, Popp, and Porte (1974) asked the respondents what percentage of the time in a graduate-level business communication course should be devoted to each of three forms of communication. The respondents would devote an average of 34 percent of the time to written communication and 36 percent to oral communication; the respondents would devote the remaining time (30 percent) to "nonverbal" communication.

Another indication of the relative importance of writing and speaking abilities is the contribution each makes to the promotions and raises a person recevies. In Hetherington's (1982) survey of employers in business, industry, and the professions in three counties surrounding Charleston, South Carolina, 51 percent of the respondents said that in their organizations promotions or raises have resulted, at least in part, from skill in speaking. In contrast, only 41 percent said that promotions or raises have resulted from skill in writing.

In contrast to the several studies that indicate that skill in oral communication is more important than skill in written communication, three surveys seem to indicate that the opposite is true. These three surveys may not be comparable to the others, however, because two of the three—and perhaps the third as well—asked specifically about "public speaking," not the more general category of oral communication. Consequently, in answering questions, the respondents may have left out of account some of the other speaking skills that Swenson found to be important for at least some groups of workers. In the first of these three studies, Steinbruegee, Hailstones, and Roberts (1955) asked personnel officers in 70 manufacturing firms in the Cincinnati, Ohio, area to rate twenty-one subjects in terms of their importance to college programs. The respondents gave the highest rating to a subject called "English, Grammar, Literature, and Composition" and the third-highest rating to business letter writing. Public speaking received the fourth-highest rating. Similarly, when Benson (1983) asked personnel managers for 59 large employers in Wyoming to rate twenty-two courses in terms of their value in preparing students for positions in management and administration, the respondents gave the highest rating to written communication and the fourth-highest rating to public speaking. Interestingly, in another part of his survey, Benson asked the respondents to rate twenty-four factors and skills in terms of their importance in helping business graduates obtain employment. In this list he included "oral communication skills" (instead of "public speaking"); the respondents rated oral communication skills highest of all twenty-two, including written communication, to which they gave the second-highest rating. Perhaps the respondents believed that oral communication skills are more important for obtaining a job than for earning a promotion, or perhaps they distinguished between the importance of what they think is taught in a public speaking course and the oral communication skills they believe to be most important on the job.

The third survey in which the respondents seem to indicate that writing ability is more important than speaking ability is Spretnak's

(1982) survey of 595 engineering graduates of the University of California at Berkeley. Seventy-three percent of the respondents indicated that their writing skills had aided their advancement, and only 60 percent indicated that their "speaking" skills had helped. But, like the question by Steinbruegee et al. and the first of the two questions by Benson, Spretnak's question may also have asked specifically about "public speaking," not about the full range of oral communication skills used on the job (Spretnak's report is not clear about the wording of her question).

In sum, survey research shows that although writing is not the only ability that is very important in the workplace, it certainly is one of the most important—at least for people with college degrees in business, science, technical, and service fields.

Composing Processes

In a few studies, researchers have asked respondents about the methods and procedures they use when writing at work and about the conditions under which they write. Although the results of these studies present only a sketchy account of composing on the job, they indicate that the survey can be a useful tool in investigating those aspects of the writing process about which people can report accurately. (On the other hand, the survey will not be useful in studying the details of the cognition of writing at work; for a discussion of this limitation of surveys, see chapter 13.)

1. *Workers devote a substantial effort to each of these three stages of the composing process: planning, drafting, and revising.* Four surveys have asked questions about the processes by which people write at work. Two of these studies provide insights into the *overall* composing process of some workers. In the most detailed study of composing processes, Roundy and Mair (1982) asked a series of open-ended questions addressed to a sample of 70 people that included 30 workers, 30 students, and 10 students who were working part time in industry.[6] All 70 of the respondents reported engaging in all three of the kinds of writing activities identified by Rohman (1965): *prewriting* (which includes "inventing" and "organizing"), *writing* (or "drafting"), and *rewriting* (or "revising"). Some information about the relative amount of time that workers devote to each of these stages is provided by Paradis, Dobrin, and Bower (1984, personal correspondence) through their survey of 265 professional employees at twenty research and development organizations (the

respondents worked for twenty organizations that responded to a published invitation to participate in a study of writing practices: see Lampe, 1982). These respondents reported spending 22 percent of their time organizing (planning), 42 percent of their time drafting, 21 percent of their time revising. The respondents devote the remaining 15 percent of their time to a fourth category listed by the researchers: procrastination.

Both the survey by Paradis et al. and that by Roundy and Mair indicate that many different composing processes are used at work. Through a closed-ended question, Paradis et al. found that when writing to communicate a decision, 34 percent of their respondents make the decision, then write it out; 39 percent make a firm decision, then work out the details as they write; 19 percent rework, improve, or change the decision as they write; and 6 percent begin with a general feeling about what they are going to say, but make the decision as they write. Through their open-ended questions, Roundy and Mair discovered that their respondents adjust their composing processes to the task at hand. When the respondents are preparing documents longer than ten pages, they spend substantially more time prewriting and revising than they do when composing shorter documents. Also, when preparing longer documents they are more likely to treat prewriting and revising separately from writing (rather than prewriting and revising simultaneously with their actual writing activities.)

Concerning prewriting activities specifically, Roundy and Mair report that all 70 of their respondents use outlines, at least for longer documents, and that none "invented"—that is, none searched for or created new knowledge when writing. (This finding is somewhat at odds with another finding: the researchers say that 67 of their 70 respondents indicated that while writing they frequently discover and add information they had not intended to use and perhaps had not fully articulated to themselves.)

Some additional insight into the prewriting activities of workers is gained through studies by Aldrich (1982a and b) and by Glenn and Green (1979). Aldrich asked 165 top-level and middle-level managers in several government agencies and private think tanks to indicate the order in which they perform eight tasks associated with pre-writing, including such things as "define purpose" and "research the subject." Overall, the respondents had no single, preferred order: from respondent to respondent, the orders differ considerably—most being at odds with the order Aldrich believes to be best.

In their survey of 181 people who earned associate degrees from Cincinnati Technical College, Glenn and Green (1979) asked two questions about prewriting, both concerned with audience analysis. Their first question was, "When planning a written communication, do you try to identify your audience as individuals or do you write to a general audience?" Sixty-eight percent of the respondents said they identify specific individuals, and 26 percent said they write to a general audience. Nine percent indicated they do not consider audience when planning a written communication. Glenn and Green obtained almost identical results in response to their second question about prewriting: "When planning the structure of a communication, do you design the structure and content to fit the needs of specific individuals or do you write to a general audience?" Sixty-five percent of the respondents replied that they design for individuals, 28 percent that they design for a general audience, and 7 percent that they do not consider audience when they design their communications.

Concerning revising activities, Roundy and Mair found that all 70 of their respondents engage in such activities as adding, rearranging, substituting, and deleting material, both during and after drafting. In addition, all 70 respondents reported that they examine their drafts for "logical progression."

2. *The amount of time workers spend writing each page is often substantial, but varies considerably.* In a study involving 122 professional and managerial personnel in a midwestern power company, Kelton (1984) collected reports that his respondents had prepared as part of their normal duties and he also asked the respondents to tell him how long they spent writing the reports. For these reports, which averaged 9.2 pages, the respondents reported spending an average of 3 hours per page—but the range was astonishingly large: from 1 to 79 hours per page. In another analysis of his data, Kelton found that the average number of hours per page spent on reports *without* appendixes was 3.5, whereas the average number for reports *with* appendixes was only 1.6. Although Kelton does not speculate on the causes of this difference, it is possible that the appendixes are sometimes photocopies of documents already written, so that these appendixes increase the length of the document without requiring any additional writing time.

3. *Workers differ in terms of the times and places they use for writing.* In a survey of 46 businesspersons, primarily managers, in the South Bend, Indiana, area, Weinrauch and Swanda (1975) found that their respondents spend more time writing in the afternoon than in

the morning. In contrast, in their survey of 265 employees in research and development organizations, Paradis et al. (personal correspondence, 1984) found that 41 percent of their respondents do most of their writing between 9:00 A.M. and noon, and another 14 percent do most of theirs before 9:00 A.M. Interestingly, 10 percent do most of their writing after 5:00 P.M., 3 percent between 9:00 P.M. and midnight. Overall, the respondents to the survey by Paradis et al. complete 80 percent of their writing during normal working hours, and the remaining 20 percent at home or working late.

Paradis et al. also asked their respondents to identify the conditions they find most conducive to writing. Seventy-five percent named "at work, in total seclusion"; 15 percent named "at work, in close proximity to others"; and 16 percent named "at home." When asked to identify "writing inhibitors," 63 percent named interruptions, 50 percent named getting started, and 29 percent named insufficient time; 16 percent named trouble organizing, and 16 percent named "multiple rewrites" (each respondent could indicate more than one inhibitor).

4. *Many workers collaborate when they write.* There are many ways that workers can collaborate when they write—ranging all the way from working as a co-author with others to delegating their writing tasks to others. Some surveys have inquired about *collaboration* in general (without specifying any particular meaning for the term), and others have asked about particular collaborative activities.

One of the studies to ask about collaboration in general is Paradis et al.'s survey of 265 professional persons in twenty research and development organizations. These respondents said that, on average, 19 percent of their writing is collaborative. In their survey of 200 college-educated workers in a cross-section of job categories, Faigley et al. (1981) also asked their respondents to tell what percentage of the writing they do on the job is prepared in collaboration with one or more other persons. Only 27 percent of the respondents reported that they never collaborate. The average percentage of their writing that is collaborative is 25 percent. Faigley et al. indicated, however, that this average is misleadingly high because a relatively small proportion of the respondents write collaboratively almost all the time; the median is 10 percent.

In a survey of approximately 250 graduates of Christopher Newport College, Harwood (1982) asked specifically about the sort of collaboration that involves critiquing drafts. Ten percent of his respondents reported that in the previous two weeks they had asked people to critique their drafts, and 60 percent indicated that in the previous two weeks they had been asked to critique drafts prepared by others. Similarly, in a survey of 595 engineering graduates of the University of California at Berkeley, Spretnak (1982) found that, on the average, the respondents spend 11 percent of their time supervising the writing of others. (Spretnak also found that 5 percent of her respondents work regularly with technical editors.) In Davis's (1977) survey of 245 people listed in *Engineers of Distinction*, the respondents reported that they spend an average of 30 percent of their time "working with the writing of others." Perhaps Davis's respondents spend so much more time than do Spretnak's in working with the writing of others because, first, more of Davis's respondents (who are prominent engineers) have risen to high-level positions; they must assume greater responsibility for the writing of others. But that explanation is merely speculative.

Another form of collaboration occurs when one person directs another to do his or her writing. Outside academe, some writers have the opportunity to delegate their written work in this way, often to a secretary or administrative assistant. In her survey of 89 managers at three levels in the San Diego area, Flatley (1982) found that 18 percent delegate between 31 percent and 70 percent of their routine composition tasks, and another 18 percent delegate 71 percent or more of their routine tasks. Further, 73 percent of the managers indicated that they *would delegate* over 70 percent of their routine composition tasks if they had a competent person to write this material once they had explained its general nature to the person.

5. *Many college-educated workers compose with word processors.* Two surveys have inquired about the use of word processors. In their survey of 200 college-educated workers in a cross-section of job categories, Faigley et al. (1981) found that just over a quarter (26 percent) compose on a computer or use a computer for word processing. Of the respondents who use computers, 47 percent reported that they do so frequently. Similarly, in their survey of 265 professional workers in research and development organizations, Paradis et al. (personal correspondence, 1984) found that 26 percent of their respondents use word processors regularly, and another 19 percent use them sometimes. Of the respondents who use word processors, 93 percent use them at work and 23 percent use them at home.

Investigating the uses of word processing among three levels of managers in private companies in San Diego, Flatley (1982) discovered that this equipment is used more widely at lower levels: 42 percent of the lower-level managers use a word processor or terminal, whereas only 21 percent of the middle-level managers and 19 percent of the upper-level managers do. Interestingly, about 70 percent of both the lower-level and the upper-level managers predicted that they would be using this method of composing five years after the date of Flatley's study.

Paradis et al. (personal correspondence, 1984), asked their respondents about the *way* they use word processing. Of the respondents who use this equipment, 10 percent use it only for final editing and formatting, 28 percent use it for revising after a workable first draft is written out and then entered into the word processor, and 53 percent use word processing for all aspects of writing, from drafting to preparing the final version. Through another set of closed-ended questions, Paradis et al. learned about the ways word processing affects the writing of their respondents: 72 percent indicated that it "greatly" increases the speed with which they produce documents, 46 percent said that it "greatly" improves the accuracy of spelling and punctuation, and 42 percent said that it "greatly" improves organization.

6. *Many workers dictate.* Several studies have shown that a considerable number of workers, though far from a majority, dictate when they compose. In Faigley et al.'s (1981) survey of 200 college-educated workers in a cross-section of job categories, 26 percent of the respondents said that they dictate. So do a much larger proportion (47 percent) of the 837 business graduates of Miami University (Ohio) who were surveyed by Storms (1983); those who use dictation equipment reported that they dictate an average of 41 percent of their written work. Treece's (1972) survey of 565 certified professional secretaries found that even 16 percent of them regularly dictate material to be transcribed by other people.

Some comparative analyses conducted by Storms indicate that there is no significant difference among the six business departments included in his survey either in terms of the percentage of respondents who dictate or in terms of the percentage of their work that they dictate. He did, however, find a statistically significant relationship between amount of dictation and amount of job experience: whereas about 54 percent of the respondents with more than six years on the job use dictation, only 30 percent of those with six or fewer years on the job do so. Furthermore, those respondents who dictate and who have more than twenty years of experience use dictation for a significantly greater portion of their writing (48 percent) than do either those with six to twenty years experience (36.9 percent) or those with less than six years of experience (36 percent).

Flatley (1982) found a much lower incidence of dictation, but a similar pattern. Of the 87 managers in private business in the San Diego area who responded to her survey, 30 percent of the upper-level managers dictate, whereas only 8.3 percent of the middle-level managers and none of the low-level managers do so.

7. *Some workers often write under pressure of deadlines.* In her survey of 595 graduates of the College of Engineering at the University of California at Berkeley, Spretnak (1982) found that 62 percent of the respondents usually or always write under the pressure of deadlines.

Writing Skills Needed

Several studies have asked what writing skills are needed at work. In the following discussion of the results, I distinguish between *general* writing skills, which might be applied to any form of written communication, and skills in creating *specific* forms of communication (such as the memorandum or the article for publication).

1. *At work, workers need to have the skills required to: write clearly, write concisely, organize well, write grammatically, and spell correctly.* When asking respondents what writing skills workers need to possess, most survey researchers have relied only on closed-ended questions. Consequently, it is difficult to generalize broadly from the results of the surveys except where more than one of them include similar skills in the lists they present to respondents.

Three of the surveys have included several of the same skills in their closed-ended lists, although each of the lists also contains several unique items. Further, with respect to the relative importance of five *general* writing skills, the results of these three surveys are in striking agreement, as table 1-2 indicates.

The conclusion that these five general writing skills are very important to workers is supported by the results of questions that ask respondents to recommend topics for college writing courses. At the

Table 1-2
Ranking of General Writing Skills Needed at Work[a]

	Stine and Skarzenski (1979) 13 General Writing Skills Listed	Storms (1983) 11 General Writing Skills Listed	Barnum and Fischer (1984) 5 General Writing Skills Listed
Clarity	1	1	NL[b]
Conciseness	2	4	NL[b]
Organization	3	3	1
Grammar	4	(5)	3
Spelling	5	(5)	2

[a]Excluding skills in preparing specific types of communication.
[b]NL = Not Listed

top of the resulting lists are four of these same items, usually in the same order: clarity, conciseness, organization, and grammar. (These results are reported in detail in the section on "Workers' Attitudes and Beliefs Concerning Education about Writing.")

There is also evidence that certain other general writing skills are also important on the job. For instance, in Storms's survey of 837 graduates of the School of Business Administration at Miami University (Ohio), the respondents gave the second highest ranking to "clearly stating your purpose to the reader," a skill not inquired about in the other surveys. Also, in a survey of 181 people who earned associate degrees from Cincinnati Technical College, Green and Nolan (1984) found that 79 percent of their respondents or their respondents' supervisors use graphic and visual aids, such as drawings, schematics, and tables. Finally, in a study by Angrist (1953), 273 managers in fifteen companies identified the following four items (out of a list of fifteen) as having "high value":

- "Write my own communications (notices, letters, speeches, etc.)." (These respondents seem to find it easier to have someone else do their writing; see the discussion of collaboration earlier.)
- "Use my own individual style, language and phrasing in my writing instead of some standardized, uniform business style ('businessese')."
- "Avoid using pat phrases, trite ways of saying things, in my written communications."

- "Write the same message in different ways to fit the education, position, attitudes or point of view of the different persons who will receive it."

These results by Storms, Green and Nolan, and Angrist point out one problem that arises when researchers rely solely on closed-ended questions to inquire about such things as the writing skills used on the job: the lists include only the items that the researcher has already decided are important enough to list. Consequently, some items that the respondents think very important will escape notice until (and if) some other researcher thinks to include them in another study.

Interestingly, in a survey by Bataille (1982) that did use an open-ended question, about 180 graduates of Iowa State University mentioned *clarity* and *conciseness* as the qualities their writing most needed to exhibit; the third quality they mentioned frequently was *precision*. Bataille observes that there seems to be a relationship between the nature of the audience addressed and the specific qualities that respondents cited as being most important. Respondents whose most important writing was intended for superiors (who, presumably, have little time to read) seem to place conciseness first; those whose most important writing goes to readers outside the respondent's organization seem to place clarity first; and those who often write to hostile audiences (for instance, when answering employee grievances) often mentioned precision.

2. *Also important to workers are the skills used to write various specific kinds of communications, especially memos, letters, and reports.* The respondents to three surveys indicate that the skills needed to write memos, letters, and reports are more important than those needed to write any of the other kinds of communications listed by the researchers. However, the three studies disagree about which of these three skills is most important. In Stine and Skarzenski's (1979) survey of 83 executives of companies with offices in Iowa, the respondents ranked the three forms this way: letters, memos, reports. In Andrews and Sigband's (1984) survey of managing partners in 38 of the largest CPA firms in the United States, the respondents ranked the forms this way: memos, reports, letters. And in Swenson's (1980) survey of 45 business executives from *Fortune 500* firms, the respondents ranked the forms this way: memos, letters, reports. Not surprisingly, these three forms are the same ones that workers identify as the forms they most often write at work (see the discussion later of the kinds of communications written at work).

In a survey of 50 executives from firms listed in the *Thomas Directory of American Manufacturers*, Rainey (1972) distinguished between the skills needed to write "routine" communications and those required to write "persuasive" ones. The skills needed to write persuasive letters were rated highest of the seven items in his list, followed by the skills needed to write proposals submitted within the company and by those needed to write proposals submitted outside the company.

It may be that at work certain general writing skills are perceived to be more important than the skills required to write *any* of the specific forms of communication. For example, Stine and Skarzenki's (1979) list of skills included both kinds of skills. The business executives who responded ranked skills in clarity, conciseness, and organization ahead of those required to write letters or any of the other forms. The precedence of general writing skills probably should not surprise us because those skills can be applied when writing any form of communication. On the other hand, the respondents to Stine and Skarzenski's survey rated letter-writing skills higher than skills in grammar, spelling, and word choice. Similarly, in Barnum and Fischer's (1984) survey of 305 graduates of Southern Technical Institute, the respondents ranked the skills in using report formats behind organization, but ahead of skills in sentence structure, spelling, and punctuation.

Audiences Addressed

Only four studies have inquired about *audience*, a key element in the workers' rhetorical situation. Nevertheless, from these four studies, an important generalization can be derived.

1. *At work, writers typically must address a variety of kinds of readers, not just one or two kinds.* The readers addressed at work may be classified in several ways. Readers *within* the workers' organization may be classified according to the readers' level in the organization: above the workers' level, at the same level as the workers, and below the workers' level. In my survey (described earlier) of 841 graduates of departments in science, applied science, and service fields at Miami University (Ohio), 70 percent of the respondents reported that they write to readers at all three levels "sometimes," "often," or "always" (i.e., more often than "rarely" or

"never"). Kelton (1984) obtained similar results in his survey of 122 managers and professional persons in a large midwestern power company. Kelton asked each of these respondents to supply him with a report the respondent had written and also to indicate (among other things) the number of people who had received the report and the level in the organization of those recipients. Kelton found that the reports had an average of 28.6 readers: 10 (35 percent) above the respondent's level, 11 (38 percent) at the respondent's level, and 7.6 (27 percent) below the respondent's level.

Another way to classify readers is according to the use they will make of a document. Respondents to the survey by Kelton indicated that, for the average report, 3.7 readers (11 percent) would decide whether to approve or reject the report, 2.5 readers (8 percent) would transmit it to someone else, 14.6 readers (50 percent) would take action based upon the report, and 9.5 readers (31 percent) would merely read and file it.

Still another way to classify readers is according to their level of knowledge of the writer's specialty. Sixty percent of the respondents to my survey (reported earlier) indicated that they "sometimes," "often" or "always" address readers with all four of the following levels of knowledge: more knowledge than the respondent about the respondent's specialty, about the same knowledge, less knowledge, and no knowledge about the respondent's specialty. Similarly, in response to a survey by Stine and Skarzenski (1979), 83 executives of businesses with offices in Iowa indicated that their workers write a considerable percentage of the time to each of these two, much different audiences: expert (41 percent of the time) and nonexpert (58 percent). Also, in Bataille's (1982) survey of 180 graduates of Iowa State University, the respondents indicated that they often write both to readers inside their area of expertise and to readers outside their area of expertise.

Finally, readers can be classified according to their location inside or outside the respondent's organization. In their study of 200 college-educated workers in a cross-section of job categories, Faigley et al. (1981) found that their respondents regularly address both internal and external readers. To readers *inside* the organization, the respondents write medians of 2.9 letters and memos per week and 2.4 reports per week; to readers *outside*, they write medians of 5.2 letters (no memos) per week and 0.4 reports per week. In their survey of 181 people who earned associate degrees from Cincinnati Technical

College, Glenn and Green (1979) asked specifically about the communications the respondents write for the purpose of requesting information. Eighty percent of the respondents said that either they or their supervisors write *outside* the company for information, and 68 percent said that they or their supervisors write *inside* the organization for information.

Unlike Faigley et al. and Glenn and Green, I found (in the survey reported earlier) a fairly sharp distinction between the amount of writing that workers send to readers outside the organization and the amount they send to readers inside. My respondents (graduates of departments in science, applied science, and service fields at Miami University, Ohio) write significantly more often to readers at each of the three levels within their organization (above them, at their level, below them) than they write to any of the following groups of outside readers: customers, vendors (who sell products to the respondents' organizations), legislators and other government officials, and the general public. Of the four groups of outside readers, the group most often addressed is customers.

One result of a study by Angrist (1953) provides an interesting comment on the finding that workers must address a variety of kinds of readers. Angrist asked 273 people at all levels of management in fifteen companies to indicate the relative difficulty, value, and frequency of 110 communication activities, including 15 that pertained specifically to writing. The only writing activity that they rated as having both *high difficulty* and *high value* was "write the same message in different ways to fit the education, position, attitudes or point of view of the different persons who will receive it."

Kinds of Written Communications Prepared

The several studies that have inquired about the kinds of communications people write at work suggest the following four generalizations:

1. *At work, the typical worker prepares many different kinds of documents.* A precise discussion of how many types of documents workers typically prepare is not possible because there is no single way of classifying types. Thus what one investigator calls a single type (e.g., the memo) may be subdivided into different types by another investigator. Nevertheless, survey results do make clear that

most college-educated workers regularly use several different types of documents. In their survey of 200 workers in a cross-section of job categories, Faigley et al. (1981) found that their respondents write an average of 8.5 *different types* of letters, memos, and reports per week. Similarly, Storms (1983) found that more than 50 percent of his sample of business graduates from Miami University (Ohio) write seven different types of communications at least "sometimes" (more often than "rarely" or "never")—and that is without letters and memos being classified into subcategories. Similarly, my study (described earlier) of graduates in science, applied science, and service departments at Miami University (Ohio) showed that more than 50 percent of my respondents write seven kinds of documents at least "sometimes," again without classifying letters and memos into subcategories.

2. *The most commonly written kinds of documents are letters and memos.* Almost all the surveys agree in finding that of the various forms written at work, the most frequently prepared is the letter or the memo: Barnum and Fischer (1984), Bataille (1982), Bennett (1971), Cox (1976), Faigley et al. (1981), Flatley (1982), Harwood (1982), Rader and Wunsch (1980), Stine and Skarzenski (1979), Storms (1983), Treece (1972), and my own study (described earlier). There are, however, some exceptions.

Two of these exceptions concern graduates of two-year colleges. In Walde's (1975) study of 112 people who had graduated with technical degrees from Eau Clair Community College about three to six years earlier, higher percentages of the graduates reported that they write daily or weekly reports (50 percent) and complete order forms and requisitions (50 percent) than reported writing either interoffice memoranda (24 percent) or business letters (15 percent). Likewise, in Skelton's (1977) survey of 257 graduates of three two-year programs in southeastern Michigan, a higher percentage of his respondents reported completing standardized forms than reported writing either memos or letters. According to Skelton's study, these standardized forms are used for a variety of purposes, such as providing progress reports, supplying data, and communicating suggestions on policy and procedures.

Two other exceptions concern graduates with bachelor's degrees. In one, Andrews and Koester (1979) surveyed two groups: 183 firms that employ certified public accountants and 157 recently graduated accounting majors. The results showed that recently graduated accounting majors spend a greater amount of time writing both numerical reports and nonnumerical reports than they spend writing either letters or memoranda. Similarly, in a survey of about 180 people who graduated from Iowa State University in six disciplines, Bataille (1982) found that sociology alumni write reports more often than they write either letters or memos.

In sum, the kinds of documents most commonly written in the workplace overall are letters and memos, although some groups of workers write one or two other forms more often.

3. *Other forms that many workers appear to write very often are short reports and instructions.* In several surveys, respondents have identified either short reports or instructions or both as forms that they write often: Barnum and Fischer (1984), Cox (1976), Faigley et al. (1981), Paradis et al. (personal correspondence, 1984), Stine and Skarzenski (1979), Storms (1983), Treece (1972) and my own study (described earlier). Some of the other forms that are identified in one or another study as being written regularly by many workers may be varieties of short reports: the status report (Faigley et al., 1981), the progress/status report (Stine and Skarzenski, 1979), and personnel-management and employee-relations reports (Faigley et al., 1981).

4. *Forms that, typically, are written very rarely include articles for professional journals, press releases, and advertising.* Studies that support this generalization are: Cox (1976), Paradis et al. (personal correspondence, 1984), Stine and Skarzenski (1979), Storms (1983), and my study (reported earlier). A puzzling exception is Erickson's (1975) survey of about 130 industrial companies in Wisconsin, Iowa, and Minnesota. These companies reported that technicians (graduates of two-year programs) spend an average of 11 percent of their time at work writing technical articles for publication, a finding that seems to be directly at odds with what all the other surveys would lead one to expect.

5. *The forms that workers typically write may be related to several factors, including college major, job category, and level in the organization.* The relevant survey results are as follows.

LEVEL IN THE ORGANIZATION. Flatley's (1982) survey of 89 managers at three levels in private companies in the San Diego area suggests that people at different levels in an organization may rely on different forms of written communication. For example, both high-level and middle-level managers use memoranda more than they use letters, reports, or preprinted forms. In fact, more than 50 percent of the high-level managers and more than 45 percent of the middle-level managers reported using memoranda 41 percent or more of the time they write at work. In contrast, only 14 percent of the lower-level managers use memoranda 41 percent or more of the time; in fact, they use memoranda less than any of the other forms named by Flatley (letters, reports, forms).

Flatley discovered other differences with respect to the types of memoranda, letters, and reports the respondents write. For example, all three levels write "informational" memoranda more often than they write either "persuasive" memoranda or "directive/policy statement" memoranda; in comparison with lower-level managers, however, middle-level and upper-level managers write "persuasive" and "informational" memoranda more often and "directive/policy statement" memoranda less often. Differences of these kinds may be related in some way to the differing responsibilities of managers at different levels.

COLLEGE MAJOR. The studies by Storms (1983) and me (reported earlier) indicate that although graduates of various departments of Miami University (Ohio) generally agree about the types of communications they write most often and least often, they disagree about how often they write some other forms. For example, whereas only 4 percent of the Chemistry alumni in my survey reported that they write advertising at least "sometimes," more than ten times as many (41 percent) of the Home Economics alumni indicated that they write advertising at least "sometimes." It seems likely that further studies will also find evidence that college major is related to frequency with which college-educated workers write various forms of communication.

JOB CATEGORY. No one has systematically investigated the relationships between job category and forms of communication used. One interesting feature of several surveys, however, is that they ask their respondents about kinds of documents that seem to be relatively specific to the job categories in which the respondents may be presumed to work. For example, in their survey concerning recently graduated accounting majors, Andrews and Koester (1979) list "statements and schedules" (numerical reports)—a form that one might presume engineers and scientists rarely use. Likewise, in their

survey of people in technical and research firms, Paradis et al.
(personal correspondence, 1984) list the "patent application," a form
of little use to accountants. Also, since graduates from different
departments typically enter different job categories, the likelihood of
a relationship between college major and kinds of documents
prepared at work suggests a similar relationship between job
category and kinds of documents.

6. *The forms that are most often written are not necessarily the
most important ones.* In their survey of 200 college-educated workers
in a cross-section of job categories, Faigley et al. (1981) asked their
respondents to tell not only how often they write a variety of kinds of
communications, but also how important each kind is to the
respondents' overall job performance. The forms that the respondents
write most often are not all the same ones they identified as being the
most important. For example, of eight forms addressed to readers
outside the organization, the letter of response to requests is the one
most often written, but only 46 percent of the people who reported
writing such letters gave them the highest "importance" rating. In
contrast, the letter designed to sell products or services is ranked
fourth in terms of how often it is written; 77 percent of the people
who write such letters gave them the highest importance rating.

Paradis et al. (personal correspondence, 1984) obtained similar
results in their survey of 265 professional employees in twenty
research and development organizations. These respondents spend a
greater amount of their time writing progress reports than they spend
on any of the other fifteen forms listed by the researchers, yet nine
other forms received higher importance ratings.

Functions of Writing

Only one study has asked respondents about the functions that
writing serves at work (Paradis et al., personal correspondence,
1984).

1. *At work, writing serves a variety of organizational functions.*
In their survey of 265 professional employees at twenty research and
development organizations, Paradis, et al. presented their respondents with a list of ten functions that are served by communications
written at work; they asked the respondents to indicate the importance of each of those functions. The following functions were

identified as being "vitally important" by more than 50 percent of the respondents: to provide answers to specific questions (69 percent); to keep others informed about major activities (60 percent); and to help plan and coordinate the activities of the individual and the organization (52 percent). Functions identified as being "vitally important" by between 33 percent and 49 percent of the respondents were:

1. To objectify a situation so that its essential elements and interrelationships can be analyzed (49 percent).
2. To instruct others (47 percent).
3. To enable individuals to make contact with others who are higher up in the organization or on the outside (45 percent).
4. To establish accountability (38 percent).

In all probability, this question by Paradis et al. only begins to indicate the functions of writing that would be rated as "vitally important" by college-educated workers. One reason for believing so is that the list contained only two other possible functions for respondents to rate—both of which were rated as "vitally important" by at least 25 percent of the respondents. Further, the list left out many other functions that might have been inquired about, especially those pertaining to communications sent outside the organization. The wide variety of other functions that could be inquired about is hinted at by the functions inherent in the titles of some of the kinds of documents mentioned in some of the surveys cited earlier: letters that sell products and services, letters that make inquiries, employee evaluations, specifications, job descriptions, patent applications, and so on.

Quality of Writing

From the various surveys that have inquired about the quality of writing in the workplace, we can draw two conclusions about quality.

1. *Many college-educated workers believe that in general the writing done in the workplace is of poor quality.* In every survey that has asked about the matter, a substantial number of respondents have indicated that poor writing is a problem in the workplace. Different surveys, however, obtain different results concerning the severity of

the problem. A survey that produced one of the most favorable views of writing in the workplace was conducted by Rainey (1972), who asked 50 executives from firms listed in the *Thomas Directory of American Manufacturers* about the quality of writing in their companies. Thirty-eight percent said that the writing is "outstandingly good," but a slightly larger proportion of the respondents, 40 percent, said that poor written communication is costing their companies a significant amount of money in lost sales or contracts.

In their survey of 200 college-educated workers in a cross-section of job categories, Faigley et al. (1981) asked respondents to indicate, on the basis of the writing that crosses their desks, whether they think writing is: not a problem, a real problem, or a serious problem. Only 22 percent said that it is not a problem, whereas 51 percent said that it is a real problem and 27 percent reported it to be a serious problem.

An even less favorable view of the quality of workers' writing emerges from two surveys that asked specifically about the writing of recent college graduates. In a survey of 38 companies from among the 105 largest accounting firms in the United States, Andrews and Sigband (1984) asked the respondents to rate on a four-point scale the ability of "new" accountants (new college graduates) in writing six kinds of communications (e.g., reports, memos). On average, 70 percent of the respondents gave the new accounts the lowest rating ("inadequate") for all six kinds of communications; *none* gave the highest for *any* of the kinds of communications. Kimel and Monsees (1979) obtained similar results when they asked some national employers and also some Kansas City members of three professional engineering societies to evaluate recent engineering graduates. When asked to indicate the importance to professional engineering practice of thirteen areas of competence (most of them technical), these respondents ranked "writing and speaking" as the *most important* area of competence in both civil engineering and electrical engineering, and second in mechanical engineering. In all three engineering fields, these same areas of writing and speaking were identified as the ones in which recent engineering graduates are *most deficient.*

Kimel and Monsees grouped *writing* and *speaking* together. Therefore, when their respondents identified this broad area as one in which engineering graduates had major deficiency, it is possible that the respondents were thinking more of deficiencies in speaking than deficiencies in writing. At least, that possiblity is raised by the results of a survey by Cox (1968), who asked 112 managers in the St. Louis area, "What causes you trouble in your job?" Eighty percent indicated communication, many more than chose "inefficiency" (69 percent) and absenteeism (54 percent), the only other possibilities checked by more than half the respondents. But when asked whether they consider written communication or oral communication the more troublesome, 68 percent indicated oral, and only 32 percent indicated written. On the other hand, Cox (1976) received evidence of more pervasive problems with written communication in a survey of people who had taken his business-communication class during the previous fifteen years and earned an A or a B in it. Seventy-seven percent indicated that the people they work with encounter problems in preparing written communications. Further, 93 percent responded "yes" when asked whether they thought "that the people you work with would be able to do their work better if they had more training in communication."

Several surveys asked for specific information about the kinds of writing problems that are seen at work. Stine and Skarzenski (1979) asked executives of 83 businesses with offices in Iowa to tell how often they see each of twenty writing problems in the paperwork that crosses their desks. The respondents indicated that the problems they see most often are (in order): wordiness, grammar, sentence structure, spelling, clarity, and organization. When asked to rank several grammatical problems in terms of how often they see them, the respondents placed run-on sentences first, followed by fragments, tense shifts, and subject-verb agreement.

Finally, in their survey of 200 college-educated workers in a cross-section of job categories, Faigley et al. (1981) invited their respondents to identify the effects of the bad writing they encountered in the workplace. One hundred thirty-four respondents accepted that invitation; according to the researchers' classification of the responses, 58 percent cited misunderstanding, 49 percent cited loss of time, and 40 percent cited bad public image. Other effects cited are lack of impact (23 percent), loss of business (17 percent) and "impedes professional advancement" (10 percent).

Taken together, these surveys indicate that the writing done at work is often perceived to be of poor quality. If so, why don't managers do something about it? In his survey of 150 people who had taken his writing class in the past fifteen years and earned an A or a B in it, Cox (1976) asked that question. Sixty-one percent of his respondents indicated that managers do not have the time required to supervise rewriting; 37 percent indicated that the managers, although they do recognize poor writing, are unable to identify the fault with it.

Workers' Perception of Their Own Writing Ability

From the few surveys that have asked questions about the workers' perceptions of their own writing ability, two tentative conclusions can be drawn.

1. *Generally, workers seem to believe that they are relatively good writers, but these feelings may be qualified by other, less self-confident attitudes.* Three surveys have found that many workers seem to have a fairly high opinion of their own writing abilities. Of the 165 managers surveyed by Aldrick (1982a and b), 96 rated themselves as "excellent" or "above average," more than three times as many as rated themselves "below average" (29). Similarly, in Harwood's (1982) survey of approximately 250 alumni of Christopher Newport College, "an overwhelming majority" of the respondents reported that their writing competence is "satisfactory for the demands they had met." Only 6 percent viewed themselves as less skillful writers than most other college graduates they know.

There are some signs, however, that at least some workers are not as self-confident as those results would seem to imply. In examining the survey questionnaires returned by the 165 managers, Aldrich (1982a and b) found an interesting reaction. Seven of her questions were essentially test questions that asked the managers to do such things as correct the faulty parallelism of a sentence. A substantial number of the self-designated "excellent" and "above-average" writers wrote critical and often hostile comments next to these questions; the self-designated average and below-average writers did not make such remarks. Aldrich interprets these comments as defensive reactions.

In a related survey, Aldrich found that most of the respondents in six writing courses she taught for government and private organizations think highly of their ability as writers. However, she also found that they have a negative attitude toward writing. More than half (55 percent) indicated that they approach writing tasks with "apprehension," "reluctance," "dread," or "downright hate." Only 29 percent reported the positive reactions, "enthusiasm" and "joy"; the remaining respondents recorded ambivalent reactions.

2. *New employees may tend to have a higher estimation of their own writing abilities than do their managers.* In a survey of partners in CPA firms and recently graduated accounting majors in those same firms, Andrews and Koester (1979) asked their respondents to evaluate "the basic communication skills (oral and written) of recently graduated accountants." Whereas 63 percent of the recent graduates rated their writing as "effective," only 32 percent of the partners did so. Andrews and Koester obtained similar results when they posed the same questions to experienced and new accountants in private corporations and in federal agencies. Similar results seem to have been obtained by Huegli and Tschirgi (1974). These researchers surveyed 101 recent college graduates in business and engineering fields and the supervisors of 35 of those recent graduates. Although very few of the recent college graduates considered themselves to be "poor" or "very poor" as communicators, almost all the supervisors indicated that the recent graduates were deficient in communication skills. Unfortunately, the researchers did not distinguish between written and oral communication skills in reporting this finding.

3. *Some workers think that their writing has improved since they started work.* In their survey of 265 professional persons in research and development organizations, Paradis et al. (personal correspondence, 1984) asked respondents to compare their writing abilities at the time of the survey and when they were in college. More than three out of four (77 percent) said that they were better writers at the time of the survey; 16 percent said that they were the same as when in college; and only 6 percent said they were worse. This finding corresponds to one obtained by Treece (1972) in her survey of 565 certified professional secretaries. Treece asked her respondents to place a checkmark beside each of the eighteen areas that caused them difficulty with writing when they began their careers and to place another checkmark beside each that continued to cause them problems at the time of the survey. For every area, fewer people indicated they had trouble at the time of the survey than indicated they had had trouble at the time they began their careers.

Nevertheless, some workers believe they can still improve their writing ability. Persing et al. (1977) asked 36 people who had taken a business communication course at various colleges and universities around the nation whether they felt the need to strengthen their communication skills; 81 percent said yes.

Workers' Attitudes and Beliefs Concerning Education About Writing

Several surveys have asked respondents about education in writing. The results of these surveys suggest six generalizations.

1. *Workers believe that people can learn how to improve their writing ability through on-the-job experience.* In their survey of 265 professional persons in twenty research and development organizations, Paradis et al. (personal correspondence, 1984) asked their respondents to rank various writing experiences and training "according to which has been most useful to you." Seventy-one percent of the respondents cited "on the job experience" as the most useful, and only 26 percent cited "writing courses" as the most useful. This result coincides with the finding (mentioned earlier) that 77 percent of the respondents to that same survey said they were better writers at the time of the survey than they were in college. It also coincides with results obtained by Bataille (1982) when he asked about 180 graudates of Iowa State Univesity, in an open-ended question, to tell what training (other than English courses in writing) had helped them develop their writing skills. The largest group of respondents (26 percent) specified on-the-job experience (or practice); then came precollege training (20 percent), mostly in English courses where writing and grammar were stressed, followed closely by company-sponsored writing courses (17 percent). Fourteen percent mentioned graduate school—usually work on their theses or help from their major professors.

The results cited in the preceding paragraph suggest that as a source of knowledge about writing, on-the-job experience may be at least as important as formal instruction in writing courses. It remains unanswered whether on-the-job experience is so important because of deficiencies in college writing courses or because the writing done at work simply cannot be taught adequately in the classroom.

2. *Employer-sponsored training in writing is available to many workers, but not to a majority.* One form of on-the-job education is the employer-sponsored training course. Four surveys have produced

widely different results concerning the percentage of employers who offer such courses in writing. The highest percentage (49 percent) was obtained by Wasylik, Sussman, and Leri (1976) in a survey of 59 members of the Pittsburgh chapter of the American Society for Training and Development, a professional organization for training specialists. The lowest average (16 percent) was obtained by Golen and Inman in a survey of 136 supervisory personnel attending the Louisiana Banking School for Supervisory Training at Louisiana State University. The other surveys that asked such a question are Denton (1979) and Meister and Reinsch (1978).

In a survey involving training managers for 316 employers listed in the *College Placement Annual*, Denton (1979) gathered information about the characteristics of the employer-sponsored training courses in which workers study writing. Enrollment ranges from 3 to 30 participants, with an average of 15.6 and a median of 18. The number of student-teacher contact hours ranges from 4 to 35 hours, with an average of 16.5 and a median of 12. Denton reports that the typical class meets for two-hour sessions twice weekly for four weeks. Thirty-six percent of the courses are taught by members of the employer's training staff, 19 percent by college faculty hired as consultants, and 10 percent by professional consultants; the remaining courses have some other arrangement for instructors, often involving a combination of types of individuals. Seventy-three percent of the courses are "individualized," which means that they have been designed specifically for the sponsoring organization. Among these courses, the most common type is the "general course in writing skills" (31 percent), followed by technical-report writing (20 percent), business-report writing (19 percent), business-letter writing (19 percent), and proposal writing (6 percent). The remaining 5 percent includes a variety of titles. Some companies reimburse employees for the costs involved with taking writing courses offered by colleges and universities. However, no survey research has been conducted into the extent or details of this practice.

3. *More company-sponsored writing courses seem to be needed.* In their survey of 136 people attending the Louisiana Banking School for Supervisory Training, Golen and Inman (1983) found that whereas only 16 percent of their respondents work for banks that offer writing courses, 81 percent of the respondents said that the banks should offer such courses. Likewise, in a survey of training directors at 261 manufacturing firms in Illnois, Meister and Reinsch (1978) found that

only 25 percent offer writing courses, but 42 percent feel that their new trainees are deficient in writing. Similarly, in Denton's (1979) survey of training managers for 316 employers listed in the *College Placement Annual*, 86 percent of respondents reported that they foresee increased demand at their organizations for writing courses over the next five years.

4. *Many workers consider writing courses to be an important part of college curricula.* In Davis's survey (1977) of people listed in *Engineers of Distinction*, 81 percent of the 245 survey participants indicated that technical writing should be included as a required course in scientific and engineering curricula, and an additional 16 percent said that it should be included as an elective that students are encouraged to take. In Rainey's (1972) survey of 50 executives selected from the *Thomas Directory of American Manufacturers*, 78 percent thought that colleges should require a formal course in report writing "even if it means a reduction of one course in the amount of work taken in a student's specialty." Cox (1976) obtained similar results in his survey of 150 people who had taken his business-communication class during a fifteen-year period and earned an A or a B; when Cox asked whether a course in written business communication should be required of all business majors, 96 percent of his respondents said yes. In their survey of 136 people attending the Louisiana Banking School for Supervisory Training, Golen and Inman (1983) found a much lower percentage of respondents—only 46 percent—recommending that a course in business report writing be included in college curricula. Nonetheless, this is an interesting result because the highest degree earned by 69 percent of the respondents is a high school diploma.

The important place of writing courses in college curricula was also indicated by the respondents to two surveys that asked about the overall design of college programs. In a survey by Bond, Leabo, and Swinyard (1964), 66 chief executive officers of major U.S. corporations were asked to rate about fifty subjects as being "very important," "fairly important," or "not appropriate" in college programs that prepare students for business leadership. English composition was identified as being "very important" by 65 percent of the respondents; only two subjects were identified as being "very important" by more respondents: business and government (76 percent) and principles of economics (71 percent). Interestingly, business report writing received the ninth-highest rating, being identified as "very important" by 48 percent of the respondents. Similarly, when Steinbruegee, Hailstones, and Roberts (1955) asked 70 personnel directors in manufacturing firms in the Cincinnati, Ohio, area to rate twenty-one subjects as being "essential," "advisable," or "unnecessary" in college programs, the respondents gave the highest rating to a subject called "English, Grammar, Literature and Composition." Eighty-two percent said that this subject was essential to a college program preparing students to work for them. The respondents gave the third-highest rating to business letter writing; their second choice was mathematics.

One survey asked the respondents to evaluate the writing courses they did have: the American Business Communication Association (Persing et al., 1977) asked 36 respondents from around the nation to evaluate their business-communication course during their senior year, during their first year on the job, and during their second year on the job. When asked (as seniors) how they rated the quality of the course in comparison with their other business courses, the respondents gave it a mean rating of 6.4 on a scale from 0 (low) to 10 (high). When asked (as seniors) to rate the course as preparation for a career, they gave it a mean rating of 6.6. Two years later, the responses they gave to these two questions were *not* significantly different from those they gave as seniors.

5. *Workers recommend that a wide range of writing skills be taught in college writing courses; ranked highest by workers are the skills needed to write clearly, write concisely, organize well, and write grammatically.* Several surveys have asked the respondents to tell what skills they think should be taught in college writing courses. Table 1-3 lists the skills ranked highest in three surveys. All three asked open-ended questions; Davis asked a closed-ended question also.

This table of the skills most highly recommended for courses is especially interesting because it resembles so closely the list of skills ranked highest in response to questions about the skills that are important on the job (see Table 1-2 in the section on "Writing Skills Needed At Work"). The resemblance between the two lists is especially striking because Table 1.3 involves open-ended questions: even when the respondents are free to name any skills they choose, these are the skills they name most often.

The respondents to these three surveys also recommend many other writing skills for inclusion in college writing courses. For the

Table 1-3
Ranking of Writing Skills Recommended for College Writing Courses

	Stine and Skarzenski (1979) Open-ended Question	Davis (1977) Open-ended Question	Davis (1977) Closed-ended Question	Faigley et al. (1981) Open-ended Question
Clarity	1	1	1	1
Conciseness	2	2	—	5
Organization	3	3	3	3
Grammar	4	—	4	2

most part, the various researchers group these other skills under headings that make it difficult to compare any one survey with others. But the lists for all three of the surveys cited do have at least one item that involves audience analysis and adaptation: such an item ranks second on Davis's closed-ended list; fourth on his open-ended list; seventh on Stine and Skarzenski's list, and eighth and tenth (two separate items) on Faigley et al.'s list. In addition, in Golen and Inman's (1983) survey of 136 people attending the Louisiana Banking School for Supervisory Training, the respondents ranked "adaptation to the reader" fourth in a list of twenty items that might be included in a business report writing class (routine letters and memos were to be excluded from consideration).

In a survey using a closed-ended question, Harwood (1982) presented about 250 graduates of Christopher Newport College with a list of writing skills that were expressed in terms more familiar to freshman English than to career-related writing courses; Harwood asked his respondents to tell which of these writing skills should be emphasized by all college teachers, not just English teachers. The respondents ranked the skills as follows: organization, content, development of ideas, mechanics, diction, spelling, logic, originality, and style. Of particular interest is the low ranking given originality and style—topics that often receive considerable emphasis in general composition courses—and the high ranking given to organization.

Finally, in a survey of certified public secretaries, Treece (1972) asked a question that could be considered an indirect method of gathering information about what might be included in career-related writing courses. Although she did not ask her respondents to recommend topics for writing courses, Treece did ask them to place a checkmark beside each of several writing skill areas that gave them trouble when they started their careers and to place another checkmark beside each area that continued to give them trouble at the time of the survey. As mentioned earlier, the respondents indicated that they were less troubled with writing problems at the time of the survey than when they began their careers. The same four areas, however, headed both lists—areas that presumably could be covered in writing courses: writing without wasting time (start 63 percent; now 23 percent); avoiding trite expressions (start 54 percent; now 15 percent); conciseness (start 40 percent, now 12 percent); and "psychological approach" (start 36 percent, now 17 percent).

Unfortunately, it is difficult to interpret precisely what respondents (and researchers) mean by the terms they use to identify the general writing skills they recommend for college writing courses. As Faigley et al. (1981) point out, when respondents recommend *clarity*, they might be expressing a concern for the plain style of writing, for good organization, or even for the underlying conception of the piece of writing. Similarly, the term *grammar* might refer to any of various aspects of sentence structure, including not only correct grammar but also correct punctuation, variety in sentence structure, and pleasing cadence.

6. *Workers suggest that writing courses should teach skills in writing a variety of kinds of documents; chief among these are letters, memos, and reports.* Survey researchers have gathered little direct information about the kinds of communications workers recommend be taught in college writing courses. (It seems that researchers sometimes intend to obtain advice about the kinds of communications to teach by asking which kinds are most often written or most important at work.) However, all the studies that have inquired about the specific forms that are recommended produce the same results: letters, memos, and reports. Surveys supporting this conclusion include: Bennett (1971), Golen and Inman (1983), Persing et al. (1977), Rainey (1972), and Swenson (1980).

Two of those surveys, both using closed-ended questions, gathered information about what their respondents feel should be the relative emphasis given to those three forms (neither survey included in its list any form other than letters, memos, and reports). In

Bennett's (1971) survey of 35 business executives of *Fortune 500* companies based in California, 57 percent of the respondents indicated that report writing should receive strong emphasis in a business-communicaton course, 43 percent indicated that letters should, and 43 percent indicated that memos should. In Persing et al.'s (1977) survey of 36 workers who had taken a business-communication course at four-year colleges around the country, the respondents recommended (on average) that 20 percent of the time in a business-communication course be devoted to letter writing, 10 percent to short reports (5 pages or fewer), 6 percent to long reports (6 pages or more), and 5 percent to interoffice memoranda.

A curious point about the surveys mentioned in the two preceding paragraphs is that they all use closed-ended lists that required the respondents to make a specific judgment on the desirability of teaching the forms the researchers included in the lists. In response to open-ended questions, respondents rarely recommend that college writing courses include skills needed for writing specific kinds of communications. In fact, they pay so little attention to these skills that in reporting the recommendations made by 83 executives of businesses with offices in Iowa, Stine and Skarzenski (1979) did not include any category about kinds of communications in their list of ten items. Similarly, in reporting the recommendations made by 245 people listed in *Engineers of Distinction*, Davis (1977) included no such category in his list of four topics. In contrast, in their survey of 200 college-educated workers in a cross-section of job categories, Faigley et al. (1981) included an omnibus category called "specific business and technical formats," but it was ranked sixth in their list of thirteen recommended topics. They reported that instruction in specific kinds of communications had been recommended by 24 percent of their respondents. In contrast, 43 percent of the respondents had mentioned clarity, 42 percent had mentioned grammar, mechanics and usage, 33 percent had mentioned organization, and 26 percent had mentioned conciseness ("brevity").

It is not clear why skills involved with writing specific kinds of communications receive so little attention in responses to open-ended questions that solicit recommendations about the contents of writing courses. Perhaps the respondents believe these skills are easy to learn on the job, or perhaps they assume these skills will be taught and therefore decide not to mention them. In any event, it is evident that when responding to such open-ended questions respondents think primarily of *general* writing skills that can be used when preparing any specific form of communication.

IMPLICATIONS FOR TEACHING

Knowledge about the writing that is done on the job can be very helpful to teachers of career-related writing courses. These teachers can gain important insights into ways to design their courses by learning the purposes writers at work try to achieve, the circumstances under which these writers write, the expectations and conventions that pertain to writing at work, the features that distinguish communications that succeed in that environment, and the composing processes writers customarily rely on there (presumably because those processes are efficacious).

In this section, I briefly present the implications—or suggestions—for teachers that seem to be warranted by the surveys I described earlier. In this list, I have included only points that can be supported by results from several studies, and I have included only advice based on what we seem to know about broad groups of workers—not just a small group of specialists in one field or kind of employment. Because almost all the existing surveys involve college-educated workers, I address all my suggestions to teachers of college students, without knowing whether any of the suggestions would also be useful to high school teachers or to instructors of company-sponsored writing courses for employees without a college education.

Finally, all my suggestions concern strategy rather than tactics, general objectives rather than specific pedagogical practices. The individual teacher must decide how to pursue these objectives.

1. *Career-related writing courses should explain to students that writing will probably play a large and important role in the students' careers, regardless of the students' majors.* If college students fail to perceive the relevance of writing to their careers, they may invest less time, effort, and enthusiasm than they should in their writing courses. Students should know that college-educated workers devote a substantial amount of their time on the job to writing and that the ability to write well is an important factor in determining the success of college-educated workers. Further, students should know that new college graduates are generally perceived as writing poorly—some-

thing that presumably hampers the graduates' progress during their first years on the job.

2. *Career-related writing courses should focus on general writing strategies that students can apply in a variety of work-related rhetorical situations.* More than anything else, the information provided by survey research indicates that typical college graduates must be able to write effectively in many different kinds of situations—to many kinds of readers—in many forms of communication.

3. *Career-related writing courses should teach students how to write communications that people in the workplace will perceive to be clear, concise, well-organized, and grammatically correct.* Certainly any writing course is likely to aim to teach students these same skills. That fact should not distract teachers of career-related writing from the importance these skills have to people in the workplace.

Teachers should also keep in mind that the precise meanings of clarity, organization, and conciseness may be substantially different in the workplace than they are, for instance, in a freshman composition course. What makes for a well-organized academic term paper might not make for a well-organized business report; similarly, what a professor sees as a concise report from a student may be very different from what an employer may see as a concise memorandum. In suggesting such comparisons, I am of course straying beyond the body of knowledge that survey literature has provided. Yet we need to be able to make these kinds of comparisons, and we need the sort of research that will enable us to do so with confidence.

4. *Career-related writing courses should provide students with instruction and practice in writing for a variety of kinds of readers.* Survey research clearly shows that college-educated workers must be able to address a wide variety of readers. Therefore, career-related writing courses should teach students how to adapt general writing strategies to the diverse rhetorical situations they will encounter on the job. Students should learn, for instance, how to write clearly to fellow specialists, and they should learn the very different ways of writing clearly to someone outside their specialties.

5. *Career-related writing courses should provide students with instruction and practice in writing a variety of kinds of communication.* Whereas some career-related writing courses focus exclusively on business-letter writing or technical-report writing,

survey research indicates that the typical college-educated worker needs to be able to use a wider variety of forms. At the least, teachers should consider covering the three forms used most often on the job by college-educated workers: memos, letters, and short reports. In addition, various fields have their own specialized forms, such as the sales letter, the audit report (in accounting), the test report (in laboratory research), and the case report (in social work). Teachers should learn what special forms their students will use at work (these may not be the same ones the students use in courses in their major departments), and the teachers should then determine whether these forms, too, should be included in their courses.

These four suggestions identify general objectives based on what we know through survey research about college-educated workers in general. Teachers can learn about additional objectives that they might adopt for their own particular career-related writing courses by studying more closely the surveys that concern people in the specific kinds of jobs their own students will hold. For instance, teachers who instruct students in business fields at schools similar to Miami University (Ohio) and the University of Arizona can derive additional insights into what to teach from looking more closely at the surveys by Storms (1983) and Rader and Wunsch (1980). By studying these surveys, such teachers of business will be reminded (for instance) that many of their students will use dictation equipment after graduation, and so may benefit from instruction in the special skills needed to compose using that technology. Likewise, teachers who instruct students in technical fields at schools similar to Miami University (Ohio) may decide (based on the findings of my survey, described earlier) that their courses should cover unsolicited communications, not just solicited ones. Teachers intending to study some of these surveys more closely may find it helpful to read chapter 13, which aims to help people untrained in social science research methods read survey research critically. That chapter is also intended to aid teachers who decide that they want to conduct their own survey research projects.

CONCLUSION

In this chapter, I have explored the knowledge that survey research has so far provided concerning the writing people do at work. At the same time, I hope that this summary suggests that there is much, much more that we can still learn through surveys. In an important sense, all the studies I have cited are exploratory. True, they have provided us with some important insights, despite their limitations and flaws. Even more important, however, the existing surveys have supplied us with preliminary findings to be tested, with a few general conclusions to be extended and refined, and with a sense that many areas—such as the composing habits of workers—lie essentially unexamined through survey research. Further, the existing surveys hint that many aspects of writing in the workplace cannot be fully understood except through the continued use of this research method. We have and will continue to have use for the special power surveys give us to generalize, to determine whether there is a wider truth in what we observe locally, perhaps through other research methods.

Acknowledgments

For their assistance, I am grateful to professors Donald H. Cunningham, Lester Faigley, Jone Goldstein, Jeanne Halpern, Steve Hinkle, John Skillings, and C. Gilbert Storms. Also, I am grateful to professors James G. Paradis and David N. Dobrin, and to David Bower for permission to cite some of the results from their unpublished study (which also contains many other interesting findings). In addition, I wish to thank Christopher Anderson, Dennis Romans, and Keith Shute for helping me locate the surveys treated here, and I wish to thank Rick Bastyr, Jennifer Kerch, and Deb Schoenberg for helping me process the data from my survey of alumni of Miami University (Ohio). That survey was supported by a grant from the university's Committee on the Improvement of Instruction.

Notes

1. I will gladly share a more detailed report of these survey results with persons who request to see it.

2. This note is addressed to readers knowledgeable about statistics who desire to know why in many of my analyses I treated ordinal-level data as if it were interval-level data. (For a definition of the levels of data, see Chapter 13.) My reasons for using the analysis-of-variance F test and Duncan's multiple range test for variable response (rather than the Friedman test for randomized block design) are explained in my section on data analysis in Chapter 13.

For all the analyses in which I compared the ways that two groups of respondents answered a single question, I performed both the Student's t-test and the Wilcoxon test. They produced very similar results. For instance, when comparing the responses made by alumni with and without graduate degrees, the Student's t-test found statistically significant differences at the .05 level for 17 of the 26 questions studied; the Wilcoxon test found statistically significant differences at the same level of confidence for all 17 of those questions and for only 2 others. Further, the differences between the results of the Student's *t*-test and the Wilcoxon test do not affect any of the general conclusions I report in this chapter. I chose to report the results of the Student's *t*-tests for the sake of consistency: like the *F* test and Duncan's test, the Student's *t*-test is parametric; the Wilcoxon is nonparametric.

3. Excluded from this summary are surveys that concern the writing done by people who are employed as writing specialists, such as technical writers and editors (Green & Nolan, 1984) and people responsible for conducting business correspondence in companies that engage in international business activities (Kilpatrick, 1984). Also excluded are surveys that inquire about communication at work without distinguishing between written and oral communication (e.g., Educational Relations Service, General Electric Company [1978]; Hildebrandt, Bond, Miller & Swinyard, [1982]; and Sylvester, [1980].

4. Although this study involved college faculty, I have included it in this chapter on writing in nonacademic settings because the respondents were asked about kinds of communication tasks encountered in any organization, not about communication tasks peculiar to academe.

5. The sample used by Faigley et al. (1981) deserves special comment. Although flawed, it is the most ambitious sample used in any of the surveys mentioned in this chapter. In this sample, Faigley et al. undertook to represent the entire populations of college-educated workers in the United States; the researchers' strategy was to construct a sample of 200 individuals that had the same proportion of workers in various job categories (agriculture, technical, etc.) as has the entire college-educated work force in the United States (according to the U.S. Departments of Labor and of Commerce). They achieved that goal, but in doing so, they used convenience techniques to locate the particular individuals in each category whom they would interview, and all their interviews took place in one fairly small region: the metropolitan areas of Austin, Houston, and Dallas, Texas, and Shreveport, Louisiana. An additional limitation of this sample is that it includes too few people for some of the observations the researchers wished to make. Nevertheless, this sample comes closer to representing the entire population of college-educated workers than does the sample of any other single survey of writing at work. Of course, many of the other studies use samples that more faithfully represent various smaller populations of interest, such as the population of workers who graduated from a school of business administration or the population of prominent engineers.

Incidentally, many of the results of this study are also reported in Faigley and Miller (1982).

6. Because Roundy and Mair (1982) do not report separately the responses of the workers in their sample, it is not possible to draw many specific conclusions about the composing practices of that subgroup of the sample. Nevertheless, some of Roundy and Mair's results appear to apply to all or nearly all of their respondents; those are the results I report here.

References

Accreditation Research Committee, American Assembly of Collegiate Schools of Business (1980). *AACSB Bulletin, 15*(2).

Aldrich, P. G. (1982a). Adult writers: Some factors that interfere with effective writing. *The Technical Writing Teacher, 9*, 128–132.

Aldrich, P. G. (1982b). Adult writers: Some reasons for ineffective writing on the job. *College Composition and Communication, 33*, 284–287.

Andrews, J. D., & Koester, R. J. (1979). Communication difficulties as perceived by the accounting profession and professors of accounting. *Journal of Business Communication, 16*(2), 33–42.

Andrews, J. D., & Sigband, N. B. (1984). How effectively does the "new" accountant communicate? Perceptions by practitioners and academics. *Journal of Business Communicaton, 21*(2), 15–24.

Angrist, A. W. (1953). A study of the communications of executives in business and industry. *Speech Monographs, 20*, 277–285.

Barnum, C. M., & Fischer, R. (1984). Engineering technologists as writers: Results of a survey. *Technical Communication, 31*(2), 9–11.

Bataille, R. R. (1982). Writing in the world of work: What our graduates report. *College Composition and Communication, 33*(3), 226–283.

Belohlov, J. A., Popp, P. O., & Porte, M. S. (1974). Communication: A view from the inside of business. *Journal of Business Communication, 11*(4), 53–59.

Bennett, J. C. (1971). The communication needs of business executives. *Journal of Business Communication, 8*(3), 3–11.

Benson, G. L. (1983). On the campus: How well do business schools prepare graduates for the business world? *Personnel, 60*(4), 61–65.

Blue, J. L., Breslin, A. B., Buchanan, A. S., & Leingany, R. L. (1976). *Occupational communications skills analysis.* Olympia: Washington State Commission for Occupational Education. (ERIC ED 134 823).

Bond, F. A., Leabo, D. A., & Swinyard, A. W. (1964). *Preparation for business leadership: Views of top executives.* Ann Arbor: Bureau of Business Research, University of Michigan.

Cox, H. L. (1968). Opinions of selected business managers about some aspects of communication on the job. *Journal of Business Communication, 6*(1), 3–12.

Cox, H. L. (1976). The voices of experience: The business communication alumnus reports. *Journal of Business Communication, 13*(14), 35–46.

Davis, R. M. (1977). How important is technical writing? A survey of the opinions of successful engineers. *The Technical Writing Teacher, 4*, 83–88.

Denton, L. W. (1979). In-house training in written communication: A status report. *Journal of Business Communicaton, 16*(3), 3–14.

Educational Relations Service, General Electric Company. (1978). What they think of their higher education. In G. H. Mills & J. A. Walter (Eds.), *Technical writing, fourth edition,* (pp. 191–212). New York: Holt, Rinehart and Winston.

Elfert, D. L. (1977). A follow-up study of engineering graduates. *Engineering Education, 68*, 181–182.

Erickson, H. P. (1975). English skills among technicians in industry. In D. H,. Cunningham & H. Estrin (Eds.), *The Teaching of Technical Writing* (pp. 153–160). Urbana, IL: National Council of Teachers of English (NCTE).

Faigley, L., & Miller, T. P. (1982). What we learn from writing on the job. *College English, 4*, 557–569.

Faigley, L., Miller, T. P., Meyer, P. R., & Witte, S. P. (1981). *Writing after college: A stratified survey of the writing of college-trained people.* Austin: University of Texas at Austin.

Flatley, M. E. (1982). A comparative analysis of the written communication of managers at various organizational levels in the private business sector. *Journal of Business Communication, 19*(3), 35–49.

Glenn, T. J., & Green, M. M. (1979). Re-evaluation and adaptation—revising a course to meet graduates' needs. *Proceedings of the 26th International Technical Communication Conference* (pp.E50–E55). Washington, DC: Society for Technical Communication.

Golen S., & Inman, T. (1983). An analysis of business report writing activities of supervisory banking personnel. *Journal of Technical Writing and Communication, 13*, 221–228.

Green, M., & Nolan, T. D. (1984). A systematic analysis of the technical communicator's job: A guide for educators. *Technical Communication, 31*(4), 9–12.

Harwood, J. T. (1982). Freshman English ten years after: Writing in the world. *College Composition and Communication, 33*, 281–283.

Hetherington, M. S. (1982). The importance of oral communication. *College English, 44*, 570–574.

Hildebrandt, H. W., Bond, F. A., Miller, E. L., & Swinyard, A. W. (1982). An executive appraisal of courses which best prepare one for general management. *Journal of Business Communication, 19*, 5–15.

Hinrichs, J. R. (1964). Communications activity of industrial research personnel. *Personnel Psychology, 17*, 193–204.

Huegli, J. M., & Tschirgi, H. D. (1974). An investigation of communication skills application and effectiveness at the entry job level. *Journal of Business Communication, 12*(1), 24–29.

Kelton, R. W. (1984). The internal report in complex organizations. *Proceedings of the 30th International Technical Communication Conference* (pp. RET54–RET57). Washington, DC: Society for Technical Communication.

Kilpatrick, R. H. (1984). International business communication practices. *Journal of Business Communication, 21*(4), 33–44.

Kimel, W. R., & Monsees, M. E. (1979). Engineering graduates: How good are they? *Engineering Education, 70*(2), 210–212.

Kinsey, A. C., Pomeroy, W. B., & Martin, C. E. (1948). *Sexual behavior in the human male.* Philadelphia: Saunders.

Klemmer, E. T., & Snyder, F. W. (1972). Measurement of time spent communicating. *Journal of Communication, 22*, 142–158.

Lampe, D. R. (1982). Writing in an R & D group: The invisible activity. *The MIT Report, 10*(9), 1–2.

Lull, P. E., Funk, F. E., & Piersol, D. T. (1955). What communication means to the corporation president. *Advanced Management, 20*, 17–20.

Meister, J. E., & Reinsch, N. L., Jr. (1978). Communication training in manufacturing firms. *Communication Education, 27*, 235–244.

Middendorf, W. H. (1980). Academic programs and industrial needs. *Engineering Education, 70*, 835–837.

Miller, C. R. (1984). Genre as social action. *Quarterly Journal of Speech, 70*, 157–178.

Paradis, J., Dobrin, D., & Bower, D. (1984). Personal correspondence (Massachusetts Institute of Technology.)

Penrose, J. M. (1976). A survey of the perceived importance of business communication and other business-related abilities. *Journal of Business Communication, 13*(2), 17–24.

Persing, B., Drew, M. I., Bachman, L., Eaton, J., & Galbraith, E. (1976). Student evaluation of the basic course in business communication. *Journal of Business Communication, 12*, 1–10.

Persing, B., Drew, M. I., Bachman, L., & Galbraith, E. (1977). The 1976 ABCA follow-up evaluation of the course content, classroom procedures, and quality of the basic course in college and university business communication. *ABCA Bulletin, 40*(1), 18–24.

Rader, M. H., & Wunsch, A. P. (1980). A survey of communication practices of business school graduates by job category and undergraduate major. *Journal of Business Communication, 17*(4), 33–41.

Rainey, B. G. (1972). Professors and executives appraise business communication education. *Journal of Business Communication, 9*(4), 19–23.

Reckless, W. C. (1933). *Vice in Chicago*. Chicago: University of Chicago Press.

Reinsch, N. L., Jr., & Lewis, P. V. (1984). Communication apprehension as a determinant of channel preferences. *Journal of Business Communication, 21*(3), 53–61.

Rohman, G. D. (1965). Pre-writing: The stage of discovery in the writing process. *College Composition and Communication, 16*, 106–112.

Roundy, N., & Mair, D. (1982). The composing process of technical writers: A preliminary study. *Journal of Advanced Composition, 3*, 89–101.

Schiff, P. M. (1980). Speech: Another facet of technical communication. *Engineering Education, 71*, 180–181.

Simonds, R. H. (1960). Skills businessmen use most. *Nation's Business, 48*(11), 88.

Skelton, T. (1977). A survey of on-the-job writing performed by graduates of community college technical and occupational programs. In T.M. Sawyer (Ed.), *Technical and professional communication: Teaching in the two-year college, four-year college, and professional school* (pp. 17–23). Ann Arbor, MI: Professional Communication Press.

Spretnak, C. M. (1982). A survey of the frequency and importance of technical communication in an engineering career. *The Technical Writing Teacher, 9*, 133–136.

Steinbruegee, J. B., Hailstones, T. J., & Roberts, E. E. (1955). Personnel managers evaluate a college business program. *Collegiate News and Views, 8*, 7–11.

Stinchcombe, A. L., Adams, R., Heimer, C., Scheppele, K., Smith, T. W., & Taylor, D.G. (1980). *Crime and punishment—changing attitudes in America*. San Francisco: Jossey-Bass.

Stine, D., & Skarzenski, D. (1979). Priorities for the business communication classroom: A survey of business and academe. *Journal of Business Communication, 16*(3), 15–30.

Storms, C. G. (1983). What business school graduates say about the writing they do at work: Implications for the business communication course. *ABCA Bulletin, 46*(4), 13–18.

Sudman, S. (1983). Applied sampling. In P. H. Rossi, J. D. Wright, & A. B. Anderson (Eds.), *Handbook of survey research* (pp. 145–194). New York: Academic Press.

Swenson, D. H. (1980). Relative importance of business communication skills for the next ten years. *Journal of Business Communication, 17*(2), 41–49.

Sylvester, N. D. (1980). Engineering education must improve the communication skills of its graduates. *Engineering Education, 70,* 739–740.

Thrasher, F. M. (1927). *The gang.* Chicago: University of Chicago Press.

Treece, M. C. (1972). Business communications practices and problems of professional secretaries. *Journal of Business Communication, 9*(4), 25–32.

Van Dijk, T. A. (1980). *Macrostructures: An interdisciplinary study of global structures in discourse, interaction, and cognition.* Hillsdale, NJ: Erlbaum.

Van Dyck, B. (1980). On-the-job writing of high-level business executives: Implications for college teaching. Paper presented at the annual meeting of the Conference on College Composition and Communication, Washington, DC (ERIC: ED 185-584.)

Walde, E. E. (1975). A survey to determine the effectiveness of a communication skills course for trade and industrial graduates of a technical vocational school. In D. H. Cunningham & H. Estrin (Eds.), *The teaching of technical writing* (pp. 161–181). Urbana, IL: NCTE.

Wasylik, J. E., Sussman, L., & Leri, R. P. (1976). Communication training as perceived by training personnel. *Communication Quarterly, 24*(1), 32–38.

Weinrauch, J. D., & Swanda, J. R., Jr. (1975). Examining the significance of listening: An exploratory study of contemporary management. *Journal of Business Communication, 13*(1), 25–32.

Winkler, V. M. (1983). The role of models in technical and scientific writing. In P. V. Anderson, R. J. Brockmann, & C. R. Miller (Eds.), *New essays in technical and scientific communication* (pp. 111–122). Farmingdale, NY: Baywood.

Describing and Improving the Structure of Discourse

II

Perceiving Structure in Professional Prose
A Multiply Determined Experience

2

GREGORY G. COLOMB
JOSEPH M. WILLIAMS
University of Chicago

Of all the characteristics of continuous prose discourse, we probably understand least well that which we casually call *form*. We understand style at the level of the sentence better, largely because we have a rich terminology based on a well-developed tradition of grammatical and rhetorical scholarship. Two thousand years of detailed analysis of words, phrases, and sentences have given us a vocabulary that lets us discuss word choice, figures of rhetoric, and sentence structure. In the last two decades, that tradition has been enriched by scholarly research in linguistics, psycholinguistics, and cognitive psychology.

At the same time, we have become increasingly certain that we understand individual sentences not in isolation, one by one, but rather by interpreting them in context. By *context*, we mean not just physical text but also the human context in which the text functions—the social and rhetorical situation, the local universe of tacit conventions and understandings that govern what counts as acceptable style, acceptable terminology, acceptable argument, acceptable form. Context must also include a complex web of intentions: the intention the reader has in reading; the intention the reader believes the writer had in writing; the intention the writer has in writing; and the intention the writer believes the reader will have in reading.

Context must even include the knowledge and presuppositions brought to bear on the text by writer and reader. We do not simply lift meaning off the page. We construct meaning. In the last decade, sociolinguists, psycholinguists, cognitive psychologists, and ethnographers of language have contributed much to our understanding of how writing functions in this fuller pragmatic context.

So rich a fabric of text, convention, setting, cognition—it defeats exhaustive analysis of even a few short sentences. To account for what we might call the cognitive event of texts as brief as a short paragraph, we must account for almost everything simultaneously. For when we read, we bring to bear on what we are reading all these aspects of the event: not just the words and the grammar of the sentence, but who the writer is, what we and the writer share, what we already know about what the writer is writing about, what conventions of reading and writing we and the writer tacitly observe. All these components interact simultaneously. To understand any of this in even the most rudimentary way requires an analysis so dense and extensive that it serves only to emphasize how complex is the act of reading.

Yet even if we do manage to understand that cognitive event in those terms, we will not come to grips with its full complexity until we understand the component of discourse we first mentioned: we are far from understanding in even a rudimentary way what constitutes that middle-level epiphenomenon we call a sense of form, a sense of structure and coherence—that land beyond the sentence where the familiar terminology of subject and verb, noun and adjective, predicate and complement give way to the almost useless generalities of topic sentence and paragraph, of beginning, middle, and end. We simply do not understand in any clear way what writers do or readers experience when we try to describe what constitutes form, structure, organization, design, disposition in discourse.

Consider just the inconsistent terminology. Some of the language we use to describe form comes from names associated with literary genres: dramatic form, narrative form, meditative form. Or we take the names of the parts of forms from the generic professional forms of writing: scientific paper—introduction, methods and materials, results, discussion, summary; legal memo—statement of issue, brief answer, statement of facts, discussion, conclusion; classical speech—exordium, narratio, confirmatio, refutatio, peroratio. There are forms associated with rhetorical devices: comparison and contrast, cause and effect, definition, classification. There are forms associated with affective psychology—most important to least important (or vice versa); with logic—syllogistic; with scientific method—inductive and deductive; with objects and shapes—funnels, triangles, spirals, straight lines. Finally, of course, we draw on brute experience: beginning, middle, and end.

In this chapter, we propose to lay out in clearer relief what goes into this perception of form in professional writing or, perhaps more accurately, what keeps us from experiencing its absence. For we ordinarily become conscious of the form of a text only when we are troubled by it. The phenomenology of reading is most strikingly captured in our disappearance into a text. When we are most caught up in reading, we lose consciousness of the particular words, the form of the paragraphs, the organizational strategy. We simply read, slipping out of touch with almost everything but the experience of the world the text creates. This happens most strikingly when we read an engrossing fiction, but we have all experienced it while reading an intensely interesting report, memo, letter. By no means do we assert that in that experience, form disappears. Quite the contrary: form is at its most potent at just those moments. But in a curious way, we become most aware of the role of form at those moments when we lose track of it. As a consequence, we will explore form here largely by contrasting well-formed and ill-formed snatches of professional discourse.[1]

We cannot account here for all aspects of form, or text structure. (We shall refer to form as *text structure* because we want a term that is not cluttered with other associations.) But we do intend to account for its most crucial components and to suggest how those components work together to create a sense of design, of overarching structure. To do that, we are going to propose a new way of looking at the structure of continuous prose. We will describe something we claim is a basic unit of text structure, a unit of structure so fundamental that it transcends all genres, all types of discourse, all fields of inquiry.

We will not, however, offer a single principle that will account for our sense of textual coherence, because that sense of coherence is *overdetermined*. That is, so many different aspects of text contribute to the experience of coherent structure that no one principle of text structure will suffice to explain the total experience. Indeed, it is precisely that excess of structural signaling that allows us to be less than perfect in constructing a text. We can depend on one set of signals at the expense of others and still seem coherent. Only when a substantial part of the entire system breaks down does a reader begin to flounder. Therefore, we will treat text structure as a *layered* experience, with multiple strata contributing to the experience of coherent text structure.

Our examples will come from our work in a wide range of professional fields: medicine, law, engineering, corporate management. The examples have been taken from books, scientific articles, internal memos, legal briefs, reports. Our analysis could encompass the literary essay, the meditation, the sermon. The absence of those types of writing means only that we chose not to include them in an article intended for publication in a volume devoted to "professional" writing (though what could be more professional than a sermon or a literary essay?).

We will describe the following aspects of text structure, integrating them into an organized, coherent, logical, focused, followable—pick the word—text.

1. *Functional Sentence Perspective*: By this we mean the way a writer sequences the individual units of information in a sentence.
2. *Topic Strings*: By this we mean the way a writer begins each sentence in a *series* of sentences.
3. *Lexical Strings*: By this we mean those repeated words that continue to remind the reader of the universe of reference the writer is working in.
4. *Units of Discourse*: In the least familiar, most innovative part of this chapter, we will offer a new account of text structure that we believe explains much more about texts than does any talk about paragraphs and topic sentences.

We will, finally, suggest some of the implications we see in our proposal and speculate about some of the research problems it might raise.

FUNCTIONAL SENTENCE PERSPECTIVE

Functional sentence perspective (FSP) considers how a writer orders ideas within a sentence. First formulated as a principle of syntactic organization in Eastern Europe in the 1930s and 1940s, it has recently been supported by empirical psycholinguistic research into the way we read. Simply put, in the canonical English sentence, the writer puts first that information already referred to, information that is more familiar, less surprising, more "accessible."[2] The writer then introduces information that is relatively newer, more surprising, less inferable from the previous discourse or from the context.

Here is a pair of passages that differ in important ways:

(1a) Mucosal and vascular permeability altered by a toxin elaborated by the vibrio is one current hypothesis to explain this kind of severe dehydration. (1b) Changes in small capillaries located near the basal surface of the epithelial cells, and the appearance of numerous microvesicles in the cytoplasm of the mucosal cells is evidence in favor of this hypothesis. (1c) Hydrodynamic transport of fluid into the interstitial tissue and then through the mucosa into the lumen of the gut is believed to depend on altered capillary permeability.

(2a) We can explain this kind of severe dehydration by the hypothesis that the vibrio elaborates a toxin that alters mucosal and vascular permeability. (2b) In favor of this hypothesis are changes in the small capillaries located near the basal surface of the epithelial cells, and the appearance of numerous microvesicles in the cytoplasm of the mucosal cells. (2c) It is believed that altered capillary permeability allows fluid to be hydrodynamically transported into the interstitial tissue and then through the mucosa into the lumen of the gut.

Consider how the second pair of sentences open:

(1b) Changes in small capillaries located near the basal surface of the epithelial cells, and the appearance of numerous microsvesicles in the cytoplasm of the mucosal cells. . . .

(2b) In favor of this hypothesis . . .

Sentence (1b) opens with information the reader would probably not anticipate: it is the evidence the writer offers to prove his hypothesis. In its conclusion, the sentence refers to information offered in the first sentence: *this hypothesis*. In (2b), on the other hand, the words that refer to the previous sentence, *In favor of this hypothesis*, locate the reader in familiar territory. The end of the sentence conveys the new information: *changes in the small . . . mucosal cells,*.

We can describe the first and third sentences in the same way. Sentence (1a) opens with a hypothesis that no reader could anticipate and ends by referring to what has already been mentioned—*this kind of severe dehydration*—and to something that any journal reader would take as a generic presupposition: medical articles offer hypotheses to explain biological events. On the other hand, sentence (2a) opens with what the reader can take for granted, with what the reader has already read. Sentence (1c) opens with more information that cannot be assumed and ends with two familiar concepts: it indirectly refers to the concept of hypotheses, *is believed*, and directly states another concept mentioned earlier, *altered capillary permeability*. Sentence (2c), on the other hand, begins with another reference to hypotheses and to capillary permeability, and ends with the new information.

The appropriate ordering of information in a sentence is one basic stratum of the cues we rely on to perceive form, one stratum of text structure. A reader who must begin sentences *out of context* will be disoriented because he or she will have to process new information before he or she knows how the new information is connected to information already assumed or assimilated.

The problem with understanding this stratum is that its effect depends on what the reader already knows. Consider these two passages:

(3) An appreciation of the effects of calcium blockers can best be attained by an understanding of the activation of muscle groups. The proteins actin, myosin, troponin, and tropomyosin make up the sarcomere, the fundamental unit of muscle contraction. The thick filament is composed of myosin, which is an ATPase, or energy producing protein. The thin filament consists of actin, tropomyosin, and troponin. A close association exists between the regulatory proteins tropomyosin and troponin, and the contractile protein actin in the thin filament. The interaction of actin and myosin is controlled by tropomyosin. Troponin C, which binds calcium; troponin I, which participates in the actinmyosin interaction; and troponin T, which binds troponin to tropomyosin constitute three peptide chains of troponin. An excess of 10^{-7} for the myoplasmic concentration $C++$ leads to its binding to troponin C. The inhibitory forces of tropomyosin are removed and the complex interaction of actin and myosin is manifested as contraction.

(4) The contraction of muscle depends on calcium. If we can understand how calcium activates muscle groups, we can appreciate how those groups are affected by calcium blockers.

The fundamental unit of muscle contraction is the sarcomere. In the sarcomere are two filaments, one thick and one thin. They contain proteins that prevent contraction and proteins that cause contraction. The thick filament contains the protein myosin, which is an ATPase, or energy producing protein. The thin filament contains the protein actin, which contracts, and the proteins tropomyosin and troponin, which regulate contraction. The troponin consists of three chains of peptides: troponin I; troponin T, which binds troponin to tropomyosin; and troponin C, which binds calcium. When a muscle is relaxed, tropomyosin inhibits the actin in the thin filament from interacting with the myosin in the thick filament. A muscle contracts when the myoplasmic concentration C++ in the sarcomere exceeds 10^{-7}. At that point the calcium binds to troponin C. The tropomyosin no longer inhibits the interaction of actin and myosin, and the muscle contracts.

We have been told by doctors familiar with the cellular mechanics of calcium blockers that the first passage is well written and that the second is obviously written for a popular audience. On the other hand, lay persons and even some doctors unfamiliar with sarcomeres, troponin, and tropomyosin find the first "full of medical jargon" and "hard to understand"; and, although they find the second taxing because of the vocabulary, they report that it is relatively clear and straightforward, much easier to read. Yet there is no information in the second that is not either explicitly or inferentially contained in the first. In other words, for some readers, there is no new information in the first passage; for others, there is too much in the wrong places. In the first case, too much information is presupposed too early in each sentence; complex syntactic and lexical bundles of information are distributed throughout the sentence, rather than being contextualized. In the second, the complex bundles are located at the ends of sentences, preceded by information explicitly asserting information based on what has gone before or what has to be asserted explicitly.

This leads to a generalization that may set the boundaries for how we understand text structure. On the one hand, at the level of the sentence, a sense of structure begins with the appropriate arrangement of information that is old and new, assumed and surprising, presupposed and unexpected. On the other hand, a sense of text structure also depends on what a reader already knows about the subject matter. A reader thoroughly familiar with a topic will be considerably more forgiving in constructing for him- or herself the experience we call coherence. A reader who is entirely knowledgeable about a subject needs fewer text signals out of which to construct a sense of form. A reader who is not knowledgeable about a subject needs many.

In short, the arrangement of ideas at this most microanalytical level of sentences depends on what the reader already controls at the macroanalytical level of knowledge. In some cases we can assert confidently that for all readers, one arrangement is better than another—as in our first pair of examples about mucosal permeability. But in other cases we cannot, as in our examples about calcium blockers. In other words, what might appropriately signal referential coherence for one reader may lead to confusion and a sense of incoherence for another.

There are relatively few generalizations to make concerning professional writing and FSP. This is a principle of style that is independent of all genres. Bad professional writing on any subject frequently exhibits the characteristics of the first calcium blocker passage.

TOPIC STRINGS

As important as the old/new principle is for individual sentences, it becomes crucial when a reader has to read sentence after sentence. A reader will feel considerably better oriented toward the whole discourse if he or she consistently begins in familiar territory, rather than having to begin sentence after sentence anew, out of context. In fact, when we step back from individual sentences to examine a series of connected sentences, we have to acknowledge a new principle of coherence, an emergent property that arises from the way a writer starts each sentence in a group of sentences.

Topic

To get to that principle, we have to introduce another concept, that of topic. By topic, we mean only what the reader takes a sentence to be about. The problem here is that we can take about to mean two things. Consider this sentence:

The reasons for this are difficult to understand.

On the one hand, this sentence is about not understanding reasons, but that phrasing of its "aboutness" focuses on what we might take to be the *point* of the sentence, its gist. There is another meaning of *about*, one closer to the traditional definition of grammatical subject.

Consider this sentence,

We believe that the computations are correct.

in answer to either of these questions:

Where do YOU two stand in regard to these figures?
What about the computations?

Depending on the question, the "same" answer is "about" us or "about" the computations. This is a sense of *about* different from the gist or point of a sentence. In this sense, *about* means the concept we are going to comment on: you asked about us, we'll tell you about us. Or you asked about the computations, we'll tell you about the computations (though with a qualification). As we said, this notion of *about* is captured in a familiar schoolroom definition of the subject of a sentence. The problem is that we cannot simply define topic as subject because of sentences like these:

With regard to funds, we will have a problem.
The reasons for this we do not understand.
We believe the computations are correct (in answer to a question about the computations).

Usually, subjects are also topics, but since sometimes they are not, we need a distinct term to refer to the idea in a sentence that we want to comment on, say something *about*. We will use the term *topic* to refer to whatever comes at the beginning of the sentence that the reader tacitly takes to be the *psychological* subject of the sentence, even if that psychological subject is not the *grammatical* subject (as in *The reasons for this we do not understand*).

To return to the problem of that emergent principle of coherence mentioned a few paragraphs before: when a reader moves through a sequence of sentences that begin with old information, that reader will not feel repeatedly dislocated from his or her knowledge. Consequently, he or she will not feel confused, out of focus, or lost, and will therefore not feel that the *text* is without structure. But in addition to that individually repeated feeling, a larger, emergent sense of coherence results when sentence after sentence begins not only with older, more familiar information, but also with a *consistent string of topics.*

Because there is not enough space here to illustrate these principles, we will have to refer back to the examples we have already used. Consider the mucosal permeability example. Here are the topics of the two passages, side by side:

(1a) Altered mucosal ... vibrio	(2a) We (can explain) the vibrio ...
(1b) Changes ... cells	(2b) This hypothesis
(1c) Hydrodynamic ... gut	(2c) It is believed ... altered capillary permeability

Note that in (1) the topics do not constitute a consistent string (except, perhaps, to someone who already knows all this information). In (2), the topics and subtopics consistently invoke concepts referring to hypotheses and belief, to information already mentioned (*permeability*), or to information a reader could be expected to know (*the vibrio*).

The Role of Prior Knowledge

Topic strings constitute the semantic units by which readers organize their understanding of what a text is about. If those topic strings are consistent, then the understanding will be coherent. If they are inconsistent, then the understanding will be less coherent. But again, this consistency cannot be inferred strictly from the page. Refer again to the two passages on calcium blockers. The topics in the second will seem consistent to almost any reader. The topics in the first may or may not be *perceived* to be consistent, depending on what the reader knows. A reader innocent of cellular biology will never be adequately oriented in that text and, as a consequence, will be more likely to construct a less well organized text structure. In the construction of form, we cannot overemphasize the importance of preknowledge and of how texts invoke it from the reader.

The lesson is self-evident, especially for professional writers who often have to write for audiences less than entirely familiar with their special knowledge: when writing for such an audience, make sure that what would count for them as new information goes at the *end* of a sentence, and make sure that sentences begin with information you have just recently mentioned or with information readily available in the body of knowledge you share with your readers.

Comment

Now we can present this principle in more schematic form. We have named two parts of a sentence, the *Topic* and our *Comment* on it. They are always in a fixed order because that is how we read: we take as *Topic* one of the first noun phrases we read, usually the subject noun phrase. What follows is the *Comment*—the verb and everything attached to it:

TOPIC	COMMENT

We also have the components of *Old* and *New* information. But as we have seen, they are *not* fixed. Indeed, one of the problems with bad writing is that the New sometimes precedes the Old. In a canonical sentence, however, the old roughly coincides with Topic and the new roughly coincides with Comment. We can make the box a bit more complex:

TOPIC	COMMENT
OLD	NEW

(In the scholarly literature, the Old is often called *theme*, and the New *rheme*.) When we add the grammatical structure to this outline, we make it even more complex:

TOPIC		COMMENT
OLD		NEW
SUBJECT	VERB	COMPLEMENT

Keep in mind that this is strictly a canonical schema. In actual sentences, Old and New may appear in reverse order; in some sentences the Topic is something other than the subject. Moreover, there are, of course, different conventions for topicalizing the writer. In internal reports, memos, etc., the use of *I* or *we* is entirely common. In scientific writing, the folklore is that writers should not topicalize themselves, though even a casual glance at well-written scientific prose reveals, especially in introductory sections, many instances of multiple authors using *we* and, in some instances, even *I*. These qualifications notwithstanding, we assert that the topic/comment structure is a characteristic of style that is independent of genre or subject matter.

LEXICAL STRINGS

Consider the following passage:

(5) Occasionally, a patient who enters a hospital in an emergency refuses treatment, even though a doctor informs him that he may be committing a fatal error. If the patient is competent, the doctor may not force treatment on him. But if the patient is incompetent, the doctor faces a problem. This happens most often when a doctor wishes to give medication to a patient who is suffering from acute schizophrenia, mania, or psychotic depression. Some physicians have argued that a psychotic patient is like an unconscious patient, unable to make a rational decision about his treatment. But others have argued that even the psychotic patient may refuse treatment. The physician who must decide this matter faces a difficult problem. Every physician should understand the underlying concepts of such a situation.

This passage was part of an article submitted to a legal journal. The editor returned it because this passage and what followed seemed "disconnnected" to the point of the whole article—what lawyers ought to know about recent developments in malpractice suits. It takes only a moment to recognize the problem: the writer had assumed that a lawyer would recognize the issue of civil rights in regard to the involuntary administration of medication. But the editor knew that readers other than lawyers would read this article and might wonder how this material fit into the overall intention of the article. If so, the reader would sense disorganization—a breakdown in text structure.

Now read an edited version of the same passage:

(6) Occasionally, a patient who enters a hospital in an emergency refuses treatment, even though a doctor informs him that he may be committing a fatal error. If the patient is legally competent, the

doctor may not force treatment on him. But if the patient is legally incompetent, the doctor faces a difficult problem in civil rights. This happens most often when a doctor wishes to give medication to a patient who is suffering from acute schizophrenia, mania, or psychotic depression. Some physicians have argued that a psychotic patient is like an unconscious patient, unable to make a rational decision about treatment. But others have argued that even the psychotic patient is within his civil rights to refuse treatment. The physician who must decide this matter faces a difficult legal problem. The wrong decision can lead to malpractice litigation over deprivation of civil rights. Every physician should understand the underlying legal issues of such a situation.

The topic strings are virtually identical. The only difference is that we have dropped in a few key words invoking the universe of the law and civil rights, *beginning with the end of the opening segment.* The opening three sentences announced the *issue* of this section, and the end of this opening segment—perhaps the most crucial spot in a unit of discourse at least as large as a paragraph—established a string of related words that locates the passage in the universe of the law. Such a string of related words is called a *Lexical String.* A *Topic String* is a kind of Lexical String that happens to coincide with Topics. There are other lexical strings in this passage: strings associated with medicine and with mental incompetence. But without the third string that locates the reader in the universe of the law, this passage will not serve its purpose: to inform lawyers *and doctors* about the legal consequences of forcing medication on seemingly incompetent patients.

Again we see the power of invoking a universe of knowledge to help the reader make sense of a passage. A few words introduced at strategic spots bring the passage into focus. It now reveals an intention of the writer that *meets the intention of the reader*: to learn something about handling or avoiding malpractice suits based on these problems, and eventually about how to earn more money.

But most important, we have also seen the crucial role of the *Comment* in an important sentence: the Comment of the third sentence states clearly a new body of information—*civil rights*—that announces a universe of reference that will be consistently invoked in one of the major lexical strings of the passage. Together with a consistent set of Topics, the Lexical String contributes to making the passage seem significantly more coherent than it otherwise would. All this depends, however, on more than a mechanical mention of certain words in certain places. It must reflect a coincidence between two intentions: the perceived intention of the writer and the actual intention of the reader. If a reader had read this passage in order to learn how to give medication to unwilling patients, that reader would have felt the passage to be off the point, unfocused, finally disorganized, without structure. And to that reader, it would have been, because that reader would have constructed a passage that did not reflect either the reader's or the author's intention.

UNITS OF DISCOURSE

At this point we have the beginnings of a relatively rich vocabulary that not only speaks about form in specific ways but also correlates our perceptions to features of text structure. But that vocabulary is still incomplete. Consider the following paragraph:

> (7) Students at the University of Chicago tend to be interested in medicine more than any other professional field. Medicine is such a popular choice because it offers the power, prestige, and money which University of Chicago students desire above all else. But to obtain these rewards of money and fame, he must suffer many sleepless nights grinding out Chemistry assignments. The hard long hours of studying chemistry is more than just rewarding financially, it gives one the feeling of doing important scientific research. And the university stresses how important careers in research are to the general welfare of society. However, while the University promotes careers in research, they also feel that careers in academics contribute greatly to the welfare of society. Finally, since all students must enter society after completing their education, we see the importance of the University's commitment to preparing a wide range of career choices for its students.

In this paragraph, the opening or Topic position of the sentences consistently includes older, recognizable, thematic information. The paragraph also contains a consistent Topic String and fully developed, appropriate Lexical Strings. Yet we can agree that this paragraph is confused, loose, muddled, wandering—in short, incoherent. The point of the example is this: those textual features we have described so far do not exhaustively account for our perceptions of form. Texts with all those features can still seem formless. We need, then, a way to account for these more basic perceptions of form, perceptions we normally describe with such adjectives as *confused, incoherent, off the point.*

Most generally, what paragraph (7) lacks is a controlling intention. We know this because the paragraph was written, one sentence at a time, by seven authors, each of whom saw only one other sentence. Several groups of seven advanced college students were asked to write a collective paragraph on "Careerism at the University of Chicago." Each student wrote one sentence on an index card, and then the stack of cards was passed to the next student, but with only the last-written sentence visible. In this situation, only a remarkable coincidence (or ESP) could give those seven students one, shared, controlling intention. Thus, despite the presence of consistent Topic and Lexical Strings (which the students were encouraged to create), the paragraph is hard to follow. We don't know what to expect, where we and the paragraph are going, how one part relates to the next. The paragraph is, we say, incoherent, at odds with itself.

But what does it means for a text *not* to be at odds with itself? Such terms as *controlling intention, coherence,* and *where the paragraph is going* only describe our perceptions. What we lack is a consistent, systematic vocabulary that correlates perceptions of coherence with features of text structure.

Shaping a Reader's Expectations

Look again at the last example of the previous section:

(6) 1) Occasionally, a patient who enters a hospital in an emergency refuses treatment, even though a doctor informs him that he may be committing a fatal error. 2) If the patient is legally competent, the doctor may not force treatment on him. 3) But if the patient is legally incompetent, the doctor faces a difficult problem in civil rights. 4) This happens most often when a doctor wishes to give medication to a patient who is suffering from acute schizophrenia, mania, or psychotic depression. 5) Some physicians have argued that a psychotic patient is like an unconscious patient, unable to make a rational decision about his treatment. 6) But others have argued that even the psychotic patient is within his civil rights to refuse treatment. 7) The physician who must decide this matter faces a difficult legal problem. 8) The wrong decision can lead to malpractice litigation over deprivation of civil rights. 9) Every physician should understand the legal issues underlying such a situation.

Earlier we noted that the first three sentences announce what's at issue in the paragraph by establishing a Lexical String ("legally competent . . . legally incompetent . . . civil rights") that locates the passage in the universe of the law.

Discourse Topic

Now, taking the point of view of the whole unit, we can rephrase that description: the opening three sentences announce what's at issue in the paragraph by announcing the *Discourse Topic* of the paragraph. *Discourse Topic* we define as that complex of ideas out of which flow the dominant Topic and Lexical Strings—in the case of this paragraph, something like "the problem in civil rights when incompetent patients refuse treatment." We also said that the paragraph as a whole announces what's at issue in the article as a whole. Now we can see that it does so by announcing the Discourse Topic of the essay: "legal issues when a psychotic patient refuses treatment." We can also rephrase our analysis of why the editor of the journal was dissatisfied with this paragraph: the opening of the article seemed inadequate because it did not announce the Discourse Topic of the article explicitly enough for a nonlegal audience. The notion of a Discourse Topic unifies, at the level of wholes or units, the scattered phenomena of the Topic and Lexical Strings.

D-Unit

The reason for unifying these phenomena under a single term lies in the structure of units of discourse, or *d-units*. A *d-unit* is any stretch of continuous text—a whole text, a section, a paragraph, even a small group of related sentences—that functions as a unit and whose parts are more related to each other than to those outside the d-unit. Note that in paragraph (6) those three opening sentences that announce the Discourse Topic of the paragraph are more closely related to each other than to the rest of the paragraph. In a sense, after these three sentences announce the Discourse Topic of the paragraph, the paragraph starts over—here moving from a general description of the matter at hand to an account of particular cases.[3] A reader forced to divide the paragraph into two parts would almost certainly divide it at this point. This division, between an opening, announcing segment and a closing, developing segment, is an essential aspect of text structure at the level of units of discourse.

Issue and Discussion

All well-informed units of professional discourse fall into two well-defined constituents. The first is an opening segment or *Issue*, which generally signals those expectations that the reader will use to construct a coherent whole and which specifically announces the Discourse Topic—what is "at issue" in the d-unit as a whole. The second is a main segment or *Discussion*, which explains, describes, illustrates, draws conclusions from, or otherwise develops the matters established in the Issue.[4] We can represent this structure as follows:

ISSUE	DISCUSSION

Strictly speaking, the relationship between the Issue and the Discussion is reciprocal—it makes as much sense to speak of the Discussion developing the Issue as it does to speak of the Issue setting up the Discussion. But so powerful is the effect when a segment simply comes first that in almost all situations it is more useful to treat the Issue as the primary, functional constituent of a d-unit. Certainly the Issue is the more important of the two constituents of a d-unit in generating the reader's perceptions of form. For it is the Issue that establishes those crucial expectations—for the Discourse Topic, for the bases of Lexical Strings, for the relevant universes of knowledge—upon which readers construct the coherence, the form of a discourse. Readers are much more likely to register a sense of formlessness or incoherence when the Issue of a d-unit generates expectations that are not met—or, more fully, when the Issue of a d-unit generates expectations that are not rich or pointed enough for the reader to recognize or (if they are lacking) to supply those connections, continuities, and indications of relative importance that are the bases of our perceptions of form. In short, we see the greater importance of the Issue in the fact that when the Issue of a d-unit does create expectations that are rich and to the point, readers will create for themselves a coherent discourse, *even if the text of the Discussion does not do so.*

Returning, then, to the example of paragraph (6), we see that the Issue (sentences 1–3) establishes, *at the end,* a "problem": the civil rights of legally incompetent patients who refuse treatment. The

Discussion (sentences 4–9) develops this problem by specifying it: the patients in question are psychotic patients, who may or may not be legally competent, and the problem in question is malpractice suits. Nowhere in the Discussion does the text explicitly address the legal competence of psychotic patients, and nowhere does it say that malpractice suits are a problem. But, given the expectations the Issue generates and the universes of knowledge it calls forth, every member of the prospective audience for this article—doctors and lawyers—can and will make those connections and so will find or make this a coherent, well-formed d-unit.

The structure of units of discourse is also recursive: d-units can be composed of other, smaller d-units and in turn can compose parts of larger d-units. Paragraph (6) is a d-unit with an Issue and a Discussion. It is also a part of a larger d-unit, the article it opened. That larger d-unit is itself composed of an Issue, paragraph (6), and a Discussion, all the rest of the article. Because the structure is recursive, we are able to construct rich, multilevel analyses.

Importance of Expectations

But we must also take care to keep separate the effects of the various levels of discourse structure. The problem with the original version of paragraph (6)—the problem that led the editor to find it an inadequate opening—is not primarily a matter of the internal structure of the paragraph. The problem is instead a question of the ability of the paragraph as a whole to serve as the Issue for the article as a whole. The original paragraph did not generate the expectations the prospective audience would need to find coherence in the text. Paragraph (6) is a more successful Issue paragraph because it establishes, *at its end*, a Discourse Topic—the underlying legal issues when a psychotic patient refuses treatment—which leads the reader to invoke the universes of knowledge appropriate for understanding the d-unit (the article) of which it is the Issue. It is also more successful because it gives the reader a reason—malpractice suits—to care about what the article will say.

Note that this crucial expectation-generating information is stated at the end of paragraph (6), at the end of the Issue of the whole. Note also that the crucial expectation-generating information in the internal structure of paragraph (6) is stated at the end of its (internal)

Issue. In both cases the most important sentence of the Issue is the last. If, for example, we were forced to use only one of the first three sentences to stand as the Issue of the paragraph, we would clearly choose a slightly expanded version of sentence 3: "If a legally incompetent patient refuses treatment, the doctor faces a difficult problem of civil rights." Similarly, if we were forced to use only one sentence in the paragraph to stand as the Issue of the entire article, we would choose a slightly expanded version of sentence 9: "Every physician should understand the underlying legal issues when a psychotic patient refuses treatment." In both cases the opening would seem to be much too abrupt (because too much new information is introduced too quickly). But the resulting one-sentence Issues would still serve adequately to announce the Discourse Topic and to generate the necessary set of expectations.

The lesson here is this: again we see that coherence is not an inherent feature of texts. Readers create coherence and, for the most part, are eager to do so. They will do so when the texts they encounter allow them to generate appropriate expectations for what is to follow—when the text announces early on what will be the Topic of the discourse, what words or ideas will form the basis for the major Topic and Lexical Strings, what areas of knowledge are relevant to the matters developed in the text, and why the reader should care about reading the text at hand. Thus successful texts will compromise and be constituted by well-formed units of discourse that fall into two clearly defined constituents: an *Issue*, which performs all these announcing functions, and a *Discussion*, which develops the matters announced in the Issue. And of all the parts of the Issue, the end will most fully and most explicitly encapsule the matters announced to the reader.

Making Points

Let us look one last time at paragraph (6). In the previous section, we said that if the author were forced to save only one of the first three sentences, he would undoubtedly save the last. And if he could save only one sentence of the paragraph, he would save the last one. These last sentences would also be given in answer to a pair of different but related questions. Suppose some obtuse or careless reader, finding the first three sentences difficult to understand, asked:

"What are you saying here? What's the gist of this? What's your point?" In this situation, too, the answer would be the third sentence: "My point is, 'If a legally incompetent patient refuses treatment. . . . '" Similarly, if this uncomprehending reader asked of the whole paragraph, "What's the point?" the answer would isolate the last sentence of the paragraph: "My point is that 'Every physician should understand . . . "

ISSUES AND POINTS. In the last section we explained these answers in terms of the principle that the end of the Issue is particularly important for establishing the Discourse Topic of a d-unit. But that does not mean there is any necessary connection between the Issue segment and the Point of a d-unit: that is, Points need not be and often are not expressed in Issues. Consider another example, a paragraph that did not in its original context open its d-unit, that was not itself an Issue or even part of an Issue. The paragraph was written by a young attorney to a major executive in a large corporation; it discusses the fines the corporation had been paying as a result of minor weights-and-measures violations in California:

> (8)   1) At the outset this sum may not appear to be particularly onerous. 2) However, the troublesome provision is not the $500 fine, but the "six months in county jail." 3) Even though no jail sentences have been rendered against Abco so far, the fact that these violations are criminal in nature causes serious concern. 4) And our concern over the criminal aspects of these violations is only deepened by California's emphasis on consumerism and the growing mistrust and hostility toward large, international corporations. 5) In view of these dangers, we should consider reviewing the way these alleged violations are dealt with.

Since it is a d-unit in its own right, this paragraph exhibits the standard structure of d-units: the Issue consists of sentences 1–2 and the Discussion of sentences 3–5. The Issue establishes the Discourse Topic—something like *criminal sanctions for these violations*—and what is "at issue" or "at stake" for the reader—going to jail. Note that here, too, there is a significant emphasis at the end of the Issue, in the very highly stressed New information in the Comment position, *six months in county jail*. Note also that this very vivid statement of the Discourse Topic sets up a rhetorically effective Topic String (*this sum . . . troublesome provision . . . "six months in county jail" . . . no jail sentences . . . violations . . . concern over the criminal aspects of these violations . . . these dangers . . . alleged violations)*—one that is indeed likely to focus the reader's attention.

So far, this is all in keeping with what we saw in example (6). If we asked of this paragraph our two questions—"Which sentence would you keep?" and "What's the point?"—the answer would once again isolate the last sentence: "The point is, 'In view of these dangers, we should consider reviewing the way these alleged violations are dealt with.' " Again, the most important, or *Point* sentence of the d-unit is the last. But here we cannot explain that fact by recourse to the principle that the end of an Issue is particularly important. Nor can we jump to the conclusion that the last sentence of any d-unit is the most important.

Consider two more sample paragraphs. The first is a paragraph (again not itself an Issue or even part of an Issue) from a book about discovering fossils:

(9) 1) Equally important, Clark's practice of carefully mapping every fossil made it possible to follow the evolutionary development of various types through time. 2) Beautiful sequences of antelopes, giraffes and elephants were obtained—new species evolving out of old ones and appearing in younger strata, then dying out as they were replaced by still others in still younger strata. 3) In short, evolution was taking place before the eyes of the Omo surveyors. 4) And it could be timed. 5) The finest examples of this process were in several lines of pigs which had been extremely common at Omo and had evolved rapidly. 6) Unsnarling the pig story was turned over to paleontologist Basil Cooke. 7) He produced family trees for pigs whose various types were so accurately dated that pigs themselves became measuring sticks that could be applied to finds of questionable age in other places that had similar pigs.

Here the Issue of the paragraph is composed of sentence 1, and the Discussion of sentences 2–7. And, as we have come to expect, the key elements of the Discourse Topic—*following the evolution of various types through time*—are stated at the end of the Issue. But here the answer to our two questions, the Point of the paragraph, is expressed not in the last sentence but in the first. In (9) the Issue of the d-unit expresses its Point; the Issue and the Point sentence are one and the same.

The next example is from a book about legal reasoning:

(10) 1) *McPherson v. Buick* renamed and enlarged the danger category. 2) It is usually thought to have brought the law into line with "social considerations." 3) But it did not remove the necessity of deciding cases. 4) Later the New York courts were able to put into the category of things of danger or probably dangerous a defective bottle and another coffee urn, although one less terrifying than the coffee boiler of 1909. 5) But for some reason or other, admission was denied to a defective automobile when the defect was a door handle which gave way, causing one of the doors to open with the result that the plaintiff was thrown through the door and under the car. 6) The defective handle did not make the car a "thing of danger." 7) And if one is comparing cases and examples, it has to be admitted that a door handle is less closely connected with those things which make a car like a locomotive than is the wheel on which it runs.

Here the Issue is composed of sentences 1–3 and the Discussion of sentences 4–7. As usual, the end of the Issue expresses the key element of the Discourse Topic: "deciding cases," which for a legal audience means something like "deciding on a case-by-case basis rather than by deductive, categorical rules." Here the Point of the paragraph is expressed in sentence 3. Thus in (10) as in (9) the Point of the d-unit is expressed in the Issue. But in (9) the Issue was composed of only one sentence, so that the Issue and the Point sentence were the same. In (10) the Point sentence is only a part—the end—of the three-sentence Issue.

RELATION OF POINT, ISSUE, AND TOPIC SENTENCE. Those familiar with traditional methods of describing text structure will no doubt have noticed, especially in paragraph (9), a similarity between our Issue and standard accounts of topic sentences—those initial sentences that state the *topic* and the *thesis* of the texts they begin. Though there are similarities, it is the differences that are crucial. First, the Issue is not a sentence (or group of sentences) but a fixed discourse position or slot, one of two correlated constituents in the structure of all units of discourse. An Issue is composed of or filled by the sentences or larger stretches of discourse that occur in the Issue position. Second, d-units range in size from pairs of sentences to the largest texts, and their Issues vary accordingly. Even at the level of paragraph-sized d-units, Issues are as often as not composed of two or more sentences rather than a single topic sentence. Third, and most important, the traditional concept of the topic sentence conflates two distinct discourse functions: to announce the Discourse Topic and to make the Point. As our four examples have shown, although some paragraphs do announce the Discourse Topic and make the Point in the same sentence (i.e., in a one-sentence Issue), most do not. Many paragraphs make their Point outside the Issue entirely (i.e., at the end of the Discussion). Those paragraphs that do make the Point in the Issue often have complex Issues composed of several sentences, only one of which expresses the Point. And when the d-unit in question is larger than a paragraph, the structure is still more complex.

LOCATION OF THE POINT. These four examples also show that there is a consistent and recognizable pattern in how and where Points are made. In these examples, as in all well-formed d-units, the Point is made either at the end of the d-unit—that is to say, at the end of the Discussion—or at the end of the Issue. With this pattern we have the basis of a relatively rich way of describing the textual features that correlate to our perceptions of form: every unit of professional discourse is composed of two major constituents, an Issue and a Discussion.[5] The function of the Issue is to generate for the reader those expectations that will be the basis for whatever lexical coherence the reader finds or constructs in the text. The most important of the expectation-generating features is the Discourse Topic, which is commonly stated, especially in d-units paragraph-sized or larger, at the end of the Issue in the Comment of the final sentence, and which is manifested throughout the d-unit in the form of Topic and Lexical Strings. The function of the Discussion is to develop the material announced in the Issue. Just how the Discussion develops from an Issue is a complex and not very well understood matter that will be explored in our later discussion of "Conventions of Order."

POINT AND DEVELOPMENT: The centerpiece of our perceptions of form, and in some sense the reason for all this structure, is the Point— that information that controls the whole, establishes the canons of relevance, and draws all else together, that information which all the rest was written to convey. A Point is expressed in a Point sentence (or Point paragraph). The "all the rest" that was written to convey the Point we call the Development. The Development is expressed in whatever is not a Point sentence (or paragraph). Point sentences or paragraphs occur in one of two positions: at the end of the Issue or at the end of the Discussion. We can illustrate this structure with the

following diagram (the parentheses indicate that the location of the
Point is optional):

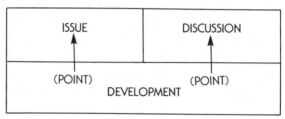

Locating Points

In the abstract, when we deal with d-units isolated from their
context, the choice of where to locate Points is a free one—a Point
will do just as well near the beginning of the d-unit, at the end of the
Issue, as it will at the end of the d-unit, at the end of the Discussion.
But when we look at d-units in the contexts in which they are actually
used, are put to work, the situation is different. Contexts—both
textual (where the d-unit occurs in a text) and situational (how the
text is produced and used)—make the choice of where to locate the
Point much less free.

We have already seen one way in which context constrains the
location of Points: when a d-unit is also an Issue of a larger d-unit,
then its Point will invariably be expressed at the end of the
Discussion. In such d-units the Point sentence will make the fullest,
most explicit statement of the Discourse Topic of the larger d-unit.
Consequently, the principle that Discourse Topics are normally stated
at the end of the Issue causes us to put the Point of the smaller d-unit
at the end of its Discussion, so that the Discourse Topic can appear at
the end of the Issue of the larger unit.

Other contextual constraints on Point locations, not all of which
we yet understand, are many and various—so various that we cannot
discuss them in detail here. But we can make some observations
about the effects on readers of locating Points in Issues or in
Discussions, effects that undoubtedly underlie all the various particular patterns of Point location.

EFFECTS ON READERS. The most general of these effects concerns
the state of the reader's knowledge and expectations as he or she
works through the d-unit. When the Point is expressed at the end of

the Issue, then not only does the Issue generate the reader's expectations, it also confirms them. Thus as readers work through d-units whose Points have been made at or near the beginning, they are able to assimilate the information in the Discussion relatively quickly and easily because they already know how that information relates to the Point, what the information will come to.

When the Point is reserved for the end of the Discussion, the end of the unit, then the expectations generated by the Issue must be continually tested and refined as the reader uses each new bit of information to construct provisional accounts of what the Point might be, what the information will finally come to. Thus as readers work through d-units whose Points are made at the end, they assimilate the information in the Discussion more slowly, with less sureness, and with more care because they do not know where they and the text are headed. And so writers who reserve the Point for the end of the d-unit are often led to offer provisional, partial Points in the Issue.

CONSEQUENCES. These differences in effects on readers have important consequences. Readers who are pressed for time or who for other reasons are unwilling to give their time to the writer tend to prefer Point-first structures, since these structures make the reading process as quick and efficient as possible. Not only does this structure make the actual reading easier, but it also makes possible speedy and reliable skimming: Having gotten the Point in the Issue, the reader is in a position to make an informed judgment of the value—given the circumstances and the purpose of the reading—of reading the whole of a particular section or paragraph.

On the other hand, readers who are willing or who must give their time to the writer and who expect in return the kinds of pleasures we associate with fine, belletristic writing generally feel more rewarded by Point-last structures, since only in such structures are they accorded the pleasures of the chase. Not only does this structure demand a greater engagement from the reader, but it also makes possible a richer and more complex unfolding of the Point, so that the reader gets the Point only after it has already been fully developed.

Each of these patterns of Point development carries with it serious costs. The Point-first structure encourages readers to be somewhat less attentive. Details are more likely to be lost in the shuffle, especially with readers who feel comfortable with the topic at hand. Readers not familiar with the topic are more likely to feel rushed by Point-first structures, especially when the Issues tend to be relatively short: these readers will often misunderstand or only partly understand a Point that has not been prepared for them, so that it is often necessary to repeat the Point at the end as well as near the beginning. And all readers will feel invited to skim texts dominated by Point-first d-units.

On the other hand, the Point-last structure forces all readers, even those who cannot or will not, to be more attentive in order to get the Point. This structure runs the risk of at best alienating and at worst losing those readers who are unable or unwilling to give the writer the care and attention the text demands. Here the danger is less that details will get lost in the shuffle than that Points will. Very few readers in professional settings are willing to allow writers the kind of claim on their time and energy that is inherent in Point-last structures. And texts dominated by Point-last d-units will defeat all but the most accomplished skimmers.

The range of contexts in which professionals write is so various that we can offer no one optimal pattern for developing Points and constructing d-units. At the level of the paragraph, paragraphs that come first or last in a larger d-unit tend to have Point-last structures, and paragraphs that come in the middle tend to have Point-first structures. But there are many variations, depending on local conventions, the particular situation in which a text is produced, and the role the paragraph plays in the overall design of the text. At the level of the largest d-units (texts and large sections of texts), most professionals find that the need for efficiency demands Point-first structures. But here, too, there is much variation. Some professions have conventional genres and formats, many of which correlate well with the general principles we have outlined here, but some of which—for reasons of particular circumstances or, more often, historical accident—do not. Other professions have loose, often unstated conventions for structuring texts. Still others value originality. But what does not vary is that successful professional writing, of whatever kind, manifests one or another of the possibilities represented in the model of discourse structure presented here and manifests them in such a way that the particular realization suits the needs and aims of the participants in that communicative exchange.

CONVENTIONS OF ORDER

We have postponed until now the most conventional ways of discussing *order* because we think we can best explain order on the basis of what has gone before. In the previous sections we have claimed that discourses are constituted out of d-units whose major constituents are an *Issue* and a *Discussion*, analogous to a *Topic* and a *Comment*. We have discussed how that fixed structural level interacts with the variable meaning-level of *Point* and *Development*. We have discussed how and where Points appear, how they shape our understanding of Discourse Topics, and how they correlate with Topical and Lexical development.

What we have not yet discussed, however, is the nature of the logical, semantic, rhetorical *connections* between an Issue and a Discussion, between a Point and its Development. That is, Topic and Comment relate to one another as psychological topic and psychological predicate; Familiar and New Information relate to one another as psychologically more and psychologically less present or available. In this section, we want to explore some of the ways Issue and Discussion, Point and Development relate to one another. We want also to explore some of those more conventional terms for order and text structure and how those concepts may or may not be compatible with our proposal. Unfortunately, we can sketch only the outlines of how we think our proposal can subsume traditional terms such as narration, comparison and contrast, inductive and deductive, and the like. Merely to summarize how others have described text structure would require a chapter twice this length. We will have to ask our readers to entertain as at least plausible what may seem a series of assertions lacking full substantiation.

Content versus Structure

First we must distinguish between describing the content of the discourse and describing its structure. In professional writing, units of discourse are often signaled by headings that contain key words from Topical or Lexical Strings. Such headings have appeared in this chapter. They signal new units of topical content, but they do not describe the structural *function* of the unit (abstract, introduction, discussion, conclusion, etc.), the role the unit plays in the discourse as a whole. Such topical headings invoke and reinvoke the universe of lexical reference the writer is asking the reader to construct. If the reader is generally familiar with that reference, with the subject matter, then the reader can rely at least in part on the structure of his or her knowledge as perhaps the basic stratum of structure that contributes to the experience of coherence.

On the other hand, what may appear to be more functional names of categories in conventionalized discourse may in fact only name the category of information typically found in that discourse, information that could be represented as topical or lexical strings. That is, a scientific paper typically has a section called "Methods and Materials," a category name for specific content; legal briefs, a section called "Cases Cited"; many contracts, a section called "Definitions." These units of the discourse have functions, but their conventional names do not signal what that function is. Nor do they stipulate a necessary position in a discourse. We easily imagine that a unit called "References" could come first, not last; "Methods and Materials" could come in an appendix (a structural name, incidentally); "Cases Cited" need not appear at all. All these are local names for units that convention decrees must appear in certain discourse genres. They are not universals in the universes of discourse.

Rhetorical Action

Few categories of discourse structure have been more intensely studied than conjunction, signaled by small function words such as *and, however, for example, indeed,* and so on. On the one hand, it is tempting to take these words as the primary data. We would, as many others have done, taxonomize the words into categories—additive, adversative, alternative, causative, and so on—categories that almost always correlate very closely with the coordinating conjunctions *and, but, or, so/for.* But if we look closely at the ways those categories are themselves named, we can recognize easily enough that the names of the categories in fact are the names of actions: *add, oppose, alternate.* The category *causative* obscures the action of stipulating a cause, condition, or effect for the preceding or following proposition or statement. Taken in this sense, the primary functional category, then, is not the name of the category of words but the name of the category of action, presumably of universals of linguistic, or rhetorical, actions.

To locate what we will refer to as *functional* universals, then, we might look first to names that designate common rhetorical actions: *introduce, discuss, conclude, summarize, append, abstract.* We might also consider more local rhetorical actions such as *state, restate, develop, elaborate, restrict, qualify, deny, digress, define, classify, compare and contrast, narrate, describe.* We must assume that actions such as these characterize all nonnarrative discourse, regardless of profession or situation.

One recurrent principle of linguistic structure is that of a bilevel unit of analysis: one level is structural and fixed; the other level is semantic and variable. This same bilevel pattern appears to characterize actions of the sort described here: those that seem appropriate to the fixed structural level of Discourse units (Issue and Discussion), and those that seem appropriate to the variable, meaning-relevant level (Point and Development). What we have in fact done is tacitly assert that (making a) Point is as much an action as Development; that (announcing an) Issue is as much an action as Discussion.

SYNTAGMATIC ACTIONS. Those rhetorical actions that would characterize the relationship between an Issue and its Discussion would be essentially *syntagmatic;* that is, they would depend on, indeed be defined by, the *order* in which they occur. Syntagmatic actions are those that a writer could perform only *after* invoking the Issue or *before* initiating the Discussion. They would be the actions that can have as their objects *only* a preceding or *only* a following unit of text.

For example, once a writer STATES (we will use capital letters to indicate rhetorical actions), the writer may RESTATE, DEVELOP, ELABORATE, RESTRICT, EXPAND, CONCLUDE, and so on. It makes no sense to say a writer *first* ELABORATES and *then* STATES. We might see this relationship as a simple left-right sequence:

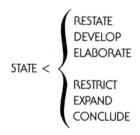

In fact, the relationships are more complex than this, for if we consider for a moment the implicational relationships among these words, we recognize that some of these actions imply others. When we RESTATE, for example, we may be RESTATING in order to perform the more specifically motivated action of RESTRICTING or ELABORATING. We RESTATE *in order to* RESTRICT or ELABORATE. We do *not* RESTRICT or ELABORATE in order to RESTATE.

Let us clarify with an example: Under ordinary circumstances, do you wave your hand with the intention of signaling someone, or do you signal someone with the intention of waving your hand? In fact, you perform both those actions simultaneously: It is *in* waving a hand that you signal, and *in* signaling that you might be waving your hand. But when we cast the relationship between the two actions as an implicational one, it is clear that under ordinary circumstances, signaling is in some sense hierarchically more important than waving a hand (i.e., closer to some defining, ultimate intention—being rescued, for example). You wave your hand in order to signal; you do not ordinarily signal in order to wave your hand.

On these grounds, we can structure this array in a more complex and revealing way, because many rhetorical actions are performed *in order to* perform a *hierarchically more salient one:*

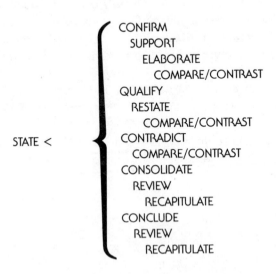

STATE <
CONFIRM
SUPPORT
ELABORATE
COMPARE/CONTRAST
QUALIFY
RESTATE
COMPARE/CONTRAST
CONTRADICT
COMPARE/CONTRAST
CONSOLIDATE
REVIEW
RECAPITULATE
CONCLUDE
REVIEW
RECAPITULATE

We shall simply assert here that these rhetorical actions roughly sketch the variety of syntagmatic relationships between Issue and

Discussion. That is, once a writer makes one STATEment, and then another, the two will relate in one of the ways specified. Moreover, the step-wise relationship, we claim, indicates the implicational relationship under ordinary conditions. At least on the basis of the way ordinary English allows us to state these relationships, we RESTATE in order to QUALIFY; we do not QUALIFY in order to RESTATE. We REVIEW in order to CONCLUDE, we do not CONCLUDE in order to REVIEW, and so forth.

Admittedly, this array represents the actual state of things too schematically and neatly. It requires only a little investigation to recognize that the ordinary language lexicon of rhetorical action is shifty, ambiguous, resistant to neat taxonomies of this kind. We present this formulation for two reasons: First, simply categorizing conjunctions (our rhetorical actions) serves no purpose beyond classification. Once we classify conjunctions as additive, adversative, causal, and temporal (with however many subclassifications), what useful information do we have about conjunction/rhetorical action? Second, the kind of syntagmatic/hierarchical classification suggested here comports well with the kind of discourse unit we have been describing: the initial STATEment (and perhaps QUESTION) corresponds to Issue, and the hierarchical array to Discussion. Indeed, we will simply assert now that Issue generically names STATEment, and that Discussion generically names the syntagmatically anterior actions: CONFIRM, QUALIFY, CONTRADICT, CONCLUDE.

It should be noted that these connections exist not merely between two consecutive sentences that constitute the Issue and the Discussion of a two-sentence d-unit, but also between Issues and Discussions, each of which may comprise several sentences or paragraphs. Thus one section of a text (itself constituting a complex d-unit) might REVIEW, RESTATE, RESTRICT what is in the previous segment (also comprising a d-unit). The previous segment can itself be taken as a complex STATEment.

NONSYNTAGMATIC ACTIONS. We may now turn to those rhetorical actions that are not syntagmatically defined, that need not be performed in a particular order but, rather, may precede or follow the object of that action. For example, one may ILLUSTRATE a concept either before the concept has been STATED, or after. One may CLASSIFY the elements of a concept before the concept itself has been STATED, or after. One may PARTICULARIZE a concept before the concept itself is articulated, or after.

In fact, these are the variably ordered *semantic* relationships that we claim *generally* obtain between Point and Development. Ordinarily, the Point is the element ILLUSTRATED, DEFINED, PARTICULARIZED, CATEGORIZED.

That this is not always the case complicates this superficially attractive division between syntagmatic and nonsyntagmatic actions. The exception usually comes in sequences of the sort that introduce a d-unit substantially larger than the d-unit containing our exception. In such cases, a particular element typically appears last in the sequence with certain associated signals, and thereby is promoted to the rhetorical Point of the d-unit:

> There are many reasons for preferring tax exempt bonds over industrials. First, ... Second, ... *But the most important reason is that* they are tax free investments that ... [This introductory paragraph will go on to discuss the advantages of tax free investments.]

These nonsyntagmatic actions may also be assembled into an implicational and hierarchical array of the sort we postulated for syntagmatic actions:

$$
\text{ACTION-X} \left\{
\begin{array}{l}
\text{SUMMARIZE} \\
\text{GENERALIZE} \\
\text{DEFINE} \\
\text{CATEGORIZE} \\
\text{PARTICULARIZE} \\
\text{STATE CAUSE/EFFECT}
\end{array}
\right.
$$

In this case, we leave the first element unnamed because it will be defined by the action that is associated with it. That is, ACTION-X may be a group of particulars, which is then DEFINED. Or one might DEFINE, then follow with a series of PARTICULARIZations. This kind of rhetorical action is not directional (i.e., syntagmatic), but rather conceptual; we may not infer from the sequence, *ACTION-X* < ... anything about the possible *actual* order of the elements in the text.

We do not stipulate the hierarchical relationship between the syntagmatic and nonsyntagmatic actions beyond claiming that they comprise the inventories of rhetorical actions assignable to the two levels of a d-unit: syntagmatic actions constitute the Issue-Discussion stratum, nonsyntagmatic actions the Point-Development stratum. The two stratified actions together constitute the full rhetorical action. *The two strata together constitute the nuclear unit of discourse in nonnarrative prose.*

It is perhaps interesting to note a few other characteristics of these actions: the nonsyntagmatic actions, of course, are the traditional *topoi* of rhetoric; the syntagmatic actions are closer to the *partitio* of the classical oration. Note, too, that they have qualitatively different entities as direct objects of their actions. The syntagmatic actions take as direct objects propositions: RESTATE, SUMMARIZE, RESTRICT the *meanings* of sentences. The nonsyntagmatic actions, ILLUSTRATE, DEFINE, CATEGORIZE, take as their direct objects entities that seem closer to the *referents* of the sentences: I ILLUSTRATE not the proposition *you are intelligent*, but the reality, reference, substance of your being intelligent.

EXTRATEXTUAL ACTIONS. Taken together, these two types of actions are hierarchically subordinate to another set of actions that themselves constitute a hierarchy:

Action	Outcome		
I PERSUADE	you of X so that you will	DO	X
I CONVINCE	you of X so that you will	BELIEVE	X
I EXPLAIN	X to you so that you will	UNDERSTAND	X
I INFORM	you of X so that you will	KNOW	X

It is these actions that the syntagmatic and nonsyntagmatic actions are in the service of. That is, I ELABORATE in order to SUPPORT, I SUPPORT in order to CONFIRM, and I CONFIRM in order to INFORM. I may INFORM in order to EXPLAIN (not vice versa); I EXPLAIN in order to CONVINCE (not vice versa); I CONVINCE in order to PERSUADE (not vice versa). Note, too, that these actions (1) take as their direct or indirect object the name of the audience and (2) are paired with the name of a rhetorical outcome. These are, of course, the names of the traditional rhetorical modes, with two exceptions: NARRATE and DESCRIBE. Neither NARRATE nor DESCRIBE has a naturally paired outcome, and neither seems to take the audience as a natural object. In this regard, they are much closer to the d-unit syntagmatic and nonsyntagmatic actions, which also do not imply an audience; that is, what natural successful outcome do we associate with RESTATING or DEFINING? Compare the natural successful outcome of INFORM or EXPLAIN: KNOW and UNDERSTAND.

We thus have the following relationship among rhetorical actions:

Pragmatic level:

Extratextual action (INFORM/EXPLAIN, etc.)

Text level:

Intratextual action	Syntagmatic action (RESTATE, etc.)
	Nonsyntagmatic action (DEFINE, etc.)

There are many other problems and implications of this way of dealing with rhetorical actions, but to address them all is not possible here. There are rhetorical actions other than those described. We have tried to be not exhaustive, but indicative. There may even be actions with no common name. We assert only that whatever those other actions may be, they can be incorporated into the kind of schema we propose.

OTHER CONJUNCTIONS. Some readers may have noted that we have left out perhaps the most frequent forms of rhetorical action— those signaled by the words most often used to illustrate the three common taxonomies of conjunctions: the coordinating conjunctions *and, or,* and *nor.* We have omitted these from our implicational array because these are never simple actions. When we coordinate, we must always first have performed one of the actions listed in the array; if we then go on with an *and, or,* or *nor* (in their simplest sense), *we simply perform that action again.* It therefore makes no sense to add COORDINATE or ALTERNATE to the list of rhetorical actions, since every act of coordination is simply one of the more complex acts performed at least one more time. (We assume that *or* and *nor* are simply expressions of the *and* relationship with one or both members of the coordination negated; that is, *or* means one or the other but not both; *nor* means not one or the other; *and* means both.) This is not to say that coordination is not *some* kind of rhetorical action, only that it is more like a function sign that indicates *iterate*. The other so-called coordinators—*but/yet*, and *for/so*—are qualitatively different. *But* and *yet* signal, roughly, the rhetorical action QUALIFY or DENY. *For* and *so* roughly signal the rhetorical action INFER, forward or back. (We omit the legion of qualifications and nuances of those words.)

What, then, is the nature of the relationship between Issue and Discussion, Point and Development? It is simply the generic relationship between syntagmatic and nonsyntagmatic actions. Issue and Discussion, Point and Development are the generic names for those actions.

Large-Scale Form

Finally, we must address the issue of the large-scale ordering of discourse—those kinds of organizations called inductive and deductive, more important to less important, chronological, spatial, and so on. It is not at all clear how—or even whether—this matter can be mapped onto what we have already described. There are, we believe, roughly three kinds of large-scale order. The first originates in experience, the second in historical convention, the third in something we will very crudely characterize as logic.

ICONIC ORDER. The first we will call *iconic order*. Iconic order bears some direct or indirect connection to that to which the discourse refers: perceived temporal order; perceived spatial order; perceived order of affect (more or less important, obvious, intense, etc.); perceived metonymic or metaphoric connection. The temporal and spatial principles, which we can think of as roughly extrinsic, obviously enough interact with the affective or intrinsic principle: a writer might pick out in a description a series of details not necessarily connected in the entity, but in the writer's own experience of them. This principle of ordering characterizes meditative discourse, belletristic descriptions, casual letters, so called free writing. The characteristic rhetorical action is that of PARTI-CULARIZation iterated either on the basis of the Topic of the previous sentence, or expanding associatively on the Comment. That is, a person begins to reminisce, one thought simply suggests another roughly coordinate with it, that thought leads to another, and so on. This is not to say that other kinds of rhetorical actions do not also occur, only that the overall structure is more associative and coordinate than logical or conventional (unless the associative form has itself become conventional).

Such iconic order characterizes the worst professional prose: the order of information follows the associations of the writer, or the sequence of inquiry the writer engaged in, or the structure of the object under discussion. It typically manifests itself in a document in which a writer discusses both sides of a question and comes to a conclusion in the last paragraph, roughly coterminous with his or her discovery of it.

CONVENTIONALIZED ORDER. In most professional writing, this reflective order must yield to the second kind of large-scale order, *conventionalized order*. A conventionalized order is determined by the historical tradition of the genre. For example, as we have said, in most professional writing the main Point of the entire discourse comes at the end of the Issue of that discourse. In much belletristic writing, such as literary criticism, the writer saves the Point until close to the end. A good many columnists, editorialists, and student essay writers do the same because that order seems to reflect the discovery of a Point—and in those contexts, the working of the writer's mind is at least as important as the product, or so many would like us to believe. Whether a writer chooses to make a Point first and thereby write what we call a *deductive* paper or to make it last and thereby write what we call an *inductive* paper is therefore partly a matter of convention. On the other hand, it is widely believed that if one is writing for an audience not entirely ready to accept a controversial point, then one is more likely to lay down an argument first and derive the Point at the end. We can make no broad generalizations about the relationship between various kinds of rhetorical actions and conventional orders.

We must point out, however, that a unit of discourse may be deductive at the Issue-Discussion level and inductive at the Point-Development level. This next paragraph, for example, opens with a very general Issue, which is expanded in the Discussion:

(11)   Let me tell you about Dr. Johnson. He was a renowned literary critic. He edited many volumes of literature. He is one of the great social critics of the English speaking world. His greatest achievement is unquestionably his Dictionary of the English Language. Dr. Johnson was undoubtedly one of the greatest polymaths in English history.

In the Issue, the writer STATES a general intention; the sentences that follow DISCUSS the proposition contained in the Issue. But the last sentence is the Point of the paragraph. We can therefore argue that the paragraph is simultaneously deductive and inductive. Again, the most interesting conclusion from this is that we can dispense with the vexed issue of Topic Sentence. Issue replaces the notion of topic, and Point replaces the notion of thesis. The Point may coincide with the Issue, and thereby express a thesis in the first sentence, constituting a canonical topic sentence. Or the writer might move the Point at the end, as in the example paragraph about Dr. Johnson. But we could move the Point to the beginning:

> Let me tell you about Dr. Johnson, undoubtedly one of the greatest polymaths in English history. He was a renowned literary critic. He. . . .

We now have a canonical topic sentence, a sentence that is simultaneously the Discussion and the Point of its own little two-sentence d-unit, and the Point of the larger d-unit.

There are a great variety of conventional orders. It may seem that genre parts and functions are immutable by nature, but we can imagine a great variety of other possibilities. What does not vary, however, are the structures we have denominated Issue/Discussion and Point/Development. The opening segment of a unit of discourse *will* be taken to establish a universe of reference. We claim readers will *always* tacitly look for points in nonnarrative discourse. (In fact, the presence or absence of an overtly expressed point is what distinguishes *pure* narrative from narrative in the service of something else.) The strata of discourse units of the kind described in the previous section are not iconic or conventional.

PRINCIPLED ORDER. Thus conventional order must yield to the third kind of large-scale order, principled order. Principled order is the order determined by the inherent demands of the human communicative situation. It covers both the semantic content and the rhetorical actions. For example, it is conventional in legal memos to provide a section called "Statement of the Facts" before a section called "Analysis" or "Discussion." But that convention depends on the inherent need for the reader to know what happened before the writer analyzes what happened. In a scientific paper, the section called "References" conventionally comes last, but it could come first. Where it may not come is in the middle, between "Methods and Materials" and "Results" (though one could imagine a plausible scientific paper in which the references followed each section). That is a principle of organization determined by the inherent structure of the discourse and the situation: d-units may not be interrupted by semantically peripheral elements.

IMPLICATIONS AND SPECULATION

We have left many questions unanswered, many more unasked. The most important remaining question is what any of this has to do with the phenomenology of reading. It is inconceivable that any reader can keep track of the extraordinarily complex structuring of multiply embedded Issues and Discussions our analysis implies. What is not inconceivable, however, is the phenomenon of local processing in the context of maximum units of analysis. That is, we do keep track of local sentence relationships, perhaps up to the paragraph level (this may be the principal reason paragraphs exist at all). From the top down, we do keep track of the overall Point and the general progression of an argument. But the middle game is a muddle.

Suppose this brief (and artificial) paragraph appeared as the introductory segment to a new section inside a much longer text:

(12)   (a) But these issues pale beside the matter of nuclear war. (b) Nuclear war would mean the end of civilization as we know it. (c) The greatest immediate effect would be on the weather. (d) There would be an immediate "nuclear winter." (e) During this period, the atmosphere would be so filled with smoke, dust, and debris that temperatures would fall to freezing.

We might represent (12) as in figure 2-1.

Sentences (a)–(b) constitute a small d-unit with its own Issue-Discussion structure, with the point located in (b). Sentences (c)–(e) constitute the Discussion for Issue (a)–(b), which is itself another embedded d-unit. Its Issue is (c), its Discussion (d)–(e), with the Point in (d). Sentences (d)–(e) constitute another Issue-Discussion unit with the Point in (d).

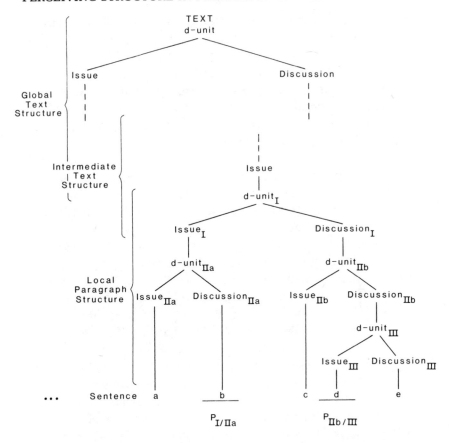

Note: The roman numerals indicate the level of the d-unit within the unit under discussion. The lower-case letters indicate the particular d-unit within any level. The roman numeral/lower-case letter associated with P indicates the d-unit with which the sentence in a point is associated. In this case, the same sentences serve as points to both higher and lower d-units.

Figure 2-1

At this microstructural level, a reader would probably be able to hold this degree of complexity in mind, as he or she was processing it. Once past it, though, the reader would dump the content into the semantic memory, erasing short-term rhetorical relationships. But unless we assume that at the same time the reader is maintaining some sense of how this unit fits into the overall structure of a text at the higher levels, we could not account for how readers treat texts as globally coherent discourses. That is, readers follow in detail the complexity of units of some unspecified, but relatively brief length, in the context of the largest Issue-Discussion units. But the relationships that link the smaller units to the largest ones cannot be as complex as our notation, fully transcribed, would indicate.

Perhaps this is why many good writers use headings that combine functional and topical elements to *anticipate* a relationship a reader would otherwise have to *reconstruct.* That is, lacking overt structural signals such as *for example* or *therefore,* and lacking any obvious generic structure, the reader can never know *in advance* how any d-unit relates to a subsequent one. The reader must always reconstruct the relationship after the sentence or section has begun. The writer, on the other hand, presumably knows (though usually tacitly) how any subsequent sentence or group of sentences relates to the previous ones *before* he or she begins that unit. In these cases, readers are always catching up to the intention of the writer.

Given the premium on clarity and efficiency in professional prose, it is not surprising, then, that professional writers would use frequent semantic and functional signals and informational and structural headings. We understand the relationship among parts as well as the writer does only when we know in advance what that relationship is, just as the writer presumably did. We might therefore conclude that the most effective use of these signals would be simultaneously semantic and functional headings indicating both the significant Topical and Lexical Strings and the function of the unit in the discourse, its rhetorical action: "Introduction: Three Examples of Abusive Tax Shelters."

An interesting problem that we have not yet finished pursuing is the relationship between rhetorical actions and the assertion of Point, which is obviously itself a rhetorical action—indeed, the most important one. Some rhetorical actions may or may not be Points—the first item in a list of examples, for instance. The second item, however, may never be a Point.

One predictable signal of at least a local Point is a CONTRADICTion beginning with *but, however, nevertheless, regardless.* A sentence introduced with any of these words is a Point that takes precedence over any other sentence in the immediate d-unit. That is, if we assert something and then deny it, the denial will always be the Point of the two. There are other correspondences and variations like these, but we have not yet determined which are only tendencies or conventionalized sequences and which are principled correspondences.

The most vexed question, however, is the way in which all these strata interact. Which are the most crucial? What are the limits of degradation in each? How do they reinforce or interfere with one another? What combinations constitute conventional genres? Are there impermissible combinations? What constitutes the most readable combination? Are some combinations appropriate for some rhetorical situations and not for others?

And, of course, the crucial issue is whether any of these structures are represented in the discourse of other cultures.

Notes

1. In using the term *professional discourse*, we hope to isolate a group of texts that we can provisionally (and without controversy) claim are isolable as a category of discourse and that we can later claim are exemplary instances of a broader category defined within a general theory of discourse. Provisionally, we characterize professional discourse as that discourse created to bring about, by means of informing some person, some end beyond the experience of the discourse—a category most readily exemplified in the kinds of discourse generated within such professions as business, the law, medicine, and academics. Our more systematic definition of the general kind will emerge from our description of certain discourse structures found in those kinds of professional prose.

2. By *canonical* we mean an idealized base form against which we may perceive variations. This base form is defined by a variety of criteria: the most psychologically readable form; the form that appears most often in competently written prose; the form that, when compared with others, is preferred by both experienced and inexperienced readers. It is only partly a form created for theoretical convenience, unlike those remote structures on which transformational grammarians of a variety of persuasions base their surface forms.

3. The general description of the matter at hand is best captured by the Discourse Topic: "the problem in civil rights when incompetent patients refuse treatment." When the paragraph shifts from the opening three sentences to the rest, the "problem in civil rights" is specified as "legal issues," and the "incompetent patients" are specified as "psychotic patients." Thus the paragraph and the article shift from the general to the more specific. This shift from general to specific is only one, albeit a very common one, of many ways in which d-units "start over" after the opening move.

4. There is a complex analogy between the discourse-level Issue-Discussion structure and the sentence-level Topic-Comment structure. The Issue position is in many ways like the Topic position, and there is at the level of discourse a stress-last phenomenon roughly analogous to the stress-last structure of sentences. But the Discussion position is much less closely analogous to the Comment position. At this point, we are reluctant to discuss this analogy in any detail.

5. This account is somewhat oversimplified. There appears to be at the end of every d-unit a wild-card slot in which writers are free to violate the normal constraints on relevance. This wild card slot, which we call the Coda, is most often used to

recapitulate the Point of the d-unit or to add particularly interesting but otherwise irrelevant observations (often in the form of quotations). Writers usually mark Codas by using heightened diction or prose that is otherwise "rhetorical." For the sake of simplicity and brevity, we have not included Codas in this discussion: Codas do not materially alter those aspects of discourse structure we do discuss. Example (10) includes an instance of what we take to be a Coda that recapitulates the point of its d-unit.

Making Information Accessible to Readers

3

JANICE C. REDISH
ROBBIN M. BATTISON
EDWARD S. GOLD
American Institute for Research,
Washington, D.C.

Most writers, when asked to improve a document, focus on changing specific words and sentences. Studies of both student writers and writers in nonacademic settings have consistently shown that most revision takes place at the level of words and sentences. Very little revision takes place at the level of the document as a whole.

Problems in word choice and in sentence structure are certainly common in nonacademic writing; in many documents, however, the most critical problem is a larger one—the document is not organized to help the reader. Short, active sentences and common, everyday words are not enough to make a document useful. If readers can't find the information they need, the well-written sentences may go unfound and unread.

As a reader, you have probably encountered many documents with inaccessible information. For example, suppose you have had an accident and need to make a claim against your automobile insurance policy. You get the policy out of your files and look for the information on how much coverage you have and how to file a claim. You discover that the policy has no index—so you can't find the relevant sections that way. The policy does not have a table of contents—so you can't find the information that way. As you scan the pages, you see that the paragraphs do have headings, which are set out by themselves in the left margin, so you think that perhaps you can find the answers to your questions by glancing through the headings. Here are the first eight headings in a "new, readable" policy that addresses the insured as "you" and talks about the insurance company as "we."

Agreement
Definitions
Liability Coverage
Supplementary Payments
Exclusions
Limit of Liability
Out-of-State Coverage
Financial Responsibility

At this point you are likely to give up in frustration and call your insurance agent. The document doesn't give you easy access to the information; it needs a human interpreter—who probably also got the information from another human interpreter and not from a document. Even if the information in this document is in readable English, you probably won't read it because it is too difficult to find the information you need. You went to the document looking for answers to questions like "Was my accident covered?" "For how much?" "How do I file a claim?" But all you found as points of access to the information in the policy were lots of multisyllabic nouns.

Let's look at a second example: You're a computer programmer working on a machine that is new to you. You think you've got everything working, but your program crashes. When you go to the Computer Science Center for help, they hand you a manual with a table of contents that begins like this:

1. Introduction
  1.1 General
  1.2 Command Format
2. Basic Commands
  2.1 Output Commands
    2.1.1. ALPHA(A)   <start>, <number>
    2.1.2. ASCII(AS)   <start>, <number>
    2.1.3. DOUBLE(D)   <start>, <number>
    2.1.4. FLOATING(F)   <start>, <number>
    2.1.5. INTEGER(I)   <start>, <number>
    2.1.6. OCTAL(O)   <start>, <number>

2.1.7.	PROGRAM(PR)	\<start>, \<number>
2.1.8.	LPROGRAM(LPR)	\<start>, \<number>
2.1.9.	TDATE(TD)	\<start>, \<number>
2.1.10.	DTIME(DT)	\<start>, \<number>

An alphabetical list of commands like this one is a typical organization for a computer manual. The problem with this organization is that you must already know which command you need before you can use the book. If you come to the manual because you have a new problem to solve, you have to guess which command will solve your problem. Even the technically trained computer programmers who are the audience for this manual will find it impossible to get to the correct information unless someone who already knows the program tells them which command to use.

Both the automobile insurance policy in the first example and the computer manual in the second example have a *content-based organization* rather than a *reader-based organization*. That is, the writers have focused on presenting a certain set of facts, not on making those facts accessible to the reader.

As these examples show, making information accessible is crucial to successful business and technical communication. Writing in nonacademic settings is seldom meant to be read and savored like a novel. It is meant to be used, when needed, to gain information. Most nonacademic writing is meant for busy people who want to get in, get what they need, and get out of the document as quickly as possible. They do not want to have to hunt for the right section, read irrelevant information, or spend time figuring out how one part of the document relates to the other parts.

This chapter is about organizing, writing, and designing documents so that information is readily accessible to readers. In the following sections, we will:

- Illustrate the problems in two typical documents.
- Suggest some techniques for making the information in documents accessible to readers.
- Discuss some of the reasons that nonacademic writing is so often poorly organized.
- Consider the implications of these findings for teachers of composition.

- Explore the need for further research on nonacademic writers and the documents they write.

WHAT MAKES INFORMATION INACCESSIBLE?

To show how documents often hinder readers from finding the information they need quickly and efficiently, we offer two brief case studies from our work at the Document Design Center.

We have used government documents for both case studies because they are in the public domain. The problems in these documents, however, are typical of writing in both the public and the private sector. The first example, the Federal Communications Commission's rules for using two-way radios on pleasure boats, illustrates problems found in many manuals—computer manuals, technical manuals, and employee benefits handbooks, as well as regulations. The second example, a fact sheet about crash testing new cars, is similar to many memos and reports we have seen from private companies.

Case Study #1: Rules for Using Two-Way Radios on Pleasure Boats

If you own a boat with a two-way radio on it, you must follow the government's rules for using the radio. You are required to have a license, to keep a log of calls you make or receive, and to use specific channels on your radio for different types of calls.

Picture yourself on a boat on your favorite lake or bay. Suddenly you find that you're in trouble. You know you can use your radio to report the emergency, but you don't remember which channel to use. Which source would you rather have for the information: a book that is several hundred pages long with a table of contents that looks (in part) like this:

SUBPART B—APPLICATIONS AND LICENSEE
83.20	Station authorization required
83.22	General citizenship requirements
83.24	Eligibility for station license

. . .

SUBPART F—   DISTRESS, ALARM, URGENCY AND SAFETY
      83.231   Applicable regulations
      83.232   Authority for distress transmission
      83.233   Frequencies for use in distress
      83.234   Distress signals

or an eleven-page booklet with a table of contents like this:

2—How to Get a License
    VHF Marine Rule 3—Do I need a license?
    VHF Marine Rule 4—How do I apply for my license and for my
    RP?
    VHF Marine Rule 5—May I operate my marine radio while my
    applications are being processed?
    . . .

4—Emergency Operation Requirements
    VHF Marine Rule 21—What are the marine emergency signals?
    VHF Marine Rule 22—What is the marine distress procedure?
    . . .

To analyze the accessibility of the information in any document, we must first consider:

- *Who* will use the document?
- *What* purpose does the agency or company hope to achieve by writing the document?
- *How, when,* and *why* will *readers* want to use the document?

We must then judge the adequacy of the content and organization (as well as the writing and design) for the audience, the purpose, and the readers' tasks.

In the case of the marine radio rules, the audience is people who own pleasure boats. Most of these people are willing to abide by the government's rules, but they don't want to spend their leisure time carting around heavy tomes or poring over rules.

From the agency's point of view, the most important purpose of the rules is to save lives in an emergency—to let boat owners know how to report and respond to an emergency quickly and that they should leave the emergency channels open. One secondary purpose is to get boat owners to comply with the law voluntarily—to get their licenses and to keep good records (which may be needed in an investigation of an emergency). Another secondary purpose is to promote considerate use of the radio, since many people may want to use the same channel at the same time.

If radio owners read the document at all, they are likely to skim through it when they first get it. After that, they will probably only go back to it when they need a specific piece of information. **That's how people use manuals.**

Considering the audience and the purpose, it is clearly crucial to help users get correct information quickly and with little effort. That wasn't easy with the original document. Four major problems hindered readers from using the rules easily:

1. The original rules were printed in the same book as many other rules on other topics. They were not available by themselves. The very size of the book was enough to keep most readers from ever looking up the relevant rules.

2. The rules for this audience (ordinary citizens who happen to own two-way marine radios) were embedded in the rules for other radio owners (on ocean liners and merchant ships). Some of the information for these other audiences was extremely technical. The owner of a pleasure boat had to wade through pages of technical information without even being able to tell clearly which rules to follow and which rules to ignore.

3. The table of contents to the original rules did not help the reader find needed information quickly. The headings were nouns or strings of nouns, such as "retention of radio station logs" or "transmitter measurements." The grammatical structure of the headings varied widely, making it difficult for readers to follow the logic of the document.

4. The original set of rules had no overview for the reader—no way of letting the reader know at the beginning of the document what it covered or how it was structured.

In revising the rules, the Federal Communications Commission considered accessibility a primary goal. They reduced the size of the document by separating out the rules for pleasure-boat owners from the more technical information needed by the other audiences. They then organized that information into a series of questions and answers that pleasure-boat owners would be likely to ask. They began by telling readers what the document was about and how it was structured. They made the emergency procedures into short steps that are easy to find and follow:

VHF MARINE RULE 22   What is the marine distress procedure?

Marine Distress Communications Form
Speak Slowly—Clearly—Calmly

1. Make sure your radio is on.
2. Select VHF Channel 16 (156.8 MHz).
3. Press microphone button and say:
   "Mayday—Mayday—Mayday."

. . .

They published the new set of rules as a document by itself—and allowed radio manufacturers to enclose the new booklet with the equipment, thus assuring that new radio owners would at least get a copy of the rules.

Case Study #2: A Fact Sheet about Car Crash Testing

If you are about to buy a car, you might be interested in knowing how well different models protect you and your passengers in crashes. The Department of Transportation tests new cars each year by crashing them into barriers and measuring head and chest injuries to specially constructed dummies. They release the results to the public in a fact sheet.

The fact sheet on 1981 cars began like this:

Legislative Authority

Title II of the 1972 Motor Vehicle Information and Cost Savings Act requires the U.S. Department of Transportation to publish comparative information on new cars by make and model in three areas: crashworthiness (how well cars protect their occupants in crashes), damageability and ease of diagnosing and repairing damage.

Goals

The intent of the legislation is to increase consumer awareness of safety and performance differences among various automobile makes and models.

The two-and-a-half page fact sheet had five headings in all:

Legislative Authority
Goals
The New Car Assessment Program
Changes in the Program
Program Responsibilities

Charts like the one shown in figure 3-1 followed the fact sheet; the explanation of how to interpret the results appeared on the back of the chart.

In order to determine if the information is accessible, comprehensible, and useful, we have to look again at audience, purpose, and readers' tasks. The primary audience is the general public—anyone who is interested in buying a car. As in the case of the FCC rules (and as is true for almost all documents in both the public and the private sectors), the writer must satisfy other audiences as well. These include the agency's lawyers, who want to be sure all the information is technically accurate and legally defensible. For the fact sheet on the car crash program, the audiences also include two other groups: consumer organizations, who want the public to know every statistic that shows a potential danger, and automobile companies, who want to emphasize that their cars meet legal safety requirements.

The agency's purpose in putting out the fact sheet is to allow consumers to make informed choices by being able to compare results for different cars easily, quickly, and accurately. The agency also has a secondary purpose. It needs to protect itself from lawsuits and adverse publicity by being careful to state the limitations of the testing and the conditions under which the testing is done.

But the consumer will probably only skim the prose and try to read the chart for a quick comparison. Again, each reader decides whether to spend time with the document on the basis of his or her own assessment of the question, "How easy is it to find the relevant information?"

And again the answer for the original document is, "Not very easy at all." The problems we found in the fact sheet are typical of many memos and reports:

- It stressed content that the primary audience did not need and left out content that they did need. Instead of helping readers

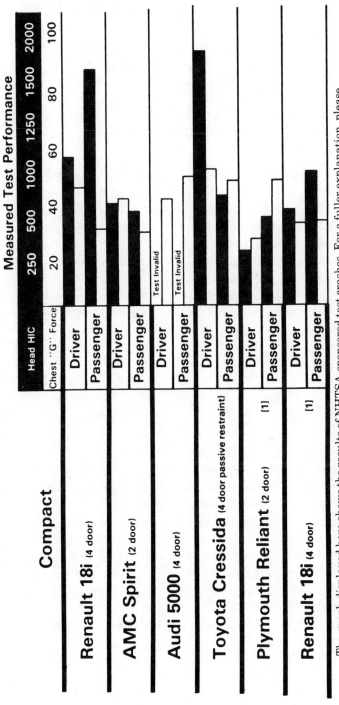

Results of 1981 New Car Assessment Program*

Measured Test Performance

	Head HIC	250	500	1000	1250	1500	2000
	Chest "G" Force	20	40	60	80		100

Compact

Renault 18i (4 door)
- Driver
- Passenger

AMC Spirit (2 door)
- Driver
- Passenger

Audi 5000 (4 door)
- Driver — Test Invalid
- Passenger — Test Invalid

Toyota Cressida (4 door passive restraint)
- Driver
- Passenger

Plymouth Reliant (2 door)
- Driver [1]
- Passenger [1]

Renault 18i (4 door)
- Driver [1]
- Passenger [1]

The graph displayed here shows the results of NHTSA-sponsored test crashes. For a fuller explanation, please see the reverse side of this graph. An attachment to these displays provides the actual values obtained from instrumented readings taken from test dummies.

■ Dummy head injury level   ☐ Dummy chest injury level

[1] Right hand frontal oblique   * September 1981 Results

Figure 3-1

interpret the charts, it gave a historical narrative about the program.

- It buried critical points in long paragraphs of text.
- It was organized for lawyers, not for consumers; it began with the legal basis for the testing. (How many consumers would continue reading after that?)
- Once again, the headings were few and uninformative.
- The graph was very difficult to decipher.

1. It combined two different scales on the same chart. (Look at the black bar labeled "head HIC" and the white bar labeled "Chest 'G' Force" in figure 3-1.)
2. It did not indicate whether a high rating on either scale was good or bad.
3. The combination of a white bar on white paper made the graph very difficult to read.
4. The scale for the critical variable (head injuries) was not correctly proportioned—the scale read 250, 500, 1000, 1250.

Figure 3-2 (pp. 140–142) shows the information and first graph from the revised fact sheet for 1982 cars. Working with lawyers and technical specialists at the agency, Joanne Landesman of the Document Design Center revised the fact sheet by:

- Using questions as headings.
- Beginning with a brief explanation of what the program does.
- Stressing the two critical constraints by putting the key words in boldface and setting off the paragraphs.
- Putting the explanation of the graphs on the front page.
- Eliminating references to the legal basis for the program. (This information does not have to appear on the fact sheet!)
- Simplifying the graphs to show only one indicator of potential injury—the one that the agency's technical staff told us was critical.
- Focusing the graph on the risk of injury, not on the names of the cars.
- Making it easy to see at a glance that shorter bars on the graph mean less risk of injury.

HOW CAN A WRITER MAKE INFORMATION ACCESSIBLE TO READERS?

Analyzing Audience, Purpose, and Content

In the past six years, we have developed and revised dozens of documents in which readers need easy access to information. This experience has taught us how crucial it is to understand who the audience is and how the audience will use the material, and then to plan the document's content and organization for that audience. Here are four general principles to follow in planning a document. After these, we will present eight specific techniques for making the information in a document easily accessible to readers.

1. *Look at the material from the reader's point of view.* The first step is to consider the document's audiences. The plural here is deliberate. There almost always are several audiences, and it helps to name them as specifically as possible. It is difficult to visualize "the general public" or "the average person on the street." It is easier to picture "the consumer who is looking for a new car," "the financial aid officer who is filling out these forms," "the boat owner who has just bought a two-way radio," or "the professor whose computer program isn't working."

Once you have named the primary audience, you can usually find the secondary audiences by thinking through the life cycle of the document. Who else will come across this document between the time you write it and the time it is filed away forever? A college course catalogue needs to serve not only "students deciding which courses to take," but also "counselors and professors who are advising students" and "prospective students who are comparing colleges."

2. *Consider how the audience will use your document.* A critical planning step is to understand how the readers are going to use the document. Students are used to writing narratives, essays, or reports that they expect people to read from cover to cover. In work settings, however, almost all documents longer than letters and memos are used primarily for reference. The reader goes to the document looking for an answer to a particular question, for a particular piece of information, or for instructions on how to do a particular task. The reader's goal is to get in, get the answer, and get out as quickly as possible.

U.S. Department
of Transportation

**National Highway
Traffic Safety
Administration**

Office of Public Affairs
Washington, D.C. 20590
(202) 426-9550

Testing How Well New Cars Perform In Crashes

April 1983

What is the New Car Assessment Program?

The Department of Transportation has an experimental program in which it tests cars to see how well they perform during a crash. NHTSA (the National Highway Traffic Safety Administration) is the agency within the Department of Transportation that conducts these tests. NHTSA publishes this fact sheet to give consumers information that can help them to compare the relative safety of cars they may be planning to buy.

Every new car sold in the United States must meet minimum safety standards that are set by the Federal government. NHTSA's crash test program goes beyond these minimum standards. It tests cars at 35 mph, a much stricter test than the 30 mph test that is required by the standards. A 35 mph crash is about 35 percent more violent than a 30 mph crash.

The graphs that come with this fact sheet show how different makes and models compare in the way they perform during these high speed crashes. In interpreting these test results, it is important to remember two points:

(1) **Drivers and passengers should always wear safety belts.** The human-like dummies used in the crashes are wearing safety belts. These tests measure how cars perform, not how people perform. The crashes are intended to illustrate potential injuries to people who are **properly seated and belted** in the car. Fifty percent of the deaths from road accidents could be avoided if drivers and passengers wore their safety belts.

(2) **Large cars usually offer more protection in a crash than small cars.** These test results are only useful for comparing the performance of cars in the **same size class.**

What do the graphs show?

The graphs show how badly a person's head could be injured in a head-on collision between two identical cars, if both were going at 35 mph.

In general, the lower the score on the head injury criteria, the **less** likely drivers and front-seat passengers will be to be seriously injured or killed in a frontal crash at 35 mph. If a car model scores substantially higher than 1,000 on the head injury criteria, human drivers and front-seat passengers in that model will be **more** likely to suffer a serious head injury or be killed in a frontal crash at 35 mph.

How does NHTSA select the cars it will test?

NHTSA tests about 25 cars every year. The graphs show the test results for a variety of cars. Because NHTSA buys its test cars off the lot, just as you would, the tests cannot begin until after a new model year has started. Test results on new cars generally begin to be available in the late winter of each year.

NHTSA chooses the cars it will test to give useful information to as many consumers as possible. For example, a popular model is more likely to be chosen, because information on that model would be of interest to many consumers. For the same reason, very expensive cars are not tested as often.

What happens when model years change?

If a car that NHTSA has already tested remains essentially the same for the new model year, it will probably not be tested again. But a car that undergoes substantial changes in the new model year will be likely to be retested. In using any crash test data, you should always check the model year that was tested and whether NHTSA believes that the test results should be used to evaluate other model years.

Figure 3-2

Head Injury Levels During Crash Tests
New Car Assessment Program
1982 Subcompact Cars

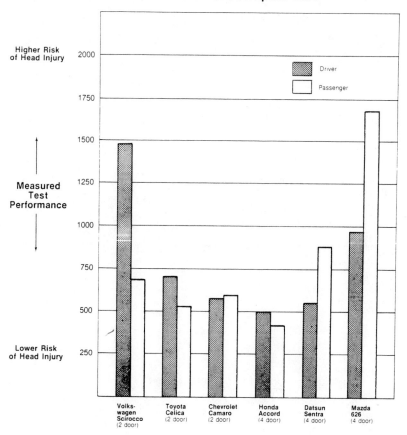

This graph shows results from NHTSA's crash tests. A lower number on the graph means a lower level of potential head injury. For a fuller explanation, please read the information pages. A chart enclosed with this fact sheet shows the actual values that NHTSA obtained from instruments that were attached to the test dummies during the crashes.

Figure 3-2 continued

How are the cars tested?

· NHTSA crashes cars head-on into a rigid barrier (a "frontal" crash). In this test, the cars are going 35 mph. A crash like this is equivalent to a head-on collision between two identical cars, each going at 35 mph—a very violent crash.

The measurements of potential head injuries that you will see on the graphs are taken during these crashes. In addition to the graphs, there is a chart enclosed with this fact sheet which shows information about potential injuries to the chest and femur (thigh bone), as well as the head, during frontal crashes.

To measure what could happen to people in the cars, NHTSA places dummies shaped like human beings in the driver's seat and the front passenger seat. These dummies are very sophisticated scientific devices, with instruments to measure the forces to the head, chest, and femur during the crash.

What can we learn from these crash tests?

During the crashes, the instruments attached to the dummies measure how much force has been exerted on the dummies.

The graphs show the most important measurement, the "Head Injury Criteria," or "HIC," for each dummy and car. HIC units tell how far and how fast the head has moved in the crash. This motion itself may cause injury. The head can only tolerate so much of this motion without suffering damage, whether or not the head strikes anything.

Do these crash tests have limitations?

Crash tests can give scientists and consumers a good idea of how individual car models might do in real road accidents. But the conditions in these tests cannot be exactly the same as the conditions in real accidents. You should consider these points:

(1) The test results on the graphs are actual measures of the forces exerted on the dummies during the crashes. Although these dummies were designed to react in the same way that people would during a crash, there is disagreement about how well they actually do.

(2) The test procedures, the conditions of the tests, or the facilities used for the tests vary to some extent. These variations account for some of the differences between test results on different cars.

(3) Differences between test results and actual injuries in road accidents are likely to occur because the conditions in the crash tests are not exactly the same as the conditions in road accidents.

NHTSA is currently doing research to find out if the tests can be made more reliable. Up to now, only one sample of each car model has been tested. NHTSA's present research involves testing more than one sample of a given car model. This kind of research will help NHTSA scientists to determine whether some of the differences in the test results come from variations in the test procedures or variations in how the sample cars were manufactured.

Figure 3-2 (continued)

3. *Organize the material logically from the reader's point of view.* Here are two useful techniques for organizing reader-based documents:

- Put yourself in the place of the reader and ask the questions a reader would be likely to ask. Then order the questions logically. (When you look at a list of questions for a reference document, there is almost always a logical order for them—by importance, timing, or location in a sequence of steps in a procedure.)
- Do a task analysis of the procedure you are describing. If possible, do the task. Write down the steps of the task in logical order.

4. *Include only the content that the audience needs.* Most writers overwrite. Programmers, for example, usually want to include every

nuance of the neat ways they've worked out to make a computer do something, even if the average user only needs to know the best or safest way. The writer needs to keep in mind how the reader will use the manual. Readers don't need (or want) to know the history of automobiles or the details of how an engine works in order to start their cars. They only need to be told where to put the key and how to turn it.

After applying these four principles for planning the document, the writer might well decide that more than one document is needed. The content and the appropriate organization for a manual on how to set up and install a computer are different from the content and appropriate organization for a manual on how to use the computer every day. Two books might serve better than one. The content and appropriate organization for a tutorial on a word-processing program are different from the content and appropriate organization for a general reference manual. Again, two books might serve better than one.

Organizing for Ease of Access to the Information

Once you have selected the appropriate content and organized by readers' questions or tasks, you need to implement that organization and make it explicit to the readers. Here are some specific techniques.

1. *Set the context.* At the beginning of a document, set the overall context by telling your readers what's in it, why they might choose to read parts of it, and what you expect them to get from it.

When you get down to procedures and details, set the context again (and again). Don't just tell people how to do something. First tell them why and under what circumstances they might choose to do that procedure, rather than something else. Here's an example from the beginning of a computer manual:

> There are two ways to bring part of another file into the file you are now editing. Use the first way if you already know the line numbers you want to bring in. Use the second if you're not sure of the line numbers.

2. *Set up signposts.* The way you organize the document won't help readers unless you also tell them what the structure is. Tell your

readers where you're taking them and how you've laid out the information. Tables of contents, indexes, and side tabs all help readers find their way. Even within sections, you can give directions about the structure of the information that follows. For example, after setting the context in a procedural manual, you might write:

> We explain the first method on this page and the second method on page three.

3. *Limit the amount of organizational information you give at any one time.* If you provide too much organizational detail, your readers may miss the big picture you want them to see. For a large document like a procedural manual or a benefits handbook, include only the chapter titles and, perhaps, one level of subheadings in the table of contents at the front of the book. Put a more detailed table of contents at the beginning of each chapter. This allows readers to move through the material in a treelike fashion to get to the right section. Within the text, use no more than four levels of headings: chapter, section, major topic, and minor topic. If you need more levels, you probably should break the text up into more chapters.

4. *Write informative headings.* Research on how people read and understand has shown the obvious: headings help readers see the organization and understand the text. Research has also shown something that is not so obvious: vague or general headings can be more misleading than no headings at all. The most helpful headings are those that match the readers' questions. In fact, using questions themselves as headings is an effective technique. Here are examples from an insurance benefits handbook we revised:

> *Old Heading:* Coordination of Benefits
> *New Heading:* What if someone is covered by two group health plans?
> *Old Heading:* Conversion Privileges
> *New Heading:* Can I convert my coverage to an individual policy?

Here is an example of useful headings from a task-oriented computer manual:

2. How to Use Magnetic Tape

2.1 Choosing an appropriate tape

2.2 Assigning the tape to your run @ ASG

2.3 Positioning the tape at the beginning @ REWIND

2.4 Copying information to and from the tape @ COPY

2.5 Marking the end of a file on the tape @ MARK

2.6 Moving a tape @ MOVE

5. *Organize the material for more than one audience.* If different audiences need to use different parts of the document, make it easy for everyone. For example, you can often use a table to tell people which parts of the document to use:

For this situation	Fill out these forms
You are requesting funds for 1983–1984	FISAP, Part I: Identifying Information and Certifications
	FISAP, Part II: Application to Participate
You received funds for 1981–1982	FISAP, Part I: Identifying Information and Certifications
	FISAP, Part II, Section D: Application to Participate, Maintenance of Effort
	FISAP, Parts III, IV, V, and VI: The Fiscal Operations Report

Even in a single document, you will rarely write for a single audience. Some readers will just want to learn the basics. Others already know quite a lot but want to clarify details. Be gentle with the novice, but set up fast tracks for the experienced reader. Charts, summary lists in the text or on a separate card, diagrams, and notes in the margin are good ways to condense information for more knowledgeable readers.

6. *Make the organization of the material graphically explicit.* Readers should be able to perceive the document's organization at a glance. As a writer, you can help the reader by making the organization clear. For example, you can use type size, position, or color to distinguish different levels of headings. You can use pictorial

or thematic symbols to cue readers visually that they are moving from one section to another. However, you should also be consistent in your organization and graphics from section to section and from chapter to chapter, so that the same graphic cue always means the same thing. Allow enough white space on your page layouts to give room for your graphic cues to work. Provide page numbers and running heads or feet so that readers can skim the pages and always know where they are.

7. *In a large document, use tabs for easy access to chapters.* The side tabs should have the chapter number, name and picture on *both* sides. Use many small chapters rather than a few general dividers so that each topic can be located easily.

8. *Include both a table of contents and an index.* Every reference book, report, or lengthy insurance policy needs both an index and a table of contents. Both are keys to the book, but in different ways. One doesn't replace the other. Some people prefer to use the table of contents; some prefer the index. Some use both—at different times, for different purposes. When you write questions, statements, or verb phrases as headings for sections, you are helping readers find answers and procedures. If they need more details, they will find the key phrases in the index. Unfortunately, however, many indexes are of little use.

The traditional index is made up mostly of nouns—the names of people, places, and events. Procedural manuals, however, aren't history books. In a book that walks readers through a process, verbs play an important role, and verbs should show up in the index, too. Multiple entries like the following may be the answer:

adding	changing	records
fields	fields	adding
files	files	changing
records	records	erasing

When you are writing plain English procedures or policies, you may be faced with another problem. If you index only the words that actually occur in the text, you may be omitting the words that some of your readers would customarily use to find information. You may be putting your more technical or experienced readers at a disadvantage, unless your index includes jargon and technical terms that the experts are familiar with and are likely to look up (the very terms you spent so much time translating into ordinary English!).

WHY DO SO MANY DOCUMENTS STILL
HAVE INACCESSIBLE INFORMATION?

There is little experimental evidence showing the value of re-organizing and rewriting documents, in part because once the new document exists, everyone thinks it's wonderful. In numerous workshops and presentations in which we have shown befores and afters like the examples in this chapter, we have had virtually unanimous agreement that the changes are great improvements. People tend to breathe a sigh of relief when they see the revised versions. Yet more documents remain inaccessible to the reader than have been revised. Why isn't more change happening?

We have written elsewhere about the various pressures that support and hinder change in document design (Redish, 1983; Redish, 1985). Let us briefly review some of them here and add information from our more recent experience in working with computer manuals.

Change seems to occur primarily through one or a combination of four motivations: altruism, legal requirements, economics, and pressure of competition. Early changes by a few companies in insurance and banking were spurred by the altruistic belief of a few individuals that consumers are entitled to readable documents. Of course, altruism can be turned into a publicity advantage and the (perhaps short-lived) competitive edge of being the first with a consumer-oriented document. But altruism does not engender wide-spread change.

External legal requirements have spurred most of the change in the insurance and consumer credit field. But because the standard for plain English in insurance documents is a particular readability score, the changes have, for the most part, been limited to the sentence and word level. Few changes have focused on making the information more accessible.

Change seems to occur most often when top management is convinced that economics favors it or that competition requires it. Thus change is happening rapidly in the computer field, where so-called user-friendly documentation has become a strong selling point and better documentation can reduce the cost of supporting toll-free telephone lines to answer consumers' questions. *User-friendly* means not only manuals in plain English, but also task-oriented manuals in which ease of access to the information is a major consideration.

Forces that hinder change are as various as those that promote it. Documents are sometimes made obscure on purpose. One can argue that the information in a typical product warranty or recall letter is not easy to locate or understand because the manufacturers do not want people to use the services being described. Again, economics is a critical factor: fixing products under warranty or under a recall costs the manufacturer money.

Many lawyers believe that the function of a legal document is not to be accessible to the user but, rather, simply to state the legal agreements. They consider only the risk of legal problems. They also believe that not enough consumers read their insurance forms or banking notices to justify the cost of changes.

Access to information is also sometimes deliberately denied because information is power: controlling access to information means controlling power. Some lawyers do not want their documents to be easy to understand because that would reduce their power to control legal knowledge.

As the number of plain English legal documents grows, these attitudes are changing, but the change is slow. Many documents now exist that are both legally accurate and accessible to readers. The predicted lawsuits have not occurred; to the contrary, consumers have won cases in court because their insurance policies and claims letters were not understandable. The cost of revising documents goes down as more examples become available to use as models.

Although obscurity is sometimes intentional, in many more cases we have found that writers don't mean to be obscure. The problem is that they have not thought about the readers' needs, they don't know how to write for the reader, or they are hindered by other factors.

Even the writer who wants to produce a document that is easily accessible to the readers may have difficulty. We have found four major ways in which writers are hindered:

- Company standards require a more traditional style.
- The writers aren't given the time to do the job well.
- The computer program or company policy changes as the manual is being written.
- The writers don't have adequate training in how to organize a document so that the information is easily accessible.

Many companies and government agencies (particularly the military) have specifications for their manuals that are based on traditional formats. These specifications often focus on technical accuracy to the exclusion of accessibility and comprehensibility. In many cases (the military, for example), comprehensibility is measured by a readability score, although a readability formula will not measure any of the organizational factors that promote accessibility.

Our initial projects with new clients are often conducted as exceptions to company standards. This requires a strong project leader on the client's side who will justify the exception in the first place and will then work with us to convince reviewers throughout the project. After an initial project succeeds, clients are more likely to accept our innovative style. Others in the company can cite the original exception and the success of the manuals produced in the new style.

Although we have written manuals that are exceptions to company or agency standards in several fields, the new reader-oriented style has caught on only in the computer field. Marketplace pressures operate here, but they do not operate in the field of military technical manuals, government policy manuals, or employee benefits handbooks.

A second major constraint on writers is time. Few managers or technical staff appreciate the time it takes to write a useful manual. Once the computer program is written, everyone is anxious to get it on the market. Even though the program will be judged in part on its manual, and even though the users will not even be able to understand or use all the features of the program if the manual is poorly organized, everyone wants the manual to be written yesterday and printed tomorrow.

Some companies are now conducting usability testing, in which people are given the manual and a computer running the program and asked to do some of the tasks the program covers. This testing can be very effective in revealing problems in both the program and the manual. Timing, however, is a problem. Testing can't take place until the program is up and running and a draft of the manual exists. To take advantage of what is learned in usability testing, time needs to be left in the schedule for revisions after the testing. Pressure to get the product out often cuts into the time left for testing and revising. When schedules slip and testing is delayed, the revision cycle is usually the place where everyone tries to get back on schedule—at the expense of the writer's time.

A third constraint on the writer is that programs and policy do not sit still to be described neatly. Programmers and policy committees are usually tinkering long after the so-called final deadlines have passed.

Sometimes this tinkering occurs because the writer has suggested changes. The writer may be the only person working on a project who represents the naive reader. That fresh perspective enables the writer to see problems in the policy or program that the technical staff did not see. On every project we have done, we have raised questions about the policy or program we were writing about, pointed out inconsistencies or missing information, and suggested changes that would make the policy more sensible or the program easier to use. Often the technical staff resist making changes at first; but when they read the new manual and the gaps or inconsistencies become obvious, then they want to make last-minute changes.

When we write policy manuals, for example, the client may be slow to realize that the substance of the policy manual is not accurate, complete, or up to date. Indeed, a client might not realize this until after we have completed our translation from the technical, abstract original to the easily accessible, clear English revision. Therefore, the writer must remain flexible and willing to change the organization of the manual as changes occur (and the client must understand that changes in the program or policy require the writer to do more work, which takes time and money).

The final constraint on writers is expertise. The task is often assigned to a technical expert (computer programmer or policy analyst) who has little, if any, training in writing, or to an English major who has little, if any, training in writing reader-oriented manuals.

WHAT CAN TEACHERS DO?

What can composition teachers do to better prepare writers to produce well-organized documents in which information is easy to locate? They can have students write or revise a reference document. They can have students work on documents that are long enough to need informative headings, context-setting paragraphs, and other features that make information accessible. They can teach students generalizable skills rather than ways to write within a prescribed format. They can provide more realistic assignments—ones that have consequences for readers other than themselves. They can send students out of the classroom to find documents that people need to have written or revised.

In composition classrooms, most teachers concentrate on helping students to write comprehensible sentences and to link their sentences into coherent paragraphs. Students are seldom required to write pieces long enough to exhibit the problems of poor overall organization that characterize much of the writing in nonacademic settings.

When students are required to write a long piece, they are often assigned a prescribed format (a traditional feasibility study or an engineering project report). Students may learn how to fit their data into one particular organization, but they don't learn generalizable skills for making information accessible in a major document.

In our highly mobile society with its rapidly changing technology, we cannot predict where any particular student will end up. Nor can we predict which types of writing will be required ten or twenty years from now in any particular career. Therefore, the most valuable skills a student can get from a composition class are an understanding of the process of writing and basic guidelines that can be adapted to any writing task.

Teachers of advanced composition classes can also look for opportunities to send students out of the classroom to work on documents in nonacademic settings. For example, the Junior Composition Program at the University of Maryland has entered into a collaborative arrangement with the University Computer Center, in which composition students will rewrite computer manuals for the center. In the graduate program at Miami University (Ohio), each student must find a "client" on or off campus and work on a document that the client needs to have written or revised.

Opportunities for students to work on nonclassroom documents abound on any college campus and in the surrounding community. There are instructions and handbooks in the financial aid office; manuals in the computer science department; fact sheets, manuals, and catalogues in the library. There may also be manuals for word processing or other computer programs that faculty or students are supposed to use regularly. If the manuals are inadequate, some students could tackle the job of revising them.

Getting students out of the classroom enables them to see writers in action; to appreciate the extent and variety of writing that most professionals do; and to work on a document that has a real audience, that serves real needs, and that can be tested.

WHAT RESEARCH IS STILL NEEDED?

Although we know a great deal about how to organize a document to make the information easily accessible to readers, we still know little about:

- How to incorporate nonacademic writing into the curriculum.
- How writers of these types of materials view their tasks, their audiences, and the appropriate organization of their documents.

We still need to ask many pedagogical questions about the suggestion to send students outside the classroom and have them write or revise documents that will be used. Should this be a course in itself or part of a more traditional advanced composition or technical writing course? How much time needs to be given to this type of assignment? How large a document is it feasible to ask students to work on? How does the teacher as advisor to the student interact with the client (for example, the Computer Science Center)? What types of collaborative groupings of students work best to achieve both a useful learning experience and a useful document? We need to have a series of case studies from professors who have brought non-academic writing into the classroom or who have sent students out of the classroom to write in nonacademic settings.

We also need more research that focuses on writers in their nonacademic settings. Most research on writing in nonacademic settings has focused on writers of letters, memos, and short reports. It has not focused on writers working on reference documents to be used by many people outside the writer's organization.

Odell, Goswami, and their colleagues have studied writers in a county Department of Social Services (Odell & Goswami, 1982); a state legislature (Odell, Goswami, & Quick, 1983); and a state Department of Labor (Odell, Goswami, Herrington, & Quick, 1983). Using a very powerful technique called discourse-based interviews, they have been able to elicit the writers' understanding of audience, purpose, subject, and context of their writing. In general, they have found that the writers they worked with are very much attuned to their audiences and purposes.

In our own work, however, we have gotten different results. We have found that the writers we work with are not well attuned to the external (end-user) audience for their manuals or to the reader's need to have easy access to information. We have found that writers are more attuned to their internal audiences (to the reviewers in the organization) and to getting the technical information down accurately. Our evidence, however, is not based on structured interviews; it is based on analyzing many documents and on informal interviews with writers who have been clients or trainees.

Part of the difference in our impressions of our writers and the findings in the work of Odell et al. may lie in the types of documents the two groups have studied. The writers in the settings studied by Odell and his colleagues generally write memos, letters, and other short documents for which the audience is clear. The writer may have met and talked with the recipient personally.

The documents we have studied—fact sheets, instruction packages, benefits handbooks, and manuals—are usually much longer documents intended for a much less precisely definable audience.

Few of the writers we have worked with have met their audience personally. It would be extremely useful to have more rigorously gathered information on the writers and the writing of these longer reference documents. Could the discourse-based interview be used or modified to study writers of the longer documents that are the subject of this chapter?

References

Odell, L., & Goswami, D. (1982). Writing in a nonacademic setting. *Research in the Teaching of English*, 201–223.

Odell, L., Goswami, D., Herrington, A., & Quick, D. (1983). Studying writing in nonacademic settings. In P. V. Anderson, R. J. Brockman, & C. R. Miller (Eds.), *New essays in technical and scientific communication: Research, theory, practice*. Farmingdale, NY: Baywood Publishing

Odell, L., Goswami, D., & Quick, D. (1983) Writing outside the english composition class: Implications for teaching and for learning. In R. W. Bailey & R. M. Fosheim (Eds.), *Literacy for life*. New York: Modern Language Association.

Redish, J. (1983). The language of the bureaucracy. In R. W. Bailey & R. M. Fosheim (Eds.), *Literacy for Life*. New York: Modern Language Association.

Redish, J. (1985). The plain English movement. In S. Greenbaum (Ed.), *The English language today*. Elmsford, NY: Pergamon Press.

Assessing the Influence of New Technologies

III

An Electronic Odyssey   4

JEANNE W. HALPERN
Purdue University

Had you told me, when I began that 7,000-mile train ride in May 1983, that it would lead me backward in time—to consider again the arts of classical rhetoric—I would have argued: "No. I'm exploring a *new* frontier. Its landmarks are the *new* communication technologies—audio mail, dictation systems, electronic mail, teleconferencing, and word processing. I'll see a different system in action at each company I visit. I'll listen. I'll learn. And I'll share my findings with other college teachers, offering ideas for preparing students for the *new* world of electronic composing."

This was my attitude when I climbed aboard that first Amtrak train. So you can imagine how startled I was to find, after gathering my interview information and synthesizing my questionnaire results, that this twentieth-century odyssey was leading me to examine the past even as I moved toward the future. For my research showed the need for a rhetoric of electronic composing that emphasized planning (which I consider one aspect of rhetorical invention), arrangement, style, memory, and delivery. To put it differently, my research showed that students who had not mastered these five arts in college would find it increasingly difficult to succeed in an electronic work environment, an environment dominated by written and oral communication.

How I reached this conclusion is the subject of this chapter. First I will show how the new communication technologies affect the way college graduates compose on their jobs; then I will discuss the consequences of this research for teachers of college composition.

HOW DO THE NEW TECHNOLOGIES AFFECT COMPOSING ON THE JOB?

In May and June 1983, I examined first-hand the effects of the new technologies on the way college graduates compose their communications. Prior to this project, Sarah Liggett and I had completed an in-depth study of the effects of one new system, dictation for word processing, on the composing process of on-the-job writers (Halpern & Liggett, 1984). My goal in the project now being described was to examine first-hand a wider range of systems, not only to test the generalizability of our earlier conclusions but also to establish appropriate directions for the new professional writing program being developed at Purdue University. Thus my 1983 summer project had from its inception two thrusts: research and curriculum development. The purposes, methods, and results of the 1983 project are detailed in this section.

Purposes

To learn how people were composing on their jobs and to estimate how changes in on-the-job composing would affect college teachers, I investigated these four research questions:

- *Systems use.* What new electronic systems are college graduates using on the job, how much do they use these systems, what advantages or disadvantages do they find, and what specific factors influence systems use?
- *Strategies and skills.* What are the distinctive features of electronic composing, and what strategies and skills are required, irrespective of *which* system is being used?
- *On-the-job training.* What are systems users being taught on the job, how are they being taught, and by whom?
- *Interviewees' suggestions for college course work.* What general programs of study, according to those interviewed, will best prepare college graduates for communicating on the job, and what specific subjects should be emphasized in college writing courses?

Methods

Answering these questions required that I survey the current literature to determine which organizations were successfully integrating the new communication technologies in their overall operations. From the 32 organizations identified, I selected and visited 9 representative companies, each of which used at least one of the major communication technologies described in the current literature. At each site, I conducted interviews and distributed detailed questionnaires.

Variables I accounted for were organizational type, size, and geography. Before and after visiting the 9 representative companies, I also interviewed at several other sites so that my research pool would reflect the main divisions of white-collar, college-graduate employment, based on the 1980 United States Census (U.S. Census Bureau, 1981): managerial and administrative, professional and technical, clerical, service, sales. My complete list includes examples of the main fields college graduates enter (Statistical Abstract, 1983): services (i.e., hospitality, health, and education), wholesale/retail trade, manufacturing, finance, government, mining. I sought diversity in organizational size, choosing large established corporations like Atlantic Richfield and small, relatively new companies like Lee Pharmaceuticals. Finally, I sought geographic diversity. During the trip, May 28 to June 24, 1983, I visited companies along the train route in the western three-quarters of the United States and Canada, the antipodes being Los Angeles and Toronto. Before and after that trip, I also visited government agencies, educational institutions, and publishers in Albany, New York; Ann Arbor, Michigan; Austin, Texas; Indianapolis, Indiana; and Phoenix, Arizona. At each site, I conducted structured interviews, distributed questionnaires, watched people use the systems, and collected materials of many kinds— training instructions, user manuals, notes, drafts, and final products. (For a list of people interviewed, sites visited, and dates of visits, see appendix 4A.)

To investigate the main research topics listed here, I developed a 36-item questionnaire that moved from closed-ended demographic to open-ended descriptive and opinion questions. (For a copy of the questionnaire with answers summarized, see appendix 4B.) The questionnaire included five kinds of questions:

- *Demographic questions* about education, employment history, present job (e.g., "What are your main responsibilities in your present position?").
- *Systems questions* about communication media available, frequency of use, advantages, and disadvantages (e.g., "For what purposes are these systems being used?").
- *Composing questions* about critical strategies and skills in writing and speaking, difficult things to learn (e.g., "Describe the typical process you go through when you compose a message using one of the new systems").
- *Training questions* about what is taught, how, and by whom (e.g., "What do the most successful training packages contain?").
- *College course questions* about the respondents' estimates of present and future needs (e.g., "If you were going to design a college writing course . . . , what would you be sure to emphasize?").

I also included several questions to validate the results of other research in on-the-job writing. For instance, having been surprised by the Faigley and Miller (1982) conclusion that people rarely write except at work, I included a question that would show whether and what my interviewees wrote off the job.

Before distributing the questionnaire to interviewees, I conducted a small, select pretest. One faculty member, one graduate student, and one staff member at Purdue University, each an experienced user of the new systems, were asked to work through the questionnaire and point out confusing or ambiguous items; these I revised. During the research trip, I gave a copy of the questionnaire to each of the 27 interviewees and went through it with them; 20 (74 percent) completed and returned questionnaires. I then tabulated results by collating all answers and analyzed them quantitatively and qualitatively.

Results and Conclusions

The following results and specific conclusions provide a synthesis of interviews, questionnaires, on-site observations, and materials collected. After providing a demographic synopsis of those interviewed during the trip, I will summarize this study in terms of systems use, strategies and skills, on-the-job training, and interviewees' suggestions for college course work.

DEMOGRAPHIC SYNOPSIS. Interviewees ranged from corporate-level managers of huge organizations to presidents of smaller companies to middle-level administrators to entry-level trainees. The interviewees had worked for their organizations between twenty-seven years and three weeks, the mean length of time being six years and the median three years. All interviewees were involved with the new communication technologies: planning and managing their use within the company, marketing them internally or externally, writing user documentation for them, training people to use them, and/or using one or more systems. All did a variety of activities on their jobs, combining such responsibilities as managing, marketing, training, and programming. For example, an account representative at the Toronto division of I. P. Sharp Associates sold the company's electronic mail and computer conferencing services, taught people to use these services in regular classes as well as with programmed instructional units, and developed customized programs for those who use Sharp's automated systems.

The educational backgrounds of interviewees varied widely: Three had PhDs; 7 had or were working on master's degrees; and all but 3 had completed bachelor's degrees. Most surprising was the fact that nearly half (10) of those with bachelor's degrees had liberal arts backgrounds; furthermore, a quarter (5) of those with bachelor's degrees had majored in English.

Interviewees ranked the most valuable legacies of their college courses as: written and oral communication skills (14); group/people processes (5); logical/analytical thinking (5); and certain technical skills (3). They noted that experience in co-ops, internships, and extracurricular activities that emphasized communication had also helped them develop abilities necessary for career advancement.

SYSTEMS USE. According to all interviewees, the new communication technologies are being widely incorporated in organizations throughout the country—though in different ways and for different purposes. In this section, I will describe the most widely used systems, suggest the extent of their use, explain advantages and disadvantages, and discuss the key factors influencing systems use.

Widely Used Systems. According to my study as well as most secondary sources, word processing and electronic mail are currently the most widely used systems; 25 of the 27 interviewees in this study use these systems regularly. Other important systems include audio mail, dictation, and teleconferencing, which are used when available in specific organizations. These five widely used systems will be described briefly; for more complete explanations, see the *Encyclopedia of Computer Science and Technology* (Belzer, Holzman, & Kent, 1979) or any of the many dictionaries on telecommunications and computers.

- *Audio mail* allows people to send and receive messages at any time by linking telephones and voice or magnetic recorders. Callers phone when *they* wish, and receivers listen and respond to the recorded message when *they* wish (Beswick, 1984; Mertes, 1981).
- *Dictation systems* allow people to dictate messages at any time from virtually any location and have the messages efficiently transcribed by keyboard operators at word-processing centers, then returned to the dictator in draft or final form (Halpern & Liggett, 1984).
- *Electronic mail* allows people to key in messages at computer terminals and have the messages electronically transmitted to others who may answer, use, or file them (Chernicoff, 1983; Mertes, 1981; and Stein & Yates, 1984).
- *Teleconferencing* allows people in different locations to "get together" electronically for formal presentations, informal discussions, project coordination, on-the-job training, or problem-solving sessions. Teleconferencing ranges from audio-only phone conferences to various combinations of audio plus video, the most complex being two-way, full-color, full-motion, live videoconferencing (Gibson & Mendelson, 1984); teleconferencing also includes computer conferences, which allow people using computer terminals to conduct ongoing, nonsynchronous information exchanges or problem-solving sessions.
- *Word processing* allows people to compose, key in, revise/edit, and format complete documents; it often offers graphics and research support as well (Bridwell, Nancarrow, & Ross, 1984; McWilliams, 1982; Wresch, 1983; Zinsser, 1983).

These are the five main systems used by people in this survey to communicate in the workplace. Secondary sources confirm that these systems are being widely integrated in the workplace (Beswick, 1984; Chernicoff, 1983; Mertes, 1981; Stein & Yates, 1984).

Amount of Use. Interviewees in this project spend nearly twice as much of their time using electronic media as using conventional media, such as pencil, pen, or typewriter. In fact, they report spending their work days (on average) this way: communicating face-to-face accounts for 37 percent of the day; using the new media, 23 percent; using conventional media, 12 percent; and conducting other activities, 28 percent. Although I interviewed people in companies in the forefront of technological change—people with strong incentives and good opportunities to use such systems—it seems clear that, given the widespread incorporation of automation in the workplace, most white-collar workers will routinely use at least some of these systems in the near future (Toffler, 1980).

Advantages and Disadvantages. Interviewees cited many more advantages than disadvantages in using the new systems. Among the advantages noted were speed; improved decision making and business planning; collaborative problem solving; wider participation on projects; easier access to and transfer of information across geographic boundaries and time zones; greater storage capacity and therefore improved availability and manipulability of information; and preparation of higher-quality written products—that is, products with better content, graphics, layout, and accuracy. As disadvantages, several people named cost; others cited frustrations associated with learning to use new equipment and to adapt old habits of composing to new media. There was also some feeling that increased use of equipment would lead to less personal interaction and also to new organizational structures and chains of communication (Connell, 1982, 1984). In general, most advantages cited in this study were information- or product-oriented, whereas most disadvantages were personal, reflecting negative feelings about technology or insecurities associated with change.

Factors Influencing Systems Use. My results also showed that an individual's use of and commitment to the new systems depend primarily on three factors: enthusiasm from upper management, efficiency and effectiveness, and personality.

Enthusiasm from above seems to be the main prerequisite for ongoing systems use within an organization. When the president and/ or top managers in a company show enthusiasm for a new system— by using it themselves, by making it widely available, by encouraging internal marketing and training—then staff members adopt the system more readily. Successful examples of this process include the adoption of dictation/word-processing systems at the Indiana State Board of Health; the organizationwide use of audio and electronic mail at Continental Illinois Bank; the incorporation of teleconferencing at ARCO; and the use of word processing by all research personnel at Lee Pharmaceuticals (see also Gibson & Mendelson, 1984).

Efficiency and effectiveness also influence continued use. When staff members find that one system or another makes their lives easier or their work better, they request and use that system. For instance, technical writers and engineers at Boeing Aerospace consistently request training on and access to word processors for report writing because word processing enables them to collaborate with each other and with graphics and other document design people. On the other hand, Boeing managers, at the time I visited, had not shown a similar interest, preferring to maintain the habit of composing in longhand for a secretary or keyboard operator. Furthermore, people choose different systems for different purposes. For problem solving and decision making, they are likely to choose data-processing, computer conferencing, and teleconferencing systems. For inventing, reconsidering, and polishing written messages, they choose word processing or dictation drafting. For speed and convenience, they choose audio mail, electronic mail, and first-time-final dictation. When what people need coincides with what a system does well, or when an individual's capabilities are extended or enhanced by a system, then that system is generally preferred and, if available, used.

Personality is an idiosyncratic factor but also an important one. Fast adapters try new things and slow adapters don't; no matter how high the enthusiasm or how useful the system, perhaps 20 percent of staff members will resist change, according to estimates by interviewees. Their reasons may be philosophical or practical or simply personal. Nonusers may believe that the new systems encourage thought control and a "Big Brother is watching you" atmosphere (Edwards, 1983; Salvaggio, 1983; Weizenbaum, 1976). They may be frustrated by equipment—by document loss, down time, limited availability, lack of sound/picture synchronization. They may be apprehensive about technology in general; even telephones make some people nervous (Reinsch & Lewis, 1984). Or they may worry that one system or another will magnify their communication weaknesses: as one interviewee noted, "Poor grammar really shows up on electronic mail!" Personality factors like these probably have more to do with who uses what systems than does age, education, or professional level; such factors can discourage successful systems use.

STRATEGIES AND SKILLS. For many systems users, however, it is not personality but lack of adequate preparation that interferes with success. Because the systems described here require composing strategies and skills that differ in emphasis or kind from those associated with pen-and-paper composing, college graduates are often unprepared to use the new media effectively. In this section, I will identify the distinctive features of electronic composing, then outline the strategies and skills college graduates need to use the new media effectively.

Questionnaire and interview responses about composing on the systems described here show that electronic composing is a relatively linear process. It emphasizes planning and translating plans into words and generally deemphasizes revision; the exceptions are word processing and dictated drafting. Table 4-1 presents the responses of five representative users of five new systems to the request: "Describe the typical process you go through when you compose a message using one of the new systems."

Distinctive Features. Taken together, the illustrative responses in table 4-1, plus related questionnaire and interview information, point to the distinctive features of electronic composing. Clearly, planning—about purpose, audience, content, and appropriate choice of medium—is the critical component. The process is also characterized by organizing the text within the constraints of the medium chosen; by adapting style as appropriate to the medium and to the frequently collaborative nature of electronic composing; by shifting back and forth between electronic and conventional media, thereby putting pressures on memory; and by actually keying in or speaking the message rather than having someone else prepare the finished product, thereby putting a premium on strong written and oral delivery skills. These features will be explained in detail.

Table 4-1
Composing With the New Media

Dictation for Word Processing	Electronic Mail	Audio-Only Teleconferencing	Full-Color, Full-Motion Two-Way Videoconferencing	Word Processing
*Consider audiences: readers and transcriber.	*Identify purpose, addressees.	*Visualize audiences and specify intent of message/meeting.	*Make reservations, participant list.	*Jot down notes on what I'm going to write (and to whom).
*Assemble materials.	*List items to be included.	*Outline anticipated flow of information/discussion; jot down key words, phrases, concepts.	*Plan agenda; distribute.	†Compose paragraph.
*Think through/make notes.	*Prioritize.	*Note need for predistributed visuals, handouts; prepare; send.	*Prepare graphics, written materials; distribute.	†Reread paragraph.

Dictate, distinguishing between content of letter and directions for transcriber.	Compose document at terminal, editing as I compose.	Communicate on phones, speakers.	Arrive on time; do hands-on training in conference room as necessary.	†Revise paragraph.
Replay tape "to hear what it's like to listen to"; fix.	Reread on-screen for clarity and content.	*Follow up as necessary.	Follow agenda.	*Print and make changes/corrections on paper—spelling, spacing.
*Review word-processed letter; correct as necessary; send.	Send and file disc copy.		Reach decision; end on time.	Correct on screen.
			*Follow up as necessary.	*Print; send.

Note: Audio mail has aspects of both dictation and audio-only teleconferencing.
*On paper and/or in mind.
†Repeats entire process on screen as many times as necessary.

• *Planning is the critical component of composing with the new systems.* As illustrated in table 4-1, considerations of purpose, audience, and content dominate planning for electronic media, as they do for conventional media. The distinctive considerations are deciding *which* medium is most appropriate for the message, and prefiguring plans in detail *for that medium* (File, Forrest, Kuritsky, & Leidermann, 1980). Such planning decisions lead in turn to other decisions, among them organization and style, which I will discuss shortly.

Planning which medium is appropriate depends on which are available or what the intent of the message is—not to mention the political, personal, and nonrational aspects of the situation. For instance, if the options are audio mail, electronic mail, a typed memo, or a face-to-face talk, and if the intent of the message is to convey especially sensitive or unpleasant information to those affected by it, people with a strong sense of the situation would avoid the impersonal or cool electronic media and opt instead for a face-to-face (or at least a personal phone) conversation. This choice would allow the message sender to adapt the patterning, style, and tone of the message during the exchange even though the purpose, content, and audience remained the same. This choice would, in other words, incorporate considerations of *kairos,* such as propriety and timing, which are as critical today as they have been throughout the history of rhetoric (Kinneavy, 1984). Because the range of communication media is now relatively wide, the *choice of the appropriate medium* is an especially important feature of planning, a feature that requires some knowledge of the capabilities of different systems and sensitivity to their effects on people.

Planning effective messages for the new media generally requires more attention to writing notes or outlines than does planning for conventional media. For instance, because leaving a complete message on an audio mail system is essential, users of this system typically jot down details before calling—details ranging from names, dates, and topics to what action the receiver should take next. In this respect, leaving an audio mail message, which resembles talking on the phone but lacks an interlocutor, requires much more careful planning than making a phone call. Other systems similarly depend on planning. One manager, who uses audio mail and electronic mail many times a day, says that no matter which medium he uses, he has developed a series of questions that he moves through mentally:

Who's the audience? What's the purpose of this message (information, decision, action, etc.)? What information do I want to get across? What key points will the message contain? After jotting down his answers, he composes the message on the phone or at the keyboard. Another interviewee, the president of an electronics company, uses earlier documents as his planning guides for composing a new document at the word processor. He composes his monthly corporate reports, for instance, using the file disc from the previous month's report as his outline, replacing old information with current material. Whether on screen or on paper, in mental, abbreviated, or elaborated form, planning is the critical element of composing on the new systems.

• *Organizing a message within media constraints requires flexible arrangement alternatives.* We are all familiar with the process of jotting down notes, then crossing some out and marking others with stars, arrows, or numbers to prioritize the points in the message we are developing. It usually does not matter whether we are planning to write the message in longhand or type it; the organization stays the same. If we decide that building the case first and putting the main point last is the most effective strategy for a particular message and reader, we follow that strategy.

But the new media can actually influence the design of a message. Consider, for example, electronic mail. The way certain electronic mail systems work and the size of the terminal screen actually mitigate against indirect or inductive messages. Preview or scan features may present only the first line or two of a message, making it desirable to state the main point succinctly at the beginning (Stein & Yates, 1983). Similarly, a small screen size or restricted linear capacity may influence a writer to put critical information up front and abbreviate or stress key points through formatting.

Or consider an entirely different set of constraints, those of two-way videoconferencing. In a typical business meeting, the agenda and materials are usually prepared in advance. In a videoconference, however, the agenda will be much more carefully planned, with more detail and elaboration, not only because of time pressures associated with the high costs of satellite transmission but also because teleconferences do not typically invite the give and take, the responsiveness, or the spontaneous creativity that can occur around a conference table. Not surprisingly, participants in videoconferences claim to be more agenda- or topic-oriented, more polite, and more

self-conscious (Gottschalk, 1983). Because there are fewer opportunities for unplanned issues to arise, the actual organization of the
teleconference has to be more carefully arranged—in the agenda and
in the written materials that support it. As these examples suggest
and as the results in table 4-1 demonstrate, the very availibility of a
wide range of communication media to which everybody (not just the
specialist) may have access means that users need to understand
media constraints and must be able to arrange their messages in a
variety of ways for maximum media effectiveness.

• *Adapting style to the requirements of the medium and to the
frequently collaborative nature of electronic composing requires
linguistic sophistication.* Different systems require different styles
and levels of discourse. The style of a phone conversation is typically
more casual than that of an audio mail message, which in turn is
often more casual than an audioconference. One interviewee, an
administrative assistant in a public agency who is currently also a
student, described in detail the pressure she felt to be careful to stick
to the facts. She said that she "used proper sentences and always
stuck to the point so as not to get too casual and give away my real
feelings. . . . " In a recent college course, she said, she had learned to
distinguish between levels of register such as casual and formal (Joos,
1961); she was very articulate in describing her control of grammatical patterns; logical features; and even auditory cues such as
speed, pitch, frequency of interruption, and rambling—which, she
said, "are to phone talk what posture, eye contact, or fidgeting are to
visible talk."

A similar need for knowledge about discourse styles shows up in
the technologies based on writing. Electronic mail messages seem to
invite a less formal style and also less effort than do word-processed
messages. This difference is illustrated in table 4-1, where the writer
of the electronic mail message describes a process of composing that
is noticeably less rigorous than that used by the writer of the word-
processed memo. But such "effortlessness" can result in misspelling,
mispunctuation, and grammatical mistakes that make the electronic
mail message look careless rather than casual and the sender look
less than literate. Users of the new media need some background in
what combinations of mechanical, grammatical, and lexical features
will allow them to achieve the appropriate style for the message they
compose and the medium they choose.

Another reason that stylistic sophistication is unusually important in electronic composing is its frequently collaborative nature:

between dictator and word-processing personnel; among diverse project members in several locations using a computerized word processor to compose their reports; among people on an international team communicating through computer conferencing. For instance, instead of a dictator relying on a personal secretary who can produce a complete letter from a roughly dictated tape, the dictator must keep two audiences firmly in mind—the transcriber and the intended audience. That is, the dictator must anticipate the needs of a transcriber, perhaps at a remote word processing center—a person who knows nothing about the letter on the cassette or its writer and who expects the dictation to be complete. Collaboration in this context means leaving an entirely self-contained message, a message composed of two quite different levels of discourse—one perhaps a more casual level appropriate for the transcriber listening to directions, the other a more formal level appropriate to the reader of the letter (Halpern & Liggett, 1984). A dictator using the new system now needs more linguistic savvy to produce a first-time-final letter (Gould, 1980). Similarly, because word processors enable people in far-flung units of the same organization working on the same project to compose different parts independently, those responsible for final manuscript preparation need experience not only with editing and formatting, and in using computer programs that help with these operations, but also with the principles of rhetorical and stylistic consistency and cohesion. Finally, since the new media provide more options for international communication, users of these systems (especially users who do not have the help of translators at each location) need more knowledge about cross-cultural rhetorical and stylistic conventions. Although many of the difficulties with international phone calls or letters or contracts have gradually been worked out, systems like telex and international electronic mailboxes are bringing a new spate of communication problems, which require considerable linguistic and rhetorical sensitivity (Coe, 1983). To use the new media effectively, people need to know more about how language works.

• *Shifting back and forth between electronic and conventional media occurs throughout the composing process, making consistent demands on memory.* As I explained earlier when discussing planning, those who use the new media rely heavily on notes, outlines, agendas, and other prefigurations in electronic composing. Clearly, such written material—by helping to clarify purpose, content, audience needs, media choice, and situation—enables systems users to translate their plans into appropriate, well-formed messages. But using writing to plan electronic messages is just one example of a continuous and observable shifting back and forth between pen-in-hand and electronic composing. The use of both conventional and electronic media also occurs during speaking and writing. In preponderantly oral contexts, such as teleconferences, participants make notes for later use or jot down questions to ask later in the conference. In primarily written contexts, those who use word processors, according to one interviewee, "occasionally like to pull a hard copy and edit on paper." Furthermore, this media shifting continues throughout composing. Toward the end of a teleconference, people write or dictate on pocket recorders what they have to follow through on, while those at word processors edit and format printouts—because "sometimes it's hard to get a feel for how the thing reads or the page looks when it's on screen"—before keying in their final changes. Electronic composing consistently relies on habits of pen-in-hand composing. But why?

The pen-in-hand features of electronic composing are connected to memory—drawing from memory information about a message being planned, prodding memory with notes and outlines to reproduce a planned segment of discourse, and depending on memory to provide the previously stored forms—how a sentence should sound, how a page should look—that enable the speaker or writer to produce texts that conform to the expectations of listeners or readers. These electronic uses of pen-and-paper notation resemble conventional uses in several ways, such as accumulating planning material from memory and translating plans into sentences (Flower & Hayes, 1981). Experienced speakers and writers have had practice with such procedures, albeit not with the technical crossovers required by the new systems, and can generally adapt these procedures to new situations.

The more difficult or less practiced use of memory has to do with form. Remembering how a well-formatted memo should look so that it can be imitated in an electronic mail message; remembering how a simple figure should be boxed and captioned so that clear directions to a transcriptionist can be dictated; remembering how an action ending in an audio message can be spoken so that it sounds neither too rigid nor too flexible: These are some areas where memory needs to be developed and often is not. There seems, in other words, to be a difference between personal or informational memory, based on individual experience with a subject or a job, and formal or literate memory, which stores and makes accessible established forms through conscious attention during reading and listening (Hirsch, 1977). In any case, the consistent use of handwritten memory-prompting devices in electronic composing suggests the need for increased attention to memory development.

• *Keying in or speaking a message is more frequently done by the composer than by secretaries or assistants. Consequently, good written and oral delivery skills are essential.* Except in dictation for word processing, all the new media shift the responsibility for producing the final product to the writer or speaker. Those who leave an audio mail call, send an electronic memo, write a report at a word processor, or participate in a phone conference go public with their own logic and their own language. This presents new challenges to systems users. One middle-level manager, for instance, told me that he is very conscious of how he wants to come across on audio mail: He avoids "ah"s, slang terms, and rambling sentences because he wants to appear confident, precise, well spoken. Similarly, he judges the audio mail messages he receives as reflecting the people leaving them.

Answers to the question, "What specific skills or abilities does a person need to use them systems effectively?" offered some important insights into necessary delivery skills. These answers fell into two categories: technical and communicative. Among the technical skills mentioned consistently were familiarity with computing terms and some technical knowledge of the particular system or hardware being used. But button pushing and keyboard fluency did not receive as much comment from my respondents as did certain communication skills. Over and over, interviewees emphasized the need for good, clear vocabulary and syntax; knowledge of spelling, punctuation, and proofreading skills; and well-paced, articulate speech. Proficiency in written and oral delivery (Britton, 1982) is unusually important in using the new systems, probably because these skills show up much more vividly when there are fewer intermediaries to clean things up.

Underlying Strategies and Skills. What does this discussion of the five distinctive features of electronic composing tell us about the strategies and skills necessary for effective systems use? First, that because systems vary so much, specific technical training in college is probably less important than general exposure to and some experience with the technologies now being used; second, that we will want to emphasize both writing and speaking in our classes; and finally, that the most valuable strategies and skills we can offer our students are those that resemble, in outline at least, the venerable rhetorical arts of planning, arrangement, style, memory, and delivery. After describing how such strategies and skills are being addressed in on-the-job training programs and how, according to my interviewees, they might be handled in college classes, I will discuss the results and conclusions outlined here, especially as they pertain to research and teaching in composition.

ON-THE-JOB TRAINING. As shown in the 1985 Carnegie Foundation study, *Corporate Classrooms: The Learning Business*, corporate involvement in education, now totaling over $40 billion a year, is approaching the annual expenditure of all four-year colleges and graduate universities in the United States. And total enrollment in corporate programs is nearly 8 million students, making it equal to current college and university enrollments (Eurich, 1985). Furthermore, the growth rate of on-the-job training as a percentage of total adult education has nearly doubled since 1975 (*Statistical Abstract*, 1984 and 1979). Within the corporate context, as within the university context, different subjects are emphasized in different places, ranging from remedial English to MS degree work in aerospace engineering. In communications, the focus of my study, different organizations likewise set different goals for their training programs. But general patterns of training for the new systems in the companies in this study can be characterized in terms of content, activities, and teachers.

Content of Training. On-the-job training currently emphasizes technical and surface-level communication skills. Technical-skills training focuses on equipment operation; this ranges from the special dialing procedure necessary to dictate a letter over the phone, to the keyboard skills necessary to use a Lotus spread sheet, to the central panel manipulation necessary to chair a two-way audio-video teleconference. (Also, in hardware- or software-oriented settings such as Zenith and I. P. Sharp, there is training in specific computer programming languages and in software development and use.) Training is almost always hands-on, and the skills taught are always system-specific. Indeed, even when switching between units of a company or from one company to another, users often receive technical skills training for each system they use—or they find a way to acquire such training.

On-the-job training also emphasizes certain communication or delivery skills such as writing clearly, speaking effectively, and managing meetings. Boeing, for instance, has developed a text-editing program called CLEAR to make sure readability levels of proposals, manuals, and other documents are appropriate for intended audiences. ARCO has incorporated in its meeting-management course special sessions for teleconferencing. Courses are offered by audiovisual or programmed instruction, through in-house classes, and occasionally by visiting consultants.

According to my research, however, only certain trainers with backgrounds in English and/or education and some visiting consultants emphasize in their on-the-job training what we in college teaching would refer to as transferable composing strategies or broad rhetorical principles (Dvorin, 1982). For instance, in answer to the question, "What do you think the most successful training programs would include?" only one trainer and one consultant, both with strong backgrounds in language, psychology, and teaching, gave answers emphasizing aspects of the composing process. Most other respondents—teachers and learners alike—named attributes of a text such as conciseness or correctness.

At the moment, on-the-job training is very successful in solving specific technical problems and in providing hands-on solutions to surface problems in communication. It does not emphasize composing.

Activities. On-the-job training activities in the organizations visited range from formal courses taught in classrooms for several days or weeks to tutorials to audio or video self-instruction—often accompanied by printed worksheets or manuals or textbooks or computer-assisted instruction, and almost always accompanied by hands-on experience. For most systems, training involves a combination of these activities. At Continental Illinois Bank, for example, an editor described how he learned to use the electronic mail (EM) system. First came the formal on-screen instruction, during which an internal marketing person explained how the system worked. There was also a hotline service to answer emergency questions. Then, and perhaps most useful, was the trial-and-error experience and the give-and-take with other EM users, which really opened the novice's eyes to resources available on the system.

Although some companies offer formal courses, from beginning to advanced, employees tend to stick to introductory courses; it is really up to the individual how far he or she will advance. Unless users are highly motivated to learn, they may not move beyond a beginner's knowledge of the systems they use or the communication skills they develop.

Teachers. On-the-job training may be conducted in several ways, often used in tandem: by a full-time training staff, with a coordinator and training specialists; by information systems personnel who also do internal marketing; by other users within a given department; or by outside vendors or consultants. The most frequent training models at the companies in this study were: classroom courses (9), tutorials (9), and self-study (7); each of these usually included hands-on experience. The largest organizations I visited, like Boeing, have elaborate internal training staffs with people to manage, develop, and teach systems use; they also prepare their own materials, ranging from simple computerized keyboarding programs that teach engineers to type, to elaborate training programs for word-processing professionals.

But in most companies and for other, less complex systems, the training is handled by a person with many other responsiblities. For instance, dictation training is often covered in one-hour slide show sessions by a supervisor or manager who has experience with a specific system; training is oriented toward technical skills and simple communication advice: plan ahead, talk clearly, don't eat apples while dictating. In any case, most on-the-job teachers have many responsibilities in addition to teaching—responsibilities ranging from managing to technical field work to sales to keyboarding to programming.

Perhaps the most surprising (and effective) group of "teachers" are the people in any given unit or department who teach each other. The interaction between novices and their more experienced counterparts resembles peer tutoring in a writing lab; those who know a little more teach those who know a little less how to solve a communication problem. Considerations of rank do not seem to hinder or otherwise interfere with this informal teaching. An editor who has been using a word processor for a year may help a new writer who has only been around for a week; an administrative assistant will give her new boss tips on good dictation; a teleconferencing supervisor will show an executive how to use the controls for a teleconference. As the head of information and technology services from ARCO put it, "A good understanding of what people don't know and need to know goes a long way in training others right in the office." Tact helps, too.

The use of vendors and outside consultants is limited. Sometimes vendors will come in to give initial training; or, more often, selected personnel will go to vendor-sponsored workshops, then return and teach their own staff members to use equipment or software. Such training is oriented toward systems use. I did interview a few consultants who give training sessions in technical and communication skills, but the demand for such services seems unpredictable. While there would appear to be a growing field in consulting (Buchholz, 1983), in-house training arrangements for electronic media are currently more popular.

According to my study, on-the-job training is successful in teaching people to use specific systems and develop specific skills; the people I interviewed had learned to use new technologies on their jobs. Training currently emphasizes technical skills or surface features of writing and speaking, but the entry of teachers with backgrounds in English or education and the occasional hiring of experienced consultants suggests that in-house training may direct itself toward a broader view of composing in the future, especially if such an emphasis looks as though it will improve organizational communication.

INTERVIEWEES' SUGGESTIONS FOR COLLEGE COURSE WORK. In addition to soliciting information about on-the-job training, I gave respondents the opportunity to suggest what college course work would best prepare graduates to communicate effectively on the job. Within the larger educational context, they agreed that a liberal arts background was useful when tempered with strong technical courses, such as computer science or business. They also suggested that hands-on experience with the new technologies—in co-ops, internships, extracurricular activities—was helpful. However, the range of responses on this subject was extremely wide; it included these three contrasting positions:

1. "College days should be spent in mastering the finer points of literature, the arts, and civilized behavior. Only primitive peoples worship soulless and mindless machines. Time enough for students to sit at a screen after they graduate."
2. "English and history are great subjects, and despite what we read so often today about high-technitis, I would still encourage students to know great literature, history, and philosophy. But they should leaven their liberal arts major with courses in econ, finance, and a foreign language or two. *Maybe* systems."
3. "Don't take liberal arts. Take computer science, business administration, communications."

Quote 1 came from a manager with a bachelor's degree with honors in English, Latin, and French; quote 2 from a writer/editor with master's degrees in English and Anglo-Irish literature; Quote 3 from a supervisor with one and a half years of college and fifteen years of on-the-job experience. If we can generalize at all, we can say that educational background is likely to influence the views reported in this section.

General Programs and Course Work. Respondents showed considerable unanimity in specifying the features of their own educational backgrounds that best prepared them for their present work. Written and oral communication was the clear leader (14), with group/people processes (5), logical thinking/problem-solving/research skills (5), and various technical specializations (3) also cited as important. On the questionnaire and especially in the interviews, writing, speaking, and interpersonal skills were mentioned as essential for using the new systems effectively; however, respondents suggested that these skills might be applied somewhat differently with the new communication media. They mentioned, for instance, more flexible outlining strategies. Respondents also said it was useful to know technical terminology and to have a mastery of certain technical procedures.

In answer to the question about what should be introduced at the college level, all but one respondent answered that students should have some experience using the new communication systems in college. Respondents showed overwhelming interest in introducing the new technologies in a wide range of classes—especially English and communication, and also, of course, computer science, engineering, and business—to reduce technophobia, to improve computer literacy, and to provide general exposure to the new technologies.

Writing Courses. Perhaps the most interesting answers—because they revealed attitudes about writing—were responses to the question: "If you were going to design a writing course, knowing what you now know about the new communication systems, what would you be sure to emphasize?" The largest number of answers (8) are reflected in this quote: "It's all in Strunk & White: Be concise, clear, and leave out the garbage." In fact, however, those who echoed this view usually tempered their statements by suggesting that although "writing itself would not necessarily change, organization would," and so would "the way one went about writing, especially outlining." Rhetorical outlining—outlining that kept before the composer notes on audience, purpose, direction, key content points, tone—was much preferred to traditional, formal outlining. The outlines I saw were flexible, sketchy, punctuated by arrows, numbers, or exclamation points; they looked more like lists than like drafts.

Respondents (6) also emphasized the importance of teaching students how a given medium influences the message, saying that students needed to get beyond button pushing and understand how the new systems "can assist one in writing" and enable writers to "creatively meet their goals." Though these respondents emphasized conciseness and "newspaper-style writing," they also mentioned the importance of clarifying and achieving goals. The few actual assignments mentioned—impromptu writing, news writing, practice with letters and reports, and short oral presentations based on written reports—reflect the kinds of communications and communication styles interviewees considered most appropriate to on-the-job writing.

In a very broad sense, answers to the last substantive question— "How do you think the new communication systems will change jobs in your organization in the foreseeable future?"—gave a future-oriented focus to assignment-making. The answers suggested that the new communication technologies are likely to change our lives as much as the car did—by changing life-styles, employment patterns, personal interactions: "Office configurations, chains of command, and power relationships will change completely." "Managers will need much less administrative support as they handle much more of the communication themselves." "The power will be on the desks of a wide range of individuals." "Secretaries and typists will be virtually eliminated; these people will move into administrative or information-processing roles." "Most human interaction will occur electronically." "Eventually, a lot of the work presently done in offices and factories will be done in private residences via satellite links or telephone hardware." According to my interviewees, working patterns will change substantially over the next few decades. What will it take to communicate in the business environment of the future? That, too, one respondent noted, might make a good topic for a writing class.

These, then, are the main results and specific conclusions of my electronic odyssey. In the rest of this chapter, I will discuss their implications for research and teaching in composition.

WHAT ARE THE CONSEQUENCES OF THIS STUDY FOR COLLEGE TEACHERS?

I have four general conclusions. First, because of numerous advantages, the use of the new technologies is likely to become even more widespread in the next decade, altering the way people communicate on their jobs. Although systems such as audio and electronic mail can make certain kinds of communication less personal, this tendency is mitigated by personal interactions such as collaborative writing and peer teaching. At the same time, however, changes in the technical aspects of written and oral communication intimidate some people, a situation that could seriously hamper their success in the workplace.

Second, in terms of strategies and skills needed by systems users, the new technologies are bringing speaking and writing closer together; students therefore need very flexible, highly transferable composing strategies that work effectively for speaking and writing. Since on-the-job electronic composing is a fairly linear process, strategies for rhetorical planning, organizing, and choosing the appropriate style would be useful at the beginning of composing, and effective memory and delivery skills would be useful during performance—that is, during the translation of plans into messages. My research also suggests that interpersonal skills, ranging from collaborative writing to meeting management to peer teaching, are essential for electronic composing.

Third, since on-the-job training programs are generally effective in preparing employees to use specific systems, they are continuing to expand. These programs, which now address basic technical and communicative skills, could move into other areas related to written and oral composing if their benefits prove convincing.

Fourth, those who have college degrees and who manage or use the new systems continue to consider teachers of liberal arts responsible for the general education of college students, especially for preparing students to grapple with issues raised by technological change, and for developing creative, interpersonal, and problem-solving abilities. But such teachers should also encourage students to take useful technical courses and to choose work experiences that include media use. Teachers of college composition and communication are considered responsible for preparing students to be effective writers and speakers or, more specifically, for imparting communication strategies appropriate to a work environment increasingly dominated by electronic systems. However, if college teachers do not effectively prepare their students for composing effectively on the new media, then corporate trainers are likely to assume that responsibility.

Implications for Research

What does this study imply for teachers of college writing? Clearly, it implies a need for what Janice Lauer (1984) calls "the willingness to go beyond what we know." More specifically, it implies the need for additional research about the consequences of technological change for our profession—research on the pervasiveness of change, on the consequences for on-the-job writers and speakers, on historical insights that can illuminate current change, on the strong points of on-the-job training, and on appropriate professional responses to technology.

DESCRIPTIVE STUDIES. My research suggests that the new media are having and will continue to have profound effects on the teaching of writing. But my project was relatively small and my sample drawn from organizations publicized as leaders in the use of new technologies. Additional descriptive research, based on surveys, interviews, site observations, and secondary sources, is needed to show whether the changes I have described here are as pervasive as my research suggests and, if so, whether they are having the effects I have outlined.

CASE STUDIES. We also need a closer look at the composing process of on-the-job writers and speakers who use the new systems. We need case studies of people using all the new technologies to illuminate the effects that specific media have on composing. Bridwell, Nancarrow, and Ross (1984) have shown that it is possible to adapt the protocol analytic method to word processing without actually intervening in the composing process; it would be good to have similarly close studies of composing on other media in the workplace. Since my own research was based largely on self-reports and general observations, case studies or intensive interviews, like those conducted by Odell and Goswami (1982), would be valuable resources for additional information on the strategies and skills on-the-job writers need to communicate effectively using the new systems.

EXPERIMENTAL STUDIES. Our profession would also benefit from a closer investigation of on-the-job teaching. In this connection, our tendency has been to move in the opposite direction; as consultants, we have adapted our college classroom goals and methods to the marketplace. But studying what works well in on-the-job contexts (Eurich, 1985; Moskey, 1983) and devising experimental studies to test the effectiveness of similar methods in our own classes might prove useful in developing our classroom resources for teaching electronic composing.

HISTORICAL STUDIES. It would also be useful to consider the strategies and skills I have identified from a historic perspective. When I first noticed the coincidence between the strategies necessary for electronic composing and Aristotle's outline of the arts of rhetoric, I reexamined the classical texts for the light they might cast on observations I had made. Indeed, I learned that we have not come very far in our knowledge of certain topics, such as the development of memory, since *Ad C. Herennium* (Yates, 1966; Norman, 1969) in Cicero's time. We should use the past to help us understand and prepare for the future. Historical studies might be interpretive, like those of Ong (1977, 1982), alerting us to the effects technologies have had on composing processes in the past. Or they might be pedagogically oriented—helping us, for example, to define alternative planning heuristics appropriate for the new media (Ewing, 1983; Young, 1978).

THEORETICAL STUDIES. Finally, we would benefit professionally from theoretical discussions of our own professional roles. For many English teachers, a study of the kind described in this chapter is not in tune with the goals of our profession; it is somehow too applied. It would be useful to know why many of us teach writing without reference to how our students, once they leave college, will use what we teach. It would also be useful to ponder which of the several prevailing theories of composition—the current-traditional, the romantic, and the new classical—would provide a workable framework for research in electronic composing (Kaufer & Young, 1984). For instance, it might be especially productive to apply Kinneavy's (1984) work on *kairos* to media choice in electronic composing.

In general, then, research related to the effects of technological change could be descriptive, experimental, historical, or theoretical. It could occur in business or industry, in the classroom, or in the library. And it could cover a wide geographic area or analyze one person composing an electronic message. The main point is that looking at what is occurring in the world around us is likely to improve the quality of the decisions we make for the students we teach.

Implications for Teaching

This study suggests the importance of bringing issues and materials and equipment associated with the workaday world into our classrooms. Some of the larger issues touched on in this study have to do with how new technologies will affect international communication, organizational policies, and individual lives. These issues, treated in stories like Harrison's "Rollerball" (1980) or books like Toffler's *The Third Wave* (1980), deserve to be discussed in our classes; they can serve as provocative introductions to the technologies our students will use. Other, more concrete suggestions point to more specific action—in recommending that students take media-related courses or technology-related college jobs, and in helping students develop interpersonal and oral skills through presentations, collaborative projects, and peer tutoring (Payne, 1981). Finally, the most concrete suggestions indicate a need for some hands-on experience with the new technologies in our classes. But these are secondary recommendations and should be taken as such.

The primary recommendation of this study is that composition teachers should emphasize the media-related strategies and skills that students will need once they graduate. These include: planning, arrangement, style, memory, and delivery.

PLANNING. To make effective plans, students will have to understand the advantages of specific systems for specific tasks. They will require some knowledge of the capabilities of different systems and some sensitivity to their effects on people. To make appropriate media choices based on an understanding of these systems, students will need planning heuristics that structure considerations of purpose, audience, content, and situation. And to enable them to translate their plans into spoken and written form, students will need to learn quick, flexible, rhetorical (as opposed to traditional) outlining strategies.

ARRANGEMENT. Students need enough knowledge about the media to understand the constraints they may impose on organizing a message. Mainly, however, students need flexible arrangement options that allow them to adjust a message to a wide range of media—paper-based, screen-based, audio-based, video-based options; inductive and deductive options; audience-based, writer-based, subject-based options. Students should be able to make intelligent, logical choices about the most effective way to organize a message for a specific system, audience, purpose, and situation.

STYLE. Students need more linguistic sophistication—a wider view of style than we typically convey when we discuss words, sentences, paragraphs, and figures. They need to know the differences between spoken and written discourse so they can use both effectively (Schafer, 1981); to understand concepts of register and formality and politeness so that they can adapt them in writing as well as in speech; to develop a conscious awareness of what consistency and coherence mean so that they can effectively collaborate on projects; to develop a sensitivity to nuance, pace, tone, and other auditory features so that they can interpret vocal "gestures" as they now interpret body language; and to learn to assess the stylistic expectations of those they work with and the stylistic levels appropriate to the media they use.

MEMORY. Students need experience using memory during composing—by searching it for content or rhetorical information; by storing in it planned sentences to be triggered by notes and outlines; by relying on it for format and grammatical, lexical, and mechanical information. They should learn to attend to what they read and hear so that this information is available to them when they plan or translate plans into writing. And they should practice—with notes or other mnemonic devices—drawing on their memories in planned and impromptu communication situations (Hirsch, 1977).

DELIVERY. Students need some experience composing on the new media—that is, speaking or keying in their own messages (Liggett, 1982). They need practice hearing each other and hearing themselves send articulate and complete audio mail messages. They need practice, if possible, with composing at an electronic mail or word-processing terminal. They need, especially, diagnoses or evaluations of their performances and remedial help as necessary with such matters as diction, articulation, grammar, spelling, punctuation, and format. In general, they need to develop the confidence that they can speak and write appropriately and correctly.

Do these suggestions for preparing students for electronic composing sound familiar? Surely in outline they resemble the rhetorical arts, and in content they resemble much of what we already emphasize in our teaching—but with a new slant. Though not medium-specific, these strategies and skills do orient the student's composing process toward planning for and translating plans into messages on the new media. This distinction, this media slant, can serve as a timely and important guide for composition teachers.

Larger Professional Implications

The history of oral and written communication has witnessed very few periods of change as pervasive as the current one. But lessons from the past and evidence from the present suggest the challenge of the future. In *Interfaces of the Word* and also in *Orality* and Literacy: The Technologizing of the Word, Walter Ong demonstrates that changes in communication technology inevitably bring about changes in communication processes and products. Writers in related fields also provide a useful historical perspective. Classicist Eric Havelock (1982), for instance, the The Literate Revolution in Greece and Its Cultural Consequences, shows not only that "the content of what is communicated is governed by the technology used, but that this same technology may have a causative function in determining how we think."

Although Havelock's conclusion is based on the effects of alphabetic writing in post-Homeric, pre-Aristotelian Greece, it applies as well today. One reason we as teachers and researchers should pay attention to electronically mediated composing in the workplace is that it may prompt us to reconsider things we thought we knew for sure—for example, that revision is a consistently important feature of composing (Emig, 1977; Perl, 1980; Sommers, 1980). The research cited here suggests that what Murray (1978) called "re-envisioning" may, indeed, occur in dictated drafting and in word processing; it is, however, the exception rather than the rule in on-the-job composing. Just as alphabetic writing altered the way people conceived of oratory, and just as the printing press altered the way people conceived of writing, so the new electronic media are likely to alter the way we conceive of composing.

If this is so, and there is increasing evidence in this direction, then the results of studies of on-the-job communication may change our professional certainties—about what we explore in our research and what we teach in our classes—as much as Apple's Macintosh is changing the way we think about typing. The challenge of charting a new rhetoric of electronic composing would certainly be an exciting professional challenge, one worthy of a modern-day Odysseus.

Acknowledgments

This chapter was supported by a 1983 grant from the Purdue Research Foundation and was prepared with help from the Department of General Business, College of Business Administration, University of Texas at Austin, and the Department of English, Purdue University. I am indebted to all those who so generously and cordially gave me interviews and especially to my consistently helpful readers: David Gibson, Janice Lauer, and Sarah Liggett.

References

Belzer, J., Holzman, A., & Kent, A. (Eds.) (1979). Encyclopedia of computer science and technology. New York: Marcel Dekker.

Beswick, R. W. (1983). Office technology: Voice store-and-forward. In R. Beswick & A. B. Williams (Eds.), Information systems and business communication (pp. 1–7). Urbana, IL: American Business Communication Association.

Bridwell, L. S., Nancarrow, P. R., & Ross, D. (1984). The writing process and the writing machine: Current research on word processors relevant to the teaching of composition. In R. Beach & L. S. Bridwell (Eds.), New directions in composition research (pp. 381–398). New York: Guilford.

Britton, J. (1982). Shaping at the point of utterance. In A. Freedman & I. Pringle (Eds.), Reinventing the rhetorical tradition (pp. 61–65). Conway, AK: L & S Books, University of Arkansas.

Buchholz, W. J. (Ed.). (1983). Communication training and consulting in business, industry, and government. Urbana, IL: American Business Communication Association.

Chernicoff, S. (1983). Electronic mail. Popular Computing, 2, 46–53.

Coe, R. M. (1983). Chinese and American discourse: Some contrasts and their implications. Paper presented at the Conference on College Composition and Communication, Detroit.

Connell, J. (1982). Managing human factors in the automated office. Modern Office Procedures, March 3, 51–64.

Connell, J. (1984). Office technology and organizational relationships. New Management, Spring, 1–6.

Dvorin, D. (1983). Tele-Skills: The people factor in teleconferencing. Satellite Communications, May 4, 44–45.

Edwards, D. (1983). 1984 looming closer: Secret Service computers pose dangers. Computers and Society, 13, 2–3.

Emig, J. (1977). Writing as a mode of learning. College Composition and Communication, 28, 122–128.

Eurich, N. (1985). Corporate classrooms: The learning business. Princeton, NJ: The Carnegie Foundation for the Advancement of Learning and the Princeton University Press.

Ewing, D. P. (1983). Needed research in business writing. In J. W. Halpern (Ed.), Teaching business writing: Approaches, plans, pedagogy, research (pp. 183–199). Urbana, IL: American Business Communication Association.

Faigley, L., & Miller, T. P. (1982). What we learn from writing on the job. College English, 44, 557–569.

File, K., Forrest, R., Kuritsky, A., & Leiderman, S. (1980). The future of video-conferencing: There's more than the meeting to consider. In Teleconferencing and interactive media (pp. 37–43). Madison, WI: University of Wisconsin Extension, Center for Interactive Programs.

Flower, L., & Hayes, J. R. (1981). A cognitive process theory model of writing. College Composition and Communication, 32, 365–387.

Gibson, D., & Mendelson, B. (1984). Factors that influence corporate teleconferencing and pedagogical implications for university business communication. In S. J.

Bruno (Ed.), *1984 Proceedings, Southwest American Business Communication Association Spring Conference* (pp. 137–147). Houston: University of Houston, Clear Lake.

Gottschalk, E. C., Jr. (1983). Firms are cool to meetings by television. *Wall Street Journal*, July 26, 31–32.

Gould, J. D. (1980). Experiments on composing letters: Some facts, some myths, and some observations. In L. W. Gregg & E. R. Steinberg (Eds.), *Cognitive processes in writing* (pp. 97–127). Hillsdale, NJ: Erlbaum.

Halpern, J. W., & Liggett, S. (1984). *Computers and composing: How the new technologies are changing writing.* Carbondale: Southern Illinois University Press.

Harrison, W. (1980). Rollerball. In T. Dodge (Ed.), *A literature of sports* (pp. 9–19). Lexington, MA: Heath.

Havelock, E. A. (1982). *The literate revolution in Greece and its cultural consequences.* Princeton: Princeton University Press.

Hirsch, E. D., Jr. (1977). *The philosophy of composition.* Chicago: University of Chicago Press.

Joos, M. (1961). *The five clocks.* New York: Harcourt.

Kaufer, D. S., & Young, R. E. (1984). Literacy, art, and politics in departments of English. In W. B. Horner (Ed.), *Composition & literature: Bridging the gap.* Chicago: University of Chicago Press.

Kinneavy, J. (1984). *Kairos:* A neglected concept in classical rhetoric. Paper presented at the Ninth Annual Rhetoric Seminar, Purdue University, W. Lafayette, IN, June 5. (Available from J. Kinneavy, English Department, University of Texas at Austin, Austin, TX 78712.)

Lauer, J. (1984). Introduction to current theories of teaching composition. Paper presented at the Ninth Annual Rhetoric Seminar, Purdue University, W. Lafayette, IN, May 28. (Available from J. Lauer, English Department, Purdue University, W. Lafayette, IN 47907.)

Liggett, S. (1982). *Preparing business writing students to use dictation systems: An experimental study.* Unpublished disseration. Purdue University. (Available from University Microfilms, Ann Arbor, MI 48104.)

McWilliams, P. A. (1982). *The word processing book: A short course in computer literacy.* Los Angeles: Prelude Press.

Mertes, L. H. (1981). Doing your office over—electronically. *Harvard Business Review, 59*, 127–135. (a)

Mertes, L. H. (1981). The professional environment in the 21st century. *Computerworld, 15*, 31–38. (b)

Morgan, M. (1983). The uses of dictation at Purdue University. Unpublished report to Vice-President Struther Arnott, October 22. (Available from M. Morgan, Department of English, Purdue University, W. Lafayette, IN 47907.)

Moskey, S. (1983). Delivering corporate training in writing. In W. J. Buchholz (Ed.), *Communication training and consulting in business, industry, and government* (pp. 183–201). Urbana, IL: American Business Communication Association.

Murray, D. (1978). Internal revision: A process of discovery. In C. Cooper & L. Odell (Eds.), *Research on composing: Points of departure* (pp. 85–103). Urbana, IL: National Council of Teachers of English.

Norman, D. A. (1969). Memory and attention: An introduction to human understanding. New York: Wiley.

Odell, L., & Goswami, D. (1982). Writing in a non-academic setting. Research in the teaching of English, 16, 201–223.

Ong, W. J. (1977). Interfaces of the word: Studies in the evolution of consciousness and culture. Ithaca, NY: Cornell University Press.

Ong, W. J. (1982). Orality and literacy: The technologizing of the word. New York: Methuen.

Payne, D. (1981). Integrating oral and written business communication. In B. Kroll & R. J. Vann (Eds.), Exploring speaking-writing relationships: Comparisons and contrasts (pp. 184–197). Urbana, IL: National Council of Teachers of English.

Perl, S. (1980) Understanding composing. College Composition and Communication, 31, 363–369.

Reinsch, N. L., Jr., & Lewis, P. V. (1984). Telephone apprehension: An initial study of etiology. In S. J. Fruno (Ed.), 1984 Proceedings, Southwest American Business Communication Association Spring Conference (pp. 149–163). Houston: University of Houston, Clear Lake.

Salvaggio, J. L. (Ed.). (1983). Telecommunications: Issues and choices for society. New York: Longman.

Schafer, John. (1981). The linguistic analysis of spoken and written texts. In B. Kroll & R. J. Vann (Eds.), Exploring speaking-writing relationships: Comparisons and contrasts (pp. 1–31). Urbana, IL: National Council of Teachers of English.

Sommers, N. (1980). Revision strategies of student writers and experienced adult writers. College Composition and Communication, 31, 378–387.

Statistical Abstract of the United States 1984, 1983, 1979. Washington, DC: U.S. Department of Commerce, Bureau of the Census, 1983, 1982, 1978.

Stein, J., & Yates, J. (1984). Electronic mail: How will it change office communication? In R. Beswick & A. B. Williams (Eds.), Information systems business communication. Urbana, IL: American Business Communication Association.

Toffler, A. (1980). The third wave. New York: Bantam.

United States Bureau of the Census. (1982). Population profiles of the United States: 1981 (Current Population Report 13, Series P-20, No. 374). Washington, DC: U.S. Government Printing Office, 43–45.

Weizenbaum, J. (1976). Computer power and human reason: From judgment to calculation. New York: W. H. Freeman.

Wresch, W. (1983). Computers and composition instruction: An update. College English, 45, 794–799.

Yates, F. A. (1966). The art of memory. Chicago: University of Chicago Press.

Young, R. E. (1978). Paradigms and problems: Needed research in rhetorical invention. In C. Cooper & L. Odell (Eds.), Research on composing: Points of departure. Urbana, IL: National Council of Teachers of English.

Zinsser, W. (1983). Writing with a word processor. New York: Harper.

Master Interview List 4A

RESEARCH TRIP, MAY–JUNE 1983

1. Brightman, Jody
Manager, Corporate Planning
Atlantic Richfield Company
Los Angeles, CA
13 June 1983

2. Clarke, Grant V.*
Publications Manager
I. P. Sharp Associates
Toronto, ON, Canada
31 May 1983

3. Clogston, Thomas L.*
Technical Training Manager
Boeing Aerospace Company
Seattle, WA
7 June 1983

4. Cooke, Bill*
Education Program Coordinator
Toronto Branch
I. P. Sharp Associates
Toronto, ON, Canada
31 May 1983

5. Dvorin, Diane*
President
TeleMedia International, Inc.
Denver, CO
16 June 1983

6. Fenster, Kathy
Electronic Data
  Processing Analyst
Boeing Aerospace Company
Seattle, WA
6 June 1983

7. Hager, Faye P.*
Manager, Word
  Processing Services
Boeing Aerospace Company
Seattle, WA
6 June 1983

8. Hartman, Larry
Zenith Data Systems
Chicago, IL
20 June 1983

9. Huck, John
Manager, Microcomputer
  Projects
Zenith Data Systems
Chicago, IL
20 June 1983

10. James, Jack*
Assistant Director
Research Dental Products
Lee Pharmaceuticals
South El Monte, CA
13 June 1983

*These people completed questionnaires as well as interviews.

11. Josephson, Hal*
    Executive Vice President
    Corporate Development
    Starcom, Inc.
    Denver, CO
    16 June 1983

12. Kayser, Leslie*
    Supervisor, ARCOvision
    Services
    Atlantic Richfield
    Los Angeles, CA
    13 June 1983

13. Lake, Bill
    Management Consultant
    Office Systems
    Conspector Group
    Denver, CO
    16 June 1983

14. Laskey, Marlene*
    Administrative Manager
    I. P. Sharp Associates
    Toronto, ON, Canada
    31 May 1983

15. Lee, Henry*
    President, Administration, and
    Acting Vice President, Research
    Lee Pharmaceuticals
    South El Monte, CA
    13 June 1983

16. Marovino, Nancy*
    Account Representative
    Toronto Sales and Support
    I. P. Sharp Associates
    Toronto, ON, Canada
    31 May 1983

17. Michalopoulos, Elaine*
    Programming Trainee
    Zenith Radio Corporation
    Chicago, IL
    20 June 1983

18. Priest, Janie
    Documentation Equipment
    Operator

Boeing Aerospace Company
Seattle, WA
6 June 1983

19. Rahbar, Holly*
    Marketing Representative
    Office Automation
    Continental Illinois Bank
    Chicago, IL
    21 June 1983

20. Reynolds, Patrick*
    Associate Writer
    Continental Illinois Bank
    Chicago, IL
    21 June 1983

21. Rodriquez, Henry
    Administrative Assistant
    Continental Illinois Bank
    Chicago, IL
    21 June 1983

22. Spenner, Dale*
    President/General Manager
    CTS Keene, Inc.
    Paso Robles, CA
    10 June 1983

23. Teigler, Dian*
    Director of Documentation
    Lee Pharmaceuticals
    South El Monte, CA
    13 June 1983

24. Tompkins, Scott*
    Software Documentation Writer
    Software Development Group
    Zenith Data Systems
    Chicago, IL
    20 June 1983

25. Troxell, Jerry*
    Manager, Corporate
      Information Technology
      and Services
    Atlantic Richfield Company
    Denver, CO
    17 June 1983.

26. Von Bergen, Jean*
Supervisor
Information Systems Training
Zenith Radio Corporation
Chicago, IL
20 June 1983

27. Wundrum, Edward*
Financial Information Officer
Office Automation
Continental Illinois Bank
Chicago, IL
21 June 1983

SUPPLEMENTARY INTERVIEWS
BEFORE AND AFTER RESEARCH TRIP

1. Clark, Richard
Controller
Matthew Bender Publishers
Albany, NY
26 March 1984

2. Galler, Bernard
Editor-in-Chief
Annals of the History of Computing
University of Michigan
Ann Arbor, MI
28 July 1980

3. Hollis, Lois R.
Texas Bureau of Financial Aid
Austin, TX
3 May 1984

4. Miel, Vicki
Manager, Word Processing Center
City of Phoenix
Phoenix, AZ
14 October 1981

5. Murchie, William D.
Director, Bureau of Management
and Services
Indiana State Board of Health
Indianapolis, IN
31 July 1980

6. Reese, Linda M.
Director of Operations
Matthew Bender Publishers
Albany, NY
26 March 1984

Research Questionnaire: 4B
Summary of Results

INTEGRATING THE NEW COMMUNICATION TECHNOLOGIES IN THE WORKPLACE

Name:	For a complete list of interviewees, titles, departments,
Title & Department:	and companies, see attachment A. Interviewees
Company:	ranged from corporate managers of huge corpora-
Address:	tions (ARCO) to presidents of middle-sized companies
	(CTS Keene Microelectronics, Lee Pharmaceuticals) to
	entry-level technical writers and programmers (Conti-
	nental Illinois Bank, Zenith Data Corporation) in the
	western two-thirds of the United States and Canada.
Date:	May 30-June 22, 1983

General Questions

1. *How long have you worked in this organization?*

   3 weeks to 27 years; average is 6 years; median is 3 years.

2. *What are your main responsibilities in your present position?*

   Majority are involved with automation: planning, developing, marketing, training, writing documentation, and using. Reponsibilities *often* overlap, though largest companies have specific staff for training and internal marketing.

3. *How often do you divide your work time in terms of different tasks? (Please given percentages.)*

Managing/administration	40%
Research/writing	25%

Marketing   20%
Training   8%
Product development   7%

4. *What other positions have you held at this organization and elsewhere?*

Teaching, technical, administrative, secretarial, programming, editorial; 0–10 years in prior jobs.

5. *What prior on-the-job experience specifically prepared you for your present position?*

Teaching, technical writing, systems and programming work, sales; communication, technical skills development.

6. *What is your educational background? College? Major? Postcollege course work? On-the-job training?*

Range: PhD to a few college and on-the-job courses.

Frequency: PhD—3
           MBA—4 (2 in progress)
           MA—3 (2 English, 1 Psychology)
           BA—13 (5 English)
           BS—6
           Other—3

Special courses noted: In-house-programming and systems; seminar planning; public speaking; dynamic learning; computer science; technical writing.
Internships noted: life crisis counseling and pastoral leadership; programming and equipment operations.

7. *What features of your educational background prepared you best for your present position?* (Rank-ordered by frequency of answers.)

Writing and oral communication
Group/people processes
Logical thinking
Technical specializations

Co-op, internship, work-study experiences
Extracurricular activities, esp. debate, public speaking, editorial work
On-the-job seminars in programming, systems, oral presentation, managing meetings

Quote: "What holds people back? Lack of good communication skills."

8. *What advice would you give a liberal arts college student interested in having a job like yours? Major? Courses? Extracurricular activities? Internships? Summer or part-time employment?*

Liberal arts background is useful if tempered with strong technical courses such as computer science or business and especially with hands-on experience in co-ops, internships, extracurricular activities. Have to develop strong people and communication skills by being enterprising in work choices during college. Range of opinion is shown in quotes:

"English and history are great subjects, and despite what we read so often today about high-techitis, I would still encourage students to know great literature, history, and philosophy. But they should leaven their liberal arts major with courses in econ, finance, and a foreign language or two. *Maybe* systems."

"Don't take liberal arts. Take computer science and business administration."

Communication Technology Questions

9. *What electronic systems are being introduced/used at your organization that were not part of your normal operation five years ago?*

Word processing (12) and data processing (8) are now the most consistently introduced systems, with electronic mail (8) used very widely where it is available. Also mentioned were: dictation, teleconferencing, computer conferencing, graphics, and audio mail systems.

10. *For what purposes are these systems being used?*

Word and data processing; financial planning and analysis; internal/external communication (electronic and audio mail).

11. *Who uses them? (Most? Least?)*

When the push comes from upper management, many or most personnel use the new technologies, no matter what the system. More typically, new systems are used by fast adapters and by those who see a *distinct* advantage in using a particular system. For instance, secretaries, writers, and engineers quickly accept and use word processing; managers don't. But some managers with financial responsibilities choose to use spread sheets such as Visicalc; people who have the appropriate teleconferencing facilities and appropriate problems to solve use video, audio, or computer conferencing; personnel who have electronic mail systems and need to keep track of or frequently exchange information use EM several times a day.

12. *Which systems do you use and how frequently? (Please check.)*

System	Occasionally	Weekly	Daily	Many Times a Day	Total
Teleconferencing	4	0	4	1	9
Audio mail	3		1	3	7
Electronic mail	3	3	3	7	16
Dictation	1	2	2	1	6
Word processing	3	4	3	7	17
Data processing/ computing	3	5	2	7	17

Others: Computer-aided typesetting, computer graphics, prospect track-ing-reporting systems, computer conferencing, on-line inquiry.

These answers confirm item 9: word and data processing and electronic mail are the most widely used systems. Least used are dictation and audio mail systems, though personal dictation for short communications and conventional phone use remain high.

13. *What percentage of your work day do you spending using these systems?*

Range: 5%–80%; average is 23%. The time people use systems is tied to jobs they hold *and* the emphasis of the company on systems use. *Highest users* are a diverse group including researchers, people in training and internal marketing, and account reps; these are in companies that emphasize systems use, with the chief executives or top managers often setting the model *and* with the company offering staff-oriented training. Second category of *highest users* is, of course, systems personnel, ranging from word-processing operators to teleconferencing supervisors to soft-ware documentation writers. Lowest users are slow adapters who are unconvinced systems will really help them or people who just don't like to be told how to communicate.

14. *What do you use these systems for? Giving and receiving short messages? Composing letters, memos, reports? Other?*

Most frequent uses of new systems (especially word and data processing or electronic mail) are producing and transmitting long, complex messages and documents (25) and shorter messages (11). Other important uses are training, holding meetings, collaborating on projects, and programming. Other uses noted: documentation, graphics, and form/list processing.

15. *What are the advantages and disadvantages of using the new communi-cation systems?*

Advantages	Disadvantages
Speed	Fear of using; reluctance to learn
Quality—accurate/neat; better planned/revised/edited	Frustrations—in learning, equipment availability, down-time and document loss
Improved decision-making and planning because of greater data availability *and* manipulability	Cost
Easier access to and transfer of information—even across time zones	Image—"poor grammar shows up" with no secretary to fix
Greater storage capacity	Less personal interaction

16. *What percentage of your work day do you spend in face-to-face oral communication?*

Range is 10%–80%; average is 37%.

17. *What percentage of your day do you spend writing using nonelectric equipment—pen and paper, typewriter?*

Range is 0%–40% average is 12%. (Interesting because three people are writers.)

18. *What do you write with nonelectric equipment?*

Letters/memos, proposals, end-of-month reports (10); drafts/outlines (5); quick notes, editorial comments, lists (5); forms (3).

19. *What writing do you typically do off the job? How often?*

Personal correspondence, occasionally (8); papers and articles (7); journal entries (3); schoolwork, class notes (4); work at home (3); lists and plans (3). (Findings are contrary to Faigley & Miller, 1982, research.)

20. *Do you have and use electronic communication equipment at home? Please explain.*

7 have personal computers at home; 1 has 2; 1 has 3.
4 have plans to get.
2 borrow loaners from work.
4 have none and didn't mention plans to get.
Dictation equipment also mentioned.

Memorable quote: "No—that's the last thing I'd want in my home. Until recently, I didn't even have a telephone."

Training Questions

21. *How are people trained to use the new systems at your company?*

Courses/classroom—9   Guides/manuals—6
Tutors—9   Hands-on/on-screen/peer help—6
Video/audio self-study—7   Vendor demonstration—2

A wide range of teaching options are used, generally in *combination*: there may be a classroom introduction for a large group, individual or small-group tutorials with manuals and printed or on-screen materials, and follow-up on-screen practice with peers available to help. (Systems for training are detailed in notes and exemplified in the materials collected.)

22. *Who does the training and what backgrounds do the trainers have?*

Peers and other users—7   Full-time training department—4
Systems or product marketing   Vendors/outsiders—2
   people—6

Only the largest organizations (Boeing, ARCO) have training staffs for electronic media; most training is done by systems people and peers. Vendors may train staff people who train others in organization, pyramid fashion. In general, training is a joint effort.

23. *Do the trainers have other job responsibilites? If so, what?*

Majority of those involved in training (12) also have other jobs in company ranging from programming to sales; a few are dedicated to training (3).

24. *How did you learn to use the new communication systems? (On the equipment? Lectures? Audio tapes? Video tapes? Slide shows? Manuals? Worksheets? Give-and-take with other employees?)*

Most learned through a combination of methods, which emphasized manuals (16), hands-on experience (11), or help by tutors or peers (11). Some attended company or vendor lectures and training sessions (10) or used audio/visual/slide shows (4) for self-instruction.

25. *After your initial training, did you receive follow-up training sessions? For what? Why?*

Yes—13   No—8

Ongoing training occurs as new products, capabilities, features become available or as individuals sense a need to learn more and request help. Nearly a third of users interviewed do not have follow-up training.

26. *Approximately how long did it take you to learn to use the systems you use?*

Varies with system, with electronic and audio mail taking a day to master technical procedures, and word/data processing taking 1-3 weeks, with a much longer time necessary to become adept at different applications and programs. A few said they just kept learning—year after year.

27. *What do you think the most successful training package would include? (Please specify the technology you're referring to.)*

All recommend a combination of methods, including manuals or floppy discs or videotapes learners can return to for reference (11), plus hands-on experience (9), lectures (6), personal (6) and on-line (6) tutorials. They emphasize providing enough time to catch on and practice-by-doing on equipment and having peers around who can answer questions.

28. *Do people at different levels of your organization receive different kinds of training? (Please explain. For example, how does training for secretaries differ from training for top management?)*

Yes—9   No—2

Different levels (beginning, intermediate, advanced) or kinds of courses are offered. Courses differ in time spent, type of delivery, objectives; these are usually associated with uses to which training will be put. Managers and executives often receive macro picture, with tutorials on request, while secretaries get much more detailed instruction to build on what they already know.

Opinion Questions

29. *How have the new communication systems changed the way you do your job?*

In addition to obvious speed/efficiency benefits, the reduction in paper-work, and the cuts in travel expenses, *qualitative* advantages are even more persuasive: more opportunity to plan, reconsider, weigh alternatives, recalculate, revise; more information at fingertips for better decision making; improvement in skills of formulating and synopsizing information; more participatory problem solving. (Also see question 15.)

30. *What were the most difficult things to learn in writing or speaking on the new systems?*

Technical skills like typing (6) seemed "most difficult" to learn, but audience/group-process interactions/communication also required new approaches.

Quote: "To make good use of silence; to learn how to solicit participation/response from others; to create rapport with less familiar people."

31. *Describe the typical process you go through when you compose a message using one of the new systems. (Please specify the system.)*

    a. (See individual forms for answers; see figure 4-1 for examples.)

    b. _____

    c. _____

    d. _____

    e. _____

    f. _____

    g. _____

    h. _____

32. *What specific skills or abilities does a person need to use these systems effectively? What writing skills? What speaking skills? What technical skills?*

    High-level (i.e., programming) and low-level (typing) *technical* skills varied with systems; but *all* agreed that writing/speaking skills are essential. Some thought these skills were the same with or without new media; others emphasized greater need for accuracy, clarity, good format-graphic sense because "secretary doesn't fix." Others noted different levels of formality for electronic mail versus external communications.

Quote from ARCO executive:	"Writing skills—for writing procedures and coordinating Speaking skills—for verbal directions and training Technical skills—to know functional operation of system enough to make technical adjustments"

33. *Do you think students should learn to use any of these systems in college? If so, how and in what classes?*

    Yes—19   No—1

    Overwhelming interest in having new technologies introduced in a wide range of classes, especially English and communication—to reduce technophobia and improve skills. Hands-on experience seems essential in class or on internships or work study. Special goals mentioned were: word processing, computer literacy, interpersonal communication. But there was another voice also. . . .

Quote: "College days should be spent in mastering the finer points of literature, the arts, and civilized behavior. Only primitive peoples worship soulless and mindless machines. Time enough for students to sit at a screen after they graduate."

34. *If you were going to design a writing course, knowing what you now know about the new communication systems, what would you be sure to emphasize?*

Strunk and White virtues were a clear first (8), with developing an openness to the new systems and how they can help second (6). Other points: choosing and using media creatively; seeing connection between message and medium selected.

Quote: "They can make you marginally more productive, but probably at some expense in creativity."

35. *How do you think the new communications technology will change the jobs in your organization in the foreseeable future? (2 years, 5 years, 10 years)*

Communication technology is likely to change our lives as much as the car: entire lifestyles, employment patterns, interactions. Example: managers will do hands-on report writing themselves; there'll be much more geographic flexibility.

Quote: "A lot of the work now being done in offices and plants will be done in private residences via satellite links or telephone hardware from residence to host companies, thereby cutting transportation costs and need for corporate office support."

36. *Other comments?*

"Graduates of accredited universities should be familiar with the new communication systems *before* they come into industry."

You have my permission to use the information in this questionnaire and the materials I gave you in your research, publication, and teaching.

Release was signed by all respondents   _____
signature   Date

Composition as Conversation

5

The Computer Terminal as Medium of Communication

DENISE E. MURRAY
San Jose State University

All the personality and humanity that show up in letters disappear on computer screens ... all the warmth and wisdom are translated into those frigid, uniform, green characters.—B. Greene, "Electronic Mail," 1983

Writing is passive, out of it, in an unreal, unnatural world. So are computers.—W. J. Ong, *Orality and Literacy*, 1982, p. 79

INTRODUCTION

The quotations above have a familiar ring to them. The sentiments have not changed; only the target is different. Plato in the *Phaedrus* (323) has Socrates point out that writing might weaken memory and writers might have the show of wisdom without the reality (cited in Scribner & Cole, 1981, p. 5). Similarly, scholars such as Hieronimo Squarciafico bemoaned the advent of print because it might destroy memory and weaken the mind (cited in Ong, 1982, p. 80).

Today, with personal computer sales doubling annually (Christianson, 1983), the guardians of the printed word and of secondary orality (a term taken from Ong, 1982) are anxious about this new medium of communication. Their anxiety is not surprising because these guardians hold key positions in the current establishment through which information is transmitted in our society. Just as the advent of writing altered the status of the epic poets as transmitters of information and the invention of printing changed the status of the scholar-priests in the Middle Ages, so too might the computer result in new institutions that will replace the radio, television, and newspaper as knowledge brokers.

Such new modalities, it is argued, have resulted in more than shifts in power. Goody and Watt (1968), for example, hypothesize that *literacy* reshapes consciousness. They claim that "The kinds of analysis involved in the syllogism and in other forms of logical procedure are clearly dependent upon writing" (p. 68). Eisenstein (1979), using historical data, shows how *print* affected society and made the modernization process possible. Although the relationship between thought and writing or thought and print is still unresolved,[1] most researchers agree that certain uses of language co-occur with literacy and yet others co-occur with print. The important question today is: What language use co-occurs with the use of the computer as a medium of communication?

The Computer as Medium of Communication

Programmers and systems analysts have used computers as a medium of communication for two decades. For them, the computer is not "passive" or "frigid"; it is a medium for sending and receiving messages, for interacting with colleagues. The alarm expressed earlier has only come into public consciousness as a result of the diffusion of personal computers since their introduction into the marketplace in 1975. Initially, hobbyists bought these computers. Since 1977, however, ownership of personal computers has grown rapidly, to 400,000 in 1980, and is predicted to reach 10 million in 1985. For most owners, computers are no longer toys, but tools for professional or personal use. Further, owners quickly begin to expand their use of the computer. In a study of personal-computer use by university professors, Case (1984) found that faculty initially purchased the computer to use as a word processor. As they became more familiar with the computer, however, there was a "dramatic increase in use as a terminal, reflecting the faculty's increased awareness of the computer as a communication device" (p. 120).

Furthermore, almost every week newspapers carry reports of computer networks. These networks serve as a means of communication for the dissemination of information. They include dating clubs, food services, and professional projects. In short, computers as a means of communication are no longer the province of technical experts, but now impinge on the daily lives of many who are not computer professionals.

Despite this widespread use, little research has been conducted to examine the characteristics of discourses where the computer is the *medium*—as opposed to the *means*—of communication. To date, research has concentrated on the use of the computer for creating extended prose (its word-processing function). Bean (1983) and Collier (1983), for example, studied whether the use of a word processor had an effect on revision patterns. In such cases, however, the computer is not a medium of communication. The final product still appears in fixed print; it is only the means of production that has changed. Some researchers have examined computer communication as opposed to word processing. For example, Carey (1980) and Levodow (1980) examined the paralinguistic devices used in computer communication. They did not, however, examine other discourse features and how they compare and contrast with those used in conversation and/or writing. The study reported here is a first attempt at examining the use of the computer as a *medium* of communication. Through an examination of both the *use* and *discourse features* of computer communication, the research provides some answers to the initial question: What language use co-occurs with the use of the computer as a medium of communication?

Computer Conversation

Computers are used for three modes of communication (to be explained in detail): documents (word processing); mail (extended text received and sent via the computer); and messages (interactive *conversation*). These modes suggest a continuum of literacy from formal to informal, with computer conversation the least formal. Computer conversation exhibits characteristics of oral discourse (such as immediacy and interaction), but is produced, transmitted, and decoded in written form. Thus it also displays features from written discourse. Documents and mail, on the other hand, exhibit features primarily from written discourse.

Thus computer conversation is an innovative use of new technology, which draws from both oral and written discourse traditions. We therefore need a description of this new mode and a tentative explanation of what motivates interactants to choose among available modes and discourse traditions. The research reported here analyzes the use and discourse features of computer conversation and shows where this mode lies on the literacy continuum. The analysis shows that interactants perceive and use computer conversation as more formal than face-to-face conversation and telephone conversation, but less formal than written memos and documents. Computer conversation draws from features of both written and oral discourse because of both the nature of the medium and the interactants' choice of voice. Computer conversation is semipermanent; can be partly planned; is subject to time delays; and lacks visual paralinguistic and nonlinguistic cues. The interaction of these characteristics results in complex turn-taking, with the turn-taking principles of oral discourse being violated; indication of topic shift; glossing of reference items to avoid ambiguity; less fragmentation than in oral discourse; and the use of graphical representations of paralinguistic cues. Interactants indicate change of voice through pronoun use, choice of diction, and graphical representations of paralinguistic cues.

After a brief discussion of methodology, the findings summarized here will be presented in detail. First, I will describe the types of computer communication and the bases on which interactants choose among them and between them and other forms of communication such as telephone conversations. Then, I will examine the discourse features of one type of computer communication: computer conversation. Thus it will be possible to show how computer conversation borrows from both oral and written traditions and what level of formality is ascribed to it by its users.

METHODOLOGY

To find the most natural use of the computer as a medium of communication, I chose a professional computer scientist. I did not, however, choose someone whose current job is programming because most of a programmer's computer use would be in program writing. Instead, I chose Peter, a manager of a data center who had been a systems analyst. Peter has worked extensively with computers since 1958. Thus I was able to observe a subject who is competent with computers but whose present position requires more communication than technical work. I was therefore able to observe samples of skilled computer communication.

In order to place Peter's computer use within the broader pattern of his orality and literacy, I observed him for a period of three weeks. In addition, I questioned him informally several times and interviewed him formally for one hour. In my interviews, I asked him to decipher codes and clarify interactions in the communication I had observed.

MODES OF COMPUTER COMMUNICATION AND THEIR USE

Modes of Computer Communication

Through the interviews and the study of work-time computer use, I was able to determine how Peter uses the three available modes of computer communication. Before examining how Peter chooses among these modes, I will describe how each functions technically. As mentioned earlier, Peter uses the computer for three different types or modes of communication: documents, mail, and messages.

•*Documents* include memos, the minutes of meetings, reports, and technical papers such as manuals. Peter sends these to recipients in hard copy (printout) but also keeps them on file, in both soft copy (computer disc) and hard copy. This mode uses the computer as a word processor, not as a medium of communication.

•*Mail* refers to extended text that Peter sends and receives via the computer only. If recipients are not logged on, the mail is stored in their file (there is also a copy in the sender's file), and they can access it when they next log on. If they are logged on, the computer displays a brief message on the screen, indicating delivery of the mail. This message indicates the sender, date, time, and origin of the mail. The recipient then must access the mail file to read the mail. The recipient may respond immediately.

•*Messages* on the other hand, are one line of text and are usually sent to a recipient who is logged on. If the sender has more than one line of text, she or he has to retype the message command and the USERID[2] of the recipient. If the recipient is logged on, the message appears on the screen, interrupting the terminal session. The message is not stored in a file. The recipient may then respond with a message, which in turn the original sender responds to, and so on, building up what I have called a *computer conversation*. Thus messages can be used to create a dynamic ongoing interaction. If the recipient is not logged on, the message is converted to mail and filed. Messages can also be used as self-reminders.

Thus in both mail and message modes, the computer is the *medium* of communication.

Use of Computer Communication

How, then, do users choose among the modes and media of communication? How does this choice reflect where users place these discourse types along the oral-literate continuum? The mode and medium Peter chooses depend on recipient accessibility, the nature of the information, and the roles of the interactants.

ACCESSIBILITY. Before deciding whether to send mail or a message, Peter determines whether the intended recipients are logged on. If the intended recipient is logged on, Peter most often sends a message. In most cases, the recipient responds immediately, and a computer conversation commences. Peter considers this a fast means of communication. If the intended recipients are not logged on, however, he knows they cannot receive a message but will be able to receive and respond to mail as soon as they do log on. Thus, for example, Peter sent mail to one of his operators who had already gone home, so that the operator would receive the information as soon as he arrived the next morning. Peter often uses either documents or typed memos. He sends hard copies of self-entered memos to colleagues who either do not use computers or use them infrequently. He may also have his secretary type a memo if he is sending it to several people (because he does not have the time to address several envelopes) and/or if the information has to be kept in the company's official chronological file.

In contrast to the other modes and media, computer conversation offers the possibility of immediate response and interaction. Thus interactants consider messages and their resulting conversations as less formal than mail. Mail implies a distancing in time and thus needs to be more explicit and formal. Hard copies are even more distanced and formal.

NATURE OF THE INFORMATION. Peter uses computer conversation when he wants an immediate response and when the information is informal but not highly complex or emotional. Computer conversation is not suitable for complex, emotional, or formal communication.

As messages are primarily one-line moves, they cannot be used for complex, technical communication. In one of Peter's computer sessions, there is a situation in which he and a system programmer are exchanging messages, but the programmer wants to convey a piece of complex technical information. He tells Peter that he will send it to him as mail and immediately goes into mail mode and sends Peter ten lines of mail. In addition to being faster, it also means that Peter now has a soft copy of this detailed explanation on file.

Computer conversation lacks the paralinguistic and nonlinguistic cues of face-to-face conversation or telephone conversation. Thus, if the communication requires negotiation and involves debate and discussion, Peter prefers to call or to speak to people face-to-face. In one instance, Peter and the same system programmer (Ted) are involved in a lengthy computer conversation, which results in a disagreement concerning manuals to help users. Peter wants Ted to provide more help for "extremely naive users," but Ted feels there is enough documentation. Rather than press the point via the terminal, Peter sends Ted the following message (Ted is logged on to his home terminal):

P: please call - we've ˙got˙ to discuss. call me when you get to work.[3]

As noted earlier, interactants consider computer conversation to be informal. Thus, if the information is very formal, Peter has his secretary type a memo or sends a memo he has typed himself using a word-processing program. If he wants to keep a record of a communication that is not very formal, he sends mail.

Thus, for formal communication, computer conversation is considered too oral—that is, too transient, casual, and personal. For possibly emotional communication, it is not considered sufficiently oral.

ROLES OF THE INTERACTANTS. In addition to accessibility and the nature of the information, the roles of the interactants determine whether Peter chooses computer conversation or another mode or medium of communication. Here I am using *role* as defined by Turner (1962) and other sociolinguists. I am not referring to a stable set of duties, rights, and attitudes resulting from the social structure, but to the identity negotiated for each situation as a result of interaction. The role taken by the interactants determines their voice. Thus, although Peter is a *manager*, in certain situations and interactions, his role could be *friend, technical colleague,* or *student.* Consequently, his voice can move across the range from writer-style to talker-style. This parallels the use of *voice* or *persona* in traditional rhetoric. "To a degree, every sane person from the age of four changes himself and his language in response to audience and subject" (Gibson, 1969, p. 52).

Traditional rhetoric, however, has been concerned with the expression of voice in writing, without the additional paralinguistic cues available in speech. In computer communication, as in writing, these cues have to be signaled more explicitly: by the use of asterisks in the preceding excerpt, for example. Furthermore, there is an additional dimension of voice not addressed in rhetorical tradition: the choice of medium. The move from writing to telephone conversation to face-to-face conversation is in itself a statement of voice. So, too, in computer communication, the choice of mail, message, or document is a statement of voice. The choice of message signals that the sender is "speaking" with a conversational, personal voice; the choice of mail signals that the sender is speaking with a more formal, but still personal voice. The choice of document is a signal of *writer-style* (Gibson, 1969), where the voice distances the author from the reader. In addition, computer communicators have the other media of communication open to them: telephone conversation and face-to-face interaction. The choice of medium and mode is determined by the role the sender intends to take, which in turn is determined by the audience and the subject. An additional determining factor is the physical constraint of accessibility to the computer, just as the use of letter writing rather than telephoning is dependent on the distance between sender and recipient. As in letter writing, the sender of mail can alter voice so it is more *talker-style* (Gibson, 1969)—that is, more message-like.

In the example referred to earlier, Peter and Ted are negotiating roles. Earlier in the same interaction, Peter asked why Ted had installed a new system before completely debugging it. He expressed annoyance once, by typing "humpf," and later, by responding "sigh," when Ted indicated that he had not installed all the necessary access codes. After more discussion that does not resolve the problems, Peter suggests the phone call. If Peter were to continue to press for more documentation in the computer conversation, he would need to take a more formal, authoritative voice. Then Ted might construe it as Peter enforcing his formal role of manager, which Peter does not want to do. Peter feels that a telephone call means their roles are of more equal status and he can use a less formal voice, full of the nuances of intonation. This choice is the result of both the nature of the information and the role relations.

Thus the interplay of accessibility, nature of information, and roles of interactants determine the mode and medium chosen. Depending on the formality of the situation, interactants choose among memos, mail, messages (computer conversation), telephone conversations, and face-to-face conversations, in that order. Thus, in actual use, computer conversation falls between memos and telephone conversations on the oral-literate continuum. We would therefore expect computer conversation to display features from both oral and written traditions. To test this hypothesis, several discourse features of computer conversation will be examined in detail.

DISCOURSE FEATURES OF COMPUTER CONVERSATION

Discourse features are a means of organizing both information and interaction in discourse. Interaction can be organized through turn-taking and expressing voice. Information can be organized through shifting topics and referencing. Although there are many other discourse features, these four will illustrate the oral/written nature of computer conversation.

Turn-taking

One distinctive feature of computer conversation is that it allows interactants to violate one of the important conventions of polite, orderly conversation, the principle of turn-taking. Further, violating this principle in computer conversation does not have the negative consequences it often does in face-to-face conversation. For face-to-face conversation, Sacks, Schegloff, and Jefferson (1974) established the following principles for turn-taking:

1. Completion of a turn unit (e.g., sentence, clause, phrase) constitutes a potential transition to another speaker.
2. Turn-allocation operates because the current speaker can:
   a. Select the next speaker.
   b. Let another speaker self-select.
   c. Continue.

These three choices are ordered as shown here and are recursive. Sacks, Schegloff, and Jefferson demonstrate how these principles account for the characteristics of conversation—for example, speakers change, one party talks at a time, and turn size is not fixed. Further, they establish turn-allocation techniques, such as sets of adjacency pairs (which consist of related, ordered pairs of utterances such as "Question/Answer" or "Complaint/Apology or Justification") and starting first.

I examined turn-taking in computer conversation to determine the ways in which it differs from these principles and what motivates these differences. To make this determination, it is necessary to distinguish between message, move, turn, and utterance in computer conversation. *Message* (defined here as one line of text) is constrained by the technology of the particular computer. *Move* refers to one speech act (e.g., a request). *Utterance* is a stretch of uninterrupted text. *Turn* refers to the sender's intended whole utterance. In face-to-face conversation, utterance and turn are usually contemporaneous. As will become clearer, *turn* is not a suitable means for describing the organization of computer conversation. Turns can, then, consist of more than one move and/or more than one message and/or more than one utterance.

In contrast to the way speakers are careful in taking turns in oral conversation, interactants in computer conversation are likely to interleave utterances and moves and to omit some turn-allocation techniques. For example, they may not respond to the first *pair part* of an adjacency pair or they may both "speak" at the same time. Computer conversation is not restricted by the physical limits of sound, which Ong (1982, p. 32) has called the "evanescence of the oral word." There is no need to negotiate for time to express an utterance. The only physical constraints are the size of the terminal screen and the time delay between sending and receiving the message (dependent on both typing time and transmission time). These constraints, however, have several consequences. The current data show four such consequences or principles that in face-to-face conversation would be considered rude but that do not have negative results in computer conversation.

1. *The sender may make a second utterance before receiving a response to the first.* For example:

T1: THEM'S REGULAR[4] ... MANUALS COVERING THE ... PRODUCT

P1: Yeah--for the product software you mean?

P2: problem is that they are not the same (product and what u have installed). that doc will only confuse the users.

P3: why has Joe hidden the documentation file?

T2: IS THAT A RHETORICAL QUESTION?

P4: no comment.

Peter's four messages are separate utterances, each having been sent separately. He does not wait for Ted's reply before continuing with another utterance. This is an example of a turn consisting of several messages (3) and several moves (5). This violates the turn-allocation technique of question/answer. Peter allocated the turn by asking the question, but then continued with his own turn.

2. *The recipient may not respond to an utterance.* Two factors operate as the cause of failure to respond.

First, responding to the utterance would deflect the recipient from his or her goal-driven plan (Wilensky, 1983). In the example, Ted responds to only the last of the three utterances. This is consistent with Ted's previous assertions that there is enough documentation.

His goal is to leave the documentation as is. To achieve this, he consistently avoids answering questions that will force confrontation. As noted earlier, Peter takes the initiative by requesting that they talk on the telephone.

In another example, Peter tries to use a computer instruction that fails. He contacts Ted and tells him the problem. Ted explains how to correct the problem, and Peter mentions another problem. The conversation continues for one minute and ten seconds on the topic of the first problem, with Peter asking questions, Ted giving suggestions, and Peter testing each suggestion. Then Peter mentions the second problem again. Again they discuss and test solutions to the first problem until, after six minutes and twelve seconds, they solve it. Peter again refers to the second problem; this time Ted responds, and they work through this second problem together. Ted's goal is to solve the first problem and then deal with the second, whereas Peter attempts to address both simultaneously. To reach his goal, Ted ignores Peter's questions about the second problem until the first is solved.

Second, the retention of the message on the screen is for the life of one screen only. Thus computer conversation displays both the transience of speech and the permanence of writing. While carrying on a technical conversation with Ted, Peter receives a message from a user, saying that "things are running better" and that they have "found what they wanted to know." Peter responds immediately by asking what they have found out and what they have done about it. He then continues the technical discussion with Ted. During this discussion, the user replies and tells Peter what they have found and what they are going to do. Before Peter has time to reply, he receives several messages (one utterance) from Ted that require immediate attention. Thus Peter responds to Ted's requests, they continue with their discussion, and the user's message gets "lost," both from the screen and from memory. In fact, Peter never responds to this message. As long as the message is in short-term memory (either screen or human), the receiver may respond (see Chapter 4 by Halpern). However, because of the transience of the message on the screen, messages may not be responded to (as above). The sender may even forget that the message was sent and not responded to. This violates the adjacency pair turn-allocation technique.

3. *A message may interrupt an utterance.* The sender may continue with the utterance or, as a result of the message, abort the

utterance or change it. In the following example, Peter's message (P1) interrupts Ted's utterance of listing systems where "it" (a particular computer program) is operating. Then Peter's message (P2) arrives before Ted has replied to P1. Thus Ted's last utterance consists of two moves: responses to two of Peter's utterances (P1 and P2).

T1: they have it running at . . . (on X)

P1: yeah—using . . . i bet!

T1: ALSO ON Y. ISN'T IT SOMETHING?

P2: what would be the effect at high speed?

T2: ALEX WAS INTERESTED IN PUTTING IT UP ON . . . (response to P1)
HIGH SPEED WOULD MAKE IT REALLY LOOK SWEET. (response to P2)

In face-to-face conversation, a new speaker self-selects as a result of cues from the current speaker. Such paralinguistic cues (pausing, eye fixation, etc.) are not available in computer conversation. Further, because of the technology, senders are often forced to pause and send a new message, not because they have reached a transition point, but merely because they have come to the end of the line on the screen. Thus new speakers may self-select by interrupting the current speaker.

4. *Adjacency pairs do not necessarily occur as pairs.* Adjacency pairs are related, ordered pairs of utterances such as question/answer or complaint/apology. In computer conversation, often only the first *pair part* occurs, or the second *pair part* comes minutes or even days later. This principle is a corollary to paragraph 2 but also includes the opening and closing pairs to which Sacks, Schegloff, and Jefferson (1974) refer. Most messages do not begin with any greeting. "MSG FROM X:" appears on the screen and functions as a form of opening. Closings do not need to be negotiated as they do in face-to-face conversation. For example, Peter concludes 45 minutes of computer conversation with the following utterance:

P: well—i gotta take off now. wife expecting me. see ya.

On other occasions, the conversation is concluded with "OK," followed by a statement of action. On many occasions, there is no signal that the conversation has ended. This is especially the case if one interactant is interrupted by the telephone or someone entering the office. Both media of communication take precedence over computer conversation. If there is a long time pause without a response, an interactant either checks to see if the other person is still there or leaves the conversation unfinished. On two occasions in these data, the recipient did not respond to the message until the following day. This is not considered rude or abnormal by computer conversationalists, who all accept that other interactions may intercept and prevent the successful conclusion of a conversation.

Thus interactants constantly violate the principles of turn-taking, but these violations do not have the negative consequences they often have in face-to-face conversation. Indeed, the concept of turn and turn-allocation as a means of organizing conversation does not apply to computer conversation. I have argued elsewhere (Murray, 1984) that we need another means for describing the organization of interaction in computer conversation.

Expressing Voice

As noted earlier, the choice of computer conversation over the other available modes and media signals a choice of voice—one that is talker-type. This implies a voice representing informal conversation. But just what are the characteristics of such conversation, and what characteristics does computer conversation share with oral and written discourse (e.g., Chafe, 1982; Schafer, 1981; Vann, 1981).

Many researchers have attempted to differentiate between oral and written discourse (e.g., Chafe, 1982, Schafer, 1981; Vann, 1981). Here I will use Chafe's distinctions—detachment versus personal involvement and integration versus fragmentation—to show how computer conversation moves along the oral/written continuum, depending on the voice of the interactant.

DETACHMENT VERSUS PERSONAL INVOLVEMENT. As in written and oral discourse, interactants in computer conversation modify their voice to suit their feelings and relations to the recipient at any given time. Unlike the case of formal written discourse, this voice may vary throughout a single communication, ranging along the detachment-personal involvement continuum. Further, as in both written and oral discourse, the choice of voice can affect subsequent interactions. Interactants, however, take on a more detached voice than they would in the same circumstances in face-to-face conversation. Thus computer conversation lies on the formal side of telephone conversation and face-to-face conversation.

The standard voice expressed in these data is personal involvement, which is characterized by use of active voice and personal pronouns; emotive and informal diction; hedging and vagueness; paralinguistic cues; and direct quotations (Chafe, 1982). Interactants use active voice throughout and choose the personal pronouns you and I (often elided) to express personal involvement. At one point in the discussion on documentation, Ted takes on a more formal teacher voice, that of manuals and documents. He replies to several questions about access rules by using "one." For example:

T: ONE MUST USE . . .

This change in voice has no effect on Peter, who continues to use a personal voice. During further discussion of the problem, Ted adopts a more personal voice, using "we" and "us." In these situations, Peter has been forgetful or inefficient over a trivial matter and Ted does not use his teacher voice, but his more humorous solidarity voice. In one such situation, Peter has forgotten a particular password, and Ted responds by referring to a program that

T: . . . WILL TELL US FORGETFUL PEOPLE

Peter says that, had the medium been face-to-face conversation, Ted would have been even more informal and would probably have responded with "dummy!" This further supports the argument that computer conversation lies on the formal side of telephone and face-to-face conversation.

Occasionally a sender will address the recipient by name. As the message goes only to the one recipient, this is not done to signal addressee as in face-to-face conversation, but to indicate friendly voice. For example, Peter uses Ted's name to introduce a request for Ted to restore an old program until its replacement is completely debugged. He also begins the request with "please" and ends it with "thanks." He is appealing to Ted as friend and colleague, rather than through his position as manager.

In one conversation, following a series of detached conversations on the same subject, Peter's choice of friendly voice results in a long, friendly interchange. Ted informs Peter that the new program he has installed is "looking pretty good." Peter responds as follows:

P1: whooppeee

P2: 'whoopppeee'—no sarcasm intended

Peter indicates his personal involvement by using informal diction and exaggerated spelling to represent the paralinguistic cues of speech. To be certain Ted interprets this as friendly voice, he repeats the message and makes a metalinguistic comment to ensure Ted reads the correct paralinguistic cues. He then tries to use the new program, and it fails. There follows an interchange in which Peter explains the problem, Ted gives instructions on how to solve it, and Peter tries them out until finally the program works. This whole interchange continues in the same tone Peter set with his original "whooppee." Ted gives informal instructions (using "you" and informal diction such as "gag me with a spoon") and Peter responds informally (also using "you" and informal diction such as "shucks"). Peter's choice of friendly voice results in a very different interchange from the discussion reported earlier in which he was trying to get Ted to keep an old program in operation. In that interchange, Peter begins with the friendly "please Ted . . . thanks," but soon takes on a more formal voice when Ted does not reply to the request to keep the old program in operation until the new one is debugged.

Chafe (1982) has shown that the more personal involvement the participant wants to display, the more likely she or he is to hedge and be vague. Written communication, on the other hand, requires detachment and definiteness. Data from the present study show only one example of hedging, the use of "maybe." As a result, even when the voice is friendly (as indicated by other discourse features), there is an impression of definiteness and, at times, almost brusqueness. This is especially evident in interchanges in *colleague* voice (neither detached nor personally involved), where the sender is asking for information and the recipient gives the required information. For example:

P1: could you give me a charge number for X currently they are under
    Y's number and he's going away

S1:   suggest using . . . as a charge number or a local number as thats all
he should be using it for

P2:   ok—i'll put him under our charge number

Unlike the case of the face-to-face conversation data Chafe (1982) examined, there is also little use of vagueness. The few examples ("one of these days," "some kind of," "seem to") seen in these data occur during very friendly interchanges. In these interchanges, the topic is technical, but neither interactant is trying to get things done. They are more like the dinner-table conversations that Chafe has described. These interchanges are also characterized by a frequent use of colloquial expressions ("look sweet," "i bet"); and friendly sarcasm ("they are *really* cheap"—where Peter also means they are useless).

Unlike oral discourse, these data have no examples of direct speech. When interactants quote other people, they use indirect speech, just as in written discourse. Computer conversation, then, lacks the excitement of verbatim accounts. Interactants appear to have adopted the more detached *reporting* voice of written discourse. Perhaps they feel it is inappropriate to use such vividness and ascribe it to someone else, in a medium where the message is written and read. This indicates some of the tension between orality and literacy that is played out in computer conversation.

Quotation marks are used frequently for the names of things and for repeating part of a message an interactant has already sent. This is very similar to the current use of quotation marks in writing. The writer uses a term that is currently in vogue, but wants to be absolved from responsibility for the term. Quotation marks signal that the words are not the writer's own (Lakeoff, 1982). Thus computer conversationalists have adopted this convention to indicate both something previously said and someone else's terminology—a convention from written discourse that signals detachment.

The use of paralinguistic cues was referred to earlier in the "whooppee" example. To simulate the personal involvement resulting from such oral cues, interactants use graphical representations of such features. For example:

1. Multiple vowels for rising intonation on questions (e.g., "sooo???").

2. Multiple exclamation marks or question marks to express sarcasm (e.g., "Forgot your password???").
3. Asterisk to indicate word stress (e.g., "*got*").

The foregoing discussion shows how computer conversation is both personal and interactive, but also exhibits characteristics of written discourse. Interactants can choose from a range of voices: *solidarity* to *friendly* to *teacher*. This can be seen in the way the use of language moves along the oral-written continuum. The sender's role shapes voice and language, which in turn may shape the response of the recipient.

INTEGRATION VERSUS FRAGMENTATION. Although oral discourse exhibits more personal involvement than written discourse, its language also shows greater fragmentation. Largely as a result of the greater amount of planning time available for written discourse, writers are able to compose ideas using more complex and integrated sentence and discourse structures. Chafe (1982) characterizes integration (typical of written discourse) as the presence of nominalizations, participles, attributive adjectives, conjoined phrases, series, complement clauses, and relative clauses. These characteristics include what Gibson (1969) calls periodic sentences, parallel structure, and complex subordination. These features occur most in academic writing and least in the dinner-table conversations Chafe studied.

Computer conversation reflects the nature of the medium: there is more time for planning and organization than in oral discourse, but less time than in written discourse. Thus computer conversation exhibits greater integration than oral discourse but less than written discourse. These data indicate that computer conversation lies between talker-style and written-style. There are many examples of integration. For example:

- Nominalization and attributive adjectives (e.g., "error correcting capability").
- Participles (e.g., "using . . . i bet").
- Complement clauses and relative clauses (e.g., "the reason i'm concerned about making this tidy is that the new . . . ").

There are, however, many characteristics of oral discourse, such as ellipsis and contractions. For example:

- Auxiliary deletion (e.g., "wife expecting me").
- Subject deletion (e.g., "found out what we wanted to know").
- Subject and verb deletion (usually with copula or auxiliary) (e.g., "take any action on it?").
- Determiner deletion (e.g., "problem is that ... ").
- Contractions (e.g., "what's").

There are very few examples of complex subordination (see the complement, relative clause example earlier). Thus computer conversation can be viewed as falling between academic writing and dinner-table conversation, on the oral-literate continuum.

Topic Shifting

The content of discourse can be organized through the discourse strategy of topic shifting. In written discourse, topic shifts need to be signaled explicitly for the reader, but can be chosen by the writer. In computer conversation, as in oral discourse, topic shifts need to be negotiated by the interactants. However, by the very nature of the medium and the lack of turn-taking conventions, shifts can be ignored or can pass unrecognized. To overcome this potential miscommunication, interactants usually choose to mark topic shifts explicitly, as in written discourse. The conventions used, however, are different.

Kinneavy (1971, p. 2), among others, claims that "The aim of a discourse determines everything else in the process of discourse." This aim can vary from creating a feeling of solidarity, as in chat, to getting things done, as in instructions and requests. In the work environment, computer conversation is used to get things done: to ask for and provide information; to make requests; to make decisions; and to solve problems. For this to be accomplished efficiently, interactants need to focus on the same topic. Thus most computer conversationalists choose to mark a change in topic so that the recipient is aware of the shift. If shifts are not marked overtly, time can be wasted as interactants pursue different goals. Interactants, however, can actively avoid marking topic shift and following turn-taking principles in order to follow different goals. In the previous discussion of Ted and Peter's problem-solving strategies, we see an example of interactants with different goals: Ted wants to solve one problem first, whereas Peter wants to address both simultaneously. When Peter first introduces the second topic, he uses "also" as a marker and explains the problem as something being "funny." On his second attempt to introduce this topic, he does not use a marker. He explains what he means by "funny," but without reference to his previous comment. In the final (and successful) introduction of this topic, he again does not use a marker. This time, however, the other problem has already been solved, and he asks Ted a direct "What do you do when . . . " question. The "when" part of the question is a gloss on his previous explanation of "funny." Thus, although he did not mark the topic, he used a gloss as a means of reintroducing an ignored topic.

In interview, Peter supported the foregoing explanation of these data. He said that he wanted Ted to pursue both goals simultaneously but did not want to adopt a managerial voice. Thus he kept returning to the second topic, but not in a heavy-handed way. Again we see the tension operating between orality and literacy in computer conversation.

In most cases of successful topic shift, the sender marks the new topic. Markers are "also," "by the way" (often abbreviated to "BTW"), and "however." "However" is used to indicate a return to a topic previously introduced but not satisfactorily concluded. It is usually preceded by the closing of the previous topic. For example:

P: everything you do is slick. however— . . .

In this example *however* indicates a topic shift to which Ted responds. After several messages, they conclude this topic, and Ted offers to give Peter a demonstration of the "slick" tool. Ted does not mark this as a new topic because it is an integration of the topic just concluded and the previous one. Thus Peter recognizes the topic shift and responds immediately to the offer. However, when topic shifts are not marked explicitly or are not expansions of the current topic, the recipient does not always recognize the shift.

Reference

In face-to-face conversation, the addressee can usually determine the item being referred to as a result of both the context and the shared knowledge of the interactants. Writers, on the other hand, often make the referent explicit by using "this + noun" or a phrase instead of "here," and so on. Writing requires explicit contextualization. Because computer conversation falls along the oral-written continuum, situations arise in which the referent can be determined as in speech. But situations also arise where the referent is not clear. This is largely the result of interleaving turns. In the example quoted earlier, in the section on turn-taking (reproduced here in part), Peter glosses "they" by putting "product and what u have installed" in brackets.

> T1: THEM'S   REGULAR . . . MANUALS   COVERING   THE . . . PRODUCT
>
> P1: yeah—for the product software you mean?
>
> P2: problem is that they are not the same (product and what u have installed). that doc will only confuse the users.

He does this because Ted's previous message referred to documentation; thus "they" could be interpreted as referring to different forms of documentation. Again, when Peter finally gets the new program to work, he says:

> P: . . . that was it. i was linked . . . !!!

He glosses "that" and "it" (in the first sentence) by explaining (in the second sentence) what caused the program not to work. He does this because several minutes have passed since Ted's information that linking to X causes problems. In the intervening time, Peter has tested Ted's suggestion, and Ted has sent other messages. Without the gloss, the meaning of "that" and "it" would not have been clear.

Because computer conversation lacks some of the visual contextualization of face-to-face conversation and turn-taking is complex, interactants use strategies from written discourse to make their meanings explicit.

CONCLUSION

Peter and his colleagues use computer conversation for a variety of purposes. They have developed a form of communication that is not devoid of "personality and humanity" or "warmth and wisdom" as

Greene (1983) claims. In fact, they are deliberately trying to build different ways of conveying meaning in a two-dimensional system. Nor is their communication "passive," as Ong (1982) claims. Peter and Ted solve problems, discuss news, and express emotional reactions in their computer conversations.

Computer conversation, however, has not replaced either oral communication or writing and print. This mode of communication straddles the literacy continuum. In terms of both linguistic features and choice of medium, computer conversation is more formal than face-to-face conversation and telephone conversation, but less formal than written memos and documents. But it does not occupy a static place on the oral/written continuum. As interactants change voice, computer conversation moves back and forth between writer-style and talker-style. Interactants respond to voice and topic. Computer conversation is context-dependent because reference items can be interpreted only by reference to the context. However, ambiguous reference items are often glossed by the sender. Thus most computer conversationalists have little difficulty reading and correctly interpreting a log of a computer conversation in which they did not participate. In other words, like written discourse, computer conversation can be interpreted by outsiders, given some contextual information (of the genre).

To use computer conversation efficiently, these interactants use discourse features from both oral and written discourse. They change voice and indicate this range of personal involvement through pronoun use, choice of diction, graphical representations of paralinguistic cues, and the use of quotation marks. They indicate topic shifts to keep the conversation on topic. They gloss reference items if there is ambiguity. They use less fragmented language than in oral discourse: their messages exhibit evidence of some forethought (Lakoff, 1982). In addition, they have learned to operate complex turn-taking and to communicate in a medium over which other media take preference. Thus they make more than one move in a message, repeat lost messages, and accept unanswered messages.

Although these data indicate a relatively efficient set of strategies, there are sources of potential breakdown resulting from tensions between the oral and written traditions: nonexplicit referencing, unmarked topic shifts, possible brusqueness, and use of quotation marks. Further, because of the absence of turn-taking principles, interactants with differing problem-solving strategies can continue along different paths for some time. We have seen these problems emerge with proficient computer conversationalists. They are likely to be magnified when interactants are relatively naive users of this mode of communication.

Since computer conversation has the purpose of providing information and solving problems—that is, of getting things done—interactants need to use strategies to prevent such breakdowns. Already Flores and Ludlow (1981) have tried to design a system to make managerial decision-making more efficient. This system requires managers to specify the speech act (e.g., request, report) of the message. The goal is for both sender and recipient to be more aware of the intent of the message and thereby speed responses and prevent miscommunications. Windt (1983) has written rules for courteous use of computer conversation. In using messages herself, she found many social-interaction problems and attempted to address them by defining rules of conduct. We can see from these two examples that computer conversationalists are becoming increasingly aware that this mode of communication is not identical with face-to-face conversation. Nor is it acquired along with the spoken language in childhood. Like written discourse, it needs to be learned if it is to be effective. In addition, it has limitations: interactants choose other media for a more personal or a more formal voice. For people to learn the skill of computer conversation, both the business community and speech and writing classes may need to include computer conversation in their teaching programs. We cannot do this, however, until we have a better description of the use of discourse features of *all* modes of computer communication. This chapter has provided a skeleton of the use and features of only one mode, computer conversation, based on data from a limited number of interactants.

Further research is needed to provide us with a more elaborated answer to the original question: What language use co-occurs with the use of the computer as a medium of communication? Several more specific questions should motivate any such further research. Which modes and media of communication are the most effective for which particular tasks? Why are they the most effective? How do interactants cope with breakdowns and misunderstandings? Who chooses to use each mode and medium? Why do they make such choices? Why do some people resist some modes and/or media? How do learners acquire computer communication skills?

These questions can be answered through several lines of research. First, we need to compare and contrast the use and features of the three modes of computer communication (research that I am currently conducting). Second, we need to compare the computer as medium with other media, such as face-to-face conversation, telephone conversation, and memos. Third, we need a research team to study several interactants in different environments to determine general usage patterns. Fourth, we need a longitudinal study of the acquisition of computer communication by several learners: people from different occupations, some familiar with computers, some proficient writers, some proficient typists, some naive computer users, some poor writers, some unable to touch type. These are some of the factors that could affect level of acquisition and resistance to different modes and media.

As indicated earlier, however, we need more than a description of current discourse features and use. We need to find more efficient ways of using this medium of communication as well as ways to teach it. This requires the cooperation of interested professionals from business, computer science, education, and linguistics. With such a joint effort, we should be able to devise the most suitable discourse strategies for this medium and, as a result, create software and hardware tools to aid the user and techniques for teaching these new linguistic and computer skills. This process could lead to a redefinition of computer literacy.

Notes

1. Olson (1977), among others, has challenged such a direct causal view and has proposed that certain types of consciousness may be antecedent to literacy rather than a consequence of literacy.

2. USERID is the name chosen by a computer user for identification by the computer system and by other users.

3. Asterisks indicate emphasis. Here and in the examples to follow, P: indicates the message sender. Messages are typed in lower case. Received messages are converted to upper case by the computer. This convention is maintained in the examples.

4. Here and in the examples that follow, " . . . " indicates confidential names of computer systems or programs.

References

Bean, J. C. (1983). Computerized word-processing as an aid to revision. *College Composition and Communication, 34*(2), 146–148.

Carey, J. (1980). Paralanguage in computer mediated communication. *Proceedings of the Association for Computational Linguistics* (pp. 61–63).

Case, D. O. (1984). *Personal computers: Their adoption and use in information work by professors.* Unpublished Ph.D dissertation, Department of Communication, Stanford University.

Chafe, W. L. (1982). Integration and involvement in speaking, writing and oral literature. In D. Tanner (Ed.), *Spoken and written language: Exploring orality and literacy.* Norwood, NJ: Ablex.

Christianson, C. (1983). *All things considered.* On KQED, October 12.

Collier, R. M. (1983). The word-processor and revision strategies. *College Composition and Communication, 34*(2), 149–155.

Eisenstein, E. (1979). *The printing press as an agent of change: Communications and cultural transformations in early-modern Europe, Vol. I.* New York: Cambridge University Press.

Flores, C. F., & Ludlow, J. (1981). Doing and speaking in the office. In G. Fick & R. Sprague (Eds.), *DSS: Issues and challenges.* London: Pergamon Press.

Gibson, W. (1969). *Persona.* New York: Random House.

Goody, J., & Watt, I. (1968). The consequences of literacy. In J. Goody (Ed.), *Literacy in traditional societies.* Cambridge: Cambridge University Press.

Greene, B. (1983). Electronic mail: Personal touch destined for doom? *San Jose Mercury News,* October 23.

Kinneavy, J. L. (1971). *A theory of discourse.* Englewood Cliffs, NJ: Prentice-Hall.

Lakoff, R. T. (1982). Some of my favorite writers are literate: The mingling of oral and literate strategies in written communication. In D. Tannen (Ed.), *Spoken and written language: Exploring orality and literacy.* Norwood, NJ: Ablex.

Levodow, N. (1980). Computer conversations: A hybrid of spoken and written English. Paper presented at the Berkeley Sociolinguistic Meeting, May 2.

Murray, D. E. (1984). Turntaking in computer conversation: Implications for language use. Paper presented at the Stanford University School of Education Forum for Research on Language Issues, May 12.

Olson, D. R. (1977). From utterance to text: The bias of language in speech and writing. *Harvard Educational Review, 47,* 257–281.

Ong, W. J. (1982). *Orality and literacy: The technologizing of the word.* London: Methuen.

Sacks, H., Schegloff, E. A., & Jefferson, G. (1974). A simplest systematics for the organization of turn-taking for conversation. *Language, 50*(4), 696–735.

Schafer, J. C. (1981). The linguistic analysis of spoken and written texts. In B. M. Kroll & R. J. Vann (Eds.), *Exploring speaking-writing relationships: Connections and contrasts.* Urbana, IL: National Council of Teachers of English.

Scribner, S., & Cole, M. (1981). *The psychology of literacy.* Cambridge, MA: Harvard University Press.

Turner, R. H. (1962). Role-taking: Process versus conformity. In A. M. Rose (Ed.), *Human behavior and social process.* London: Routledge and Kegan Paul.

Vann, R. J. (1981). Bridging the gap between oral and written communication in EFL. In B. M. Kroll & R. J. Vann (Eds.), *Exploring speaking-writing relationships: Connections and contrasts.* Urbana, IL: National Council of Teachers of English.

Wilensky, R. (1983). *Planning and understanding: A computational approach to human reasoning.* Reading, MA: Addison-Wesley.

Windt, J. (1983). Minding your on-line manners. Interview with Michael McCabe, *San Jose Mercury News,* November 30.

Viewing Writing from a Social/Institutional Perspective

IV

Nonacademic Writing 6
The Social Perspective

LESTER FAIGLEY
University of Texas at Austin

The past several years have seen a great deal of interest in the writing people do as part of their work. As other chapters in this book will indicate, this job-related writing is worthy of our interest and serious study. In exploring this sort of writing, researchers can take one or a combination of three major theoretical perspectives—the textual perspective, the individual perspective, and the social perspective. In this chapter I discuss the foundations of the social perspective and how it might contribute to research in nonacademic writing. Although the social perspective is least well established, I will argue that it can be a fruitful perspective from which to study nonacademic writing. To illustrate the three theoretical perspectives, I will refer to the following four examples of writing situations in nonacademic settings.

• An editor working for a major publisher in New York neglects to answer a query from an editor in another division. A few days later she writes a brief memo on the company's memo stationary, apologizing for her failure to respond. She uses the excuse that the request became buried on her desk. She follows the company's memo format, but she adds a letterlike closing that says: "Excavatingly yours."

• A supervisor of bank examiners in Colorado has the responsibility of teaching newly hired examiners how to write reports. Since examiners travel extensively and are not well paid, his staff is young and turns over rapidly. The supervisor is now revising an examiner's report on a small bank in southwestern Colorado that has made several questionable loans. In the margins he notes several problems with the report: the lack of reasons for several conclusions, the omission of important factual details, and general wordiness. At the end he explains to the young examiner why the overall tone is inappropriate for an examiner's report. He reminds the examiner that the report will be read at a board of directors' meeting and that it will be the basis for any reform in the bank's management. He tells him to stick to the specific regulations that were violated and to avoid derogatory remarks about the practices of rural banks.

• A nurse in Boston changes jobs and begins work at a psychiatric hospital. At his previous job at a large general hospital, the nurse's section of a patient's chart was a checklist. The psychiatric hospital, however, requires discursive notes on the chart. The nurse photocopies a few examples during his first day on the new job. He uses these examples as models when writing the chart for a schizophrenic patient. He observes that the notes are written in phrases and that certain abbreviations occur frequently, such as *pt.* for *patient*. He begins describing his patient's behavior:

> Very anxious and agitated, seclusive to room except when preoccupied with phone. Poor personal hygiene. With much coaxing, pt. finally took a bath but refused to wash hair. Pt. very paranoid. States "Someone is trying to burn down my trailer."

• A wildlife biologist works for an environmental engineering firm in Houston. She serves as project manager for an ecological survey of the proposed site for a liquefied natural-gas terminal on Matagorda Bay in Texas. She is part of a team that is preparing an environmental-impact statement for a major oil company, and she is composing on a computer the final report on terrestrial ecology. This report will be submitted with other reports on aquatic ecology and hydrology. Major subsections of the report include (1) wildlife habitats, (2) checklists of species, (3) endangered species, and (4) commercially important species. In writing the "checklists of species" subsection, the biologist relies on several master checklist files stored on computer diskettes. She loads the master checklist file for birds, a file that includes all species known to the Texas coast. She edits the file using her field notes on the birds she sighted while visiting the site, marking either "present," "absent," or "probable" beside each species. The biologist knows that the Environmental Protection Agency (EPA) gives special attention to endangered flora and fauna, and she includes in the report a separate subsection for habitats of endangered species. She documents her own findings with independently published sightings.

PERSPECTIVES FOR RESEARCH

Each of the writing situations just described—the editor's memo, the bank examiner's report, the nurse's notes, and the environmental-impact statement—differs substantially from typical classroom writing tasks. An overriding question for researchers of nonacademic writing is how these differences might best be understood and described. The three perspectives mentioned at the beginning of this chapter represent general lines of research that attempt to answer this question. They are, in fact, collections of approaches, collapsed and simplified here for purposes of comparison.

The Textual Perspective

The primary concerns of linguistics and literary criticism during much of the twentieth century have been the description of formal features in language and texts. Following from the assumptions of these traditions, much writing research has analyzed features in texts. This line of inquiry has long been dominant in the study of business and technical writing. One goal of this research has been to describe features that typify particular genres, such as what elements appear in the introduction of a marketing forecast. Another goal has been to produce more "readable" texts. *Readability* has been defined traditionally in terms of quantifiable linguistic features such as sentence length and word length—the basis for the popular read-ability formulas of Flesch and Gunning (reviewed in Selzer, 1983). Only recently have discussions of readability included factors such as the suitability of texts for potential readers (see Redish, et al., chapter 3, this volume).

If researchers who take the textual perspective were asked to examine the four situations I cited at the beginning, they would collect and analyze the texts the writers produce. They might, for example, compare the specialized vocabularies of the environmental-impact statement, the examiner's report, and the nurse's notes. They might compute T-unit length and clause length for each example. They might analyze the topics of individual sentences and determine how these sentence topics form topical progressions. They might, for example, study documents' tables of contents in order to identify conventions of organization. They might look at errors in the nurse's writing and measure "improvement." And they might comment on stylistic variations such as the closing of the editor's memo. Results of these studies would be used to make generalizations about specific kinds of texts—generalizations that are sometimes stated prescriptively as rules for style and format.

The Individual Perspective

This perspective has been strongly influenced by recent theory and research in psychology. For much of this century, linguistics and psychology in the United States were dominated by behaviorism, which declared mental strategies to be unobservable and beyond scientific investigation. During the 1950s and 1960s, however, behaviorist assumptions encountered serious objections. In linguistics, Noam Chomsky argued persuasively that behaviorist theory could not account for the complexity of human language acquisition, and thereby changed the direction of American linguistic research. In psychology, further challenges arose from several sources, two of which later became important in the study of writing. The European cognitive-developmental tradition—best known through the work of Jean Piaget—influenced American researchers studying the development of the thinking reflected in children's writing. A second tradition of cognitive psychology in the United States engaged researchers in creating general theoretical models of the reasoning that attends the writing process. Both these new lines of inquiry in psychology directed the attention of some writing researchers to strategies writers use in composing. For example, Emig (1971) tried to identify some of the strategies high school students used when they composed. Emig's work was followed by numerous other studies of the composing processes of elementary, secondary, and college students. The 1970s movement toward process-oriented inquiry into how children and young adults learn to write eventually led to studies of how nonacademic writers compose (e.g., Gould, 1980).

For researchers who take the individual perspective, a text is not so much an object as an outcome of an individual's cognitive processes. The primary attention shifts away from the text to an individual writer's emerging conception of the writing task. Researchers taking the individual perspective would likely examine how writers make certain choices during composing. They would inquire about writer's goals in composing, either by retrospective interviews or by asking writers to voice their thoughts while they composed. They would consider how an individual's formulation of a writing task directs the production of the resulting text. For example, researchers might observe how the biologist divides the task of writing the environmental impact statement into segments and what she hopes to accomplish in each section. They might observe how the editor at a publishing house goes about creating a persona as she writes the memo and how she understands that persona to fulfill a larger purpose—in this case, gaining the reader's acceptance of an oversight. They might study protocols of the nurse's composing or consider the time he devotes to each stage of writing (e.g., Does he ever revise?). They might take the bank examiner's case as an example of failure to develop an appropriate sense of audience. One goal of these studies would be to describe the processes that are effective and those that are ineffective so that effective strategies can be taught to ineffective writers.

The Social Perspective

The social perspective also focuses on the process of composing, but this perspective understands process in far broader terms. In the social perspective, writing processes do not start with "prewriting" and stop with "revising." Researchers taking a social perspective study how individual acts of communication define, organize, and maintain social groups. They view written texts not as detached objects possessing meaning on their own, but as links in communicative chains, with their meaning emerging from their relationships to previous texts and the present context. The social perspective, then, moves beyond the traditional rhetorical concern for audience, forcing researchers to consider issues such as social roles, group purposes, communal organization, ideology, and finally theories of culture.

If we consider the examples at the beginning of the chapter, we see that neither the textual perspective nor the individual perspective gives us a way to understand how a wildlife biologist learns to write an environmental-impact statement, or why the nurse's section of a patient's chart at one hospital would not require any writing, or how the supervisor's editing of the bank examiner's report affects the audit of the bank and its consequences, or even why the editor's closing is funny. These questions all involve social relations, tensions, or conflicts that go beyond the text as a physical object and the writer as an isolated strategist. To ask these questions is to assume that writing, like operating a jackhammer, arguing a lawsuit, or designing an office building, is a social act that takes place in a structure of authority, changes constantly as society changes, has consequences in the economic and political realms, and shapes the writer as much as it is shaped by the writer. Questions like these could be avoided as long as researchers studied student compositions, but they arise as soon as we leave the academic setting with which we are familiar. Consequently, a writing researcher taking the social perspective needs not only new methods of research, but also a theory that explains how we can participate daily in an all-encompassing social world and yet still see the structure of that world. Before turning to questions of research methodology from the social perspective, I first will look at how such a theory might be constructed.

FOUNDATIONS FOR A SOCIAL THEORY
OF WRITING

A central tenet of the social perspective is that communication is inextricably bound up in the culture of a particular society. Consequently, a researcher of writing who takes the social perspective must have some way of defining and describing that society in terms broader than the traditional rhetorical conception of audience (see Nystrand, 1982). For those of us who have been trained to appreciate literary texts as works of solitary artistic genius rather than expressions of a culture, the task of describing a society seems formidable—if not impossible. There is some comfort, however, in knowing that others ill equipped in theory and method have stumbled onto vast social questions concerning language and have not only survived but even changed basic notions about how we communicate. One such group of explorers—an appropriate metaphor here—were anthropological linguists who attempted to describe the languages of Africa and Asia during the years following World War II. They found that traditional definitions of language and methods of linguistic analysis were no better suited for the astonishing diversity of language in newly emerging nations than was the wool clothing earlier explorers wore to the trophics. These linguists met speakers of the "same" language living a few villages apart who could not understand each other. In many small villages they found that everyone was fluent in two languages or dialects, and that a speaker's choice of one of them often conveyed the social standing of the speaker or listener.

To cope with this diversity, linguists developed the notion of a *speech community*, which Gumperz (1971) defines as "any human aggregate characterized by regular and frequent interaction by means of a shared body of verbal signs and set off from similar aggregates by significant differences in language usage" (p. 114). This notion of a speech community became a basis for the new discipline of *sociolinguistics*. Sociolinguists employed the idea of a speech community to examine how language is used to maintain social identity. For example, Blom and Gumperz (1972) studied a small Norwegian village where all residents spoke both Bokmål, one of the two forms of standard Norwegian, and a local dialect. They found that choices between the two dialects varied among speakers within the community. In some cases, choices between the two dialects signaled certain attitudes and beliefs. A similar phenomenon occurs in my neighborhood in Austin, Texas, where most residents are bilingual in English and Spanish. My neighbors typically greet each other in Spanish, then often switch to English if they wish to engage in prolonged conversation, then signal the conclusion of the conversation by returning to Spanish. Differences in language use can establish social identity even among speakers of the same language (cf. Hymes, 1972). For example, speakers of English would likely understand the literal meaning of utterances of inner-city blacks such as "Your momma so black, she sweat chocolate," but they might not understand that such insults comprise a form of verbal play called the "dozens" (Labov, 1972).

Although the notion of a speech community offers us some insights into the social dimensions of writing, the concept of a community connected by writing must be defined by different criteria. Many of the linguistic markers of speech communities (e.g., differences in pronunciation) do not have simple parallels in written language. Further, written language is actually a collection of genres. Written language is composed in and comes to us through many forms—in shopping lists, in newspapers, in dictated letters, in scripted newscasts, in signs, in receipts. As many commentators on literacy have noted, written language can be understood outside the writer's immediate community or outside the writer's lifetime (which is also true for electronically recorded spoken language).

We need, therefore, an alternative concept to accomodate some of the special circumstances of written language—a concept we might label a *discourse community*. In one sense, all persons literate in a language constitute a discourse community. But few, if any, texts are written for everyone who is capable of deciphering the words. Texts are almost always written for persons in restricted groups (cf. Bazerman, 1979). Persons in these groups may be connected primarily by written texts, as is the case with scholars on different continents who participate in a scholarly debate. Or they may belong to the same organization that has an in-house language and certain local discourse conventions. The key notion is that within a language community, people acquire specialized kinds of discourse competence that enable them to participate in specialized groups. Members know what is worth communicating, how it can be communicated, what other members of the community are likely to know and believe to be true about certain subjects, how other members can be persuaded, and so on.

Scholars for a long time have recognized that academic disciplines are a type of discourse community, each with its own language, subject matters, and methods of argument. In this seminal book, *The Uses of Argument*, Toulmin (1958) theorizes that although arguments have basic structural similiarity, they also are distinguished by fields. He offers academic disciplines as examples of fields, pointing out that patterns of arguments in fields such as physics are very different from those in disciplines such as history or law. Willard (1983) broadens Toulmin's account of a field to include instances of ordinary discourse. In addition to academic disciplines, which Willard calls *normative fields*, Willard distinguishes *encounter fields* (communication among strangers), *relation fields* (communication among associates, friends, and spouses), and *issue fields* (schools of thought that often cross disciplines such as Freudianism). Willard describes fields as rhetorical in operation. Fields sanction what knowledge is accepted, what subjects might be investigated, and what kinds of evidence and rhetorical appeals are permitted.

The academic discourse communities receiving the most study to date have been the sciences, with most attention coming from an extensive research program in the sociology of science (reviewed in Bazerman, 1983). Following Merton's (1957) observation that the growth of scientific knowledge reflects its social organization, many researchers have examined groups, subgroups, and hierarchies among scientists. Researchers have considered how scientific articles serve the social organization as both a means of communication and a means of earning rewards. Hagstrom (1965) drew the analogy of the scientific article as a form of primitive "gift giving," where the scientist offers the "gift" with the expectation of receiving some sort of later recognition from the community. Latour and Woolgar (1979) argue for a different model, where scientists publish to earn credibility, which in turn furthers their interest in the "game" of science. Another issue in this research program is the nature of scientific knowledge. The old notion of an independent and rational body of scientific knowledge has collided with many demonstrations of the human construction of scientific facts (e.g., Feyerabend, 1975; Toulmin, 1972), and "new" scientific knowledge has been shown to emerge from an agreed-on body of old knowledge (e.g., Price, 1963).

It is tempting to import wholesale the research issues raised in the sociology of science for the study of nonacademic writing. But before any such ambitious research program can begin, certain questions of definition must be addressed. One of the most crucial is how to differentiate academic and nonacademic writing. In examining nonacademic writing, we find many overlapping communities. For example, the biologist writing an environmental-impact statement abides not only by certain disciplinary conventions in biology, certain legal forms determined by the Environmental Protection Agency, and certain unstated and stated conventions particular to her company, but also by a complex set of conventions of political language (consider the use of the term *endangered species*). If the notion of discourse communities is to be illuminating, it must not be used without attending to how such communities might be identified and defined and how communities shape the form and content of specific texts. Chapter 9 by Miller and Selzer in this volume suggests how analyses of texts written in specific communities might proceed.

In the case of academic or professonal discourse, it is relatively easy to see writing as a social activity. It is more difficult to see how a "private" act of writing, such as an entry in a diary, might be construed as a social act. Take an extreme example, where the writer of a diary encodes her entries in a cipher that only she knows. Theoreticians of the social perspective, such as Lev Vygotsky, would argue that such a coded diary entry would be no less a social act than the environmental-impact statement. Vygotsky (1962) contends that there is no such thing as "private" language, or even "private" thought:

> Thought development is determined by language, i.e., by the linguistic tools of thought, and by the sociocultural experiences of the child ... The child's intellectual growth is contingent on his mastering the social means of thought, that is, language ... Verbal thought is not an innate, natural form of behavior but is determined by a historical-cultural process [p. 51].

The historical-cultural process to which Vygotsky refers is simply that children do not learn words from a dictionary but through hearing them uttered in social situations to convey specific intentions and to achieve specific ends (see Bizzell, 1982). Words carry the contexts in which they have been used. Granted, Vygotsky does discuss "inner speech," but his conception of inner speech is not the same as private language. Although inner speech is not voiced, it consists of fragments of speech the speaker has drawn from the community in which he or she lives. More important, inner speech takes the form of a dialogue, which implies the continuous presence of an "other."

Vygotsky's contemporary, M. M. Bakhtin, applied these same notions to written texts. It is not clear whether Bakhtin and Vygotsky knew each other or influenced each other. (Bakhtin remains mysterious in other ways as well. Apparently some of his works were published under the names of his associates.) In *Marxism and the Philosophy of Language*, originally published under the name V. N. Vološinov in 1929, Bakhtin claims the textual perspective (which he calls "abstract objectivism") distorts the nature of written language by separating a text from its context. Bakhtin goes on to say that the textual perspective mistakenly assumes that meaning can be separated from a specific situation, that the textual approach inevitably emphasizes parts at the expense of the whole. He also faults approaches that center on the individual; these approaches he claims, miss the nature of language. Like Vygotsky, he insists that language is dialogic, that a text is not an isolated, monologic utterance, but "a moment in the continuous process of verbal communication" (Vološinov, 1973, p. 95). A text is written in orientation to previous texts of the same kind and on the same subjects; it inevitably grows out of some concrete situation; and it inevitably provokes some response, even if it is simply discarded. In short, the essence of a text—any text—is inextricably tied up in chains of communication and not in the linguistic forms on the page or in the minds of individual writers.

RESEARCH ON WRITING FROM
THE SOCIAL PERSPECTIVE

A broadly defined research program that explores writing from the social perspective would first examine what constitutes a discourse community. It would probe the fluid and multiple nature of discourse communities, and how communities overlap and change. Such a research program would examine how a particular discourse community is organized by its interactions and by the texts it produces (see chapter 8 by Paradis et al. in this volume). It would examine what subjects are considered appropriate in that community and how those subjects are determined. It would examine how genres evolve within a community. Finally, it would investigate how a community sanctions certain methods of inquiry.

Such a research program would *integrate* considerations of individual writers and particular texts into a broader view of the social functions of writing. It would explore how individual writers come to know the beliefs and expectations of other members of the community, and how individuals can alter the community's beliefs and expectations. It would consider how individuals cope with texts—how they learn to read texts and how to make meaning in texts in a particular community. It would investigate how conventions shape and are shaped by the processes of writing and reading. It would examine not only how individuals learn to represent themselves in a text, but how that representation emerges in response to a specific situation. In addition to the familiar aspects of the composing process, this research program would consider how all language is interaction, how all texts entail contexts, and how texts accomplish interactions between writers and readers rather than embodying meaning entirely by themselves. Consequently, this research program would not only examine an individual's composing processes, but would also follow the completed text, examining how it is disseminated, who has access to it, who reads it and who doesn't, what is read, what actions people take upon reading it, and how it influences subsequent texts.

Moreover, this research program would not separate the study of texts from the study of technologies used to create texts. These technologies include not only writing implements, but also symbol systems and the knowledge to interpret those systems. New technologies arise in response to needs, and members of discourse communities must know how to apply new technologies to existing functions for writing (see chapter 4 by Halpern in this volume; see also Faigley & Miller, 1982; Halpern & Liggett, 1984; Williams, 1981). For example, in writing the endangered-species subsection of the environmental-impact statement, the biologist uses computer software to form a pie chart that illustrates the percentages of wildlife habitat affected on the proposed site. The knowledge that readers use to interpret the pie graph is as critical a technology to this particular writing act as the technology that led to the development of the computer hardware and software.

The central questions for research taking the social perspective are ones that concern the contexts in which texts are written and read. These questions will be addressed in theoretical, historical, and empirical research. Theoreticians who adopt the social perspective can look to a long tradition of scholarship in rhetoric and more recent work in semiotics (e.g., Barthes, 1968); literary criticism (e.g., Fish, 1980); the philosophy of science (e.g., Popper, 1963); social psychology (e.g., Vygotsky, 1962); and cultural anthropology (e.g., Geertz, 1983). Historians can examine the functions of writing in small communities or the effects of literacy on large ones. Empirical researchers must be able to connect theoretical approaches to the mundane writing events of everyday life.

POSSIBILITIES FOR EMPIRICAL RESEARCH

In the social study of language, two major lines of empirical inquiry have emerged—one quantitative and the other qualitative. Both quantitative and qualitative approaches can be valuable in studying nonacademic writing. The quantitative approach is exemplified by work in sociolinguistics, such as Labov's (1966) findings that certain linguistic features are stratified by social class. The qualitative approach is exemplified by research in anthropology that is collectively known as *ethnography* (see chapter 14 by Doheny-Farina and Odell in this volume). Because qualitative research offers the potential for describing the complex social situation that any act of writing involves, empirical researchers are likely to use qualitative approaches with increasing frequency.

But if researchers take a qualitative approach, what do they examine? Let us consider again the situations posed at the beginning of this chapter. In the case of the editor, researchers might begin with the apparent tension between the constraints of the memo form and the tone sought by the editor—a tension that prompts innovation. Examining the causes of this tension leads to issues of the use of language by those whose business is the production of language, the use of language between two people at the same level of the corporate structure, and the use of language to personalize an apparently impersonal form. For example, researchers might collect instances of personalization (e.g., handwritten additions, capitalization or underlining, second-person address, private references) and ask writers why they chose to make personal additions.

In the case of the bank examiner, researchers might observe, over the course of a year, the supervisor's interaction with three or four trainees. In teaching the trainees how to write examiners' reports, the supervisor must also teach the trainees about the social organization of a bank. By understanding the social organization, examiners can help to correct the problems they uncover. To study how this social knowledge is transmitted, researchers would record the oral as well as the written communication between the supervisor and the trainees. They likely would interview trainees at different times to discover how social understanding evolves, and they would be sensitive to the reactions of bankers to the examiners' reports.

The case of the nurse also concerns the way writers under someone else's authority learn the conventions of a community. At one hospital, nurses are allowed only a checklist. At the other, they can—and must—write; but at the same time, they must use certain conventions associated with the practice of psychiatric medicine and with the particular hospital. Researchers should be interested in how nurses acquire and internalize these conventions. Researchers might also wish to observe how these written reports are used by physicians in diagnosing and treating patients.

In the case of the environmental-impact statement, a researcher who takes the social point of view might try to identify the sources of the set format for such documents. One might also want to consider the effects of this format on the kinds of information that can and cannot be considered. Ohmann (1976), for instance, has analyzed the conventions of the Pentagon papers and their effect on U.S. policies in the Vietnam War. Or one might consider ways in which a specific report differs from the conventional format of the environmental-impact statement. Is there a tension, traceable in the structure of the statement, between the format and the issues of the particular case? For instance, is one section much longer than usual? Is the tone of the opening different from previous statements? What is revised in the course of writing, and by whom? What cannot be revised?

All these lines of inquiry spring from three general questions:

1. What is the social relationship of writers and readers, and how does the text function in this social relationship?
2. How does this kind of text change over time?
3. How does the perspective of the observer define and limit the observation of this text?

This last question forces researchers to consider what it means to observe and what it means to interpret. Debates over these issues have occupied cultural anthropologists for the past two decades. Anthropologists have developed two broad notions of ethnography: an older notion concerned with observation and a newer notion concerned with interpretation. Both notions are important to the study of nonacademic writing.

The older notion is useful for its focus on how to observe. One anthropologist says that enthnography involves the attempt to "record and describe the culturally significant behaviors of a particular society" (Conklin, 1968, p. 172). He goes on to say that ideally, this description, an ethnography, requires a long period of intimate study and residence in a small, well-defined community, knowledge of the spoken language, and the employment of a wide range of observational techniques including prolonged face-to-face contacts with members of the local group, direct participation in some of that group's activities, and a greater emphasis on intensive work with informants than on the use of documentary or survey data [p. 172].

In a traditional conception of ethnography, an anthropologist lives (usually for a year or longer) in the culture being studied (usually a technologically primitive culture) and collects copious data by observing, interviewing, charting patterns, and collecting case studies. Although not every method might be used, the ethnographer will surely use more than one method in collecting data, and the chief data source will be the ethnographer's diary. The ethnographer tries to avoid value judgments and abandons assumptions from his or her own culture. Hymes (1980) says that ethnographic investigation is always open-ended.

The newer notion of ethnography is sometimes called *interpretative anthropology*. One of its chief practitioners is Geertz, whose essay, "Thick Description: Toward an Interpretative Theory of Culture" (in Geertz, 1973), argues that a culture can be "read" not by starting with abstract concepts but by first microscopically examining the culture's most salient activities. Geertz's famous essay on the Balinese cockfight (1973) demonstrates how a single event can provide "a metasocial commentary upon the whole matter of assorting human beings into fixed hierarchical ranks and then organizing the major part of collective existence around that assortment" (p. 448). The function of the cockfight "is interpretative; it is the Balinese reading of Balinese experience, a story they tell themselves about themselves" (p. 448). In a similar way a researcher of nonacademic writing can "read" in a manager's striking out the formal salutation "Dear Mr. Wittenburg:" and inserting by hand "Kent—" in a memo to a subordinate a great deal about how the community of the workplace is socially organized and maintained. As Geertz says, "Small facts speak to large issues" (p. 23).

The potential for qualitative research in nonacademic writing is great, but researchers should heed the warnings of anthropologists. One of the most critical is the insistence on a cross-cultural perspective. Some anthopologists question whether valid ethnographies are possible by members of the same culture. These anthropologists argue that the experience of living in another culture makes the ethnographer aware of how much a sense of belonging to a culture depends on shared knowledge and beliefs. Although very few writing researchers will attempt enthnographies of the kind done by anthropologists, the need for contrastive analysis still exists. Researchers of nonacademic writing must continually reflect on their own perspective—on what they are likely to observe and not observe, and on how their own assumptions about writing and the world affect how they interpret what they observe (see Boon, 1982; Clifford, 1983).

Researchers should also be aware of the history of writing systems. Contemporary archaeologists have found that the development of writing systems grew out of economic necessity. The purposes of writing for the first five hundred years apparently were strictly commercial and administrative (Driver, 1948). Most surviving tablets record the property and accounts of temples; religious, historical, and legal functions for writing came later. Today we are in the midst of large-scale changes in the nature and uses of writing systems—changes brought about by electronic technology and again stimulated by changing economic and social needs. Computerized information services were first established to provide immediate access to financial news and other economic information, but these data bases quickly spread to more general kinds of information and even to hobbies. Electronic mail is as old as the telegraph, but with the advent of computer and satellite technology it has become an increasingly pervasive communications system, extending rapidly beyond the workplace. The point here is that writing technologies arise from perceived needs within communities. If world trade were less complex, the need to develop electronic communication technologies would be proportionately less. Consequently, the changing nature of nonacademic writing cannot be understood without examining changes in communities that produce nonacademic writing.

Researchers who take the social perspective show us that writing in a complex society is diverse and that our definitions of literacy must necessarily be pluralistic. They show us that writing is an act not easily separated from its functions in a particular discourse community. They increase our awareness of the social importance of what we teach. In chapters that follow, Odell (chapter 7); Paradis, Dobrin, and Miller (chapter 8); and Miller and Selzer (chapter 9) explore some of the complex relationships between writing and the social, organizational, and professional contexts in which that writing is done.

Acknowledgments

I am grateful for the responses of Phyllis Artiss, Charles Bazerman, Patricia Gambrell, Greg Myers, Martin Nystrand, Walter Reed, and Beverly Stoeltje to earlier drafts of this chapter.

References

Barthes, R. (1968). *Elements of semiology*. (A. Lavers & C. Smith, Trans.). New York: Hill and Wang.

Bazerman, C. (1979). Written language communities: Writing in the context of reading. (ERIC Document ED 232 159.)

Bazerman, C. (1983). Scientific writing as a social act: A review of the literature of the sociology of science. In P. V. Anderson, R. J. Brockmann, & C. Miller (Eds.), *New essays in technical writing and communication: Research, theory and practice.* Farmingdale, NY: Baywood.

Bizzell, P. (1982). Cognition, convention, and certainty: What we need to know about writing. Pre/Text, 3, 213–243.

Blom, J. P., & Gumperz, J. J. (1972). Social meaning in linguistic structures. In J. J. Gumperz & D. Hymes (Eds.), *Directions in sociolinguistics.* New York: Holt, Rinehart and Winston.

Boon, J. A. (1982). *Other tribes, other scribes.* Cambridge: Cambridge University Press.

Clifford, J. (1983). On ethnographic authority. *Representations, 1,* 118–146.

Conklin, H. C. (1968). Ethnography. In D. Sills (Ed.), *International encyclopedia of the social sciences.* London: Macmillian.

Driver, G. R. (1948). *Semitic writing from pictograph to alphabet.* London: Oxford University Press.

Emig, J. A. (1971). *The composing processes of twelfth graders* (NCTE Research Report No. 13). Urbana, IL: National Council of Teachers of English.

Faigley, L., & Miller, T. (1982). What we learn from writing on the job. *College English,* 44, 557–569.

Feyerabend, P. (1975). *Against method: An outline of an anarchistic theory of knowledge.* Atlantic Highlands, NJ: Humanities Press.

Fish, S. (1980). *Is there a text in this class?* Cambridge, MA: Harvard University Press.

Geertz, C. (1973). *The interpretation of cultures.* New York: Basic Books.

Geertz, C. (1983). *Local knowledge: Further essays in interpretative anthropology.* New York: Basic Books.

Gould, J. D. (1980). Experiments on composing letters: Some facts, some myths, some observations. In L. W. Gregg & E. R. Steinberg (Eds.), Cognitive processes in writing. Hillsdale, NJ: Lawrence Erlbaum.

Gumperz, J. J. (1971). Language in social groups. Stanford, CA: Stanford University Press.

Hagstrom, W. O. (1965). The scientific community. New York: Basic Books.

Halpern, J., & Liggett, S. (1984). Computers and composing: How the new technologies are changing writing. Carbondale, IL: Southern Illinois University Press.

Hymes, D. (1972). Introduction: Toward ethnographies of communication. In P. Giglioli (Ed.), Language and social context. Baltimore: Penguin.

Hymes, D. (1980). What is ethnography? In D. Hymes (Ed.), Language in education: Ethnolinguistic essays. Arlington, VA: Center for Applied Linguistics.

Labov, W. (1966). The social stratification of English in New York City. Arlington, VA: Center for Applied Linguistics.

Labov, W. (1972). Language in the inner city: Studies in the Black English Vernacular. Philadelphia: University of Pennsylvania Press.

Latour, B., & Woolgar, S. (1979). Laboratory life: The social construction of scientific facts. Beverly Hills, CA: SAGE Publications.

Merton, R. K. (1957). Social theory and social structure. New York: Free Press.

Nystrand, M. (1982). Rhetoric's "audience" and linguistics' "speech community": Implications for understanding writing, reading, and text. In M. Nystrand (Ed.), What writers know: The language, process, and structure of written discourse. New York: Academic Press.

Ohmann, R. (1976). English in America: A radical view of the profession. New York: Oxford University Press.

Popper, K. (1963). Conjectures and refutations: The growth of scientific knowledge. New York: Harper & Row.

Price, D. J. (1963). Little science, big science. New York: Columbia University Press.

Selzer, J. (1983). What constitutes a "readable" technical style? In P. V. Anderson, R. J. Brockmann, & C. Miller (Eds.), New essays in technical writing and communication: Research, theory, and practice. Farmingdale, NY: Baywood.

Toulmin, S. (1958). The uses of argument. Cambridge: Cambridge University Press.

Toulmin, S. (1972). Human understanding (Vol. 1). The collective evolution of scientific concepts. Princeton, NJ: Princeton University Press.

Vološinov, V. N. (1973). Marxism and the philosophy of language. (L. Matejka & I. R. Titunik, Trans.). New York: Seminar Press. (Original work published 1929)

Vygotsky, L. S. (1962). Thought and language. (E. Hanfmann & G. Vakar, Trans.). Cambridge, MA: MIT Press. (Original work published 1934)

Willard, C. A. (1983). Argumentation and the social grounds of knowledge. University, AL: University of Alabama Press.

Williams, R. (1981). Communications technologies and social institutions. In Contact: Human communication and its history. New York: Thames and Hudson.

Beyond the Text

7

Relations between Writing and Social Context

LEE ODELL
Rensselaer Polytechnic Institute

In the past decade all of us in the field of composition have become increasingly aware of the importance of rhetorical context. We have begun to see how a writer's sense of audience, voice, and purpose influence the features of a text (Rubin & Piche, 1979; Crowhurst & Piche, 1979) and also the process of composing (Flower & Hayes, 1980; Matsuhashi, 1981). Further, we have begun to realize that an awareness of rhetorical context might influence our evaluation of a text (Lloyd-Jones, 1977; Odell, 1981). In other words, teachers, theorists, and researchers have begun to look beyond the written text. But we may not have looked far enough. With some notable exceptions (e.g., Clark & Florio, 1983; Kantor, 1983; Bazerman, 1983; Witte & Faigley, 1983; Bartholomae, 1985; Herrington, forthcoming), we have tended to ignore the larger contexts in which writing is done. We have avoided looking at writing, to use Lester Faigley's terminology, "from a social point of view" (see chapter 6, this volume); we have given too little thought to ways a "discourse community" (see Bizzell, 1982) might influence writers' attempts to formulate and express their ideas. For writers in nonacademic settings, we have paid too little attention to the organizational context in which they do their writing. We have not considered the relationships between the process of composing and the knowledge, values, and experiences that writers share with others in their office.

This becomes a significant problem, not only in light of the theory Faigley discusses, but also in view of recent work in composition and in organizational theory. We have reason to believe that the process of composing may entail a great deal of social interaction. For example, Jack Selzer (1983) found that for the engineer who took part in his study the composing process relied heavily on "communal brainstorming" (p. 180) in the form of telephone conversations with advisors in other offices and formal and informal conversations with colleagues in the engineer's own office. Selzer's results are supported by survey research (see Faigley & Miller, 1982) indicating that people in various occupations often have to write collaboratively, that some sort of human interaction may be important to the production of a written text. Moreover, we have reason to suspect that a writer may be influenced not only by interaction with colleagues, but by something much less readily observable—by what Terrance E. Deal and Allen A. Kennedy (1982) call the "culture" of the organization in which the writer works. That is, writers who are members of an organization (a corporation, a bureaucracy, a school, a club) may have internalized values, attitudes, knowledge, and ways of acting that are shared by other members of the organization. This culture, Deal and Kennedy assert, influences "practically everything" in the life of the organization.

This assertion, combined with indications that interaction and collaboration are important for writers, make it seem essential that we explore the organizational context in which nonacademic writing is done. Does this context influence the writing people do as part of their job? If so, in what ways are writers affected by their interactions with others and by their awareness of their organization's culture— its widely shared attitudes, knowledge, and ways of operating?

To investigate some of the relations between organizational context and writing, I conducted an ethnographic study of workers in a state bureaucracy. Participating in this study were a small group of supervisors and administrative analysts, all of whom worked in an office where the principal tasks were to assess proposed legislation and to design procedures to implement legislation and agency policy. As a result of interviewing these writers, observing their daily work routines, and recording and analyzing a number of their group discussions, I want to suggest the following:

- In *judging the appropriateness of choices* that appear in their writing, writers in this study relied on their awareness of attitudes and prior experiences that are shared by others in their organization.
- In *assessing their audience*, writers in this study sometimes created their reader in their own or their supervisors' image; writers' perception of their audience reflected not only their knowledge of the intended reader but also, in some cases, their understanding of their own job and their familiarity with procedures characteristic of the office in which the writers themselves work.
- In *conducting the process of inquiry*, writers in this study appeared to be influenced by the demands of their job and by the concerns or attitudes of the particular office in which they work.

It is important to be cautious about generalizing from these observations. Behavior noted in this study may not be typical of administrative analysts in other branches of state government, let alone of writers in general. Consequently, I shall follow my report on writing done by administrative analysts with suggestions for further research that will test and refine my tentative conclusions. But since these conclusions seem consistent with theory (see Faigley, chapter 6, this volume; Moffett, 1968), and with other research (see, especially, Selzer, 1983; Heath, 1983), I shall conclude by speculating about possible implications for teaching.

JUDGMENTS ABOUT CHOICES OF CONTENT

Following a procedure used in earlier studies (Odell & Goswami, 1982; Odell, Goswami, Herrington, & Quick, 1983), I asked writers to provide copies of writing (memos, letters, analyses of legislation) they typically did as part of their job. I identified points at which they had chosen to elaborate on their assertions, and I subsequently interviewed writers about their willingness to delete these elaborations. With each interviewee, I emphasized that I was not suggesting that the elaboration was inappropriate and that I was simply interested in the writer's reasons for being willing or unwilling to delete a particular passage. (For an analysis of assumptions underlying this procedure, see Odell, Goswami, & Herrington, 1983.) Over a four-month period, I interviewed each analyst about six or more different pieces of writing.

As previous studies (e.g., Odell & Goswami, 1982) would lead one to expect, the analysts gave several different types of justifications for their choices. Some justifications were based on the analysts' assessment of their audience, others on the nature of the subject they were writing about. The analysis of these interviews, however, reflected a concern that has not been observed in previous studies. The analysts in this study frequently referred to elements of the culture in which they worked. Specifically, they referred to:

- Widely shared attitudes or values, in their own office or in other branches of the agency.
- Prior actions or previously held attitudes.
- Ways in which the agency typically functioned.

Attitudes and Values

Some of the comments about attitudes or values had to do with the specific topic the analysts were addressing. For example, one analyst did not want to delete a bit of elaboration because:

> I think once again it just gives a little more emphasis to the point that we want to make about the security of the . . . system. It adds more emphasis . . . we see [security] as being the major advantage of [the new system].

In other instances, analysts referred to ongoing concerns of their office, concerns that are applicable to more than just the topic at hand. One analyst refused to delete a passage because:

> That's something that would strike somebody reading the memo: "Yeah, that's something that we really have to consider." And I want to emphasize that.

When asked how she knew that a reader would likely have that reaction, she replied:

> In this department, one of our main concerns is the effect on our district offices. What will this change actually do to that person standing in line or that person working in the office? That's a point that shouldn't slide through, "Oh, this won't have that much effect," or whatever. Yes, it *will*

have that much effect and we should sit back and take a look at what the effect will be.

Another analyst reflected her awareness of the attitudes of other departments in her agency. During one of the interviews, the analyst had indicated that she wanted to meet with a group that included a representative from the Office of Field Investigations (OFI). Anticipating my question, she said:

> And why do [I] want someone from OFI? Because security has to be investigated.

When asked how she knew this investigation was necessary, she explained that she was setting up a procedure that would require a nongovernment office to print and mail out certain forms:

> OFI inspects the offices of printers who produce these forms to see if they are secure. I'm talking not about a security document but about contracting out to someone else to do our mailing. I know that these [OFI] types are going to want to decide whether it's secure for us to do that.

Prior Actions or Circumstances

In addition to commenting on attitudes, the analysts also justified choices by mentioning prior actions or circumstances:

> We've taken a stance in the past of just responding to particular problems voiced by other people . . . and this is my attempt at a more active role.

In at least one case, a sense of history and attitudes appear together:

> There's a history of reluctance on our part in this department to trust [another branch of state government] to do what they're supposed to do accurately. And without actually saying that, I'm trying to convey it.

Agency Procedures

Finally, the analysts justified some of their choices by revealing their knowledge of how things worked in the agency. Some of this knowledge pertained to the ways analysts were supposed to carry out a particular type of writing assignment. One analyst, for example, was unwilling to delete a reference to a program's ability to generate revenue and achieve a break-even point; that sort of information, she said, is:

> ... one of the required pieces of information under [the section headed] "Fiscal Impact"—whether there's revenue generated and how much [the proposed program] is going to cost us.

In other cases this knowledge pertained to the ways in which the agency functions, what its formal procedures are, and how long they take:

> The point I wanted to make here is that we're going to have a very tight time frame with this bill. It's already mid-March now. The bill probably will pass around the beginning of April and will become effective June 1. And there's a certain amount of work that has to be done—a certain amount of programming that has to be done and then polling and printing renewals. There's not much time to get all of that done. So I wanted to point out that even though the bill has not passed yet, could we start?

Finally, one analyst remarked on a more informal—but apparently prevalent—mode of operation:

> Though you're confident of your information, you can't always say that you're 100% correct. [In fact,] you can never say you're 100% correct. You take the information you get, you analyze it, and you say these are the facts I've gotten and this is the way it looks to me. But somebody else can take those facts and massage them a different way and say, "Well, it looks very different to me."

In all these preceding examples, the analysts' awareness of social context related directly to the decision about whether to delete information from what they had written. There were, however, a few comments in which social context had a more indirect effect on decisions about writing and appeared to have been as important for reading as for writing.

Indirect Influence of Context

One analyst, for example, made an observation that showed how her awareness of office history influenced her reaction to something she had read, and how that reaction in turn influenced her decision about deleting a particular bit of elaboration. She had been assigned to write a response to a letter criticizing the agency. She felt the criticism was unfair:

> We have made it clear in any information we've ever given to the legislature or anyone else about this program that we have fully looked into issues involved. We have gone to other states, we have gotten written information. It's not a decision that we ever made frivolously— to choose this system.

This understanding of the agency's prior actions led to this reaction to the criticism:

> And to me . . . in 1983, [for the letter writer] to say, "we question the sagacity of the Department's decision"—to me it's insulting. . . .

This reaction, in turn, made her unwilling to delete a sharply worded bit of elaboration. This particular elabortion was important because:

> . . . if you get something like this [letter] . . . then you want to seriously and emphatically respond to it that "No, this is not the case."

Another analyst explained how her knowledge of office procedure did more than influence her choice of a particular bit of information. She reported that, on being asked to write an analysis of some proposed legislation:

> I called the legal bureau and said to one of the secretaries, "Which lawyer drafted Bill_____?" And she said, "_____." This is SOP [standard operating procedure] for doing any of the bill analyses. Go talk to the lawyer that drafted it.

Later in this chapter, I shall examine this discussion in some detail, noting ways in which it was a part of both the reading and the writing process. My point here is that the analyst's knowledge of office procedure enabled her to identify appropriate help in formulating the ideas she would express in her written analysis of a piece of legislation.

PERCEPTION OF AUDIENCE

As noted earlier, analysts frequently justified their choice of content by referring to the reader to whom their writing was addressed. In some instances the analysts' sense of audience seemed to be based on their experiences with or personal knowledge of the person to whom their writing was addressed. It was relatively unusual, however, for analysts to report this personal knowledge of their audience. Instead, analysts' comments suggest that their understanding of their audience was a projection based on the immediate organizational context in which the analysts do their writing. In other words, the analysts' perceptions of audience are often based not so much on their experience with the intended reader but rather on the analysts' experiences in the office where they themselves work and on the nature of the work the analysts do.

Paradoxical Comments about Audience

On the face of it, analysts would seem to have a very strong sense of the person to whom they are writing. They refer to the reader's knowledge of the subject at hand or to the ways a reader might react to their writing. More specifically, when asked if they would be willing to delete certain bits of elaboration, the analysts occasionally imagined a dialogue in which the reader might raise any of the following types of questions:

QUESTIONS ABOUT SPECIALIZED TERMS
OR UNFAMILIAR REFERENCES.

—I suppose that it's not really essential for the reader to know. It's just a possible question: "What does manual issue order mean?" It's a nitty-gritty type piece of information that I believe the readers of this wouldn't know the answer to. [Before writing this memo] I didn't know what a manual issue order meant, so I asked.

—Anybody reading this will say, "Well, what temporary license?" I know it's been mentioned previously, but it's not necessarily something they've committed to memory.

QUESTIONS ABOUT PROCEDURE.

—No, I wouldn't [delete a passage] because once again this [memo] did also go to Charlie, who didn't know anything of what transpired that day. So it would be good for him to know. If I'd just left that out, he might say, "Well, what did we do? Just leave it in the air? Did you let anybody know about it?"

—I think the question would come back. There would be questions like "How are you working with the other bureaus?" . . . As far as I'm concerned, it's a logical question to say, "This program is going to be operational involving these [other] groups. Are you getting them involved?"

QUESTIONS ABOUT RATIONALE.

—Once again, the person reading it might be thinking, "Well, why couldn't we just stay with our present system? Why would we have to go to all the expense of going to a terminal system?" And right up [here], this will tell him why. This will give him the information he needs.

In transcribing these questions, it is impossible to convey the urgent tone of voice in which they were expressed. This tone suggested a certain immediacy to the writer-reader relationship, as though writer and reader were engaged in a face-to-face conversation in which the reader was trying—not always patiently—to find out exactly what the writer was getting at or what factual basis the writer had for a particular assertion. Yet this sense of immediacy seems inconsistent with other comments analysts made. For example, the analysts reported relatively little direct contact with their intended audience; only one analyst indicated that he had talked with the reader he was addressing before writing a draft. Further, the analysts had relatively little to say about the personal characteristics of the person they were addressing. Even when the analysts referred to the audience's knowledge of the subject at hand, they rarely talked about what the reader actually did know. Rather, they usually spoke about what the reader might or should know (or not know) about the subject at hand. Finally, in almost half their comments about audience, analysts referred not to the specific person to whom their writing was addressed, but instead to "the reader" or "the person who reads this." In one interview, an analyst mentioned the name of the person she was writing to but went on to say, "Take away the name —— —— —and insert the reader or whomever; you [still] must explain why you recommend a certain action."

In summary, then, the analysts' sense of audience seems a bit paradoxical. In one sense, there is an immediacy about the writer-reader relationship. Yet in another sense the analysts seem quite remote from their intended readers.

Influence of Office Setting

This paradox is partially resolved if one understands the office setting in which the analysts worked. Consider this excerpt from an interview in which an analyst explained why she would not be willing to delete some explanatory material:

> *Analyst*: No, it tells the reader how I came to a figure of 3,500 notices handled a day.
>
> *Interviewer*: But suppose you didn't tell them how you came to that figure?
>
> *Analyst*: Somebody would ask, "Where are you getting this from?"
>
> *Interviewer*: [All the analysts] seem to have a clear notion of when somebody would ask and what they would ask.
>
> *Analyst*: It's probably from the days when you first start. You tend to be brief and cursory in your writing. Anyway, I did. I learned from my mistakes. I insert those things in any report that I do which, I've been told before in the past, to put it in. It saves the reader a lot of trouble and it saves a lot of phone calls from people who are reviewing this asking how and why. I guess it's just experience.
>
> *Interviewer*: Is that something that [an office supervisor] insists on?
>
> *Analyst*: No, it's just . . . remember the hierarchy of people that review these things. Depending on who it's going to, there's a possibility for it to be reviewed by _____, by_____, by _____ _____ and his staff and by Commissioner _____ and his staff. So when that many people are reviewing your work there's all kinds of questions they have. And just over the years you get an instinctive feeling on what to include and what not to include. It's instinctive based on past experience. I know I'm on the right track with this because nobody deleted anything from this report and nobody added anything.

As was common with all the analysts, this analyst had almost no contact with the high-level administrator to whom the memo was addressed. Indeed, she had only infrequent contact with Commissioner_____, the person whose name would appear as the writer of the memo. But she had frequent contact with the three supervisors who worked in her office and who reviewed her writing. Further, these supervisors often responded to the analysts' writing in conversation, as well as in writing. On occasion, I overheard some conversations in which a supervisor responded to an analyst's work, and analysts sometimes reported to me the gist of these conversations. My own observation plus the analysts' reports suggest to me that the questions the analyst imputed to her intended reader are, in fact, the questions that are likely to be raised (again, not always patiently) in conversations with the people who review her writing before it reaches the intended audience.

Influence of Analysts' Job

Another way to account for analysts' paradoxical sense of audience is to consider the nature of their job. Although they sometimes have little knowledge of their intended reader, the analysts have extensive personal knowledge of the demands of their job, which requires that they deal with facts and logistics. In anticipating a reader's questions, analysts often reflect these concerns. This is especially true for two of the types of writing analysts do most frequently: explanations of procedures for carrying out policy and analyses of pending legislation. In writing procedures, the question analysts face is not, *Should* we implement the program? but *How* do we implement the program? Similarly, when they analyze proposed legislation, analysts tend to think in terms of logistics: How much will this cost? How many personnel will be involved? Can we do it? Further, in answering these questions, analysts often acquire information that is not common knowledge within the agency and, therefore, is probably not readily available to their readers. In explaining why they would or would not delete certain passages from their writing, the analysts often assumed that their reader shared the analysts' understanding of the nature of the analysts' work and would want answers to the sorts of questions the analysts had asked in preparing a piece of writing. Although this assumption may be well founded, it still seems worth testing, for reasons suggested later on. My point here is that the analysts' conception of their audience sometimes seems to reflect their own understanding of their role in the agency. The analysts understand that role and hypothesize a reader who also understands and accepts it.

THE PROCESS OF INQUIRY

As we have already seen, when an analyst was assigned to assess the strengths and weaknesses of a piece of legislation, it was "standard operating procedure" for the analyst to discuss the legislation with the lawyer who had drafted it. In other words, the organization in which the analyst worked encouraged discussion and collaboration not only on this sort of topic, but on others as well—as a part of the process of inquiry. In this section I shall examine in detail a particular discussion, one in which a lawyer and an analyst are considering a new piece of legislation. This discussion suggests that organizational context influences the process of inquiry in at least two ways.

- Since the organization places such emphasis on discussion and collaboration in the process of inquiry, analysts are virtually required to develop some sort of interpersonal strategies that will help make a discussion productive.
- The offices in which the analysts and lawyers work are likely to influence the kinds of questions or analytic strategies analysts and lawyers bring to an exploration of a topic.

Interpersonal Strategies

Throughout the discussion with the lawyer, the analyst used several interpersonal strategies that seemed well suited to draw out the lawyer, to find out what he knew and thought. Since she was attempting to understand a text that left her "in a complete fog," the analyst did not come to the discussion with a point of view that she felt obliged to defend. Moreover, there had been other occasions on which she had discussed other pieces of legislation with this lawyer, and she was confident of his knowledge and his willingness to be helpful to her. Thus she displayed interpersonal strategies that are useful for one type of discussion. In other circumstances (e.g., with someone who was less reliable, less knowledgeable, less disposed to be helpful, more disposed to be argumentative), she occasionally displayed somewhat different strategies. But in this conversation she seemed to be well served by the following:

- Paraphrasing or summarizing the lawyer's comments.
- Acknowledging her lack of knowledge or indicating an area in which she needed help.
- Avoiding arguments. At one point where disagreement arose, she did not attempt to defend her assertions against the lawyer's objections but, rather, indicated her willingness to check on the source of her information.
- Varying her role in the discussion. At times she allowed the lawyer to determine the direction of the discussion, but at other times she was very assertive about how the conversation would proceed and carefully tested the lawyer's assertions.

In describing these interpersonal strategies, I do not mean to suggest that the organizational context led the analyst to use these specific strategies. Other strategies might well be equally appropriate, and certainly these strategies might be equally useful in other organizational contexts. By emphasizing collaborative inquiry, however, this organization requires analysts to develop strategies for working effectively with others. In other words, the nature of the analysts' work often places them in situations where they must use these interpersonal strategies to complement the analytic strategies needed to explore the topic at hand.

Analytic Strategies

In the course of their discussion, both the analyst and the lawyer used readily identifiable analytic strategies—in effect, sets of questions that, with little or no modification, could be used in assessing almost any proposed legislation. These strategies reflected the differing perspectives of the offices represented by the analyst and the lawyer.

Perhaps predictably, since she was seeking information from the lawyer, the analyst asked a number of questions during the discussion:

- How does the bill relate to other texts? Is it consistent or inconsistent with, similar to or different from: comparable bills, position papers or statements of agency policy, federal guidelines, existing law?

- What distinctions are implicit or explicit in the bill?
- At what points does the lawyer's knowledge exceed her own?
- Are there disparities between what the law does and what it should or could do?
- Are there disparities between what the law might do and what she (or someone else) wishes it would do?
- What are the intended consequences of the bill? What will it require citizens to do? What will it require the agency or the state to do?
- What are possible unintended consequences of the bill? How might law enforcement officials react? How might interested citizens react?
- Are there any existing data on which one can base one's inferences about consequences? How reliable are these data?

In addition to answering the analyst's questions, the lawyer, explicitly or implicitly, considered the following:

- How does the bill relate to other proposed legislation on this topic?
- Are there problems with related bills? Are there important things they fail to do?
- What is not included in or not affected by the bill?
- What do I know that the analyst does not know and has not thought to ask about?
- How does this bill relate to present operating procedures?
- What is the rationale for the changes proposed by the bill?
- How did this bill get produced? What is its background? What is the intent of the author?

As suggested by these two lists of questions, the analyst and the lawyer tend to approach a topic with somewhat different analytic strategies. We find further differences when we see how the analyst and the lawyer use what might appear to be the same strategy—considering how a piece of legislation is located in a sequence of events. The analyst is concerned chiefly with the future, especially with long-range consequences that may have some unexpected impact on her agency. The lawyer, however, never initiates discussion of this sort of sequence. When he talks about the future, he considers only the immediate future, usually by describing scenarios of actions to be performed by a person who is arrested for violating the law established in the bill. When the lawyer initiates some discussion of sequence, he usually refers to past sequence—the events that led up to the drafting of a bill or the intent of the people who are sponsoring the legislation.

Both the analyst and the lawyer are simply reflecting the concerns of their respective offices and the experiences they have had in those offices. The lawyer was one of several people in his office who helped draft the bill under discussion. Consequently, he is most knowledgeable and concerned about how the bill was formulated and what reasoning and intentions guided those who drafted and sponsored it. The analyst, on the other hand, belongs to a group whose principal responsibility is to anticipate ways in which a new law or policy may affect the agency in which she works. From her experiences with previous analyses, she knows that her reading of the bill will not be complete until she understands what these consequences may be, and her writing will not be acceptable until she has explained these potential consequences.

Dynamics of the Inquiry Process

The foregoing lists of strategies only begin to suggest the complex ways in which the various strategies interact. Consequently, I want to look closely at several episodes from the conversation in order to show how analytic and interpersonal strategies interact with each other and lead to a thorough exploration of the subject at hand.

INTERACTION OF STRATEGIES. Near the outset of the conversation, the lawyer reads a passage from the bill under discussion.

Analyst: So there's a distinction here between [two groups of people who are affected by the bill].
Lawyer: Right. That's the difference between our bill and [another bill on the same issue]. Because underlying both bills [lawyer explains a provision of both bills].

This passage reflects an analytic strategy that the analyst uses very rarely in this conversation; she makes a distinction between groups of people who are affected by the bill. The passage also reflects one of the analyst's most frequently used interpersonal strategies. She paraphrases either the provisions of the bill or a statement the lawyer has made. Then she waits for him to say whether her interpretation is correct and gives him the opportunity to expand on what she has said. Frequently she writes notes about her paraphrase and inserts the lawyer's comments.

This brief exchange is particularly interesting because the interpersonal strategy of paraphrasing prompts the lawyer to elaborate on the analyst's paraphrase by using a new analytic strategy— contrasting the bill at hand with other, related bills. Further, the paraphrase-elaboration sequence provides closure on this specific topic. Both parties now know that the analyst understands what the lawyer has been saying and that it is appropriate to go on to a new topic. Consequently, when the lawyer finishes his explanation, the analyst begins a new line of inquiry:

> Analyst: You've told me already that the DAs [district attorneys] have said "go ahead." Do you think the DAs will do a number on it, or do you think that was implicit consent?

> Lawyer: They will support it fully. Because they know that if they don't, then we're going to go back to [an earlier bill to which the DAs objected]. It's not really extortion. It's just that if we can't get something both of us agree on, then we might as well hold to our original concept.

> Analyst: What about_____ [President of a citizens group that has taken a position on the topic addressed by the bill]? Does _____ support this?

> Lawyer: _____ is apparently not real happy about the commissioner's support of this.

> Analyst: _____ liked 36? [an earlier version of the present bill].

> Lawyer: From trying to sell this to the commissioner, [I believe that] he acknowledges the political realities and says, "This does a lot of what we want to do so let's get something rather than nothing."

> Analyst: What about the federal guidelines? Does this meet [pause] you know, the hearings that you went down to testify at?

> Lawyer: I don't really know. Somebody like _____ _____ would be in a better position to answer that. Because I don't know what's happened with the rule-making in those guidelines, anyway. I mean, they want a ninety-day hard suspension, and I don't know what a hard suspension means anyway.

> Analyst: They also want a jail sentence [. . .] what else do you think I
> need to know about [this bill]? Answer my questions before I ask
> them [laughs].
>
> Lawyer: The way I see it—and I'm not trying to do your job.
>
> Analyst: [interrupts] That's all right. Do my job.

Early in the preceding passage, the analyst considers the political context for the bill by trying to determine what future actions the bill is likely to prompt. How will governmental officials react to the bill? How will concerned citizens react? The lawyer, as he is likely to do, responds to the analyst's questions about the future by drawing on what he knows of the past: What events or actions preceded the writing of the bill? Further, the analyst uses another important strategy, one that both she and the lawyer use later in the discussion: How does this bill relate to other texts—in this case, federal guidelines? The episode concludes with the analyst using her interpersonal strategy of asking—only partly facetiously—for the lawyer's help.

CHANGING FROM PASSIVE TO ACTIVE ROLE. The analyst's comments "What else do you think I need to know . . . ?" and "Do my job" give the initial impression that the analyst is playing a rather passive role in the discussion. But this impression is misleading. The dialogue immediately following her remark "Do my job" shows that her remark signals the acceptability of a change in topic and allows the lawyer to introduce topics that the analyst lacked the information to raise herself. In other words, the paraphrase does more than signal understanding; it helps move the discussion ahead to new issues. Further, as soon as the lawyer begins explaining the new topics, the analyst assumes an obviously active role in the discussion. Having provided the lawyer an opportunity to introduce new information, the analyst uses this information as a basis for initiating a new series of questions ("Does this mean . . . ?") about the intended consequences of the bill. Here is the dialogue that immediately follows the request "Do my job."

> Lawyer: What the bill creates, above anything else, as far as the
> department is concerned, is one additional personal contact with [a
> particular law enforcement official]. [The lawyer goes on to explain
> procedures stipulated in the bill.]

Analyst: This does not mean that as soon as [a motorist] gets his suspension that he can enroll in [a rehabilitation program]?

Lawyer: What it does as far as driver improvement is concerned is [the bill] simply moves forward the point at which [officials] have to review the guy's eligibility.

Analyst: Does this mean they'll review the guy's eligibility at the time he requests?

Lawyer: [*Interrupts, corrects her interpretation.*]

Analyst: Okay, why? We're [the state agency the analyst works for] going to set up a whole new class of license?

Lawyer: [*Responds, explains procedure.*]

Analyst: So all they'd have to do is [*paraphrases previous statements*].

Lawyer: [*Explains.*]

A similar movement from passive to active participation appears later in the discussion. The analyst and the lawyer have begun discussing a bill that is closely related to the one she will have to write about.

Analyst: I don't understand this one, so I'll go and get my *V & T* [*Vehicle and Traffic Law*] and [*unintelligible*].

There is a moment of discussion based on the analyst's memory of a passage in the *V & T*. She then goes to get her copy of the *V & T*, returns, opens the text, and indicates a specific passage:

Analyst: Paragraph A, subdivision 2.

Lawyer: [*Reads passage aloud.*] Okay, first of all, this [the bill they are discussing] is another one that's drafted wrong. Because you've already got . . . all they're talking about is the time of revocation. They don't have to provide for a new revocation, because there's already a mandatory revocation in here for DWI [*reads*]. So what they *should* be doing here is amending 510(b) to say revocation is mandatory hereunder based upon a second conviction [*reads*].

Analyst: Read that slowly. "Should amend 510(b) to say . . . "

Lawyer: To say . . .

Analyst: Let's find 510(b) [*thumbs through V & T*].

> *Lawyer:* Now you've got all these provisions in 510(b); it says [reads] the general rule is that where revocation is mandatory, *they'll lose their license* for at least 6 months. Okay. What they [the authors of the bill] should be doing is amending 510(b) to say, "Where revocation is mandatory hereunder, based upon second conviction . . . No new license shall be issued for at least one year thereafter." Which is . . . part of our Bill 32 . . . [?]
>
> *Analyst:* Okay. Has 32 come over here?
>
> *Lawyer:* Uh-huh.

As in the passage beginning, "What else do you think I need to know?" the analyst begins the preceding passage by acknowledging the limitations of her own knowledge. As before, however, she quickly takes an active role in the discussion, directing the lawyer's attention to specific passages in the *V & T*. After reading the passages aloud, the lawyer goes on to note disparities between what the legislation should have done and what it actually did do.

EVALUATING DATA. Near the end of the conversation, the analyst indicates how she will proceed in analyzing the bill at hand. On the basis of that procedure, she raises a new question, one that focuses on the numbers of people who will be affected by the bill:

> *Analyst:* I assume that I'm going to spend the bulk of my time figuring out [this bill], contrasting it with [a competing] bill and then briefly talking [pauses] . . . The rest of [the analysis will be] numbers which will impact us. Do you have any numbers? You know what kind of numbers I'm talking about?
>
> *Lawyer:* Not at this point.
>
> *Analyst:* The number of arrests, convictions, which will in turn translate themselves into suspensions, which are impacts on the department.
>
> *Lawyer:* [*Borrows cigarette.*] You know I think we start from the same base [used for analyzing another related bill].
>
> *Analyst:* Nobody objected to the 70,000—or did they?
>
> *Lawyer:* Nobody but me.
>
> *Analyst:* Did you have better numbers?

Lawyer: No, I don't think they're better; I think they're more realistic. I don't think the 70 is real solidly premised on any solid facts we have.

Analyst: Yeah, _____ explained to me where the 70 came from . . . without taking down a lot of notes, there was a fudge factor built in for increased arrests, etcetera, etcetera. _____ _____ sent me some figures . . .

Lawyer: That's where I think the best figures come from, because I think those are the only hard figures we've got.

Analyst: His contention was that certain groups of motorists act differently than others. I don't know where we get the rest of the information. The only thing that held true on his figures were [unintelligible]. . . . That was the only thing I could say that someone accurately projected.

Lawyer: So, the way I look at it—we're probably getting away from the point, but you've gotta get to it eventually—we don't know [about _____'s data].

Analyst: He claimed that they did. I've gotta call him and find out what he's basing that on; I promised to get back to him with my reaction.

Lawyer: There's only two important sources of numbers. I think in a couple of months you can go down to Clarence and say, "What's our arrests? What's our conviction rate?"

Analyst: You don't think he's got it yet.

Lawyer: I don't think so.

The preceding passage is important partly because it shows one way the analyst goes about answering a basic question: How will the proposed legislation affect the agency I work for? To answer the question, she must consider other questions, implicitly or explicitly: Do numerical data exist that allow me to anticipate the extent to which this legislation might affect the agency? Has anyone noted weaknesses in these data? Does anyone have more reliable or well founded data? In short, this passage shows some of the strategies the analyst uses in trying to evaluate a set of data. Perhaps more important, it shows interpersonal strategies that allow the analyst and the lawyer to avoid arguing or placing each other on the defensive. These strategies permit a relatively dispassionate assessment of the data.

AVOIDING ARGUMENTS. One of the first interpersonal strategies is that displayed by the analyst when she shows herself willing to check on her own assumptions ("Nobody objected to the 70,000. Or did they?"). The lawyer tries to remove some of the sting from his objection to the analyst's statement, by making a distinction that may have more to do with courtesy than with reality: he declines to say that he has figures that are "better"; they are just "more realistic." A more substantive strategy comes from the analyst. Instead of trying to refute the lawyer's implied claim that the figure 70,000 is not realistic, she remembers a statement that appears to corroborate the lawyer's point of view; someone had told her that the figure 70,000 included a "fudge factor." Finally, rather than assert the correctness of the figure she has, she simply indicates her willingness to recheck her source of information.

It may be that circumstances forced these interpersonal strategies on the lawyer and the analyst. Neither had a solid basis for defending his or her conclusions about the validity of the data. Nonetheless, both of them—especially the analyst—behaved in such a way as to encourage new information. In this manner, the analyst increased her chances of obtaining information that would let her do an important part of her job—assessing the ways in which the legislation might affect her agency.

IMPLICATIONS

As noted earlier, the conclusions I have drawn from this study invite testing and refinement. Consequently, I shall suggest some of the questions that might direct research both in nonacademic settings and in classrooms. Encouraged by pedagogical theory (e.g., Moffett, 1968) and by research (e.g., Selzer, 1983; Heath, 1983) that suggests social interaction can be important for the processes of reading and writing, I shall also suggest ways in which the social interaction I have observed might inform the teaching of writing.

Research in Nonacademic Settings

In proposing questions for research in nonacademic settings, I shall be guided by the topics explored in this study: writers' justifications for choices, writers' perceptions of audience, and means by which writers carry out the process of inquiry.

JUSTIFICATIONS FOR CHOICES. In this study, I examined only the justifications writers gave for their decisions to include or exclude a certain type of content. In earlier studies, however, colleagues and I have examined writer's justifications for other types of choices—the various ways writers chose to address a reader, for example, or to express a command or request. In one of these studies, we found that different types of choices tended to elicit a preponderance of certain types of justifications (Odell & Goswami, 1982). In another study, we found that justifications for a given type of choice may vary widely according to a writer's position in an organization's hierarchy (Odell, Goswami, Herrington, & Quick, 1983).

Results of these two earlier studies suggest that we need to consider the following questions:

- Is awareness of organizational culture more important for some types of choices than for others?
- How is one's place in a hierarchy reflected in the justifications one gives for choices? If we were to interview people on various levels of a hierarchy, would we find that their justifications reflect more (or less) attention to culture? Would these writers have different perceptions of their culture?

PERCEPTIONS OF AUDIENCE. As was noted earlier, all the analysts had a very definite sense of questions their readers might ask. These questions, of course, provided the analysts with a good bit of guidance. But such guidance may be a mixed blessing. It suggests ways in which to proceed, but—since we can attend to only so many things at one time— it may also lead us to overlook other possibilities. In focusing our attention, we may also limit our investigation of a given subject. This limitation becomes important in light of Karl E. Weick's work on organizational communication (1979). Weick has pointed out "the important role that people play in creating the environments that surround them" (p. 5). Since both individuals and groups of people are continually selecting, modifying, and interpreting the phenomena around them, Weick claims that "organizations have a major hand in creating the realities which they view as 'facts' to which they must accommodate." Consequently, Weick asserts, "Limitations exist because they have not been tested" (p. 150).

If one agrees that a sense of audience limits as well as guides a writer's efforts, Weick's arguments raise several kinds of questions:

- How were these limits conveyed to the analysts who took part in this study? How are these limits reinforced? By whom? More generally, how does any organization help writers understand how they must conceive of the audience(s) for whom they write? What are the formal means of instruction? What are the informal means?

- What would happen if a writer were to test those limits? Who would notice? What form(s) would their response take? How would writers assess this response?

- How valid are these limits? Are they consistent with what members of the intended audience actually do when they receive a piece of writing? Does the intended audience actually read the document? If the intended audience actually does read the document, are there passages that they either skip entirely or dwell on at length? How does a reader decide to pay little attention to some passages and examine others carefully? Would an understanding of those decisions change writers' perception of their audience?

THE PROCESS OF INQUIRY. To explore this process, I have examined ways in which an organization's culture influences discussion between two members of that organization. In some respects, this discussion is very typical. For almost every writing assignment, analysts are expected to formulate their ideas by talking with people from other offices in their organization. In several respects, however, the discussion may be slightly atypical. First, this was a dialogue rather than a group discussion. The analyst had to elicit and evaluate information from only one source, not several. Further, the analyst was talking with a well-informed, trusted colleague, someone she knew was able and willing to help her accomplish her goal of analyzing a piece of legislation. Intuition and casual observation suggest that other discussions may require the analyst to use somewhat different interpersonal and analytic strategies. Finally, the discussion reflects the strategies of only one analyst and one lawyer. Even if we assume that other analysts might have to consider the same questions that this analyst raised, we do not know whether they would display the same interpersonal strategies.

The apparently unique qualities of the dialogue between analyst and lawyer give rise to several questions:

- What types of interpersonal and intellectual strategies does the analyst (or, indeed, any writer) use in discussions where people are, say, less well informed or less disposed to be helpful? In other words, what repertoire of strategies does one need in order to function effectively within the culture of this agency? How does that repertoire differ from what other cultures require?
- What interpersonal strategies do other analysts use? Do these strategies reflect such personal characteristics as gender, attitude, or job experience?

So far, my observations and questions have pertained only to what happens during a discussion. Yet surely this is just a starting point, especially if the discussion is confusing or inconclusive. For example, the analyst who met with the lawyer to discuss a piece of legislation also discussed this legislation with administrators in another branch of the agency in which she worked. Back at her desk after this discussion, the analyst said she was going to "think about" what she had learned at the meeting. I asked her to think out loud and to allow me to observe the process she went through in assessing the discussion.

She began by trying to resolve the disagreement about how the bill related to existing law.

> The first thing I have to do is figure out what we disagreed about. Since the conversation was fast and furious, it left me in the dust. It has to do with two sections of the bill which I think are somewhat linked, and [administrators] disagreed. [Looks back at notes.] So what [the administrators] were saying was that [summarizes, paraphrases their comments], Okay, the intent of the law [states intent]. And they're saying . . . I'm not sure what they're saying.

Up to this point, the analyst is relying on her ability to paraphrase, an ability she used frequently in her dialogue with the lawyer. In this instance, however, paraphrase is used for a new purpose. Instead of paraphrasing to make sure she understands the lawyer's comments, she is paraphrasing two sources of information (the law and the administrators' comments) in order to see where the two disagree.

The analyst continues paraphrasing for a few minutes and then concludes:

Now this is where [administrators] and I disagree [reads law]. If I draw myself a little chart, this will come clear. [Writes out summary of one section of law; then, in another column, writes out summary of other sections of the law. Looks back and forth between the two summaries.] Oh, oh. I see what he's talking about. We're both right. I think. I've gotta ask [the lawyer]. I think what this means is that [paraphrases bill]. However, I think that the administrators are ignoring [a provision of the bill].

In this passage, the analyst's paraphrase serves yet another purpose—that of answering the following questions: How are different sections of the law related to each other? Are there passages in the law that justify what the administrators are saying? In other words, could it be that "We're both right"? Are the administrators ignoring some provision of the law or an important relation between two sections of the law?

Having considered these questions and, thereby, formed her own conclusion about the validity of the administrators' reasoning, the analyst decides to check on her conclusion.

I think I'll have to talk to [the lawyer who took part in the dialogue cited earlier]. I may call [administrator] back and see if that's what they're actually telling me. . . . That's all I can come up with right now. Probably I should show them my chart. [Summarizes law.]

This brief analysis makes it clear that (1) not all discussions are immediately helpful to the process of inquiry, and (2) in assessing such discussions, an analyst may need to consider questions that may or may not have come up in the discussion. Consequently, we need to ask:

- How does one assess, interpret, make use of discussions that might not immediately seem clear or helpful? What strategies are important for this process?

Classroom Research

In the preceding section, it was easy to talk at some length about implications for research in nonacademic settings. Since this is a relatively new area for research, it is easier to think of new questions than it is to arrive at definitive conclusions. Consequently, I want to be cautious in suggesting implications for the classroom. Certainly there is no basis for suggesting that all the findings of this study should influence our teaching. Indeed, one of the main implications of this study is not that we should adopt certain teaching procedures but, rather, that we need to begin doing research with our own students.

Although there is much we do not yet understand about the relation between writers and their culture, there is reason to believe that organizational culture can be very important for both readers and writers. If we accept this belief and if we further assume that a school (elementary, secondary, or postsecondary) may have an organizational culture, we are faced with this sort of question:

- What aspects of our school's culture are important for students in our classes? What are the shared beliefs or patterns of behavior that influence an individual student's writing and reading? In other words, what is going on out there in our schools and classrooms, and how does it relate to what our students do when they read and write?

Stated thus, the question is probably unanswerable. If we subdivide the question, however, it becomes a little less intimidating. Thus we might follow Stephen Witte and Lester Faigley's suggestion (1983) and examine the institutional context in which our classes exist:

- What institutional policies and goals might bear upon what we do or ask our students to do?
- Are the stated goals and policies actually consistent with the way the school is run?

Or, to take a slightly different approach, we might ask:

- Is there a dominant ethos for the students at our school?

At the school where I teach, for example, over 75 percent of the undergraduates are majoring in engineering or computer science. As a group these students are extremely bright, hard-working, ambitious, and competitive. Further, my impression is that they prefer to deal with well-defined problems, especially quantitative problems, that can be solved by the use of algorithms. Consequently, these students seem a little dubious about courses in writing. This may be due in part to the fact that these courses raise questions for which there are no "right" answers. Also, these courses may not seem to bear any relation to the student's conception of what an engineer is or does.

This speculation about causes is probably premature. After all, I have only impressions of an ethos the undergraduates seem to share. The first set of questions is:

- Are these impressions justified?
- Do students at my school or in my classroom really share the characteristics and attitudes I attribute to them?

If the answer to these questions is yes, we also need to ask:

- How does this ethos influence the processes they engage in as readers and writers?
- How does it influence their perceptions of the work I ask them to do in my undergraduate writing classes?

Even if there is no schoolwide ethos, we need to know more about the culture in which our students exist.

- Are there any widely held beliefs about the multisection courses our departments offer? What is the reputation of the specific sections we teach? How is that reputation reflected in the work students do for our courses? Do students in our classes share any common perceptions of or attitudes toward the work we ask them to do for our courses?
- Do students make use of any social resources when they do our assignments? That is, are there people (classmates or students in other courses) with whom they discuss topics they are reading or writing about? Are there people whose critical opinion they especially trust (or distrust)? Are any of these people particularly influential? What analytic and interpersonal strategies do students display when they talk with these people?

Classroom Teaching

Perhaps the clearest implications for teaching appear in the discussion of the analyst's process of inquiry. Here the analyst's strategies most closely parallel two teaching practices already used by many composition teachers: (1) the practice of teaching students sets of questions that can guide their exploration of a topic and (2) the practice of asking student writers to engage in discussion and work collaboratively with their classmates. The analyst's work may reinforce our commitment to these practices. What we learn from this analyst, however, may modify our teaching in several ways.

For one thing, the analyst's performance suggests that we may need to change the kinds of analytic procedures we teach students to use. Usually we try to teach procedures that are simple yet also widely applicable. Thus we are likely to select a procedure such as Burke's Pentad (see Irmscher, 1981) or elements of the tagmemic analytic procedure (see Young, Becker, & Pike, 1970). Our hope, understandably, is that the procedure will suggest a relatively limited number of cognitive operations that will be useful in exploring any sort of subject matter. Writing is a complex process, and we do not want to complicate it further. Further, it is probably true that we can describe conscious intellectual activity with a relatively brief list of terms. It may be, however, that in trying to reduce cognitive complexity we unwittingly increase it.

Almost inevitably, a simple yet widely applicable analytic procedure will have to be stated in relatively general terms. Thus it is not enough for a writer to know the terms of the analytic procedure; the writer must also be able to translate those terms into specific strategies or questions that will enable him or her to investigate a particular subject matter. Furthermore, the way one applies an analytic procedure may vary widely, reflecting not only the subject at hand, but also the organizational culture in which the writer must work. For example, both the analyst and the lawyer made reference to *sequence*, one of the *topoi* of classical rhetoric and an element of Burke's Pentad and of tagmemic theory. But the specific application of this *topic* differed greatly. The lawyer's conception of sequence (the short-term consequences of a proposed law; the law's immediate effect on an offender) was not adequate for the analyst's purposes. She had to be concerned with the law's long-term implications for her agency. In order to function effectively in their respective jobs, it would not be enough for either the analyst or the lawyer simply to consider *sequence*; each of them must know a specific application of that topic. By understanding this application, they reduce some of the cognitive complexity they encounter when they read and write.

That complexity is reduced further because neither lawyer nor analyst tries to use all the elements of any analytic procedure; instead, they use only those elements that are specifically appropriate to the task at hand. For instance, both analyst and lawyer consider a topic that is easily recognized as part of Burke's Pentad; both consider who will be *affected* by the legislation they are discussing. And both analyst and lawyer consider elements of the tagmemic model: *sequence, classification,* and *contrast.* But they do not refer to *change* or *physical context.* In other words, each person has an eclectic procedure that is useful for the task at hand.

The thought of using such an eclectic procedure may be troubling. After all, by limiting our use of an analytic procedure, we increase the chances of limiting unduly our investigation of the topic at hand. But some limitation, some focus is necessary. Not all questions are equally useful for exploring all subject matters. Different academic disciplines—even different topics within a discipline—may make somewhat different intellectual demands on a writer (see Maimon et al., 1981; Odell, 1980) Consequently, I want to propose this implication for teaching:

- Instead of teaching students a generalized analytic procedure, we need to help them understand the specific questions that can help them explore the topics they must write about.

In addition to suggesting a change in the way we teach analytic procedures, the analyst's discussion with the lawyer seems to have some bearing on the way we use discussion in our classes. For one thing, the success of the analyst-lawyer dialogue seems to stem from the analyst's interpersonal strategies. She understood how to conduct herself so as to make the discussion profitable. Students need to have the same sort of understanding. They need to acquire the interpersonal strategies that will be important for eliciting information and formulating ideas. Moreover, students could benefit from discussion throughout the composing process. For the analyst, discussions with the lawyer (and, indeed, discussions of other topics with other groups) were not restricted to an analysis of a written draft. These discussions helped at the earliest moments in the composing process, when she was just beginning to sort out her ideas on the topic she had to write about. Students also can learn to benefit from this sort of help. They can and, I think, should learn how to benefit from others' help while in the process of formulating ideas. This observation leads to the following suggestion:

- We need to help students make the process of inquiry a social process, one that begins well before students have written a draft.

However, the ability to engage in a social process presupposes certain skills, which students may either lack or fail to use in what most of them will probably think of as a novel situation. Thus it seems likely that:

- We need to give students frequent opportunities to practice the interpersonal skills that will enable them to function effectively in a dialogue or in a group discussion. It will not be enough to ask students to work in groups; we will have to make sure that they know how to do so effectively.

WHAT IS AND WHAT OUGHT TO BE

These last suggestions indicate that as we come to understand how organizational context influences writing, we might also see how to modify our teaching. But these suggestions also invite caution. To reiterate a point from the "Introduction" to this book, we must be careful not to confuse *what is* with *what ought to be*. Indeed, we must be careful with our assertions about *what is*. We have scarcely begun to understand how organizational context relates to writing, and we have almost no information about which aspects of that relationship are helpful to writers and which are harmful. Thus we must test each new finding in this area, trying to reconcile it with our best intuitions as classroom teachers and with our best theory about how and why people write and about what it means to be a mature, effective writer. As a result of this testing we will improve our understanding of both what is and what ought to be. Perhaps we will also reduce the disparity between the two. Surely we will improve our teaching and our conception of our discipline.

References

Bartholomae, D. (1985). Inventing the university. In M. Rose (Ed.), *When a writer can't write: Studies in writer's block and other composing process problems* (pp.134–165). New York: Guilford Press.

Bazerman, C. (1983). Scientific writing as a social act. In P. Anderson, R. Brockman, & C. Miller (Eds.), *New essays in scientific and technical writing* (pp. 156–184). Farmingdale, NY: Baywood.

Bizzell, P. (1982). Cognition, convention, and certainty: What we need to know about writing. *Pre/Text, 3*, 213–243.

Bruffee, K. (1983). Writing and reading as collaborative or social acts. In J. Hays, P. Roth, J. Ramsey, & R. Foulke (Eds.), *The writer's mind: Writing as a mode of thinking* (pp. 159–169). Urbana, IL: National Council of Teachers of English.

Bruffee, K. (1984). Collaborative learning and the "conversation of mankind." *College English, 46*, 635–652.

Clark, C. M., & Florio, S., with J. Elmore, J. Martin, and R. Maxwell (1983). Understanding writing instruction. In P. Mosenthal, L. Tamor, & S. Walmsley (Eds.), *Research on writing*. New York: Longman.

Crowhurst, M., & Piche, G. L. (1979). Audience and mode of discourse effects on syntactic complexity in writing at two grade levels. *Research in the Teaching of English, 13*, 101–110.

Deal, T., & Kennedy, A. (1982). *Corporate cultures: The rites & rituals of corporate life.* Menlo Park, CA: Addison-Wesley.

Faigley, L., & Miller, T. (1982). What we learn from writing on the job. *College English, 44*, 557–569.

Flower, L., & Hayes, J. R. (1980). The cognition of discovery: Defining a rhetorical problem. *College Composition and Communication, 31*, 21–32.

Heath, S. B. (1983). *Ways with words.* Cambridge: Cambridge University Press.

Herrington, A. J. (forthcoming). Writing in academic settings: A study of the context for writing in two-college chemical engineering courses. *Research in the Teaching of English.*

Irmscher, W. (1981). *Holt guide to English: A comprehensive handbook of rhetoric, language, & literature* (3rd ed.). New York: Holt, Rinehart & Winston.

Kantor, K. J. (1983). Classroom context and the development of writing intuitions: An ethnographic case study. In R. Beach & L. S. Bridwell (Eds.), *New directions in composition research*. New York: Guilford Press.

Lloyd-Jones, R. (1977). Primary trait scoring. In C. R. Cooper & L. Odell (Eds.), *Evaluating writing: Describing, measuring, judging.* Urbana, IL: National Council of Teachers of English.

Maimon, E. et al. (1981). *Writing in the arts and sciences.* Cambridge, MA: Winthrop Publishers.

Matsuhashi, A. (1981). Pausing and planning: The tempo of written discourse. *Research in the Teaching of English, 15*, 113–134.

Moffett, J. (1968). *Teaching the universe of discourse.* Boston: Houghton Mifflin.

Odell, L. (1980). The process of writing and the process of learning. *College Composition and Communication, 31*, 42–50.

Odell, L. (1981). Defining and assessing competence in writing. In C. R. Cooper (Ed.), *The nature and measurement of competency in English.* Urbana, IL: National Council of Teachers of English.

Odell, L., & Goswami, D. (1982). Writing in a non-academic setting. *Research in the Teaching of English, 16,* 201–223.

Odell, L., Goswami, D., & Herrington, A. (1983). The discourse-based interview: A procedure for exploring the tacit knowledge of writers in non-academic settings. In P. Mosenthal, L. Tamor, & S. Walmsley (Eds.), *Research on writing.* New York: Longman.

Odell, L., Goswami, D., Herrington, A., & Quick, D. (1983). Studying writing in non-academic settings. In P. V. Anderson, R. J. Brockman, & C. R. Miller (Eds.), *New essays in technical and scientific communications: Research, theory, and practice.* Farmingdale, NY: Baywood.

Rubin, D., & Piche, G. L. (1979). Development of syntactic and strategic aspects of audience adaptation skills in written persuasive communication. *Research in the Teaching of English, 13,* 293–316.

Selzer, J. (1983). The composing processes of an engineer. *College Composition and Communication, 34,* 178–187.

Weick, K. (1979). *The social psychology of organizing* (2nd ed.). Reading, MA: Addison-Wesley.

Witte, S., & Faigley, L. (1983). *Evaluating college writing programs.* Carbondale and Edwardsville: Southern Illinois University Press.

Young, R., Becker, A., & Pike, K. (1970). *Rhetoric: Discovery and change.* New York: Harcourt, Brace & World.

Writing at Exxon ITD   8
Notes on the
Writing Environment of an
R&D Organization

JAMES PARADIS
DAVID DOBRIN
Massachusetts Institute of Technology

RICHARD MILLER
Exxon Chemicals Corporation, Houston

Written communication takes up a considerable part of the industrial employee's time and thus represents a major financial investment for many research organizations (see Davis, 1978; Olsen & Huckin, 1983; Faigley & Miller, 1982). Yet in-house writing and editing remain hidden activities in industry: as the saying goes, they just get done. We rarely ask what motivates research and development (R&D) employees to write and edit their internal work documents or how the industrial environment influences the way in which employees carry out these processes.

One consequence of this neglect is that, on the whole, the functions of in-house writing are not understood. Writing is commonly viewed as a pragmatic routine of transferring and archiving information—the afterthought of serious research activity (see Latour & Woolgar, 1979; for a discussion of information theory and communication, see Dobrin, 1982). Managers and supervisors often do not appreciate that editing documents provides them an important means of managing the work of employees—defining tasks, assigning them, and calling them in—as well as shaping work results to fit established company objectives. Staff engineers and scientists often do not appreciate that their writing is part of a larger social process by which they create and maintain significant professional relationships with colleagues (for a review of the literature on this subject, see Bazerman, 1982). In short, many R&D employees have trouble seeing how the writing-editing cycle they repeat so frequently can deeply influence the inner workings and success of their organizations.

In an effort to examine how individuals interact to produce work-related documents in an R&D environment, we spent a week observing the writing activities of 33 engineers and scientists at the Exxon Chemicals Company in Baton Rouge, Louisiana. These professionals made up most of the staff and management of the Intermediates Technology Division (ITD), an R&D division conducting process and product research for the larger organization. The individuals in this group were quite diverse. They had been educated at Emory, Texas A&M, Massachusetts Institute of Technology, Rensselaer Polytechnic, the University of Virginia, Louisiana State University, to name only a few; their degrees ranged from BS to PhD; and their fields were in the sciences and applied sciences, as well as in management. In professional experience, one-third of the group fell in each of the following categories: <4 years, 4–12 years, >12 years. Hence, small as it was, the group represented a good mix of educational and experiential backgrounds.

The main concern of the ITD R&D division was the production of phthalate esters, which are widely used as plasticizers in the polyvinyl chloride (PVC) industry. Manufactured at the large Baton Rouge plant, phthalate esters are used in PVC product manufacturing to control a range of characteristics, chiefly flexibility, that make PVCs conform to various processing and performance requirements. The ITD group carried out process R&D, gave nonroutine technical support to the local manufacturing operation, provided marketing support for technical products, and developed new products and applications. Much, but not all, of their work was proprietary.

Briefly, we took the following approach. Before our week of interviews began, we administered a questionnaire and writing test to 33 professionals. During our week-long visit, we interviewed 26 people, talked to several small working groups, observed work patterns, inspected documents, and met several times with supervisors and managers. We pursued two lines of inquiry:

- What roles do writing and its associated activities play in the life of an R&D organization?
- How do individuals interact in an industrial environment to produce internal documents?

By asking these broad questions, we sought to examine what kind of writing environment the R&D organization provided writers and editors.[1] In what follows, we describe some of our findings and suggest some of the possibilities for future research.

WRITING AND JOB RESPONSIBILITY

Employee estimates of the time they spent writing at ITD were substantial at all levels of the organization, averaging between one-third and one-half of a given individual's job-related time. Our personal interviews with staff, supervisors, and managers confirmed the questionnaire estimates shown in figure 8-1. On our questionnaire, we broke writing activities down into three categories: (1) writing and editing one's own documents, (2) editing and reviewing the internal documents of others, and (3) preparing oral presentations. Hence, the estimates of figure 8-1 do not include the informal oral communication that occurs in offices and hallways and on telephones. Nor do they include general reading of documents from outside the local group. The values of figure 8-1 are based on individuals' perceptions of the time they spend on writing-related activities. On the basis of these crude estimates, we calculated that our 33 respondents were spending about 22,270 hours annually on writing and allied activities—or about 13.5 hours each per work week. Some of this time, as we will note, was spent before or after official working hours.

Different kinds of ITD writing activities were associated with different levels of organizational responsibility. Although nearly everyone at ITD felt he or she spent much job-related time on writing, the amount and kind of writing varied markedly as one moved from the basic staff level, to the intermediate supervisory level, to the upper managerial level. As ITD employees moved up this organizational ladder, they gave steadily smaller proportions of their job-related time to composing their own documents and ever more time to

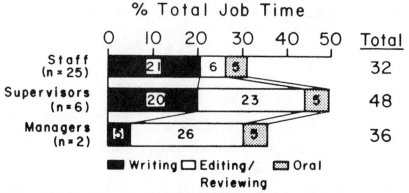

Figure 8-1   *Percentage of Job-Related Time Spent at ITD on Writing and Allied Activities*

editing and reviewing the documents of other employees. These shifting patterns, shown in figure 8-2, were further substantiated in our follow-up interviews with staff, supervisors, and managers.

To the ITD staff engineers and scientists, documents were instruments for initiating projects, reporting on their progress, and bringing them to a conclusion. Documents thus promoted the fundamental progression of industrial R&D work, in proposals, progress reports, and final research reports. Collectively, these three kinds of documents accounted for about half the time employees devoted to writing-related activities (see table 8-1 later in the chapter). Although staff members were the composers of most of these basic (or *stem*) documents, supervisors and managers usually assigned the documents or gave subordinates the go-ahead to prepare them. Staff members' writing-related time was given mainly to composing documents, but about one-fifth of their time was spent reviewing the documents of fellow staff members. This informal reviewing helped colleagues obtain technical accuracy, proper coverage, and sharper ideas.

Supervisors—middle-management—had by far the most diverse job responsibilities and the most complex writing loads. As figure 8-1 shows, they spent, on the average, half their job-related time just writing and editing documents. As did staff members, they conducted their own project research and wrote all the accompanying stem documents. As did managers, they directed the work of subordinates and wrote administrative memoranda both to them and to higher

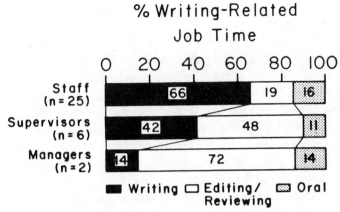

Figure 8-2 *Percentage of Breakdown of ITD Employee Time Spent on Writing and Allied Activities*

management. Supervisors were responsible for assigning most staff writing and for making sure that it got done. In addition, they were the main agents of document *cycling*, the editorial process by which they helped staff members restructure, focus, and clarify their written work. Nearly half the supervisors' writing-related job activities were devoted to this editorial procedure (see figure 8-2). Unlike the reviewing that staff members did for one another, the supervisors' cycling review was often obligatory, somewhat formal, and quite rigorous. Document cycling provided supervisors a powerful means of carrying out their job responsibilities of adapting the work of subordinates to an environment of needs and priorities created by the ITD and broader Exxon management.

ITD managers, of whom we interviewed only two, spent only about 5 percent of their job-related time writing and editing their own documents. Their writing was largely devoted to preparing administrative memoranda—informing subordinates of policies and decisions and reporting to upper management on ITD process toward Exxon R&D objectives. Three-quarters of the managers' writing-related time, as shown in figure 8-2, was given to the editorial-review process. Unlike supervisors, however, managers did not engage in the cycling process of close editing. Rather, managers reviewed finished internal documents mainly to gather information and to monitor progress toward large objectives set by top management. In other words, they oversaw the production of documents in the broadest terms of setting work objectives and deadlines, but they rarely got involved in the composition-editing process itself. Both managers we interviewed relied more heavily than did other ITD employees on meetings and informal oral communication. These two forms seemed more suited to their responsibilities of interacting with many individuals at different levels of the corporation.

The ITD hierarchy found that the language of writing tasks provided useful metaphors for focusing and directing labor, which often could conveniently be construed as *composing, editing,* and *reviewing* activities. Hence, writing activities provided effective means of dividing job responsibilities among the individuals at different levels of the organization. This approach to dividing tasks was not always followed; some experienced staff engineers and scientists actually wrote, edited, and distributed their own documents. But the patterns of figure 8-1 were clearly the norm. It was the staff engineer's job to produce high-quality data; it was his or her supervisor's job to show how the group's activity was part of a coherent program; and it was the manager's job to make sure that this cycle of knowledge production was meeting corporate needs and making the best use of available resources. Many of these goals, we found, were most aptly discussed as problems of document production.[2]

WRITING AND PRODUCTIVITY

Given the scale and importance of writing activities at ITD, we were surprised that writing was neither commonly discussed as a technique nor widely recognized as a key work activity. In interviews, many individuals, uncertain about the legitimacy of writing as a work activity, felt uneasy about the amount of time they spent writing.

Writing is not, by nature, a highly visible activity. Whether composing, editing, or reviewing, the individual needs solitude in order to do an effective job. On the questionnaire, nearly three-quarters of the respondents (24 of 33) indicated that they preferred to write at work, in total isolation. From our interviews and observations, we concluded that writing and its related activities were most successfully carried out at work behind closed or partly closed doors during the quiet hours of early morning and late afternoon. Hence, the writing process itself would not be the subject of common observation and easy group discussion; writing technique was difficult for most individuals to discuss, even in private interviews.

Much employee ambivalence about the techniques and functions of writing in the R&D environment was the result of so little consensus in the organization about the goals, standards, and processes of writing. This lack of consensus about writing made it very difficult for people to discuss—let alone agree on—the objectives of the document-cycling process referred to earlier. Certainly, university training had not established for this group much of a shared idea of the minimal requirements for clear, effective documents. Although most of the respondents (80 percent) had completed college courses in writing or writing-intensive subjects, many felt that their training had not stayed with them or that it had only limited application in the R&D environment. (Only 4 individuals had taken courses in technical communication.) When asked what training and experiences were most useful in teaching them how to write, employees most commonly cited on-the-job experience (49 percent), followed by company courses (18 percent) and university courses (15 percent). Clearly, the work environment is an effective training ground for R&D writing. The most common complaints about college training in writing were that there was not enough of it, that it rarely dealt with real situations and requirements of writing on the job, and that it stressed the finer points of stylistics at the expense of the techniques of organizing material and revising drafts. We did not systematically probe these complaints.

Additional ambivalence among ITD employees about writing arose in the means-ends controversy. Many individuals held the view that documents were not ends, but merely means to ends. Those ends were engineering tasks: a project go-ahead, a new process, a set of data, a policy implementation, and so on. This view tended to deflect the writer's attention from the document to its goals, obscuring issues of document structure and style and writing methodology. It also tended to obscure the fact that at ITD, as in any R&D organization, documents can *themselves* be information products. Whether the R&D worker encodes information in a physical object (hardware) or in a verbal artifact (software), both are the constructs of human physical and intellectual labor.[3] Both require time, and thus dollars, to complete, and both get listed as company objectives. For example, one ITD supervisor, in a memorandum to his staff and manager, listed 11 out of 22 of his November 1982 objectives as documents that had to be produced—final reports, feasibility studies, cost estimates, and the like.

Although employees had trouble coming to terms with the idea that writing is a form of labor and that documents are legitimate R&D products, this idea, quite unexpectedly, played an important role in the employee review process. The ITD employee review process was structured around the "Appraisal Review Form," a company-confidential form that listed 22 criteria for employee job performance. People we interviewed spoke of the form with considerable respect. To writing specialists, like ourselves, the connection between job performance and communication skills implicit in this form was striking. Of 22 major categories on the form, only one, labeled *communications abilities*, was explicitly identified with an individual's ability to write. Yet, communications abilities had much more weight than 1/22 of the total, because supervisors rated employees for other categories by referring to employees' documents. For example, categories such as *quality of work, quantity of work,* and *analytical ability* could often be judged accurately, managers and supervisors told us, only by reviewing the employee's document file. Documents formalized elements of the individual's work record—its character, sequence, and volume as well as its quality. Document analysis thus provided management an important technique for assessing employee job performance. In the questionnaire responses, more than half the respondents—and *all* the managers and supervisors—could cite situations in which a person's writing influenced seriously his or her chances for promotion.[4]

WRITING AS INFORMATION TRANSFER

ITD employees, like many R&D workers, viewed writing almost exclusively as a means of transferring and archiving information. The industrial organization depends for its problem solving on the knowledge and experience of its professional staff; hence it also depends on the ability of that staff to pass along its expertise to others. Expertise can be passed on by word of mouth, a process in the R&D environment that has been studied by Allen (1977). Expertise can also be passed along in writing, a mode that is widely accepted in industry. For example, Shuchman, in her national survey of engineers, found that most engineers disseminate their information as "internal reports" (1981, p. 19). Written communication, she noted, is one of the more important resources for local problem solvers.

Although oral communication might seem the more immediate and convenient method of passing along information and ideas, written communication offers many advantages. A document is, first of all, permanent and serves as a memory. Written messages can be retrieved at will in their exact original form; hence written forms are required when an accountability for precise detail is critical. For the details of a contractual agreement or a rocket housing or polymer design, it would be futile to depend on word of mouth. In addition, documents, unlike spoken words, are *objects*. Their physical quality enables the author to work over and reconstruct the detail until an effective scope and level of complexity are achieved. In effect, documents free their authors from the message. This decoupling not only makes ideas into moldable objects that can be built up and refined, but it also makes co-authorship and other forms of collaboration, including document cycling, possible. Readers can also study a message in its physical form. Hence, writing can accommodate more comprehensive and complex messages than can oral communication (see also Joos, 1967, pp. 41–43). Finally, the fact that documents are portable means that individuals can do work (i.e., construct and review documents) out of the immediate R&D environment. At ITD, nearly everyone extended his or her work time in this manner (see figure 8-3).

Because of its special characteristics, written communication played several key roles in the internal operation of ITD. The informational functions of internal documents conformed to the work responsibilities of staff, supervisors, and managers. For example, staff members tended to spend most of their writing time on *stem* documents, which correlated with the primary phases of the research cycle—proposing, tracking, and summarizing research. As noted in table 8-1, this kind of writing accounted for nearly half the ITD employee writing time. Supervisors and managers, on the other hand, wrote most of the miscellaneous memoranda (which would include correspondence). These documents had mainly administrative functions. As can be seen in table 8-1, very few individuals wrote refereed articles and symposium papers. This had less to do with lack of publishable material or individual ability than with the proprietary nature of most ITD research and the fact that job performance is not linked, as it is in the university, to publication in

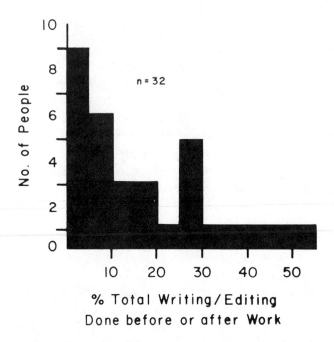

Figure 8-3 *Writing-Related Work Accomplished Outside Regular ITD Working Hours*

the refereed literature. Industrial R&D groups are very different from academic research units in this respect.

Technical Analysis

Since technical analysis was one of the most tangible and important results of their work activities—a primary product, so to speak—ITD staff members considered it one of their best ways of making a contribution to the community. Preparing an analytical report was often a critical step in solving a problem. An analysis in a document enabled an employee to respond to a question posed at some other organizational level—a customer query, for instance. Written analysis often required the employee to decide what the problem was; to develop approaches to a solution; to generate and evaluate information; and, finally, to suggest solutions. Hence, the writing process was a problem-solving process.[5] Analytical reports at

Table 8-1.

Percentages, as Estimated by ITD Employees, of Writing Time Given to Certain Kinds of Documents

Kind of document	Percent writing time[a]	Perceived importance[b]
Stem Documents		
Internal proposals	10	2
Progress reports	22	2
Final research reports	17	3
Process and Design Guidelines		
Design reports	4	4
Patent applications	2	4
Specifications	3	4
Operating process instructions	4	4
Test procedures	4	4
Administrative Documents		
Miscellaneous memoranda	19	3
Trip reports	4	4
External Documents		
External proposals	6	3
Consulting reports	2	5
Refereed articles	0	5
Papers at symposia	1	5

[a]Percentages are averaged.
[b]1 = extremely important; 5 = not important.

ITD studied the mechanics of materials production; chemical reaction rates under given conditions; the effect of structure A on process B; data from experimental production units; and the mechanics and finances of catalysts. These documents were critical instruments of analysis, because they revealed the objective elements of complex situations so that they could be independently evaluated. Documents showed the structure of problem solving and thus opened up decisions to the review process and to collective judgment.

Process and Design Guidelines

A great variety of short, miscellaneous documents, many of them 1–4 pages long, provided design and procedural information both to staff and to management. In the questionnaire, these documents did not rate very high in average time commitment or perceived importance to their authors' job responsibilities. Yet, collectively, they amounted to around 17 percent of ITD employee writing time (see table 8-1). They included design reports, patent applications, specifications, operating or process instructions, and test procedures. Many of these documents played key roles in the ITD operation because they embodied the design information on which the industrial processes themselves depended. A written analog existed for every piece of plant apparatus and every industrial process at ITD. This crucial standardizing role of documents was integral to the ITD operation, which could not otherwise have proceeded. Indeed, all industries are built upon such documents.

Administrative Information

A third class of informational documents concerned the administrative operation of the R&D group. Largely written by supervisors and managers, these nontechnical documents treated the gamut of operations from political etiquette to research goal-setting. Documents with titles such as "Ground Rules: Responding to Questions from Upper Management" and "November Objectives of the BN Program" set policies and procedures and provided basic administrative information to members of ITD. Using documents rather than word of mouth freed up the manager's time and also reduced possible misunderstandings that might result from inconsistent reporting or from staff or management forgetfulness. In an operation as complex as that of ITD, such written measures, when properly used, save time and, therefore, translate directly into cost savings.

WRITING AS A SOCIAL ACTIVITY

Professionals in R&D groups need a steady flow of new information to meet their own work objectives. Because industrial R&D writing is such an obvious means of passing ideas and data on to others, internal documents are often seen solely as vehicles for *transferring messages*. Yet, quite apart from their informational uses, ITD documents, we found, had enormous impact on the personal status of employees and on the growth and maintenance of group relationships. The content of any document has a context—that is, a specific audience and informational objective—but the *activity* of writing the document also has a context. In industry, the R&D writer must interact with many other individuals and take into account a complex organizational *environment*. Very little is known about writing as a group or organizational behavior.[6]

At ITD, the personal or social functions of writing were virtually unrecognized. Yet personal interviews made it clear that individuals often wrote for reasons that had nothing whatever to do with passing along technical information. Several individuals told us, for example, that their writing forced them to stay abreast of other developments, in order to coordinate their work with that of other employees. Conversely, the writing in any given week constituted an important updating process by which work completed was now made available to the community. Hence, the activity of writing demanded that its practitioners develop a kind of social consciousness of the organizational environment. In addition, writing made individuals take the measure of their own fit in the R&D organization, because it made them evaluate their work, their attitudes, and their relationships with colleagues. One's documents also kept one's profile up among colleagues, giving writers the opportunity to show their accomplishments to their colleagues. Documents were a means of self-analysis and self-projection.

Work Management by Documentation

Fitting work to the objectives of the organization posed some of the most difficult problems anyone had to solve at ITD. R&D data and other results rarely come in usable verbal packages; a great deal of hard intellectual work must be done to mold data into meaningful terms that reflect the specific interests of others in the organization. At ITD, the writing and editing cycle appeared to play a key role in making the individual's work advance the organization's established objectives.

In a common, yet mostly unspecified process we have called document *cycling*, a document passed back and forth between a staff member and supervisor. Many individuals at ITD had no idea that they routinely engaged in such a process, yet they invariably agreed it took place, once we described it to them. The most common—but not the sole—pattern was as follows. A document was assigned to an employee, often as a means of calling in work. Usually, but not always, the supervisor was the initiator of this process, largely because middle management was responsible for keeping projects to deadlines. At various stages of writing, staff would pass the document on to a supervisor, who reviewed the document and then called for certain revisions (see figure 8-4). Most of the document drafts we inspected had marginal notes calling for revisions of technical information, rearrangement of material, and changes in the scope of the document. Very little of this criticism had much to do with stylistic or grammatical questions. The document was then returned to the author, who was usually required to send the revised version back to the supervisor. This cycle could sometimes be repeated more than half a dozen times, although it usually did not go beyond three. As several employees noted, increasing the number of cycles also increased staff tensions.

Cycling was a collaborative, if sometimes stormy, process of managing work. Much supervisory time was spent getting writers to hone their work down to terms that embodied the organization's priorities. One supervisor observed that document cycling was his main means of establishing *leverage* over the timing and substance of his staff's labor. Assigning a document enabled him to divide work into tasks, to distribute them among his staff, and to call work in when he felt it was time. Specifying documents enabled him to establish work objectives without telling people exactly how to accomplish the work. Document drafts, another supervisor observed, "show project weakness." By reading the draft, he could identify work that had to be redone or extended and ask the staff member to revise his or her work accordingly.

Staff, on the other hand, were far less clear about the purpose of document cycling. At a group lunch session we had with younger staff, several thought the process arbitrary. It was agreed that those who did not interact with supervisors in the planning stage of the writing process generally had trouble at the editorial stage. Several of these junior staff members thought cycling painful, immensely time-consuming, and even mystifying. Yet most agreed that, carried out conscientiously, cycling encouraged early planning and gave the writer a feeling that his or her work was on target. Solid, constructive comments on a document draft were regarded as being extremely helpful. A sense of supervisory support and understanding seemed to

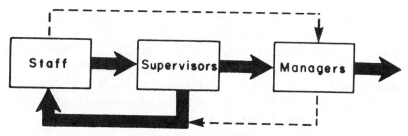

Figure 8-4   The Document-Cycling Process

be the one factor mentioned most by these junior people as an aid to their writing.

Self-Promotion by Documentation

The activity of writing was fundamental to the generation and transmission of ideas in the R&D group, because it enabled the employees to package and project their physical and intellectual labor. "Work I did at first was lost," one young staff engineer mused, "because I didn't write it up." She didn't mean that the benefits of her work were lost to the organization but, rather, that they were lost to her, because no one (including herself) could remember exactly what role she had played in certain projects. This observation underscored the widespread notion among ITD staff that the activity of writing is one of the principal means an individual has of projecting his or her work into the R&D community. The same engineer observed that she now "maintained" her position in the community partly by means of her documentation. Like many of her peers, she viewed her writing as a means of establishing a claim to her work among her peers. Writing, in this respect, not only fixes ideas but also *binds* them to individuals. "Results can still be useful if they're not written up," one supervisor noted, "but not writing them up does hurt the individual."

Another supervisor viewed documents as a way of establishing the right of his group to exist and of maintaining the competitive standing of his group in the organization. "Group competition is real," he noted: "We're a small outpost in a big empire." This supervisor felt it essential to write, in order to protect his group's work and to maintain contact with key individuals at divisions around the country. Documentation was, he noted, partly a political activity—a way of gaining visibility for his own group and for himself. At the same time, he noted, it was crucial to know when *not* to write. "Management wants original ideas," he observed, "and weak or confused documents simply call attention to incompetence." This supervisor's objective was to contribute a memo each month about some original idea or key development.

It was clear from many of the interviews that employees felt their writing activities put them "on the map," as one staff member put it: "Documents show what you're doing and also show your competence in doing it." Hence, to this employee, a document was a legitimate way of selling one's ideas in the organization. Even the most routine document was felt to offer the individual a chance to record his or her own attitudes, ideas, and work. Beneath this and similar talk was the notion of *legitimizing* oneself. "A document helps to fit a person into our organization," one supervisor noted. By writing, an individual becomes a visible part of an enterprise. Indeed, a poor response to one's written work was felt by staff to raise questions about one's contributions and legitimacy.

Networks and Writing

Each person at ITD operated in association with a small network of people. This network of colleagues, which varied in size from a few individuals to as many as a dozen individuals, was considered a valuable source of information and support. Members of one's network could contribute valuable ideas, promote one's projects, and generally give one the important sense of fitting into the community. Yet a network is also restricted to individuals who are within the physical compass of one's daily activities. Hence, the staff member or supervisor sometimes found his or her network limited to a group of individuals who only partly represent the intellectual domain of his or her interests. Writing and circulating documents offered employees an important means of extending their networks to other, less available individuals. In one interview, a supervisor and his staff noted that documents and formal oral presentations were among the few means available to employees of making contact with individuals in other research groups or with individuals who were two to three levels up the organizational ladder. Indeed, one manager noted that he liked to attend the weekly seminars to see how new members of the R&D group, whom he rarely had the chance to meet personally, handled themselves in front of an audience.

The emphasis on self-promotion by writing also led to many cautions, especially by supervisors, about its liabilities. Long, self-regarding documents, extensive cc lists, and poorly thought out documents were uniformly viewed as harmful. At a meeting of ITD supervisors, it was broadly agreed that inappropriate documents could harm an individual's standing in the organization. These included recommendations that impinge in some way on other individuals' territory, writing over-long documents, and writing for the sole sake of self-advertisement (see also Hays, 1984).

Documents and Accountability

Although group discussion is probably the best mode of communication for arriving at an actual R&D decision, writing is frequently the preferred mode of conveying the decision. Important research decisions must often be presented in such a way that the financial, technical, and administrative factors of the decision can be assessed by all concerned parties. Only then can the expertise of the organization be brought to bear, and only then can the decision makers and their supporters be given full credit and responsibility for their actions.

Since the document traces work to an individual or a group, it also records the lines of accountability in an organization. Staff evaluation, a critical process in the dynamics of any organization, is difficult and touchy. No one was prepared to say that one's documents were the ultimate sign of productivity, but both staff and management admitted that they were among the most convenient and objective ways to fix an individual's activities in time. Hence, the willingness and ability to write up one's work is an important characteristic of the successful R&D worker.

All the supervisors felt that proposals, progress reports, and final reports revealed the quality of a staff member's contributions: how the individual framed the question, brought data to bear, and considered options.[7] "Writing reflects the quality of my staff's minds," one supervisor observed. A staff scientist observed, "New people tend to get pegged in their first two years on the basis of their documents—for the management track or for horizontal movement." In and of itself, however, a document was not evidence of an individual's value. "If I'm arguing for an individual's promotion," a manager said, "I will be helped or hindered by documents."

Writing as a Means of Stimulating Ideas

Writing played a special role at ITD in generating new ideas. The employee networks noted earlier not only increase an individual's store of information, but also stimulate the growth of new concepts and applications. The activity of writing, one manager noted, was "one of the fastest ways to jell an issue." At ITD, the writing of a document sometimes created a good deal of ferment, political argument, and intellectual exchange. Almost all the employees we interviewed circulated drafts of their documents in order to get insights on their work. Since a document is physical and forces comments from others who may be affected by it, a whole train of collaborative development is set in motion once a document begins to circulate.

Internal circulation to colleagues at ITD frequently generated a quantity of marginal comments that extended ideas, added relevant facts, and altered focus and organization. Such activities kept ideas floating in the organizational environment. Circulating drafts was a means of cross-fertilizing projects with important new concepts in the making.

Writing as a Mode of Education

Writing and its related activities also had important educational functions both for employees and for the organization. This education was not merely a matter of becoming informed; something much more profound took place as individuals wrote and reviewed their own and other's documents.

Writing, first of all, provided a measure of continuity in the organization by providing employees new to a position essential background on the work of their predecessors. One supervisor observed, for example, that documents left behind by a departing employee provided the recruit a concrete introduction to the job—

what technical areas were of most concern, how policy had shaped the group's approach to those areas, and what the dynamic of the group had been in recent times. By reading the file, the new employee could assess how his or her own interests and abilities could contribute to the group's effort. This sort of written record is especially important in organizations where employee mobility is high. Although the ITD staff was extremely experienced, our questionnaire data indicated that 22 individuals (66 percent) had occupied their present positions for three years or less. Such mobility, common in most modern R&D groups, gives documents an extremely important educational role in maintaining the continuity of the organization.

Not only documents, but writing itself, played a significant educational role in the organization. To write effectively about a subject, the author has to get a firm grasp of the subject matter and its importance to others in the organization (see also Emig, 1977). An employee has to learn how to think within the framework of R&D objectives before he or she can write proposals or progress reports. Many new ITD employees we interviewed felt they were learning their fields anew as they wrote their documents. They were reconstructing their basic knowledge around real R&D applications, and learning to project their knowledge within the working environment of an industrial R&D operation. Although we were unable to study this process systematically at ITD, it was clear that some supervisors were using the document-cycling process as a mechanism to promote employee self-education.

CONFLICTS IN THE WRITING PROCESS

We have suggested that writing was both a necessary step in knowledge production at ITD and also a social process that helped individuals to fit themselves into the work community. We have also suggested that there was little consensus about the purpose of writing, the features of good writing, or the procedures for preparing documents. Little effort had been made, for example, to rationalize the cycling process. Writing and its related activities were submerged in the working environment. The invisibility of such a strategic activity made it probable that the preparation of any given document at ITD would give rise to conflicts. Indeed, document cycling did create internal tension among employees. Some of this tension was quite constructive, because it helped individuals focus and tighten up the results of their labor; some of it was counterproductive, because it developed into serious employee disagreements.

Because the cycling process of close editing was a key to producing documents at Exxon ITD, it was also the focus of certain employee conflicts. Typical conflicts between supervisors and staff over writing and editing are summarized in figure 8-5. During the cycling process, the personal goals of the staff writer are weighed against the needs and thrust of the larger organization; the experience of the supervisor helps to shape the intellectual labor of the staff researcher. As R&D work takes its final written form, the supervisor thus becomes an *editor*, because his or her managerial activities are exercised in the shaping of an information product. The supervisory process is carried out on the pages of a document draft.

Predictably, the cycling process was viewed from very different perspectives, because it concerned so many different personal and organizational priorities. The most common source of conflict was the failure of supervisor and staff to discuss matters of organization, purpose, and audience before the document was written. After much labor had gone into writing a document, criticism came very hard to most employees. People who had no notion that the editorial stage was an important phase of document production were inclined to give and take criticism negatively. Hence, differences of view that were based on managerial priorities and experience were often interpreted by writers as mere editorial whims. Managers sometimes assumed that the writer's task was simple and straightforward, when, in fact, the writing task was unfocused and difficult. The opportunities for confusing motives in document preparation seemed endless.

Younger employees often thought that the important thing in writing a document was to show how sound their approach to a problem was, a holdover attitude from the college environment. Student lab reports, for example, are rarely of any practical consequence to anyone at all; instructors are more interested in *how* students get their results (see also Barton & Barton, 1981). On the other hand, R&D supervisors in industry often need data to solve real problems; they want *results* and *recommendations*—save the logic for later. As Souther showed in his Westinghouse study (summarized in Souther & White, 1977), management rarely wants to review how

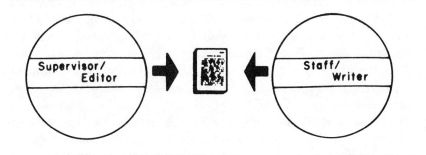

1. I have to fix a lot of bad prose	1. He tries to put it in his style
2. He throws rough drafts at me	2. He won't tell me what he wants
3. It takes three or four recycles	3. I don't understand his criticisms
4. He doesn't spend any time writing	4. I spend too much time writing
5. It takes forever to edit this stuff	5. It sits on his desk forever
6. He's reluctant to write up results	6. I can't get to writing, because he's always giving me something else to do
7. This needs to advance company objectives	7. I want to show what I've been doing
8. This better be good, because my boss is looking at it	8. I don't know who/what this is for
9. I don't know how good this needs to be	9. I don't know how good this needs to be

Figure 8-5   The Conflict between Supervisor and Staff

one solves a problem, nor do they usually expect an extensive catalogue of the results. In short, the novice wants to reproduce the process of problem solving, whereas the supervisor wants to see what the results are and how they promote established goals.

This conflict was illustrated in an afternoon seminar at ITD that we devoted to reviewing a single-spaced, eight-page report that analyzed the economics of two competing catalysts for a plant process. The young engineer was praised by both his supervisor and his manager as a very bright and potentially effective researcher. Yet neither of them liked the report. In our seminar, it gradually came out that the author had buried his recommendations in the final section of the report. Yet the author vigorously defended his document, because it *showed* the logic leading up to his decision. In this way, his reasoning could be reviewed, he said: the logic was as important to him as the recommendation itself. This concern reflected the author's desire to get his superiors to share his logic and, thus, the responsibility for his decision. Both the supervisor and manager felt, on the other hand, that the author should have given his findings and recommendation first. Neither felt the academic urge—nor did they have the time—to review the fine points of the author's reasoning. "If he's wrong, we'll find out, and he'll hear from us," was the hidden message.

When neither side appreciates the other's motives, each is inclined to think the other's actions arbitrary. An instance of this conflict arose over a young chemical engineer's documenting of a long project in a long report. He was preserving what he saw as the organization's investment in his research. Only a lengthy report of nearly seventy-five pages could do his work justice, he felt, so he spent personal time writing the project up. After submitting his document, he was told it was uneditable and impossible to use, and was then asked to cut the report to five pages, with a data sheet tacked on. The supervisor was genuinely troubled that the author expected him to edit such a long, ragged, confusing document. The author clearly had no idea what kind of effort it took to read, let alone edit, long documents.

Many younger employees, just out of the universities, have been accustomed to thinking that quality of writing *effort* counts. This university norm can lead to confusion later on. A young chemist, for example, showed an interviewer a paper written for a college course and then observed, with some puzzlement, that the professor had given her an A. The paper treated a theoretical problem in catalysis, came to about twelve typed pages, and included forty-two references. The professor's written comments were: "Good paper—well-written, easy to read. Shows considerable amount of 'extra work,' with a proper distribution of coverage between early work, summary of this paper, and subsequent work." The paper, modeled on the peer-reviewed research paper, was graded partly for quality of effort. It was the kind of paper, the chemist noted, that should not be written in an industrial R&D organization, but she was at a loss as to what to write instead.

The organizational savvy required to write successful documents may take, if our interviews are any indication, up to three or four years for a person to acquire. Younger staff at ITD rarely received systematic guidance about how writing functions in the R&D environment, possibly because few people know how to articulate the process. Hence, a frequent complaint from younger staff members was that their documents had to be political—that is, shrewdly tailored to the social environment, in which many unknown interests were competing. This political factor, many studies have shown, is part of the daily operation of an industrial unit (see Hays, 1984, pp. 16-20; Mathes & Stevenson, 1976, pp. 18-19). As we moved up the administrative line, writing ability significantly improved, which could mean that such ability may be one of the factors in the selection process that moves people into higher administrative roles. It is equally likely, however, that people learn how to write as they gain experience. People at the senior level understood their organization better and seemed to understand who their audiences were and what these audiences needed. Unlike beginners, experienced employees were not writing to abstract positions or levels. They were writing to real people, whom they often knew by first name. This makes a difference.

HOW CAN INDUSTRIAL R&D
WRITING BE IMPROVED?

Although they seemed to write about as well as their counterparts in academia, ITD employees were eager to learn how to write better. Indeed, we had trouble maintaining our research stance through the entire week, because employees wanted us to drop the research and help them with their writing. Many employees flatly stated that their college training did not adequately prepare them to communicate in the R&D environment. Usually, this was not a complaint about college English or writing departments; it was more a reflection on modern science and technical education, which rarely teach students how writing and editing activities contribute to the industrial enterprise. Core engineering and science curricula, undergraduate or graduate, rarely feature writing and editing; they differ markedly, in this respect, from core humanities and social science curricula. Moreover, instructors of engineering or science writing often don't know much about the environments in which their students are going to work. Hence, one way of improving R&D writing is to seek ways of modifying university curricula. Such modifications should be based on studies of industrial environments.

How much the university can accomplish remains an open question, since writing responsibilities and audiences appear to vary greatly from industry to industry and from job to job. The university can teach students how to solve writing problems in general, but it can hardly anticipate the full gamut of demands that industry makes on individuals. When we recall that ITD employees felt that their job experiences taught them their most valuable lessons about writing, we need to think of in-house education as a major strategy for improving R&D writing. Companies can help by developing a formal program that will draw employee attention to the role writing and editing play in the organization.

Such a program should be organized around specific objectives, rather than the generic goals of most packaged short courses. Analysis of the writing environment should always precede curriculum design. A formal in-house program should begin with careful study of the roles writing and its associated activities play in the life of the organization in question. Internal courses in communication can then be built on actual company priorities, and employees can study writing and editing as they work on their own projects-in-progress.

Companies like ITD can gain much simply by strengthening mentorship. For example, supervisors should be responsible for assigning document planning conferences and instructing junior members in the forms and functions of in-house documents. Short, nonprescriptive communications manuals can effectively inform new employees about the role of writing in the organization, provide guidelines for editorial conferences, and present sample documents.

One primary objective is to improve the editorial cycle. Supervisors and managers should be encouraged (1) to make presubmission conferences on the scope and coverage of a document standard practice, especially for new employees; (2) to establish (and adhere to) carefully considered editorial priorities in their criticism, possibly with the aid of a communications manual; (3) to plan and participate in a course for supervisors and managers on in-house editing.

FUTURE RESEARCH

By exploring the attitudes of employees and the mechanisms of their writing and editing, we can understand much about the formal and informal roles of writing in the modern R&D organization. We stand also to gain much new knowledge about how language and human labor—words and actions—are converted to one another. The study of writing environments, in short, provides us a critical window into the operations and social climate of a modern organization.

Several interesting kinds of writing research might proceed along the lines set out in this study. These include:

1. *Submerged nature of writing.* Although it is clear that writing and editing cycles belong to the nonrationalized domains of most industrial operations, we should know more about why this is so. How does writing *operate*, when it proceeds underwater, so to speak? Are industrial writing practices best left unanalyzed? What happens when organizations attempt to specify writing practices to employees?

2. *Time investment in writing.* Far more time is spent on written communication than is generally realized by people in industry. Subsequent studies carried out at MIT indicate that the time investment at ITD was consistent with another twenty R&D groups in major industrial organizations (see Lampe, 1984). What does it mean, however, to say that an employee spends one-third to one-half of his or her work week on writing-related activities? What kinds of work are done? How does this work promote the objectives of the organization? What are the cost implications of this kind of time investment? We also need more information about actual writing behavior: Where and when do people write? How does this behavior change with the style of the organization?

3. *Writing and productivity.* Many employees think of writing and editing as nonproductive activities, even when documents are the sole deliverables of their labor. We need to study the phenomenon of writing as labor more carefully from both the theoretical and the empirical standpoint. If writing is labor, then how can it be quantified in the manner of other forms of labor, and what are the implications of this? What are the mechanisms by which documents are converted to labor? Do documents store labor? How does the writing cycle in industry compare with academic cycles of publishing?

4. *Dual function of writing.* To many R&D employees, the function of writing is to transfer and archive information. But writing also has many important social functions, both organizational and personal in scope. We need to explore this dual function in detail in order to determine how employees are motivated. What is the hidden agenda of in-house R&D writing assignments? Can we get a clearer idea of their modes of operation?

5. *Editing as managing.* The purpose of editing is often thought to be the checking and repairing of documents, but editing also has important organizational functions. During editing, documents and—by proxy—project results are fitted to the organization's needs. We need a better understanding of how this process actually takes place. What options for managing labor does the writing and editing cycle open up for managers and supervisors? What are the best practices for cycling documents?

6. *Writing and self-education.* Finally, writing may be one of the least acknowledged, yet most significant modes of employee self-education. Can we establish one or more simple models—possibly through protocol analysis—for how writing obliges the author to construct new knowledge out of old? What are the social, financial, and policy implications of this educational process for industrial organizations?

Acknowledgments

The authors wish to thank the Exxon Chemicals Company for its cooperation and support in providing travel, expenses, and company time for our research effort. Without this assistance, we could not have entered into the project.

Notes

1. In his article, "Linguistic Responsibility" (1977), Joseph Williams asks, "What Counts as Good Writing at EXXON?" That question assumes a unity of opinion that is difficult to imagine in the industrial world, where writing has such a profusion of forms and functions.

2. Latour and Woolgar apply this principle in *Laboratory Life* (1979) to research scientists working for noncommercial organizations; see pp. 72–80.

3. In her *Information Transfer in Engineering* (1981), Hedvah Shuchman notes, "In-house reports are the work products of the largest group of engineers in our sample."

4. The existence of this selection process is supported by Davis's questionnaire findings (1977).

5. Young, Becker, and Pike (1970) discuss writing as problem solving. See also Flower, "Writing about Problems" (1981, pp. 19–34).

6. One aspect of environment, the so-called *ethos*, is discussed by Miller (1980, pp. 184–191).

7. Mathes and Stevenson (1976, p. 13) make this point a criterion of successful audience analysis.

References

Allen, T. (1977). *Managing the flow of technology*. Cambridge, MA: MIT Press.

Barton, B., & Barton, M. (1981). The nature and treatment of professional engineering problems: The technical writing teacher's responsibility. *Technical communication: Perspectives for the eighties* (NASA Conference Publication 2203, Pt. 2, 511–522).

Bazerman, C. (1982). Scientific writing as a social act. In P. Anderson et al. (Eds.), *New essays in technical and scientific communication* (pp. 156–184). Farmingdale, NY: Baywood.

Davis, R. (1977). Technical writing: Who needs it? *Engineering Education*, November, 209–211.

Davis, R. (1978). How important is technical writing?—A survey of the opinions of successful engineers. *Journal of Technical Writing and Communication, 8*(3), 207–216.

Dobrin, D. (1982). What's wrong with the mathematical theory of communication? *Proceedings of the 29th International Technical Communication Conference*. Boston: STC. (E-37-40).

Emig, J. (1977). Writing as a mode of learning. *College Composition and Communication, 28*(2), 122–128.

Faigley, L., & Miller, T. (1982). What we learn from writing on the job. *College English, 44*, 557–565.

Flower, L. (1981). Writing about problems. *In Problem-solving strategies for writing* (pp. 19–34). New York: Harcourt, Brace.

Hays, R. (1984). Political realities in reader/situation analysis. *Technical Communication, 31*(1), 16–20.

Joos, M. (1967). *The five clocks: A linguistic excursion into the five styles of English usage*. New York: Harcourt, Brace.

Lampe, D. (1984). Communications skills: A top priority for engineers and scientists. *The MIT Report, 12*, 1–2.

Latour, B., & Woolgar, S. (1979). *Laboratory life: The social construction of scientific facts*. Beverly Hills: Sage Publications.

Mathes, J. C., & Stevenson, D. W. (1976). *Designing technical reports*. Indianapolis: Bobbs-Merrill.

Miller, C. (1980). The ethos of science and the ethos of technology. *Proceedings of the Technical Communications Sessions, 31st Conference on College Composition*.

Olsen, L., & Huckin, T. (1983). *Principles of communication for science and technology*. New York: McGraw-Hill.

Shuchman, H. (1981). *Information transfer in engineering*. Glastonbury, CT: The Future's Group.

Souther, J., & White, M. (1977). *Technical report writing* (2nd ed.). New York: Wiley.

Williams, J. (1977). Linguistic responsibility. *College English, 39*, 13.

Young, R. E., Becker, A. L., & Pike, K. L. (1970). *Rhetoric: Discovery and change*. New York: Harcourt, Brace.

Special Topics of Argument in Engineering Reports

9

CAROLYN R. MILLER
North Carolina State University

JACK SELZER
Pennsylvania State University

In a recent essay on the relationship between writing and the academic disciplines, James L. Kinneavy (1983) has called for detailed study of the rhetorical conventions of specialized discourse communities. He recommends that rhetoricians "make some general study of the methodologies, definitions, criteria of evidence, general axiomatic systems, and views of value systems" in various disciplines. As a discussion of writing-across-the-curriculum programs in universities, his essay focuses on disciplinary discourse within academic settings. Nonacademic discourse, although not so obviously divided into disciplines, also occurs in communities with particular conventions, purposes, and institutions; such discourse can be subjected to similar study.

Kinneavy is not alone in calling for study of what he calls the "ethnologics" of various discourse communities. In the past few years many scholars have reminded us that meaning is dependent on situation, that interpreting discourse requires understanding the social context in which it is produced and used. Thus written documents produced by individuals and groups in everyday work situations can best be understood within the contexts of the particular communities in which those documents have their uses. In order to follow and appreciate the arguments of literary critics or molecular biologists or transportation engineers, we must attend not only to the language and logic of those arguments but also to the rhetorical contexts and conventions that shape the argument. Indeed, Stanley Fish (1980) has argued that the main business of English studies ought to be to investigate the nature of discourse communities and the effects of those communities on written prose. The work of Stephen Toulmin, especially *The Uses of Argument* (1958), has provoked inquiry into how arguments differ according to their subject matter. Charles Bazerman (1983) has called for research on the distinctive features of prose in specific disciplines, so that students might be taught the issues, values, and lines of argument likely to be persuasive in particular forums. And Patricia Bizzell (1982) has suggested that "composition studies should focus upon practice within interpretive communities"—on exactly how conventions work in the world and how they are transmitted—so that students can be taught to write, reason, and argue within their own disciplines.

Several people have already begun the work of explicating the conventions of specific discourse communities, particularly those defined by academic disciplines. In "The Rhetoric of Economics," Donald McCloskey (1983) has explored and critiqued the argumentative methods of contemporary economists. Bazerman (1981) has discussed the tactics and conventions employed by scholarly articles in three academic disciplines. Anne Herrington (1983) has studied various features of the academic discourse produced by student chemical engineers, including the typical lines of reasoning used. Marie Secor and Jeanne Fahnestock (1982) have catalogued the conventions that recur in literary argument.

Critical studies of specific texts have been infrequent, however, and appropriate methods for those studies are still being developed. Moreover, little attention has been given to the question of how (or indeed whether) the discourse of nonacademic communities is informed by the conventions of those communities—for example, how working engineers and managers employ the conventions of identifiable discourse communities when they write reports, proposals, and other on-the-job documents. This chapter, therefore, has two related aims. First, we will propose a method for rhetorical analysis of on-the-job writing, a method that is intended to highlight the discourse features that are specific to a community. Building on Kinneavy's suggestion that the study of specialized discourse might proceed by the analysis of how it uses the rhetorical topics of classical theory, we propose that analyzing the topical basis of discourse will help us to understand the community-specific conditions of successful argument. We will further propose that there are three kinds of such topics—those specific to a genre, those specific to an organization or institution, and those specific to a discipline. Second, we want to illustrate how this method might be used to analyze a particular (and important) kind of contemporary practical discourse: technical reports. The topical analysis of such discourse, we hope, will interest not only those who teach practical rhetoric but also those seeking to understand the functions of specialized discourse within the wider context of contemporary society.

SPECIAL TOPICS IN TECHNICAL DISCOURSE

Systems of *topoi*, or topics, were central to invention as classically conceived and to the early teaching of practical rhetoric. Throughout its history, invention has been alternatively treated as the mechanical finding of content (as *inventory*) or as the creating of arguments. Topics can thus be conceived, alternatively, as pigeonholes for locating already existing ideas or as patterns of thought or methods of analysis that can be called on in the construction of arguments. In practice, these alternative versions are conjoined: by learning a mechanical system of pigeonholes, one masters patterns of thought that then become habitual and spontaneous. Quintilian therefore emphasized the value of topical systems as training devices for apprentices, as Michael C. Leff has noted in his discussion of topical systems in the classical tradition. "Approached in this spirit," Leff says, "the topics can enhance native ability and enlarge the capacity to recognize the argumentative possibilities in any case whatsoever" (Leff, 1983). Topics thus make explicit for the learner what is implicit for the expert: patterns of concepts that are material to gaining the assent of an audience.

Classical theory, however, does not lend itself directly to the study of the specialized discourse of technical reports. As conceived by the Greeks and Romans, discourse addressed to a specially qualified audience and involving specialized knowledge was considered to be scientific demonstration, not rhetoric. Demonstration proceeds not from topics but from undisputed or self-evident premises, via syllogistic logic, to indisputable conclusions. Because demonstration dealt with certainties, it did not need topics, which were used to establish probable arguments when certainty was not possible. Topics were elements of rhetoric, which was understood as public discourse on issues of concern to all citizens, and of dialectic, the method of rational discussion on general questions (Kennedy, 1980, pp. 66, 83).

To Aristotle, then, the *sciences* (or what we would call *disciplines*, whether they are scientific disciplines or not) involved a kind of discourse wholly different from rhetoric or dialectic. Contemporary philosophers and historians of science, however, have called into question Aristotle's separation of the sciences from rhetoric suggests the possibility of a similarly expanded conception even a scientific one, are often disputed and that syllogistic logic is insufficient to account for the development of a discipline (Kuhn, 1970; Toulmin, 1972). Since the premises of science are matters for debate, the discourse of the disciplines (including scientific and technical disciplines) has become part of the contemporary conception of rhetoric. This conception blurs the distinction between rhetoric and dialectic (as methods of argument) and restricts demonstration to artificial axiomatic systems like mathematics. As Chaim Perelman (1982) sees it, "argumentation, conceived as a new rhetoric or dialectic, covers the whole range of discourse that aims at persuasion and conviction, whatever the audience addressed and whatever the subject matter" (p. 5). This expanded conception of rhetoric suggests the possibility of a similarly expanded conception of topics.

The topical systems described by Aristotle and by subsequent classical rhetoricians drew their power from their general utility in a great many typical rhetorical situations. Thus, what Aristotle called the common topics were strategies for finding premises or reasons that are applicable to any situation, strategies like *comparison* and *possibility*. What Aristotle called the "special" or "particular" topics were those heuristic strategies "derived from propositions which are peculiar to each species or genus of things" (*Rhetoric*, I.2.1358a21). As he illustrates them, special topics concern the rhetorical problems typically encountered in the civic occasions for public speaking. These topics locate issues to be addressed in speeches of accusation and defense, praise and blame, and exhortation and dissuasion on the civic and political subjects about which Athenian citizens engaged in public discourse.[1]

The Aristotelian special topics have two aspects. They can be considered genre-specific, for they are peculiar to a situation-dependent complex of subject matter, rhetorical convention, and purpose which characterizes a genre. And they can be considered institution-specific, for they require Athenian political institutions to make complete sense. Other institutional arrangements, other relationships between citizens and the state, would require the rhetor to address different issues to make a sound case. So when Aristotle discusses speeches of exhortation and dissuasion (deliberative rhetoric), for example, he announces that there are five subjects that enter into such deliberations: ways and means, war and peace, defense, imports and exports, and legislation. This topical scheme presupposes a specific and limited function for deliberation, one predicated on the organization of the Athenian *polis* and on clearly delineated occasions for public discussion of political decisions (deliberation does not concern, for example, environmental impact or technical questions of scientific validity). Thus both the political institutions and the generic functions of public discourse underlie the Aristotelian special topics. In Aristotelian rhetoric these two aspects are bound together because of the limited social functions for rhetoric (on this point, see Kaufer, 1979). We believe they can be separated into two distinct kinds of special topics that may or may not occur together: those suggesting materials for persuasion in a given genre and those suggesting materials for persuasion in a given institutional environment, regardless of genre.

In addition, we believe that Aristotle's *Rhetoric* suggests a third kind of special topic for contemporary theory, a kind based on the specialized knowledge of disciplines. Because he distinguishes sharply between matters of knowledge and matters of opinion, Aristotle understands rhetoric (and dialectic) as sharply distinct from disciplines. But he recognizes that this distinction is easy to violate in practice. Although rhetoric itself has no subject matter, Aristotle says, it is closely concerned with the disciplines of politics and ethics (*Rhetoric*, I.2.1356a7). Further, he postulates a close relationship between the special topics (the *eide*) and the first principles (*archai*) of disciplines: "As to the specific topics, the happier a man is in his choice of propositions, the more he will unconsciously produce a science quite different from Dialectic and Rhetoric. For if once he hits upon first principles, it will no longer be Dialectic or Rhetoric, but that science whose principles he has arrived at" (*Rhetoric*, I.2.1358a21–22). In other words, first principles may masquerade as topics if the boundary between rhetoric and disciplines is not observed carefully.[2] If we deny the existence of a boundary at all, if we adopt the perspective of the new rhetoric, which makes argumentation a dimension of all discourse, even the most specialized, we can postulate an identity between *eide* and *archai* and thus a category of topics that is discipline-specific. One of us has argued this point elsewhere, that Aristotelian *archai*, or key technical concepts, underlie the shape and effectiveness of specialized argument by serving as special topics (Miller, 1983).

Toulmin's work provides a useful contemporary perspective on the role of specialized concepts in disciplinary discourse. In *Human Understanding* (1972), Toulmin defines concepts as the "skills or traditions, the activities, procedures, or instruments of [our] intellectual life and imagination . . . through which . . . human understanding is achieved and expressed" (p. 11). Disciplinary communities are defined by their "collective concept-use" (p. 361). That is, disciplines use concepts to build intellectual enterprises, which have explanatory goals, as well as to build practical enterprises like the crafts and technologies, which have productive goals; the concepts that evolve in the latter are not laws and theories but recipes, techniques, manufacturing processes, and the like (p. 365). Since concepts are central to such efforts, as both tools and products, we conclude that they must inevitably serve as material sources for persuasion. That is, the specialized concepts of a discipline help to form the issues and problems of disciplinary discourse and become, through their evolution, the resources for resolving those issues and problems. Further, according to Toulmin, collective concept-use has two manifestations: the discipline, or "communal tradition of procedures and techniques for dealing with theoretical or practical problems"; and the profession, or "organized set of institutions, roles, and [people] whose business it is to apply or improve those procedures and techniques" (p. 142). These two aspects underlie the two kinds of special topics we call discipline-specific and institution-specific.

To use special topics as a method of understanding (and explaining) how arguments are conducted within discourse communities, one must imaginatively reinvent the argument to find the sources of persuasion. Interpretation, whether by intended audience or by intruding analyst, requires the interpreter to share with the rhetor a conceptual network that defines the terms and goals of the argument. If topics operate in invention prospectively, as conceptual places where a rhetor can find sources for arguments, they operate in analysis retrospectively, as places where audiences can find the sources of the persuasiveness of those arguments. Both analyst and audience seek within the discourse reasons for belief, gauging the potency of those reasons by their sources in the conceptual network the argument presupposes. For the outsider, the analyst, learning what concepts yield cogent reasons uncovers the intellectual framework of the rhetor and audience—that is, of the discourse community to which they belong.

Since an arguer is not always aware of where ideas come from, we can establish only the probability that a concept served as a topic for the rhetor or that it will serve in the audience's reconstruction. We can attempt to identify topics in two ways. First, textual analysis can show where a reason is being offered. Anne Herrington (1983), for example, describes a method that enabled her to identify three general kinds of reasons in student lab reports: error analysis, theories based on "the literature," and data plots of students' own lab results. Toulmin's textbook suggests the kinds of reasons that are typically used in reasoning in science, law, management, and other large discourse communities (Toulmin, Rieke, & Janik, 1979). Other reasons are associated with technical terminology or organizational vocabulary. Such reasons are likely to have their sources in topics, either common or special.

A second method of attempting to identify topics is by questioning writers and readers to learn what they actually consider to be material contributors to the potency of an argument and where, conceptually, those contributions came from. A writer might be asked why he or she included (or decided not to include) a certain passage, or what inspired a given section or paragraph, or where a certain reason has its source. A reader might be asked what he or she finds persuasive (or missing) in a given document—and why. If a writer or reader's explanation is based on logical analysis or on common sense, then the topic used is not specific to a discourse community but is common to the patterns of human thinking or to many discourse communities. If, on the other hand, the explanation is based on the expectations and conventions surrounding a particular type of rhetorical interaction, or if it is tied to the insider's vocabulary of an organization or institution, or if it is bound into the conceptual network of a discipline, it probably identifies a special topic. In the next section, we aim to demonstrate how special topics contribute to the arguments of several engineering reports.

TOPICAL ANALYSIS OF ENGINEERING REPORTS

We have defined special topics as patterns of thought deriving from specific genres, institutions, or disciplines—patterns that are material to gaining the assent of an audience within a particular discourse community. To illustrate further what special topics are and to demonstrate concretely how they can be exploited to help explain the substance and shape of particular arguments, let us now turn to some writing by professional engineers. The premises of this section are that scholars and teachers will gain a better perspective on arguments in on-the-job writing if they consider the contribution that special topics make to the nature and effectiveness of those arguments; and that those special topics themselves might be better understood if they are classified according to their origin: generic considerations account for certain conventional arrangements and lines of argument in reports and proposals; institutional or organizational consider-ations affect arguments constructed by members of those institutions; and the concepts, methods, and assumptions of particular disciplines influence arguments relevant to those disciplines. The pedagogical implication here is that teachers will be able to guide students better if they understand the contributions that special topics make to scientific and technical prose.

Generic Special Topics

The special topics that are perhaps easiest to acknowledge and recognize are those that can be tied to specific genres—to the established conventions of proposals, recommendations, environ-mental impact statements, progress reports, and so forth. In fact, those conventions are already so widely acknowledged that they typically make their way into textbook chapters that list what proposals or progress reports or other established genres ought to include. The conventionalizing of report contents—and even of the arrangement of the contents—is a widespread tendency in technical discourse. One of us, for instance, has shown that a proposal writer relies partly on previously written examples in the company files to determine the contents and arrangement of subsequent proposals (Selzer, 1983). The other of us has noted that the Council on Environmental Quality's list of eight points to be covered by Environmental Impact Statements has come to be taken as a virtual outline of the major sections in impact statements and thus as a generic topic determining the adequacy (and persuasiveness) of impact statements (Miller, 1980). Because generic conventions are widely recognized, we will give here only a rather general account of the conventions of two specific genres: transit development plans (reports prepared by consultants that recommend transit policies and plans for local governments); and the proposals that won the contracts to develop those plans.

Consider first the tables of contents for two different transit development plans (see figures 9-1 and 9-2). Even though these plans were developed five years apart by two different writers and though the plans address the needs of widely different localities (urban South Bend, Indiana, and rural Mercer County, Pennsylvania), they still present their arguments in very similar, very conventional ways. Note that both reports follow a problem-solving pattern. Both writers offer the same kinds of introductory chapters, focusing on background information, problems addressed, and study purposes. Both next give accounts of "Existing Services" and "Ridership Analyses" that are based on previously collected data and surveys of the local population. Both make their major recommendations (based on a consideration of several alternatives) in chapter 5, and both recommend management tactics in separate chapters (chapter 6 in the South Bend study, chapter 4 in the Mercer County report). Finally, note that both documents conclude with advice for financing, marketing, and evaluating the transit systems (chapter 7 of the South Bend plan, and the final three chapters in the Mercer County report). The similar content and arrangement of the two reports derive from the generic conventions of this kind of report; our survey of the contents of many other transit development plans nearly always turned up the very same topics, nearly always in the very same order.

Transit plans by convention include other generic special topics, too. The plans always provide in some way for the elderly and handicapped, not only because they are important customers but

Figure 9-1 Table of Contents for "Transit Development Plan and Program for the South Bend Urbanized Area"

Figure 9-1 (continued)

because federal and state legislation requires that transit companies attend especially to the needs of those riders. For that matter, references to legislation and regulations are made throughout the reports since local transit plans must conform to those regulations in order to qualify for state and federal funds. There are also other criteria—constantly referred to—on which transit recommendations are based: cost (including discussion of initial investment, fare schedules, ridership levels, potential for attracting new customers, maintenance costs, operating costs, and so forth) and service

Figure 9-2   Table of Contents for "Mercer County Rural Transportation Study"

Figure 9-2 (continued)

(including discussions of scheduling, efficiency of transfer from one route to another, flexibility, and frequency of service). As one of the authors remarked, "All these should be in any good transit plan." We would even suggest that certain graphics have become conventional features of transit plans: readers can expect to see organizational charts; tables filled with survey and cost data; and maps of land use, of present and proposed routes, and of population densities and distributions. According to the writers we interviewed, all the conventions we have mentioned in the past three paragraphs derive ultimately from Urban Mass Transit Administration (UMTA) regulations codified in the early 1970s.[3] Just as the Council on Environmental Quality listed the points to be covered in Environmental Impact Statements, UMTA prescribed specific points that transit plans were expected to cover if they were to be successful. Even though the Reagan administration has required less formal adherence to federal guidelines (and permitted more flexible standards to be developed by states, local communities, and consulting engineers), the formats and contents of transit reports nevertheless remain predictable, for by now the conventions of the genre have become firmly established.

The proposals that won these engineering projects in South Bend and Mercer County also illustrate nicely how generic considerations guide writers in the development of their arguments. In fact, as their tables of contents show, proposals in the field of transportation engineering are even more conventional than final transit plan reports, for at least two reasons. First, the criteria for selecting among proposals are relatively fixed by the same guidelines that prescribe the contents of final transit plans: the scope and management of a project are largely determined by the request-for-proposal that a city planning officer sends out, and contracts are awarded on the basis of the qualifications and capabilities of the proposer, the work schedule, and of course the budget. Second, the proposals that are funded are quickly imitated by other firms anxious for a share of the market; in this way, progressive engineers and engineering firms are responsible for establishing generic conventions very quickly. Hence, even though the proposals in figures 9-3 and 9-4 were composed by different writers for different projects, they again include the same contents, though not in exactly the same order (since the authors want to emphasize different things to their different readers). Within twenty pages both proposals specify a work program and work

DE LEUW, CATHER & COMPANY
ENGINEERS AND PLANNERS
165 WEST WACKER DRIVE
CHICAGO, ILLINOIS 60601
FINANCIAL 6-0424 · AREA CODE 312

July 18, 1975   OUR REF. 0126990

Mr. Cleveland Brown
Director of Planning
Southeastern Michigan Transportation Authority
211 Fort Street West, Suite 1600
P.O. Box 333
Detroit, Michigan 48231

Dear Mr. Brown:

In response to your invitation of June 30, 1975, and subsequent staff discussions we are pleased to submit our proposal to furnish consulting services to the Southeastern Michigan Transportation Authority for an immediate action Bus Services, Policies, and Standards Work Program.

This Proposal is intended to be fully responsive to the transit needs of the SEMTA Area. Input provided by the SEMTA Board and staff, the Southeastern Michigan Council of Governments (SEMCOG), and other municipal entities would be an integral part of the overall project. It is intended that the final product will be a joint effort between the above groups and De Leuw, Cather & Company. We have been offered local assistance by Professional Engineering Associates when required on local problems and issues relating to this study. The proposal is organized as follows:

Scope of Work and Methodology

Consultant's Qualifications and Personnel

Time Schedule and Study

The opportunity to be of assistance to the Southeastern Michigan Transportation Authority is sincerely appreciated. We look forward to your favorable response to this proposal.

Very truly yours,

DE LEUW, CATHER &
COMPANY

Walter A. Barry, Jr.
Vice President

Figure 9-3   Transmittal Letter Showing Contents for South Bend Transit Proposal

INTRODUCTION	1
STUDY PHILOSOPHY	2
PROPOSED WORK PROGRAM	3
WORK SCHEDULE, MEETINGS, AND REPORTS	14
PROJECT STAFFING AND MANAGEMENT	16
PROPOSED BUDGET	18
QUALIFICATIONS OF THE CONSULTANT	19
CONTACT PERSONS	21
VITA	22

Figure 9-4 Table of Contents for Mercer County Transit Proposal

schedule; both set forth a budget; and both detail the qualifications of key personnel with commentary, resumes, and references to past clients. The contents of these proposals, of course, correspond to the contents of most proposals in general. A well-known textbook, for example, defines a technical proposal of any kind as "a written offer to solve a technical problem in a particular way, under a specified plan of management, for a specified sum of money" (Mills & Walter, 1978, p. 274).

Generic special topics can be found in the specific sections of the two proposals as well. Both open with short accounts of the goals and philosophies of the proposer, accounts that emphasize practicality over theory. "It is important that the goals and objectives are not a compendium of well-meaning, idealistic statements applicable in almost any situation," says the author in the South Bend proposal. "Rather, they should express the concrete and achievable end states applicable" (p. 1). The Mercer County proposal makes the same sort of claim: "Mercer County does not need an abstract, long-range study. What is needed is a short-range, operations-oriented planning effort which outlines specific steps" (p. 2). And both describe their proposed work plans in similar terms: they will specify goals and objectives; analyze various alternative transit plans according to specific criteria; assemble and evaluate local and regional information pertinent to the study; survey demand for transportation service; develop evaluation programs; and so forth.

Not everything is similar in these transit proposals and reports, of course. Each project requires different work programs and activities; each consultant conceives of a transportation project in slightly different ways and brings different resources and expertise to it; and each evaluator of a proposal calls for different emphases. Moreover, those who write transit plans proposals and reports exploit common topics as well as special ones, and institutional and disciplinary special topics as well as generic ones. Nevertheless, the more we compared various transit proposals and reports and the more we talked to their authors, the more we saw how remarkably conventional those reports and proposals are, and the more we realized that the conventions have been so fixed that they actually require authors to call on recurring patterns and issues. If a report or proposal fails to address these—fails to use these special topics—its effectiveness is diminished because the generic conventions establish a set of potential conditions that an argument in a given generic situation is expected to satisfy. Thus any proposal that does not describe a work program and a work schedule (for example) will be less persuasive as a proposal because it will be understood as incomplete, inadequate to the rhetorical task of its genre.

Institutional or Organizational Topics

Those who write engineering reports are undoubtedly influenced by the conventions of the particular genre they are working with. But they are also influenced by the institutions and organizations that provide the contexts for their discourse. In the words of March and Simon (1958), "the world tends to be perceived by ... organization members in terms of the particular concepts that are reflected in the organization's vocabulary" (p. 165). When such concepts and vocabulary are sources of arguments, we call them institutional special topics.

Some scholarship has already been done on institutional topics. In their chapter on "Reasoning about Management," for example, Toulmin, Rieke, and Janik (1979) have noted that support for arguments about management derives from systems analysis and computer modeling; from the values and objectives of business organizations; and from organizational definitions of efficiency, productivity, cost control, and the like (pp. 303–304). In addition, one of us has shown how certain terms in the National Environmental Policy Act became, through judicial interpretation, topics for the preparation of legally adequate Environmental Impact Statements. These terms, such as *major, significant,* and *human environment,* in the phrase "major Federal actions significantly affecting the human environment," acquired specialized significance based in congressional intent, case law, and official interpretation by the Council on Environmental Quality (Miller, 1980). In interviewing a proposal writer, the other of us found that the writer spent a great deal of time thinking about how his company's resources could be adapted to a particular client's needs; we suspect that such thinking is guided in part by institutional topics (Selzer, 1983). Finally, elsewhere in this book and in a 1983 essay, Lee Odell and his colleagues recount their experiences with legislative analysts for a state legislature (Odell et al., 1983). They note that certain institutional considerations have become heuristics for those who compose "bill memos" for state legislators. The analysts believe a "good" bill memo should cover certain topics: the direct consequences of the legislation, its relationship to existing laws and regulations, its effect on certain constituencies, the likelihood of its achieving the sponsor's intent, its procedural comprehensiveness, and so forth. Because these topics have to do with the institutional purposes, methods, interests, and attitudes of those who write or defend legislation, we consider them not as common topics (*consequence, relationship,* etc.) but as institutional special topics—as products of the insider's perspective.

One easy way to illustrate how institutional topics can influence written work is to compare two letters of transmittal prepared by a proposal writer at Henningson, Durham, and Richardson (HDR), an Omaha-based engineering firm. The proposals competed for two rather different contracts—one to plan the expansion of the Waukegan, Illinois, airport; and one to execute a traffic circulation study for Rockford, Illinois. In listing the reasons that HDR should be awarded the Waukegan airport project, the letter of transmittal suggests (among other things) that HDR "has made a strong corporate commitment to provide professional resources in Illinois to build a major office" and that HDR believes in "maintaining a close client/ consultant working relationship throughout the duration of the project." The letter submitted with the Rockford proposal is supported by very similar language: HDR "has made a transportation production commitment to Illinois through our Des Plaines office" and is interested in "maintaining a close working relationship with you, the client, throughout the entire duration of the project." The engineer who wrote those proposals reported to one of us that the appeals were suggested by his manager. Because its Des Plaines office was only recently opened, HDR wanted to call attention to that fact; and because HDR makes a special effort to achieve "close client/consultant working relationships," the company suggests that the topic be mentioned explicitly in its proposals. These points thus become company-specific sources of persuasion.

Quite often, in fact, an organization will specify that particular things be included in its proposals and reports, things that go beyond superficial matters of format and appearance. "Every company has something unique it wishes to emphasize," says one manager. That something might be codified in company guidelines or manuals. Or, like the topics that were mentioned in the previous paragraph, it might be explicitly directed in meetings between managers and top executives. Or it might be imposed by a manager whose responsibility is to oversee all report-writing functions (at HDR, for example, the personnel resumés that accompany proposals are prepared by a centralized office, thus ensuring that standardized items are included in all of them). At other times institutional topics are the product of a supervisor's wishes. Note in figure 9-5 how the intervention of a supervisor at HDR influenced the writer of a particular user manual. Even though the technical language of the memo is more disciplinary than organizational, the supervisor's request for the inclusion or elaboration of these disciplinary concepts (*modal split, volume/capacity ratios, generation rates*) is based on organizational considerations. And the need for such organizational attention is due to wider institutional relationships between three groups: HDR, "the mass transit people," and the users of the manual.

Institutional and organizational topics can often be discovered by surveying and comparing both the documents prepared by specific organizations and also the internal directives that accompany those documents. Nevertheless, finding institutional special topics requires some ingenuity. Sometimes they can be turned up through a detailed comparison of many documents produced by a firm; institutional language will recur in many kinds of writing produced for many different occasions. But more often some external evidence must be sought. If a company provides written guidelines for its writers, those can point to institutional topics. If the files and internal correspondence for a project are available, marginalia and memos to writers (like the one just discussed) can reveal institutional topics. If the writer of a document is available, he or she might be interviewed about institutional constraints, policies, and values. If the writers

To   Doug Bulter   From   Ken Nelson

Subject   Review of User Manual   Date   Jan. 12, 1983

Overall, I think this draft of the User Manual looks extremely good. I like the format, contents—I think it will be a very usable document for them. Although you stated it was rough, I think it is in darn good shape. Therefore, I went ahead and did some minor editing to it. As far as I am concerned, besides a few comments that I will make below, it is ready to go.

I have put numbers on the areas that I would like to comment on as follows:

1. I hate to dismiss modal split as negligible, or nearly zero. I would rather get a total number of daily transit trips, compare that roughly to the total number of trips made per day in the Rockford area, and calculate a percent. If this percent turns out to be, say, less than 3%, it can be stated as such and then dismissed. At least in this way, we will not offend the mass transit people. Also, it is very easy for someone to take the total number of trips and multiply them by a factor, regardless if that factor is .75 or .99.

2. I think we need one more paragraph here concerning what to do once we finally calculate the capacity. It would be good to talk about volume/capacity ratios, and possibly the minimum ratio that would be acceptable, based on level of service. I don't see a need for a detailed discussion on level of service, but we have to give them some type of ratio to look at to determine whether or not they have a problem.

3. Before we get to recommendations, I think there are two other options available here. Number one, there should be a iterative type process where they go back and assign the trips, as possible, to adjacent roads. Due to the lack of a complete road network in downtown Rockford, many times this will not be possible. However, this is how the traffic would actually flow. Also, it should be stated in here that a change in location could drastically change or negate the need for any improvements. Therefore, the whole idea of this analysis is to determine what improvements will be associated with each location of a potential development. Therefore, at

Figure 9-5 Internal Memorandum Reviewing Preparation of a User Manual

this point, we may state that consideration should be given to another location, or at least that these improvements are only associated with that particular location of that development.

The only other comment I have concerns the land use. As I wrote on the example, your example is described as a general office building, but under your procedure you stated that this type of description is too general. You go on to say that you should state whether it is a medical or a governmental office. Are there actually different generation rates for these two types of uses? Maybe when describing use, under the Generator Description, you may want to refer them to the Trip Generation Book for a list of uses.

cc: Rockford Downtown Circulation Study File

Figure 9-5 (continued)

have worked for other institutions, they can explain how different organizations contribute different institutional attitudes and interests to various documents. When all those methods are employed together, we can obtain a good sense of how the arguments of writers at work are influenced by institutional considerations.

Disciplinary Special Topics

While generic and institutional special topics account for many of the lines of argument used in engineering reports, the special topics that arise from particular disciplines are just as important—but may be more difficult to recognize and assess. Disciplinary special topics, as we have defined them, are bound up in the conceptual framework of a particular discipline; they depend not on recurrent features of specific genres or on the values and interests of particular institutions but on the shared concepts of particular disciplinary communities. Hence they are not always accessible to analysis, especially if those doing the analysis are unfamiliar with the discipline involved.

Nevertheless, the job of explicating the special topics of various disciplines has already begun. Toulmin, for example, has assessed the arguments characteristic of the legal, scientific, business, and artistic discourse communities (Toulmin, 1958; Toulmin, Rieke, & Janik, 1979). Bazerman (1981) and Herrington (1983), as we mentioned earlier, have studied the topics used in the physical sciences; and Secor and Fahnestock (1982) have explored the lines of argument common in literary criticism. Two sociologists, Gilbert and Mulkay (1981), have pointed out that scientists in research laboratories describe their methods by means of general formulae and methodological rules that only members of the particular research community can appreciate. Here we want to demonstrate three points: (1) that certain topics in the writing of transportation engineers are products of the conceptual network of their discipline; (2) that transportation engineers use disciplinary special topics when they argue in proposals and reports; and (3) that those topics can be uncovered through rhetorical analysis.

The reports and proposals we discussed earlier make their points with the help of discipline-specific topics as well as common, generic, and institutional ones. The ridership surveys in the South Bend and Mercer County reports, for example, may be required on generic grounds; but the surveys themselves are handled according to disciplinary norms, with accounts of origin and destination patterns, profiles of typical riders, and attitude measures. The recommendations in chapter 5 of the South Bend report are also reinforced not only by common topics (like *consequence* and *comparison*) and by the generic topics we looked at earlier, but also by topics specific to the transportation engineering discipline. One transit alternative, for example, is recommended because it will provide for its riders a "memory schedule" (i.e., regular and easily remembered intervals between buses); because it will permit "coordinated scheduling" and "pulse scheduling" (both concepts understandable to transportation engineers but undefined in the report); and because it will allow "headway" (i.e., proper time between buses) and "streamlining" (pp. 7–11). Cost criteria are described in terms of "revenue/cost ratios" (or "R/C ratios"), "productivity analyses," "efficiency analyses," "low productive route loops," and "low productive loop segments" (pp. 11–12). The recommendations would not be persuasive without the inclusion of these disciplinary topics. Similarly, recommendations in the Mercer County report are based on "headway," "coordination," and "memory scheduling" (pp. 60, 77, 80). Its cost recommendations are backed by references to a "zone fare structure," and its service alternatives are classified as "fixed route service," "deviated fixed route service," and "demand responsive service." All these concepts depend on the reader's and writer's familiarity with a particular discipline; they imply or designate accepted principles, data, and conclusions that the writers believe support the claims made in these reports.

What we mean by disciplinary special topics and what these topics contribute to arguments will become even clearer if we examine them in an engineering report where they are more prominent and where they cooperate with common topics and generic ones. Such a report is a traffic engineering study submitted in September, 1983, by Henningson, Durham, and Richardson (HDR) to the city of Highland Park, Illinois. The purpose of "Traffic Engineering Study: Clavey Road and U.S. 41 Intersection" was "to develop a range of alternatives, including both short- and long-term recommendations, that will reduce . . . the high accident rate that has occurred at the intersection in recent years." The intersection is dangerous because the Edens Expressway north of Chicago terminates suddenly at Clavey Road, where it becomes U.S. 41.

As figure 9-6 shows, the argument of this report essentially follows the conventional problem-solving pattern that we discussed in the section on generic topics. First, the introduction identifies the aim of the report. Next, in chapters 2 through 4, background information is detailed and particular problems are identified. In chapters 5 and 6, short-term, low-cost improvements are explored. Chapter 7 considers the feasibility of long-term, major changes at the intersection. Chapter 8 is essentially an appendix intended to support a recommendation made earlier in the report, and chapter 9 puts the report in the context of some related work being done by the Illinois Department of Transportation.[4] Chapter 10 explicitly states the report's recommendations.

This brief outline, however, only begins to suggest the shape of the argument. As chapter 10 makes clear, the real aim of the report is to discourage the long-term "improvements" listed in chapter 7 and to argue in favor of the suggestions in chapters 5 and 6:

> The overall results of this traffic engineering study allow one to draw a number of general conclusions. The construction of a grade-separated

Figure 9-6   Table of Contents for "Traffic Engineering Study: Clavey Road and U.S. 41 Intersection—Final Report"

Figure 9-6 (continued)

interchange, although capable of eliminating the existing intersection-related accidents, has extensive impacts, including significant property acquisition and relocation, elimination of access driveways and the construction of new access roads, and the strong potential for increased accidents at West Park Avenue. Based on the in-depth analysis performed in this study linking types and numbers of accidents to traffic movements, geometric design and signal hardware, it appears that a full series of low-cost improvements can be made that can account for and have the potential to eliminate a significant number of accidents. Equally as important, the potential for severe accidents will be reduced.
[p. X-1]

In other words, the report argues both implicitly and explicitly that Highland Park should pursue the "full series of low-cost improvements" detailed in chapters 5 and 6 and reject the other alternatives, all of which require "the construction of a grade separated interchange" and which therefore have "extensive impacts." Interestingly, the topics that support these recommendations in chapter 7 are largely common ones; in chapters 5 and 6, however, the authors rely on a number of disciplinary special topics.

To discourage readers from pursuing other alternatives, all of which would require the elimination of the Clavey Road intersection in favor of a grade-separated, limited-access interchange, the authors essentially argue in chapter 7 from a common topic: *consequence*. In the case of each of the seven alternatives, the authors skip quickly over advantages and concentrate instead on one or more of these damaging consequences: "that the elimination of the intersection at Clavey Road will most likely increase the number of accidents" (p. VII-1) at the next intersection down the road (West Park Avenue), where the road again would inevitably narrow; that the change would "add to the congestion" on the roads involved and create delays for motorists; that the costs of acquiring property and constructing the interchange would be prohibitive; and that the change would significantly inconvenience residents, businesses, police, and firefighters. Alternative number one, for example, "will reduce the level of service" by creating congestion and "increase the potential for rear-end accidents" at Clavey Road (p. VII-4). Alternative number two would eliminate the accidents, but it would be "inconvenient for the western Highland Park residents using the Park District and shopping facilities" (p. VII-5) and negatively "affect non-local trips originating in Highland Park" (p. VII-7). Moreover, "Highland Park police and fire services will be negatively affected" (p. VII-5), the additional traffic on other roads would require improvements themselves, and the traffic diverted "will create several problems": "added trip lengths," "additional pressure on other roads," and "additional delays" (pp.VII-7–VII-8). The other five alternatives in the chapter are similarly dismissed by catalogues of undesirable consequences: "additional time" (p. VII-9), expensive acquisition of land (pp. VII-11, VII-13, VII-16), increased noise levels (pp. V-12, V-15), and prohibitive construction costs (pp. VII-12, VII-15, VII-16). Note that the arguments in chapter 7 are easy to follow even for someone unfamiliar with transportation engineering: by using common topics like *consequence*, writers make their cases accessible to everyone.

Chapters 5 and 6, however, are much more difficult for outsiders because the arguments within them are often supported by reasoning from discipline-specific topics. Chapters 5 and 6 essentially develop a series of recommendations—for traffic signal adjustments, signing and marking improvements, increased law enforcement, and so forth—based on general analysis of causes and consequences. But because the writer understands those common relationships *through* the technical concepts used in the analysis, the argument is supported by special topics that are much more accessible to people in the discipline of transportation engineering. The recommendation for "improvements in traffic signals," for instance, is supported by theories and assumptions particular to transportation engineering— by "the lack of sight distance" in the area (i.e., the inability of motorists to see low traffic signs); by the lack of "back plates" to solve visual problems; by faulty "traffic signal phasing" in the area; and by the fact that "the optical programming of the signals makes them extremely difficult to read" (pp. V-1–V-2). The "paving marking improvements" that are recommended next depend on technical studies recorded in scientific journals and footnoted in the report: traverse pavement markings are suggested because they "have been used effectively in Kentucky . . . and Maine to slow traffic" (p.V-7); and raised pavement markers are suggested because the engineering literature indicates that they "can be effective in reducing accidents at an exit ramp area" (p. V-8). Because no support for those assertions is given beyond the footnote references, those references may be considered special topics, the cogency of which would depend on the reader's familiarity with the literature. Finally, when the report recommends that speed limits be enforced more diligently, it resorts again to a special topic—to a disciplinary theory that "a revision to the speed limit is expected to raise the speed of the slower vehicles and tighten up the overall range of speeds, therefore contributing to a safer driving environment" (p. V-8).

The rather brief chapter 6, in recommending three "Minor Construction Improvements," also depends on disciplinary special topics. The first recommendation, to extend "the existing length of the third lane of U.S. 41 north of Clavey Road," is supported only by statements deriving from common topics: the change would have the consequences of "decreasing delay and backups through the Clavey Road intersection" and of eliminating "conflicting [and dangerous] weaving movements" by cars (p. VI-1); and an alternative proposal is rejected on account of its negative consequences: it would cause "extensive backups and delays," "force traffic to adjacent parallel routes," and "further aggravate the rear-end accident problem" (p. VI-2). However, the second recommendation (that the exit ramp of northbound U.S. 41 be revised) is justified by a reference to a disciplinary concept whose implications will be clear only to a transportation engineer: the revision "will allow for more storage" (p. VI-4). And the third recommendation ("that the east leg of Clavey Road be channelized") is also supported by disciplinary special topics. The "channelization" is suggested because of "traffic volumes" (p. VI-4) noted in early chapters of the report; no acceptable traffic volume is spelled out in the report, for that volume is an assumption of the disciplinary community. Moreover, the "channelization will reduce the amount of green time required for Clavey Road"—a topic that makes sense to traffic engineers but that is not readily accessible to outsiders. Clearly, the engineer making these arguments relies heavily on explanations and evidence and reasoning that are part of the conceptual network of his discipline.

Other sections of the report also depend on disciplinary special topics. Chapter 2, an account of "The Existing Study Area" that establishes assumptions for later chapters, defines the area's roadway types in disciplinary terms: "freeway level design," "grade-separated interchanges," "principal arterial facility," "at-grade signalized intersections," "high-volume traffic corridor" (p. II-1). The existing physical situation is described in terms of "four-lane cross sections" and "five-lane cross sections" (p. II-2). Traffic volume is based on "Average Daily Traffic (ADT)" and calculated in accordance with disciplinary conventions. Notice how the first sentence of this final section of chapter 2 is supported by concepts like "total access control," "full freeway-level cross section," "right-of-way," and "freeway-level facility environment," whose full implications are dependent on an insider's knowledge of transportation engineering:

> Overall, the perception a driver has as he travels northbound on U.S. 41 from Lake-Cook Road to West Park Avenue is confusing. He first encounters a low speed limit (40 MPH) in the section of U.S. 41 from Lake-Cook Road to Clavey Road where there is total access control and a

full freeway-level cross section. As he travels north of Clavey Road, the speed limit goes up to 50 MPH but the width of the roadway and right-of-way narrows. He encounters commercial and residential development with associated access driveways. Further north, he approaches the Deerfield Road interchange, where the right-of-way widens and there is little development directly adjacent to the roadway. Once again, the driver is in a freeway-level facility environment. Finally, approaching West Park Avenue the right-of-way begins to narrow, a driveway is encountered to an automobile dealer and West Park Avenue is encountered with a signalized intersection and development with direct access to U.S. 41. (p. II-8)

Chapters 3 and 4 ("Data Collection" and "Data Analysis and Problem Identification"), which argue that certain particular problems need to be solved by the study, also make liberal use of disciplinary special topics. Data is collected according to the discipline's conventions—from "As Built" plans and "orthophotos" (p. III-1); and from traffic counts that monitor " 'Z' and 'U' maneuvers" (p. III-2). Speed studies are based on the "85th percentile speed rule" (p. III-3), a "rule" of the discipline that requires speed limits to be set at a point where 15 percent of the drivers exceed it. The problems identified in chapter 4 are tied to "roadway geometrics" (p. IV-7), "inconsistent cross sections," "capacity" (p. IV-8), "signal cycles," "optical programming of signals," "tangent sections," and "sight distance" (p. IV-9). Finally, the speed limits that are established in chapter 4 and assumed later in the report are defended not by arguments in the report but by a reference to journal literature (p. IV-10).

In short, "Traffic Engineering Study: Clavey Road and U.S. 41 Intersection" is a complex argument that relies on a variety of tactics to find material support for its generalizations. Its overall problem-solving structure is predicted by its genre. One of its chapters (chapter 9) is included at least in part for institutional reasons. Several of its recommendations, especially in chapter 7, depend on common topics easily accessible to any reader. And other recommendations are supported by disciplinary special topics—by theories, assumptions, and formulas current in transportation engineering (and often signaled in a text by the use of specialized vocabulary); by references to the research literature of the field; and by the special methods and diagrams current in transportation engineering. The variety and complexity of the argument can be attributed in part at least to the variety and complexity of its audience. Like many technical reports, this Traffic Engineering Study must satisfy a variety of readers—everyone from local citizens and officials to HDR's own managers to professional engineers who work for local and state agencies. The writers of reports like these often choose their common, generic, institutional, and disciplinary appeals in order to succeed with this varied readership.[5]

CONCLUSION

This chapter has suggested some new directions for teachers and scholars interested in writing in nonacademic settings, especially those interested in technical discourse. The premise of our presentation has been that discourse in particular communities is shaped by the generic, institutional, and disciplinary conventions of that community. Our aim has been to suggest a particular way of conceiving of those conventions and to demonstrate how that method can bring about a better understanding of the arguments of one particular type of discourse, transportation engineering reports. This method emphasizes the complexity of such discourse, especially the variety of its connections to its context and the ways in which those connections contribute to its effectiveness. For scholars, we hope this essay suggests both the continuing relevance of classical rhetoric and the rhetorical interest of technical discourse.

For teachers, we hope we have provided a way of connecting the necessarily general concerns of the writing course to the diverse specializations of students. Our work implies that discussions of argument have an important place in technical writing and business writing courses—and that those discussions ought to include more than an account of the common topics used in public discourse for general audiences. It further implies that teachers will need to be familiar with generic, institutional, and disciplinary constraints before they can advise technical or business writers with complete confidence. It suggests a method for doing rhetorical analyses of technical documents that should have practical applications in the classroom. Finally, it may even suggest a rationale for a sequence of writing courses in the college curriculum—a sequence perhaps analogous to one proposed by James Kinneavy: a general composition course, another course "in which the mature student explains his or her discipline to the general reader in a common university dialect," and a third course "in which students can write as subtly and esoterically as they wish in the genres of their careers to an audience of peers or superiors" (Kinneavy, 1983, p. 16).

Our effort has only been a start, however. Next we must test and refine our conclusions against the results of other analyses in other disciplines. Do "special topics" truly exist? Should they be defined as we have defined them—in terms of the system of classical rhetoric? Are there other, perhaps more efficient, ways that those topics can be conceived of and discovered? Do special topics in fact derive from generic, institutional, and disciplinary sources? Are there other sources of special topics? Only the evidence of many more rhetorical analyses and many more discussions with writers can provide the answers. In addition, we hope to investigate a number of other questions that occurred to us in the course of our work. Are there hard and fast distinctions between generic, institutional, and disciplinary topics, or is there (as we came to suspect) considerable overlap? Do generic, institutional, and disciplinary considerations guide the use of common topics? Would it be possible to develop a complete taxonomy of special topics that would be analogous to Aristotle's taxonomy of common topics? And how does our method of analyzing arguments compare with other methods, especially Toulmin's scheme for analyzing the claims, grounds, warrants, and backing of arguments? We hope others will join us in investigating these questions.

Notes

1. In dialectic there are no special topics. The dialectical topics are a series of general concepts applicable to any subject matter; the concepts include four predicables (definition, property, genus, and accident) and ten categories, such as quantity, quality, place, time (Kennedy, 1980, p. 83).

2. See also I.iv.136a13 and I.i.v.1359b5-7 in the Rhetoric.

3. See, for example, UMTA's External Operating Manual: Program Information for Capital Grants and Technical Studies Grants, U.S. Department of Transportation, 1972.

4. Interestingly, chapter 9 was included in the report largely for institutional reasons. Because the engineers at HDR commonly work with the Illinois Department of Transportation and respect the professionals at IDOT, HDR's engineers wanted to refer to IDOT's related work in the Highland Park area. The remainder of the report and our conversations with Kenneth Nelson at HDR make very clear, however, that HDR was working for Highland Park on the Clavey Road project—not for or with IDOT—and in a very independent way.

5. We are grateful to Kenneth Nelson of Henningson, Durham, and Richardson and to James Miller of the Transportation Institute at Penn State for sharing their work with us, for discussing it in detail with us, and for allowing us to quote from it in this chapter.

References

Aristotle. (1975). *Rhetoric.* (Trans. John Henry Freese.) Cambridge, MA: Harvard University Press.

Bazerman, C. (1981). What written knowledge does: Three examples of academic discourse. *Philosophy of the Social Sciences, 11,* 361-387.

Bazerman, C. (1983). Scientific writing as a social act: A review of the literature of the sociology of science. In P. V. Anderson, R. J. Brockmann, & C. Miller (Eds.), *New essays in technical and scientific communication: Research, theory, and practice.* Farmingdale, NY: Baywood.

Bizzell, P. (1982). Cognition, convention, and certainty: What we need to know about writing. *Pre/Text, 3,* 213-243.

Fish, S. (1980). *Is there a text in this class? The authority of interpretive communities.* Cambridge, MA: Harvard University Press.

Gilbert, N., & Mulkay, M. (1981). Contexts of scientific discourse: Social accounting in experimental papers. In K. D. Knorr, R. Krohn, & R. Whitley (Eds.), *The social process of scientific investigation.* Dordrecht: D. Reidel.

Herrington, A. (1983). *Writing in academic settings: A study of the rhetorical contexts for writing in two college chemical engineering courses.* Unpublished PhD dissertation, Rensselaer Polytechnic Institute.

Kaufer, D. (1979). Point of view in rhetorical situations: Classical and romantic contrasts and contemporary implications. *Quarterly Journal of Speech, 65,* 171-186.

Kennedy, G. A. (1980). *Classical rhetoric and its Christian and secular tradition from ancient to modern times.* Chapel Hill, NC: University of North Carolina Press.

Kinneavy, J. L. (1983). Writing across the curriculum. *Profession 83* (pp. 13-20). New York: Modern Language Association.

Kuhn, T. S. (1970). *The structure of scientific revolutions.* Chicago: University of Chicago Press.

Leff, M. C. (1983). The topics of argumentative invention in latin rhetorical theory from Cicero to Boethius. *Rhetorica, 1,* 23-44.

March, J. G. & Simon, H. A. (1958). *Organizations.* New York: Wiley.

McCloskey, D. N. (1983). The rhetoric of economics. *Journal of Economic Literature, 21,* 481-517.

Miller, C. R. (1983). Fields of argument and special *topoi.* In D. Zarefsky, M. O. Sillars, & J. Rhodes (Eds.), *Argument in transition: Proceedings of the third summer conference on argumentation.* Annandale, VA: Speech Communication Association.

Miller, C. R. (1980). *Environmental impact statements and rhetorical genres: An application of rhetorical theory to technical communicaton.* Unpublished PhD dissertation, Rensselaer Polytechnic Institute.

Mills, G. & Walter, J. (1978). Technical writing. (4th ed.). New York: Holt, Rinehart & Winston.

Odell, L., Goswami, D., Herrington, A., & Quick, D. (1983). Studying writing in non-academic settings. In P. V. Anderson, R. J. Brockmann, & C. R. Miller (Eds.), New essays in technical and scientific communication: Research, theory, and practice. Farmingdale, NY: Baywood.

Perelman, C. (1982). The realm of rhetoric. Notre Dame, IN: University of Notre Dame Press.

Secor, M. & Fahnestock, J. (1982). The rhetoric of literary argument. Paper delivered at the Penn State Conference on Rhetoric and Composition, University Park, PA.

Selzer, J. (1983). The composing processes of an engineer. College Composition and Communication, 34, 178–187.

Toulmin, S. (1958). The uses of argument. Cambridge: Cambridge University Press.

Toulmin, S. (1972). Human understanding: The collective use and evolution of concepts. Princeton: Princeton University Press.

Toulmin, S., Rieke, R., & Janik, A. (1979). An introduction to reasoning. New York: Macmillan.

Moving from Workplace to Classroom— and Back

V

The Writing Teacher in the Workplace
Some Questions and Answers about Consulting

10

DWIGHT W. STEVENSON
Professor of Technical Communicaton
College of Engineering
The University of Michigan

I said I'd think about it, but I knew even before I hung up the phone that I would do it. Here was a state agency offering me $300 for one hour's work, and on my 1971 salary as an associate professor of English that sounded like an enormous sum. Never mind that I knew nothing about the topic they had asked me to speak on: writing appellate judicial opinions. And never mind that I had not met an appellate judge before I was to face an audience of sixty of them from a five-state area surrounding Michigan to tell them how they should structure their written opinions. And never mind that I would have to spend three weeks in the law library preparing the lecture. I liked the sound of that fee for "just one hour's work," and I knew I was going to do it. And later, after calming my excitement, I called back and accepted.

That was my introduction to consulting. Looking back, I am amazed by the accidental nature of it all. I am amazed that I was asked. I am also amazed both by my audacity in accepting the assignment and by the naivete with which I approached it. I had never talked to anyone about consulting before then, and certainly I had never read anything about it. I knew nothing about the whys or the hows, the values or the pitfalls. I just jumped in and did it because I wanted that consulting fee.

I do not regret my decision to take that first job. In fact, it opened up a whole new area for me in research, publication, and teaching; and it led indirectly to my continued consulting on legal writing for more than ten years now. Yet I do think that I could have done a better job if I had been more aware of consulting at the outset and had asked the right questions before getting involved.

There are a number of issues for writing teachers to consider before seeking or accepting consulting work. Certainly it offers important opportunities. Certainly it provides an excellent way of testing classroom theory. Certainly it provides opportunities for developing both research and teaching materials. And, yes, it does pay well. Yet there are some questions that I would urge any writing teacher to ask and answer before beginning to do consulting work, some issues to consider before becoming overly attracted by those fees. And that is the purpose of this chapter: to raise questions that writing teachers should ask about consulting and to try to answer them as well as I can both from the available literature and from experience.

I will begin with a definition of *consulting* and then will organize my list of questions as follows: First, do you want to consult? Second, if you do want to consult, how do you get started? And third, after you are started, what do you do? As I go along, I will try to anticipate and address a number of subordinate issues under each of those general headings.

A DEFINITION OF *CONSULTING*

Before we launch into the first question, it is important to agree on what we mean by this pompous-sounding term, *consulting*. For many people—especially those in liberal arts disciplines—it is a vague term, one that conjures up images of boardrooms, executives dressed in "power suits," and discussions of corporate secrets. After all, relatively few academics in liberal arts disciplines serve as consultants, and many have no contact with colleagues who consult. Indeed, one study of the consulting work of American academics (Marver & Patton, 1976) points out that although humanities disciplines contain 20 percent of all American academics, together they account for only 11 percent of all consulting work. Yet, as the study points out, among academics generally, the proportion who regularly engage in consulting work is over 50 percent. Moreover, my own research convinces me that among some writing teachers—specifically, technical-writing teachers—the proportion who consult regularly is higher than the proportion in the liberal arts generally. For example, a recent study of the activities and accomplishments of twenty-four national leaders in the field of technical communication (Stevenson, 1984) revealed that all but three of the twenty-four members of the study group had consulted during the past five years. Among them, the twenty-one consultants had spent a total of 1,182 days consulting during the five-year period—an astonishing total of 3.2 person-years of continuous consulting. Among the professors in the study group, the average for the five-year period was 62 days of consulting; among associate professors the average was 36 days of consulting during the study period. And that does not tell the whole story, for the most active members of the group consulted more frequently than the averages indicate: the range was from zero to 150 days and zero to 90 days, respectively, for the two ranks. In short, although consulting may be unfamiliar to some academics in liberal arts disciplines, for others, and at least for some writing teachers, consulting is a familiar and frequent activity.

What, then, is *consulting* by writing teachers? I use the term here to refer to communication-related, income-producing activities carried out in business, industry, and government by otherwise full-time academics. Specifically, I am using the term to encompass a number of different sorts of paid work on written and oral communication: research, counseling, management advising, contract writing and editing, and teaching. The work to which I refer is done by academics employed temporarily on salaries or fees to work for business, industry, and government. The fees and salaries are term-based; that is, they are paid for a specific period and carry none of the normal fringe benefits that go with academic salaries. Moreover, these fees always originate outside the academic institution. That is, I exclude from consideration here off-campus work compensated by academic institutions and work that is rewarded—as academic consulting is— by *honoraria*—that is, token fees derived from academic budgets.

DO YOU WANT TO CONSULT?

I started by mentioning my own economically motivated entrance into consulting, and the question of fees *does* seem to be high on everyone's list of questions when consulting is discussed. So let me go immediately to the question of pay. An important point to stress, however, is that the economic incentive should not be the chief reason for consulting, nor are the economic benefits as substantial as they might first seem. Moreover, let me emphasize that other benefits seem to me to outweigh the economic benefits. But more about that later.

Financial Considerations

What *do* consultants earn? The answer to that question is, of course, not a simple matter. I know writing consultants who are being paid as little as $150 per day. I know others who are paid as much as $2,000 per day. In one case I know a writing consultant who was paid $5,000 for two day's work. Yet these extremes are misleading, or so it seems to me. A much more likely range is between $300 and $600 per day—with *day* defined as any significant portion thereof, and with the amount separate from expenses—the travel, hotel, and meal charges associated with being on site for a day's worth of consulting.

Normally, consultants are paid by the day rather than by the hour, and normally they are expected to travel on their own time. Thus a consulting job in a city five hundred miles away might require half a day's travel each way, but the fee would be for only those days spent on the site. Of course, the expenses associated with the trip—mileage to and from the airport, air travel, car rental, hotel, and meals—would be paid by the client, but time for that travel would not. Also, the consultant might write into an agreement that a certain number of preparation days "off site" will be paid. This is a good point to remember. In my eagerness to get my first job, I didn't think of the three weeks it would take me to get ready, so my actual pay for that "$300 hour"was really more like $15 per day. I have now learned to charge for preparation days—and I still tend to underestimate the required time. As a rule of thumb, I estimate that a minimum of two days off-site is *always* required, no matter what the job, and quite frankly I ask for as many preparation days as I think I can get, depending on the nature of the job and the client. To encourage clients to pay the preparation time, I usually set a differential rate; that is, I charge less for a day off-site than for a day on-site. In general I find that clients understand the necessity for research and preparation time—particularly since they do not want a "canned" presentation—and they usually agree to the number of preparation days asked for. At least it is a subject for negotiation.

It is fair to acknowledge some variation in the fees that individual consultants are paid depending on the nature of their clients. Some federal and state agencies, for example, are limited by law as to the amount that they may pay consultants. In some cases, the amount was set years ago. (For example, one agency's limit of $135 per day was set by law in 1968.) Naturally, this tends to make it difficult for these agencies to find consultants. As a result, they tend to be cooperative in paying off-site preparation days to boost the actual fee into the $500 or $600-a-day range that many consultants charge. Other organizations may allow much higher daily fees but tend to be less willing to pay off-site time. Thus, depending on the client, the fees may vary quite a bit. As a result, most consultants would be hard pressed to quote one fixed rate.

The beginning consultant should attempt to be reasonable in setting his or her daily rate, recognizing that to overprice the time may be unrealistic, but also that to underprice it may make clients worry about what they are getting. After all, a company that hires a consultant is not doing so for the first time; to come in absurdly under the normal price raises questions of one's competence and general awareness of consulting. I would not suggest dropping the price below a reasonable level—perhaps $300 or $400 per day—but neither would I suggest that the beginning consultant try to start at the top of the scale.

Of course, these amounts do sound attractive. But remember that the amounts are quite unlike similar amounts in an academic paycheck. They include no fringe benefits—often another 18 or 20 percent at most schools. More important, they are amounts from which no tax will be withheld. They are before-tax dollars that will be taxed at a rate determined by the consultant's total income unless the consultant is incorporated as a business. In the case of a married taxpayer who files jointly, the total earnings of two wage earners might set a tax rate over 40 percent, and the consultant's fee will be taxed at that rate. In other words, a dollar isn't a dollar; it is 60 cents—maybe less. And the $300 or $400 day becomes a $180 or $240 day—in hourly figures, $22.50 or $30.00 per hour.

That isn't all. If the consultant's earnings reach even $1,000, which can happen with two or three day's consulting, the IRS will express an enthusiastic interest in being paid estimated tax on a quarterly basis. They not only want to be paid; they want to be paid in advance. In other words, before that $300 check can be spent, a fair chunk of it will have to be sent to the IRS, or there will be a penalty at the end of the year for failing to file estimated tax.

I have said that consultants generally are paid by the day, in the range of $300 to $600. But it is also true that under the umbrella of consulting is some "job shopping" or contract work that is paid by the hour or by the "piece." A large number of clients, particularly those interested in having writing and editing work done on a one-time basis, expect to pay job-shoppers a flat hourly fee or piece-rate. Typically, this fee is paid without any of the travel expenses or preparation time associated with consulting, and typically the job-shopper has all the job security of a migrant farm laborer. But certainly there is writing and editing work to be done, particularly locally, by consultants who would like to do contract writing and editing. The fees vary considerably, as is indicated in *1983 Writer's Market* (Schemenaur, 1983). For an advertising copywriter the range is $10 to $35 per hour. For associations and groups, $5 to $15 per hour for small groups and up to $60 per hour for large groups. For technical writing, $15 to $30 per hour. For general business writing, $20 to $50 per hour. For corporate histories, up to 5,000 words, $1,000 to $3,000. For sales brochures of 12 to 16 pages, $750 to $3,000. For sales letters, $150 for two pages.

In general, fees of from $15 to $35 per hour for contract writing (that is, $120 to $280 per day) are reasonable. However, in estimating the time necessary to produce a product (or the piece-rate fee for that product), there is more to worry about than the actual writing and editing time. There is the research time and the time necessary for layout and working with a printer to see the final product through to production. From the client's point of view, of course, the job is not done until it is physically produced. Although those production aspects of writing and editing may be unfamiliar to many English teachers, they are normally a part of the contract writer's job and must be taken into account in setting piece rates or in estimating the numbers of hours required to complete a project. Again, as with preparation time, this aspect of the job is often underestimated and thus should be an area of special care for the new consultant.

Along with the fact that he or she must take taxes into account and must plan wisely for preparation time and perhaps for production time, the consultant also must face the simple fact that making money will cost money. That is, few consultants who do more than occasional consulting can do so without spending money on things they customarily take for granted in an academic environment. They must print up some letterhead, business cards, and perhaps brochures. They must pay for the secretarial services academics expect for free. They may need to acquire some equipment such as a good typewriter or a personal computer. (Understandably, schools tend to frown on the use of their supplies, equipment, and personnel for profit-making activities.) And perhaps they will even have to spruce up their wardrobe. (The customary campus look of turtlenecks, baggy cords, and tweeds is mildly unsettling to many clients and a cause for outright consternation among others.) Moreover, for consultants who actually produce a product for their clients, there is the added need to protect themselves with liability insurance. Yes, written material is definable as a *product* under the law. Thus a great deal of the product liability litigation that has exploded in the courts in the past twenty years has centered on the adequacy of the written documentation accompanying the hardware that we usually have in mind when we use the word *product*, (Driskill, 1981). The contract writer—indeed, any serious consultant—should consider liability insurance because, if sued by a consumer, the client in turn can very easily sue the consultant who produced the product in question. Although many consultants ignore this risk, it should be an issue for their concern. And it is an expensive issue. For example, the Association of Professional Writing Consultants recently sought bids on liability insurance for its members.[1] The annual premium rate was $750 per year per $500,000 of insurance. And $500,000 is hardly any insurance at all in the field of liability insurance.

Finally, for the serious consultant, there is the cost of setting up and operating a consulting company. Of course, clear tax advantages and legal protection derive from setting up even a one-person company. The company can own equipment; it is taxed at corporate rates, not personal income rates; it can put the consultant's family on the payroll; and it can provide various tax shelters such as retirement plans and medical insurance plans for its "employees" (you and your family); it can even own a "company car" that is leased to an employee (you) for private use during a reasonable portion of the time. However, there are costs associated with setting up and running a company. Incorporation is not expensive, but the necessary legal and financial advice that follow incorporation can easily add up to several hundred dollars per year.

In simple terms, then, the answer to the question "How much do consultants earn?" is something like $300 to $600 per day (plus expenses) or $15 to $35 an hour (without expenses), depending on the type of work. Both these rates probably sound pretty attractive to underpaid English teachers. As we have seen, however, the simple answer is really quite misleading and the amounts are not quite what they first appear. As a result, to earn over $10,000 per year in consulting really requires a major commitment of effort.

Demands of Consulting

In simple terms, then, the answer to the question "How much do is also the practical reality of what the job entails. On a simple human level it requires a good deal of traveling and worrying about airlines and dry-cleaning schedules. It requires living more than one would wish in hotels and eating hotel restaurant food. It requires working on an intense schedule that sometimes sends you back to the classroom on Monday morning exhausted. And, of course, it requires careful planning and administration of your materials and time. Not only do you have to plan your regular classroom work around consulting trips, you also have to plan your trips so that without your filing cabinet or a secretary you have the transparencies you need in Oshkosh on Tuesday afternoon. From one perspective, consulting is a second job—moonlighting that will tire you out, tax your organizational skills, send you to places you don't really want to be, and require you to live at least part of your life uncomfortably away from home.

But more important to consider than any of these creature-comfort issues is the fact that consulting will compete, as a second job, for time you need professionally to spend on research and teaching. Make no mistake, consulting is an activity that may be smiled upon by some academic administrators; but it is also an activity that ranks significantly below teaching and research in most administrators' minds. No one ever got tenure for consulting.

Admittedly, in technical institutes and other technical environments, consulting tends to be routine. For example, the dean of the Engineering College at Michigan said this about consulting: "Although we are certainly an academic program like physics, chemistry, and so forth, we are also a professional school. Many of our faculty have very strong professional obligations as engineers. Their consulting activities and service on various state and federal committees are roughly akin to scholarship in other units."[2] In other words, consulting is tolerated and even encouraged, as is service work generally, but service work of a special order. Yet, even in such an environment, consulting is *rewarded* only if it results in direct contributions to research and teaching. The consulting work itself is regarded as necessary to stay in touch, a responsibility that carries its own reward. But only when it results in funded research, in publication, and in direct impact on the classroom does it become a rewardable form of academic performance. (I make this observation only after surveying the chairs of a number of technical departments in which consulting is done.)

In an English department, consulting may be even more problematic for the new consultant. In engineering, consulting is encouraged because it is expected to lead to research and publication, whereas in English it often is seen as *preventing* research and publication—or as producing publications of unrewardable types. Let me quote, for example, the letter of one candidate for tenure. He asks, "Can I use material I wrote for money—in one case a 600-page book—as evidence of scholarship? Would my time have been better spent banging out an article this summer rather than working with the XYZ Corporation?"[3] The answer, I am afraid, is obvious: in most English departments, writing the refereed journal article would have been a better way to spend his time. Even in an engineering school, the act of writing that 600-page book should have led to further research (that is, funded research), to publication, or to direct impact on his teaching before it became a major issue in a tenure review.

In sum, the lure of consulting fees and interesting work may cause the consultant to lose sight of the normal reward system that operates in academic life. Consulting may take away the time necessary for publication. It may not contribute to teaching in evident ways. As a consequence, it may ultimately prevent professional advancement. At the very least, the consultant should recognize that consulting is normally seen as an appropriate stimulus to research, publication, and innovative teaching; it is seldom (perhaps never) seen as an alternative to them.

The economic rewards may not be all that they appear to be, and for various practical and professional reasons consulting may not be the best choice for everyone. But what are the positive answers to the question, "Do you want to consult?"

Benefits of Consulting

In my view, there are several strong positive answers. First, the alert consultant will always bring back far more than he or she takes into industry, business, or government. Consulting presents a rich opportunity to learn from the experience of others, to discover new ways of doing things, to find fruitful new research areas. For example, much the most interesting research being done anywhere concerning on-line documentation (electronic texts) is being done in superbly equipped laboratories in industry. No university laboratories even come close. Similarly, some of the most interesting and useful publications on communication are now being done by research scientists in major companies such as IBM or Bell Labs. Often these publications are in-house research reports, but they represent the cutting edge of work in cognitive psychology, human-factors engineering, and other communication-related disciplines. To have first-hand access to such work is one of the chief benefits of consulting.

Another benefit is that consultants have a steady supply of example materials to be used in research, teaching, and publication. Although constrained by confidentiality agreements, consultants have access to real-world documents that other writing teachers may not even know to exist. For example, what is a PSI report? Have you ever seen one? Ever heard of one? Do you have any idea what the law requires they contain? Chances are that you do not know any of these things; yet in Michigan alone there are 700 agents of the Michigan Department of Corrections who, collectively, write 20,000 Pre-sentence Investigation (PSI) Reports per year for use by judges in sentencing convicted felons. (And similar reports are written in every state, a million per year nationally.) The reports are typically five or six single-spaced pages containing specific sorts of information arranged according to specific guidelines. In many states they are governed by rigorous disclosure rules and must be able to stand up in court under cross-examination. Writing teachers who have social work students or criminal justice students in their classes right now are probably training writers who will eventually write these reports. Yet examples of these reports are found in no textbook that I am aware of. Without consulting work, perhaps you would never see this sort of report.

In addition to helping the consultant learn what is happening in the field and providing him or her with a supply of example materials for use in publication and teaching, consulting also helps the consultant to develop new theory and to test current theory. It puts the consultant into a situation where the problems are distinctive and frequently not amenable to stock solutions. It requires facing tradeoffs of quality, time, and money. Recently, for example, a proposal submitted late by one company caused them to be disqualified from bidding on a twenty-six million dollar construction job (Moorhead, 1984). Could a writing teacher have helped with the planning, writing, and scheduling of the bid preparation? (The development of such a proposal is an extremely complex and expensive undertaking.) Or in another instance, a badly written three-page report cost one company $75,000 in wasted research.[4] Could a writing teacher have helped the writer to have handled it better?

The point is that consulting work puts you on the spot. It forces you to learn quickly, to adapt, to integrate, to make trade-offs, but to get results. It forces you to test your theory and to develop new theory to deal with unfamiliar situations. But in doing so, it provides perhaps the greatest reward in teaching: the excitement of a new challenge and the exhiliration that comes with meeting it successfully.

A final positive benefit to consulting is, quite frankly, that it helps to increase your credibility with your students, and perhaps with your colleagues. Students are understandably suspicious of teachers who never venture off the campus. They wonder about the applicability of writing instruction to the needs of what they commonly call "the real world." And they give at least some credence to the old saw, "Those that can, do . . . ," etc. If you bring into your classroom new writing assignments modeled on "real world" problems which you are learning about in your consulting, if you can show students "real life" examples rather than generic examples, if you can enlist their help in trying out different solutions to real problems, your stock goes up. Particularly with business and technical students this suspicion of the isolated academic can be a problem for the non-consulting writing teacher. After all, most of the students' other professors consult and use consulting problems in their teaching. The Chemical Engineers on our campus, for example, take a design course in their senior year. The problems are always real, and the affected companies send visitors to participate in the class planning, occasionally in lecturing, and even in evaluating the design reports which result. I cannot imagine teaching those students in a writing course without connecting in some way to the experience that they are having in the design course. Conversely, I know from experience that to work closely and realistically with those students concerning the rhetorical aspects of their design work is to gain their willing cooperation and respect; they work hard at what they care about. If there were no other benefit to consulting work, that benefit might be enough to justify it for the writing teacher.

To conclude, the question is "do you want to consult?" The answer, as I hope I have shown, is not obvious. Certainly it should not be the answer to which I alluded at the beginning, my own first answer, "Yes. I need the money." In my view, the money may be the smallest reward for consulting, and certainly there are other, more important benefits for the beginning consultant to consider. If your answer is to be, "yes, I want to consult," at least let the answer be based upon substantive reasons.

HOW DO YOU GET STARTED?

The beginning consultant faces the same dilemma faced by the first-time job hunter: you need experience to get a job, but you need a job to get experience. If you are willing to take time and to work at it, however, there are a number of methods of getting involved in consulting. In all likelihood it isn't something that will happen in a few weeks, but there are opportunities for those who are willing to work at finding them.

Make Personal Contacts

One point to recognize at the outset is that the first method chosen by many beginning consultants—direct mail solicitation—is probably the least likely to get results. They print up some letterhead stationery, business cards, and perhaps a brochure (at a cost of several hundred dollars), and then mail these sales pitches to every organization in the immediate area. "Jones Communication Consultants, Inc., is pleased to announce a new service in this area . . ." and so forth.

Unfortunately, that tactic is probably going to produce very little unless you really stick with it, mailing out large volumes of direct mail and spending substantial amounts of time at it. First, every company is constantly buried in unsolicited sales pitches; thus they regard these proposals in the same way the homeowner regards "Occupant" mail—as an annoyance to be swept aside as quickly as possible. While the beginning consultant might hope that the company will carefully read his or her expensively prepared and carefully written material, it often is quickly "processed"—that is, trashed. Second, even if the mail is read, it is likely to be read by the wrong people. That is, it probably will not reach the managers who have both a need for the consultant's services and the decision-making authority to do something about meeting that need. Third, because the unsolicited proposals are written with no knowledge of specific needs, they are likely to be so general as to be of little interest to a decision maker, even if by luck they do happen to reach the right desk. For example, if a manager's biggest headache is that his or her employees do not know how to compose effective Telex messages for use in the Japan office, it does little good to provide a two-page list of generic information about all the writing problems you are prepared to deal with. The manager's need is specific; the unsolicited proposal is necessarily general.

There is an analogy here to the advice we give our students about job hunting. We tell them not to write to personnel departments because those departments have no decision-making authority to hire salaried employees. Personnel departments, we tell them, have three functions: (1) to deselect as many applicants as possible, (2) to pass along to decision makers those few that match posted needs, and (3) to process the paper work and make arrangements once the decision has been made to interview or to hire. In other words, to write the personnel department is to miss the decision maker and to fall into the protective screen companies erect between applicants and decision makers.

It is the same with unsolicited proposals. To propose consulting work to companies without knowing anything about their internal workings is to lump the proposal together with the rest of the junk mail and miss getting to the people in the company who have communication problems to be solved and a budget to solve them with. Although a training department may administer a project, it seldom originates that project. The trick, then, is to reach the right people and to know in some specific detail what their communication problems are.

Of course, if the beginning consultant has friends who work in local companies, he or she can probably learn the names of specific managers and perhaps even something about their specific needs. If so, the unsolicited proposal has a higher chance of success. But you may not have that inside access to companies and may feel awkward about using it even if you do. Furthermore, even if you reach the right person with something specific, from his or her point of view you are still an unknown. Thus you must find other ways to learn about the inside workings of prospective client companies and to meet the people who make the decisions in them.

Perhaps one of the best ways of doing this is to take advantage of the local chapters of the various professional societies in your area. Probably there are monthly meetings of the Society for Professional Engineers, the Society of Automotive Engineers, the Society of Naval Architects and Marine Engineers, and the like. Attending these meetings will be a professionally active cadre of technical specialists representing a cross-section of companies in the area—clearly the people to meet and talk to in order to learn about needs for consulting work and, specifically, about who has those needs.

Finding the professional societies is a simple matter. The reference desk at the public library or the local Chamber of Commerce is almost certain to have a listing—arranged by occupational specialty, including information about where and when meetings are held, and providing the name and telephone number of a local contact person. It took me only two telephone calls and less than five minutes to obtain such a listing for my own area.

Once you have found the list of professional societies, it is a simple matter to call up and ask to be allowed to attend a monthly meeting. Of course, it is much too soon to indicate an interest in consulting work; but it is quite reasonable to explain that you teach writing at the local university and are therefore interested in chatting with some of the participants about what they think you should be working on with your students. (That, by the way, is a clear benefit of attending these meetings.) Indicate that you will not interrupt the meeting in any way but that you would just like to observe, talking to participants during the coffee break or at the social part of the meeting afterwards. Almost certainly you will be welcome to attend.

The next stage is to do just what you have said you will: attend the meetings, meet people, talk to them when you can about writing and about their own particular areas of concern at their various companies. Don't rush it; just take time to get to know them and to let them know you, remembering that they are likely to be interested in you but uncertain about why an English teacher would want to attend a meeting of the Association of Computing Manufacturers. Above all, *listen*: you are there to learn from them, not to teach.

After you have gotten to know people and have acquired a fairly specific sense of what they see as their writing problems, you are ready for the next phase. Approach the program chair and offer to work up a little talk for the next meeting—a talk in which you will give a writing teacher's advice on how to handle a specific problem that you have heard about during earlier meetings. If the program chair is like most people with such assignments, he or she will be delighted to have a part of a program taken care of, and you will find yourself on the program for the next meeting.

Now, of course, you have to deliver. That is, you really do have to provide something that they will find useful. You have to entertain them. You have to arouse their interest. But if you have really been listening during the earlier meetings, by now you should have a feel for what will work, and you should know the people to ask for help in finding a few examples that you can use in your talk. Again, you should have no problem. In fact, as soon as you ask most managers if they have any examples of bad writing, you will find yourself with more material than you can cover in the short time you will talk. But you must keep the talk both short and reasonably light. A classroom lecture won't work for professionals who have been out of school for many years and who have already put in an eight-hour day before they hear you. The trick is to leave them with the solid impression that you know what you are talking about, that you really do have some specific solutions to real problems, and that you can handle yourself well in a professional context.

If the talk has gone well, you will know it. But don't expect to receive offers that evening or to sit down to write proposals the next day. Getting started is a slow process of becoming known, of learning, and of meeting the people who may become clients. If you do get some feelers, of course, follow them up. Offer to send a paper based on your talk for use in the company newsletter. Offer to deliver the talk at another meeting or in a company. Offer to come in for a closer look in a particular company, to conduct some unpaid research and perhaps to provide advice or guidelines they might find useful. Just keep doing what you have been doing—learning, getting to be known, and offering to help. Sooner or later you will get a nibble, and then you can folow it up with a specific proposal written to the right people and addressing the right problems. You can present yourself as a known person. You can visit companies and talk face to face about what needs to be done and what you are able to offer.

This route to consulting may seem tediously long to the eager beginner, but it is an effective route. This is because *companies* don't hire consultants; *individual decision makers* within companies do. They hire consultants to meet specific needs, not general ones. And they much prefer to deal with people whom, through first-hand observation, they have come to regard as competent. In my own case, a talk given at a Law Clerk's Conference and a paper presented at an Earthmover's Conference (Society of Automotive Engineers, heavy-equipment manufacturers division) have provided numerous contacts, which in turn have led to consulting opportunities for me over the years. (These two presentations thus indirectly paid for the college education of one of my two children.) It may be a slow route, but it works.

Invite Professionals to Campus

A second way to get involved in consulting is very much like the first, but instead of attending professional society meetings, you get the professionals to come to the school and become involved in the planning of writing instruction. A number of schools use advisory boards to work in close association with their technical writing programs (see chapter 3 by Couture et al., in this volume). Often, arranging contact through the Society for Technical Communication, these schools have organized groups of technical specialists to help in setting objectives for courses, in developing teaching materials, in organizing internship programs, and in evaluating students' work. Although my own school does not have an advisory board, my colleagues and I have had the opportunity to call professionals a number of times, and we have always found them willing to help. On at least a dozen occasions, a company has paid all the costs for its employees to spend significant amounts of time working with us without charge. On three occasions I have traveled (at their expense) to visit companies that had something they wanted to share with us. I am referring here not to short trips into Detroit, 50 miles away, but to trips to California, Florida and Minnesota. Companies, of course, see this activity as good public relations and as an opportunity to influence the training of future employees. Beyond that, they seem to be genuinely interested in establishing mutually beneficial contacts.

From the point of view of the prospective consultant, the principle here is the same as in the first method: get to know people in companies, let them come to know you, and acquire some specific knowledge of their needs. As you can see, this strategy will provide several benefits beyond the possibility of developing a consulting relationship with various companies. Both research and curriculum design can be helped by university-industry exchange. It may also produce an offer for consulting. For example, one of my colleagues had a number of interactions over a period of about three years with a manager for the technical information department of one of the large automobile manufacturers. Through that association, the manager had learned of my colleague's expertise in the area of teaching technical English to nonnative speakers. Since in this particular company (as in many) a large proportion of the research engineering staff are foreign-born, this association led to a request for a proposal and, ultimately, an extended consulting appointment.

Of course, this second method still requires some initial contact between a school and a company. Most large companies have college relations officers who will be happy to refer inquiries to the appropriate individuals. To illustrate, one telephone inquiry to the college relations office of a large computer manufacturer contributed to a three-year chain reaction of events: (1) his visiting our campus twice to meet with us; (2) his sending two employees—one from Florida and another from Chicago—to be interviewed on videotape for use in our classes; (3) invitations to participate in two corporate meetings; (4) four visits by two senior managers of the company; (5) two visits by the department heads within the company; (6) the summer-long paid visit of one of our faculty to the company; (7) approximately $20,000 worth of consulting contracts over a three-year period, including work on both coasts, on northern and southern borders, and in Europe; and (8) two contracts for research totaling $120,000.

The point is that contact must be established between representatives of a school and representatives of companies. In the first method, you go out to establish the contact; in the second, you invite them in. From the experience within my department, I would say that both methods do work and both ultimately result in consultations.

Publish in Appropriate Journals

A third method that is almost certain to get results is the obvious one for writing teachers: publish. There is no better way to become known to prospective clients than to publish articles that catch their attention in professional journals. Admittedly, this method is a little difficult to use without other sorts of contact with industry, business, and government. That is, without such contacts, you probably do not know what subjects are appropriate, and you may not know where to publish in order to catch the eye of prospective clients. Certainly an article in *College English* or in *College Composition and Communication* is unlikely to catch the attention of prospective clients. But if you take advantage of every opportunity to appear in print in places where business, industry, and government people will see your work, almost certainly you will be contacted for consulting sooner or later.

Turn that talk you gave for the professional society into a little article. Then ask your friends in the professional society for a list of appropriate places to send it. No doubt the society has a journal, and, if your talk went over well at the local meeting, perhaps it would go over well in the journal also. Or consider sending it as a proposed paper for the national meeting of the society. Since professional societies in the sciences and technology often have excellent *Proceedings*, your article may attract quite a bit of attention if presented in this way.

Because the outlets for publication tend also to be specialized, your article will have the best chance for publication if it is fairly specialized, too. For example, there is a journal for military surgeons and one for military hospital administrators. An article on medical writing might be of considerable interest to one of those journals but of no interest at all to the other. Similarly, an article on legal writing might find a large and interested audience in a journal like *Judicature* but go quietly unnoticed in a journal like the *Vanderbilt Law Review*. Thus you may have to search around. But a number of professional journals in different disciplines have carried articles on communication in the past and will no doubt be receptive to them in the future.

Again, from my own experience and that of my colleagues, the evidence is that publication in industry, business, and government contexts produces consulting offers, although sometimes the direct connection may be difficult to trace. Nonetheless, it is worth pointing out here that to publish articles related to writing in the workplace also serves other purposes than attracting potential clients. It will provide an evidence of relations between theoretical research and application, an issue appropriately of interest to tenure and promotion review committees. Naturally, from the academic administrator's point of view, publications in journals such as *Personal Computer Age* are not equivalent to publications in refereed academic journals. Such publications, however, let a consultant begin to connect research, consulting, and publication and, in that light, are worth doing.

Apply for Specific Jobs

A final way to find consulting work is simply to treat it as a summer job to be found, as such jobs are, by direct application. This is perhaps a little different from the sort of consultation we normally have in mind, but it is a way to get started and to establish some credentials.

Earlier I mentioned job-shopping—that is, contract writing and editing carried out on an hourly or piece-work basis. Such work can be found in the "help-wanted" section of the newspaper or in the directories that job-shoppers use as their guides. It may surprise you to know that such directories exist, but many free-lance writers who make their livings entirely by job-shop work depend on these directories. Sometimes the jobs last a few days, sometimes they extend for years. But always they go to people who are willing to go where the work is, to work on an hourly basis, to give up fringe benefits, and to have no job security beyond the immediate writing project.

This sounds like a difficult life, and no doubt it is. But there is work to be had for the beginning consultant—and probably there is no better training ground. As Donald H. Cunningham has said after his experience in job-shopping (Cunningham, 1984), it will provide twice as much money as you can make in a summer of teaching; it will take you to different locations; it will provide professional challenges; it will give you understanding of the work world into which you are sending your students; and it will increase both your competence as a writer and your credibility with colleagues, students, and clients.

To find such work, submit your resumé and a letter of application directly to as many contract firms as you wish. These are easy to locate through the directories I mentioned earlier. These directories are available from Contract Engineering Publication,[5] an organization that publishes several trade publications such as *Directory of Contract Service Firms*, the monthly *Contract World*, and the weekly *Newsletter of Job Openings*. As Cunningham points out, the firm even has a resumé-mailing service to which you can subscribe.

There are many other ways to get started in consulting. You can put your name on the mailing list for Requests for Proposals published by federal and state agencies. You can ask ex-students to alert you to possibilities within their companies. Finally, you can offer to do unpaid research in companies to help them to diagnose communication bottlenecks. Any of these methods will work—and have worked for colleagues of mine.

Whatever approach you use, however, there are two important points to remember. First, consulting work does not come to people who stay on the campus and who are unknown in the workplace. It comes only to those who, by some mechanism, have established a bridge of mutual knowledge, respect, and interest. Second, once consulting work has started, there is very little difficulty in finding further consulting work. Indeed, most academic consultants discover that they have so many repeat consultations and referrals that they no longer need to seek consulting actively. Some consultants find that they do not have time to take care of the consulting offered to them. In some cases this has presented a conflict of values for consultants: they have wanted to hold onto the academic life, but the consultant's life is appealing, too. In other cases, consultants have found the consulting opportunities so numerous that they have had to choose between the two lives and have gone into full-time consulting. In any case, the first jobs are perhaps a little difficult to find, but after that there is no shortage.

WHAT DO YOU DO?

Experienced consultants or not, we have all spent a lifetime in studying the uses of language and how to perform and to teach those uses. Thus the appropriate answer to the question, "How do you consult about writing?" may be simply, "Do what you already know how to do, and do it in your own way; just do it in a different place." This is particularly true if the job is either writing, editing, or advising rather than research or teaching, because it is only with research and teaching that detailed methodologies can be developed. In the other types of consulting the consultant really has to roll with the punches. Even with teaching and research, despite the fact that numerous articles present detailed methodologies for in-house courses,[6] I suspect there really are no universally applicable trade secrets here, no patented techniques.

Yet if I am uneasy about focusing on the particulars of method, I am also convinced that underlying the variety of appropriate methods in consulting there is a general process that might be usefully examined. Thus I will focus on that process in my approach to this final question. Specifically, I will explore each of the ten stages that I see as appropriate in consulting work, offering, as I go along, suggestions for the successful management of those stages. First, however, I would like to approach a threshold issue that all consultants must consider in every stage of the consulting process: consulting ethics.

Consulting Ethics

Before this book appears, a Code of Ethics, now in draft form, will have been published by the Association of Professional Writing Consultants (APWC). My strong suggestion is that beginning consultants request a copy of the APWC code from the president of that association, Lee Clark Johns[7].

Although I do not know the final form of the APWC code, other sources suggest a number of appropriate guidelines. Many of the hundreds of consulting associations listed in the *Encyclopedia of Associations* have such codes. Numerous articles have been written on the subject by scholars in a variety of fields (see especially Benne, K. D., 1969; Pfeiffer, J. W. & Jones, J. E., 1977). Moreover, a useful synthesis of these codes and articles is presented in a book which I recommend, *The Profession and Practice of Consultation*, by June Gallessich (1983).

Gallessich provides a detailed discussion of twenty-eight principles of consulting ethics which I will summarize here only briefly. These are:

1. Consultants place their clients' interests above their own, in all actions supporting the interpretation of the official representative of the client organization on matters of company policy and interest.

2. Consultants are responsible for safeguarding the welfare of their client organizations.

3. Consultants present their professional qualifications and limitations accurately.

4. Consultants do not make unrealistic promises about the benefits of their services.

5. Consultants are obliged to express their observation of unethical behavior on the part of a client to official representatives of the client organization.

6. Consultants avoid entering into relationships with competing companies, relationships that can create conflicts of interest and jeopardize confidentiality.

7. Consultants avoid manipulating consultees and instead seek to increase their independence and freedom of choice.

8. Consultants accept contracts only if they are reasonably sure that the client will benefit from their services.

9. Consultants establish clear contracts with well-defined parameters.

10. Consultants provide all the services agreed on, being careful to do so within the time boundaries of the contract.

11. Consultants strive to evaluate the outcome of their services.

12. Consultants assume responsibility for assisting administrators in establishing and observing confidentiality policies relative to the consultation.

13. Consultants seek to maintain the highest standard of competence in their profession, keeping abreast of new theoretical, empirical, and technical developments that are related to consultation.

14. Consultants know their professional strengths, weaknesses, and biases; they avoid allowing their particular professional "sets" to distort their approaches to the needs of their clients.

15. Consultants are aware of personal characteristics which predispose them to systematic biases—issues of age, ethnic origin, sex, and social status that may distort their perceptions and recommendations.

16. Consultants do not enter into contracts with companies or clients whose values are antithetical to their own.

17. Consultants regularly assess their strengths and weaknesses.

18. Consultants advertise and promote their services accurately.

19. Consultants serve public interests by providing their services free of charge to publicly based consultees who are unable to pay.

20. Consultants contribute to the growth of knowledge through their own research and experimentation.

21. Consultants seek to protect the public welfare; if client company policies and actions are harmful to that welfare, the consultant will seek to change that behavior by discussing it with the client. The consultant should also be prepared to resign and even to take public action against a client company if the harmful behavior does not cease.

22. Consultants contribute to the training of less experienced consultants.

23. Consultants behave so as to protect the reputation of their profession.

24. Consultants cooperate with other consultants and with members of other professions.

25. Consultants stay within the normative range of fees for consultants in their area of expertise and geographical location.

26. Consultants who observe unethical behavior by other professionals should first discuss it with those individuals and, if no change occurs, should report that behavior to another professional or professional group for review.

27. Consultants contribute to their profession by participating in activities of peer associations and supporting their standards.

28. Consultants take active steps to maintain and increase their effectiveness; in the event that either their physical or their mental health interferes with normal functioning, they suspend or terminate their services.

It may be stating the obvious to say that writing consultants, like writing teachers in any context, should be ethical in all aspects in the process of their work. Yet the competitive business and corporate context in which consulting is carried out almost inevitably will confront the consultant with unfamiliar ethical issues.

For example, consider the issue of confidentiality. In a classroom context, of course, we respect the basic need for *personal* confidentiality in our dealings with our students. Yet how many of us have not made use of examples from student papers without the students' permission? How many of us have not discussed—without permission—situations, problems, and particular solutions that we have found in student work? I confess that I have done so in class *this week*, and I submit that the evidence of our textbooks and our conference papers is that many writing teachers do so commonly, even in print.

Yet surely there is a difference between the classroom context and the corporate context in this regard. In the classroom we can protect the *person* even though we may use some of the person's work as illustration. In the corporate context, it is the *work itself* that often must be protected. For example, I have often read documents and talked to people in companies about market-sensitive issues. I have a foot-high stack of confidential company papers within two feet of me as I write this sentence. On my bookshelf three feet away is a draft volume describing what was, a year ago—when I received it—an unannounced product in the computer industry; the competition would have loved to see that. Last summer I reviewed a document describing the defense strategy in a product liability case in which my host company was being sued—the plaintiff would have killed to see that. And so on. In these cases, clearly I cannot use even sanitized examples drawn from my client's work. Not only would it make me legally vulnerable, it would be a breach of ethics to reveal to others work that I have seen.

And it *is* frustrating! I have several wonderful examples that I would love to share with my students and to write about. Yet there is just no alternative here. The context for these examples is not the university context, where knowledge is free and shared; it is the corporate context, where knowledge—even apparently trivial knowledge—is often high-priced and jealously guarded. To the writing teacher that may seem an unreasonable constraint; to the writing consultant it cannot. Academic freedom is an *academic* concept, not a concept that pertains to industry and business.

In sum, a threshold issue that must run through every stage of the consulting process is the issue of consulting ethics. In important respects the ethics of the consultant's world are distinctive, and thus merit consideration. Indeed, I believe the topic merits further reading by consultants.

But let me turn now to discussion of the stages of the process of consulting.

Stages of Consulting

In all, I see ten likely stages in many consulting relationships (Gallessich, 1983, pp. 253–254; see also Whalen, 1980):

- Seeking consultantships.
- Making initial contact.
- Preparing a preliminary proposal.
- Reaching an agreement.
- Conducting research.
- Preparing the design.
- Presenting it to management.
- Preparing the materials.
- Presenting your results.
- Following up afterward.

The first stage, *seeking consultantships,* has been covered in the earlier discussion, so let me take up the stages that follow that first stage.

MAKING INITIAL CONTACT. At this stage, solicited or unsolicited, an invitation is made either for work or for a bid on work. Usually the invitation will come in the form of a telephone call rather than in the form of a Request for Proposal, a letter, or a direct personal contact. Moreover, often it will come from a person other than the person who has made a decision to hire a consultant and for whom the work is to be done—from a staff person, perhaps the head of an in-house training department.

From both parties' point of view, the fact that the contact often comes in the form of a telephone call is an advantage. In fact, if the initial contact comes in the form of a letter or a Request for Proposal (RFP), as it sometimes does, there is good justification for following it up with a telephone call (and, if possible, with an interview) before a proposal is written. The letter is not likely to say much beyond the fact that the company is considering having you as a consultant, that they want to receive a proposal from you, and that they would perhaps like to have your services at some specific period of time. An RFP is likely to focus more on the appropriate *form* of the proposal than on the *reasons behind the request*. A telephone contact (or interview), on the other hand, gives the client this advantage: a good deal can be said to the consultant with little expense in time. Another advantage for both the client and the consultant is that telephone contacts and interviews are interactive. Both client and consultant can get preliminary responses to a number of particular questions that will have to be resolved before the consultantship is carried out. For the consultant especially, this provides a good deal of help. It provides the basis on which the next stages are to be carried out. Accordingly, it is good practice to take some time to "pump" the client's contact person as much as possible to get solid information about what the specific problems are, who needs help, why—and about how the proposal should be written. But most important, an initial telephone call will provide an opportunity for the consultant to find out in particular who the decision maker is behind the decison to seek a consultant's services.

That latter point strikes me as important. Seldom have I been directly approached by the person who is really hiring me. Yet in most of these cases I have found that a decision maker behind the contact person is by far the best source of information to be used in drafting a proposal and carrying out work. The contact person may not actually know too much about the specifics of the situation. Moreover, although sometimes the decision maker will have delegated the task of reviewing proposals to someone else, often the proposal will be read and evaluated by the decision maker himself or herself. Thus to base the proposal on information gained solely from the contact person, or even from an RFP, is to risk missing crucial details relating to specific objectives (see Dickson, 1982).

Again, I will recall my own first telephone contact for a consultantship. I was so flattered to be asked, so excited about the prospect of that $300 fee, that I hardly asked anything. I just sputtered profuse thanks for the invitation and hung up. The call probably lasted no more than two or three minutes: not a very solid basis for planning what was to be done.

The danger here is that you may want the first job so much that you will not take time to be businesslike. Certainly you would not base the decision to buy or sell a used car on no more than two or three minutes of discussion over the telephone; yet the price of the consultantship may well exceed the cost of that used car several times over. Does it not merit equal and careful discussion?

I have made an assumption here that may or may not hold—the assumption that the work is to be done at a distant location. (That has been my experience, but for others it may be different.) If that is not the case—if the work is to be done locally—the obvious thing to do is to ask immediately for an interview with the contact person and with the decision makers so that the details of the consultantship can be discussed before a proposal is written. In cases where face-to-face interviews have been possible for me, I have sought them. In one instance, I even traveled as far as four hundred miles for an interview, with no guarantee that I would recover my expenses.

During this initial contact stage many issues must be resolved by both the prospective client and the consultant. The consultant needs hard information to use for preparing a proposal; the client needs affirmation of the preliminary decision that there may be a good fit between the consultant and the company. In my view, the best way to meet both needs is by substantial telephone contact with the decision maker and contact person or by face-to-face, preliminary interviews with both of them.

PREPARING A PRELIMINARY PROPOSAL. Depending on the degree to which this stage is guided by a detailed RFP and by sufficient face-to-face or telephone interviews, this stage can be relatively easy or very difficult. Also, it will be greatly affected by the extent to which a decision to hire has already been made. In many cases the hiring decision will already have been concluded; in other cases the competition is just beginning. (Perhaps contrary to expectation, I find that most of my proposals are written after I have been tentatively hired, not before.) A starting point, then, is to decide whether the purpose of the proposal is to win the contract or to establish a basic plan for the consultation. In the former case, a full-blown, persuasive proposal will be necessary; in the latter case, a relatively short letter will be sufficient to review and clarify for the record what has been talked about so far with the client at the initial contact stage.

If the proposal is to sell the consultation, in addition to the obvious matters of schedule, budget, materials, and equipment needs, a package of credentials information is needed: full vita, sample publications, sample course materials, testimonial letters, sets of course evaluations from industry courses, and the like. It is useful here to consider the advice that one industry person gives to managers about hiring writing consultants from the academic community. Looking at the issue from the industry side, Frederick M. O'Hara tells managers to seek a consultant who has proven experience not just in teaching but also in writing. He says: "A good teacher of writing should be a good writer as well as a good teacher. Ask to see . . . lists of publications and some examples of his or her writing . . . Ask to see evaluations of the courses that have been performed and what the results were. Contact the consultant's previous employers. . . . Ask to see any instructional materials the consultant is considering using" (1983). In other words, he advocates that managers really check up on the prospective consultant. His advice is intended for managers, but it can be helpful to consultants too. After all, both the interview stage and the proposal stage can make the manager's job easier if they furnish—without the manager's request—the information needed to do the checking that O'Hara recommends.

If the initial contact has established that a contract will be given, then the purpose of the proposal is to present the details of a preliminary plan; the explicit "selling" information can be omitted from the proposal. What should not be omitted, however, is reasonably detailed consideration of all of the following:

- Statement of the general purposes of the project and identification of its preliminary objectives (these will later be particularized in the fully developed plan)

- Statement of the respective responsibilities of the client and of the consultant
- Schedule
- Budget
- Rudimentary plan for implementation

Of these several matters I would rate *purposes, budget,* and *schedule* as the most important. The problem-solving plan is yet to be developed; in fact, there is a danger of committing too early—before research—to do work in a particular way. (More about the research and planning stages later.) The other preliminary issues, however, will be the basis for a contract and thus need to be understood at the outset.

In developing a preliminary proposal, it is important to agree on what the basic problems are. If they are not well understood, even the most rudimentary plan for solving those problems may be flawed. For example, as I mentioned earlier, I was once approached by a state agency that wanted to improve the writing of 700 of its field agents. The problem, they told me, was "bad writing." But I found in face-to-face preliminary interviews that the problem was really twofold: first, the "writing" was really transcribed *dictation*, which, because of time constraints, could not be significantly edited; second, because of a new law requiring public disclosure, the documents under discussion had to be "lawyer-proofed." In other words, the real problems were that they had no effective heuristic for dictation and that they did not know what features of their documents would not stand the scrutiny of public disclosure. To develop a plan to address those two particular issues obviously was quite different from developing a preliminary plan to address "bad writing" generally.

Issues of budget and schedule are especially important to get straight from the beginning. If, for example, you expect to bill secretarial time, equipment rental, telephone calls, travel and living expenses, you need to say so now. Later on it won't do to say, "Oh, I thought you would cover those things." Also it is imperative to establish a schedule that permits research and paid preparation time, as well as full cost for materials and presentation. Here, I think, many beginning consultants make mistakes. The obvious one is that they don't ask to be paid for everything that will cost them money and time. The less obvious one is that they assume—I believe incorrectly—that they can use materials from the classroom or from prior consultations.[8] I believe that you should bill for research time on site and off site, for preparation and materials-development time off site, and for all overhead expenses—as well as for presentation time and for the obvious expenses of travel and housing. As I indicated earlier, a differential rate can be charged for research and preparation time to make the proposal more attractive, but I think it is essential to charge for that time. Precisely this research and particularized preparation will allow the consultant to avoid the problem much commented on in the literature: canned presentations by consultants who do not do their homework. To quote O'Hara again: "Consultants often try to sell you what they have available, not necessarily what you want or need . . . canned presentations in an industry setting, where the needs of many and different clients must be met, are just not the answer" (1983, p. 10).

REACHING AN AGREEMENT. Again, both formal and informal approaches are common. Some companies will send back a formal contract that incorporates elements from the proposal and inserts elements that the company lawyers use for protection. Other companies will call up and say, "Fine, go ahead with it." In both cases a little prudence is appropriate. If it is a formal contract, read the fine print. You may find a clause that gives your client sweeping controls over your materials. For example, I refused this clause in a contract: "Consultant agrees to assign, and hereby assigns, to (company name) ownership of any copyright for any work prepared during the period of this agreement and fixed in any tangible medium of expression (including, without limitation, reports, drawings, prints, records, notebooks, manuals, computer programs and print-outs, and specifications)." In other words, whether I did work for them or not, they owned it. Another contract, also refused, included a clause that—interpreted literally—would have given exclusive use of the name "The University of Michigan" to one company in Japan. You can see the problem!

If the agreement is informal, nonetheless you should ask for a written confirmation of the agreed-on terms. A handshake and verbal agreement are nice, but hard copy is better. Again, consider that used-car deal.

Although as academics we may tend to be innocent about these business matters, we shouldn't be. Gallessich (1983) recommends that the written agreement (formal or informal) contain all of the following:

1. General goals of the consultation.
2. Tentative time frame.
3. Consultant's responsibilities: services to be provided; methods to be used; time to be committed; evaluation of accomplishment, including types of evaluation, nature of reports, and dates for submission.
4. Client responsibilities: Nature and extent of staff support; fees to be paid.
5. Consultant's boundaries: contact person; persons to whom access is to be given; access in terms of departments, meetings, and documents; conditions for bringing in others; confidentiality rules.

I would add one other appropriate detail: time of payment. Frequently government agencies and some companies will keep you waiting for six months if you do not put in a clause requiring payment within thirty days. With whopping expenses on your charge accounts, you can't wait six months.

All this may seem rather legalistic. Still, as Mark Twain said, "Put your eggs in one basket, but watch that basket."

CONDUCTING RESEARCH. Before a consultant can deliver well-suited solutions to industry problems, he or she must spend the time necessary to research those problems. Precisely this feature distinguishes the consultant from the off-campus academic, the consultation from off-campus instruction. The writing consultant brings his or her expertise to a client and applies it to the client's particular needs; the off-campus academic brings only what he or she already knows and offers stock solutions. As O'Hara (1983) warns managers, "... an academic's idea of teaching your employees to write might be to give a standard rendition of English 103" (p. 11).

Of course, research provides benefits to the consultant beyond those necessary for the consultation. That is, research provides an opportunity to test and to develop theory, a fact that should return benefits in the form of scholarly research, publication, and pedagogy (Skelton, 1984). Yet, my real interest here is in the benefits that research provides for carrying out the consultation in an effective manner. In simple terms, I believe that the research allows the consultant to define specific problems, to set priorities among problems, and to develop a set of illustrations of the problems and appropriate solutions within the context of the client company.

To carry out in-house research, four strategies may be useful: interviews, data analysis, case studies, and surveys. At the interview stage it is important to talk in detail to as many of the affected parties as possible. It is not sufficient to talk only to the contact person or even to the manager who has decided to invite you as a consultant. The perceptions of problems may be quite different when viewed from individual roles. Joseph Baim warns that "within the same company, standards can differ markedly from manager-to-manager, division-to-division, and even from year-to-year" (1977). It is thus imperative to interview more than just a few people, at more than just one level, and at more than a limited depth. As an illustration, for a recent consultation with a state agency I have visited the agency twice, talking to three managers at different levels. Later, off site, I conducted interviews three additional times—with one, two, and six people, respectively—again at different levels. In all, I conducted perhaps ten hours of interviews.

Along with the interviews it is useful to review substantial amounts of written material illustrative of the types that one has been called in to investigate. Although consultants are often given a handful of examples that, in a manager's view, illustrate the problems, it is much better practice to seek access to a randomly selected, large data base of materials for analysis. In one case, for example, in a company of several hundred employees, I used copies of all materials submitted to the word-processing pool during one day. In other instances I have reviewed stacks of materials that would fill a small suitcase.

The objectives during this review of sample materials are simply to get a feel for the way things are normally done, to begin to spot evidences of difficulties that have been identified during the interviews, and to begin to collect examples that can be used either to explain to managers what needs to be done or to instruct writers.

Sometimes the volume of materials at this stage seems prohibitive. Sometimes, in fact, I have paid graduate student readers to help me sift through the piles. Yet substantial review of materials seems to me to be essential.

Following the review of materials, it may be useful to focus on a small set of case studies. It helps to particularize problems if one studies the rhetorical situations of specific, illustrative documents in detail. For example, in one company I tracked three documents through the system, interviewing for each document all the people on the distribution lists as well as the writer and the writer's managers— twenty people for one of the documents. In each case, I scheduled interviews with the appropriate people, gave them a copy of the document to refresh their memories, and interviewed them for up to one hour each. I asked questions—chiefly about how they used the documents, but also about their opinions of the effectiveness of the documents. From these interviews I was able to develop extended illustrations that helped particularize problems not apparent during my first reading, problems of audience need and document function that perhaps no single individual in the company could have summarized for me. These case studies later became a basis for both management briefings and instruction that has now been going on once a year for five years.

Surveys can also be useful to reveal information that a small number of cases may not reveal. As illustration, William J. Rothwell (1983) explains the procedures and illustrates the questionnaires used for a two-stage survey research project on writing for the Illinois Department of Personnel's Division of Employee Development. The surveys, ultimately used as a basis for planning instruction open to 100,000 state employees, were administered to all managers in a representative unit with 500 employees and to an additional 200 managers in one of the state's largest agencies.

My own experience with surveys has been very limited; I can think of only two that I have done specifically for consulting purposes. In preparing a presentation for military hospital administrators, I surveyed some seventy U.S. Army officers who manage hospitals. In another case, preparing for a job with the Detroit-area court system, I surveyed thirty-three judges and asked them to mark up a copy of a Presentence Investigation Report that I circulated to them, asking them to indicate with a felt-tip marker the data in the report that they would actually use in sentencing a convicted felon. In both cases, the surveys provided materials that I was able to use for management briefings and for writing exercises.

This research stage, though neglected by some off-campus academics, is in my view the key component of the entire consulting process. It is, in fact, the component that distinguishes consultation from off-campus instruction.

PREPARING THE DESIGN. Here, of course, the activities depend on the "product." If a management briefing is the intended product, one simply has to decide what to present and to prepare it in a format that managers will find convenient. I suggest a formal briefing of no longer than one hour—shorter if possible—although, in the case of some particularly complex problems, briefings can be longer. (Keeping them short is a good idea, however; managers, unlike college students, tend not to sit still for long.) I also suggest that the briefing be done with simple, professionally prepared graphics that are shown on transparency and/or on slides. And I suggest that a set of handout materials be prepared to supplement the briefing, materials that succinctly define and illustrate the problems and appropriate solutions. This formal briefing can usually be supplemented with additional individual conferences with selected managers.

If writing or editing is the product, the design stage simply involves doing the writing and editing, although it is a good idea to prepare a briefing that presents the plan before the product is actually developed.

For many writing consultants, however, the product will be in-house instruction. Here the planning and preparation must take into account several features not characteristic of conventional, on-campus instruction, where we have a generous schedule, broad educational objectives, and general populations of students.

First, the objectives should be specifically related to the problem-solving purposes of the instruction—in other words, to the high-priority problems identified in the research stage. Focus, not breadth, is a desirable characteristic for in-house instruction. If writing titles is a problem, then teach title writing—otherwise skip it. If abstracting causes problems, teach abstracts. If paragraphing causes problems, teach paragraphing. If punctuation is a problem, teach the types of punctuation that people really have problems with; skip the general survey of all possible nuances of punctuation. Set priorities among the problems and focus on the immediate and serious ones. In other words, adopt an instrumental, problem-solving focus on a focused set of objectives that are possible to accomplish in a reasonably short time. Use a triage approach to in-house instruction: treat only the wounded; treat only their wounds; and don't waste too much time on those that are impossible to save. That may sound reductive, but in my experience the most effective and best-received in-house instruction has been instruction with clearly defined, focused objectives and identifiable outcomes. Most consultants, I think, will agree.

Second, in terms of selection of participants, there is also a difference between industry and academia. On campus we describe a course and take whoever enrolls. In industry, we design the selection process and take only those we choose. That strikes me as a key part of the design. Left to choose the participants, a manager may send people to take a course simply because they are between projects: anything to fill up the time. (A consultant friend of mine tells about his worst in-house course. It was for strike-idled participants who actually did no writing on their jobs. The company simply wanted to keep them busy.) Another manager may send someone who is coasting toward retirement. (Despite my best efforts, I had three such participants among the last forty in classes at one company.) Still another manager may send participants who do not write but who may do so at some time in the future. Yet if it is to be successful, the industry course must address people who really do write and really do have problems. It also helps if they know they have problems and want to be in the class. I would add that a reasonable mix of different backgrounds, ages, and departments is always a good idea. It helps to avoid the "everyone knows this" syndrome that develops within limited company contexts. In any event, the design needs to include the design of the participant-selection process.

Third, there is the issue of class contact hours. Numerous articles have been written about different designs of in-house courses. Max Weber, for example, describes an in-house course for the Argonne National Laboratory in which the course met two nights per week for twelve weeks, with two-hour sessions—a forty-eight hour course (cited in Kachaturian & Estrin, 1983). Armen Kachaturian and Herman Estrin describe an eight-week course for a large engineering construction firm, a course that met once a week for eight weeks, with six class hours at each meeting—again forty-eight hours (1983). John Mitchell (1976) mentions the popularity of a "one afternoon a week for ten weeks" model—a forty-hour model. Richard Davis (1982) recommends a limit of fifteen to thirty hours, warning that if the instruction is to exceed thirty hours "it may become a chore for the people in the class."

Although I am confident that different course lengths are possible, I think there are arguments in favor of a relatively small number of contact hours and a condensed schedule, as Davis suggests. For me, the typical model is twenty contact hours spread over no more than two weeks.

In favor of a small number of contact hours is the fact that if the objectives are well defined and selected, a small number of hours is possible. Don't use more time than is needed. A more practical matter is that a class offered either for a small number of hours over a long time or for a large number of hours in a short time will tend to be very disruptive of the company's normal functioning. Participants travel and have ongoing projects; thus many will find it almost impossible to stick with a long course. Indeed, I have found that long courses work for me only when the participants are all taken off site to a place where they can be held "captive" for the duration. With the American Academy of Judicial Education, the Michigan Judicial Institute, IBM, and various other agencies, I have been involved in numerous such off-site programs that have worked exceptionally well. But the key was to get the people away from their work routines and telephones for the necessary time, usually a full work week. As a lure—at least in the American Academy of Judicial Education— resortlike conference sites were always used. That is, of course, an expensive practice and unlikely to be used except for top-brass classes.

A fourth feature of the design is to work out a good mix of different types of activity. Industry audiences are not accustomed to being at one task for long; they are not accustomed to lectures; and they tend to like the variety and discontinuity that typifies the rest of their work lives. Thus in the design phase it is a good idea to work up a plan that includes lecture, in-class exercise, out-of class exercise, at-home reading, peer critique sessions, and individual consultation.

A final feature to consider in the design phase is class size. Most college writing courses have about twenty-plus students. The assumption might be that the same pattern should hold for industry courses—and perhaps it should for most instruction. But I think there is a danger of making the assumption that writing instruction can be useful only if it is in college-sized classes. The fact is that depending on the objectives, the size can appropriately be much larger or much smaller. For example, I am designing a course for supervisors in one company, focusing it on the issue of evaluating writing and giving feedback to writers. The course is to be a concentrated, two-and-a-half-day design. However, the nature of the objectives and of the activities of the course will permit much larger than typical audiences. In fact, the audience size is limited only by the size of the auditorium in which the course is to be offered—120 seats. (I *think* the design will work.) Conversely, a one-week course in opinion writing for judges, frequently and successfully offered, has a student/teacher ratio of five to one. It has even been offered with four students per instructor. In other words, size is a function of course objectives; it need not be, as it is on college campuses, a function of "FTEs," tradition, and section-to-section consistency. A variety of sizes will work.

PRESENTING IT TO MANAGEMENT. I have already spoken about presenting the design to management if the product is to be advice. The same holds true if the product is to be instruction. The design for the course should be presented to management before the course is offered to anyone else. This is important because the consultant should not try to teach without management's support for what is to be taught. Nothing helps an in-house course more than saying, "Here is what your top managers say you should do in this case." Nothing hurts an in-house course as much as a comment from the back row like, "My manager doesn't agree with you on how that should be done."

My own practice is to schedule a management briefing after the design stage and before an in-house course is offered. I present a one-hour explanation of what I will do and how I will do it. In addition, I say, "Tell me now if you disagree with anything I have planned to do. If we disagree, I will try to convince you. If I cannot convince you, you may convince me, and I will try to adjust. If I cannot adjust, we will call it quits before the course is offered." For what it is worth, I have never gone into an industry course without the prior approval of management, and I have yet to cancel or radically alter a planned course. Perhaps the management briefing is not really necessary, but the leverage it provides to you and the understanding it provides to management makes it worth one hour of everyone's time.

Richard Davis (1982) adds another comment on the value of this precourse management briefing: "It lets them see that you have incorporated some of their suggestions and gives them the feeling that they have participated in both the development and approval of the course (p. 70). In other words, for political reasons as well as for substantive reasons, a management briefing is a good idea. Consulting, by the way, *does* put you into a new political arena.

PREPARING THE MATERIALS. For an on-campus course, we have the luxury of having our file cabinets and equipment at hand and plenty of time to prepare materials as we go along. We can adapt to what is happening in class day by day. Thus even though I have a seventy-five page syllabus and course-pack (plus a textbook) for an on-campus technical writing class, I can add material when I need it. I can make transparencies at the last minute, or work up a new handout. I have to plan the industry course more carefully: all the needed materials must be put into a self-sufficient, complete, and presentable form.

If the research stage has been well done, there should be no shortage of sample materials. These, along with appropriate explanation, should be prepared specifically for each course and put into a convenient format. Typically, I prepare a workbook of 150 to 200 pages for each in-house course. I also prepare a full set of framed transparencies for use on an overhead projector—the normal mode of industry instruction. (Note: I prepare both the workbook and the transparencies for use on an overhead projector—the normal mode of industry instruction. (Note: I prepare both the workbook and the transparencies; the company does not prepare them for me nor am I typical course, the workbook is spiral-bound or punch-bound, has an attractive cover with the appropriate company logo, and contains everything I will use during the course. It is all attractively typed on a high-quality text-processing system, with computer graphics, lots of white space, and provision for note-taking by the participants. Along with the sample material, I provide identification of the specific objectives of every component of the course, explanation, workshop exercises and assignments, and suggested reading. Occasionally I supplement this workbook with a text and/or a handbook, but usually the workbook is the entire set of course materials.

Three points strike me as important for the consultant to consider in preparing his or her materials. First, whatever is to be used should be planned for and prepared ahead of time. Second, the materials should be prepared in a very professional manner, with first-quality print and graphics—far more presentable than the materials we commonly accept as normal on campus. Third, almost no materials should be drawn from sources outside the company.

The reasons for the first and second of these points should be apparent: the industry course must be self-sufficient and attractively presented. The level of expectation that professionals have about how materials are prepared considerably exceeds the expectations of undergraduates (and English teachers). Many participants will be accustomed to typeset text, professional artwork, and high-quality reproduction; mimeographed materials prepared on a portable typewriter with dirty type just won't do. On campus, where we worry excessively about costs, we tell our students to look only at the content, not the form. In industry that won't work. And of course the cost in industry is high. For example, I recently spent over $700 for an in-house workbook used with forty students. I also had the company buy two additional books for each participant—another $1,200. But no one in the company blinked at the expense. On campus, my request would have caused my department's administrative assistant to have a stroke.

In relation to the third point, the reasons may be less apparent. After all, materials from a variety of sources theoretically could be used in any industry course, just as they are in on-campus courses and textbooks. Yet I think most experienced consultants will agree that the appeal of an in-house course rises as the number of in-house examples increases. Donald Dickson (1982) says, "The sooner we can use something written on their letterhead to illustrate a particular problem, the more interested they usually become and the more they seem to learn" (pp. 14–15). I would further suggest, as Dickson does, that it is best to move from these in-house examples to theoretical principles, rather than the reverse. On campus I frequently teach in a deductive fashion, but in industry I invariably use an inductive approach, starting with their own examples. I have even taught industry courses that used materials drawn entirely from the work of the participants themselves. Unbelievably time-consuming to prepare and a bit tricky in terms of tact, that technique nevertheless arouses enough interest to make it *almost* worth the effort.

If the product is to be instructional material, that material should be prepared with attention to every detail of substance and form. The same holds for any materials used in management briefings, in writing and editing jobs, or just in informal discussions with individual managers. After spending some time in industry and business, many writing consultants are embarrassed by hastily written, poorly edited, and crudely reproduced materials. That may be the academic norm; it is not the business and industry norm.

PRESENTING YOUR RESULTS. For management consulting or for writing and editing, the results are presented either by a prepared briefing—as we have already discussed—or by simply turning in the work to the appropriate manager. With in-house instruction, the work is presented just as an on-campus course would be, with all the appropriate variations in individual teaching techniques. As I said at the outset, we are all experienced teachers; we don't need to be told how to teach. My advice is just to do what works for you and try to be sensitive to the different mores of your world and theirs.

Nevertheless, I can't resist quickly listing three tips on technique that have helped me in my own industry work.

1. *Learn names.* you should learn the names of all appropriate managers as well as the participants in your classes. Effort will be required because you have only a short time in which to do this, but you can do it. After watching a colleague learn names on a consulting job when I first started consulting, and after mastering his simple memory technique, I discovered that I can learn forty names in one day. Of course, I forget them as soon as I move on, but at least for the week I am in a company I can know all of the people with whom I must deal. You can do it too, and I assure you it gives you all sorts of advantages in working with your classes. I can't recommend it enough.

2. *Learn the organization and its products.* You will work with people who speak a language you don't understand and who live in a country whose map you have never seen. They will talk knowingly about such things as "the 2260" or the "T02-test." They will refer to locations such as "the tenth floor" or "PPG" or "downtown." They will identify managers by first name, assuming that you understand who those people are and what their roles are. All these things have legitimate meanings in their world; as well as you can, you should learn them. Davis (1982) indicates that nobody really expects you to be an expert on local practice (pp. 73–74), and he is right. But, oh, what an advantage if you are at least reasonably familiar with the company and its products: rather like speaking a little Japanese in Japan, it will carry you a long way.

3. *Keep the class entertaining, but make it all business.* On-the-job people crave humor just as much as undergraduates do—maybe

more. They are pragmatists, however. They are there because profit is to be gained. They want to use the time and to use it productively. Keep them refreshed and laughing, but keep them working hard and learning things that they can use immediately. Remember that students on campus come because they have to; in industry, to a great extent, each class session determines tomorrow's enrollment. As one manager commented to me recently after he had looked into my class, "It must be going well; they were all there and it is already Wednesday." He was only partly kidding.

FOLLOWING UP AFTERWARDS. Whatever the nature of the job, it should be followed up with an evaluation and debriefing. In courses, formal written evaluations by the participants should be taken and should be sent to and discussed with the appropriate managers. Similarly, efforts should be made to solicit reactions and suggestions from audiences, managers, and co-workers on writing and editing jobs and management advisory jobs. In every case, the consultant should seek to learn as much as possible about the outcomes of the work and to assure that those outcomes are made known to the appropriate people in the compnay. Not only will this help the consultant to learn from experience, it will also help people in the company to know the impact of the consultation and to follow it up in their own way. In addition, it often leads to further consultation.

In the follow-up evaluation it is appropriate to consider more than the simple question, "Did I perform well?" A more helpful list of topics might include several of those mentioned by Gallessich (1983):

- The degree to which the desired goals were reached.
- The factors that contributed to both positive and negative outcomes.
- Interim feedback about how an intervention is progressing.
- The cost/benefit ratio of interventions.
- The consultant's overall effectiveness and effectiveness in the various stages and processes of consultation, such as contracting and diagnosis.

These general issues can be explored in written form and in brief conferences with managers. Yet it is a good idea to go beyond that, not only for political reasons but for substantive reasons as well. I try to follow my consultations with letters to the managers and to selected participants—ones from whom I think I can learn something and with whom I want to stay in contact. Before I leave the company, I also invite phone calls and make sure that everyone has my phone number. (You would be surprised how many do stay in contact and how much mutual benefit there is in those contacts.) Further, I sometimes write into the contract a paid follow-up period during which, at home, I continue to receive and evaluate work. In one series of consultations during the early 1970s, that was a standard feature: ten months of once-per-month evaluation. For an individual job that was an extremely valuable feature, but when jobs piled up it became an impossible scheduling problem.

In the follow-up, whatever its form, it is important to be tough-minded and candid, but it is also important to stay away from evaluation of people as much as possible. Class participants should be told that the objective of the class is to help them do their jobs more effectively, not to develop information about individuals that will be reported back to managers. Similarly, in writing and editing and management advisory jobs, the follow-up should focus as much as possible on the processes and products, not on the contributions of individual people to those processes and products. It is the company's job—not yours—to hire, evaluate, reward, and punish people. Evaluate the *work*, not the *people*.

Admittedly, at times it is difficult to stay away from personalities. In one company, for example, my research made it quite evident that the "failure" of one piece of writing was not so much in its author's failure as in the failures of three separate managers in their uses of the writing: one clearly did not read it; one read it superficially, failing to recognize that he had responsibility for matters covered in the document; and one used the document more for self-promotion than for instrumental purposes. The writer and the document might be said to have failed, but my personal assessment was that out of eighteen readers and users of the document, three were guilty of slipshod work. Of course, I did reach very strong opinions about these three people. I had a hard time keeping a straight face in one of the interviews. Yet I did not report back to the company that they had at least one incompetent person, if not three; that really would have gone beyond the scope of my agreement with them. My job was to evaluate the writing behavior, not the reading behavior, and certainly not the people who did the reading.

Whatever strategies the consultant and the company choose to use for follow-up—assuming that the results are positive—it is good practice to get the company to go on record as being satisfied with the consultation, if they are. Again, a letter is better than a phone call. Not only will the letter be useful in getting further consultations, it may actually prove useful on campus during merit, promotion, and tenure considerations.

CONCLUSION

Judging from the available articles and from late-night bull sessions, writing teachers who have consulted tend to be like any enthusiasts with a new interest: they tell their friends, they testify to the values of the experience, and they become salespersons and advocates, trying to convert everyone who hasn't yet tried consultation.

In closing, I must say that I have a strong urge to do just that. Consulting has been a rewarding, exciting, interesting series of experiences for me and for many of my colleagues. It has helped us in our classrooms and our studies—as well as, incidentally, in our checking accounts. I can't imagine what my career would have been like for the past decade without consulting, nor can I imagine giving it up in the future, even though at times I feel the two-job pressure of the campus and the workplace to be more demanding than I can manage.

Yet I want to resist the temptation to oversell consulting. Consulting is probably not good for all writing teachers, nor are all writing teachers good for consulting. As we have seen, consulting involves values and activities that conflict with, as well as contribute to, campus values and activities. It carries unquestionable rewards, but it also involves a kind of commitment that many writing teachers may find difficult to make.

Let me end, then, not with a call for all writing teachers to march into the workplace. Rather, let me end with the observation that for writing teachers who wish to consult, a need for their services exists in the workplace. Meeting that need, though time-consuming and demanding, will yield benefits to the writing teacher, to the client, and to the profession. I hope this chapter has provided a balanced and informative view of both those benefits and what is involved in obtaining them.

Notes

1. The Association of Professional Writing Consultants was formed in 1981 as an outgrowth of interactions among consultants at the Conference on College Composition and Communication. Its president is Lee Clark Johns. Its address is: 3942 South Troost, Tulsa, Oklahoma 74105. Liability insurance, negotiated by the association with Bowes and Company of Minnesota, is available to members.

2. Dean James J. Duderstadt, interview published in the College of Engineering *Newsletter*, The University of Michigan, 1981.

3. Personal letter sent to Dwight W. Stevenson (1983) in response to survey research questionnaire.

4. A research project I conducted in one company in 1979 revealed that the only written record of a $75,000 testing project carried out by the company failed to answer ten specific questions of fact that various readers of the documentation had. The record of that testing, marked for five-year retention in the company library, remained the only record of the testing when its author, the test engineer, left the company.

5. Contract Engineering Publication, Box A, Kenmore, Washington 98028. Telephone: (206) 485-7575.

6. Detailed syllabi and explanations for in-house courses are to be found in Kachaturian and Estrin (1983), Rothwell (1983), and Weber (1975). In addition, the reader should see "The In-house Teaching of Technical Communication," special section in *Technical Communication*, 30(1), (1983), 4–13.

7. See note 1 for the address.

8. Here I disagree with Richard Davis's otherwise excellent advice when he comments that "Basic patterns can be repeated from course to course with relatively little modification, and examples and exercises developed in one can be used in another" (p. 66). Although I am confident that *patterns* can be repeated from course to course, *materials* seem to me to be appropriately particularized for different clients. This point is discussed in detail later.

References

Baim, J. (1977). In-house training in report writing: A collaborative approach. *The ABCA Bulletin*, December, 6.

Benne, K. D. (1969). Some ethical problems in group and organizational consultation. In *The planning of change*. New York: Holt, Rinehart & Winston.

Cunningham, D. H. (1984). Preparing your course: consulting. In Conference on Teaching Technical and Professional Communication, *Workbook* (4.7-8 through 4.7-11). Ann Arbor: The University of Michigan.

Davis, R. (1982). Presenting courses in government and industry. *The Technical Writing Teacher, 9*(2), 65–74.

Dickson, D. R. (1982). Planning for the in-house writing seminar. *ABCA Bulletin*, June, 14–16.

Driskell, L. P. (1981). Trends in liability affecting technical writers. In J. C. Mathes & T. E. Pinelli (Eds.), *Technical communication: Perspectives for the eighties* (pp. 597–

608). Hampton, VA: National Aeronautics and Space Administration Scientific and Technical Information Branch, Publication 2203.

Gallessich, J. (1983). *The profession and practice of consultation: A handbook for consultants, trainers of consultants, and consumers of consultation services.* San Francisco: Jossey-Bass.

Kachaturian, A., & Estrin, H. (1983). Teaching in-house technical communication courses. *ABCA Bulletin*, June, 42–48.

Marver, J. D., & Patton, C. V. (1976). The correlates of consultation: American academics in the "real world." *Journal of Higher Education, 5,* 319–335.

Mitchell, J. H. (1976). Professional educators as communication consultants. *Journal of Technical Writing and Communication, 9,* (1), 36.

Moorhead, A. E. (1984). *The rhetorical design and function of the proposal.* Unpublished Doctor of Arts dissertation, The University of Michigan.

O'Hara, F. M. Jr. (1983). Hiring a private consultant. *Technical Communication, 30*(1), 11.

Pfeiffer, J. W., & Jones, J. E. (1977). Ethical considerations in consulting. In *Annual handbook for group facilitators.* San Diego: University Associates.

Rothwell, W. J. (1983). Developing a writing course for state employees: A case study. *Journal of Technical Writing and Communication, 12*(2), 103–113. (a)

Rothwell, W. J. (1983). Developing an in-house training curriculum in written communication. *Journal of Business Communication, 20*(2), 31–44. (b)

Schemenaur, P. J. (1983). How much freelancers charge. In *1983 writer's market.* Cincinnati: Writer's Digest Books.

Skelton, T. (1984). The in-house course as a research tool for technical communication. Unpublished conference paper, Conference on College Composition and Communication.

Stevenson, D. W. (1984). Evaluating technical communication faculty: Some empirically-based criteria and guidelines. *Resources in Education*, September.

Weber, M. (1975). Teaching an effective course in technical writing in private industry. *The Technical Writing Teacher, 3*(1), 8–20.

Whalen, T. (1980). Techniques for developing an effective in-house course in business and technical writing. *ABCA Bulletin*, September 27–28.

Building a Professional Writing Program through a University-Industry Collaborative

11

BARBARA COUTURE,
JONE RYMER GOLDSTEIN,
ELIZABETH L. MALONE,
BARBARA NELSON, AND
SHARON QUIROZ
Wayne State University

Writing teachers in colleges and universities attest that the best way to inform a curriculum on writing for the workplace is through first-hand experience with the contexts, processes, and products of written communication on the job. Thus veteran teachers of technical communication encourage new teachers to work as technical writers or as consultants in business and industry to gain that first-hand perspective (see Stevenson, chapter 10, this volume; Barnum, 1983; Anderson, 1977). At the same time, experienced technical-writing faculty rely on theoretical and empirical studies of technical discourse to gain broad and detailed perspectives on the complexities of communication for the workplace, and they encourage new instructors to do likewise. However, the task of assimilating actual and vicarious experience with writing for the workplace is for many teachers a time-consuming enterprise, adding to the already pressing burden of teaching practical writing classes.

A relatively new approach to assimilating both first-hand experience and empirical research on writing for the workplace is to establish a university/industry collaborative for research and curriculum development in professional writing. Our purpose here is to describe and evaluate a model collaborative effort, Wayne State University's Professional Writing Project (PWP).[1] The PWP has joined the communicative expertise of experienced teachers of writing and of professionals from business, government, and industry to address three needs yet unmet by current approaches to the development of professional writing curricula:

- The need to obtain detailed empirical research on the products and practices of technical/professional writing.
- The need to characterize aspects of technical/professional writing relevant to the wide variety of work settings that college graduates enter.
- The need to base technical/professional writing instruction on this empirical research, rather than on conventional wisdom or individual on-the-job experiences.

This chapter describes a process by which a university can collaborate with business and industry to improve research and curriculum development in professional writing. We will illustrate this process by referring occasionally to conclusions we drew from our own work. Primarily, however, we are interested in describing in a basic process rather than drawing conclusions about research or pedagogy in professional writing. Detailed conclusions of our collaborative research will appear in forthcoming publications.

DEVELOPING RESEARCH AND CURRICULUM WITH CORPORATE AND GOVERNMENT ADVISORS: A MODEL PLAN

At the time we first considered collaboration at Wayne State, the university offered a full complement of advanced writing courses, including expository writing, technical writing, business writing, and specialized courses in research writing for prelaw students and nurses. We felt, however, that teaching additional specialized courses for writing in specific careers might not be the best way to ensure that students are prepared for the diverse communication tasks outside the university. We wanted students to learn what distinguishes writing on the job from the writing they do in most college classes and to master those skills *generic* to written communications in the workplace. We are well aware, of course, that only a little research has been done on the varieties of writing tasks in the workplace and that discovering any generic qualities of these tasks would require a comprehensive research project. Bringing together both expert teachers and practitioners would enable us to explore the common aims and characteristics of writing tasks in the workplace with implications for teaching on-the-job writing skills in our current writing courses.

To achieve this overall goal, we planned five procedures to integrate academics' and practitioners' perspectives on professional writing:

1. *Establish a collaborative team of faculty experienced in the research and teaching of writing and nonuniversity professionals knowledgeable about effective writing practices in their individual work settings.* Our collaborative team would assess the teaching of professional writing at the university and the practice of writing in various work settings and would provide numerous contacts with other professionals who could tell us about writing in occupations predicted to be open to college graduates in the next decade. This team would have the potential to establish an expert view of professional writing practice through collective discovery of those skills all writers must master to communicate effectively in work settings.

2. *Motivate the collaborative team toward **cooperative investigation** of the theory, research, teaching, and practice of professional writing.* To ensure that our faculty and advisors from the workplace functioned as a team, we had to orient each group to how the other speaks about issues of writing practice and establish common terminology. We had to foster respect for differing perspectives and encourage collective problem-solving to achieve a truly *cooperative investigation.* Our goal was to help members from both groups to act as a cohesive community of experts on professional writing.

3. *Employ our collaborative resources to do research on writing in the workplace.* Our contacts outside the university would help us conduct research on writing in the workplace, expanding the breadth and depth of current studies. With their cooperation and endorse-

ment, we planned to collect detailed information on writing practice from employees in targeted occupations and to conduct comparative studies with implications for teaching writing skills important for all professionals.

4. *Design goals and objectives for professional writing instruction in a* **process-oriented, interactive forum** *for university/industry exchange.* We believed that all representatives in the collaborative effort would best express and clarify their individual views in a *process-oriented, interactive forum.* In such a forum, we could explore alternative perspectives while constructing a common "goals and objectives" document for a professional writing curriculum. Working collectively would ensure that this draft represented the views of the collaborative team and would also translate meaningfully to teachers and students not connected with our project.

5. *Develop, revise, and test curriculum in an atmosphere of collaborative problem solving.* Our purpose in this activity was to ensure that *both* faculty and advisors could be involved in every stage of developing, producing, and testing instructional materials. The ideal result would be curriculum materials that could be adapted to our current writing courses and that would prepare our students to communicate effectively in a broad range of organizational situations.

In the remainder of this chapter, we elaborate our perspectives in approaching each of these tasks, describe our actual procedures, and evaluate the effectiveness of each activity in achieving our overall goals for the university/industry collaboration.

Establishing a Collaborative Team

Our collaborative team brought together professionals from quite diverse rhetorical communities who are experts in the practice and pedagogy of professional communications. This team consisted of two groups distinguished by their relationship to the university: an internal Project Team of professors and graduate student researchers; and an external Advisory Board of managers, trainers, writers, and editors from business, government, and industry. The composition of this collaborative team was our key to discovering generic aspects of effective professional communication in a variety of work settings.

The internal Project Team represented technical and business writing faculty from the English Department and the School of

Business Administration. This team worked closely with a group of university advisors including deans of colleges whose students are required to take advanced writing courses in the English Department (School of Business Administration, College of Engineering, School of Nursing) and the chair and literature faculty from the English Department—the university community that claims expertise in the evaluation of written discourse. As our ultimate aim was to create a curriculum that would be taught by a range of members from this group, this internal team had to represent not only teachers/scholars of exposition, but also teachers/scholars of literature, who, if not called on to teach professional communication, at least influence its status as an area for scholarly study. Besides including teachers of composition, business writing, technical writing, and literature on our internal team, we involved graduate students in our PhD in Writing Program. As neophytes in the academic community of composition research, these students often called into question university attitudes toward transactional communication, thus sharpening experienced academics' awareness of the English Department's perspective on the teaching and practice of professional communications. In short, in constructing the internal Project Team, we attempted to recreate as faithfully as possible the academic rhetorical community that passes judgment on written communications practice and pedagogy.

The notion of representing rhetorical communities that evaluate professional discourse also directed our selection of the Advisory Board. We assumed that the effectiveness of writing at work is not measured quantitatively or by some objective criteria, but rather by subjective criteria established by a working community.[2] Hence, rhetorical communities defined by professions and organizations can best evaluate generic aspects of effective writing in work settings. We selected for our team rhetorically competent professionals in leadership positions, reasoning that these persons would be self-aware of criteria for communicative competence in their workplaces.[3] In addition, we recruited writers and editors who, almost by definition, combine an awareness of language with an awareness of organizational needs. We believed that a community of diverse professionals who are competent to evaluate written discourse could help us both interpret empirical research on the writing behavior of technical/managerial professionals and assess writing practice in several occupations, making sophisticated judgments about tasks common to many. They could collectively establish an expert view of professional writing practice and ultimately construct the generic features of writing practices in quite various settings.

HOW WE LOCATED OUR EXPERT ADVISORS. Very pragmatic considerations guided our selection of advisors from business, government and industry. We looked for personnel who could characterize the writing of professionals in positions likely to be held by our graduates. To target professions and organizations that may employ such candidates, we correlated statistical projections of employment possibilities for college graduates from the *National Job Outlook*, employment statistics published by the Michigan Employment Securities Commission, and lists of occupations open to college graduates in the Detroit area, specifically those for which Wayne State trains students. Enlisting the help of the Wayne State Placement Services, our own faculty, deans of professional schools, and members of local professional organizations (e.g., the Society for Technical Communication), we then established contacts in business, industrial, and government organizations.

We asked our initial contacts to recommend from their individual organizations people whose authority derived in some part from rhetorical expertise, who were familiar with a wide variety of communications from different professional communities within their organizations, and who were sophisticated and articulate about rhetorical practice. Besides these qualifications, we required that our representatives hold positions that gave them access to documents in their organizations and the authority to request that other workers cooperate with PWP research efforts. Persons who met our qualifications in most cases were training directors, personnel administrators, communications directors, writers, technical writers, or editors.

HOW OUR FACULTY AND ADVISORS WORKED AS A COLLABORATIVE TEAM. Our Project Team and Advisory Board were to cooperate in three tasks: conducting an extensive survey of the writing practices of college-educated professionals in targeted professions; locating skills generic to the practice of professional writing in several occupations, and then translating these skills into teaching goals; and developing and testing a professional writing curriculum to teach those skills. We insured interaction among all participants in these efforts by conducting highly organized bimonthly conference sessions, replete with specific agendae, prepared and spontaneous large- and small-group activities, and break time for informal conversation. Sessions were tape recorded and reproduced as written transcripts.

The conference sessions located shared values among our expert representatives of diverse academic and professional nonacademic communities. Our collaborators collected and evaluated writing samples, exchanged narratives of individuals' writing processes, and described significant aspects of professional writing tasks, thus pinpointing the boundaries of "competence" and "effectiveness" for their own communities. As later sections of this chapter show, the conference sessions proved to be the most important vehicle for debate and self-reflexive evaluation of individual contributions and of collaborative work. They encouraged conferees to deliberate and solve problems, extending each participant's personal contacts with other professionals representing the world the group was debating, as well as developing each member's resources for reacting critically to that world.

We believe that our Project Team and Advisory Board achieved a level of interaction that made it possible for participants to assert three somewhat different perspectives: their individual points of view, the authority of the communities where they worked, and the "expert view" of a new community—the collaborative team forged by their participation in the PWP.

Differences between academics' and other professionals' perspectives heightened all members' awareness of their own approaches to writing, thus focusing discussion explicitly on that intersection of specific current practices and generalizations about those practices that we wanted to examine. But such focus was not the spontaneous outcome of our bringing faculty and outside professionals together; we had to apply specific techniques to make the collaboration work.

Motivating the Collaborative Team toward Cooperative Investigation of Professional Writing

To make our collaborative team function as researchers and curriculum developers, we first had to turn this conglomerate into a cohesive community motivated to reach consensus about effective writing practice for the workplace. Faculty and advisors were simultaneously both well and ill prepared to function as we planned. Certainly, both groups were motivated to seek ways to better prepare college students for on-the-job writing and to gather and assess information about writing in the workplace. But they were not ready to work together to achieve these ends.

Our faculty came to the collaborative team prepared to discuss writing processes and products; they were familiar with traditional and current taxonomies of the writing process, and with the varieties and characteristics of expository prose. We could not assume, however, that our collaborators in business and industry would speak of writing in similar terms or make the discriminations that composition teachers are trained to make. Furthermore, despite their expert status, our advisors were less likely than our faculty to speak as detached observers about writing practice in the workplace. In fact, the exigencies of particular communication problems made it difficult for some advisors to attend to common concerns.

Still, most advisors from business and industry came to the collaborative team accustomed both to working in an organizational setting and to applying group problem-solving techniques. This was not the case for the academics. Our graduate students, though versed in research on professional communication, of course, were inexperienced in behaving either as authorities on writing research or as participants in organizational activity. Even many professors on the Project Team had scant experience with group work: faculty typically work independently on research projects and, in the classroom, operate as leaders of activity rather than cooperative participants. Furthermore, the process of problem solving by consensus is to some degree antithetical to the process of research in the humanities, where scholars establish competing points of view and value dialectic as the impetus for considered thinking and the core of "truth" itself.

HOW FACULTY AND ADVISORS WERE PREPARED FOR COOPERATIVE INVESTIGATION OF WRITING PRACTICE. To prepare this diverse collaborative team for cooperative investigation, we applied conventional techniques for motivating group problem solving and even devised new techniques appropriate for our particular mission to create a cohesive community of evaluators of written discourse.

We oriented academics to group work through structured meetings with well-defined group activities. For instance, we asked our experienced instructors and our graduate students to construct lists of writing skills to be emphasized in professional writing classes, based on their reading and experience in technical writing research and pedagogy. In small-group discussion they compared their lists, negotiated terminology, and argued the relative importance of various skills (e.g., creating logical structure versus effectively addressing an audience).

To prepare these academics for the extensive group composition they were to do later on in the project, we conducted several activities that shifted and distributed individuals' responsibilities for team work. Faculty members took turns chairing their meetings with our advisors and shared responsibility for developing program agendae. Team members individually developed meeting handouts and plans for small and large group activities, and then brought their work to the group for critique and revision. Individuals wrote to the advisors memos that summarized faculty discussion and requested more information of them. Because the entire Project Team was involved in program planning, producing program materials, and writing to the Advisory Board, members naturally began to think of their work as representing the group instead of themselves as individuals. This attitude, conventionally assumed in organizations, is not fostered by the typical academic tasks of teaching and writing scholarly papers in the humanities.

To assist further in the faculty's orientation to organizational behavior, we provided opportunities for faculty to give oral presentations as practiced in the workplace: Project Team members gave prepared talks to the Advisory Board, explaining principles of technical communication advocated by textbooks and confirmed or denied by research. Through these presentations, faculty members— who were more experienced in formal presentation for academic audiences than for business professionals—learned to communicate information about their area of expertise to a nonacademic audience. At the same time, our Advisory Board members were brought up to date on current research and teaching practice in professional communications.

Although we did not need to orient the advisors in quite the same way to group work and organizational oral presentation, we did have to mediate their efforts to speak as peers with faculty members. We found that a great deal of residual "student" behavior surfaced when board members communicated with faculty. Some tended to see faculty as "the scholars" of writing in the workplace and themselves as "the students"; others tended to talk about writing in the ways they thought English teachers expected to hear (e.g., commentary about poor mechanics or incorrect usage); and still others thought that we were, in fact, going to teach them rather than collaborate with them. At first we tried to dispel these tendencies and behaviors by accomodating the incipient student/teacher roles through the faculty-to-advisors lectures described earlier (thus allowing both groups to assume roles with which they were already familiar). We insisted, however, that the content of the lectures be a by-product of our collaborative activity. For example, advisors provided samples of writing from their workplaces and annotated those samples with their comments on the writing's effectiveness. The faculty, in turn, used the annotated samples to illustrate principles of effective technical communication confirmed by conventional wisdom and empirical research. When advisors and faculty became comfortable working in this fashion, we reversed the leadership roles, having advisors speak to faculty on their perceptions of what factors influence effective written communication in the workplace. Finally, we moved to sessions in which both faculty and advisors worked together in small groups to define perspectives on technical communication.

Our graduate student researchers were oriented to their new collaborative roles in a special graduate seminar, "Approaches to Professional and Technical Writing," where they discussed interpretations of recent research; developed questions to ask advisors; and later, as the Project Team presented the teaching materials for review to the Advisory Board, were coached in professional writing and oral presentation techniques. The seminar instructor served as mentor to these students. Other faculty on the Project Team worked with them as peers while they developed curriculum objectives and created teaching materials.

HOW OUR EFFORTS WORKED TO MOTIVATE A COLLABORATIVE IN-VESTIGATION OF PROFESSIONAL WRITING. Our structured activities for faculty and advisors created a cohesive group of problem solvers, but the process took time. Our faculty and graduate students eventually became a working unit cooperating in team planning, team writing, and team revision of group work. We now believe that the success of university/industry collaborative work is contingent on careful orientation of all participants to the subject matter they will investigate, the language each uses to describe concerns about written communication, and their problem-solving roles as collaborators. As we will now show, these orientation efforts were crucial to moving individuals toward collective research of rhetorical practice and development of a professional writing curriculum.

Employing Our Collaborative Resources to Do Research on Writing in the Workplace

Our collaborative team of faculty and advisors from industry ensured the success of the first of our project tasks—to conduct a formal investigation of commonalities and differences in the writing practices of professionals in a variety of work settings. Through this research project we hoped to generalize about large groups of competent writers and at the same time investigate in detail aspects of planning, drafting, and revision of professional discourse as reported by individuals. Hence, we needed to devise a research instrument that could achieve both these aims. Furthermore, we needed to conduct our research within a context that would facilitate a valid interpretation of our findings.

Our solution was to create a lengthy, detailed survey instrument that not only would reach large numbers of professionals in multiple settings, but also would investigate specific aspects of professional writing unexamined by previous survey research—aspects that require the respondent to devote considerable time and effort to completing a questionnaire. As the following sections explain, involving the Advisory Board in administering the survey and in ensuring cooperation of the respondents made this research plan possible. Furthermore, the rich resources of the PWP Team provided an interpretive context to assist us in analyzing the survey results. Our faculty researchers knew the writing practices advocated by texts, the conventional wisdom and principles of composition, the theoretical studies of technical rhetoric, and the methodologies and results of empirical investigations of writing on the job. Our advisors from industry, on the other hand, represented the collective experience of writing practices in a wide variety of professions and organizations: Each representative had experience with a different context and had access to writers in several professions working in that context. The professional experience of our combined faculty/

advisory group, we believed, would help us assess the findings in the fullest and most meaningful way.

HOW WE DESIGNED AND CONDUCTED OUR FORMAL RESEARCH PROJECT IN COLLABORATION. Our research design responded both to needs perceived by our writing faculty for specific kinds of data on professional writing practice and to the opportunities created by our collaborative team. To date, studies of writing practices in the workplace have tended to be detailed observations of a few subjects (see, for example, Selzer, 1983a) or very broad-based surveys of kinds of writing (see, for example, Anderson, this volume; Faigley & Miller, 1982; Storms, 1983) or of the significance of writing on the job (see, for example, Davis, 1977). Most studies have not examined more specific aspects of the writing practices of large numbers of professionals or identified practices of those deemed to be competent writers by their organizations.[4] Quite clearly scholars and teachers need in-depth research on the writing practices of large populations of writers from various professions situated in many organizational contexts. We need empirical and naturalistic studies of several types, using diverse methodologies and approaching writing practices from multiple perspectives to achieve a true picture of the phenomenon of professional writing practice—a view that preserves the inherent complexity of the communicative act (see, Halloran & Whitburn, 1982; Couture, 1983; Odell, Goswami, Herrington, & Quick, 1983a, pp. 34–35, 1983b, p. 19).

Our faculty researchers wished to add to the now growing body of data on professional writing practice through an empirical investigation of writing practice in the work settings of our Advisory Board members. Yet at the same time, they wished to avoid the narrowly scientific tendencies reflected in some empirical writing research.[5] The PWP research effort attempted to define common assumptions about writing practice in the workplace, assumptions that direct the behavior of writers and teachers of professional communication; it did not presume to quantify characteristics of effective professional communication. In an effort to achieve a balance between strict empiricism and subjective analysis, our faculty researchers planned a detailed yet broadly based research project—first, articulating theories about writing practices and written products that we believe are reflected in common knowledge and current research on writing in the workplace, and second, testing these assumptions against the asserted practices of a large, diverse group of professionals who write.

Our faculty, versed in research methodologies in linguistics, composition, and technical writing, realized that the problems of testing language behavior in business and industry are legion. Writers' behaviors reflect their positions in organizations, and each organization represents a community comprising many separate but interacting subcommunities—departments, units, professional groups. To study these practices in detail requires a great commitment by investigators in observing, interviewing, and reading. It also requires a great commitment of business time by employers in identifying the appropriate populations, arranging access to them, and clearing any proprietary information. Furthermore, such studies require a commitment of time and effort by each professional subject.

The Advisory Board members' collaboration allowed us to surmount these problems. Because the board representatives were experts with an overall perspective on the language communities in their organizations (performers who knew the rules, conventions, and operations of language groups from the inside), they could provide us with the requisite knowledge of writing practices and contexts in each individual workplace. They could also identify and provide access to competent writers in specific professions. Our design, implementation, and analysis of the formal research thus was dependent on a dynamic process of dialogue between faculty and these industry representatives. Advisors initiated faculty into the mysteries of their individual language communities, thereby providing researchers with something of the insiders' perspective in each context. Faculty researchers, familiar with scholarship on communication in the workplace, formulated research questions that would help teachers and practitioners define more concretely the characteristics of writing practice reflected in their individual rhetorical standards.

Devising a Survey Questionnaire. Through informal discussions with the Advisory Board members, faculty confirmed their decision to develop an *in-depth, written questionnaire*—what had been, in fact, the first choice as the research instrument. This would best suit the research objective to study writers' processes and products in various professions and contexts. It also would receive strong support from participating organizations. Survey results can be generalized, verified, and compared; and they can best array differences in practice across various rhetorical communities. Written questionnaires, however, are frequently plagued by a lack of respondent cooperation prompted by a variety of causes, ranging from questions that are too lengthy, complex, or numerous to the absence of special incentives to respond (see Young, 1966, pp. 193–202; Simon, 1969, pp. 117–120). Here is where the advisors' investment in our project played a key part. They, together with management in their organizations, agreed to secure the required respondents and provide released work time to complete the survey. With the requisite cooperation from a large, diverse population, we could thus design a comprehensive writers' survey to investigate complex areas of on-the-job practice.

Our faculty composed a complex thirteen-page instrument, posing multiple-choice (using a Likert scale), short-answer, and open-ended questions exploring writing practices confirmed by conventional wisdom and research. This survey instrument was intended to provide detailed data on such questions about composing as: Do professionals revise their on-the-job writing? If so, at what point in their processes do they choose to revise? What strategies do they favor? What tasks do they believe require revision?

The structure of this survey reflected to some extent the design of previous surveys of writing in the workplace, but also differed in some significant ways. We collected demographic data on the writers' occupations, organizations, educational background, and training in business or technical writing. We also collected information on the amount of time professionals spend writing several specific kinds of documents. All these data can be compared with information gathered by other researchers who have surveyed professional writers. Our survey is unique in that we asked each writer to designate his or her most typical "routine" writing task and most typical "special" writing task. For each of these tasks, writers indicated the frequency of particular behaviors such as writing according to employer guidelines, using readability indexes, using formatting devices to signal change of subject matter, and getting feedback on writing from others. Hence, we could compare such behaviors across groups and by writing types. In addition, the survey collected information on stylistic preferences, in an effort to reveal tendencies that may characterize writing in certain professions.[6]

Selecting the Sample Population. Faculty members worked together with the advisors to *select a sample* of employees to survey. Using techniques employed to choose appropriate representatives for our Advisory Board, faculty and graduate student researchers again correlated data from *Michigan Statistical Abstracts*, the *U.S. Job Outlook Quarterly*, and Michigan Employment Security Commission job statistics to create a prioritized list of occupations likely to be held by college graduates over the next decade. This list was then matched with areas of study offered to undergraduates at Wayne State in order to come up with a group of fifty targeted occupations. The industry representatives identified employees in their organizations in each targeted occupation. When advisors found insufficient employees in certain targeted occupations, we sought additional organizations to participate in the PWP. Final employee selections were limited to competent writers with six or fewer years of job experience (primarily because we wanted to study writing in occupations open to new graduates).

We stressed the selection of *competent* writers in our directions to the advisors, yet we did not define what competency means. Instead, we stipulated that their employing organizations should determine who were competent writers among their employees in the targeted categories and suggested that advisors rely on their organizations' reviewing personnel: managers, supervisors, persons in training and human resourses, and (when appropriate) themselves. We believed that reviewing personnel in each organization were most qualified to evaluate competency within the individual corporate communities because of their own status (achieved through performance) and because of their overall knowledge of the language community and its requirements.

Administering the Survey. The Advisory Board members gained organizational approval for the research and access to the selected respondents for survey distribution. Board representatives secured released work time for the employees to complete the lengthy questionnaire (approximately 40 minutes) and conveyed the organizational support for the study, both through supervisory personnel and their own offices. They also distributed and collected surveys, completed anonymously. The sponsorship of the employer was therefore twofold: the contact person for the research project with the respondent was an employee, not an academic; and the questionnaire was completed on company time and with management's blessing.

Analyzing the Survey Results. After spending several months entering our massive survey data in computer files, we ran some preliminary statistical analyses on our data to see if clear patterns differentiated the writing practices of respondents in two large groups: those we identified as *writers*, respondents whose primary job responsibility involved writing or editing, and those we called *professionals*, respondents who held professional positions that involved writing, but who were not writers per se. Our first conclusions based on these statistics both confirmed and contradicted our expectations about the writing behavior of "writers" and "professionals."

To help us interpret these conclusions, we consulted with our advisors, who elaborated the findings in the light of their own professional experiences in a wide variety of situations. Involving the advisors in the interpretation of survey results, in fact, helped us to maintain a holistic view when examining findings from the analytic survey instrument. Their commentary reasserted a particular subjective perspective on our statistical data—a perspective that reflected their specific work and writing environments as opposed to our own generalized view. In presentations at the joint meetings of our Project Team and Advisory Board, faculty researchers presented both survey questions and results to the advisors, who then commented on how survey subjects responded to questions about their writing behavior. In listening to several individuals' interpretations of results, we became aware both of the different conventional ways that the faculty and advisors regard and speak about writing practice and of the wide range of interpretations inspired by our different work contexts.

A brief review of advisors' responses to results from one of the multiple-choice survey items illustrates how their commentary assisted our interpretation. Respondents named two most typical and frequent writing tasks, one that they regarded as "routine," and one that they regarded as "special"—categories that the questionnaire clearly defined for them; they then reacted to several survey statements describing explicit strategies by telling how frequently they applied these strategies to their routine and special tasks. Here is a sample statement:

> Question 12—I use a standard readability index (such as Gunning's Fog or the Flesch) to help me revise my writing.

On a five-point Likert scale, respondents indicated how often this statement applied first to their routine and then to their special writing: "never," "rarely," "sometimes," "often," or "very often." If the statement was "not applicable" at all, they could indicate this as well.

The responses to the statement about readability indexes were surprising to us both as researchers and as teachers of professional writing. Here is what our "professionals" said about using readability indexes when doing "special" writing: only 9 percent use readability indexes with any frequency ("sometimes," "often," or "very often") when they revise their writing, with a mere 1 percent claiming to use them "very often." Two thirds of the professionals claimed that they never use readability indexes, with 14 percent designating the question as not applicable. This response pattern was very similar for "professionals" applying the statement to their routine writing, and for "writers" applying the statement to both their routine and special writing. In short, very few "professionals" or "writers" are using readability indexes to revise their writing at work.

For us as faculty researchers, these results seemed to confirm that the writing practice of writers at work was in accord with the empirical research discrediting the indexes as revision tools and even questioning their validity as predictors of readability level (see Redish, 1980; Karlinsky and Koch, 1983; Selzer, 1983b). Perhaps, we thought, the indexes that had once been so widely promoted were now in disfavor among most writers in the workplace. The advisors, however, interpreted these results quite differently in applying them to their own specific work settings.

Some advisors explained that the low figures for using readability indexes reflected the *limited applicability* of these tools: "If you're writing . . . technical manuals, then you'd use [them]. . . . Other than that . . . [they're] really useless." Others saw the indexes as *guarantees of readability level* to meet client demands: "We do [use them] in my business when a client asks us to gear to a certain grade level. . . . That's probably the only thing we use [them] for. . . . " But still other industry representatives implied that the indexes were, in fact, a guide to revision and that computer word-processing systems incorporating them may ensure that they are widely used in the near future; as one member said:

> You're under deadline pressure, and you really don't have time to sit down and spend a half hour [to use an index] to analyze a page . . . Now as people start using more and more wordprocessing . . . and start to use, like UNIX, which has . . . style and diction programs that help you to change your writing style, I think . . . we'll see a resurgence in the popularity of those [indexes].

Clearly this advisor—and others who readily agreed with him—does not believe that the scant use of readability indexes indicates that their value is rejected by many professionals; the indexes may simply be regarded as unwieldy, a difficulty soon to be resolved by computerized readability analysis. Commentary such as this brought new perspectives to the interpretation of survey data, perspectives formed by the very writing contexts we were examining.

HOW THE COLLABORATIVE EFFORT WORKED TO IMPROVE OUR RESEARCH. The collaborative effort of the Advisory Board and the Project Team enabled the PWP to collect an enormous data base on the generic processes and products of writing on the job and on practices of specific professions. We believe these results will allow for a humanistic portrayal of writing practice in specific contexts, generalizations about common practices, and comparisons of differences among occupational groups. This data base forms a valuable resource for the PWP researchers, for the Advisory Board members (many of whom manage training and editing staffs in their companies), and for scholars and practitioners elsewhere. Most important, the entire process of conducting collaborative work on a formal research project served to solidify the advisor's participation in our new community of evaluators of professional writing practice, making this community a responsive, goal-directed group—a result that enabled us to use the advisors in some instances as co-interpreters of our research results. As a side benefit, the creation of a purposeful, committed collaborative team positively influenced our process of curriculum design.

Designing Goals and Objectives for Professional Writing Instruction

Our task of developing goals and objectives for a professional writing curriculum drew upon the detailed and diverse descriptions of professional writing practice that surfaced in meetings between our faculty and our advisors throughout the two years of our project. In these sessions, the collaborative team strove to define and describe skills that any professional writing curriculum must address to prepare students for writing in varied work settings. From these skills descriptions, our internal Project Team identified goals and objectives for a model professional writing program and published these goals and objectives in a document that was discussed with the advisors and then revised by the Project Team.

Our greatly elaborated collaborative process of developing the goals and objectives document with numerous planners and writers reflected in many ways the process any single writer undergoes when addressing a complex writing task: defining the problem; gathering information; generating ideas; determining a message; and planning, drafting, and revising the document. But our group, unlike a single writer, had to unify multiple, diverse perspectives on the content generated in each of these process stages. Most important, in its progress through these stages, our group had to make the intellectual movement from writer-based to reader-based considerations that a single writer makes when moving from first to final draft. For instance, our early lists of writing skills reflected concerns about who we were, what we were saying, and what we meant to say. Our revised statement of goals and objectives had to reflect outward concerns about who we wanted to reach, what they would think about our approach, and what they would likely do with our document.

Our ultimate objective was to create a document for writing instructors as a guideline for developing professional writing curriculum. The document's authenticity and credibility were to come from the combined perspectives of our team of expert evaluators of professional communication.

HOW WE FORMULATED OUR GOALS AND OBJECTIVES. In formulating the curriculum goals and objectives, we responded to two problems: first, the need to move from thinking in terms of writing skills our students need and that competent professionals have to writing program guidelines for instructors, and, second, the need to unify the diverse perspectives of our collaborative team throughout this whole process. Each of these concerns affected every stage of formulation, from defining the problem to drafting and revising the final document.

Defining the Problem. As our faculty had developed curriculum guidelines for other programs before, we had some knowledge of the task before us. Our approach to defining our problem was closely linked to our perception of what the final product of our investigation would be. We thought an effective goals and objectives document for a professional writing curriculum had to do two things: (1) define those skills that students must master in order to write effective professional communications—*our goals*; and, (2) suggest specific activities that students could perform in the classroom to learn the skills and demonstrate their mastery of them—*our objectives*. In our initial thinking about these categories, we assumed that *goals* would probably name skills for mastery such as "employing audience analysis" or "creating clear and logical organization." *Objectives* would probably name activities that demonstrate these skills, such as "writing two documents covering the same information, each of which addresses a different audience" or "distinguishing decision-making readers from several different readers of the same document."

To ensure the validity of these guidelines, we planned at the beginning of the project to base them on past research in the practice and teaching of professional writing as well as on the considerable body of informal research on writing practice that we would gather through numerous meetings and communications with our advisors from business, government, and industry. The goals and objectives would reflect, in short, descriptions of professional writing skills defined by faculty and advisors and based on their combined experiences of teaching student writers, training writers in the workplace, writing in specific professional settings, and conducting and studying research on professional communication. The goals and objectives would also reflect our faculty's detailed discussions with advisors about the requirements of specific writing tasks typical in each of their own work settings. Our long-range plan after completing the guidelines was to corroborate them with our own survey research on the practices of competent writers and the future research of others.

As we defined the kinds of information we needed for teaching guidelines, we also tackled the problem of how to complete our task with the full participation of our large collaborative team. In gathering information about skills writers need, we believed it was best to begin by asking participants to draw upon those contexts most familiar to them, whether the workplace or the classroom. Later we would ask them to relate these skills to a context the whole group could share—that is, those generic aspects of the professional writing process that all could agree must be addressed by a writing program.

Gathering Information. We began gathering information on skills writers must have to write successfully in the workplace by surveying individual advisors and teachers. To elicit specific information, we encouraged individuals through our questioning to articulate perspectives that were imposed by their work settings. A few examples from work sessions with our faculty and advisors illustrate this point.

We asked advisors to choose effective and ineffective examples of writing from their workplaces and to annotate them, noting skills or deficiencies the examples illustrated. Commentary from the advisors on the writing samples revealed a distinctly corporate stance: "blunt and no nonsense"; "changes clearly spelled out"; "flowery"; "too weak for our purposes"; "need to know who will enforce action, who will decide, will there be a follow-up memo." Similarly, we asked our faculty to describe skills to be emphasized when teaching practical writing. We encouraged them to base these descriptions on their experience with student writers, research in composition and technical writing, and review of textbooks on writing for the workplace. Their responses, though complex and varied, typically reflected the academic view: writers need to know how to "classify items and terms," demonstrate "analytical thinking," write with a sense of "ethos." In short, the terminology used by all participants asserted their various professional interpretations of the situations we posed. Our next task was to translate these contextualized remarks into concrete perspectives about effective writing that spoke significantly to everyone and that suggested teaching goals—that is, skills a student must master to do effective on-the-job writing.

Generating Ideas. We developed concrete ideas through two procedures: (1) trying to relate the writing skills identified by faculty and advisors to key processes that all participants could agree were typical of professional writing practice: and (2) asking them to describe skills as they articulated these processes.

Although the combined lists of skills constructed by our faculty and by our advisors were long and varied, many different terms expressed the same ideas and related to the same writing processes. For instance, a faculty member's concern that students understand the role of "ethos" in writing, clearly related to the businessman's concern that writing be "blunt and no nonsense." Yet we had to find language that communicated this connection to both groups. Naming a writing process that related to both perceptions—in this particular case, "developing professional style—made it possible for faculty and advisors to see the connections between the two groups. Our task was somewhat analogous to what Linda Flower and John R. Hayes (1977) have described as finding rich "bits" or key "terms" to stand for meaningful information.

We eventually settled on four key processes that described aspects of the professional writing addressed in the skills lists of both our advisors and faculty:

1. Analyzing readers and purposes.
2. Manipulating the writing process.
3. Designing graphics and format.
4. Developing professional style.

Having settled on these areas, we went back to individual participants and asked them to articulate their ideas about needed skills once more, now elaborating them in terms of personal experiences with these activities. These personal experiences would provide the raw material for our objectives, our descriptions of activities students must complete successfully to demonstrate they had mastered our goals. Figure 11-1 displays a sample of the questions the Project Team developed to guide this next stage in our process of formulating goals and objectives.

Determining a Message. The process of determining the message for our goals and objectives document translated to discovering the unified inside perspective on professional writing practice that we had generated through the continuous collaborative work of our faculty and advisors. That perspective would come through, we felt, if we went back to the team and asked for more specific information about the factors that influenced effective writing in their organi-

Readers and Purposes

How do writers find out information about internal audiences?

Do writers in organizations write to individuals or to personal roles? Is position in the organization more important than personal traits?

Can studying previous documents as models teach writers about readers? How?

Writing Process

Do you outline? What do you do before beginning to draft a document?

How do you assess a writing task? Do you have a set of questions which you ask yourself?

Have you changed your writing process in the time you have been working? How? Why?

Graphics and Format

What do you see as the main function of a graphic aid?

How do you decide when to include a graphic aid?

How does a consideration of audience dictate the kind and complexity of a graphic aid you might include?

Professional Style

Where and how do employees get a sense of the writing style which is important in their writing roles?

Is professional style mostly distinguished by a profession? A particular type of document? A particular institution?

What is it that professionals value when they say a document is written in the correct style?

Figure 11-1 Questions for Elaborating Professional Writing Skills

zations, but this time emphasizing the perspective of their role as collaborators with university faculty in curriculum development. We asked individual advisors to relate their own work experiences with professional writing as they were relevant to each of the four writing process areas we had identified earlier. Their responses this time certainly reflected their increased sense of belonging to a community of professionals whose goal was to identify guidelines for instructors of professional writing.

One advisor who described her experiences with audience analysis gave a detailed picture of the process of analyzing audiences when writing computer documentation manuals. She said that audience analysis not only was guided by what a reader needs to *know*, but also by what a reader *should not, in fact, be told*. For instance, manuals for computer operators should not enable them to alter programs—that information should only be available to programmers. This perspective inspired hot debate among advisors and university faculty about the role of information management in audience analysis.

We debated the process of audience analysis and many other issues inspired by advisors' narratives of work experience, and then followed discussion with a written questionnaire to all participants inviting more commentary. We found that written responses in some cases were more detailed; a few advisors felt more comfortable expressing their views on paper than they did in speaking in front of the whole group. For instance, in commenting on the experiences that advisors had related to illustrate "varieties" of professional writing in our discussion of professional style, one advisor wrote:

> Another kind, which I don't have a name for immediately, is a kind of "organizational relations" writing—memos, letters, PR pieces, project proposals (surprised?), that are basically to persuade or convince others. I want you to do your job better, I want you to be more enthusiastic about the firm, I want your work behavior to improve, I want you to know that I am doing my job as best I can, but I'm being stalled by some other person or group who are out of my control, someone you can speak to in your higher position in the firm (and, in any case, whether you speak to them or not, I'm now off the hook, because—I've told you, in writing, that I have a problem which you must solve—I've transferred the monkey).

Not surprisingly, after evaluating narratives of personal experience gathered in the interactive forum and the reflective written commentary, we determined new categories of the overall professional writing process that better covered the experiences we had now reviewed:

1. Gathering information for documents from nonlibrary sources.
2. Integrating technical/managerial problem solving with the writing process.

3. Adapting to special writing constraints.
4. Writing with collaborators.
5. Analyzing readers and purposes.
6. Arranging and formatting documents.
7. Incorporating graphic aids.
8. Developing a professional style.

Formatting a Statement of Goals and Objectives. To select the best format for presenting goals and objectives in the eight major process areas, we evaluated the needs of our principal readers: the Advisory Board who would evaluate our finished draft against their experience; instructors who would use it to plan activities in their classes; and students who would be required to meet the objectives we specified. To produce a document that would seem meaningful to all groups, we had to contextualize the information by describing job-related writing situations that required the skills we were emphasizing. Therefore, we planned to relate some of the experiences mentioned by the advisors in separate introductions to the goals and objectives in each of our eight areas, thus focusing skills more clearly, documenting the need for these skills, and demonstrating to our advisors that their expertise had been a valuable resource. (Figure 11-2 shows an introduction written for the "Adapting to Special Writing Constraints" section of our goals and objectives document.) After relating real work experiences to illustrate the need for skills in each of our eight areas, we began the process of writing *goals* that named skills students should master in each process area and *objectives* that described the kinds of classroom activities students must complete successfully to demonstrate that they have reached the instructional goal. Writing separate goals and objectives for each of our eight process areas allowed us to assign individual writers to draft different portions for review, making the initial drafting productive and efficient.

Drafting, Revising, and Editing the Document. We have asserted that a gradual movement from writer-centered to reader-centered concerns was reflected in each stage of our writing the goals and objectives document. This movement was particularly evident in drafting. Responsibility for composition was assigned to five Project Team members. In the initial meetings of the team writing sessions, the co-writers were more defensive about their writing than in later

Professionals who write must produce effective documents under the pressure of deadlines. This pressure can affect all aspects of the writing process, including how writers gather and confirm information, how and when writers consult with others prior to writing, whether or how they construct an outline or other written plan, how they integrate previous documents related to this communication into the text, how they format the text, whether and how they incorporate "boiler plate" passages, how they revise the document, and how they edit. For example, a professional who is writing a constuction company bid proposal in response to a request for bids from a developer may choose to incorporate passages from previous bids to save time. A busy sales representative may need to write documents confirming phone conversations immediately at the typewriter and use them as final drafts. An engineer who must file a report of job activities at the end of each week may keep a daily journal of notes so that all information to be summarized in the weekly report is handy when the final document must be written. In short, professionals may be obliged to alter their writing processes in several different ways to one end: to meet an inflexible deadline.

Figure 11-2 Introduction to "Adapting to Special Writing Constraints" Section of the Goals and Objectives Document

meetings—a change dramatized when the Project Team evaluated a draft of goals and objectives written by a team member who had not attended the initial meetings. When the other members each critiqued the draft offering suggestions for revision, this new member felt personally attacked. Others had come to expect criticism and were prepared to adjust their writing to meet the group's consensus.

The movement away from egocentric concerns also became apparent when we discussed the draft document with the advisors. In small groups at earlier planning meetings, the advisors and faculty pontificated more often than responded to one another. At later meetings, both groups interacted freely. Advisors, in particular, were better able to connect their experiences to those of others. A portion of the dialogue from one of our final meetings of the collaborative team reported in figure 11-3 illustrates this improvement. The advisors were discussing skills needed to gather information orally, from other people, rather than from printed material. The quoted passage shows them relating their own personal experiences and at the same time making an effort to categorize and define skills required to perform writing tasks in several professions—for instance, the information-gathering skills of listening attentively,

Advisor #1: All you can teach is interviewing skills. You can't really teach the skills, you can teach the theory, and then you can just have them interview each other until they drop. You can teach listening skills, because most of interviewing is listening: "I don't understand that; can you tell me more about it."

Advisor #2: [And] assertion skills. Once they get out there—I won't say in the real world, because it's all real—but once they get out in the business world, they're going to have people, source people, who say, "No, don't write it that way. Use these words because I'm the technical specialist." And you have to be ready to push back . . . and say, "Right, but you aren't the writer. I'm the writer and I'll write it, and then you tell me if it's technically accurate. And IF it's technically accurate, then SHUT UP." But you have to say that in a way that you're not aggressive to them. You have to be ready to push them back and ASSERT yourself. Because you're going to have people . . .

Advisor #3: Students can't do that. When they first get up . . . they'd get creamed.

Advisor #2: Well, but if they have the assertion skills, and the listening skills— because that's really what it is, is listening to someone. . . . If a software person comes up to me and blows up at me because I wrote some things wrong, I'm going to sit there and I'm going to say, "Yea, OK." And I'm going to listen to them, and eventually they're going to run out of steam. And when they're out of steam, then I can say, "All right. Now, rationally, what needs to be made right. How do we go about doing that? What ideas do you have?"

Figure 11-3 Dialogue from Collaborative Team Meeting

asserting a position, and getting feedback on the accuracy of gathered data. They are moving from their personal views of situations toward relating those views in terms shared by others.

HOW WELL THE PROCESS-CENTERED APPROACH WORKED. Our strategy of involving all collaborative participants in the entire process of writing the goals and objectives document not only helped us write a more effective document, but also solidified participants' commitment to the team research and curriculum development effort. The interactive forums helped us to move toward creating a unified "expert view," which in turn enabled us to specify clearly skills that are crucial for the beginning professional writer. Achieving this view meant coming to terms with the diverse terminology and perspectives of the individuals on our collaborative team—a process that led our PWP participants to a phenomenological understanding of professional writing practices while writing the goals and objectives. Finally, the experiences and examples recounted by our advisors gave credibility to our guidelines, demonstrating their generic applicability to many professional writing situations.

Writing, Revising, and Testing Curriculum Materials

In developing goals and objectives, our Project Team and Advisory Board ultimately were concerned about the shape of the end document—how well it would function as a set of teaching guidelines and, at the same time, reflect the standards of effective writing and competent writing practice developed by the PWP collaborative team. These concerns also dominated the PWP's teamwork in writing, testing, and revising curriculum materials to meet our objectives in the writing class. In handling these latter tasks, however, we had to meet some additional criteria: the teaching units had to be immediately usable in the classroom, had to appeal to students, and had to improve students' preparation for on-the-job writing. After all, our major goal in collaborating with industry was to make research-based teaching techniques more accessible and usable for the classroom teacher. Whereas our goals and objectives suggested teaching directions, our teaching units had to translate these guidelines into day-to-day activities.

To meet this demand, the Project Team had to take the goals and objectives abstracted from the multiple writing tasks and contexts described by the Advisory Board and *recontextualize* them, applying them to practices appropriate for the college writing classroom. Faculty had to reconcile academic purposes with our advisors' perceptions of the demands on beginning writers in the workplace in order to create curriculum materials that are apt and flexible—inits that remain in process, gaining continued enrichment from teachers, theorists, professionals in the workplace—and, of course, from students.

HOW WE PLANNED CURRICULUM UNITS TO TEACH GENERIC WRITING SKILLS FOR THE WORKPLACE. We developed individual units to be integrated into existing courses singly or in conjunction with other units. A collection of units would serve as a resource for beginning and experienced instructors, a place to go for assignment sequences, suggested readings, concepts, and activities on which to begin building a new syllabus or enriching an existing one.

Through participatory conferences with the Advisory Board, graduate students, and full-time faculty, faculty identified several areas in which curriculum units would be developed that reflected the writing skills and activities suggested in our goals and objectives. These areas included: *using logic in writing, revising and editing, analyzing readers, writing with collaborators, using graphic aids, assuming authority in technical/professional writing, and adapting to specific communication situations.* These foci for curriculum units, decontextualized from the many individual comments and responses of both the Advisory Board members and our faculty, were to be elaborated and recontextualized in assignments and activities that would develop skills that students could apply when they entered the workplace. In turn, we planned to write assignments and activities for each unit that could fit within the context of any of our instructor's classrooms. We would do so by offering alternative approaches that match several teaching styles and a range of student abilities.

HOW THE COLLABORATIVE TEAM DEVELOPED CURRICULUM. As with the goals and objectives, the collaborative team helped the PWP create teaching materials that would address three diverse and equally relevant audiences: instructors, Advisory Board members, and students.

Faculty on the staff of the PWP proposed the units, drafted them, and then carefully scrutinized them, suggesting changes, additions, and new directions. Senior faculty who teach literature as well as advanced writing reviewed early presentations of unit outlines and read drafts of the developing curriculum materials, evaluating the strengths and weaknesses in each unit. Out of these dialogues, the Project Team developed a format for structuring the units for easy teacher orientation: each unit would contain a summary of relevant goals and objectives, a day-by-day schedule, assignment sheets for students, background materials and lecture suggestions for instructors, and an annotated bibliography. Working within this format, our faculty writers fleshed out units covering each of the topic foci we introduced earlier to meet the criteria for successful units that we had established in our collaborative planning.

In each of our teaching units, we met our criterion of re-contextualizing the skills (or teaching goals) identified by our Advisory Board and Project Team by relating these skills to writing research and pedagogical approaches that are familiar and/or easily accessible to teachers. For instance, from our advisors' descriptions of actual professional writing tasks and situations, we had abstracted generic "reader analysis" skills such as "understanding how reader analysis can direct what the writer says about the same information to different readers." In our reader analysis teaching unit, we related this skill or teaching goal to textbook discussions and current research on audience analysis listed in the unit's annotated biblio-graphy. We also created scenarios for writing assignments that reflected the kinds of reader analysis situations that our advisors described.

We met our criterion of making units adaptable to different teaching styles by creating, in all units, activities that involved lecture by the instructor, class discussion, small-group work, and a wide range of writing and reading tasks. For instance, in the reader analysis unit, we gave teachers suggestions for lecturing about the differences between audience analysis in the classroom and the same task on the job; we gave students assignments with clearly specified audiences as well as guidelines for analyzing these audiences and for assessing the appropriateness of their own writing as it responded to these readers. One assignment asked students to compare annual reports as they reflected different audiences, another to compare several technical articles on the same subject as they responded to different journal readerships, and still another to complete the audience-specific writing task of requesting an exemption from a certain graduate requirement from a particular college admini-strator.

When we first presented plans for our reader analysis unit and the other teaching units to the Advisory Board, inherent differences between the perspectives of teachers and professionals in the workplace on these materials were exhibited in force. Advisory Board members' critiques highlighted contrasts between the class-room environment and the workplace environment. Underlying some advisors' commentary was a wish not only to stimulate but actually to replicate workplace tasks in the classroom. One Advisory Board member even suggested giving students two or more writing tasks during the same class hour, both "rush jobs, of course, then having a telephone ring and create other workaday interruptions"—those situations would give students a real feel for what writing on their jobs would be like. Some asserted that the classroom should become, as much as possible, a mini-workplace. Faculty, on the other hand, defended the protected atmosphere of the university, where writers have the liberty to reflect on the full meaning and consequences of their communications in ways the workplace often cannot allow.

As we continued to work together, other advisors spoke against making the classroom just like the workplace. As one put it:

> I really still believe that a university has to maintain a certain element that a business does not really need to maintain. . . . I really think [it] is pretty impossible . . . to duplicate what goes on in business at a university. . . . My feeling is that if you're not going to get a little bit of theory in a university, then you're not going to get it in   most [workplaces].

One board member put his defense of emphasizing theory in the writing class even more strongly:

> I am concerned that we not stand on our heads to hide Toulmin (1958) [whose rhetorical theory figures strongly in one of our units]. We have, in recent years, reacted to . . . classical subjects by pretending they don't exist or, the most damaging lie of all, that they aren't practical. Believe me when I say there is nothing, NOTHING more practical than the quadrivium and the trivium.

The debate between the virtues of theory and practice continued throughout the PWP collaboration, and the dynamic of Advisory Board and Project Team interaction forced curriculum developers to make more explicit the connections between classroom activities, skills developed, and on-the-job applications. Unit writers ultimately incorporated more workplace-like writing tasks and openly asserted the teaching units' connections with the workplace, but they did not attempt to turn the classroom into the workplace.

HOW WE TESTED THE CURRICULUM UNITS AND EVALUATED THEM. In testing our teaching materials in Wayne State writing classes, we wanted to find out from teachers whether the units emphasized appropriate writing competencies, whether they required extensive teacher input, and whether they worked in the classroom. We wanted to find out from the students whether or not the assignments were challenging and interesting and whether they could perceive connections between what they were doing in the classroom and what they would have to do on the job.[7]

We interviewed each instructor after he or she taught a curriculum unit and also collected written comments. Because we had monitored the teaching of all units throughout the pilot process, the interviews at the end gave many instructors a chance to summarize responses they had given us in bits and pieces earlier. For some, this was a cathartic process; we had no need to question them specifically about aspects of the unit they taught, since they were quite willing to tell us its successes and failures with little prompting. In fact, we believed that beginning the interviews with broad, open-ended questions and continuing in this fashion until a teacher had nothing more to say *before* making specific inquiries helped us obtain the most detailed and honest responses. However, we did prepare a list of specific interview questions to ask when necessary to ensure that all our concerns about unit flexibility, appropriateness, ease of use, appeal to students, and relevance to teaching objectives were addressed.

The interviews were a particularly rich source of suggestions for revision, alternative assignments, and expansion. Teacher comments documented the particular importance of using examples of professional writing in our units, both student papers and workplace documents, and reiterated the importance of creating clear contexts for each workplace writing activity we presented.

In assessing student response, we collected student papers and open-ended evaluations of unit assignments, and conducted a pre- and posttest of professional writing skills. The open-ended responses to units showed that students valued the opportunities to confront workplace writing tasks in the classroom. For example, in directly evaluating the assignments from a case that our faculty designed to simulate on-the-job problem-solving resulting in written reports,[8] students remarked that the assignment was "challenging because there was not just one clear solution" and that it "gave . . . a complete new perspective on what a real work situation might be like."

The process of writing, revising, and testing curriculum to incorporate both work and academic perspectives helped PWP faculty to create teaching units rooted in the demands of on-the-job writing, but also firmly grounded in rhetorical theory and proven pedagogical strategies. The dynamic of the interaction between faculty and professionals from industry, in particular, enabled us to achieve this end.

EPILOGUE

We have described in this report a step-by-step process of university-industry collaboration that we believe has worked successfully to improve research and curriculum development in professional writing. We used our collaborative team specifically to research writing practice and to develop a curriculum that concentrates on generic skills applicable to writing in many professions. Other institutions may wish to adopt some of our procedures on a smaller scale to begin the process of university-industry dialogue that can enrich their writing programs.

With the major mission of the PWP complete, we at Wayne State are now making plans to continue meetings of our faculty and Advisory Board to discuss issues of professional communication on a regular basis. To further this end, we have invited our advisors to select other interested professionals to join our collaborative team and have established an initial list of topics for continuing forums. We have also solicited Advisory Board members to employ students in our English Department student intern program, which gives English majors the opportunity to work as writers in local organizations for college credit. In short, we have found great value in continuing our collaboration as an ongoing tool to keep faculty informed about real-world writing practices, to improve university-industry relations, and to better prepare our students for their careers beyond the university.

We believe our experience has demonstrated that university-industry collaboration *can work successfully* to increase research and curriculum development opportunities in professional writing and encourage others to adopt our model. The success of such collaboration, however, is contingent on developing in all participants a collective commitment to the goal of improving professional writing instruction—a commitment that will come from a sense of belonging to a community of experts that is especially qualified to evaluate the practice and teaching of professional writing.

Notes

1. The PWP was sponsored by Wayne State University's English Department and funded by the U.S. Department of Education's Fund for the Improvement of Postsecondary Education (project co-directors, Barbara Couture and John Brereton).

2. Our assumption echoes Kuhn's (1970) theory of the scientific community as assessors of the credibility of scientific truth; Toulmin's assertions of rhetorical competence as a function of field specific knowledge; and, of course, the entire body of research on reader-response criticism, which asserts that a reading community determines the aesthetic value of literature.

3. Individuals often advance in organizations because they have superior communication skills. Surveys of management in a variety of organizations consistently show that communication skills often rank far above basic technical and functional skills as competencies crucial to an employee's success. See Davis (1977) and Hildebrandt, Bond, Miller, and Swinyard (1982).

4. A few studies have revealed more detailed information about the writing practices of numbers of professionals. See, for example, Roundy and Mair (1982) and Odell, Goswami, Herrington, and Quick (1983a, 1983b).

5. We share Robert Connors' misgivings about composition research that is a "barren enactment of imitation science," ignoring the complexity and subjectivity of human discourse: "In our laudable desire to improve our discipline we must not lose sight of the danger of falling into scientific fallacies and trying to enforce empirical canons that must, if they are to be useful, grow naturally from previously-solved puzzles" (1983, pp. 20, 19).

6. The Writers' Survey, developed by Barbara Couture and Jone Rymer Goldstein, was constructed according to survey design guidelines and distributed under controlled conditions to a select sample representing the target population. Details of the survey and discussion of results will appear in future publications.

7. Over two semesters, Wayne State faculty piloted five of six curriculum units (more are being developed at the writing of this report) with more than 300 students of professional writing majoring in engineering, nursing, business, the sciences, liberal arts, journalism, and education. Classes included Technical Report Writing I and II, Advanced Expository Writing, and Techniques of Expository Writing. Instructors were both full- and part-time members of the faculty. The U.S. Department of Education (Fund for the Improvement of Postsecondary Education) has awarded a dissemination grant to the Professional Writing Project to redevelop the PWP curriculum for future publication.

8. A case is a narrative detailing the problem-solving processes of a technical professional at work that lead to his or her writing a report.

References

Anderson, P. V. (1977). Teaching the teacher what government and industry want from technical writing. In T. M. Sawyer (Ed.), *Technical and professional communication* (pp. 65–78). Ann Arbor: Professional Communication Press.

Anderson, P. V. What survey research tells us about writing at work, Chapter 1, this volume.

Barnum, C. M. (1983). The technical writing teacher as bridge builder—from classroom to boardroom. Paper presented at the 1983 MLA Convention.

Connors, R. J. (1983). Composition studies and science. College English, 45(1), 1–20.

Couture, B. (1983). Toward a holistic analysis of writing quality. Michigan Academician, 15(3), 353–368.

Davis, R. M. (1977). How important is technical writing?—A survey of the opinions of successful engineers. The Technical Writing Teacher, 4(3), 83–88.

Faigley, L., & Miller, T. P. (1982). What we learn from writing on the job. College English, 44(6), 561–569.

Flower, L. S., & Hayes, J. R. (1977). Problem-solving strategies and the writing process. College English, 39(4), 435–456.

Halloran, S. M., & Whitburn M. D. (1982). Ciceronian rhetoric and the rise of science: The plain style reconsidered. In J. J. Murphy (Ed.), The rhetorical tradition and modern writing (pp. 58–72). New York: MLA.

Hildebrandt, H. W., Bond, F. A., Miller, E. L., & Swinyard, A. W. (1982). An executive appraisal of courses which best prepare one for general management. The Journal of Business Communication, 19(1), 5–15.

Karlinsky, S. S., & Koch, B. S. (1983). Readability is in the mind of the reader. The Journal of Business Communication, 20(4), 57–70.

Kuhn, T. (1970). The structure of scientific revolutions (2nd ed.). Chicago: University of Chicago Press.

Odell, L., Goswami, D., Herrington, A., & Quick, D. (1983). The discourse-based interview: A procedure for exploring the tacit knowledge of writers in non-academic settings. In P. Mosenthal, L. Tamor, & S. A. Walmsley (Eds.), Research on writing: Principles and methods (pp. 220–236). New York: Longman. (b)

Odell, L., Goswami, D., Herrington, A., & Quick, D. (1983). Studying writing in non-academic settings. In P. V. Anderson, R. J. Brockmann, & C. R. Miller (Eds.), New essays in technical and scientific communicaton: Research, theory, practice (pp. 17–40). Farmingdale, NY: Baywood Publishing Company. (a)

Redish, J. C. (1980). Readability. In D. B. Felker (Ed.), Document design: A review of the relevant research (pp. 69–93). Washington, DC: American Institutes for Research.

Roundy, N., & Mair, D. (1982). The composing process of technical writers: A preliminary study. Journal of Advanced Composition, 3(1–2), 89–101.

Selzer, J. (1983). The composing processes of an engineer. College Composition and Communication, 34(2), 178–187. (a)

Selzer, J. (1983). What constitutes a "readable" technical style? In P. V. Anderson, R. J. Brockmann, & C. R. Miller (Eds.), New essays in technical and scientific communication: Research, theory, practice (pp. 71–89). Farmingdale, NY: Baywood Publishing Company. (b)

Simon, J. L. (1969). Basic research methods in social science. New York: Random House.

Stevenson, D. W. The writing teacher in the workplace, chapter 10, this volume.

Storms, C. G. (1983). What business school graduates say about the writing they do at work: Implications for the business communication course. *The ABCA Bulletin*, 46(4), 13–18.

Toulmin, S. (1958). *The uses of argument*. Cambridge: Cambridge University Press.

Young, P. V. (1966). *Scientific social surveys and research*. Englewood Cliffs, NJ: Prentice-Hall.

Workplace and Classroom

12

Principles for Designing Writing Courses

DAVID A. LAUERMAN,
MELVIN W. SCHROEDER,
KENNETH SROKA, AND
E. ROGER STEPHENSON
Canisius College

During the past several years at Canisius College, we have designed and taught five new advanced composition courses: "Business Writing," "Writing for Social Service," "Technical Writing," "Writing for the Humanities," and "Writing for Learners." In this work, we assumed that our teaching of writing should be informed not just by the assignments given in other academic disciplines but by the kinds of writing tasks that students will do when they enter the workplace. We further assumed that these writing tasks are complex and challenging and that they would allow us an opportunity to deal with rhetorical and intellectual issues that are important for any liberally educated person.

Our efforts to devise these courses took us into the actual writing worlds of business (manufacturing, sales, and banks, especially); social services (hospitals and social agencies); science and technology (industrial and research labs); public life (newspapers, television studios, public relations and advertising firms, law offices, and cultural institutions); and education. It may seem strange to

427

include education in our list, but we did so for two reasons. First, we wanted to devise an advanced composition course for prospective teachers. And second, we discovered that teachers in almost every discipline do more writing than one might expect and that these teachers write for contexts that are much more varied and complex than the writing tasks those same teachers tend to set for their students.

Although we did not try to establish the formal administrative structure described in the preceding chapter by Barbara Couture and her colleagues, we did make extensive use of our contacts with local businesses, industries, and governmental agencies. In this chapter we will explain briefly how we established these contacts and how we gathered data to use in planning our courses. Then we will explain some of the principles that can guide this work and illustrate those principles with examples of assignments we have created for our new advanced composition courses.

ESTABLISHING CONTACTS
AND GATHERING DATA

To establish contact with writers in nonacademic settings, we relied heavily on our contact with Canisius graduates, especially English majors. Luckily, our English majors work in an astonishing variety of jobs in the Buffalo area. While our Alumni Office was helpful, we most often began by telephoning friends among our recent graduates; we began with English majors now working in social services, in business, in research, in law, or in teaching. We explained our project, described our need for access to working writers, and asked for the name of a contact person. We gave each contact person a one-page description of our research, and asked the contact person to find us people competent in their work and willing to give us some time—two one-hour interviews. The warm feeling that our city has toward our college students and their teachers moved people to cooperate; we had only a very few refusals. Where we needed to extend our contacts in technical areas, we called on colleagues in departments active in consulting and in providing student internships: Chemistry, Political Science, Education, Communication. These academic contacts worked as well as our personal contacts.

Once we had identified participants in various offices, we did research that was both intensive and extensive. We opened the process by conducting an initial interview with writers on the job, using a questionnaire that covered, among other issues, the types of writing tasks; methods and problems; and the institutional, personal, and professional significance of the writing. From all participants, we also collected a portfolio of the most frequent and important kinds of writing that they did on the job. After studying that material, we returned for an "analytical interview" that focused on particular features of selected pieces of writing.

Upon completing a series of interviews with people in a given area (e.g., business), we held a workshop involving the researchers and consultants, as many as possible of the work-world writers, and Canisius College faculty members from the departments most related to the individual research sequence. At these workshops, we informed participants about our approach to field research and showed them examples of writing and transcripts of interviews. We asked workshop participants to help us speculate on ways of using these materials in our courses, and we concluded the workshop by asking participants to help us draft goals for our new courses. This helped us both to inform colleagues (and their students) about our new approach to writing and also to suggest that they sponsor writing in their own courses. The nonacademic writers helped to retain our work-world orientation.

For our immediate consideration in designing new advanced composition courses which were to have strong relationships to writing on the job, and for subsequent study through the years, we amassed through our research project a wonderful "hoard" of materials: the initial questionnaires, the numerous portfolios of work-world writing, the analytical interviews (on tape and typed), and typed and taped records of the concluding workshops. What we want to do in the remainder of this chapter is to illustrate some of the principles that guided us in trying to collect and use these materials in designing our advanced composition courses.

PRINCIPLES AND ILLUSTRATIVE ASSIGNMENTS

Explore the Context(s) for Work-related Writing

Throughout the rest of this chapter, we will describe assignments that are based on samples of writing that people had done as a normal part of their daily work. But these assignments are not based solely on our analysis of the written texts themselves. Rather, our assignments are based on our understanding of the rhetorical, organizational, and interpersonal contexts in which the writing was done. To gather information about these contexts, we relied heavily on the analytic interviews, mentioned earlier.

In preparing for these interviews, we selected six pieces of writing that participants had labeled typical and important for their jobs. Then we identified places at which the writer had made decisions about style or content. Consider, for example, the following letter by an English teacher who was protesting an assistant principal's high-handed (or at least thoughtless) request for information:

March 21, 19__

Dear [Ms. Jackson]:

A problem has arisen which is causing a bit of comment, so much so that I feel I must write to you about it.

Yesterday, a group of teachers volunteered to evaluate the material which was sent in by teachers for [our literary magazine]. I was appreciative of their willingness to come to the District Office and go over this material. I was astounded when Mr. [Jones] asked these teachers to write down the names of teachers who submitted material and the number of pieces they submitted. First of all, teachers should not be asked to write down other teachers' names, and, secondly, these teachers were here for the purpose of evaluating the material, not for the purpose of keeping track of who sent how many things in. I hope you agree that teachers should not keep track of other teachers.

Besides this, I feel that a compilation of teachers' names and the number of contributions per teacher is not a valid statement of anything meaningful. The reasons why I feel this way are based upon what I saw yesterday. Some teachers may hand in 10 writings based on the same assignment; in this case, only the best 1 or 2 should be sent in for consideration, since printing all 10 of the same thing would not be practicable. Another teacher may send in a folder of 30 writings which have not even been proofread or looked at previously. A third teacher may send in 2, which may represent the very best of many he/she has considered. And so on the various possibilities go. So, to say that in the above examples, teacher 1 sends 10, teacher 2 sends 30, teacher 3 sends 2 does not prove anything about which teacher has put forth the best effort for [Say It Now]. This does not prove that teacher 2 is the best or teacher 3 is the worst.

It appears then that in compiling statistics, the underlying realities of the matter are lost in the figures. So, I feel that this type of statistic is meaningless and should not even be recorded.

I think you would agree with me that in producing something like [*Say It Now*] the utmost co-operation from the faculty is vital to its success. Yet, this type of statistic-seeking produces the opposite effect. Underscoring this fact is the dubious value of these statistics. I think that our present task in promoting [our magazine] is to seek co-operation, not to inspire alienation. I hope you can agree with this.

Sincerely,

*Bracketed materials are altered from the original.

From our reading of this letter and other examples of the teacher's writing, we identified the following kinds of decisions:

1. The teacher had decided to address this reader in rather formal terms (Ms. Jackson); in other letters, she had addressed her readers more informally.
2. She began the middle paragraph with a strong personal opinion; in other pieces of writing, she was less direct in expressing opinion.
3. In the middle paragraph she chose to provide a fairly elaborate hypothetical case.
4. In the fourth paragraph her sentence structure was relatively simple, especially when compared to the more highly embedded sentences we occasionally noted in her other pieces of writing.
5. In the last sentence of the letter, she phrased her request rather mildly, much more so than she had phrased other requests.

To explore the context for these decisions, we interviewed the teacher about the following altered draft of her letter.

March 21, 19__

1. A. Dear Ms. Jackson:
   B. Dear Elizabeth:
   C. Dear Beth:
   D. Memo: To: Ms. Jackson
            From:

A problem has arisen which is causing quite a bit of comment, so much that I feel I must write to you about it.

Yesterday, a group of teachers volunteered to evaluate the material which was sent in by teachers for our [literary magazine]. I was appreciative of their willingness to come to the District Office and go over this material. I was astounded when

2. A. Mr. Robert Jones
   B. Mr. Jones
   C. Robert Jones
   D. Bob Jones

asked these teachers to write down the names of teachers who submitted material and the number of pieces they submitted. First of all, teachers should not be asked to write down other teachers' names, and, secondly, these teachers were here for the purpose of evaluating the material, not for the purpose of keeping track of who sent how many things in. I hope you agree that teachers should not keep track of other teachers.

Besides this,

3. A. I feel that a compilation of teachers' names . . .
   B. It should be obvious that a compilation of teachers' names . . .
   C. A compilation of teachers' names . . .
   D. In my opinion, a compilation of teachers' names . . .

and the number of contributions per teacher is not a valid statement of anything meaningful. The reasons why I feel this way are based upon what I saw yesterday.

4. A. Some teachers may hand in 10 writings based on the same assignment; in this case, only the best 1 or 2 should be sent in for consideration, since printing all 10 of the same thing would not be practicable. Another teacher may send in a folder of 30 writings, which have not even been proofread or looked at previously. A third teacher may send in 2, which may represent the very best of many he/she has considered. And so on the various possibilities go.
   B. Some teacher may hand in 10 writings based on the same assignment. Another teacher may send in a folder of 30 writings which have not even been proofread or looked at previously. A third teacher may send in 2, which may represent the very best of many he/she considered.

So, to say that in the above examples, teacher 1 sends 10, teacher 2 sends 30 and teacher 3 sends 2 does not prove anything about which teacher has put forth the best effort for [Say It Now]. This does not prove that teacher 2 is the best or teacher 3 is the worst.

5. A. It appears then that in compiling statistics, the underlying realities of the matter are lost in the figures. So, I feel that this type of statistic is meaningless and should not even be recorded.

   B. Since the underlying realities of the matter appear to be lost in compiling numbers, I feel that this type of statistic is meaningless and should not even be recorded.

I think you would agree with me that in producing something like [Say It Now] the utmost co-operation from the faculty is vital to its success. Yet, this type of statistic-seeking produces the opposite effect. Underscoring this fact is the dubious value of these statistics. I think that our present task in promoting our magazine is to seek co-operation, not to inspire alienation.

6. A. I hope you can agree with this.

   B. I hope something will be done to prevent this sort of thing from happening again.

Sincerely,

As we did in all our analytic interviews, we began by assuring this writer that all the alternatives (1) were derived from decisions she had made in other pieces of job-related writing and (2) were grammatically correct. We told the writer that we were interested in the reasoning that would lead her to prefer a given alternative to the others.

The teacher's responses provided this scenario. She was moderator of the literary magazine; the administrator had asked which teachers had forwarded student entries, and how many. She had decided to approach the problem by addressing her friend, Ms. Jackson, in a formal way. Her response to item 1 explains a bit about her sense of purpose and her relation to her reader: "It's not entirely personal, . . . I had a complaint I was trying to voice in a rather polite way. She was my superior." Her terse closing sentence explains further: "I wanted her to . . . prevent this from happening again," but she wanted to do it "subtly." She definitely implied—but did not wish to state—a request for action; and she had gotten action. In this context, she hung onto her preference for the very elaborate middle paragraph (paragraph 4). Nevertheless, she wanted to make it clear (paragraph 3, "I feel") that this was a matter of opinion. This veteran writer recognized how elaborate her explanation was and how indirect her language was, and she would not have changed a thing. She also explained at some length her sense of the situation in which the request had been made and of how the principal's request was inappropriate for that situation.

Use Your Knowledge of Context in Creating Writing Assignments

Having come to an understanding of the context for the letter to the assistant principal, we devised the following writing problem for students in an advanced composition course for prospective teachers.

> You are in charge of *Say It Now*, the anthology of student writing that is published by your district each year. Some time ago you sent a memo to all the teachers, asking them to send you samples of their students' work.
>
> Yesterday a group of volunteer teachers met with you in the district office to go over this material. To your surprise, Mr. Robert Jones, the high school curriculum coordinator, came in and asked you and the others to prepare a list of all the teachers who sent in papers and the number submitted to each.
>
> You strongly object to his request for three reasons:
>
> 1. The meeting was not called for that purpose.
> 2. Teachers should not be asked to evaluate or report on other teachers.
> 3. The statistics would be meaningless. Some people submitted everything they had, while others submitted only the best.

You decide to write to the superintendent to voice your feelings. Draft your letter.

Ask Students to Consider the Choices Writers Have Made

Having presented students with the writing problem, we could proceed in any of several ways. For one thing, we could show students the altered version of the letter and ask them to make their own choices. In subsequent discussions, we could ask students to compare their choices and reasons with choices and reasons given by the writer. Having sent students back to their own tacit knowledge of writing, this discussion might elicit at least a review of various dimensions—audience, persona, subject—of a complex writing situation.

We could also begin by setting the writing problem before our group as an impromptu assignment. This too would send our students back to their tacit knowledge of such a situation and their ideas about the approximate approach and tone for handling it. Follow-up discussion might elicit a demonstration that various approaches work rather well, and that there is probably no ideal text (or hidden agenda) up some teacher's sleeve.

Frequently, we combine these strategies by setting the problem, asking students to produce a piece of writing. Then we talk about their approaches and their decisions, and eventually introduce the original letter and review the writer's decisions. The spirited discussions that follow (as a rule, for example, few people are willing to adopt the approach used by the writer of the preceding memo) let the group observe and discuss what happens when one writes. This is the point from which our class begins and to which it must return every day.

Insist That Students Accept the Constraints Implied in the Context for Their Writing

A writing problem such as the one we have just described provides a good bit of rhetorical context. It also imposes constraints that make student writers uncomfortable and that make the writing task very difficult. Consider the following sample assignments, the Inventory Directions Memo and the Toiler Memo.

The Inventory Directions Memo

Instructions to Students:

You are a supervisor of workers; and you are responsible for the company's annual physical inventory. (You have, of course, many other year-round responsibilities.)

You are to write a memo to the persons who will be doing the inventory. There are 150 of them: about 30 will be doing this for the first time; about 60 have done it for five years (ever since you've been using the present system); the rest have done it anywhere from one to four times.

Every worker will receive a copy of this memo. Also, it will be posted on every one of the numerous bulletin boards in the buildings where these people work.

These are production workers of many sorts. Once a year, for several days, they become inventory workers, whatever their job the rest of the year. (During the inventory, you are the immediate and crucial supervisor of these people—but for the rest of the year very few of them are directly under your supervision.)

Along with this memo, every worker receives a thorough set of directions for taking inventory—six long and packed pages. These directions have been issued every year you've been using the present system for inventory. (The system is a good one, and there is not a weighty reason to change.)

Even with full directions, there is one part of the process that does not go perfectly. And so even though this part is thoroughly explained in the full directions, you want to use this memo to try to make the errant part go perfectly this year. (It went perfectly one year—the first year of the present system.)

You are also using this memo to announce the days of the inventory: April 6 through 9, 198__.

The problem: At the outset of the inventory work an enormous number of inventory tickets get issued—many to each worker. These tickets are used in recording the quantity and classification of objects. Every one of these tickets should be turned in by the end of the inventory process. Otherwise the computerized summarizing of the human counting gets messed up. (The computer knows about every ticket issued for openers; and the computer, being even less tolerant than humans about human errors, expects to get back every last ticket.) Every year, except the very first, tickets disappear. Workers are careless and lose tickets. Or they deliberately discard tickets when they've made mistakes on them, filled them out wrong. (What they should do with a flawed ticket is mark it as a flawed ticket and turn it in along with all the other tickets.)

Modest though it may seem, this assignment challenges students in a number of important ways. For one thing, students do not have the clear and fixed sort of authority that they might have in other situations. They do not know the persons involved very well, nor can they get to know them better. Students also know that they are facing quite a range of reading skills in their audience, as well as a variety of attitudes toward the writer and toward this special annual task of inventory.

These challenges often tempt students to add to the scenario. They sometimes want to create new authority for themselves—new powers to coerce and even punish, which are not really allowed by the scenario. Even more frequently, they want to add positive factors. They want to promise picnics, parties, bonuses, prizes, and days off as incentives to insure that the inventory goes right this time. This impulse to embellish seems natural enough. For one thing, it is a kind of retreat from the difficulties inherent in the task, the writing that might do the job in relation to the scenario as it is. But no matter how much we might sympathize with this impulse, the limits and frustrations of the scenario are not purely fictional. The real situation within which the actual piece of work-world writing was originally done was very close to the one we wrote into this scenario. Consequently, we forbid students to add to the scenario. We want to press them to deal with the complications through their writing, their designing of the memo, not by eliminating the complications. We want them to realize that this assignment reflects some very real issues of the work world. And we like the way they have gotten inside the lesson. We do not have to lecture to them about what we know about problems that can make writing on the job difficult. They seem to live inside that lesson as they produce their memos.

The Toiler Memo

Instructions to Students:

This is a memo you are writing to Mr. Thomas Toiler, who heads the homeowners policies division of the large insurance company for which you both work. You are a sort of coordinator in this situation. Mr. Toiler has written you, asking that you arrange for his division to be given a much larger share of the company's computer capacities. Up to now, his division has had to issue policies through methods that are somewhat slow and cumbersome, and that involve quite a bit of manual labor in typing and keeping records and filing. (Some of the company's divisions have very appreciable shares of the computer capacities: thus they enjoy speed and efficiency not possible without computer resources.)

In this memo, you have to tell Mr. Toiler that he cannot get what he wants. For one thing, there is a waiting list of other divisions that want more of the computer capacities, just as he does. For another thing, higher administrative offices of the company are planning to review and upgrade the computer system—and so the company is not willing to spend time and money now to integrate more of its divisions into the present system. All of the divisions, Mr. Toiler's included, would share the advantages of an upgraded computer system. But that ideal situation could be more than a year away.

Another aspect of the situation: through no fault of your own, Mr. Toiler has had to wait quite a long time for this reply to his request. Other offices, both above and below you in organizational structure, have been slow to respond to your request for information and advice concerning Mr. Toiler's desires. One of these dilatory offices is headed by a Mr. Oscar Procrast. Mr. Procrast heads the "Planning Division," and he is one of the persons who will be getting a copy of this memo. (Only two other persons get copies: Mr. John Friendly, your immediate superior, and Mrs. Myra Digit, who runs the computer system.)

Mr. Toiler has been with the company fifteen years. He is very good at his work. He is a valuable and valued employee, and you think highly of him. You are not a personal friend—but you do have a lot of respect for him and for his accomplishments.

As with the Inventory Directions Memo, this is very close to the actual situation one of our participants faced in writing for his job. For the inventory memo, one needs to find a way to be clear and concise, and transmit successfully, to a rather messy mixture of readers, a relatively simple and limited message. To do well with the Toiler Memo, one has to deal with a smaller audience. More is known about each person involved—for example, students have some sense of their rank as the writer of the memo and where they stand in relation to the others who will be reading the memo. The scenario requires that the writer send Mr. Toiler bad news. The writer needs to include a relevant selection from the information offered. The writer should also strike a tone of respect, if not also of some sympathy, without sounding condescending or effusive. Because of the distribution of the memo, the writer cannot pass the buck for the decision or the delay in replying to Mr. Toiler's request. There is some temptation here to make oneself, as writer, look good by making others look bad. But given the total scenario, the writer needs to resist that temptation.

This assignment poses a situation for which even a good piece of writing might fall short of the results desired. But there is considerable clarity: one can see the difficulties, if not the solutions. We feel that in the academic world, the difficulties of a given writing assignment too often lie hidden. They are neither directly nor indirectly taught to the students before they begin to write the paper. And too often, the students discover too late what their struggle really was—as they sit with the graded and annotated paper, perhaps. Much of what has gone into those annotations should probably have been delivered, somehow, at the start. So we reiterate a basic point here: *one must design assignments that directly and indirectly teach the writer about the difficulties and dangers within a given writing task.* We find ourselves trying to reverse what we think of as the more usual, traditional academic pattern, wherein we often tend to demand a result without teaching much about what stands between the start of the paper and success in the writing task.

Students have found the Toiler Memo fairly difficult. They sense the complications that stem from the distribution of the memo, and they understand that one should address Mr. Toiler's feelings, somehow, without going too far with emotions. They know that in writing to the affective need here, there is some danger that the writer will cloud or distort the basic message: Mr. Toiler cannot have what he wants.

As with the Inventory Directions Memo, students often want to add to the scenario. They want to call Mr. Toiler on the phone or see him face to face. They look for ways to get him computer capacities from somewhere. One student once offered to surrender some of his own computer resources. We forbid them such embellishments, of course. We want them to have to use writing to do the job—exactly as the real writer in the work world had to do.

The Toiler Memo has proved itself a valuable assignment. Younger student writers do not always produce good memos—but they do see into the problems they must try to solve through their writing. Older writers, especially those with work-world experience, tend to do better in understanding the challenge and problems, and in producing effective memos. From these same older and experienced writers, this assignment has received some interesting praise and approval. They find it very real.

Create Data Sheets to Introduce
Students to Unfamiliar Topics

In our regular composition courses, we rarely ask our students to generate text from facts with which they are not very familiar. When we ask them to perform writing tasks using new material, it is usually part of a research experience. "Research subject A," we tell them. "Then take those new facts and organize and present them in a coherent manner." We expect they'll read secondary material with some care and come to a fairly thorough understanding of those new facts. But our writing research shows that work-world writing often involves handling unfamiliar material in very limited time frames and for very specific purposes. Advertising copy-writers, for instance, very often find themselves with this situation. Technical writers do too. One way we can approach this matter in the classroom is through the *data sheet* assignment.

To set the task, we use material from a work-world situation somewhat like those described earlier. In those cases, we had abstracted a scenario from the writing sample and interview; we then provided this context to students and asked them to write. In this case, we provide a data set from the writing sample, preceded by a brief scenario.

Instructions to Students:

The Miron Problem

You are a copy-writer for the Public Relations section of General Chemical Company. Your boss, the Director, presented you with the following data and told you to write a draft of a press release—for local and, ultimately, for national distribution. Members of the local community are very upset about prior instances of chemical contamination of the environment. Consequently, your press release will have to be informative and will also have to allay people's fears without seeming self-serving. Your boss and various corporate officers will write the final press release itself.

Miron Data Sheet

Miron: A pesticide used in southern states to control fire ants.

1967: Company stopped manufacturing Miron.

1975: Company stopped processing (packaging and shipping) at Riverside plant.

1976: Department of Environmental Conservation and Environmental Protection Agency took samples from waste streams coming from the Company's plant on East River; on each day samples were taken, DEC and EPA found up to $1\frac{1}{2}$ pounds of Miron in these streams.

Company is still storing 147 tons of Miron

- in sealed drums
- in secured warehouse

Now: New study done on samples from same streams; the Company began this study after Miron had been reported in fish taken downstream, from nearby Grand Lake. Study conducted by three laboratories:

- Environmental Protection Agency Laboratory
- Company's own laboratory
- Laboratory run by Dr. John L. Laser
  - Laser is
    - Chairman of Department of Biological Sciences at State University.
    - Leading authority in field of water analysis.

Procedures of Present Study

- These techniques
  - are very precise.
  - can detect very low levels of chemical compounds.
  - identify molecular structures by their "fingerprints."
  - have been used in an extensive study of fish in Grand Lake; the Company began this study after Miron had been reported in fish taken from Grand Lake.

Results of Present Study

Results of Present Study

- The three labs haven't found any Miron in waste streams leading from the plant to Easter River or in city sewage system.
- Reports from the three labs were presented at a technical meeting held in State Capital last March. Present at the meeting were representatives from Company, EPA, and State Department of Environmental Conservation.
- No government action is being taken against the Company at this time.

You'll want to present the facts as accurately as you can, of course. But you'll want to present the company in as positive a light as possible. Remember, your *boss* will be your first reader. One typed page will suffice.

As we send students off with this task, we ask that in addition to writing the draft they record the five questions or problems they thought were most important in completing the assignment. When students return to class, they typically report having had as many problems with audience as with subject matter. Most writers worry about their "boss"; some worry about other corporate officers. Knowing what a volatile issue pollution is for the chemical industry, they want to be true to the facts yet make the company (and themselves) look good. Most writers see public hostility as a major concern for themselves as writers—even knowing that their copy would be edited by higher-ups.

The subject matter presents students with some major difficulties. Many are likely to feel that they do not have enough data. They feel the need to know more about Miron toxicity, for example. Other students may think they have too much information. They are not sure how much of the data is essential to presenting the company in a favorable light. The fact that there are no ideal answers to these questions is likely to make them feel a bit more secure in handling difficult new material.

A follow-up task can focus on a continuation of the scenario. Students can become the public relations directors. Now they must examine each other's drafts with an eye toward editing for public consumption. Obviously, as roles change, so do the demands of the task. In our follow-up, students learn to tailor the data—unfamiliar though it is—to the needs of multiple audiences. They learn to summarize and organize difficult information. And they learn to project themselves as writers, even when the material they are asked to present comes from somebody else.

Design Sequences of Increasingly Demanding Assignments

Two of the assignments in the preceding section of this chapter are always given in the same sequence as they are presented here, first the Inventory Memo and then the Toiler Memo. We follow this sequence because the Toiler Memo is the more difficult of the two tasks. In the Toiler Memo, the process of defining one's persona and audience entails complexities that are not present in the Inventory Memo assignment. The task of deciding what information to include (and exclude) is also trickier. Both these assignments are given relatively early in the semester. The next assignment is given at the end of the semester.

The Hotstuff/Scorcher Letter

Instructions to Students:

Your company is G. Hotstuff, Inc., 444 Vista Ave., Buffalo, New York 14000. It manufactures and sells heating elements for industrial furnaces of many sorts.

You are a "Product Manager." You are responsible for many of the issues and problems that occur after elements have been bought and while they are being used in the manufacturing furnaces of your customers.

You must write a letter to B. Scorcher, Inc., of 123 Wasteland Ave., Cleveland, Ohio 15222.

For two years now, Scorcher has been buying and using your model EX-111 element. And for most of those two years, your company has been refunding quite a bit of money and replacing without charge quite a few elements, because the elements are not functioning well or lasting long enough in Scorcher's furnaces.

You have just been put in charge of this account. This is a big account, and it would be a very profitable one, were it straightened out. (As of now, however, you are losing money on the account because of all the refunding and replacing you've been doing.) You want to keep Scorcher as a customer. And turn Scorcher into a profit-maker for your company.

Your research in your own plant and your quality control make you confident that you are not selling Scorcher a flawed product. And so you feel that the problems are Scorcher's fault.

The EX-111 serves very well and lasts much longer at the many other factories where it is being used. Scorcher is your only EX-111 customer where the element is doing so poorly.

For a year now, you have been trying to get from Scorcher a comprehensive packet of data involving operating temperatures, variations of operating temperatures, installation procedures for the EX-111, maintenance schedules and procedures for the furnaces, and the electrical loads being fed to the elements.

Scorcher has not flatly ignored your call for data. But they cannot seem to get their act together. They have never sent the data on the regular schedule you want (once a month); and the data have never been as complete and comprehensive as you wish. You do not feel that you are facing dishonesty here. Rather, you are dealing with organizational and managerial weakness at Scorcher.

As of the date of this letter, Hotstuff, Inc., will make no more refunds or free replacements to Scorcher, until Scorcher furnishes the sort of data that you need, and until those data are studied and the problems with the EX-111 elements pinpointed with technical accuracy.

Two weeks ago, Mr. Andrew Undershaft, of Scorcher, Inc., came to Hotstuff to discuss the EX-111 problems with you. Mr. Undershaft delivered by word of mouth a scenario of the two years of bad performance of the EX-111. You did get to show him the EX-111 being made at your plant, but you did not argue your side of the situation.

Copies of this letter go to your superior, John G. Fromage, and to the office of production engineering, headed by Harold Bildung.

This has worked very well as the final business writing task of the course. This memo is considerably more difficult than are the Inventory Directions Memo and the Toiler Memo, and the stakes are higher. The challenge to turn a bad account into a highly profitable one is the most difficult and complex of the writing problems we assign; and, coming at the end of the semester, it becomes a sort of exam on much of what has gone on throughout the semester.

For the work-world writer who was the actual source of this scenario, this letter was the piece of his portfolio that interested him most and also troubled him most. He had worked very hard on the letter, yet it had not produced the desired action and understanding with the errant customer firm. He had then circulated the letter among some of his peers, all of whom thought his work adequate for the situation. And yet it had failed.

Among the important elements for this writing task are: delivering information; establishing context and reviewing some case history; announcing bad news for the recipient; and managing to be firm without insulting or alienating the Scorcher people. The basic business task is to turn the account into the highly profitable sort it has been and could be again. How to handle the audience, what kind of persona to create, how to accomplish the basic task—these are all rather complex and heavy challenges. They make this letter a good late or final assignment.

The facts and the difficulties are all pretty much available for the student: the demands become clear with a careful study of the scenario. In a sense, the more one notices and understands, the more intimidating the writing task becomes. Students are not as eager to embellish this scenario as they are the earlier ones. For one thing, they have learned that we will not allow it. When they do it early in the semester, it is merely something to be warned against; if they do it late in the semester, it is a clear and dangerous mistake, and must affect the grade they get for the assignment. Further, we think that the numerous and complex challenges of this scenario tend to draw the students into the situation, whereas an earlier and relatively simple scenario like the Inventory Directions Memo tends to push them outward, looking for a scenario they would like better. In effect, they seem to have learned to live with the given reality—not a bad lesson for persons who hope to write well in the business world.

As with the Toiler Memo, the Hotstuff/Scorcher Letter is often seen as a very real and relevant assignment, especially by student writers with some experience in the work world. Most of them seem to have encountered their own version, larger or smaller, of a task like this.

Don't Restrict What You Know to Composition Courses

Although our primary concern was creating assignments for advanced composition courses, we realized that much of what we learned about writing in business and industry might be useful in almost any course. For example, much of the job-related writing we have examined involves collaborative writing, a single writing task performed by several writers. In two county government offices, a group of employees prepared a department manual, and a team of ghost writers for the county executive prepared campaign literature, graduation speeches, and press releases. As a social service agency, a group of writers drafted a Fair Housing Ordinance for the City of Buffalo, an ordinance that was subsequently submitted to the Common Council for amendment, redrafting, and voting. At the offices of the Buffalo Philharmonic Orchestra, several writers prepared the public relations materials for the annual fund drive. The evaluation of all these collaborative writing tasks came first from the team writers who passed oral and written judgments on the drafts and final copies of their own writing. We have adapted such professional collaborative writing for use in our new writing courses and discovered that it can be a valuable teaching aid in freshman composition courses and upper-level literature courses as well.

Although we know collaborative writing assignments are being made in more and more classrooms, we want to describe a somewhat novel form of collaborative writing, one that is applicable in a wide range of courses. This form of collaboration, which we refer to as the group quiz, multiplies the occasions for freshmen and upperclassmen to write, without increasing the burden of reading and grading for the instructor. As a rule, teachers use quizzes to police—to find out who is preparing for class regularly. The audience for such writing is limited to the teacher as evaluator. The only other function of the quiz—beyond the instructor's accumulation of evidence—is to assure the student that he or she has survived another hurdle in the course or, if the student stumbles on the quiz, to serve as a warning to prepare better. Quizzes are summative, transactional writing tasks of limited value because their purpose usually ends with the grade. The group quiz, however, includes but goes beyond such a transactional function by expanding the quiz into an occasion for learning through collaborative writing. Students work in groups of four or five; they prepare a single written statement per group; and each student in the group receives the group grade.

Group quizzes benefit the student in several ways. They multiply the audience for the task by including the class members as well as the teacher. The social dimension of group quizzes encourages more responsible preparation and fosters more pride in one's work since they require real and often difficult cooperation with one's peers in creating a document that will bear the group's signatures and will be read by the other groups in the class. Most important, the process of preparing the group response allows students to discuss, write about, and thereby learn the material. Teachers benefit as well. A group quiz can become the basis for a rich class discussion. And since twenty-five students produce only five documents, the group quiz decreases the burden of grading and allows the teacher to use the device more frequently. Although it functions in part as a conventional quiz, the group quiz also transforms such transactional writing into a more valuable, yet still manageable, in-class learning procedure.

We have used the following samples of group quizzes suc-cessfully in the classroom. Each is an exercise in interpretation, description, and analysis—three of the fundamental reading and writing processes that composition courses attempt to develop and that literature courses demand in more subtle and complex ways. Although we have used the group quiz only in literature classes, it would seem possible to modify this activity so that it entails intellectual processes that are appropriate for other disciplines and for nonliterary types of subject matter. Sample 1, which follows, and other group quizzes like it dissolve the barriers that often hinder students from working well as a group of learners. Rotating group members, discussion leaders, and scribes familiarizes class members with each other and allows each to play a number of roles that demand varying degrees of responsibility. Reading the group responses aloud focuses the discussion that follows, makes it more comprehensive, and thereby assures the efficient use of class time.

Sample 1: A Victorian Literature Group Quiz

Eng 311: Victorian Literature
Dickens, *Bleak House*—Strive, seek, find, yield!

Group Members' Names:

1	2	3	4

Often in *BH* the omniscient narrator reminds us of the tangled web of relationships that make up the novel's world: Sir Leicester is a "glorious spider" who "stretches his threads of relationship," and others think "how strangely Fate has entangled this rough outcast [Jo the crossing sweep] in the web of very different lives."

Create an illustration, or a diagram, in which you group the novel's characters in their various immediate associations and then weave the web of interrelationships among the various groups by drawing lines between the appropriate individual characters. Happy spinning!

Creating the "tangled web of relationships" on paper recalls the novel for the writer; but, more important, it is a way for the writer to learn the novel. Even if some of the students have not completed reading the book and even if no one student remembers all the characters, creating the diagram gives the class valuable practice in prewriting, which they later can use in more polished and elaborate papers about the novel.

Samples 2 and 3 afford students two more types of discovery, one more directed than the other. The group quiz on Robert Browing accomplishes three goals: (1) it moves students from an understanding of a part of a poem to the whole; (2) it helps to unravel a series of difficult works; and (3) it enables students eventually to comment on "Browning's poetry" without relying on vague overviews. The Thomas Hardy group quiz moves the students from the personal choice of a "memorable scene or incident" to speculation about the power of the scene or the bias of the reader, to conclusions about the novel as a whole. Again, these group quizzes emphasize the learning process—the way mere information changes shape to become our evolved understanding.

Sample 2: A Variation—Group Quiz on the Poetry of Robert Browning:

In small groups, discuss the following passages from Browning. Choose a Scribe and a Reader for your group—one person for each job; former discussion leaders are ineligible. The group should prepare for the class a report which answers the following questions:

1. How would you paraphrase your group's passage?
2. How is the passage related to what the poem does as a whole work?
3. What questions would you have to take into consideration if you were trying to convince a non-English major to read the poem?

The group answers to these questions should be written out in a statement which will be read to the entire class.

Group #1:

... This grew; I gave commands;
Then all smiles stopped together. There she stands
As if alive.

Group #2:

And as yon tapers dwindle, and strange thoughts
Grow, with a certain humming in my ears,
About the life before I lived this life,
And this life too, popes, cardinals and priests,
Saint Praxed at his sermon on the mount,
Your tall pale mother with her talking eyes ...

Group #3:

Give us no more of body than shows soul!

Group #4:

Ah, but a man's reach should exceed his grasp,
Or what's a heaven for?

Group #5:

A. Ah, Just when I seemed to learn!
   Where is the thread now? Off again!
B. "Love Among the Ruins" (the title)

You will turn in your group statements at the end of class. I will make copies of them all for us to share and discuss.

Sample #3: A Second Variation—Group Quiz on Thomas Hardy's Jude the Obscure:

1. For the first part of this exercise, work by yourself. You may use your text. Choose a specific incident or a specific scene from *Jude* which has impressed you or which you consider memorable (for whatever reason). On the back of this paper, tell the location of the scene or incident (give the book, chapter, and, if you're using the Riverside edition, the page). Then briefly summarize the scene/incident and tell why you selected it.

2. For this part of the exercise, work in five small groups of four persons each. Choose a Scribe to list the four individual scenes/incidents which the members of your group selected. Then discuss the reasons for those individual choices. Given the choices and the reasons, prepare a conclusion which your group can offer to the class about Hardy's novel.

3. At the end of your work, you should have: (a) the individual statement of choice and the explanation for that choice; (b) a group statement which lists the four individual scenes/incidents chosen by the group members and the conclusion which your group has drawn about the novel. Be sure to include the names of all group members on (b). All these documents will be handed in at the end of class.

We believe that group quizzes can extend a writing task beyond the usual bare transactional function of the classroom quiz. Their speculative nature makes them valuable beginnings for understanding and for preparing subsequent papers. Beyond these benefits they allow the instructor in literature to give students valuable experience in the kinds of collaborative writing so frequently required of professionals in the work-world. Collaborative writing in the classroom mirrors the social reality of work-world writing— engaging oneself in working with one's colleagues, creating a text, and sharing the successes and failures of the task.

CONCLUSION: A CHANGED PERSPECTIVE

Our research in the work world has changed our approaches to teaching, research, and writing in important ways. Moving off campus was the most basic factor in this change. We discovered there a very purposeful orientation among writers in business and government; these writers were using writing to get a job done, and they were very good at it. Yet their concerns were somewhat different from ours, and we began to reorient ourselves accordingly.

This reorientation made us look at writing in new ways; it made us especially aware of the complexity of writing situations. These off-campus writers knew who they were writing for, and it was never "the general reader." Audience response was their overriding concern. They got feedback from their readers, and they reacted to it. They practiced; they wrote daily. And they expected to be rewarded for writing well. In their world, writing is heady business, not just "grammar"; it involves serious decision making with serious consequences.

Returning to our campus, we began to see how classroom writing could be enriched in these very respects: we could set up real and multiple audiences; ask readers for feedback; require written reports and analyses at each step of a developing activity; and reward successful writing with a smile, recognition, and applause. This made us alter some preconceptions: writing became practice, rather than a test; prose models were replaced by samples; rules gave way to strategies. The classroom became a workroom, a busier and noisier place.

We may think of consequent changes in our own reading and teaching of literature as a happy accident, arising from our enhanced awareness of the writer's situation. Yet we all write with clearer purpose and greater pleasure, and with a new sense of the job that prose (even academic prose) ought to do.

Conducting
Research

VI

Survey Methodology   13

PAUL V. ANDERSON
Miami University, Ohio

Surveys have emerged as a prominent and useful tool for studying the writing people do outside academe. Much of the systematically gathered, empirical information that we possess about writing in the nonacademic workplace has been provided by the fifty surveys that have asked one or more questions on this subject. In chapter 1, I summarize the findings of these surveys and discuss their implications for teaching. In this chapter, I explain the methodology of the survey.

AIM OF THIS CHAPTER

The aim of this chapter is to provide readers who are untrained in social science research with an introduction to the conceptual foundations and technical aspects of survey design, administration, and analysis. This introduction can be useful to such readers in two ways.

First, it can help them be more critical in their reading of published accounts of surveys of writing in nonacademic settings. Many of these surveys present substantial challenges to the reader because they deviate from the model of the "ideal" survey in ways that are not readily apparent to someone who does not understand the methodology involved. These challenges are especially complicated because (in most cases) the deviations are not so serious as to render the surveys entirely useless. Therefore, the reader, instead of having the relatively simple chore of deciding whether or not to ignore a particular study, must perform the more complicated task of determining to what extent and in what ways the methodological deviations limit the conclusions—whether conceptual or practical—that can be drawn from the survey.

Second, the information in this chapter will aid people who have no training in social science research but still desire to undertake survey research of their own. Some of these people may be nonscientists who desire to conduct original empirical studies that increase our general understanding of writing. To such people, the survey can be an appealing methodolgy because it is particularly amenable to collaborative efforts in which social scientists provide technical assistance while still leaving the nonscientist with considerable opportunity to contribute significantly to the research project. Thus a social scientist might plan and conduct the data analysis; a humanist could take the lead in such crucial activities as defining the issues to be studied, designing the questions to be posed, and interpreting the results.

Others who may want to conduct survey projects include teachers of business technical, and other occupational writing courses. Because these courses aim to prepare students for the writing they will do in their careers, the teachers can gain important insights into what and even how they should teach by studying the writing people do in nonacademic settings. They can obtain this information in many ways. For example, they can read reports of surveys that have gathered information from people who now hold roughly the kinds of jobs their students will one day fill. But the best information the teachers could possibly obtain would be that gathered from graduates of their own schools. Each school's alumni typically find employment in particular types of jobs, with particular kinds of employers, in a particular region of the country. Thus, by surveying graduates of their own schools, teachers can gain very precise information about the writing that their students can be expected to do in their careers. Teachers untrained in social science research may find the thought of conducting such alumni surveys especially attractive because they can engage in these projects without having to create their own study designs. They can adapt or simply copy someone else's—substituting graduates of their own institutions.

Although this chapter falls far short of providing a complete instruction manual for conducting survey research, it can serve as a useful introductory guide for people interested in undertaking their own survey projects. To people interested in conducting an original study, this chapter offers an overview of the kinds of things that survey researches must think about. To people who choose to imitate someone else's study design, the chapter provides information that will help them select wisely the design they adapt or copy—and the chapter will alert them to the kinds of changes they can make to strengthen the original study design (if it needs strengthening) and warn them of the kinds of alterations that would weaken the design.

In order to meet the needs of both the reader who would like to conduct survey research and the reader who would like to read published surveys more critically, I have divided this chapter into three parts. In the first, I describe the major elements of a survey. My discussion mixes theoretical with practical considerations, emphasizing how the careful handling of each element of a survey contributes to the ability of researchers to answer their research questions, and also explaining how various commonly encountered deviations from sound methology diminish the confidence that can be placed in a survey's results. In the second part of this chapter, I summarize the chief limitations of survey research, and in the third I discuss ways of integrating the survey with other research methods within broad research programs where the strengths of the various methods complement one another.

ELEMENTS OF A SURVEY

A survey is an empirical investigation in which naturally occurring phenomena are studied by asking predetermined sets of questions. The earliest and plainest form of survey is the census (Rossi, Wright, & Anderson, 1983; Young, 1949). Used to tally the populations and wealth of the Egyptian kings even before the pyramids were built (about 3000 B.C.), such simple head counts continue in use today, for instance in the decennial census that is used to apportion the United States into districts containing roughly equal numbers of voters.

In recent history—most dramatically since 1930—survey research has changed greatly, largely as a result of three factors.

1. Techniques have been developed for generalizing about very large groups of people by obtaining responses from a very small proportion of these people. For example, preelection polls use

information obtained from only a few thousand individuals to predict, with great accuracy, the outcome of elections in which tens of millions participate.

2. Developments in computer hardware and software have permitted the use of analytical techniques not feasible earlier and have greatly increased the ease with which a survey may be conducted.

3. The ability to ask questions that produce valid, reliable responses has been refined immensely, partly through accumulated experience and partly through the development of analytic tools for assessing questions. As a result of these developments of the past several decades, the survey has become a very sophisticated research tool.

The survey may be thought of as having five basic elements:

Purpose
Research question
Respondents
Survey instrument
Data analysis

The next five sections of this chapter discuss the five elements of the survey and their relationships with one another. In these sections, I refer to many sources, three of which will be particularly useful to the readers who want to study surveys further (complete bibliographic citations are supplied in the references at the end of this chapter):

- D. A. Dillman, *Mail and Telephone Surveys: The Total Design Method* (1978). A how-to book concerning survey design and administration (but not data analysis). Bibliography.
- L. H. Kidder, editor, *Research Methods in Social Relations* (1981). A textbook made up of chapters by several authors who provide helpful introductions to most matters related to survey research.
- P. H. Rossi, J. D. Wright, and A. B. Anderson, editors, *Handbook of Survey Research* (1983). Essays that treat procedural matters at an advanced level, discuss theoretical considerations, and include substantial lists of references.

PURPOSE

At a general level, the purposes of most modern surveys are the same: *to make valid generalizations about large groups of people by systematically gathering information from a small portion of the individuals in those groups.* Most of the technical features of survey design may be thought of as techniques used in the service of making valid generalizations. Deviations from established survey practice are criticized chiefly because they hinder researchers from achieving that general goal.

In addition to the general purpose of making valid generalizations, any individual survey is informed by the researchers' special purposes in undertaking that particular study. It is crucial for both researchers and readers of survey results to consider carefully these special purposes because many aspects of a survey can be shaped, either deliberately or inadvertently, by the use to which the researcher intends to put the results.

Multiple Purposes

With respect to purpose, a survey project is not necessarily unified in the way that many other types of research are. A single survey may serve several distinct purposes simultaneously. In fact, to lower the costs of administering surveys, researchers often combine into one survey the questions from two or more unrelated studies that are both designed to gather information from the same group of people (e.g., middle-income consumers in rural areas in midwestern states). Although researchers who study *writing* have not combined independent studies in this way, many of their surveys include a variety of questions, some serving one purpose, others serving quite different purposes. Further, the responses to most survey questions can be put to several uses, even if the researcher had one use primarily in mind when framing the question.

Typical Purposes

Keeping in mind the risk of oversimplification in attributing only one purpose to a particular survey or survey question, it is nonetheless useful to consider typical purposes that underlie survey research about writing in nonacademic settings. These fall into four categories.

The major purpose of most of the surveys is to provide a basis for improving the teaching of writing—a fact that should not surprise us because most of this research has been conducted by educators, especially teachers of business, technical, and other functional writing courses. As mentioned earlier, the aim of such courses is to prepare students for the writing they will do in their careers; consequently, these teachers are very interested in learning about the writing performed by persons now employed in those jobs. To whom do these employees write? What forms (reports, proposals, etc.) do they use? What strategies of composing do they rely on? By obtaining the answers to such questions, teachers hope to establish a sound basis for determining what to include in their courses.

A second purpose of survey research about writing on the job is to help writers in the workplace (not those in the classroom) improve their writing. For example, Paradis, Dobrin, and Bower (personal correspondence, 1984) conducted a survey in which they asked individuals in several organizations about their writing habits. Once the data were tabulated, these institutions received reports that compared the responses from their employees against the responses obtained from all participants in the study. The force of such a presentation is to suggest to organizations and individuals who are dissatisfied with their writing that they might look for the causes of the problem in areas where their responses differ from those of the entire pool of respondents.

A third purpose for conducting survey research about writing in the workplace is to add to the body of knowledge about an intrinsically interesting area of human activity. Although writing lacks some of the fascination of the activities investigated in their surveys by Kinsey and his associates (1948), writing at work is sometimes studied simply to extend our understanding of people and our interactions in the social (i.e., work) structures we create for ourselves.

Finally, some survey research is conducted for essentially persuasive—even political—purposes. Connors (1982) has pointed out that at varous times throughout this century, technical writing courses and faculty have been held in low esteem even in the technical and engineering departments whose students the courses serve. Partly in response to this attitude and partly in response to the difficulties of inspiring some engineering students to take their technical writing courses seriously enough, Davis (1977) surveyed people listed in *Engineers of Distinction* about the importance of writing. The results of the survey were never in doubt for Davis, who assumed from the beginning that "The importance of effective written technical communications to the technical man (or woman) is obvious to just about anyone who has ever been in industry, business, or government" (p. 83). The problem, as Davis saw it, is that this importance is not so obvious to "many people in academia." Davis's survey bore out his assumption about the importance of writing, so it is often quoted to students, and it is cited in the opening chapters of some recent technical writing textbooks (e.g., Olsen & Huckin, 1983). Davis suggested that his results should also be shown to advisors who help students choose courses; in addition, teachers might present the results to college administrators and colleagues in other fields in an effort to win a larger place for technical writing courses in curricula and to win recognition of the importance of technical writing courses and their instructors.

Naturally, a desire to persuade others of the importance of writing in the workplace will lead to somewhat different survey strategies than will a more disinterested curiosity about this realm of human behavior. Moreover, any purpose, even the most disinterested, will shape the strategies that a survey researcher employs. Thus, leaving aside the question of whether survey research can ever be *entirely* disinterested, it is still important both for those who conduct surveys and for those who read about them to ask, "Why is this particular study being undertaken?"

RESEARCH QUESTIONS

In pursuit of their purposes, survey researchers—like any other kind of researchers—seek to answer questions, which we might call *research questions* to distinguish them from the specific inquiries (or *probes*) that are posed to the respondents in a particular survey project. In survey research, the research questions fall into two broad categories, descriptive and explanatory.

Descriptive Research Questions

When they ask *descriptive* research questions, researchers desire to compile facts, very much in the manner of a census taker, about the incidence and distribution of the phenomena under study. To answer questions about *incidence*, the researcher merely tabulates the number or percentage of respondents who reported a certain phenomenon (e.g., x percent of the respondents reported that they spend at least 20 percent of their time at work writing). To answer questions about *distribution*, the researcher reports how the incidence of a phenomenon is distributed among various subgroups of respondents (e.g., y percent of the respondents under twenty-five years old and z percent of the respondents twenty-five and older reported that they believe writing is "very important" on the job).

Explanatory Research Questions

When they ask *explanatory* research questions, researchers are concerned with the ways that various phenomena relate to one another. The following list illustrates some of the categories of explanatory research questions that can be investigated through surveys concerning writing in the workplace.

- *Comparison within groups.* "Do graduates of four-year colleges write more often on their own initiative or at someone else's request?"
- *Comparison between groups.* "Do graduates of college programs in home economics find writing to be less important than do graduates of programs in chemistry?"
- *Covariance among phenomena.* "Is an increase in the number of years of job experience accompanied by an increase in the percentage of time at work spent writing?"
- *Cause and effect.* "Will the growing use of word processors create a fundamental change in the ways people compose at work?" (The use of survey research to study cause and effect is relatively unknown to people who are not social scientists. For a discussion of the well-established use of panel studies—a type of longitudinal survey—to investigate cause and effect, see Rigsby, 1981. For a discussion of newer statistical tech-

niques for studying cause and effect, see Stolzenberg & Land, 1983.)

Most surveys about writing seek to answer several types of research questions, and many factors affect the amount of confidence that the researchers (or someone reading research results) can place in the answers that a particular survey provides to its research questions. The most important of these factors are described in the next three sections, which discuss the following elements of a survey: survey respondents, survey instrument, and data analysis.

RESPONDENTS

Surveys are used to answer research questions about some group (called a *population*) by gathering information from selected members of that group. Taken together, these members may constitute the *entire* population or they may be a subgroup of it, in which case they are called a *sample* of the population. All the survey research discussed in this chapter involves the use of samples.

Usually, the populations studied consist of people. However, it is also possible to survey other kinds of entities, such as texts. For instance, Gopnik (1972) used survey techniques to study the occurrence of certain linguistic structures in technical and scientific documents. Similarly, Odell et al. (1983) studied three types of documents prepared in a Department of Social Services in order to learn about the ways in which certain syntactic features of the writing produced in that setting vary according to rhetorical context. In this chapter, however, I deal exclusively with surveys of people.

Importance of Obtaining a
Representative Sample

In survey research it is extremely important that the sample be *representative* of the population under study. At bottom, survey research is usually inferential: the researchers create generalizations about the population based on information provided by a small sample of its members, who are called *respondents*. If their sample is not representative, the researchers have little chance of drawing valid conclusions about the population from the information that the respondents provide.

The rest of this section discusses the ways in which researchers strive to ensure that their respondents comprise a representative sample of the population they wish to study.

Defining the Population

The researchers' first step in obtaining a representative sample is to define carefully the population that the sample is intended to represent. That definition will tell the researchers where to look for people to be included in the sample. For example, if a team of researchers wants to make generalizations about the writing done at work by the population of people who earned a computer science degree from one particular two-year college, the researchers would know that their sample must consist of alumni of that school who earned that degree. In contrast, if the same researchers wanted to generalize about the population of people who earned computer science degrees from any two-year college in the United States, the researchers would know that their sample must include graduates of many schools in more than one region of the country.

Choosing a Sampling Method

Once researchers have defined the population they wish to study, they must carefully select the *particular members* of the population who will be asked to respond to the survey. The techniques for selecting these individuals are called *sampling methods*; they fall into two general categories (Chein, 1981; see also Frankel, 1983, and Sudman, 1983).

PROBABILITY SAMPLING. The most rigorous are the *probability sampling methods*, in which the following conditions are met:

1. Every member of the population under study has a chance of being included in the sample. In technical terms, this can be stated in the following way: every member of the population has a *probability greater than zero* of being included. (The

phrase *greater than zero* is important because in statistics a probability can be zero; a person with a zero probability of being included in a sample has absolutely no chance of being included in it.)

2. The probability of any member's being included in the sample *is known.*

One example of a probability sample is the *random sample*, in which every member of the population has the same probability of being included in the sample. Random samples are usually created from lists that include the name of every member of the population under study. Each person on the list is assigned a number, and then some method of choosing numbers randomly is used to select one number; these methods include using random-number tables and using computer programs for generating random numbers. The person with the number that is chosen is included in the sample. The process is repeated until enough people have been selected.

Another kind of probability sample is the *stratified random sample.* Researchers use it when they desire that the sample include a specific number or proportion of respondents from each of the subgroups of a population. (Each subgroup is called a *stratum.*) For example, a team of researchers might desire to obtain a sample that includes the same *proportion* of urban, suburban, and rural individuals as are found in the United States overall, even though the researchers will draw their sample from a state that has a much larger proportion of urban residents (and a much smaller proportion of rural residents) than does the nation as a whole. In this case, the researchers would:

1. Divide their population into the three subgroups (urban, suburban, rural).
2. Decide on the number of individuals they need from each subgroup to achieve the desired proportion in the overall sample.
3. Use random sampling techniques to select the specified number of respondents from the first subgroup, then from the second subgroup, and so on.

A particular rural resident of this state would have a greater probability of being chosen for the overall sample than would a particular urban resident; for both residents, however, the probability of being chosen would be known because random sampling is used within the subgroups.

Stratified random sampling is also used in a much different situation. As will be mentioned again later, many statistical procedures require some minimum number of respondents, particularly if subgroups of the population are to be compared with one another. Therefore, researchers often employ stratified random sampling when they want to compare subgroups but believe that simple random sampling will not provide them with enough respondents from the smaller subgroups. Such a situation might arise, for instance, in a study comparing the writing done at work by foreign-born workers with the writing done at work by people born in the United States.

A third kind of probability sample is the *cluster sample*, which involves sampling in stages. Cluster sampling is very useful where random sampling is impractical or impossible. Suppose that researchers wanted to study college graduates who had earned accredited engineering degrees in the United States in a given year. To sample that group randomly, the researchers would need a comprehensive list of all those graduates, something that would be very difficult and expensive to construct. Alternatively, the researchers could create a cluster sample. To do that, they would obtain a list of accredited schools from the accrediting agency, and then select colleges ("clusters") from that list, using either random or stratified random techniques. The researchers would complete this first stage of sampling by obtaining a list of the appropriate graduates from each of the selected schools. In the second stage, the researchers would choose from each of those lists the particular individuals from that school who would be asked to respond to the survey (again using random or stratified random sampling techniques). A similar procedure was used by the Ad Hoc Committee of the American Business Communication Association (1975) to evaluate the basic course in business communication.

A fourth kind of probability sample is the *systematic sample*, which can most easily be explained by way of an example. Suppose that a researcher wants to select a sample of 100 individuals from a population of 1,000 persons. An *intuitively* satisfying way to select that sample would be to obtain a list of the population and then take every tenth name from the list. That procedure would be *technically* sound also, provided that the researcher randomly selects the first name to be chosen. (The first name chosen is also the name that begins the cycle of selecting every tenth name.) As this example illustrates, only three things are needed to create a systematic sample: (1) a *list of the population*, (2) a *sampling interval*, and (3) a *random start*. In most cases, a systematic sample is as satisfactory as a random sample, and because of its simplicity the systematic sample is more often used in survey research than is the random sample. Systematic sampling can replace random sampling at the appropriate stages in creating a stratified sample or a cluster sample.

NONPROBABILITY SAMPLING. The second category of sampling methods is called *nonprobability sampling methods*. When researchers use these methods, they lose both the certainty that every member has *some* chance of being included in the sample and the ability to estimate the probability that any particular member of the population will be included. (If some member or members of the population have no chance of being included in the sample, then the population is improperly defined.) An example of a nonprobability sample is the *convenience sample*, in which the people included are selected because they are readily available to the researchers, for instance because they are all attending a meeting at which the researchers are present. Another example is the *quota sample*, in which (1) the researchers determine that they want the overall sample to include a certain number of individuals from each of the strata of a population, but (2) the researchers do not use a probability sampling technique to select the people from each stratum who will fill its quota.

EVALUATING SAMPLING METHODS: In survey research, nonprobability samples are much less desirable than probability samples because they do not provide as sound a basis for making inferences about the population under study. In fact, in surveys of samples whose members were selected through nonprobability methods, it is not even appropriate to employ many of the most useful statistical procedures for analyzing survey data because these procedures assume the existence of a larger population than the sample represents.

On the other hand, the selection of a truly representative sample can be difficult or even impossible, especially when special populations are under investigation. For example, through a survey discussed in chapter 1, I wanted to draw conclusions about the writing done at work by graduates of seven departments of my school, Miami University (Ohio). Ideally, I would have liked to create a probability sample of all graduates of those departments. Unfortunately, there exists no address list for all graduates, but only one of the graduates who have given their addresses to the university's alumni office. In this case, I had no choice but to use the less-than-ideal sample.

Such difficulties in creating a true probability sample are common in survey research, and the failure of a researcher to obtain a probability sample because of such problems is *not* taken to mean that his or her study is invalid or useless. On the other hand, whenever a nonprobability sample is used, researchers and readers must carefully consider the extent to which the limitations of the sample reduce the confidence they can place in the results of the survey. Readers should ask whether, under the circumstances, the researcher has done as good a job as possible of selecting a sample that accurately represents the population under study. Further, researchers and readers must consider the particular ways in which the specific limitations of the sample might affect the survey results. Sudman (1976; abridged in Sudman, 1983) describes a "credibility scale" for evaluating samples. His scale includes such factors as the adequacy of the geographic distribution of the sample, the avoidance of a convenience or an obviously biased sample, and the thoroughness of the researchers' own discussion of the sample's limitations.

Response Rate

In selecting a sample, researchers are choosing only the members of the population who will be asked to respond to the survey questions. In most surveys, some people selected for the sample decline to respond. When that happens, a second problem arises: although the sample of people asked to respond may faithfully represent the population under study, the group of people who actually respond may be unrepresentative. That would happen if the people who did not respond belonged to some significant subgroup of the population, a subgroup that will not be represented since its members refused to cooperate with the research. One might ask, for example, whether the people who refuse to respond to surveys about the writing they do at work feel differently about writing than do the people who are willing to respond to such surveys. If so, the results of these surveys are inaccurate to the extent that they do not include information from the special group of the population that won't respond.

Because they desire to ensure that the actual respondents represent the overall population just as well as the sample does, survey researchers are very concerned with a survey's *response rate* (the percentage of the people asked to respond who actually do so). Ways of increasing response rate have been studied extensively (Dillman, 1978). Some factors that have been shown to increase response rate in surveys administered through the mail are the following:

1. Designing the questionnaire in a way that makes it look easy to fill out.
2. Placing the most interesting and topic-related questions first, with potentially objectionable questions coming later and those requesting demographic information placed last.
3. Providing a prepaid envelope in which the respondents can return the completed questionnaire.
4. Including a cover letter that explains the social usefulness of the study and tells why each respondent is important to the study.
5. Printing the cover letter on letterhead stationery from the sponsoring organization.

Dillman (1978) has assimilated the results from the many studies of such matters into a plan, called the Total Design Method (TDM), that prescribes ways of handling all the details of questionnaire construction and administration. For example, one of the TDM prescriptions concerning questionnaire construction is the following: "No questions are printed on the first page (cover page); it is used for an interest-getting title, a neutral but eye-catching illustration, and any necessary instructions to the respondent" (Dillman, 1983, p. 362). An example of a TDM prescription concerning questionnaire administration is this: "The mailout packet, consisting of a cover letter, questionnaire, and business reply envelope (6⅜ x 3½ in.) is placed into a monarch-size envelope (7⅜ x 3¾ in.) on which the recipient's name and address have been individually typed (address labels are never used) and first-class postage is affixed" (p. 366). Dillman reports that by following the detailed prescriptions of the Total Design Method, researchers have obtained an average response rate of 77 percent, with the rates for some studies being greater than 90 percent; the response rates for most extant surveys of writing in the workplace are between 20 percent and 90 percent, with most below 50 percent. Even with a response rate as high as 90 percent, however, researchers must remain concerned about the characteristics of those individuals who have not responded.

Of course, it would be senseless to consider a high response rate as an end in itself. For instance, imagine that a team of researchers knew, through some professional association, a group of executives from a miscellaneous variety of business concerns. By asking each executive to distribute copies of a questionnaire to two dozen of his or her employees, the researchers might obtain a very high response rate. But it is difficult to imagine what population would be represented by the people whose answers were obtained in this manner. And, given the dubious nature of the sample's representativeness, it is difficult to imagine what kinds of generalizations could be drawn from the results.

Sample Size

When designing their surveys, researchers must concern themselves not only with strategies for ensuring that their samples are representative but with establishing a sample of suitable size. How large should a survey sample be? There is no absolute answer. Researchers need to balance two considerations:

1. *The demands of the statistical analyses that will be applied.* Different analyses require data sets of different sizes.
2. *Cost.* Each additional respondent represents an additional cost to the research project.

For the use of professional survey researchers and those who conduct large projects, Sudman (1976) provides a technical discussion of methods of weighing the cost of increasing the size of a sample against the value of the additional information that would be gained by doing so (see also Stopher & Meyburg, 1979).

For the beginning researchers, Sudman suggests that one practical way of deciding about sample size is to consider the sizes of the samples used by experienced social scientists. He observes that for national studies in a variety of subject matters (financial, medical, etc.) samples typically have 1,000 or more respondents. Regional studies typically have 100 to 700. Sudman points out, however, that an important factor is the number of subgroups that will be analyzed. Therefore, as a rule of thumb, he suggests that researchers use samples that are large enough so that there will be 100 or more respondents in each category of the major breakdowns and a minimum of 20 to 50 in each category of the minor breakdowns.

Summary

In sum, then, with respect to the respondents used in a survey, both researchers and readers need to be concerned with four things:

- The care with which the population to be studied is defined.
- The use of a sample that is large enough for the statistical *who will be asked* to respond to the survey accurately represents the population under study.
- The use of appropriate techniques to assure that the group of respondents *who actually respond* to the survey also represents the population accurately.
- The use of sample that is large enough for the statistical analyses that the researchers desire to use.

SURVEY INSTRUMENT

To gather information that will enable them to answer their research questions about the population under study, survey researchers ask the people in the sample a predetermined series of survey questions, which may be administered in writing or in person; in-person administration may occur through a face-to-face interview or over the telephone.

Survey questions can be divided into the four categories, according to the kind of phenomenon they concern (Dillman, 1978):

- *Attributes.* How people describe themselves with respect to their personal and demographic characteristics. *Example:* "What is the highest degree that you have earned?"
- *Behavior.* What people report that they do. *Example:* "How often do you write to people who are outside your organization?"
- *Beliefs.* What people think is true. *Example:* "In comparison with the writing of your colleagues, how good is your writing?"
- *Attitudes.* How people feel about something. *Example:* "Which of the following words best describes how you feel when you approach a writing task at work: apprehension, enthusiasm, boredom, joy, dread, other?" (Questions about attitudes are rarely asked in surveys about writing in the workplace; the example question is based on one asked by Aldrich, 1982.)

Operational Definitions

Regardless of the kind of phenomena they concern, survey questions are considered to be *instruments* because they are designed to *measure* something. To measure something is to follow a specified procedure (called an *operational definition*) for placing it on a scale (Kidder, 1981). Thus we measure a person's temperature by inserting a thermometer under the tongue for a certain length of time, and then reading how high the mercury in the thermometer has risen, as defined by the Fahrenheit scale. In much the same way, researchers use survey questions to obtain numerical representations of the attributes, behaviors, beliefs, and attitudes of groups of people. Even the open-ended questions used in some surveys may be thought of as instruments because they use a specified procedure to elicit an interpretable response.

One of the most basic tasks facing survey researchers is that of devising operational definitions of the phenomena they desire to study. It is particularly difficult to create operational definitions for measuring abstractions, such as beliefs and attitudes. To create such definitions, researchers follow a process that has two basic steps (for a more detailed overview of this process, see Johnson, 1977, and Wagenaar, 1981a). In the first step, researchers define as fully and precisely as possible the meaning of the abstraction they desire to study. What is meant, for instance, by "the importance of writing" or "the quality of writing" at work? Because such abstractions are complex and multifaceted, researchers define them by identifying the various dimensions of the abstractions. For example, the concept of "the importance of writing" might include such dimensions as the extent to which writing is essential to performing a person's job and the effects of writing ability on a person's prospects for advancement. In identifying dimensions, researchers seek to find all the pertinent aspects of the concept and to avoid including irrelevant ones. For example, "the amount of time spent writing" is not necessarily an aspect of "the importance of writing" because a person might write very little even though the writing he or she does do is crucial. When defining an abstraction, researchers often obtain helpful insights by reading reports by other investigators who have studied the same or similar phenomena.

The second step in creating an operational definition of an abstraction is to create the specific questions that will be asked to obtain measures along each dimension. Creating a question involves not only writing the question that will be posed to the respondent but also deciding on the form in which the person will be asked to respond. For example, will the person be asked to respond in an open-ended or closed-ended form? If the question is closed-ended, will the person be asked to check a number on a scale to indicate which of several phrases most accurately describes his or her attitude, belief, or behavior? Or will the person answer in one of the numerous other manners used in survey research?

The pool of specific questions that might be used in an operational definition of some particular abstraction is often quite varied. Consider, for example, some of the questions that might be asked concerning "the importance of writing," a topic that has been of considerable interest to researchers studying writing at work. One might ask the respondents to report their attitude concerning the importance of writing to their jobs (Barnum & Fischer, 1984). Or one might ask the subjects about their beliefs concerning the way in which writing ability has affected their own advancement (Davis, 1977); the advancement of other people in their organization (Storms, 1983); or the advancement of some class of workers in general, such as white-collar workers in their business field (Stine & Skarzenski, 1979). Or one might ask about behavior: "When you select or approve someone for advancement, . . . " (Davis, 1977).

One of the difficulties facing a researcher is deciding which questions provide the best indicators of the abstractions under study. After all, each question necessarily probes a distinct area of experience. Consider, for example, the experiences probed by the various questions that are listed in the preceding paragraph. A respondent might believe that writing ability has affected his or her advancement in a different way than it has affected the advancement of other people. And the respondent could also believe that in both cases the effect of writing ability on advancement was entirely incommensurate with the importance of writing to his or her job. Given the possibility—and even the likelihood—of such differences, a researcher (or reader of research) could have difficulty determining how well "the importance of writing" is measured by any of these questions, whether they are taken alone or together. When researchers or readers speculate about the extent to which a survey question actually measures the phenomenon it is supposed to measure, they are evaluating what is known technically as the *validity* of the question. Validity is a topic taken up later. I introduce it now to emphasize the considerable challenge of creating questions that constitute a satisfactory operational definition for an abstract concept.

Levels of Measurement

Although the variety of specific questions that might be asked in a survey is endless, all involve one of four basic methods of assigning numbers to phenomena. These methods are called the four *levels of measurement*.

NOMINAL LEVEL. Responses are gathered in mutually exclusive and exhaustive categories, and each category is assigned a number. For example, a researcher might ask respondents whether they are male or female. Respondents who said "male" could be assigned a 1, and those who said "female" could be assigned a 2. Assignment of a particular number to a particular category is arbitrary.

ORDINAL LEVEL. Respondents are asked to provide rank-order information. For example, respondents might be asked to rate the importance of some characteristics of writing (spelling, organization, tone, etc.) on a five-point scale: "unimportant," "little importance," "some importance," "considerable importance," "great importance." Their responses could then be assigned values on a scale where "unimportant" = 1 and "great importance" = 5. The more important the characteristic, the higher the number assigned to it. However, the distances between values are not equal; that is, the distance between "unimportant" (1) and "little importance" (2) cannot be shown to be the same as the distance between "little importance" (2) and "some importance" (3).

INTERVAL LEVEL. The distance between one value and the next is the same as that between any other pair of adjacent values. For example, the distance between an IQ score of 95 and one of 100 is the same as the distance between an IQ score of 105 and one of 110. With interval-level measurements, however, there is no absolute zero. For example, there is no zero amount of intelligence. Consequently, one could not say that someone with an IQ score of 120 is twice as smart as a person with an IQ of 60.

RATIO LEVEL. With ratio-level measurements, there is an absolute zero. For example, a researcher could ask respondents to give the number of memos they write in a day or the number of years of job experience they have had. Respondents could sensibly answer "zero." For that reason, one could say that a person who writes 4 memos a day writes twice as many as a person who writes only 2 per day.

Some kinds of phenomena (such as the sex of the respondents) tend to be measured at only one of these levels, but other phenomena can be measured at two or more levels. For example, researchers can measure the "amount of writing" that respondents do on the job by asking a question that measures at the nominal level ("Do you write a lot at work: yes? no?") or at the ordinal level ("How much writing do you do on the job: none? a little? a moderate amount? a lot?") or at the ratio level ("On the average, how many minutes a day do you spend writing?"). The level of measurement of a particular set of responses is important to researchers because the level of measurement is one of the key factors that determine which statistical procedures they may use to analyze those responses (this point is discussed further in the section on "Data Analysis"). For that reason, when writing their survey questions, one issue researchers must consider is the level of measurements they wish to make.

Measurement Error

A basic assumption in social science research is that all measurements involve error. The task of the researcher is to reduce that error as much as possible.

With respect to measurements in survey research, error may be defined in various ways. For questions about attributes and behaviors, error might be thought of as a discrepancy between a person's response and the information that might be obtained from some other source (for instance, a difference between the number of progress reports the subject says he or she has written in the past year and the number of progress reports written by him or her that are found in the company files). Although it may appear unlikely that errors will occur in response to questions about relatively concrete phenomena like attributes and behaviors, errors are always a possibility. For instance, when asked, "How many progress reports have you written in the past year?" some subjects may answer inaccurately because they have difficulty remembering. Similarly, when asked what percentage of their time at work they spend writing, some subjects may answer inaccurately because of difficulty in making the requested estimation: they may, for example, have trouble aggregating the sporadic moments they spend at the task, or they may be uncertain how they should define *writing* ("Does it include the time I spend on the phone obtaining information to be included in a letter?").

With respect to questions concerning attitudes and beliefs, error is thought of in much different terms. In dealing with such questions (e.g., how important do you think writing is?), researchers think of the person's response (e.g., the number that the person checks on a scale that runs from 1 to 5) as a function of some unobserved "true variable" (e.g., the person's "true attitude" toward the importance of writing). In this manner of thinking, the person's true attitude is considered to have a "true score." Error is the difference between that true score and the person's response. (The nature of the true score is problematic because true attitudes do not exist in the same way that true age does [Bohrnstedt, 1983]).

Response Effects

The questioning process that is central to measurement in survey research contains many potential sources of error. These errors are called *response effects* because they affect the response a person may give. Bradburn (1983) divides response effects into three classes:

1. Errors that arise from the respondent's desire to mislead the researcher—for instance, in order to make a good impression or to keep the researcher from finding something out.
2. Errors that arise from the respondent's inability to remember accurately.
3. Errors that arise from communication problems—for instance, when the respondent may misunderstand the question or the researcher may misunderstand the response (as might happen with open-ended questions).

Researchers have identified a broad array of factors that can produce these sorts of errors (Bradburn, 1983; see also Dillman, 1978, and Labow, 1980). Bradburn (1983) classifies these factors into three categories. The first involves the task presented to the respondent— for example, the clarity of the questions; their phrasing, length, and order; the demands they place on the reader (e.g., whether they require difficult feats of memory); their form (e.g., whether they are open-ended or not); and the method of administration (in person, through the mail, on the telephone). The second category includes the various factors that originate in the respondent, such as the tendency to provide answers the respondent thinks society would approve or the researcher desires. The third category involves the ways in which interviewers, working in person or on the telephone, can affect the responses a person will make.

Reliability

Closely allied with the concept of measurement error are the concepts of reliability and validity. At the conceptual level, *reliability* has no standard definition, although it is generally associated with the degree to which an instrument makes consistent and repeatable measurements (Wagenaar, 1981a). In practical terms, reliability is defined operationally in terms of the operations or procedures that are performed to produce the number that is the reliability of an instrument. Bohrnstedt (1983) divides these procedures into two major classes: those that measure stability over time and those that measure equivalence. *Stability* is often measured by giving the same questions to the same people on different days (*test-retest method*).

The more similar the responses on the two days, the higher the reliability of the instrument. A problem with using stability to assess reliability is that this approach can confound change with unreliability: the respondents' answers may be different the second time because of error, but the answers may also be different because the respondents' attributes, attitudes, beliefs, or behaviors have, in fact, changed.

The second approach to assessing reliability is to measure the equivalence of answers given to questions that are assumed to measure the same underlying phenomenon and are therefore assumed to have the same true score. The closer the scores on such pairs or groups of questions, the more reliable they are thought to be. One technique for measuring equivalence is the split-half method, in which the responses given to the first half of the questions about a phenomenon are correlated with the responses given to the second half of the questions. Equivalence methods for assessing reliability can be used only when the researchers pose groups of questions about the same phenomenon, something that is uncommon in the published surveys of writing in nonacademic settings.

Despite the difficulty of assessing the reliability of questions that are not grouped with other questions that measure the same phenomenon, the concept of reliability remains crucial to survey research because of the importance of using questions that can be relied on to produce the same response whenever the true score is the same.

One final point about reliability is important: an instrument can be reliable (consistent) without being accurate, as in the case of a bathroom scale that consistently measures 10 pounds light. Like that scale, survey questions can produce consistent but inaccurate results for any of the reasons listed in the section on response effects, including the respondents' desire to mislead, failure to remember accurately, or inability to understand what the researcher means.

Validity

In general terms, the validity of an instrument is the degree to which the instrument actually measures the phenomenon it is intended to measure. For example, a valid measure of "motivation to write well" is one that measures that concept and not some other concept, such as how hard the person must work at writing a communication to make it acceptable to his or her supervisor. Likewise, a valid measure of "motivation to write well" is one that measures that concept *only* and not also some other, such as a general desire to please.

Researchers use several methods for assessing validity. In the *face-validity method*, experts in the field (perhaps knowledgeable colleagues) evaluate the degree to which the instrument probably measures the concept being studied. In the *concurrent validity method*, the respondent's score is correlated with some other criterion *at the same point in time*. For example, the respondent's report of his or her motivation to write well might be correlated with his or her interest in reading books and articles that give advice about writing. In the *predictive validity method*, the respondent's score on some measure is correlated with his or her *future* standing on some criterion variable of interest. For example, the respondent's report about his or her motivation to write well might be correlated with the level of interest the person reports six months later in enrolling in a company-sponsored course in writing. Other methods of assessing validity are described by Bohrnstedt (1983), Kidder (1981) and Wagenaar (1981a).

How to Improve Measurements

Although there are methods for assessing reliability and validity after the fact, researchers should bear in mind that the best time for them to address problems involving error, reliability, and validity is when they are designing their instruments. In part, this means spending adequate time reading and thinking about the concepts they want to study and therefore must define in operational terms. It also means taking great care in writing their questionnaires and taking the trouble to train their interviewers and to pretest their surveys.

Two aspects of questionnaire design that require special attention by researchers are the phrasing and ordering of questions. Studies have shown that even minor changes in phrasing can affect the responses people give. For example, a classic study reported by Rugg (1941) and replicated many times showed that in the United States respondents gave 21 percent more support for free speech when asked, "Do you think the United States should forbid public speeches against democracy?" than when asked, "Do you think the United States should allow public speeches against democracy?" Nuances of meaning similar to that which distinguishes "forbid" from "not allow" can affect other questions, including (presumably) those that might appear in questionnaires that study writing in the workplace. Of course, other aspects of questions, such as their length and clarity, also deserve special attention by researchers.

In addition to the phrasing of questions, the order of questions can affect the answers respondents give (Shuman & Presser, 1981). For example, the National Crime Survey, conducted by the Census Bureau from 1972 through 1975, asked respondents a series of questions about crimes that had been committed against them in the preceding twelve months. Respondents who were asked these questions after first answering a series of sixteen questions concerning their attitudes toward crime reported significantly more crimes than did respondents who were not asked the attitude questions first. Similar ordering effects might influence surveys that ask respondents about the writing they do or the communications they read at work. Research also shows that the order of the responses offered to people in the closed-ended questions can affect their answers (Shuman & Presser, 1981).

For guidance in writing and ordering their questions so as to reduce the likelihood of error, researchers may turn to many sources of advice, including Backstrom and Hursh-Cesar (1981); Dillman (1978); LoSciuto, Kornhauser, and Sheatsley, (1981); Payne (1951); Sheatsley (1983); and Sudman and Bradburn (1982).

In studies that use interviewers, researchers can reduce error by training their interviewers carefully. This training may be thought of as having two purposes. The first is to develop the individual interviewer's skills and attitudes so that he or she can present survey questions in a way that will produce unbiased responses (Weinberg, 1983). To achieve this purpose, training might include, for example, instruction in the role of an interviewer, and in how to read (pacing, tone, etc.) and probe (where open-ended questions are used). The second purpose of training is to ensure that all the interviewers for a particular study follow the same procedures (Downs, Smeyak, & Martin, 1980). Training can be provided through reading, written exercises, and practice interviewing, to name a few of the possibilities. In some cases, interviewers are provided with manuals— either a general manual, such as the one published by the University of Michigan's Survey Research Center (1976), or a special manual specifically designed for the particular study at hand (Weinberg, 1983).

Once they have made their best efforts at designing their questionnaires and preparing their interviewers (if they have them), researchers should pretest their instruments. Pretesting involves presenting the questionnaire and other survey materials (cover letters, etc.) to individuals who might be able to alert the researcher to difficulties in them. These individuals might belong to any of three groups: (1) colleagues trained in survey research who understand the study's intent and can evaluate the extent to which it is likely to achieve its objectives; (2) people trained in the subject matter of the survey (perhaps potential users of the results) who can judge whether the survey is asking important questions in a way that will seem acceptable to potential respondents; and (3) people drawn from the population to be studied.

Generally, when undertaking pretests that involve the members of the population to be studied, researchers conduct dry runs in which they administer the draft version of the survey in exactly the manner they will administer the final draft to their survey sample. By doing so, the researchers can discover potential problems with all aspects of the survey, including not only the phrasing of questions and their responses, but also the length of the questionnaire, the rhetoric of the cover letters—even the logistics of locating subjects and handling data (Backstrom & Hursh-Cesar, 1981). Dry runs also provide researchers with data they can use to assess the reliability and validity of their instruments. By performing these assessments, researchers can identify concepts and questions that need to be recast before the final administration of their surveys.

Thus, through careful work at writing their questionnaires, through training their interviewers, and through pretesting, researchers can significantly reduce measurement error (but never eliminate it), and they can significantly increase the reliability and validity of their research instruments.

ANALYSIS

To be able to draw valid conclusions based on the responses to their questionnaires, researchers must analyze these responses in a way that is appropriate to the data obtained, the kind of sample used, and the research question being asked. In this section, I briefly describe the general categories of statistical tools for analyzing quantified data; I do not treat the interpretation of unquantified responses to open-ended questions. Throughout, I have attempted to explain the statistical tools in a way that will help the reader understand and evaluate the statistical procedures that are most often used in survey research.

Descriptive Statistics

The statistical tools used in survey research fall into two broad categories: descriptive and inferential statistics. Descriptive statistics summarize distributions of data. The simplest descriptive statistics are *frequency distributions*, which report, usually in tables or bar charts, the frequency with which each response was given (37 respondents said "often," 25 said "very often," etc.). Another simple descriptive statistic is the *percentage*, which provides a sense of what proportion of the subjects gave each response.

MEASURES OF CENTRAL TENDENCY. Three descriptive statistics— *mean, median,* and *mode*—provide a sense of the typical response to a survey question by identifying the *central tendency* of the group of responses. The *mean* is the average of the responses. It is generally the preferred measure of central tendency, for two reasons. First, it takes the most information into account: the exact value of every response is used to compute the mean response. In addition, the mean is generally less variable than are the other two measures, so that the mean is usually more dependable for situations in which data from the sample is used to draw inferences about the overall population.

However, the mean is not the appropriate or best measure of central tendency in all situations. For example, it is not usually appropriate for data gathered at the nominal level, where numbers are arbitrarily assigned to mutually exclusive categories (e.g., male = 1, female = 2). It makes no sense to talk about the "average sex" of the respondents. Also, means are not usually used with data gathered at the ordinal level because the intervals between the possible responses are not equal.

Furthermore, even with responses gathered at the interval or ratio level, the mean can provide a misleading impression of central tendency if a few of the responses are extremely low or high. Such a situation arose in a survey of writing at work in which Faigley, Miller, Meyer, and Witte (1981) asked 200 respondents how many letters and memos they wrote to persons inside or outside their own organization in an average week. Five of the respondents reported writing over 100 letters per week, many more than were reported by the other 195 respondents. The responses from these individuals greatly inflated the mean.

In cases like this, the researcher can gain a much more accurate sense of the typical response by using the second measure of central tendency: the *median*. The median is the value of the response that falls in the middle when the responses are arranged in order of magnitude. Thus, in the situation just mentioned, Faigley et al. found that the *median* response (8.1 letters and memos per week) provided a much more accurate portrait of the typical response than did the mean (19.7). Another common use of median is to describe the central tendency of data gathered at the ordinal level.

The third measure of central tendency is the *mode*, which is the response given most often. Attention to the mode is especially important in situations where the responses fall into two distinct groups. For example, in a survey of 245 people listed in *Engineers of Distinction*, Davis (1977) asked the respondents how the amount of writing they did at work has changed as they have advanced; 65 percent of the respondents reported that as they have advanced they have written more, and 32 percent said that they have written less. Only 3 percent said that they have written about the same amount. Clearly, the respondents fell into two distinct subgroups, each reporting a unique experience; the typical experience of the respondents could not accurately be characterized by an "average." It could, however, be characterized accurately by saying that the distribution of responses had *two* modes, each representative of one of the kinds of experience.

Thus, to determine which of the three measures of central tendency—mean, median, mode—best characterizes the typical response in a set of data, a researcher must consider both the level of measurement involved and the distribution of the responses in the data set.

MEASURE OF DISPERSION. Three other descriptive statistics are used to provide manageable summaries of the *dispersion* of the responses in a set—the extent to which they are similar to or dissimilar from one another. The first measure is the *range*, which is the difference between the highest and lowest responses. Such a measure can be very informative because a single mean can represent two very different sets of responses, one in which all responses are very similar and the other in which at least some of the responses are very different from one another. For example, a mean of 50 may represent the central tendency of a set of responses that vary only from 48 to 53 or a set of responses that vary all the way from 0 to 100. By knowing the range, researchers can tell something not only about the typical response but also about how much the various responses vary from the mean.

The range, however, does not tell whether *most* of the responses are close to the mean or whether most are far from the mean (at the extremes of the range). Another measure, *sample variance*, does do that. The variance of a sample is calculated by (1) calculating the distance of each response from the mean, (2) squaring each distance, (3) summing all the squares, and (4) dividing the total by $n - 1$ (i.e., by the number of responses minus one). As is evident from this procedure, if there is an increase in the number of responses that are far from the mean, there will also be an increase in the sample variance.

A shortcoming of sample variance as a measure of dispersion is that it is difficult to interpret. What would it mean to say that the spread of a set of responses is 7.6? Certainly, a sample variance of that size is less than one of 8.5 and more than one of 4.2, but what does a sample variance of 7.6 mean in absolute terms? The third measure of dispersion, called the *standard deviation*, provides not only a basis for comparison among different distributions but also an informative description of a single set of measurements.

The standard deviation is the positive square root of variance. This measure is useful because of the empirical finding that for the most commonly encountered distribution of responses, called a *normal distribution*, the interval between one standard deviation above the mean to one standard deviation below will contain approximately 68 percent of the responses, the interval from two above to two below will contain about 95 percent of the responses, and the interval between 3 above and 3 below will contain almost all the responses. (A normal distribution is a symmetrical distribution in which the mean response is also the most frequent response, and responses progressively more distant from the mean are made by progressively smaller numbers of subjects; represented graphically, it gives a bell-shaped curve.)

Thus, provided that a set of responses falls into a normal distribution, the standard deviation can tell a researcher how closely the responses are grouped about the mean. If the standard deviation is 3, then about 68 percent of the responses are no more than 3 units from the mean, about 27 percent are between 3 and 6 units from the mean, and the approximately 5 percent that remain are between 6 and 9 units from the mean. In contrast, if the standard deviation is 9, then about 68 percent of the responses are within 9 units of the mean, and so on.

BIVARIATE ANALYSIS. Measures of central tendency and dispersion are used for *univariate analysis*—analysis involving only one variable (i.e., the response to one question). Other descriptive statistics are used for *bivariate analysis*, which concern the association between the responses to two questions. Bivariate analysis would be used, for instance, by a researcher who wanted to determine whether a relationship exists between answers to the question, "How many years of job experience do you have?" and "How many hours a week do you spend writing at work?"

Conceptually, bivariate analysis examines cause-effect relationships; the researchers are determining the extent to which the variation in one variable (i.e., the responses to one question) can be accounted for by variation in the other variable (i.e., the responses to the other question). The variable whose variation is being accounted for is called the *dependent variable*, and the variable that may cause that variation is called the *independent variable*. Since surveys are not controlled experiments, assignment of these terms is subject to a common sense understanding of which variable could "cause" the other. For example, it seems sensible to imagine that a person's years on the job might cause the amount of writing the person has to do, but it is not sensible to envision that the amount of writing a person does causes the number of years he or she has been at work. To clarify this point, researchers sometimes say that the dependent variable is the one that can be thought of as coming *last* in a time order: the respondent has been on the job for fourteen years (independent variable) before doing the amount of writing he or she is doing now (dependent variable).

The statistics used for bivariate analysis are called *measures of association*. Used with data gathered at the ordinal, interval, or ratio level, measures of association yield values between +1 and −1. If the independent variable accounts *fully* for the dependent variable, then the value of the measure of association will be either +1 (if the two increase together) or −1 (if one decreases as the other increases). On the other hand, if there is no association whatever between the responses to the two questions, the measure of association yields a value of zero. In surveys, the phenomena under study usually have many causes, so that any one variable accounts for—at most—only a portion of the variation in another variable. For example, even if the number of years of job experience partly accounts for the amount of writing done at work, many other factors may also account for that amount, including (perhaps) amount of education, type of employer, and the respondent's attitude toward writing. Thus, in surveys, measures of association often yield values closer to zero than to either +1 or −1. According to a rule of thumb provided by Wagenaar (1981b), an association is *weak or negligible* if the measure of association is between +.24 and −.24, *moderate* if it is between +.25 and +.49 (or −.24 and −.49), and *strong* if it is +.50 or more (or −.50 or less).

There are many measures of association, and the choice of which to use depends largely on the level of the data involved (whether nominal, ordinal, interval, or ratio). The measure of association most familiar to people untrained in statistics is *Pearson's product-moment correlation coefficient*, often called simply the correlation coefficient. All measures of association are reported in the same way by researchers: with the name of the statistic (Crammer's V, Yule's Q, etc.) and the value (e.g., +.36).

MULTIVARIATE ANALYSIS. Another class of statistics enables researchers to perform *multivariate analysis*, in which they can examine the relationship among the responses to three or more questions. Multivariate analysis could be used, for example, to examine the effect that years on the job and years of education, *taken together*, have on the amount of writing done at work. Another use of multivariate analysis is to increase the researchers' confidence that one particular independent variable *does* cause variation in the dependent variable; to do this, the researchers would show that the other variables do not cause the variation.

A discussion of the many specific procedures used in multivariate analysis is beyond the scope of this chapter. Some of these procedures are described in an introductory way (without formulas) by Wagenaar (1981b). It is noteworthy that although these powerful statistical tools are commonly and helpfully used in most survey research, they are not employed in any of the published surveys of writing at work. This is one sign that ample opportunity remains for basic survey research in this area.

Inferential Statistics

From the point of view of survey research, descriptive statistics have a very serious limitation: used alone, they only summarize the responses from the sample; they do not provide a sound basis for drawing conclusions about the population from which the sample is drawn. Another broad array of procedures, called *inferential statistics*, can be used to make inferences about populations based on information gathered from samples.

STATISTICS AND PARAMETERS. To underscore the difference between the results of analyses performed on data gathered from a sample and the results that would be obtained from the entire population, researchers distinguish between a *statistic* and a *parameter*. In this usage, a *statistic* is the value obtained by performing some statistical procedure on data gathered from a sample. A *parameter* is the value that would be obtained by performing a statistical procedure on data gathered from every member of a population.

An example will help to illustrate the relationship between statistics and parameters. Suppose that a teacher of business writing wants to learn the average amount of time that the twenty-two students in her class spend per week preparing the course assignments. She could ask a sample of five students to tell her how much time each of them spends, so that she could calculate the average for the five. The average for that sample is a *statistic*. If, instead, she asked all twenty-two students to tell how much time they spend, she could calculate the average for the entire population; the resulting figure would be a *parameter*.

In one very important respect, this example situation differs from the situation facing survey researchers. Whereas the teacher has the ability to gather information from the entire population, a survey researcher does not. Therefore, survey researchers cannot calculate parameters, but only estimate them. Inferential statistics are built on the assumption that a sample statistic provides the best estimate of a population parameter—but that it does not provide a perfectly accurate estimate.

SAMPLING ERROR. To understand why statistics fail to provide perfect estimates of parameters, it is necessary to understand the concept of *sampling error*. If the business writing teacher were to calculate the average time spent on assignments by a randomly selected sample of five students from her class, it is improbable that this average would be precisely the same as the average that she would obtain if she had randomly selected a different group of five students. It is also unlikely that either of these groups would report an average that is precisely the same as the average for the entire class. The difference between a statistic obtained from a sample (in this case the average obtained from a group of five students) and the parameter that would be obtained from the entire population (the whole class) is called *sampling error*.

LEVELS OF CONFIDENCE. Because researchers cannot obtain data from the entire population and because the statistics they obtain from samples are subject to sampling error, researchers can never know the exact value of a parameter or the exact difference between their statistic and the corresponding parameter. Using inferential statistics, however, they can determine the accuracy of their sample statistics, so that they can express their *level of confidence* that the parameter falls within a specified interval from the statistic. For example, after using the appropriate inferential statistic, a team of researchers could say that they are 95 percent confident that the average age of a population falls within plus or minus two years of the average age of the sample from which they have gathered data.

BIVARIATE AND MULTIVARIATE ANALYSIS. In addition to calculating the accuracy of univariate statistics (such as averages), researchers can use inferential statistics to study relationships between two or more variables: Do college-educated workers spend more time at work writing than do workers without a college education? Do they write letters more often than they write reports, proposals, and advertisements? Do they think good grammar is more important than good organization to the success of a communication? Because such questions are so often asked in survey research, anyone working with or attempting to read about survey research should understand the logic that underlies the application of inferential statistics.

THE LOGIC OF STATISTICAL HYPOTHESIS TESTING. When researchers use inferential statistics to answer questions about relationships between two or more variables, the researchers focus on *differences between groups of responses*. Essentially, the question they are asking is this: "Is it probable that the differences we found between the responses to two or more questions in our sample data also exist in the population from which our sample was drawn?"

For example, imagine that a team of researchers has decided to investigate the writing done by graduates of a certain college. As part of their research, they desire to learn whether or not the alumni of one department spend more time writing at work than do alumni of another department. The researchers might begin by calculating the mean time spent writing by respondents from each of these two departments. Suppose they found that the respondents who graduated from the first department spend an average of 7.3 hours per week and the respondents who graduated from the other department spend an average of 7.5 hours per week. So far, they would have found a real difference between the two groups of alumni *in their sample*. However, both averages are subject to sampling error. What the researchers want to know is whether the difference between these sample averages results from sampling error or whether it represents a real difference that exists *in the population*.

Inferential statistics help researchers answer such questions by enabling them to engage in a special form of *hypothesis testing*. First, the researchers formulate a hypothesis, called the *null hypothesis*, which states that the difference found in the sample does *not* exist in the population. Then they use an appropriate statistical procedure to choose between one of two mutually exclusive alternatives: either they reject the *null hypothesis* or they do not.

However, even these statistical procedures cannot tell the researchers for certain that they have made the correct choice regarding the null hypothesis. After all, the procedures work with data provided by a sample—data that are, therefore, subject to sampling error. Consequently, instead of being stated in terms of certainty, the results of these statistical procedures are stated in terms of *statistical significance*, a term that is often misunderstood by people untrained in scientific research methods.

STATISTICAL SIGNIFICANCE. *Statistical significance* is the probability that it is a mistake to reject the null hypothesis. To put it another way, statistical significance is the probability that the difference found in the sample does *not* represent a real difference found in the population. Thus, when researchers report that they have found a difference at the .05 level of significance, they are saying that they have decided to reject the null hypothesis but that there is a 5 percent probability that their decision was a mistake—and that there is a 95 percent probability that they were correct in their decision. Similarly, a .01 level of significance indicates that there is a 1 percent probability that the researchers were wrong to reject the null hypothesis—and a 99 percent probability that they were right. As these examples indicate, the lower the level of significance, the greater the confidence that the researchers have that the difference found in the sample data represents a real difference existing in the population.

The term *significance* can be the source of considerable confusion for people unused to working with or reading about social science research. *Statistical significance* is not the same as *substantive significance*. *Statistical significance* can only tell researchers whether it is probable that a difference exists; it cannot tell researchers whether the difference is important. As Johnson (1977) cautions, to say that " 'two groups were significantly different (at the .05 level)' means only that there's a 5-percent chance we'd make a mistake in concluding that the two groups were not exactly alike. Two groups can be 'significantly different' even when the actual difference, although real, is very, very small" (p. 228). This point is especially important because level of significance is directly related to sample size; the sampling errors are greater in smaller samples. A real difference in the population might be found by a sample of 1,000 people but not by one of 100 people; the difference would be present in data gathered from both samples, but might be statistically significant in the larger sample only.

To determine whether or not a difference is substantive—one worth talking about—researchers (and readers) must look to descriptive statistics and then apply criteria originating in common sense, theory, or other sources. Thus, if the researchers just mentioned found that there was a statistically significant difference between the amounts of time spent per week in writing by the graduates of the two college departments, the researchers would have to look at the means themselves to see if the difference was large enough to matter: Is the statistically significant difference between writing an average of 7.3 hours per week and an average of 7.5 hours per week an important difference? Likewise, if the researchers found some statistically significant relationship between two variables (e.g., age and amount of writing done at work), the researchers would still have to use measures of association (which are descriptive statistics) to determine whether the relationship is a strong one.

EXAMPLE OF STATISTICAL HYPOTHESIS TESTING. The nature of the statistical hypothesis testing that is integral to the use of inferential statistics can be illustrated through the example of the researchers comparing the graduates of two college departments in terms of the time they spend writing at work. The researchers would begin their hypothesis testing by conceptualizing the respondents from the first department as being a sample from one population and the respondents from the second department as being a sample from another population. Next the researchers would frame the null hypothesis: there is no difference between the two populations in terms of the variable under consideration, namely the average amount of time spent writing. Then the researchers would determine the significance level that they desire to use as they decide whether or not to reject the null hypothesis. In survey research, the most commonly used significance levels are .05, .01, and .001. Next, the researchers would use the appropriate statistical procedure (in this case, a t-test) to answer this question: "If we assume that we are drawing samples from two populations that are identical with respect to this variable (that is, if we assume that the null hypothesis is true), then what is the probability that we will draw two samples that differ by 0.2 (7.5 minus 7.3) or more?" Next, the researchers would compare the results of the statistical procedure with the significance level they had chosen in order to decide whether or not to reject the null hypothesis. Finally, if the researchers found that the difference was statistically significant, they would review their descriptive statistics to determine whether the difference was also substantive. (For a fuller account of a similar example on which mine is based, see Johnson, 1977, pp. 225–227.)

THEORETICAL ASSUMPTIONS. A discussion of the theoretical justification of inferential statistics is beyond the scope of this chapter. It is important, however, for both researchers and readers of research to be aware that these statistics are based on the assumption that certain important conditions are met. Chief among these is the condition that the sample is a random sample and that there is no measurement error. In most instances the first condition is not met, and the second never is (for reasons explained in the section on "Measurement"). As a practical matter, the absence of these two conditions is overlooked, provided that the researchers have used *some* probability sampling method (not necessarily random sampling) and provided that they have carefully designed their questionnaire. Rigor in statistical analysis, however, cannot compensate for carelessness in sampling or measurement. The less representative the sample and the less accurate the measurements, the less confidence one can place in the subsequent statistical analyses, regardless of the significance level reported.

VARIETY OF INFERENTIAL STATISTICS. There is a great variety of inferential statistics, and additional ones are constantly being developed. Each has very specific applications that involve well-defined conditions. For example, there is one inferential statistic for determining whether two means are significantly different when the means summarize responses to *two different questions by a single group* of individuals (paired *t*-test), and there is another for use where the means summarize the responses to a *single question* by *two different groups* (Student's *t*-test). And there are inferential statistics for comparing groups of three or more means with one another (such as Duncan's multiple-range test for variable response).

An account of all the varieties of inferential statistics and their proper application would require a much longer and more technical discussion than is possible in this chapter. (Indeed, it would require a book.) Readers of this chapter who want a more complete account of inferential statistics may turn to the works cited later on in the section entitled "Additional Reading about Statistics."

Judgment in the Use of Statistics

Because there are so many statistical procedures, each designed for use under well-defined conditions, it might seem that researchers should be able to tell with absolute certainty which test would be the *right* one for a given analysis and which tests would be *wrong* ones for that analysis. On the contrary, researchers often encounter situations for which no existing statistical procedure is ideally suited. Consequently, the use of statistics requires much more judgment than people untrained in the social sciences usually realize.

For instance, I needed the informed judgment of a statistician concnerning a survey that I describe in chapter 1. In that survey, I asked alumni of seven departments of my university how often they wrote each of eleven kinds of communicatons, such as letters, step-by-step instructions, and advertising; the alumni responded by providing ordinal-level information (i.e., checking one of five responses: "never," "rarely," "sometimes," "often," "always"). To learn whether the alumni wrote some of these eleven forms significantly more often than they wrote others, I could have used either of two statistical procedures, neither of which was ideally suited for the information I had gathered. One procedure, the Friedman test for randomized block designs, seemed appropriate because it was designed for use with measurements made at the ordinal level. But the standard form of the Friedman test is useful only if every one of the possible responses has been made by at least one person. That was not the case in my survey. For some of the subgroups I wished to study, no one had checked some of the possible responses (e.g., not one of the alumni of the Chemistry Department indicated that he or she "often" wrote advertising). A modified Friedman test has been developed for use in such situations, but all the calculations must be done by hand because no one has yet prepared a computer program for it; since I had responses from more than 800 alumni, this modified version of the test was impractical.

Alternatively, I might have performed an analysis-of-variance F test followed (if the F test found a statistically significant difference among the means) by Duncan's multiple-range test for variable response. However, both the F test and Duncan's test assume that the data involved were gathered at the interval or ratio level. I could simulate interval-level data by converting the ordinal-level responses from the alumni to a five-point scale where "never" = 0 and "always" = 4; but, as discussed earlier in the section on "Levels of Measurement," the intervals between the numbers would not necessarily have been equal.

In the end, I used the F test and Duncan's test because—in the *judgment* of my statistical adviser—that procedure was more likely to give dependable results than was the standard Friedman's test. Similarly, the judgment of an expert is often required to choose the most appropriate procedure for analyzing a given set of data—and even the experts sometimes differ in their judgments.

Advice for Reading Statistical Results

Even so short an explanation of descriptive and inferential statistics as I have given here does provide a basis for some practical advice to people who do not know statistics but desire to read survey research critically.

1. *Whenever researchers state or imply that a relationship (difference, association) that they have found in a sample reflects a relationship that exists in a population, the researcher should use inferential statistics (not just descriptive ones).* According to common practice, when researchers use an inferential statistic they include in their articles and reports both the name of the statistic and the significance level they employed. In addition, they often announce the results of the procedures, usually in mathematical form, such as "$t(789) = 2.15$." A reader who finds no mention of specific statistical procedures in reports of surveys that discuss differences among responses should suspect that the necessary inferential statistics were not used.

2. *Whenever researchers use inferential statistics, they should provide evidence that the sample is representative of a larger population.* Thus a reader should look for the researchers' explanation of the details of the procedure by which the sample was selected—and the reader should evaluate the plausibility of the researchers' claim that a sample selected in that way is representative of the larger population of interest. For help in determining what kinds of sampling procedures are accepted by specialists in survey research, readers of this chapter may turn back to the section on "Survey Sample" and to the works cited in that section.

3. *All statistical results should be evaluated in light of the carefulness with which the researcher designed and wrote the questionnaire used to gather the data.* If the questionnaire is faulty, the statistical results based on it will also be faulty. For help in evaluating questionnaires, readers may turn back to the section on "Survey Instrument" and to the works cited therein.

4. *All statistical results should be evaluated in light of the care and skill with which the researchers selected the particular statistical procedures they used.* To determine whether appropriate statistical procedures have been applied by the researchers, a person who is not trained in social science research will need the assistance of someone familiar with statistics.

5. *All reports of statistical significance should be read with the knowledge that "statistical significance" is not the same as "substantive significance."* Readers should look for evidence that the statistically significant differences reported by researchers are *important* ones and that the statistically significant relationships between variables are *strong* ones.

Advice for People Undertaking Surveys

Three basic points concerning statistics are important to people who would like to undertake survey research but are not familiar with statistics.

1. *Inferential statistics are essential to any survey intended to generalize beyond the sample to a larger population.*
2. *Because inferential statistics constitute a very technical field, it is wise to enlist the advice of an expert.*
3. *The statistical advisor should be consulted throughout the work on the project, beginning with the creation of the research design.* If involved with the project early, this advisor can provide valuable help with such crucial activities as designing the sampling methods and framing the questions (so that the questions gather responses at a level that is appropriate for the desired statistical analyses).

Additional Reading about Statistics

For a more detailed (but still introductory) explanation of the assumptions, applications, and procedures of descriptive and inferential statistics, readers may turn to any of the following sources: Babbie (1973), Backstrom and Hursh-Cesar (1981), Johnson (1977), Kerlinger (1979), Milburn (1981), Wagenaar (1981b), and Weisberg and

Bowen (1977). Readers who are interested in learning to perform these procedures may start with any of the many introductory textbooks in the subject, such as Blalock (1979), Jendrek (1985), Kohout (1974), and Leonard (1976).

LIMITATIONS OF SURVEY METHODOLOGY

Like all other research methods, the survey is specialized. It is suited for looking only at certain kinds of phenomena under certain conditions and certain purposes. In particular, the key limitations of the survey are the following:

1. *When a survey is used for the purpose of making generalizations about large groups of people, the persuasiveness of the survey's results depends on the researchers' ability to construct a representative sample of the larger population under study.* For various practical reasons, researchers can have difficulty constructing representative samples. The more difficulty they have, the less confidence the researchers and their readers can place in the conclusions reached. Surveys are sometimes used with nonprobability samples to study relationships among variables (through bivariate and multivariate descriptive statistics), but even then a researcher would hesitate to generalize the findings unless there was good reason to believe that the sample accurately represented some large population.

2. *The survey is suited only for studying phenomena about which people can report accurately.* Thus, for example, the survey is not helpful in studying the details of the cognitive processes of writing. It appears that because of the nature of our short-term memory we cannot remember the small steps we perform when we write. Accordingly, other research methods (such as protocol analysis) must be employed to study this creative process (Hayes & Flower, 1980).

3. *In surveys, researchers rigidly control the kinds of information that their subjects can provide about the phenomena under study; as a result, the subjects' responses may provide distorted information about those phenomena.* When they devise operational definitions of the abstractions they wish to study, researchers necessarily impose their conceptional frameworks on those abstractions. For instance (to continue an example used in the "Measurement" section of this chapter), a team of researchers desiring to investigate "importance of

writing in the workplace" might decide that the dimensions of this abstraction are "effect of writing well on promotability, on salary increases, and on ability to perform the required work." The researchers would then devise at least one question concerning each of these dimensions, for instance, "How does the ability to write well affect promotability? decreases it, does not affect it, increases it." Such questions require respondents to talk about the phenomena under study in terms of the researchers' conceptual framework—and the questions prohibit the respondents from talking about those phenomena in other terms, even when those other terms are the ones the respondents would naturally use.

Using a different method of gathering information, the researchers might obtain much different—and perhaps much more valid—information. For instance, the researchers might visit one of the respondents to their survey and say, "Tell us about the importance of the writing you do at work—and tell us how you came to hold that view." In response, the worker might tell a story that presents "the importance of writing" in a way that is very different from the researchers' conceptualization of that abstraction. Or the worker's story might contain the dimensions used by the researchers, but couched in a way that changes their meaning. At the very least, the worker's story would explain *why* the worker answered the survey question in the way he or she did—which is something the survey itself cannot discover. Of course, this one worker's response might be idiosyncratic, nothing on which to base a generalization. On the other hand, it might be typical of a widely held way of thinking that had not occurred to the researchers.

Thus, in order to meet the formal, methodological conditions that provide surveys with their power of generalization, researchers sacrifice the ability to learn whether their respondents' natural way of looking at the phenomena under study corresponds with the researchers' preconceived framework.

INTEGRATION WITH OTHER RESEARCH METHODS

Because all research methods are specialized, each providing a view of its subject that is inextricably linked with its modality, different methodologies can be thought of as different points of view for observing the same area of study. The portraits drawn of that area by various research methods can complement and verify one another, or they can contradict and compete with one another in a way that provides an impetus to additional investigation. Accordingly, in many areas of study researchers develop broad research programs in which the results obtained through one method are used to generate the specific research questions that will be investigated through a different method. Such broad programs can arise spontaneously as researchers in a field read one another's work, or the programs may be formulated in advance by investigators who plan multistage studies. Within the broad effort to study writing in nonacademic settings, the survey has an important role to play, one that depends chiefly on the power of the survey to generalize.

The relationship between survey research and other methodologies can be explained in terms suggested by Guba (1978). Discussing the general progress of research efforts, Guba argues that investigators oscillate between two modes of inquiry. In the "expansionist or discovery" mode, they try to discover the meaning of something they want to study; they do this by developing hunches and hypotheses about it. In the "reductionist or verification" mode, they attempt to verify these hypotheses through more highly structured procedures that necessarily close them to fundamentally new insights—until they return once again to a discovery mode. In such an analysis, survey research would be associated with the "reductionist or verification" mode because of the manner in which the formal constraints of survey methodology narrow the researchers' view of the phenomena under study. At the same time, it is from these very constraints that the survey gains its particular power to test hunches that researchers develop through less formal means about people's attitudes, beliefs, and behaviors.

Working from an analysis similar to that by Guba, Morton-Williams (1978) recommends that survey researchers begin their research projects by using unstructured and flexible interviewing to explore the phenomena of interest to them. In this way, researchers can gain insights into the range of behaviors, attitudes, and issues involved, and can increase their chances of designing survey questionnaires that will avoid forcing their subjects' responses into false or irrelevant structures.

A study by Green and Nolan (1984) illustrates one way that a single research project can effectively coordinate a survey with another research method. To aid educators who want to create academic programs that prepare students for careers as technical communicators, Green and Nolan desired to obtain a detailed, accurate portrait of the job of the typical technical writer. Further, they wanted this to be a composite portrait drawn by professionals working in that field, where people's jobs vary widely. Consequently, Green and Nolan began their study by convening a panel of ten experienced, practicing technical writers, whom they asked to work as a group to perform the following activities: devise a one-sentence definition of the job of the technical writer, enumerate all the various tasks performed by technical writers, group these tasks into significant areas of activity, and then identify those tasks that seemed to be "higher-order tasks" (those that are usually performed by more advanced members of the profession). The panel devoted two full days to creating, debating, and editing their response to this assignment—thereby providing the kind of analysis of their profession that a survey could not produce. In the end, the panel identified over 200 tasks grouped under 13 headings. Then, to determine which of the tasks identified by the panel played the most important roles in the work of the *typical* technical writer, Green and Nolan presented all the tasks in a survey questionnaire sent to more than 200 practicing professionals.

A similar complementarity of research methods could exist between *separate* studies conducted by different researchers. For example, Odell et al. (1983) used a variety of research strategies—but not the survey—to gather information about their writing from an unsystematically selected group of individuals who worked in a state welfare agency. One of the fruits of this research project was a framework for classifying the reasons that writers give for their decisions about such things as the phrasing they will use to express a command or request, or the form they will use to refer to themselves ("I" or "we," for example). Further, the researchers found that there appeared to be important differences between various groups of workers in terms of the kinds of reasons they gave most often. For example, the less experienced workers explained their decisions in terms of the persona they wished to establish more often than did the more experienced employees. A survey could determine whether this and other differences found in the small group of people who cooperated with Odell et al. also exists in some larger population. Populations that might be studied include all the employees in the state agency examined by Odell et al., all the employees in all state agencies in that state (or in all states), or all college-educated employees in the United States—among other possibilities.

CONCLUSION

In these examples of ways that surveys can be integrated with other research methods, I have tried to emphasize the primary use and value of survey research: to allow researchers to make valid generalizations about large groups by obtaining information from only a small number of people who belong to those groups. The survey provides a means of distinguishing the typical from the accidental, of inferring the general from the particular. In so doing, it provides a powerful instrument through which we can increase our understanding of one of the most fascinating, complex, and significant of all human activities: our efforts at our place of work to ask and answer, enrage and entertain, persuade and placate, subjugate and inspire—indeed, to conduct any of our affairs of the mind and heart—through the written word.

Acknowledgments

I am grateful to Professors Margaret P. Jendrek, John Skillings, and Theodore C. Wagenaar for their comments and suggestions. I am also grateful to Keith Shute for assembling many of the materials used to write this chapter, for copyediting it, and for making substantive suggestions.

References

Ad Hoc Committee of the American Business Communication Association. (1975). Student evaluation of the basic course in business communication. *Journal of Business Communication, 12*(4), 17–24.

Aldrich, P. G. (1982). Adult writers: Some factors that interfere with effective writing. *The Technical Writing Teacher, 9*, 128–132.

Babbie, E. R. (1973). *Survey research methods.* Belmont, CA: Wadsworth.

Backstrom, C. H., & Hursh-Cesar, G. (1981). *Survey research.* New York: Wiley.

Barnum, C., & Fischer, R. (1984). Engineering technologists as writers: Results of a survey. *Technical Communication, 31*(2), 9–11.

Blalock, H. M., Jr. (1979). *Social statistics.* New York: McGraw-Hill.

Bohrnstedt, G. W. (1983). Measurement. In P. H. Rossi, J. D. Wright, & A. B. Anderson (Eds.), Handbook of survey research (pp. 69-121). New York: Academic Press.

Bradburn, N. B. (1983). Response effects. In P. H. Rossi, J. D. Wright, & A. B. Anderson (Eds.), Handbook of survey research (pp. 289-328). New York: Academic Press.

Chein, I. (1981). An introduction to sampling. In L. H. Kidder (Ed.), Selltiz, Wrightsman, and Cook's research methods in the social sciences (pp. 418-444). New York: Holt, Rinehart & Winston.

Connors, R. J. (1982). The rise of technical writing instruction in America. Journal of Technical Writing and Communication, 12, 329-352.

Davis, R. M. (1977). How important is technical writing?—A survey of the opinions of successful engineers. The Technical Writing Teacher, 4, 83-88.

Dillman, D. A. (1978). Mail and telephone surveys: The total design method. New York: Wiley.

Dillman, D. A. (1983). Mail and other self-administered questionnaires. In P. H. Rossi, J. D. Wright, & A. B. Anderson (Eds.), Handbook of survey research (pp. 359-377). New York: Academic Press.

Downs, C. W., Smeyak, G. P., & Martin, E. (1980). Professional interviewing. New York: Harper & Row.

Faigley, L., Miller, T. P., Meyer, P. R., & Witte, S. P. (1981). Writing after college: A stratified survey of the writing of college-trained people. Austin: University of Texas.

Frankel, M. (1983). Sampling theory. In P. H. Rossi, J. D. Wright, & A. B. Anderson (Eds.), Handbook of survey research (pp. 21-67). New York: Academic Press.

Gopnik, M. (1972). Linguistic structures in scientific texts. The Hague: Mouton.

Green, M., & Nolan, T. D. (1984). A systematic analysis of the technical communicator's job: A guide for educators. Technical Communication, 31(4), 9-12.

Guba, E. (1978). Toward a methodology of naturalistic inquiry in education evaluation. Los Angeles: Center for the Study of Evaluation, UCLA Graduate School of Education.

Hayes, J. R., & Flower, L. S. (1980). Identifying the organization of the writing process. In L. W. Gregg & E. R. Steinberg (Eds.), Cognitive processes in writing (pp. 3-30). Hillsdale, NJ: Erlbaum.

Jendrek, M. P. (1985). Through the maze: Statistics with computer applicatons. Belmont, CA: Wadsworth.

Johnson, A. G. (1977). Social statistics without tears. New York: McGraw-Hill.

Kerlinger, F. N. (1979). Behavioral research: A conceptual approach. New York: Holt, Rinehart & Winston.

Kidder, L. H. (1981). Reliability and validity. In L. H. Kidder (Ed.), Selltiz, Wrightsman, and Cook's research methods in social relations (pp. 120-143). New York: Holt, Rinehart & Winston.

Kinsey, A. C., Pomeroy, W. B., & Martin, C. E. (1948). Sexual behavior in the human male. Philadelphia: Saunders.

Kohout, F. J. (1974). Statistics for social scientists. New York: Wiley.

Labow, P. J. (1980). Advanced questionnaire design. Cambridge, MA: Abt Books.

Leonard, W. M., II. (1976). Basic social statistics. St. P☉l, MN: West.

LoScuito, L., Kornhauser, A., & Sheatsley, P. B. (1981) Questionnaires and interviews.

In L. H. Kidder (Ed.), *Selltiz, Wrightsman, and Cook's research methods in social relations* (pp. 144–197). New York: Holt, Rinehart & Winston.

Milburn, M. (1981). Data analysis. In L. H. Kidder (Ed.), *Selltiz, Wrightsman, and Cook's research methods in the social sciences* (pp. 313–341). New York: Holt, Rinehart & Winston.

Morton-Williams, J. (1978). Unstructured design work. In G. Hoinville & R. Jowell, (Eds.,) *Survey research practice* (pp. 9–26). London: Heineman.

Odell, L., Goswami, D., Herrington, A., & Quick, D. (1983). Studying writing in nonacademic settings. In P. V. Anderson, R. J. Brockman, & C. R. Miller (Eds.), *New essays in technical and scientific communication* (pp. 17–40). Farmingdale, NY: Baywood.

Olsen, L. A., & Huckin, T. N. (1983). *Principles of communication for science and technology.* New York: McGraw-Hill.

Paradis, J., Dobrin, D., & Bower, D. (1984). (Massachusetts Institute of Technology.) Personal correspondence.

Payne, S. L. (1951). *The art of asking questions.* Princeton, NJ: Princeton University Press.

Rigsby, L. (1981). Survey research designs. In L. H. Kidder (Ed.), *Selltiz, Wrightsman, and Cook's research methods in the social sciences* (pp. 58–81). New York: Holt, Rinehart, & Winston.

Rossi, P. H., Wright, J. D., & Anderson, A. B. (1983). Sample surveys: History, current practice, and future prospects. In P. H. Rossi, J. D. Wright, & A. B. Anderson (Eds.), *Handbook of survey research* (pp. 1–20). New York: Academic Press.

Rugg, D. (1941). Experiments in wording questions: II. *Public Opinion Quarterly, 5,* 91–92.

Sheatsley, P. B. (1983). Questionnaire construction and item writing. In P. H. Rossi, J. D. Wright, & A. B. Anderson (Eds.), *Handbook of survey research* (pp. 195–230). New York: Academic Press.

Shuman, H., & Presser, S. (1981). *Questions and answers in attitude surveys: Experiments on question form, wording, and content.* New York: Academic Press.

Stine, D., & Skarzenski, D. (1979). Priorities for the business communication classroom: A survey of business and academe. *Journal of Business Communication, 16*(3), 15–30.

Stolzenberg, R. M., & Land, K. C. (1983). Causal modeling and survey research. In P. H. Rossi, J. D. Wright, & A. B. Anderson (Eds.), *Handbook of survey research* (pp. 613–675). New York: Academic Press.

Stopher, P. R., & Meyburg, A. H. (1979). *Survey sampling and multivariate analysis for social scientists and engineers.* Lexington, MA: Lexington Books.

Storms, C. G. (1983). What business school graduates say about the writing they do at work: Implications for the business communication course. *ABCA Bulletin, 46*(4), 13–18.

Sudman, S. (1976). *Applied sampling.* New York: Academic Press.

Sudman, S. (1983). Applied sampling. In P. H. Rossi, J. D. Wright, & A.B. Anderson (Eds.), *Handbook of survey research* (pp. 145–194). New York: Academic Press.

Sudman, S., & Bradburn, N. A. (1982). *Asking questions: A practical guide to questionnaire design.* San Francisco: Jossey-Bass.

Survey Research Center. (1976). *Interviewer's manual, revised edition*. Ann Arbor: Institute for Social Research, University of Michigan.

Wagenaar, T. C. (1981). Measurement. In T. C. Wagenaar (Ed.), *Readings for social research* (pp. 72–75). Belmont, CA: Wadsworth. (a)

Wagenaar, T. C. (1981). Social statistics without formulas. In T. C. Wagenaar (Ed.), *Readings for social research* (pp. 281–301). Belmont, CA: Wadsworth. (b)

Weinberg, E. (1983). Data collection: Planning and management. In P. H. Rossi, J. D. Wright, & A. B. Anderson (Eds.), *Handbook of survey research* (pp. 329–358). New York: Academic Press.

Weisberg, H. F. & Bowen, B. D. (1977) *An introduction to survey research and data analysis*. San Francisco: Freeman.

Young, P. V. (1949). Development of the survey movement. In *Scientific social surveys and research* (pp. 1–61). New York: Prentice-Hall.

Ethnographic Research on Writing

14

Assumptions and Methodology

STEPHEN DOHENY-FARINA
University of North Carolina at Charlotte

LEE ODELL
Rensselaer Polytechnic Institute

Within the past decade or so, theorists and researchers have begun to argue that there is a need for ethnographic investigations of the complex relationships between writing and the social contexts in which texts are written and read (Basso, 1974; Scribner & Cole, 1981; Bizzell, 1982; Cooper & Holzman, 1983; Faigley, chapter 6, this volume). The assumption is that these investigations may contribute substantially to our present understanding of such matters as the nature of the composing process, the characteristics of "good" writing, and the ways in which readers go about making meaning out of what someone else has written. There is also the chance that this sort of research will help us expand our notions about the functions of writing. For example, it may be that, as Paradis, Dobrin, and Miller suggest (chapter 8, this volume), writing does more than reflect the social context in which it exists; it may be that writing helps shape that context.

Ethnographic research on writing is becoming increasingly popular. It has been conducted in both academic (see Kantor, 1984; Newkirk, 1983; Herrington, 1983; Clark et al. 1983) and nonacademic settings (see chapters in this volume; see also Scribner & Cole, 1981; Doheny-Farina, 1984). And results of these studies suggest that this sort of work has substantial implications for composition theory and pedagogy. However, we want to reiterate a caution raised by the editors of *Research in the Teaching of English*: there is the possibility that researchers will embark on ethnographic inquiry or will attempt to integrate ethnographic procedures with more traditional approaches "without fully understanding [ethnography's] methodological and philosophical underpinnings" (p. 6, 1984) An understanding of these underpinnings is important since, as Heath (1982) points out, one thing that distinguishes ethnography from other forms of naturalistic or qualitative research is the researcher's reliance on a set of theoretical assumptions developed by researchers in cultural anthropology. We shall begin this chapter by reviewing these assumptions. Then we shall suggest ways in which ethnographic methods can be applied to research on writing.

THEORETICAL ASSUMPTIONS

Thick Description

Ethnographers insist that their research be grounded as fully as possible in the empirical world. They stress the importance of closely observing the specific phenomena of the culture in which one is conducting research. Thus an ethnographer's observational notes (discussed later in this chapter) may contain detailed references to minute, even apparently trivial matters of how people dress and how they interact with colleagues; of whom they initiate conversations with and who initiates conversations with them; of the features of their nonverbal language. As Geertz (1973) has pointed out, "behavior must be attended to and with some exactness," for "it is through the flow of action—or more precisely, social action—that cultural forms find articulation" (p. 17).

Despite this concern with carefully observed detail, the detail is not an end in itself. The ethnographer's ultimate goal is to understand what Heath (1982) refers to as the "ways of living of a social group" or "the rules individuals within [a] society have to know to produce, predict, interpret, and evaluate behaviors in given settings or social situations" (p.34). Consequently, ethnographers are interested in obtaining not merely a description of a particular phenomenon but what Geertz calls a "thick description," one that not only lists phenomena but also indicates the meaning(s) phenomena have within a particular social context. Geertz draws on the work of Gilbert Ryle for this example: in observing a person, we may note that, at a given instant, the person's eyelid contracts. An ethnographer might record that phenomenon. But by itself that event is not very significant. So the ethnographer would be obliged to answer such questions as these: Was the behavior an involuntary muscle contraction, or was it a wink? If it was a wink, how did the person understand that act? What meaning did he or she attribute to it? Who else noticed the wink? What meaning(s) did the other observers attribute to it? Can the researcher identify additional meanings of the wink, meanings that are important to the functioning of the group being studied but that members of the group might not be able to articulate? In other words, the ethnographer is interested not only in events but also in the significance that can be ascribed to those events.

Facts

With this discussion of thick description, the complexity of an ethnographer's task begins to seem a bit more apparent: the researcher must not merely observe phenomena but also must collect data that reflect the significance of phenomena, a significance that does not exist "out there" or "in" the data but rather is to be found in the meanings people (including the researcher) ascribe to the phenomena. The task is further complicated by some assumptions about people's inability to record phenomena accurately, assumptions that are shared by theorists in other disciplines. Kenneth Boulding (1964), for example, makes the point thus: we do not "perceive [our] sense data raw . . . [there are] no such things as 'facts' . . . [there are only] messages filtered through a changeable value system" (p. 14). I. A. Diesing (1984) makes a similar point: "a sensation would be something that is just so, on its own, a datum; as such we have none. Instead we have perceptions, responses whose character comes to them from the past as well as the present occasion" (p.20).

These assertions put researchers in the uncomfortable position of having to acknowledge that their data, the very grounds for any conclusions they draw, are inherently limited and fallible, even when the researcher is dealing with apparently simple phenomena such as overt behavior. Further, some of the data are not reports of the researcher's own first-hand observations but reports of observations done by others, people whose observations are just as limited, just as influenced by their own perspective, as are a researcher's observations. As Geertz (1973) points out, ethnographers' data often consist of "our own constructions of other people's constructions of what they and their compatriots are up to" (p. 9). Thus even the most "objective" interpretations are interpretive; "right down at the hardrock, in so far as there is any, of our whole enterprise, we are already explicating: and worse, explicating explications" (p. 9). Paul Diesing (1984) makes a similar point:

> ... there are no infallible data in ethnography nor anywhere in the social sciences. Observations are always in part projections of what we would expect or like to see. Informants' statements are self-serving and project their attitudes toward other people involved. Official records and reports are interpretations which idealize or focus on salient problems or achievements.

The assumptions described thus far lead to still further assumptions—about the importance of naturalistic settings, about the relations of researchers and people studied, and about the necessity of collecting multiple types of data.

Naturalistic Context

If researchers assume that they want to understand the significance of a given action in a given social context, they will have to do their research in a naturalistic rather than an experimental setting. That is, researchers will need to investigate phenomena in the social contexts in which these phenomena routinely occur. As George Herbert Mead (1956) argues:

> The behavior of an individual can be understood only in terms of the whole social group of which he is a member, since his individual acts are involved in larger social acts which go beyond himself and which implicate the other members of that group. [p. 121]

This is so, in part, because people's interpretations of the world are, to use Shatzman and Strauss's term, "social in origin"; "they arise through an individual's interpretations of numerous instances of social interaction" (1973, p. 5). Further, we would argue, a social setting can provide resources—shared knowledge with which to approach a task, shared values, familiar procedures for analyzing data, widely agreed on criteria—which may be essential for succeeding with a given task. When a researcher removes people from the social environment in which they routinely function, the researcher may deprive them of important resources, especially when the researcher poses an experimental task that is not part of the normal social environment. Having separated people from their social resources, it may very well be that the researcher substantially alters the very behavior that he or she is trying to isolate in an experimental setting.

Research Roles

If researchers want to conduct inquiry in naturalistic settings, they must change their notions about the respective roles of researchers and the people who take part in researchers' studies. Researchers may no longer think of their work as a matter of manipulating variables and trying to predict or influence behavior. Nor may researchers continue to think of themselves as working with subjects who simply perform tasks with no real understanding of those tasks. Instead, the researcher's principal job becomes one of trying to describe and explain phenomena over which the researcher has no direct control.[1] Further, ethnographic researchers are continually working with people who are, in some ways, far more expert and knowledgeable than are the ethnographers (Blumer, 1969, pp. 21–47; Dean, Eichhorn, & Dean, 1969a, b, pp. 19–24). It is the research subjects who are familiar with the shared meanings that exist in a culture; it is they who will guide the researcher's behavior and interpretations—for example, by identifying new sources of information or alerting the researcher to an upcoming event that might have more significance than the researcher had realized. Furthermore, researchers and subjects are engaged in similar tasks. Both the researcher and subject interpret their worlds and attribute meanings to the persons, events, and objects in those worlds. Both construct realities, or ways of looking at the world. Both are capable of taking on the perspectives of others. The researchers differ in that they are particularly interested in doing the latter. Ethnographers know they are obliged to try to provide a rounded view of the activity under study, to collect all significant points of view on a given activity or issue.

Since an ethnographer's subjects have so much authority and autonomy, researchers must adopt a dual role—that of both participant and observer. As participants, researchers try to develop an empathetic relationship with the individuals they are studying. Researchers must try to see things from these individuals' point of view, becoming—at least vicariously—participants in the life of the group to which the individuals belong. Researchers, however, must also be able to distance themselves, to look at phenomena from an outsider's point of view (Scott, 1965, pp. 265–266; Blumer, 1969, pp. 35–42; Denzin, 1970, pp. 7–8). This is necessary because, paradoxically, a person who becomes too much of an insider may lose his or her ability to perceive the meaning of routine acts. This distance is important, as Wilson (1977) argues, because insiders may not always be able to articulate their perspectives; their tacit knowledge may be so deeply internalized that it is not readily available to them. Consequently,

> the researcher must find ways to cultivate awareness of the latent meanings without becoming over socialized and unaware as most participants may be. The researcher must develop a dynamic tension between the subjective role of participant and the role of observer so that he is neither one entirely. [p. 250]

Multiplicity

So far we have argued that all perception is highly selective, that all meaning is interpretive. Such a point of view inevitably raises this question: How can ethnographers collect valid data? How can they obtain a solid empirical basis for their conclusions? Ethnographers would, of course, admit that both their data and their interpretations are continually subject to reassessment and revision. Ethnographers, however, assume they can strengthen the validity of their conclusions by a process that Denzin (1970, pp. 301–313) refers to as *triangulation*. A researcher may rely on

- *Theoretical triangulation*: examining data from different theoretical perspectives.

- *Investigative triangulation*: relying on a research team rather than a single researcher: see the discussion of research teams later in this chapter.
- *Methodological triangulation*: using a variety of research methods to elicit data from a variety of sources.

Methodological triangulation is especially important. Blumer (1969) argues that ethnographers should feel free to

> use any ethically allowable procedure that offers a likely possibility of getting a clearer picture of what is going on in the area of social life. Thus, it may involve direct observation, interviewing of people, listening to their conversations, securing life-history accounts, using letters and diaries, consulting public records, arranging group discussions, and making counts of an item if this appears worthwhile. [p. 41]

We see this principle in chapter 8 by Paradis et al. in this volume. They report results based on several different sources: a questionnaire, a writing test, individual and small-group interviews, seminars, conversations, and analyses of corporate documents. Similarly, in their study of Vai culture, Scribner and Cole (1981) relied on interviews with 700 Vai adults; participant/observations of literacy in two rural towns; observations of Vai language teaching sessions; and analyses of a range of Vai documents. In his study of collaborative writing in a small, computer software company, Doheny-Farina (1984) observed and tape-recorded collaborative writing sessions; conducted open-ended interviews with a variety of informants (those who were collaborating and those who had observed the development of the company over a period of a year or so); and conducted discourse-based interviews concerning specific features of the document on which participants had collaborated. Denzin indicates the significance of such attempts at triangulation when he argues that no one research method of data collection or data analysis is "always superior. Each has its own strength and weaknesses" (p. 471). Webb (1970) concurs:

> Every data gathering class—interviews, questionnaires, observation, performance records, physical evidence—is potentially biased and has specific validity threats. Ideally, we should like to converge data from several data classes. . . . [p. 450]

The underlying logic of triangulation is this: ethnographers seek patterns in the data they collect. Triangulation at any level tests emerging patterns by increasing the possibility of finding negative cases and countering the bias of any one approach. Thus triangulation fosters more rigorous research. "The greater the triangulation, the greater the confidence in the observed findings. The obverse is equally true" (Denzin, 1970, p. 472).

METHODOLOGY

In this section we shall define the term *methodology* rather broadly. We shall begin by discussing procedures that characterize good ethnographic practice, suggesting ways to go about developing research questions, beginning a study, and carrying out a study. We shall conclude this section by describing methodologies for collecting and analyzing data.

Developing Research Questions

Whereas it is important for ethnographic research to proceeed from some general research questions, it is also important to remember that questions imply a set of expectations about the phenomena one is observing. These questions and implied expectations provide essential guidance; without them, researchers would have no way to focus their attention and energy. But this very guidance implies certain limitations. As researchers focus attention on one set of possibilities, in effect they blind themselves to other possibilities. No researcher can escape this predicament, but it is an especially important issue for ethnographers. Ethnographers assume that they are working in settings where their knowledge and expertise are limited; it is not the researcher but rather the informants who are experts. It is the ethnographer's task to uncover some of the significant features of the informants' culture, not to presume to know in advance what those features are. Certainly ethnographers have their guesses, their prior experiences, their knowlege of what they think may be relevant theory. However, ethnographers must do their best to attend to the distinctive features of the setting in which they are conducting their research (Blumer, 1969; Levine, 1970).

Consequently, it is probably a good idea to begin research with only a very general research question and then allow that question to evolve into more focused questions. For example, Doheny-Farina (1984) began his research in a computer software company guided initially by the following question: What are the rhetorical activities in which the participants in this setting engage? After a preliminary research period, Doheny-Farina began to focus his research on a more specific question: How do company executives' perceptions of the organizational context influence the writing processes of the executives? As research proceeded, Doheny-Farina began to consider the converse of this question: How do rhetorical activities influence the shape of the organization? His ultimate focus was on this reciprocal relationship between organizational context and collaborative writing processes.

Another ethnographic researcher (Newkirk, 1983) reports that he began one study of writing with a preliminary set of general research questions concerning students' ability to evaluate themselves during a composition course. As the investigation proceeded, however, Newkirk discovered that this set of questions limited his focus:

> As the study progressed it became apparent that the subjects were providing information that went beyond the initial question of evaluation. Larger issues of how writers view the writing process, and of how they view themselves as writers, were (also) explored. . . . [p. 132]

Newkirk's observations help us reiterate our point that ethnographers are continually engaged in a process of discovery. They must not limit their capacity to discover by setting up rigid, tightly focused research questions before they begin to collect data.

Beginning Research

CHOOSING A SITE. Since ethnographers should allow research questions to emerge after entering the research site, choosing such a site is very important. This choice necessarily begins the process of focusing one's research. Besides seeking a setting in which writing and reading are significant activities for the participants, the ethnographer should try to gain entrance into a site that allows for some freedom of access. Specifically, researchers should look for a site that they can visit at varying times during the day or night, and where they can collect data for an indefinite length of time. They should also be able to take various physical perspectives within the site and to observe and speak with a variety of participants.

Once a site is chosen, the investigator should begin on-site research with extreme care. The early stages of ethnographic research can be difficult and intimidating for both the participants and the researcher. During the early stages, researchers should engage in activities that enable them to (1) establish research roles; (2) minimize the disruptiveness of their presence; (3) develop physical, temporal, and social maps of the setting; and (4) develop relationships with key informants.

ESTABLISHING RESEARCH ROLES. There are four useful roles that a writing researcher can assume during data collection. A researcher may assume any of these roles at different times during the course of a study.

One researcher role is that of *complete observer* (Gold, 1969, p. 36). A researcher assumes this role when he or she enters the setting, observes and records activity, but does not interact with the participants at all. On the surface this role may appear to be an ideal way to record the natural activity of the participants without disrupting that activity. It may seem that a researcher who takes on the role of complete observer will best be able to record "what really goes on" in a setting.

Although this role can be a valuable tool when used selectively, there are two significant problems with adopting it exclusively. First, the novice ethnographer must realize that he or she cannot enter a naturalistic setting and remain completely uninvolved and unobtrusive. That is, when a researcher enters a naturalistic setting, he or she becomes a part of the activity in that setting. Unless the natural setting of the participants is already equipped with hidden cameras and one-way viewing screeens (a highly unlikely possibility), the researcher's presence will not be a secret to the participants; nor will that presence leave the participants unaffected. An investigator who does not interact with the participants may well make them uneasy. The participants may never accept a silent, mysterious observer, and they may significantly alter their customary behavior in the presence of someone they don't know or trust.

Moreover, a writing ethnographer must employ data-gathering procedures that enable him or her to explore the personal meanings that the participant writer constructs. Although passive observations of participants' conversations will provide valuable insights into their constructed meanings, the researcher will probably need to interact with the participants to further explore these meanings and their bearing on the processes of writing and reading. (We will identify some of these procedures on later in this chapter.)

A second researcher role is that of *participant-as-observer* (Gold, 1969, pp. 35). In this role, researchers interact with participants only to establish themselves as an acceptable presence to the participants and to clarify the data collected. Researchers may, for example, record a paraphrase of a lengthy statement made by a participant during a conversation. At an appropriate time, the researcher may ask what the participant intended. The researcher then records the participant's response. In the course of this exchange, brief conversations arise between participants and researcher, allowing the researcher some insight into the participant's construction of meaning, and also providing the participant with some insight into what the researcher is doing. Shatzman and Strauss (1973) note the benefits of assuming the role of participant-as-observer:

> This type of activity has two distinct advantages: it gets at meaning, and it meets the expectations of the hosts insofar as the researcher is not only an observer, but is revealed as personable and interested; through his comments or questions his apparent agenda is indicated. The agenda is understandable and appears appropriate; therefore, the observer can be thought of as at least "kind of" a member of the group. [p. 60]

Although a participant-as-observer tries to become part of "the group," the researcher must do so cautiously. Whereas the purely passive, complete observer may be perceived as a snoop, the participant-as-observer may be perceived to be an ally of one faction within the group. Wilson (1977) explains this point by example: if an ethnographer in a school setting wished to study a controversy surrounding student aggression at a particular school, the researcher would need to

> be careful about the way he entered the situation and came to be perceived. For example, he would work methodically to avoid being identified as the member of any particular subgroup. Did the teachers consider him someone the principal had sent? ... Similarly, did the students consider him to be a teacher-like person? ... The group identity of the observer is important not only because the participants might consciously withhold information from someone with the wrong identification ... but also because the participants might consciously color what they said and did [when in the presence of the observer] ... [pp. 254-255]

To avoid this sort of problem, some researchers establish their personality and competence by officially becoming insiders. That is, some researchers establish themselves not only as researchers, but also as participants (see Kahn & Mann, 1969, for a discussion of "dual entry.") For example, in their research projects in nonacademic settings, Kanter (1977), Knoblauch (1980), and Doheny-Farina, in particular, reported that interaction through this channel helped him establish himself as someone who could be trusted, even though his principal work as a consultant had ended before his research began. (For further discussion of procedures for participant-observation, see Goetz & LeCompte, 1984, pp. 109–119.)

Although the three researchers cited in the previous paragraph all reported that they had consulting arrangements with the companies that they studied, none of the three reported that they themselves had adopted a third type of role, that of *complete participant* in the group they were studying (Gold, 1969, p. 33). However, a complete participant in a setting may also become a researcher. Such a dual role may be difficult to perform by oneself, but it is possible that a complete participant may join with an outside researcher to form a research team. For example, Pettigrew, Shaw, and Van Nostrand (1981) developed complete-participant/complete-researcher teams to investigate writing instruction in eight elementary school classrooms. These teams systematically analyzed qualitative data that were collected during writing instruction. Each analysis team consisted of a teacher of a lesson, an observer of that lesson, and a third researcher who would read the observer's field notes. These analysis teams combined three types of data: (1) the participant's conception of the meanings of his or her own actions as teacher; (2) the observer's perceptions of the teacher; and (3) an outsider's perspective on the observer's interpretations.

The research roles described so far assume that the researcher is interested in minimizing his or her influence on the setting being investigated. It is also possible to take a fourth research role, that of *observer-as-participant* (Gold, 1969, p. 36). Researchers assume this role when they create data-gathering situations and take active control of those situations. Although researchers create data-gathering situations whenever they engage participants in conversation, the clearest example of such researcher-created situations is the formal interview, a procedure we will discuss later in this chapter.

MINIMIZING DISRUPTIVENESS. No matter which role is chosen, ethnographers seek to minimize their impact on the setting. Participants can easily be disturbed by the sight of a stranger watching them and then intently scribbling notes on a yellow legal pad. Consequently, researchers who are just entering a research site probably should not try to record a great deal of data in the particpants' presence. Instead, researchers should gradually increase on-site data collection activities over time, after they have begun to gain the trust of the people they are working with. For inexperienced researchers, this suggestion is troublesome; they may feel they are missing data that may ultimately be crucial to their study. As Shatzman and Strauss (1973) advise, however, the possibility of "'missing' things" early on is not a problem at all:

> The experienced observer is not overly concerned about "missing" things; most of what occurs will happen again and again. If a specific event does not get repeated, another which points to the same underlying pattern of occurances very likely will. [p. 37]

If an event occurs early on, goes unrecorded, and rarely or never again manifests its importance—that is, if it does not appear to be a part of a pattern—then the event was probably an aberration that should be of no consequence to the research.

DEALING WITH OBSERVER EFFECT. As Goetz and LeCompte (1984) point out, participants in a study may deliberately act or talk in ways that the participants think are consistent with the researcher's interests. Or the changes in behavior may be subtle and inadvertent, occasioned perhaps by motives (e.g., a desire for approval) that participants might be unaware of or unwilling to acknowledge. Whether deliberate or not, such changes constitute what Goetz and LeCompte call "observer effect." To reduce the chances of being misled by this effect and to arrive at credible, significant conclusions, one needs to follow procedures identified in this chapter and described at length in the sources we have cited. It is particularly important to follow the procedures of remaining on site for an extended period of time, talking with a variety of participants in a variety of situations, and confirming conclusions by drawing on multiple sources of data (all discussed later in this chapter). It is also important to check one's observations with people who participate in the study, asking them, for example, if one has recorded a given event accurately and fully and if the behaviors described are, in fact, consistent with what the participants know of people involved in the event (see Goetz & LeCompte, 1984, p. 225). The participants' reactions and suggestons for additions, deletions, or modifications become part of the data relating to the event in question. (We do not recommend, however, that researchers show participants the researchers' interpretations of the behaviors they have described. That practice can lead participants to try to conform to the researcher's interpretations; it can also make participants self-conscious and uncomfortable.)

We know of no way to eliminate observer effect. All researchers—whether in a naturalistic setting or in an experimental setting—must realize that the presence of an observer will have some effect on the phenomena being observed. By following ethnographic procedures, however, researchers can obtain multiple reference points against which to check their observations and interpretations. By carefully testing their observations and interpretations, ethnographers can achieve the rigor that is essential for good research.

DEVELOPING MAPS OF THE SETTING. Although an ethnographer may not be able to record a great deal of data during the very early stages of research, there are some data that he or she should seek to collect. One of the first observations that an ethnographer needs to record is the physical boundaries of the setting. For example, a researcher who has entered a large complex of offices may first draw a map of the whole complex, recording employee names and titles in appropriate places. As the researcher focuses his or her inquiry on specific sections of the office, the researcher will write descriptions of those sections.

In addition to creating this map of the physical setting, the researcher must also become oriented to both the social and temporal layouts of the setting:

> The researcher must learn the formal and informal psychic schedules and geographies of the participants . . . he must become aware of all the behavior settings in the community and their important characteristics . . . He works to become part of the various communication

networks that daily orient participants about where and when significant events are likely to occur. [Wilson, 1977, p. 256]

It will take a certain amount of time, but eventually the researcher will develop a sense of when various activities are likely to occur—of when, for example, a writer is likely to begin a new project or to receive feedback on a completed project. Simultaneously, it will take time for an ethnographer to learn who the participants are, what they do, how approachable they are, how accepting they are of the investigator, and—in bluntly pragmatic terms—how useful they are to the investigation. This last point is critical. Knowing where and when events occur in a setting will yield only limited data. Developing useful relationships with participants—that is, developing relationships with key informants—is the ethnographer's most crucial task when he or she first enters the setting.

DEVELOPING RELATIONSHIPS WITH KEY INFORMANTS. Ethnographers must seek out participants who can provide them with significant interpretations of the activities under study. For example, a key informant may be a manager who allows the researcher to follow him or her throughout a signficant time period—a staff meeting, a day's work, a year's work, a production cycle, a firing, a hiring, or any number of other activities. The choice of key informants should be based on four factors:

1. The informants should engage in activities that appear to be related to the investigator's emerging research questions.
2. The informants should be able to provide a range of perspectives on the activities under study.
3. The informants should be willing to be observed over time.
4. The informants should be capable of doing their work while being observed (see Dean, Eichhorn, & Dean, 1969b, p. 143, for a description of useful types of informants).

Writing researchers in nonacademic settings will want to choose informants for whom writing and reading form significant aspects of their daily activities. As investigations proceed and research questions emerge, researchers may add or change key informants. Of course, researchers must exercise considerable tact when adding or dropping key informants during a research project.

Carrrying Out a Study

REMAINING ON SITE FOR AN EXTENDED PERIOD. Underlying all ethnographic inquiry are the assumptions that social interaction is a process and that one of the ethnographer's primary goals is to discover patterns in this process. These patterns become apparent only as one observes for an extended period of time; during the course of several months, one's interpretation of the patterns may change, and so may the patterns themselves. For example, a researcher may enter an industrial setting and find that, during the first two months of research, the participants write often, write quickly, and rarely rewrite anything. This pattern may seem consistent with the pace of other work-related tasks in this setting. From these observations a researcher might conclude (1) that writing processes at this site are truncated, and (2) that the participants are not concerned with producing carefully crafted written products. However, over a longer period of time, say six months, the researcher may discover that the participants' writing processes are heavily influenced by the proximity of certain deadlines. The pace of the participants' work may be determined by changes in the pace of industrial production. The researcher may need to collect data that span deadlines in order to understand how the pace of production influences writing processes. By collecting such data, the researcher may gain a more complex perspective on industrial writing processes. It is impossible to predict exactly how long a researcher must spend at a given site in order to obtain these data. However, a general rule of thumb for selecting a research site is that it must be one where a researcher can spend at least six months to a year collecting data at the site (in some cases, however, the research can last much longer; see Heath, 1983).

VARYING TIMES FOR OBSERVATION. In addition to selecting a site where they can spend a great deal of time, researchers must also look for a site that they can visit at different times of the day (see, for example, Shatzman & Strauss's discussion of "overlapping times," 1973, p. 39). This is especially important early on in the investigation. For example, a researcher who visits an industrial office every other day from 1:00 to 2:00 P.M. may conclude that the employees are often distracted and listless. However, this observation may describe only a pattern of postlunch behavior. A researcher who visited the site at differing times of the day or night might observe a range of behavior. By choosing a site where it is possible to vary visitation times, the researcher may be able to better appreciate the complexity of patterns of interaction.

VARYING PHYSICAL PERSPECTIVES. In her study of male and female roles in corporate life, Kanter (1977) realized that in order to gather all the data she needed, she would need access to a number of different physical settings: people's offices, company lunchrooms, employees' homes, social gatherings. This sort of access is especially important to writing researchers since we assume that writing and reading may go on in a variety of settings and that writing and reading processes include more than just the moment at which one is engaged in encoding or decoding a message. For example, it is true that an industrial manager may write memos at his or her office desk. However, important aspects of that manager's writing process may also occur in the coffee area, at lunch, or in meetings in someone else's office. If researchers are to have a clear understanding of that process, they will have to choose a site where they can be physically present in some of the diverse situations in which the process occurs.

OBSERVING AND SPEAKING WITH A VARIETY OF PARTICIPANTS. Recent research has begun to show how social interaction is an important aspect of the composing process (e.g., Selzer, 1983; Doheny-Farina, 1984; Odell, chapter 7, this volume). If researchers are to continue to explore this interaction, they will have to select a research site where they have access not only to writers but also to writers' co-workers and supervisors—the people who assign, help develop, and review (formally and informally) the materials writers produce. Researchers will need both to observe writers' interaction with their colleagues and to interview these colleagues, trying to complement the data derived from observing and interviewing the writers themselves.

Collecting Data

Earlier in this chapter, we argued that ethnographers need to be flexible when they pose their initial research questions; they must allow these questions to evolve in ways that reflect the unique qualities of the setting in which they are working. A similar flexibility is necessary in selecting or devising procedures for collecting data. Although we shall describe some of the more widely used procedures, we must point out that not all of these procedures will be equally appropriate in every situation. Further, we want to reiterate Diesing's warning (1984) that ethnographers cannot plan to enter a setting and conduct their work by "running through a series of prearranged steps" (p. 5). Each situation is in some ways unique. Thus, as Wilson points out:

> The ethnographer must constantly make decisions about where to be, what kind of data to collect and to whom to talk. Unlike prestructured research designs, the information that is gathered and the theories that emerge must be used to direct subsequent data collection. [1977, p. 256]

In effect, there can be a reciprocal relationship between data and data-gathering procedures. While gathering data, an ethnographer may come to see the need for a new or modified data-gathering procedure. This procedure, in turn, may lead the researcher to discover new data and, possibly, the need for still other data-gathering procedures.

Bearing these warnings in mind, we shall describe several of the more widely used data-gathering procedures that strike us as currently or potentially appropriate for researchers who are studying writing in nonacademic settings. These procedures include: (1) writing field notes, (2) conducting interviews, (3) tape recording conversations, and (4) using other recording technology.

WRITING FIELD NOTES. Probably the most useful data collection procedure that an ethnographer can use is the writing of field notes. Shatzman and Strauss (1973) identify three types of field notes.

1. The first type consists of *observational notes* (ON)—statements through which a researcher attempts to accurately record observed activity. These notes "contain as little interpretation as possible, and are as reliable as the observer can construct them" (Shatzman and Strauss, 1973, p. 100).

2. Second are *theoretical notes* (TN), which are researcher interpretations that analyze the activity described in observational notes. Theoretical notes are a private declaration of meaning (that the

researcher) feels will bear conceptual fruit. (The researcher) interprets, infers, hypothesizes, conjectures; he develops new concepts, links these to older ones, or relates any observation to any other in this presently private effort to create social science. (p. 101)

3. Finally, there are *methodological notes* (MN), which are statements that serve as guidelines for future research activities. These are researchers' operational notes to themselves.

The following is an example of a page of field notes that illustrates the use of each type of note:

4/12/84   10:00AM   In-town office

ON: Greg (a programming manager) and Larry (a staff programmer) are in the computer room and Greg has turned the radio up a bit. He's tuned to a rock station and it is louder than usual. At one of the computers Greg is writing what appears to be a memo. At another terminal Larry is working on a computer program.

MN: Possibly ask Greg if he likes to write memos to music.

TN: Sometimes it appears that Greg doesn't care if what he does bothers others in the office—if he likes to write with the music up, he does so.

ON: From just outside of the computer room Dave (a programming manager) just called over to turn the music down. Greg calmly called back, "No." Dave: "It's not 2:00 in the morning; it's business hours. Turn it down." Greg: "Nope."

MN: Find out if these people sometimes work here around the clock.

ON: A minute later Dave walked in and turned the radio down. Greg smiled to himself as Dave left and Barry wondered aloud: "I wonder what kind of music Dave likes." Greg: "Barry Manilow." They both laughed and Greg went over and turned the radio back up.

TN: It appears here that Greg undercuts Dave's authority by challenging him in front of subordinate workers.

ON: I asked Greg what he was writing. Greg: "A memo about better cooperation among managers."

MN: Find out if Larry works for either Greg or Dave.

Writing these types of field notes should begin when the researcher first enters the setting and begins observing. As suggested earlier, a researcher new to a setting may wish to refrain from writing many field notes while making his or her first or second visit. However, this practice should not keep the researcher from recording extensive notes after leaving the setting. In fact, throughout a research project there may be times when a researcher is not able to make a full record of his or her observations while on site. In such cases, the researcher should write up the notes as soon as possible after leaving the site. Often, the researcher will record extensive field notes while on site, then add to those notes later after leaving the setting.

Since ethnographers may collect a massive amount of hand-written data, it is helpful to type up each day's hand-written field notes. Typing already-written notes is not a purely clerical task. If a researcher develops a routine of typing recently recorded field notes, the typing sessions can become an important analytical stage in the data collection process. When typing notes, researchers can reconsider the activities observed and note evolving concepts in additional theoretical notes. Such a practice has two benefits. It deepens the researcher's understanding of the data, and it helps to physically organize what can eventually become an overwhelming amount of written information.

CONDUCTING INTERVIEWS. Interviews in nonacademic settings may range from brief informal interviews (e.g., conversations conducted while participants are engaged in routine activities) to formal tape-recorded interviews that interrupt or supplement participants' usual work. The informal interviews enable a researcher to explore participants' interpretations of events that are occuring as they speak. If careful, the researcher can often record these interpretations without greatly disrupting the natural flow of events. More formal interviews may require a participant to interrupt his or her work-related activity. Consequently, these interviews lack the immediacy of the informal interviews; but they have the advantage of allowing a researcher to probe a topic at greater length and depth. (For a discussion of the uses and limitations of interviews, see Atlas, 1979; and Odell, Goswami, & Herrington, 1983.)

In any interview, no matter how formal or informal, the researcher's goal is not simply to confirm the researcher's own intuitions or conclusions but to find out what the participant thinks— to stimulate the interviewee to express the meanings that he or she attributes to the topic at hand. To do this, the interviewer may need to provide a certain amount of guidance by focusing the interviewee's attention (on a general topic, an event, a specific passage in a text) and encouraging the interviewee to elaborate on the meanings he or she attributes to the topic. Yet the interviewer must be careful not to provide too much guidance; the interviewer must avoid saying or doing things that somehow predict or impose a particular response by the interviewee. It is, for example, surprisingly easy to let tone of voice or nonverbal language express one's attitudes. There is also the danger of rephrasing the interviewee's comments so they reflect the interviewer's expectations ("Oh, so what you're really saying here is that the main thing you think about when you compose is the contextual factors that influence your audience's reaction").

To provide focus for an interview, one might very well come to the interview with a predetermined set of questions that reflect the concerns of the interviewer. Ethnographers, however, assume that their concerns will be shaped by what participants do and say on the spot. In relatively informal interviews, the focus—indeed, the entire conversation—may be influenced by a participant. For example, a participant's offhand remark may introduce an unexpected line of conversation. In more formal interviews, a researcher might use either a "stimulated recall" or a "discourse-based" procedure.

With the stimulated recall procedure, a researcher observes writers while they are in the process of composing. The researcher notes unusual aspects of that process (e.g., lengthy pauses) and, as soon as the writer has completed a task, interviews the writer about the thoughts, feelings, or reactions that accompanied the writer's activity. (For a fuller discussion, see Matsuhashi, 1982; Rose, 1984.)

With the discourse-based interview, the researcher focuses on places in a text where the writer has made choices of style or content. Drawing on his or her knowledge of other pieces the writer has done, the researcher identifies alternatives the writer has used in other contexts. Then the researcher asks the writer if he or she would be willing to substitute any of the alternatives for the original choice. (For a fuller discussion, see Odell, Goswami, & Herrington, 1983.)

To our knowledge, the stimulated recall procedure has not been used in a naturalistic study of writing in a non-academic setting. But it seems as though it might be readily adopted to a naturalistic setting. And like the discourse-based interview, it has the advantage of letting participants help determine points on which the interview will focus.

In attempting to get interviewees to elaborate on their comments, we have found it useful to try to respond to interviewees' statements in ways that are as nonjudgmental and nondirective as possible. Indeed, it may be that a good initial response to an interviewee's comment is to remain silent for a few seconds and give the interviewee an opportunity to elaborate. If, after a brief pause, no elaboration is forthcoming, it can be helpful to begin a sentence with the words, "So what you're saying here is . . . ," and then pause to allow the writer time to complete the sentence. Another set of strategies would be (1) to say, "I'm not sure I understand," or "Could you elaborate?" (2) to paraphrase a participant's statement as closely as possible and give the participant a chance to modify the paraphrase; (3) to listen for unelaborated terms that imply value judgments or entail a range of meanings (e.g., "It seemed important to do X") and then try to get the participant to clarify the term (e.g., one might ask, "How do you mean 'important'?" or say " 'Important' in that . . . " and allow the participant to complete the sentence).

TAPE RECORDING CONVERSATIONS. If one assumes that social interaction is an important part of the composing process, it seems useful to tape record conversations that occur in a naturalistic setting. This process (see Odell, chapter 7, this volume), may provide insight into the writer's process of invention by capturing some of the questions a writer considers in developing his or her ideas on a given topic. Indeed, a novice researcher may plan to use tape-recording equipment as a primary data collection device in a naturalistic research project.

The benefits seem clear, but we want to raise several cautions. For one, a researcher's primary concern must be the effect that tape recorders can have on participants. The introduction of any electronic recording devices into natural settings should be done gradually and carefully. The presence of such devices can intimidate and/ or irritate participants. Moreover, recordings can be very difficult to transcribe if a researcher records a conversation that includes more than two participants. Finally, the task of transcribing tapes can be expensive and time consuming. Newkirk (1983) indicates that this latter problem can be serious enough to inhibit the scope of an ethnographic project.

Yet even bearing these cautions in mind, we think that tape recording may be a useful procedure for answering certain kinds of questions. For example, if researchers want to try to identify the cognitive strategies writers use in formulating ideas, they will need to look closely at writers' conversations with colleagues, since these conversations may be important to the writer's efforts to think through a topic about which he or she must write. Transcripts of such conversations would enable a researcher to do the sort of detailed analysis that could provide categories with which to begin to describe other conversations.

USING OTHER RECORDING TECHNOLOGY. In special circumstances, it may be feasible and useful to photograph, videotape, or film the activity under study. Each of these technologies has the potential to provide a perspective on that activity. However, researchers should not assume that such recording represents a completely objective account of an event. Bogdan and Bicklen (1982, pp. 102–112) demonstrate the subjective aspects of photography used in qualitative research by showing how the composition of photographs can be manipulated. Further, the use of any type of camera for data collection will likely be conspicuous and distracting to the participants.

A possibly less intrusive recording technology may be the computer. Some recent research into composing processes has used computers as a means of exploring the writing processes of individuals writing on word processors. Cooper and Holzman (1983) discuss research in progress of Olson, who has used word-processing systems to "record every editing function that (writers) invoke: substitution, deletion, transposition; it also notes whenever (writers) re-read their text, and counts such things as word and sentence length" (p. 292). The technology used in this research and in that of Lutz (1983) could provide an ethnographer another useful perspective on writing, if, in their natural settings, participants write with word-processing systems. Of course, the feasibility of implementing such a recording system may be a major stumbling block. An ethnographer would not want this method of recording to interfere with the natural performance of the already in-use word-processing system.

Analyzing Data

The goal of data analysis is to develop a model of the activity under study. The ethnographer builds a model by first establishing provisional patterns in the data, and then testing, clarifying, and classifying those patterns. This model-building process begins the first day that the researcher enters the site and continues through to the final draft of the research report.

The analysis procedure can be classified into four stages: (1) recording on-site analysis, (2) developing categories, (3) linking categories and developing a model, and (4) integrating categories and chronology. These four stages need not be completely sequential, nor will they necessarily be distinct from each other. Although one tries to analyze data chronologically and systematically, the analysis process will be partially recursive and intuitive.

RECORDING ON-SITE ANALYSIS. This analysis is conducted by writing theoretical notes (TN) during data collection. For example, a researcher observes a collaborative writing session between a manager, John, and a staff member, Lisa. The researcher records the following observational note (ON):

> ON: Lisa suggests that the opening sentence be revised. John, angrily: "No. I wrote it. I like it." They move on to another section of the report.

Upon writing the ON, the researcher may vaguely associate this brief interaction with the other past incidents, and thus write the following TN:

> TN: John doesn't take criticism well. He uses his authority to defend and preserve his rhetorical choices. Collaborative decisions seem to reflect the relative authority of the collaborators.

Such on-the-spot analyses can help the researcher begin to uncover patterns of behavior that may be borne out through extensive analysis. Of course, a TN like this one may not link up with any others and may prove to be insignificant.

DEVELOPING CATEGORIES. After completing all data collection and leaving the research site, the researcher begins intensive, systematic data analysis. In doing this, the researcher tries to identify specific phenomena as instances of a larger class or pattern in the data. For example, the researcher might come to see the behavior recorded in the observational note just mentioned as an instance of a class of behavior that could be labeled *managerial authority*.

This process of establishing categories can be the most difficult, frustrating, time-consuming part of one's research. Yet it is extremely important. Raw data—unanalyzed and unassimilated—is by itself of limited value or interest. It is true that ethnographic research reports a great deal of primary data, detailed accounts of what people did and said. As we noted earlier, however, ethnographers are not interested merely in describing phenomena but in achieving a "thick description," one that conveys the significance of observed events. This significance becomes apparent only as ethnographers identify individual statements or actions as examples of some larger pattern of language or action, as members of a category.

In trying to understand the significance of a body of data, an ethnographer must depend in part on intuition, serendipity, inspiration; as with any other form of inquiry, there is no way to reduce the process of ethnographic inquiry to a sequence of conscious intellectual operations that lead inevitably to a profound insight. Recent work in rhetoric and composition, however, suggests that it is possible to give oneself some sort of guidance in the process of discovery. Indeed, it seems likely that the analysis of ethnographic data could be greatly assisted by heuristic strategies derived from the work of Young, Becker, and Pike (1970); Kenneth Burke (see especially Irmscher's treatment of Burke's theory, 1981); or Peter Elbow (1973). In our own work, we have found it useful to be eclectic, relying partly on intuition and partly on elements drawn from each of the theorists mentioned here. For example, we have found it useful to begin data analysis with an intuitive, impressionistic response: What interests me about the data? What aspects of the data strike me—for whatever reason? When I write down my initial impressions, what center of gravity begins to appear? In addition, we have found it useful to classify and contrast: How is this specific act or word like something I have seen elsewhere in the data? How is it like something I know from other studies or other experiences? How is this statement (or this person, or this event) different from other things in the data? How is it different from what I had expected or had hoped to find? Also, we have found it helpful to think about what Young, Becker, and Pike would call *context* or what Burke would call *scene*: When does X phenomenon occur? What led up to it? What does it

lead up to? What is the physical setting in which it occurs? Who are
the principal agents in the scene? Who is affected by this phenomenon? Who benefits from it?

This series of questions is, of course, illustrative rather than
definitive. Researchers familiar with any of the theories mentioned
here could identify many more questions that would help one analyze
data. And any of the questions mentioned here might easily lead a
researcher to raise additional questions. Our point here is that even
though ethnographic data analysis may seem like unfamiliar, even
forbidding territory, composition researchers have a repertoire of
strategies that can provide a good bit of guidance as they explore that
territory, trying to establish categories that get at the significance of
the data at hand.

As one begins to formulate categories, one must engage in two
additional activites. First, it is necessary to specify the properties of
these categories (Glaser & Strauss, 1967, pp. 36–39). For example,
having formulated a category such as managerial authority, the
researcher might go on to stipulate that one property of this category
is "power to propose or veto revisions in a document." As the
researcher identifies these properties, he or she improves the chances
of recognizing new instances of this category.

This attempt to recognize new instances leads to a second
important activity, that of constantly testing the categories the
researcher is establishing. Using what Glaser and Strauss (1967) call
the Constant Comparison Method, the researcher proposes provisional categories, tries to define their properties, and applies them
to new pieces of data, using these data as a basis for redefining either
the categories or their properties. (For a discussion of other analytic
strategies, see Goetz & LeCompte, 1984, pp. 164–207.)

LINKING CATEGORIES AND BUILDING A MODEL. The point of all this
forming, defining, and testing of categories is to develop a model—a
set of statements that describes and explains the rhetorical activities
under study. As a researcher works with the mountains of data that
have been collected, it may seem that the task is overwhelming, that
the process of categorization could easily go on until both the data
and the researcher are exhausted. What usually happens, however, is
that the researcher will begin to link significant categories and
eventually discover what Shatzman and Strauss (1973) call the "key

linkage." This discovery will enable the researcher to focus the classification process:

> For once the analyst gains a Key Linkage—that is, a metaphor, model, general scheme, overriding pattern, or "story line"—he can become increasingly selective of the classes (categories) he needs to deal with: classes to look for, to refine further, or to link up with other classes. The principal operational advantage to the researcher of creating or finding a key linkage is that, for the first time, he has the means of determining the significance of classes. Without it, he must give relatively equal attention to a vast number of the more obvious classes, and consequently will never feel comfortable enough to implement a closure process. [p. 111]

INTEGRATING CATEGORIES AND CHRONOLOGY. Even though ethnographers spend a great deal of their time trying to develop analytical categories, much of their data appears in chronological form; most observational notes, for example, are about what happened on a particular day in a particular setting. Consequently, results of ethnographic research are often reported in narrative form. Sometimes the narrative description of the activity under study dominates the analytical explanations of that activity, and the researcher can claim that the data can speak for themselves. Unfortunately, the data may not speak clearly. Thus, when writing up results of a study, it is crucial for an ethnographer to integrate the analytical with the narrative.

This point is clearly illustrated in Geertz's classic account of a Balinese cockfight. His account integrates several levels of narrative: the personal experience that Geertz and his wife had during a raid of a cockfight, as well as the native stories that surround various aspects of cockfighting. Yet the analysis of the Balinese culture is interwoven throughout these stories. Geertz does not just let the data speak for themselves. Rather, he explores the significance of the data through analytical categories that explain Balinese social structure. These categories show the cockfight to be a "paradigmatic human event" of Balinese culture (p. 450).

Similarly, a major part of chapter 7 by Odell in this volume describes a meeting between a legislative analyst and a lawyer. Rather than structuring that part of the article on a chronological account of the meeting, Odell organized his report around two analytical categories: interpersonal and analytical strategies. The analysis takes precedence over the narrative.

USES AND LIMITATIONS OF ETHNOGRAPHIC RESEARCH

Having described procedures for conducting ethnographic research, we want to conclude this chapter by reflecting on the uses and limitations of such research. Once researchers have carried out an ethnographic study, what should they be able to do? What kinds of claims should they be able to make? What purposes might they achieve by making those claims? What claims and goals are beyond an ethnographer's grasp?

Heath (1983) points out one limitation ethnographers must acknowledge: the "ethnographic present," the recorded phenomena of daily experience, "never remains as it is described." No matter how carefully and thoroughly the ethnographer studies the life of a particular group, the details of that life will continue to change. An ethnographer cannot be certain that behavior observed during the course of a particular study will still be in evidence ten years—or perhaps even ten months—after the study has been completed.

Geertz (1973) identifies additional limitations. Unlike researchers in some other disciplines, ethnographers cannot claim to have established general principles that will enable them to predict exactly how people will act if certain variables are manipulated. Further, ethnographers cannot anticipate that their studies will have a cumulative effect that will enable them, ultimately, to provide a definitive, permanent solution to a particular problem. By contrast, medical researchers can assume that if they design their studies carefully enough, each will define some small part of a much larger problem until, finally, there can be a major breakthrough that will solve the problem once and for all by eliminating a particular disease. Unless there are flaws in a particular study, medical researchers can assume that it should not be necessary for another researcher to cover the same ground or try to answer the same specific question. Ethnographers can make no such assumption. They may never have a conclusive answer to a question such as: How do reading and writing interact with the social context in which they occur? The answer may change as researchers examine new communities or bring new theoretical perspectives to bear on existing sets of data.

What ethnographers can do is illustrated in any number of classic studies, Geertz's among them (1973). But given our own interests and those of our readers, we shall try to answer the preceding question by referring to Heath's study of reading and writing in two small southern communities. As a result of her years of participation in one of these communities, Heath (1983) is able to identify a number of recurrent patterns in the way inhabitants read and write. For example, Heath notes that for adult members of one community, "reading is a social activity" (p. 196). Most of the common types of reading material (e.g., letters, newspapers, circulars) are read aloud to groups of family members and/or neighbors. The reading material is discussed at some length, with listeners supplementing the written account with their own experiences and interpretations. Heath concludes that "authority in the written word does not rest in the words themselves, but in the meanings with are negotiated through the experiences of the group."

This brief reference to Heath's work illustrates one of the claims that an ethnographer can make. The ethnographer can claim to have identified recurrent behaviors that are significant in the life of the group and that illustrate some larger principle that members of the group might not be able to see or to articulate. As we have just suggested, an ethnographer cannot claim that these patterns will necessarily continue to exist in the future. Insofar as the ethnographer has reported carefully and honestly, however, the ethnographer can claim to have provided a valid, informative account of how things were at a particular time in the history of a particular group.

The ethnographer—or subsequent researchers—can confidently use this account in several ways. For example, the ethnographer can use the account to build theory or to test claims from existing theories and research. As Heath observed the way speech could interact with and enrich the reading process, she began to raise questions about widely held distinctions between communities with an "oral" tradition and those with a "literate" tradition. Further, she was able to suggest that it may be a mistake to assume that all oral (or all literate) traditions are essentially the same (pp. 230–231).

In addition to testing existing scholarly viewpoints, results of an ethnographic study can be used to derive explanations for other phenomena. Heath was able to show how the language habits of the social community in which children live could interfere with their performance in school. This explanation in turn became a basis for trying to work with the teachers of those children.

Finally, results of an ethnographic study can become—like those of any good other good scholarly inquiry—part of the intellectual life of a particular scholarly community. For the authors of this chapter and, we hope, for increasing numbers of researchers in reading and writing, Heath strikes a responsive chord when she asserts that reading and writing may be influenced by the social context in which they occur. Consequently, we are encouraged to pursue work we have already begun, and we are able to use Heath's work to focus our own inquiry by asking such questions as: When we observe other communities, do we find that readers engage in the sort of social collaboration Heath describes? What are the dynamics of this collaboration? How do they compare with what Heath has described? In posing these questions, we do not anticipate that our studies will need to replicate Heath's findings. Her conclusions are not some sort of Procrustean bed into which our data must be forced. We do anticipate, however, that her observations will give us a starting point, a means of looking at the phenomena we encounter in communities that may be quite remote from those she has described. Perhaps we will find further illustrations of the principles she articulates. But perhaps her work will be useful by contrast; we may come to understand the significance of what we observe as we understand how it differs from what Heath observed. In other words, one important use of ethnographic research—in our view the most important—is that good ethnographic research becomes part of a scholarly conversation (Geertz, 1973, uses the term "argument"), an ongoing effort to make sense of our own experience and that of the communities in which we do our work.

Notes

1. Inevitably, the ethnographer's presence will have some influence on the behavior of participants in a study. For further discussion of this point, see pp. 515–516. Moreover, at least one anthropologist (Heath, 1982) appears not to rule out completely the use of experimental methods. Heath asserts, however, that such methods "if used at all" occupy "a much less significant role than participant observation" (p. 34). Heath further asserts: "Laboratory experiments or any non-

contextualized behaviors, *tend* [emphasis added], in the ethnographer's view, not to yield substantive conclusions generalizable to the same participants in their natural environment" (p. 34).

References

Atlas, M. (1979). Assessing an audience: A study of expert-novice differences in writing (Technical Report No, 3, Document Design Project). Pittsburgh, PA: Carnegie Mellon University. Contract No. NIE-400-78-0043.

Basso, K. (1974). The ethnography of writing. In R. Bauman & J. Sherzer (Eds.), *Explorations in the ethnography of speaking*. London: Cambridge University Press.

Bizzell, P. (1982). Cognition, convention, and certainty: What we need to know about writing. *Pre/Text, 3*, 213–243.

Blumer, H. (1969). *Symbolic interactionism: Perspective and method*. Englewood Cliffs, NJ: Prentice-Hall.

Bogdan, R., & Bicklen, S. (1982). *Qualitative research for education: An introduction to theory and method*. Boston: Allyn & Bacon.

Boulding, K. (1964). *The image*. Ann Arbor: The University of Michigan Press.

Clark, C., Florio, S., Elmore, J., Martin, J., & Maxwell, R. (1983). Understanding writing instruction: Issues of theory and method. In P. Mosenthal, L. Tamor, & S. Walmsley (Eds.), *Research on writing: Principles and methods*. New York: Longman.

Cooper, M., & Holzman, M. (1983). Talking about protocols. *College Composition and Communication, 34*, 284–296.

Dean, J., Eichhorn, R., & Dean, L. (1969). Limitations and advantages of unstructured methods. In G. L. McCall and J. L. Simmons (Eds.), *Issues in participant observation: A text and reader* (pp. 19–24). Reading, MA: Addison-Wesley. (a)

Dean, J., Eichhorn, R., & Dean, L. (1969). Fruitful informants for intensive interviewing. In G. J. McCall & J. L. Simmons (Eds.), *Issues in participant observation: A text and reader* (pp. 192–194). Reading, MA: Addison-Wesley. (b)

Denzin, N. (1970). *The research act*. Chicago: Aldine.

Diesing, P. (1984). Ethnography. *The English Record*, 2–6.

Doheny-Farina, S. (1984). *Writing in an emergent business organization: An ethnographic study*. Unpublished PhD dissertation, Rensselaer Polytechnic Institute.

Elbow, P. (1973). *Writing without teachers*. New York: Oxford University Press.

Geertz, C. (1973). *The interpretation of cultures*. New York: Basic Books.

Glaser, B., & Strauss, A. (1967). *The discovery of grounded theory: Strategies for qualitative research*. New York: Aldine.

Goetz, J. P., & LeCompte, M. D. (1984). *Ethnography and qualitative design in educational research*. New York: Academic Press.

Gold, R. (1969). Roles in sociological field observations. In G. J. McCall & J. L. Simmons (Eds.), *Issues in participant observation: A text and reader* (pp. 30–39). Reading, MA: Addison-Wesley.

Graves, D. (1981). A new look at research on writing. In S. Haley-James (Ed.), *Perspectives on writing in grades 1–8*. Urbana, IL: National Council of Teachers of English.

Heath, S. (1982). Ethnography and education: Defining the essentials. In P. Gilmore & A. A. Glatthorn (Eds.), *Children in and out of school*. Washington, D.C.: Center for Applied Linguistics.

Heath, S. (1983). *Ways with words: Language, life, and work in communities and classrooms*. New York: Cambridge University Press.

Herrington, A. (1983) *Writing in academic settings: A study of the rhetorical contexts for writing in two college chemical engineering courses*. Unpublished PhD dissertation, Rensselaer Polytechnic Institute.

Irmscher, W. (1981). *Holt guide to English: A comprehensive handbook of rhetoric, language, and literature*. (3rd ed.). New York: Holt, Rinehart & Winston.

Kahn, R., & Mann, F. (1969). Developing research partnerships. In G. J. McCall & J. L. Simmons (Eds.), *Issues in participant observation: A text and reader* (pp. 45–52). Reading, MA: Addison-Wesley.

Kanter, R. (1977). *Men and women of the corporation*. New York: Basic Books.

Kantor, K. (1983). Classroom contexts and the development of writing intuitions: An ethnographic case study. In R. Beach & L. S. Bridwell (Eds.), *New Directions in Composition Research* (pp. 72–94). New York: Guilford Press.

Knoblauch, C. (1980). Intentionality in the writing process: A case study. *College Composition and Communication, 31*, 153–158.

Langer, J., & Applebee, A. (1984). Musings. *Research in the Teaching of English, 18*, 5–7.

Levine, R. (1970). Outsiders' judgments: An ethnographic approach to group differences in personality. In R. Naroll & R. Cohen (Eds.), *A handbook in cultural anthropology* (pp. 388–397). New York: Columbia University Press.

Lutz, J. (1983). *A study of professional and experienced writers revising and editing at the computer and with pen and paper*. Unpublished PhD dissertation, Rensselaer Polytechnic Institute.

Matsuhashi, A. (1982). Explorations in the real-time production of written discourse. In M. Nystrand (Ed.), *What writers know: The language, process, and structure of written discourse* (pp. 269–290). New York: Academic Press.

Mead, G. (1956). *The social psychology of G. H. Mead*. A. Strauss, (Ed.). Chicago: University of Chicago Press.

Newkirk, T. (1983). Anatomy of a breakthrough: A case study of a college freshman writer. In R. Beach & L. S. Bridwell (Eds.), *New directions in composition research*. (pp. 131–147). New York: Guilford Press.

Odell, L., Goswami, D., & Herrington, A. (1983). The discourse-based interview: A procedure for exploring tacit knowledge of writers in non-academic settings. In P. Mosenthal, L. Tamor, & S. Walmsley (Eds.), *Research on writing: Principles and methods* (pp. 220–236). New York: Longman.

Pettigrew, J., Shaw, R., & Van Nostrand, A. (1981). Collaborative analysis of writing instruction. *Research in the teaching of English, 15*, 329–341.

Richards, I. (1965). *The philosophy of rhetoric*. New York: Oxford University Press.

Rose, M. (1984). *Writer's block: The cognitive dimension*. Carbondale: Southern Illinois University Press.

Scott, W. (1965). Field methods in the study of organizations. In J. G. March (Ed.), *Handbook of organizations* (pp. 261–304). Chicago: Rand McNally.

Scribner, S., & Cole, M. (1981) Unpackaging literacy. In M. F. Whiteman (Ed.), *Writing: The nature, development, and teaching of written communication* (Vol. 1; pp. 71–87). Hillsdale, NJ: Erlbaum.

Selzer, J. (1983). The composing process of an engineer. *College Composition and Communication, 34,* 178–187.

Shatzman, L., & Strauss, A. (1973). *Field research.* Englewood Cliffs, NJ: Prentice-Hall.

Webb, E. (1970). Unconventionality, triangulation, and inference. In N. K. Denzin (Ed.), *Sociological methods: A sourcebook* (pp. 449–457). New York: McGraw-Hill.

Wilson, S. (1977). The use of ethnographic techniques in educational research. *Review of Educational Research, 47,* 245–265.

Young, R., Becker, A., & Pike, K. (1970). *Rhetoric: Discovery and change.* New York: Harcourt, Brace and World.

Author Index

537

Subject Index

Abstract objectivism, 240-241
Academic disciplines, 238. *See also* Discourse community.
  Accessibility of information to readers, 129-153, 143-144
  in legal documents, 148
  usability testing for, 149
  use of headings for, 144-145
  use of signposts for, 143-144
Additive words. *See* Rhetorical action.
Adjacency pairs of utterances, in computer communication, 215
Administrative information, in R&D environment, 292
Adversative words. *See* Rhetorical action.
Alternative words. *See* Rhetorical action.
Analysis-of-variance *F* test, use of, 78n, 491-492
Analysis, on-site, in ethnographic research, 526
Analysts, administrative:
  analytic strategies used by, 261-263
  interpersonal strategies used by, 260-261
  study of writing done by, 251-278, 326
  use of dialogue by, 264-269, 277
Archai, 313, 314
Aristotelian special topics, 312-314. *See also* Topic.
Audience:
  addressed in writing on the job, 56-58

analysis of as aid in making information accessible, 139, 142, 145, 179
intended, consideration of in writing process, 49, 133-134, 249-252, 255-259, 412, 414, 415, 436-437, 450
perceptions of, by administrative analysts, 270-271
and social perspective on writing, 235-236, 293
Audio mail. *See* Electronic technologies.

Behaviorism, 234. *See also* Writing, nonacademic.
Bivariate analysis, 483-484, 486-487. *See also* Descriptive statistics.
Burke's Pentad, 276-277

Canisius College, course design at, 427-450
Canonical, defininition of, 127n.
Categories, use of in ethnographic research:
  development of, 526-528
  integrating with chronology, 529-530
  linking of, 528-529
Causative words. *See* Rhetorical action.
Census, 455. *See also* Survey.
Central tendency, measures of, 480-481. *See also* Descriptive statistics.
Cluster sample, 464. *See also* Sampling methods.

543